A WORLD
I NEVER MADE

A WORLD
I NEVER MADE

James T. Farrell

with an Introduction by
Charles Fanning

University of Illinois Press
Urbana and Chicago

© 1936, 2007 by Cleo Paturis
Reprinted by arrangement with Cleo Paturis,
Literary Executor for the Estate of James T. Farrell
Introduction © 2007 by the Board of Trustees
of the University of Illinois

Library of Congress Cataloging-in-Publication Data
Farrell, James T. (James Thomas), 1904–1979.
A world I never made / James Farrell ; with an
introduction by Charles Fanning.
p. cm.
Includes bibliographical references.
ISBN-13: 978-0-252-03173-1 (acid-free paper)
ISBN-10: 0-252-03173-3 (acid-free paper)
ISBN-13: 978-0-252-07423-3 (pbk. : acid-free paper)
ISBN-10: 0-252-07423-8 (pbk. : acid-free paper)
1. Irish Americans—Fiction.
2. South Chicago (Chicago, Ill.)—Fiction.
I. Title.
PS3511.A738W67   2007
813'.52—dc22   2006030907

James T. Farrell's
O'Neill-O'Flaherty Novels:
An Introduction

Charles Fanning

Background

James T. Farrell's 1935 story, "The Oratory Contest," presents George O'Dell, a middle-aged Chicago streetcar driver, and his sixteen-year-old son Gerry, who is about to compete in the senior oratorical contest at Mary Our Mother School on the city's South Side. This story opens with Gerry practicing before the bathroom mirror, "imagining the thunder of applause that would greet him at the conclusion of his oration." The scene recalls the opening of Farrell's first novel, *Young Lonigan*, published three years earlier, where Studs Lonigan strikes hard-boiled poses before his mirror on the night of graduation from eighth grade at St. Patrick's School. I believe that this is a deliberate echo, and that Farrell is making the point that two boys from the same neighborhood and Catholic school system can go in very different directions. That point would have been sharp in 1935, for the third Lonigan novel, *Judgment Day*, in which the hapless Studs dies at twenty-nine, had appeared in April, and the trilogy was published in one volume in November. The contrast is pronounced, for Gerry O'Dell is a successful student, encouraged by his teachers and considering college, although he can't afford to go unless, as his father suggests, he can "get a job and study law in the evenings downtown at St. Vincent's."

As he and his other son Michael approach the high school, George feels "increasingly timid," and realizes "that Gerry, instead of waiting for him and Michael, had gone ahead. Gerry, he suddenly felt, was ashamed of him. He argued with himself that the boy had had to get there early, and that, anyway, he had been nervous about the contest and restless, like a colt before the start of a race. But still, no, he could not rid his mind of that thought." In the ensuing competition, Gerry speaks eloquently and wins the gold medal. George O'Dell is moved to tears and "a simple and childlike joy" by his son's victory. After rushing out to a drugstore to telephone the news to his wife, he returns to congratulate his son, only to find the stage empty: "Gerry must have gone. He told himself that Gerry had known that his father would wait to see him, congratulate him, buy him a treat, and that then they would go home together. And Gerry had not waited." George O'Dell searches the few remaining faces, asks a crowd of boys if anyone has seen his son, and then the story ends: "He stood with Michael. Only a few scattered groups remained in front of the hall. Feeling blank, he told himself, yes, Gerry had gone. He solemnly led Michael away, both of them silent. He asked himself why Gerry hadn't waited, and he knew the answer to his question."[1]

When I first read this story in the late 1970s, I felt the shock of recognition, because it's my story too. My father was a school custodian, and on the night when I competed in the local high school essay contest, he was not seated in the audience, but on duty in the building, standing at the back of the auditorium. When I emerged from the hall clutching the first-prize check for $25, he was in the foyer leaning on a push broom. I remember always having been proud of how hard he worked, especially in winter when he'd have to get up at four in the morning to shovel snow. And my memory of that evening is that I went right over and shook his hand. But I could so easily have been Gerry O'Dell, and I'm sure that sometimes I was. There is no more effective rendering in American fiction of the gulf that can develop between working-class parents and their better-educated children than "The Oratory Contest." The story exemplifies the great strengths of James T. Farrell's fiction: plain-style austerity in the telling, realistic presentation of pain that can be understood but not alleviated, and a mutually reinforcing combination of clarity and compassion—the whole rendered without a scrap of condescension toward the characters and situations.

"The Oratory Contest" points straight toward the second phase of Farrell's achievement, his five O'Neill-O'Flaherty novels: *A World I Never Made* (1936), *No Star Is Lost* (1938), *Father and Son* (1940), *My Days of Anger* (1943), and *The Face of Time* (1953). His first two major cycles, the *Studs Lonigan* trilogy (published in 1932, 1934, and 1935) and the O'Neill-O'Flaherty pentalogy, share a setting (the South Side neighborhood around Washington Park where Farrell himself grew up), a time frame (roughly 1890 to 1930), and many characters. Farrell's own childhood around Fifty-eighth Street had much more in common with the experience of young Danny O'Neill in the second series than with that of Studs Lonigan. However, with a wisdom unusual in young writers, Farrell knew that in order to deal in a balanced way with his own emotionally laden personal experience, he ought to tell Studs's story first. But Farrell's eight Washington Park novels actually comprise one coherent grand design with two contrasting movements: the downward, negative alternative embodied in the passive, doomed Studs, and the upward, positive possibility embodied in Danny, who grows up to become a writer.

In June 1929 Farrell had written a publisher that he was "working on two novels. One is a realistic story of a corner gang at Fifty Eighth and Prairie Avenue of this city. . . . The other novel is a tale of a boy in a Catholic high school of this city during the early part of the jazz age." After finishing *The Young Manhood of Studs Lonigan* in 1934, Farrell reported to Ezra Pound: "one more Lonigan book to come, and I'm writing it, . . . and also am working on a long story of a family, Irish American, with a lot of autobiography, that extends from 1911 to 1933, and intends to shoot the works, and include a number of things I've held back in my other books. It may be anywhere from one to five volumes." Farrell published the first O'Neill novel, *A World I Never Made*, in October 1936. Shortly thereafter, he explained to a friend that the new series "is conceived as a complementary study to 'Studs Lonigan.' One [of] the main characters, Danny O'Neill, is planned as a character whose life experience is to be precisely the opposite of Studs." Farrell held to this conception through the writing of the remaining volumes. While finishing up the final draft of *My Days of Anger*, he wrote his publisher that "I think now, it'll come out right, and be a fitting end to the series—and a fitting companion series to *Studs Lonigan*—and that Danny and Studs will stand as I conceived them—dialectical opposites in their destinies—one goes up, the other goes down."[2] The two sequences and the many short stories that share the same South Side setting (there are at least fifty stories about Danny O'Neill) constitute a full-scale fictional chronicle of three generations of urban Americans, from nineteenth-century immigrant laborers to Depression-era intellectuals, grounded in a specific place with clear reference points like the markings on a compass. Farrell's sense of the scope and the integrity of his Chicago fiction was already clear by August 1934 when he wrote to a friend: "I hope to run to at least twenty volumes of novels and short stories attempting to describe, represent, analyze and portray connected social areas of Chicago that I have lived in, and that I have more or less assimilated. In these terms, then, the various books and stories are all panels of one work."[3]

The grandson of Irish immigrants and the son of a teamster and a former domestic servant, Farrell was born on February 27, 1904, raised in South Side Chicago neighborhoods near Washington Park, and educated at Corpus Christi and St. Anselm's Catholic grammar schools and St. Cyril's Carmelite High School, graduating in 1923. Because his parents had many children and little money, he lived from age two with his maternal grandparents and his unmarried uncles and aunts who were better off, and this double perspective of belonging to two families both enriched and complicated his youth. Farrell was first encouraged to write by his eighth-grade teacher at St. Anselm's, Sister Magdalen. He recalls sitting at the parlor window of his grandmother's apartment on South Park Avenue overlooking Washington Park on a rainy Saturday in autumn. Planning out an essay on Andrew Jackson and the United States Bank, "for the first time in my life I experienced that absorption, that exhilaration, and that compulsion which drives you to sit alone and write with the immediate world about you walled out of your consciousness and with your impulses to have fun in the present put to sleep." At St. Cyril's, which is still open at the same location at Sixty-fourth Street and Dante Avenue as Mount Carmel High School, he was further encouraged by two of the Carmelite fathers who were his English teachers, Father Leo J. Walter and Father Albert Dolan. He remembers that in his first year he wrote "an essay of two pages about two boys who didn't want to fight and who talked toughly to one another. Here was a dim forecast of my future writing." This piece became "Helen, I Love You," the first Farrell story to appear in a national publication—H. L. Mencken's *American Mercury* in July 1932. He wrote "out of passion and interest," often about baseball and the White Sox, including a long piece about the Black Sox scandal, which broke during his second year of high school, and the school magazine published his first piece of fiction, "Danny's Uncle," a vignette of the street encounter of young "Danny O'Neil" with his wealthy uncle. "We boys were naive," Farrell remembered. "We did not come from cultivated households. We did not live in a cultural milieu." And yet, under the tutelage of the Carmelites, he took his first "slow step" toward "self-expression and self-consciousness."[4]

Over the next five years, Farrell worked for an express company and as a gas station attendant, took a semester of prelaw courses at De Paul University night school, and enrolled for several quarters at the University of Chicago. In March 1927 he had resolved to be a writer, and embarked on a fierce regimen of reading and writing, in and out of schools, from which he never subsequently deviated. On February 27, 1929, he turned twenty-five. Soon after, he enrolled for what would turn out to be his last quarter at the University of Chicago, taking one course, Advanced Composition, from a favorite professor, James Weber Linn. This year also saw the first commercial publication of a Farrell story, the writing of a second and crucially important story, and the conception of the Lonigan and O'Neill fictional cycles. In June 1929, in the first number of a local little magazine, appeared the story "Slob," which describes an unnamed young man struggling with his drunken aunt in an apartment on Chicago's South Side. And a month or so previously, Farrell had written for Professor Linn's course another South Side Irish story, in which a thoughtful young man attends the wake of a former acquaintance who has died of dissolute living. Its title was "Studs." The narrating consciousness in these two stories is the precursor of Danny O'Neill.[5]

Farrell took the chance of a creative life by quitting the University of Chicago after the spring quarter of 1929. He later wrote of this "drastic step" that "there was a cost to success, and I would not pay that cost. I could not pay it, because, if I did, then I could not write." Over the next two years, unfazed by the stock-market crash (except as it would provide a certain dénouement for his novel in progress), he traveled to New York City twice, did odd jobs while living at home or flopping on couches in his friends' Hyde Park apartments, and read and wrote feverishly, day in and day out. He recalled of these years that in order to give "as much of my time as I could to study and writing, . . . in a sense, the Depression caught up with me. By early 1928, I had brought on my own Depression. I got myself jobless, not through inability to hold a job, but because I did not want one."[6] The result was, as Edgar Branch has said, that the young Farrell had, like the young Herman Melville, "swum through libraries." Among the writers he had read in depth by 1930 were "William James, Dewey, and George H. Mead, Nietzsche, Max Stirner, Bertrand Russell, Thorstein Veblen, R. H. Tawney, Sigmund Freud, Walter Pater, Ibsen, Chekhov, H. L. Mencken, Theodore Dreiser, Sherwood Anderson, Carl Sandburg, Sinclair Lewis, Ernest Hemingway, and James Joyce."[7] "There were ways," recalls Murray Kempton in his memoir of the thirties, "in which [Farrell] was the best-educated young writer of his time. He had read philosophers well outside the realm of discourse of conventional critics; he was a deep, though perhaps narrow, student of history; he had great resources in the European tradition. He was a perceptive enough critic to argue for William Faulkner in the early thirties, when Faulkner was at his peak of creation and his nadir of reputation. He was certainly better educated than Hemingway and Fitzgerald, who in many areas were not educated at all."[8]

By early 1931, Farrell had written thousands of manuscript pages of fiction, including much that would be incorporated into the *Studs Lonigan* trilogy and the O'Neill-O'Flaherty series. He got almost none of it published. In April 1931, dead broke and still without a publisher except for the smallest of the Midwest's little magazines, Farrell did the next logical thing—he got married, to Dorothy Butler, and the newlyweds sailed off to Paris for a year. There he expanded his reading by absorbing great amounts of Balzac, Proust, Henry James, Spinoza, and Trotsky. Then came his breakthrough. Shortly after arriving in Paris, Farrell learned that his first novel, *Young Lonigan: A Boyhood in Chicago Streets*, had been accepted by the Vanguard Press in New York. In April 1932, the novel was published and James T. Farrell was off and running.

What followed was one of the most extraordinary creative flowerings in the history of American letters. One thinks of Herman Melville's eight novels and several stories between 1846 and 1857, his entire fictional corpus but for *Billy Budd*, and William Faulkner's eleven books, including his masterworks, between 1929 and 1942. When he finished writing *My Days of Anger*, the fourth O'Neill-O'Flaherty novel, in February 1943, Farrell wrote a friend that "I have accomplished what I set out to. Shortly after I will have reached thirty nine, I will have accomplished my two major literary objectives—not of course that I haven't more that I want to write. But this much I have done. I have now written the books I said I would write a little over ten years ago when this seemed like a wild prediction."[9] In eleven years he had published eleven novels, four collections of short fiction, one book of literary criticism, and over 300 essays and reviews. The *New York Times* had hailed the *Studs Lonigan* trilogy as "one of the most powerful pieces of American fiction," and its inclusion in the Random House Modern Library in 1938 ensured a continuing audience of intelligent readers. As both an artist and an intellectual, James T. Farrell was a force to be reckoned with in American letters.

Farrell was far from alone in having made this sort of journey at this time in American cultural life. Although his output was uniquely prodigious, he was but one of many children and grandchildren of immigrants and the working class who made up a chorus of new voices starting out in the 1930s to expand the boundaries of American literature. Indeed, Michael Denning has argued that the extraordinary artistic and intellectual energies unleashed in that decade consti- tuted "a birthing of a new American culture, a second American Renaissance," when "for the first time in the history of the United States, a working-class culture had made a significant imprint on the dominant cultural institutions."[10] Among the new "proletarian" writers bent on bringing their experiences and those of their parents' generation to fiction were (with some of their books): Mike Gold (*Jews without Money*, 1930); Edward Dahlberg (*Bottom Dogs*, 1930); Langston Hughes (*Not without Laughter*, 1930); Catherine Brody (*Nobody Starves*, 1932); Grace Lumpkin (*To Make My Bread*, 1932); Jack Conroy (*The Disinherited*, 1933); Marita Bonner (*The Black Map*, 1933); Daniel Fuchs (*Summer in Williamsburg*, 1934); Albert Halper (*On the Shore*, 1934); Henry Roth (*Call It Sleep*, 1934); Tillie Olsen, "The Iron Throat" (1934); Nelson Algren (*Somebody in Boots*, 1935); Clara Weatherwax (*Marching, Marching*, 1935); Thomas Bell (*All Brides Are Beautiful*, 1936); Meyer Levin (*The Old Bunch*, 1937); John Fante (*Wait until Spring, Bandini*, 1938); Pietro Di Donato (*Christ in Concrete*, 1939); and Richard Wright (*Uncle Tom's Children*, 1938, and *Native Son*, 1940). These were writers who shared a faith in literature as an uncondescending chronicle of working-class and under- class lives and, at its best, a potential vehicle for social change.[11]

Farrell marked his own consciousness of this community in his April 1935 speech before the First American Writers' Congress in New York, a widely publi- cized, Communist-led event. He took as his ambitious subject "the development of literary traditions" in "a succession of patterns," using as his main illustration an inclusive look at the new African American literature and an insightful anal- ogy with the Irish tradition. The first pattern of "Negro literature" that he sees is "the Uncle Remus story of the dark-skinned Southern Handy Andy." The reference is to the stereotyped Irish peasantry in books such as Samuel Lover's *Handy Andy* of 1842, in which there is also implied "a condition of master and slave, oppressor and oppressed." The "Uncle Remus" pattern "presents a vaude-

vilized conception of the Negro, portray[ing] him as obsequious, shiftless, childishly humorous and simple, . . . the subject of comedy which, as we know, slurs
and distorts the story of the tragic history of the Negro in capitalist America."
Farrell sees this conception as still very much abroad in the land in 1935. He
cites the *Saturday Evening Post*, the movies, and the Amos and Andy radio show,
and he analyzes this pattern as "a combination of the conventions forced upon
the Negro to permit, on one hand, some harmonious interaction between the
Negro and the privileged class of whites living on his back, and, on the other, a
wish fulfillment of what that privileged class desires the Negro to be."

Farrell goes on to connect the "literature of realism and social protest which
has come to be the dominant literary tradition in twentieth-century American
writing" with "an increasingly apparent contradiction between the hopes of the
American dream and the manner in which human destinies unraveled in actual
life." In this movement, contemporary American writers have "been introducing
us to a new kind of American life, to the life of poor farmers and sharecroppers
in backward rural areas, to the scenes, sights, and dialects of the urban streets,
to the feelings of Slavic immigrants, the problems and discontents of sweat-shop
workers, the resentments and oppressions of the factory proletariat. . . . In brief,
it has been dipping us down toward the bottom of the so-called American melt-
ing pot." Farrell goes on to criticize the lack of "internal conviction" in "many
of the new revolutionary short stories." Authors "seek[ing] to express a revolutionary point of view, . . . instead of making their aim functional within the
story so that the aim impresses the reader as a natural and integral aspect of the
story, it seems to be glued on," in the worst cases, "as a slogan or revolutionary
direction sign that possesses no coherent and vital or necessary relation to the
body of the story."[12]

One conference participant who paid close attention to Farrell's speech was
Richard Wright, who had come east from Chicago, where his family was living
on the South Side at 3743 Indiana Avenue, ten blocks north of Farrell's childhood
home on the same street and twenty blocks north of the Studs Lonigan/Danny
O'Neill neighborhood. A few years earlier, Wright had lived even closer, at 4831
Vincennes. In fact, the Chicago South Side neighborhoods around Washington
Park constitute an outstanding example of the resilience of urban communities
as genius loci for artistic expression in the earlier twentieth century. Much has
been made of the disruption to patterns of living in the wake of the great migration of African Americans from the rural South to northern cities between
the two world wars. And yet, where the arts were concerned, there was significant continuity as well. It was just that the dominant art form changed from
literature to music. Among the jazz greats who came of age in the 1930s on the
same streets where Farrell and Wright had matured in the 1920s were Dorothy Donegan, Joe Williams, Johnny Board, Viola Jefferson, Milt Hinton, John

Young, Johnny Hartman, and Nat "King" Cole. Most attended DuSable High School at Forty-ninth and Wabash, where they were trained by the legendary bandmaster, Captain Walter Dyett.[13]

When he arrived in New York for the American Writers' Congress, Richard Wright was twenty-six, four years younger than Farrell, and had published a few poems and stories in little magazines. He also spoke at the conference—on "The Isolation of the Negro Writer." Michel Fabre has said that Wright "was enthralled to hear James T. Farrell speak on the revolutionary story," particularly Farrell's "true defense of art against propaganda and political tyranny." As Wright was just then becoming interested in short fiction, "Farrell's vigorous observations could not help but influence him, especially because he had his own reservations about the political demands of the Party. This was the beginning of a literary friendship that benefitted Wright enormously."[14]

Farrell spent impressive critical energies in the 1930s warning artists against the contaminating influence of politics on literature and distancing himself from those who would judge books ideologically. In 1936 he published *A Note on Literary Criticism*, his book-length analysis of the relationship between literature and Marxist cultural criticism. There, with detailed discussion of sources as varied as the Japanese *Tale of Genji*, Spinoza, Thomas Aquinas, Dickens, Proust, Dostoyevsky, and Joyce, he defended the integrity of art against the corruption of political propaganda, which he saw as an urgent threat from the intellectual left.[15] In this campaign, Farrell's was an early and very strong voice. Similarly, in his preface to the 1937 single-volume edition of his first three story collections, Farrell discussed the most conspicuous example of his era's blind faith in content: the demand in left-wing magazines such as *The Anvil* for didactic, so-called proletarian fiction featuring "a purely conceptualized, hypothetical, and non-existent worker [as] the hero. The stories produced in this movement were bad, lifeless, wooden. In place of the happy ending of *The Saturday Evening Post* variety, they had an 'uplifting' conclusion based on a sudden conversion to the sole correct faith in progress and the future of humanity." Thus, Farrell attacked distortions of content in the name of form in the mechanical "plot story" of popular magazines and college writing courses, and distortions of form in the name of content in "local color" and "proletarian" stories about minorities and the working class. There is little to choose, he declared, between fiction produced and endorsed by political standards or by short-fiction handbooks: "The former hypostasizes, narrows, and freezes content; the latter achieves a similar effect with form."[16]

Farrell's candid critique made him several enemies, and, as luck would have it, some of these people (among them Malcolm Cowley, Granville Hicks, and Alfred Kazin) went on to become influential shapers of literary reputation in the 1940s and 1950s. These New York–based critics utilized an embrace of high modernism and a "new critical" aesthetic to try to blackball Farrell from consideration as a serious writer. This vindictive crusade began with the publication of the first O'Neill-O'Flaherty novels, *A World I Never Made* in 1936 and *No Star Is Lost* in 1938. A good example of the level of much of this was the dismissal of the third novel in the series, *Father and Son*, by Edmund Wilson in *The New Republic* in October 1940. After confessing that he hadn't read Farrell's "last two or three novels," Wilson had the gall to declare that Farrell was "writing book after book about Irish boys growing up in Chicago," and "continuing to tell the same story." Instead of reviewing this new one, Wilson says, "I should like to ask you to state yourself why you expect people to go on reading your books. . . . Why do you keep on with this interminable record?" The magazine did allow Farrell to respond: "As for Studs Lonigan and Danny O'Neill," he says, "they can be pronounced alike only by a critic who could confuse Becky Sharp and Mrs. Wiggs of the Cabbage Patch." And as for Wilson's disingenuous questions: "I answer, because I have an unshakeable conviction that I have a true and representative story to tell of how people have lived, suffered and enjoyed, striven and forged ideals, loved and hated, died in my time. . . . When I began writing, I determined not to compromise with passing fads that come and go. I have rigidly tried to adhere to this intention. I have always been prepared to breast every hostile current that my books required and I am still prepared to do this. I make these statements not with any arrogance, but rather out of a full realization that each writer must find his own way in accordance with his temperament and his talents."[17]

Actually, the O'Neill-O'Flaherty novels were greeted in many of the most respected journals and newspapers as major literary events. For example, in his review of the first volume for the *Nation*, Carl Van Doren pointed out that the characters' "consciences make up nearly as much of the story as their acts. This helps to give to *A World I Never Made* that habitual tenderness which is quite as characteristic of Mr. Farrell's novels as their toughness." Further, Van Doren's sense of the overall effect of the style is fully congruent with Farrell's own aims: "He has an extraordinarily capacious mind which holds the persons and events of a novel as if they were, somehow, in solution, to be poured out in a full stream in which his own share as narrator may be lost sight of. You forget that you are seeing this life through the eyes of a selecting novelist. It seems merely to be there before you." As to subject matter, he went on to praise Farrell as the American city's "truest historian." Indeed, "Mr. Farrell seems to me to go beyond any other American novelist in his knowledge of the common life of an American city and his understanding of the city culture."[18] The novel sold over 5,000 copies in its first year, making it Farrell's most successful book up to that point.

When the fourth volume, *My Days of Anger*, appeared in 1943, Carlos Baker said in the *New York Times Book Review* that it "reveals in the author a heartening accession of philosophical gentleness and narrative power. It is in many ways a better book than Farrell has done before," and "if there is an accession of tenderness and even a kind of optimism in the present novel, there is also a gain in narrative power and incisiveness." The critics who praised the books of the O'Neill-O'Flaherty series as they appeared also included Bernard De Voto, Harold Strauss, Lewis Corey, Weldon Kees, Diana Trilling, and H. L. Mencken. In February 1937, Van Doren, De Voto, and Heywood Broun also testified in the successful court action against the New York Society for the Suppression of Vice, which had petitioned that *A World I Never Made* be banned as "obscene, lewd, and lascivious."[19]

What was missing from the criticism, however, was a developed sense of the projected scope and ultimate achievement of the O'Neill-O'Flaherty series as a whole. Had this been registered strongly in either 1943 with *My Days of Anger* or 1953, when the fifth volume, *The Face of Time*, appeared, then all of these books would be much better known. Militating against the articulation of full perspective on the series was everything that constituted the uniqueness of Farrell's accomplishment—the setting, characters, and style of his portrait of the artist in Washington Park on the South Side of Chicago. These all ran counter to the ultimately elitist hegemony of the "New Criticism" in the late 1940s and 1950s, which favored and praised high style, the veins of irony and allusion that cry out for exegesis, and an erudite controlling narrative consciousness, as in iconic works such as *Ulysses, The Waste Land,* and *To the Lighthouse.*

A clarifying visual analogy to both Farrell's achievement in the O'Neill-O'Flaherty series and the lack of critical recognition thereof is Peter Brooks's discussion of Gustave Courbet's revolutionary "Burial at Ornans" of 1849, a huge painting (ten by twenty-two feet) of a "humble" subject (an ordinary funeral in his own home village). This was the first volley in the campaign for *réalisme* in which Courbet was the salient standard-bearer. Brooks asserts that Parisian critics were scandalized both by the "heroic scale usually reserved for the grandeur of history painting" and the spectacle of a straggling parade of "low, vulgar" villagers, "in fact, portraits done by Courbet from his fellow townspeople," ranged around the "gaping hole" of a grave.[20] Similarly, Farrell chose to work on the largest literary canvas, a sequence of related novels that would reach 2,500 pages, and to take as his subject the works and days, lives and deaths of the ordinary people among whom he had grown up.

Contexts: Joyce, Proust, Chekhov, the Pragmatists

The O'Neill-O'Flaherty series is, among other things, a portrait of the growth of an artist, and in the design and ambition of his own project, Farrell's great tutelary spirits were James Joyce and Marcel Proust. With his own Irish American

Catholic background, he could hardly have failed to be affected by Joyce. After reading the galleys of *Young Lonigan* in February 1932, Ezra Pound had jibed to Farrell, "Effect a bit too much Joyce of the Portrait," to which Farrell replied, "As to the Irishness of it. I generally feel that I'm an Irishman rather than an American, and [*Young Lonigan*] was recommended at the nrf [Nouvelle Review Française, its French publishing house] as being practically an Irish novel. I had read Joyce [meaning *Ulysses*] and pretty well forgotten him in all details at least a year, and the Portrait a year and a half before even starting the book, and any similarity was all unconscious." However, upon rereading "most of the Portrait a month or so ago," Farrell continued, "I did feel that, with differences of time, climate, and country, there were certain similarities to the exterior conditions and experiences and even the personal ones portrayed there and the ones I bumped into in the course of growing up as a Catholic young man, attending a Catholic high school taught by Carmelites rather than Jesuits etc."[21]

In *My Days of Anger*, in which Danny O'Neill reaches maturity, he discusses *A Portrait* and *Ulysses* with friends at the University of Chicago. Shortly after completing that novel, Farrell wrote two essays on Joyce for the *New York Times Book Review* that were later expanded and published separately, in which he located the *Portrait* firmly in its innovative contexts. First, he insists that nineteenth-century Irish political history is necessary to understanding the book, for "Joyce was a kind of inverted nationalist," for whom "the nationalism he rejects runs . . . like a central thread." Second, he asserts that "it was Joyce who introduced the city realistically into modern Irish writing. The city—Dublin—is the focus of Ireland in his work, and in his life. We see that this is the case with Stephen [Dedalus], the genius son of a declassed family. Stephen lives, grows up in a Dublin that is a center of paralysis. Is he to have a future in such a center? Is he to prevent himself from suffering paralysis, spiritual paralysis? Stephen's painful burden of reality can be interpreted as a reality that derives from the history of Ireland's defeats and that is focused, concretized, in the very quality of the men of Dublin." Third, Farrell emphasizes Stephen's Catholicism as crucially formative: "From his considerable reading in the literature of the church the boy gained not only a sense of the past but also a sense of an ordered inner world and of a systematized *other* world. Eternity has filled his imagination." Furthermore, "his greatest sufferings are not imposed by the Dublin reality which disturbs him so much but by images of inferno as terrifying as that of Dante. He quivers and cowers before the vision of an other world which must make that of the Irish legends seem the most pale of mists. His spiritual struggle is one involving acceptance or rejection of this ordered other world."

Farrell goes on to place Joyce in the context of the European tradition of the bildungsroman, which he charts as a three-part progression through the nineteenth century. "Early in the century we see the young man—for instance Julien

Sorel of *The Red and the Black*, or Balzac's Lucien and Rastignac—seeking glory and fame. Their aim is success, and the plane of action is the objective one of society." At mid-century, "in the Russian novel—Pierre of *War and Peace*, Levin of *Anna Karenina*, Bazarov of *Fathers and Sons*, and Dostoyevsky's Raskolnikov and Ivan Karamazov—there is a shift of emphasis. These young men probe for the meaning of life; they seek to harmonize their words and their deeds." Toward the century's end, "we see the young man seeking freedom in the realm of feeling. This is the object of Frederic Moreau in *A Sentimental Education*—and of Des Esseintes (in a purely decadent fashion) in Huysmans's *Against the Grain*. Marius [Pater's Epicurean] and Stephen are both of this line; they, too, seek freedom in the realm of feeling and of culture." Farrell sees this substitution of artistic for worldly or ontological goals by fiction's protagonists as a reflection of "the evolving conditions of life in the nineteenth century. The character of public life changes and decreases the opportunities to be free. The idea of culture (as the realm of freedom) begins to grow. Thus, the logic of art for art's sake. The artist, crushed by the weight of contemporary culture, adopts the attitude that art is its own end, becomes the rebel artist." Stephen Dedalus fits here. He is "the artist as rebel, questioning the whole moral sensibility of his age."

Having recently finished his fourth and, at that point, the final O'Neill-O'Flaherty novel, Farrell must also have been locating his own bildungsroman as an advance into twentieth-century America of this venerable Old World tradition. Moreover, it is clear from Farrell's description that Stephen Dedalus and Danny O'Neill are as different as their differing places, times, gifts, and limitations dictate. Farrell notes that "almost from childhood, Stephen is an exceptional character. He is separated from others. He is aloof, lonely, different. His childhood is not a normal one in which he shares the common experiences of give-and-take between boys. He seldom participates in games; he is bookish, introspective. By the time he becomes a university student his mind is monkish, cloistered, and he regards it as such." Danny O'Neill hasn't the precocity, arrogance, or self-confidence of Stephen Dedalus. Though they are about the same age at the conclusions of *My Days of Anger* and *Ulysses*, Stephen is much further along on the road toward conviction and self-sufficiency in his vocation of artist.[22]

This distinction between the two protagonists relates to Farrell's lifelong ambivalence about Joyce, which had mostly to do with aspects of literary style. In his Joyce essay, Farrell explains Joyce's brilliant melding of style and theme in *A Portrait* by observing that "Joyce's realism is a realism of the mind, of the consciousness. Stephen's life is described in a highly concentrated and selective manner, deriving from this point of view. His own mind serves as the frame of reference for the story." Thus, "in many parts of the narrative the very style in which it is written has direct bearing on the theme." Because "the inner life of the artist is what is significant in [Stephen's] life, . . . the style, the perspective, the organization of the novel all seem to harmonize beautifully with its content." That is, Joyce makes his protagonist's exceptionalism clear by making the dominant style in the last chapter of *A Portrait* and in *Ulysses* a reflection of Stephen's brilliance, isolation, and self-absorption. In Farrell's view, this was a double-edged sword. As early as 1934, he had written that "parts of *Ulysses* seem like stunt performances to permit the author the luxury of showing off. I feel that the question and answer chapter is of such a nature. But such performances remain the privilege of genius." Farrell went even further a few years later in writing a friend that *Finnegans Wake* was "a signal of a man of genius with colossal egotism," which ultimately failed to meet John Dewey's "only demand" of an artist: "that his product be communicable in some sense to someone."[23]

Dennis Flynn has pointed out that a measure of Farrell's fluctuating opinion about Joyce is his "repeated comparison of Joyce and Proust. Early in his career, he favored Joyce's 'rigorousness, restraint, and stern dignity' as opposed to Proust's 'narrowness of range' and 'repetitive succession of agonies of heart.' Later he wrote that, though Joyce was a great genius, his work no longer seemed as stimulating. He came to reconsider his earlier estimate: 'Among writers of the twentieth century, the one whom I love the most is Marcel Proust.'"[24] Farrell had read Proust's first volume, *Swann's Way*, in Chicago in about 1927, and he went on to read all seven volumes of *In Search of Lost Time* while in Paris in 1931. The many references to Proust in *A Note on Literary Criticism*, Farrell's 1936 defense of literature against propaganda, demonstrate the strong connection between them at this early stage of Farrell's career. Farrell first mentions Proust in his summary dismissal of the extraliterary critique of literature coming from the cultural left, citing the "usual Marxmanship" of Mike Gold, Granville Hicks, and others. Class and politics be damned, is Farrell's message, for a "proletarian writer" (whatever that may mean) will be influenced by all sorts of art, by the fiction of James Joyce, bizarrely condemned by D. S. Mirsky as "inseparably connected with the specifically decadent phase of the bourgeois culture," and "by literature that is unqualifiedly non-proletarian, like Proust's works, or unqualifiedly non-revolutionary, in the political sense, like T. S. Eliot's."[25]

Overall, there are at least four areas of fruitful connection between Proust and Farrell. First is their shared focus on consciousness, especially in their shared sense of the pernicious effects on consciousness of habit. Here Proust's fiction reinforced Farrell's own philosophic roots in American pragmatism, which will also be discussed a bit later in this essay. Second, there is a clarifying similarity between Proust's concept of involuntary memory and the use of daydream and reverie in Farrell's fiction. Third is the primacy of place for both writers as the object of cathexis (the objective locus for concentration of emotional energy) through which the artist realizes his overarching aim of defeating time. Fourth is the way that Proust's narrator serves as a model for Farrell's portrait of the artist.

In *A Note on Literary Criticism*, Farrell emphasizes the centrality of Proust's view of habit in an extended analysis of a passage from Proust's second volume, *Within a Budding Grove*. Farrell cites "a most excitingly exact description of certain impressions of a railroad journey taken by the 'I' of the novels," which is followed by a passage where the narrator stresses the uniqueness of the impressions of the outside world registered by each individual consciousness and the aesthetic (and moral) falseness of generalization. Here Farrell quotes Proust at length:

> We invariably forget that these [qualities that we perceive through the senses] are individual qualities, and, substituting for them in our mind a conventional type at which we arrive by striking a sort of mean amongst the different faces that have taken our fancy, the pleasures we have known, we are left with mere abstract images which are lifeless and dull because they are lacking in precisely that element of novelty, different from anything we have known, that element which is proper to beauty and happiness. And we deliver on life a pessimistic judgment which we suppose to be fair, for we believed that we were taking into account when we formed it happiness and beauty, whereas in fact we left them out and replaced them by syntheses in which there is not a single atom of either.

By extension, Farrell asserts, "so it is with a character in a novel, no matter what class he belongs to. He is not just a copy of all the other members of his class. He is a person with resemblances to all the other members of his class, and with a difference from all the other members of that class." To explain further, Farrell again quotes Proust: "As a rule it is with our being reduced to a minimum that we live, most of our faculties lie dormant because they can rely upon Habit, which knows what there is to be done and has no need of their services." And yet, the railroad journey stimulated the narrator to use more of his faculties because, Proust explains, the sights and sounds presented "a project which would have the further advantage of providing with subject matter the selfish, active, practical, mechanical, indolent, centrifugal tendency which is that of the human mind."[26]

Here Proust supports Farrell's argument in *A Note on Literary Criticism* that politics is irrelevant or worse as motivation or measuring stick for art. I also believe that this is the heart of Farrell's own design for fiction, toward which Proust's masterpiece is a model of belief in the validity for extended artistic rendering of individual consciousness. The result is the O'Neill-O'Flaherty series—*In Search of Lost Time* in Washington Park. Farrell had no illusions, by the way, as to the potential receptiveness of an American literary audience to his emphasis on the interior life. He pointed out in a lecture that "perhaps the greatest literary tradition in modern times is that of France. . . . When the novel developed in France, there was already a very highly developed culture." He cites *La Princess de Cleves* (1678), *Adolphe* (1815), and *Les Liaisons Dangereuses* (1880s) as examples of novels in which "the characters understand a great deal about their own emotions. There is a high level of sophistication, of sophistication in a good sense, and there was an audience that could understand it." In contrast, America has been "a crude and primitive" place ("except in New England"), where "it was impossible for us to have a developed awareness, a developed consciousness of self, such as the French had, because we didn't have stabilized classes, a stabilized culture or even a stabilized language."[27]

The second link between Proust and Farrell is their shared understanding of how the mind can find release from the enslaving ballast of habit. For Proust, liberation comes only in the fresh, unbidden visitations of "involuntary memory," the most famous of which is the first—when a tea-soaked biscuit brings the narrator's entire childhood world vividly into his adult mind.[28] In Farrell's fiction, the unbidden epiphanies of involuntary memory come in experiences of daydream and reverie, and these contribute to his pioneering expansion of the possibilities for literature of the consciousness of so-called ordinary people. In his first two fictional cycles, the *Studs Lonigan* trilogy and the O'Neill-O'Flaherty pentalogy, examples include Studs Lonigan's recurrent dream of perching in a tree with Lucy Scanlan, Mrs. Mary O'Flaherty at her husband's grave, Old Tom O'Flaherty on his deathbed, Jim O'Neill dozing over Shakespeare after having suffered three strokes, and the boy Danny O'Neill drifting aimlessly through Washington Park at all seasons of the year.

The third element, place, is pervasive for both writers. When he first read *Swann's Way* in 1927, Farrell was surely struck by renderings of and attitudes toward important locations that echoed his own experience. One such is the depiction of Proust's narrator's sickly Aunt Léonie, whose "bed lay by the window, she had the street there before her eyes and on it from morning to night, to divert her melancholy, like the Persian princes, would read the daily but immemorial chronicle of Combray, which she would afterward comment upon with [her maid] Françoise." Another is the narrator's remembered perception that the steeple of the Catholic church organized the entire country town of Combray: "It was the steeple of Saint-Hilaire that gave all the occupations, all the hours, all the viewpoints of the town their shape, their crown, their consecration." Reading these passages, Farrell would have seen his own grandmother, Julia Daly, sitting at her window "reading the daily but immemorial chronicle" of Washington Park, and he would have felt the echo of his own childhood neighborhood, in which Corpus Christi and St. Anselm's churches focused everyone's works and days.

Swann's Way ends with the section titled "Place-Names: The Name," and more than half of *Within a Budding Grove* is the section called "Place-Names: The Place." In both books and throughout Proust's entire sequence of seven novels, evocations abound of place as catalyst for remembered experience. As it happens, two more of the earliest and most important also involve church steeples.

Early in the "Combray" section of *Swann* comes the lovely passage in which the narrator confesses: "And even today," if someone answers his question for directions in a strange town by pointing to a steeple, he finds himself "forgetting the walk I had begun or the necessary errand," and "remain[ing] there in front of the steeple for hours, motionless, trying to remember, feeling deep in myself lands recovered from oblivion draining and rebuilding themselves. . . . I am still seeking my path, I am turning a corner . . . but . . . I am doing so in my heart." And at the climax of "Combray," the narrator recalls one of his earliest experiences of the mystery and the power of place. While out walking, "suddenly a roof, a glimmer of sun on a stone, the smell of the road would stop me because of a particular pleasure they gave me, and also because they seemed to be concealing, beyond what I could see, something which they were inviting me to come take and which despite my efforts I could not manage to discover." And then, one day,

> At the bend of a road I suddenly experienced that special pleasure which was unlike any other, when I saw the two steeples of Martinville, shining in the setting sun and appearing to change position with the motion of our carriage and the windings of the road. As I noted the shape of their spires, the shifting of their lines, the sunlight on their surfaces, I felt that I was not reaching the full depth of my impression, that something was behind that motion, that brightness, something which they seemed at once to contain and conceal.

This time he asks the family friend who is driving the carriage for a pencil and paper, and he writes out his impressions of the steeples. The result is the narrator's first attempt to make art, and although the result is clumsy and tentative, he nonetheless recognizes immediately that the act of writing will be his weapon against time.[29]

From the outset of his writing life, place was equally important in Farrell's fiction. "Helen, I Love You," the first story, dated 1930, in his first collection of short fiction opens with "two boys . . . in front of one of the small gray-stone houses in the 5700 block of Indiana Avenue, glaring at each other." And he begins his first novel, *Young Lonigan: A Boyhood in Chicago Streets*, published in 1932, with an abundance of detailed place lore. About to graduate from eighth grade, the young protagonist Studs Lonigan defines himself in terms of "St. Patrick's" church and parochial school at Michigan Avenue and Sixty-first Street, Indiana Avenue where he walked his first girlfriend home, the "corner of Sixtieth" where he broke some basement windows, the Carter Playground where he had his first fight, and the elevated railroad structure at Fifty-ninth Street, the site of his brave acceptance of a challenge to climb a girder. This boy's reverie is followed by the stock-taking daydream of Studs's father, Paddy Lonigan, who recalls his own childhood as the son of a "pauperized greenhorn," with a wider-ranging litany of place names: Blue Island, St. Ignatius church, dances at Hull-house, "back of the yards," Canaryville, "Luke O'Toole's place on Halsted." Place is similarly paramount from the opening pages of the first O'Neill-O'Flaherty novel, *A World I Never Made*, as six-year-old Danny O'Neill stands looking "wistfully out the parlor window. He saw the vacant lot at the corner of Fiftieth and Calumet Avenue with the elevated tracks in the alley behind the lot and the advertising signboards running all around the front of the lot." He notes "an elevated train" going north, and thinks that "he rode on that train when Uncle Al took him to see the White Sox play." And when "an electric" passes, "headed for Fifty-first Street," he looks down "at the moving black roof" and "wished that he was riding in it," instead of having to get ready to go to Sunday Mass.

Indeed, the connectedness of mind and milieu infuses every page of Farrell's fiction. "No ideas but in things," as William Carlos Williams puts it, and Farrell once wrote (in an unpublished essay) that the world of Washington Park "was tremendously and vividly real to me. It was as real to me as I was to myself," and that "Santa Claus and God were real to me as a child—'There's nothing either good or bad but thinking makes it so'—as real, as true as the building off of the alley between Calumet Avenue and Grand Boulevard and set back from a gravelly, rectangular-shaped little school yard: the building was Corpus Christi School." Here, Farrell continues, "I played, and grew, and dreamed."

Thoughts such as these do not appear as often in Farrell's art as in Proust's because of the radically different narrative positions of each novelist. Proust's aim is recovery of the past from the doubled, reflexive perspective of the consciousness of one highly sophisticated narrator in full adulthood. Farrell's aim is the recovery of the past from the single perspective of the consciousness of a character living a life moment by moment—that is, recovery of the past by imagining it as the present. As Farrell put it in that same unpublished piece, "a novelist, of course, must have knowledge of many details." This is especially true of his fiction, because story, happenings, characters "are all presented from the standpoint of immediate experience."[30] In addition, even when the character is Danny O'Neill, the future artist, the insights day by day are less startling, incisive, lyrical—whatever can be said about Proust—because Danny is not looking back, but registering the moments as he lives them. Furthermore, Danny and his family are not French aristocrats and aesthetes, but working-class and lower-middle-class Irish immigrants and second-generation Americans.

And yet, despite the obvious distances between them, Proust's narrator and Danny O'Neill have much more in common with each other as portraits of the artist than either has, for example, with Stephen Dedalus. Here is the fourth way in which Proust served as a crucial, directing model for Farrell. To be sure, Proust's, Joyce's, and Farrell's large fictional projects all conclude in similar anticlimax. At the end of the seventh volume of *In Search of Lost Time*, of *Ulysses*, and of Farrell's *My Days of Anger,* none of the three protagonists has written anything of consequence. All artistic achievement lies beyond the pages with which these sequences end. This makes practical sense because the novelists would have realized that, after the artist has committed to his vocation, he's not so interesting to the prospective reader. Better grist for fiction's mill is the fits and false starts, the hard slog through the tangle of unmediated experience through which Proust's narrator, Stephen Dedalus, and Danny O'Neill fight their way toward enlightenment. The end of this inward journey marks the outer limit of the portrait in each case. But young Stephen Hero is much farther along the road than either of the other two. He knows, and thus we know, that he's definitely going to get there. In contrast, Proust's narrator is a dismayingly unprecocious seeker, stumbling, vulnerable, and maddeningly tentative in his development. So is Danny O'Neill, and Farrell got from Proust the courage of his conviction to give extended narrative treatment to so slow and painful a pilgrim's progress toward a life in art.

Thus, encouraged in so many ways by the example of Marcel Proust, James T. Farrell began fashioning a body of fiction in which the relentless, deadening force of habit faces off against the fitful, countervailing blessings of daydream and reverie. The great enemy is time, but in these novels, the characters in whose minds this war plays out are fixed in the writer's amber of fully realized place. Much in Walter Benjamin's succinct elucidation of Proust also illuminates Farrell. Benjamin declares that Proust's "true interest is in the passage of time in its most real—that is, space-bound—form." Although "there has never been anyone else with Proust's ability to show us things," he uses experience "not to drink from it, but to dream to its heartbeat," and his bass note is a "hopeless sadness" that springs from acknowledgment of "the incurable imperfection in . . . the present moment." Add to this Benjamin's assertion that "Proust approaches experience without the slightest metaphysical interest, . . . without the slightest tendency to console," and you have much of the truth about Farrell as well.[31]

Farrell's investigation of consciousness in the O'Neill-O'Flaherty novels is especially inclusive and challenging. In addition to the development of the artist's mind, he also sets out to render the inner lives of some half-dozen members of the two families from which Danny O'Neill springs, most of whom have not had the luxury of advanced education and circumstances that allow for or encourage reflection. Even in *My Days of Anger,* which focuses on the young artist's coming of age, Farrell does not abandon Danny's parents, grandmother, brothers, and sisters. All continue to contribute their individual thoughts to the interwoven pattern. It is here that the example of a third writer was crucially reinforcing for Farrell's project, an artist without either the stylistic egotism of Joyce or the focus on characters from the cultured elite of Proust. This was Anton Chekhov, whom Farrell had first read seriously in 1927 while beginning work on his own fiction. Farrell's 1942 essay on Chekhov elucidates the connection between them. He describes Chekhov's characters as "idle dreamers who live sunk in the commonplace; men and women who cannot react to cruelty, who cannot be free, who cannot lift themselves above the terrible plain of stagnation—people in whom human dignity is dissolving." Farrell emphasizes two characteristics of Chekhov's work, both noted by Maxim Gorky, which were central to Farrell's own aims. The first was Gorky's assessment that "banality always found in him a discerning and merciless judge," to which Farrell adds, "Chekhov raised the portrayal of banality to the level of world literature." The second was Gorky's statement of Chekhov's essential message: "You live badly, my friends. It is shameful to live like that." Farrell goes on to indicate the motive behind that portrayal by quoting a Chekhov letter that articulates the faith of the literary realist: "The best of [writers] are realists and paint life as it is, but, through every line's being soaked in the consciousness of an object, you feel, besides life as it is, the life that ought to be, and that captivates you. . . . Man will only become better when you make him see what he is like." Farrell underscores his sense of this passage, which also expresses his own goal for fiction: "great and good writers saturate us with a consciousness of life, and, by achieving this effect, endow us with a sense not only of what life is but also of what it ought to be."[32]

Elsewhere, in a piece on "Nonsense and the Short Story," Farrell cites a number of spurious opinions about the genre, then asks, "Which of these definitions is best suited to the stories of Chekhov?—in my opinion the greatest short-story writer who ever lived. Or which one is most applicable to the stories in Joyce's *Dubliners*? To *Winesburg, Ohio*?" Rejecting the formulaic criterion that a story should create a "*single* or a *unified* impression," he described Chekhov's "A Woman's Kingdom," as "literally, a cross section of many phases of life [in czarist Russia]. One gets from it impressions of class relationships, of characters, of moods. What, then, of the singleness of impression? In fact, Chekhov's stories are an excellent refutation of all these definitions. His stories are, in my opinion, like doors of understanding and awareness opening outward into an entire world."[33]

The idea of grafting Chekhovian concern for inclusion of the mundane on Joycean and Proustian attention to consciousness involved a dramatic change of narrative orientation for Farrell. He recalled later that his first stories came easily—too easily, and when he had first tried to write an autobiographical novel about "my boyhood and high school days" in April 1927, he had failed utterly: "I went back to my short-pants days, and attempted to create a character who had been much like myself, and who would reveal himself, and tell a story of others around him and of himself; this would be done in a stream-of-consciousness flow. In a Standard Oil filling station at Thirty-fifth and Morgan, the last of the stations in which I worked, I stood at the desk and wrote in pencil. It was a sunny afternoon in April and I thought that I had found a way of writing, one that I could do easily, rolling it off, in a swift succession of pages. But it was not that easy; it wasn't that way. I came to a dead halt."[34] Two years later, shortly after conceiving the character of Studs Lonigan, he recognized the major flaw in his early fiction to be lack of objectivity: "I analyzed my character as I considered him in his relations to his own world, his own background. I set as my aim that of unfolding the destiny of Studs Lonigan in his own words, his own actions, his own patterns of thought and feeling. I decided that my task was not to state formally what life meant to me, but to try and re-create a sense of what life meant to Studs Lonigan. I worked on with this project, setting up as an ideal the strictest possible objectivity."[35]

The result of Farrell's thinking was the reinvention of his style. Most of the proletarian realists of the 1930s had as one of their aims speaking for people for whom self-expression comes hard. This theme of tragic inarticulateness suggests a stylistic challenge, a problem of narrative voice: how to speak for people who cannot easily speak for themselves. Farrell's solution was to create a third-person-limited point of view that shifts from character to character. The result is a kind of omniscience—but with a difference. It is an omniscience of which one key aim is exclusion of the consciousness of the author. Except, of course, for the selection and organization of incidents, events, and the consciousness on which these register, this is the meaning of Farrell's often quoted goal of writing "so that life may speak for itself." This is Flaubert's "free indirect discourse," but without the irony that signals authorial control and judgment. The medium that Farrell fashioned is an austere style of scrupulous plainness that effectively renders the thoughts and speech of ordinary people. For this prodigiously gifted intellectual, encyclopedically well read and fiercely committed to the life of the mind, the forging of this style was likely a heroic effort of will. Taken in 1929, Farrell's hard decision to displace the central narrative consciousness from the sophisticated, autobiographical self to the limited other resulted in the creation of an urban plain style that is one of his great gifts to American literature. Analogues for this achievement include Mark Twain's decision to let Huck Finn tell his own story, Robert Frost's incorporation of New England idiom and rhythms into lyric poetry, and William Carlos Williams's determination to use East Coast city colloquialism in verse, including the epic.

The Farrell style can be understood in a larger literary context. Farrell has said that "I was decidedly formed and ready before the Thirties started. And I had read and been influenced by many, Ben Hecht, Maxwell Bodenheim, George Moore, James Joyce, Hemingway, Sherwood Anderson, Nietzsche, Red Lewis, etc., and not solely and simply by Teddy Dreiser." Farrell's position as a stylistic innovator with modernist roots in the twenties has been established by Donald Pizer, who credits Farrell's use of epiphany and development of stream-of-consciousness writing and links him particularly with Joyce and Anderson. Pizer identifies Farrell's stream-of-consciousness technique as a form of "indirect discourse," a third-person voice wherein "the narrator is present as reporter, structurer, and summarizer of the character's frame of mind but . . . [in which] he presents this material in the language and grammatical form habitually used by the character." And he sees *Studs Lonigan* as "a novel of the 1920s in Farrell's exploration of the inarticulate felt life of a character by means of indirect discourse."[36] Farrell's technique is notably effective in the many examples of daydream and reverie in his fiction, and his rendering of the dream life of ordinary people is part of his expansion of the literary possibilities of the consciousness of Americans. The climax of this effect in the *Studs Lonigan* trilogy is Studs's fevered death fantasy, a distorted montage of the people who have influenced his life that flickers through his failing consciousness near the end of the trilogy's 1935 final volume, *Judgment Day*. Surreal dream materials are even more prominent in *Gas-House McGinty*, his novel of 1933 set in the bustling "Wagon Call Department" of an express company, an unlikely place, before Farrell, for such literary experimentation. By the inception of the O'Neill-O'Flaherty series, these techniques were fully at his command. The result is several examples over the five novels of a hard-won, minimal eloquence that embodies Farrell's faith in the ability of relatively unreflective and uneducated people to clarify and bless their own lives, even if only in their own minds.

A final overarching influence for Farrell's fiction was the philosophy of pragmatism. In several essays and lectures in the mid-1960s, he asserted that the writings of the pragmatists William James, George Herbert Mead, and, especially, John Dewey had been the most important influence on the development of his own art. He recalls that beginning in 1929, he filled notebook after notebook with quotations and comments based on his first, excited engagement with these philosophers: "When I read book after book of John Dewey in the fall of 1929 and in 1930, I was permanently influenced. . . . John Dewey and Mead had a tremendous influence on me in the writing of *Studs Lonigan*. . . . I was concerned with how to conceive character, and I was concerned with certain general problems, both for themselves and in relationship to the writing. I was just two years a writer by then, and James on habit and John Dewey on habit in *Human Nature and Conduct* influenced me, and Mead and Dewey and the social conception of self and the personality—the social conception of individuality—and Dewey in his approach to a problem in terms of the situation rather than in an individualized way or in an abstracted generalized way."

At that time, Farrell continues, "The whole cast of my thought was really fixed and this has never changed." He recalls how much clicked into place when he read the passage from Dewey that became an epigraph for his first novel, *Young Lonigan: A Boyhood in Chicago Streets*: "While I was working on the book about a character called Studs Lonigan, I came across the following, which I quote from *Human Nature and Conduct*, which crystallized much of my thinking in reference to the book, and thinking of mine in general. 'The poignancy of situations that evoke reflection lies in the fact that we really do not know the meaning of the tendencies that are pressing for action.' And I had begun *Studs Lonigan* from the end—that is, he was going to die as a young man in his young manhood. There was actually a situation that called for reflection, I felt." He explains that Dewey, James, and Mead "saved and short-circuited" him into "a clearer conception of naturalism," a "philosophical" naturalism that differs fundamentally from that of Emile Zola, who "took two very generalized railroad-train conceptions of hered- ity and environment, and counterposed them to each other and said that hered- ity was stronger. That was the generalization of what he thought was science, and he dismissed individual opinions and impressions as lies."[37] Harry Smith has succinctly summarized the crucial distinction that Farrell makes here and at many other places in his critical writing: "Farrell was not the last great exponent of American Naturalism. Rather, he achieved the first great synthesis of realist tradition and the newer subjectivist fiction, bringing psychological exploration to social forces and the facts of ordinary life. Farrell was more concerned with consciousness, attitudes, personality, subjective time, dream and the irrational than was any 'realist' or 'Naturalist.'"[38]

In a 1966 essay, Farrell highlights what was for him Dewey's key idea of growth as a social phenomenon, which became the grounding for Farrell's own passion- ate commitment to fiction that locates character in its deepest social context:

> The pragmatists in philosophy are concerned with process and particularly with growth. The living organism must function in society. A child, for example, has inner impulses and a child has to grow, intellectually as well as physically. Growth springs from those inner impulses. Because the mind is an organ, developed in society—not set apart—knowledge is essentially cooperative in character. How an individual functions is to be tested by consequences, but, in Dewey's view, this is not the same as simple success. The fulfillments of functioning are in "shared experi- ences." He believed that certainties do not exist. Man, in a universe of peril, can reduce uncertainties that threaten him by the cooperative acquisition of knowledge and by cooperative action. In this world void of certainty, categorical imperatives are arbitrary. The only imperative, if there be one, Dewey held, was that of growth.[39]

Robert Butler has explained most usefully how the pragmatists' conceptions of time and habit also guided Farrell's fiction from the start:

> [The pragmatists] developed an idea that is crucial to Farrell's vision, that time is an organic continuum centered in human consciousness. The mind reconstructs a past to stabilize action in the present and it simultaneously imagines a future to serve as a directive for such action. This is what Mead understands as "temporal

perspective" and what James describes as temporal "equilibrium." For current action to be useful in the growth of individuals and the progress of society, it must be harmonized with the other two levels of time. Otherwise, time becomes fragmented and a fundamental loss of control over experience results. . . . Such a fragmentary experience of moments is what the pragmatists referred to as a 'specious' present—an assortment of isolated events which either drift into nothingness or eventually form a chain of repetition. But, as Dewey points out, the self can be whole and effective only if the consciousness which directs action is artfully balanced in all three levels of time.[40]

Here are the psychosocial models for Studs Lonigan and Danny O'Neill, the one caught in centrifugal drift and deadening habit, the other struggling to develop a secular, "temporal perspective" on which to ground a significant life.

Butler further explains that "both Farrell and the pragmatists saw entrenched habit as a serious human problem. Allowing the past to dominate the present rather than inviting the present to "organize" the past for its own needs, habit makes time a rigid circle of necessity, stripping the here and now of novelty and making the future a dreary set of mindless repetitions." As Butler summarizes, "These theories of time helped Farrell to imagine human experience in coherently structured terms and were, therefore, immensely useful in the formal shaping of his fiction. . . . Seen in this light, . . . his fictive world is remarkable not only for its often acknowledged power but also for its little-recognized depth of vision and formal control."[41]

In a 1965 lecture, Farrell paid homage to Mead on aesthetics, and then described how his own thinking went beyond Mead in a more positive, humanistic direction. The result is one of his most moving defenses of the artist's endeavor: "[Mead] treated aesthetics as serial processes leading to an end or a culmination. He made a distinction between the functional and the aesthetic. The functional was what you wanted in order to get on to the next step. . . . But when you pause and contemplate the pleasure and the joy and the satisfaction you will get or gain at the end of this serial process, that is aesthetic experience." And yet, while appreciating Mead's systematic approach, Farrell disagrees, especially for the artist: "I would say that all experience is both aesthetic *and* functional—or should be. . . . It is not for [the artist] to work only for himself; rather it is for him to render multiple experience as best he can—to render it with the hope that he will leave some of it to the memory of mankind, because in the first, in the last and in every analysis the memory of mankind is what sustains us. In it is the source of all belief and of all faith."[42]

I agree with Dennis Flynn, who declares that "I can think of no American novelist who begins to approach Farrell in the degree to which his work is rooted in a philosophical world view. Farrell's roots in the philosophy of pragmatism help account not only for his being realistic and dispassionate about the Catholic Church, but also for the generally experimental and innovative nature of his writing. He was able to put into fiction . . . thoughts and feelings many people have had but which had never been held worthy of inclusion in serious literature."[43] Farrell began with a solid, philosophical basis for both style and subject matter of what he wanted to write. From the outset, he committed to fiction that emphasizes consciousness as active, seeing the mind as in process, buffeted by experience, searching for "Truth" or "truths," often unaware of that distinction, often blocked by habit—the result of laziness among the comfortable or exhaustion among the underprivileged. In my view, this is most important in the O'Neill-O'Flaherty series, where the novelist's challenge is rendering the variously damaging or fruitful applications of consciousness to the placement of the self in time by a large number of characters. This philosophical justification also explains the conviction and energy with which Farrell attempted so detailed a scrutiny of the interior lives of his characters. In this deep and thoughtful context, no mind is more or less "ordinary" than any other. Novelist Thomas F. Curley put it well when he praised Farrell's "steady attempt to make art of an experience that is at once common and significant."[44]

Neighborhood, Catholicism, Childhood

Farrell's fiction is also important to American literature from the 1930s onward in its delivery of fresh and corrective perspectives in three thematic areas: city life as actually lived, the religion of ethnic Americans as actually practiced, and the nature of experience as perceived by children. Farrell recalled that the first profound catalyst for his decision to become a writer was Sherwood Anderson—in particular, *Tar; A Midwestern Childhood*, which he read early in 1927. His excited reaction mirrors that of many subsequent writers to his own work: "If the inner life of a boy in an Ohio country town of the nineteenth century was meaningful enough to be the material for a book like *Tar;* then perhaps my own feelings and emotions and the feelings and emotions of those with whom I had grown up were important. . . . I thought of writing a novel about my own boyhood, about the neighborhood in which I had grown up. Here was one of the seeds that led to *Studs Lonigan*." He goes on to explain that "the neighborhoods of Chicago in which I grew up possessed something of the character of a small town. They were little worlds of their own. Many of the people living in them knew one another. There was a certain amount of gossip of the character that one finds in small towns. One of the largest nationality and religious groups in these neighborhoods was Irish American and Catholic. I attended a parochial school. Through the school and Sunday mass, the life of these neighborhoods was rendered somewhat more cohesive. My grandmother was always a neighborhood character, well known. I became known, too, the way a boy would be in a small town."[45]

Before Farrell wrote, few American writers had presented city neighborhoods in this way. Finley Peter Dunne's "Mr. Dooley" columns about Chicago and Abraham Cahan's stories of Jewish New York in the 1890s were among the few notable exceptions. Farrell's perspective, pioneering in its balance as well as in its accurate detail, revises a number of distorted views: Stephen Crane's vision of the city as a threatening, impressionist theater set, Theodore Dreiser's view of the city as an exciting but alien destination for immigrant and rural seekers, and the local-color journalists' (Richard Harding Davis, Brander Mathews, and others) portraits of the city as a tourist stop wherein to find the quaint and picturesque. Unlike these others, the city in Farrell's fiction is a real place where daily life is presented with fullness and fairness. Crucial to that presentation is the creation of urban neighborhoods that are as richly realized as any in fiction. Farrell knew instinctively what Eudora Welty has put so memorably: "The truth is, fiction depends for its life on place. Location is the crossroads of circumstance, the proving ground of 'What happened? Who's here? Who's coming?'—and that is the heart's field."[46]

The O'Neill-O'Flaherty novels show us what it looked, sounded, smelled, tasted, and felt like to live in South Side Chicago neighborhoods, what areas such as Washington Park provided and lacked for working- and middle-class urban Americans, and how these places changed over time, specifically from the 1890s through the 1920s. Like many immigrant couples, Tom and Mary O'Flaherty begin their Chicago life in one of the city's oldest places, Blue Island Avenue, where many generations of settlers have already come and gone. In their story of internal migration to better neighborhoods, the O'Flahertys exemplify the process by which many marginally middle-class, ethnic families got ahead—young adults lived at home until they married and contributed their earnings to the family. Thus, by the time Old Tom retires from his teamster's job, his children Al, Ned, Margaret, and Louise earn enough to allow the family to move from a crowded flat on Twelfth Street to larger apartments further south. The culminating change of location in the O'Neill-O'Flaherty series puts the family in a spacious apartment overlooking Washington Park. Similarly, Farrell documents Jim and Lizz O'Neill's laborious movement toward a better life for their large family in terms of their three homes over the course of the five novels: a cold-water tenement flat, a ramshackle cottage with outhouse behind, and, finally, a comfortable apartment with indoor plumbing, gas, and electricity. The map accompanying this introduction demonstrates the congruence between these places and the homes of Farrell's parents, James Francis and Mary Daly Farrell, and maternal grandparents, John and Julia Brown Daly.[47]

The depth of neighborhood place lore in the O'Neill-O'Flaherty novels is partly because they were very much a family affair. On February 2, 1934, begins the remarkable group of letters in which, like Joyce writing back to his relatives in Dublin, Farrell asks his brothers and sisters for help. The first is to his sister Mary: "I've started the family saga, and maybe you could help me, by, without making it apparent that you're doing it, picking up whatever you can about LaSalle Street, and Mrs. Butcher, Mrs. Meyers, etc. I'd appreciate anything you can send me, and as you can get it, and so on." These letters go back and forth for the entire writing life of the series, and include questions and answers about street addresses and neighborhood characters, racing forms and "linguistic habits," and the mechanics of various jobs. "No details will be negligible, I'm sure," Farrell writes early on, "so don't hesitate any time you feel so inclined to write more."[48] It is possible that Farrell's powerful evocation of the few square blocks that make up a city neighborhood is a vestigial link with his family's Irish heritage. After all, the literature of Ireland is remarkable in this same way, and its origins are in the ancient Irish poetic tradition of *dindshenchas,* which means a poetry explanatory of place and place lore. Whatever its roots, the South Side Chicago world that emerges in Farrell's fiction is as complete and coherent as Proust's Combray, Joyce's Dublin, and Faulkner's Yoknapatawpha County.

Farrell's rendering of Catholicism is another of his pioneering contributions to American fiction. For his Irish characters, a second familiar charted boundary, at least as vital and defining as the neighborhood, is the immigrant/ethnic Catholic parish, which provided both continuity with Ireland and help toward adjustment in America, as well as religion's traditional gifts of meaning and solace. In nineteenth-century urban America, the Irish found more negative echoes of the old country than one might have assumed. Here again, they were renters—apartment dwellers to be sure, but renters nonetheless. Here again, they were living in the worst available housing—flimsy, fire-prone, overcrowded, disease-ridden tenements. (Mr. Dooley tells us that "th' Hogan flats on Halsted Sthreet" was "wan iv thim big, fine-lookin' buildings that pious men built out iv celluloid an' plasther iv Paris.") Here again, they were at the bottom of the economic ladder in terms of remuneration for labor, with destitution and beggary looming just below the surface of daily life. Here again, as Catholics, they faced prejudice and discrimination from a Protestant governing class—with the difference being that this time the Protestants were in the majority, constituting a true demographic establishment. And here again, their religion provided both spiritual comfort and social adhesive. However, in the New World, there were formidable counterweights to second-class citizenship. The Irish in America were able to practice their religion freely, they could earn wages that increased over time, and they had the opportunity to rise in the world. As a result, they soon had the economic wherewithal—albeit often by accretion of nickels and dimes—to progress from frame and basement churches to that wonder of the late-nineteenth-century American religious world, the urban Catholic parish—a strong and vibrant complex of church, school, public meeting hall, rectory, and convent, with significant outlying institutions—Catholic hospitals, orphanages, and social settlement facilities.

Farrell's Washington Park novels describe this sophisticated cultural milieu in full swing, and they also illustrate the various attitudes toward the Church among three generations of Irish Americans. Like no other American writing when he was starting out, Farrell's fiction is bursting with descriptions of what went on in Catholic schoolrooms and schoolyards, at populous Sunday masses and quotidian visits to the peaceful, empty church, at the administration of the sacraments of penance and extreme unction, and at all sizes and manners of wakes. Notable in this vivid rendering is Farrell's balanced presentation of opposing aspects of American Catholic culture. True to his realist aesthetic, these contrasts are also a significant part of the dialectical opposition in the two fictional cycles. In the *Studs Lonigan* trilogy, St. Patrick's church and its pompous and hypocritical pastor, Father Gilhooley, fail everyone. Despite his flirtations with street life, Studs remains a conventional Catholic, never questioning the teachings of the Church, and reacting typically right up to his last illness. Although he tries to save his sinking life by joining parish groups and making countless acts of contrition, nothing avails. As a child, Danny O'Neill is terrorized by the fear of everlasting perdition instilled by the nuns at Crucifixion School, and yet, Catholic education also provides him with models of spiritual, educated, and ideologically dedicated men and women who eventually inspire the boy to translate his imaginative life into words. In addition, the Church exposes Danny to positive attributes unavailable elsewhere on the South Side of Chicago: a sense of order and ritual, historical continuity, and mystery. Although far from being the only writer in the thirties raised as a Catholic, Farrell was unique in the fullness of his exploration of Catholicism as a shaping institutional force in American life, from the graduation ceremony at St. Patrick's grammar school at the beginning of *Young Lonigan* to Danny's grandmother Mary O'Flaherty's black rosary beads at the end of her life in *My Days of Anger*. In the next decade, many would follow his lead, but it is important to understand just how innovative Farrell's fiction was in this regard. He brought Catholicism into the mainstream of American literature.[49]

The consciousness observing Washington Park and its Catholic parishes in Farrell's novels is often that of a child, for whom perceptions of urban life are fresh and formative. Here Farrell is also innovative. In his critique of the sorry state of American fiction at the First American Writers' Congress in 1935, he declared that much of "the writing about children by adults" was "of the same nature" as Harris's Uncle Remus stories and Lover's Handy Andy stage Irish stereotype: "Booth Tarkington's *Penrod*, for instance, is put into the same kind of mold, and it is a combination of certain conventions necessary for the intercourse between children and certain types of parents, on one hand, and, on the other hand, of a wish fulfillment or an adult fantasy about childhood." With his deep grounding in the works of John Dewey, Farrell saw education as the central issue. He wrote of his first novels that "the story of Studs Lonigan was conceived as the story of the education of a normal American boy in this period. The important institutions in the education of Studs Lonigan were the home and the family, the church, the school, and the playground. These institutions broke down and did not serve their desired function." In their place, "the streets became a potent educative factor in the boy's life."[50] Conversely, the path of Danny O'Neill makes it clear that education broadly defined in the Deweyan sense can have opposite, positive results for a city boy from a background much less stable than Studs's. This is another contribution to the dialectical force field that connects the two series of novels.

The Five Novels

The O'Neill-O'Flaherty series is sweeping and symphonic in structure. *A World I Never Made* is the prelude in which major themes are introduced. *No Star Is Lost* is a dark movement in a shattering, minor key. *Father and Son* consists of contrapuntal variations between the two title figures. *My Days of Anger* contains a large, focused statement of the major theme of the entire series. *The Face of Time* is a lyrical coda recapitulating the opening themes. Two streams of experience mingle in these pages: the outer stream of social life, a chronicle of the works and days of three generations of Chicagoans, and the inner stream of consciousness, the perceptions of that chronicle and of themselves in the minds of several individuals living it. Throughout the series, the same two watershed experiences recur—death and illuminating reverie. Deaths in the family constitute the central events of the outer stream and emphasize the social themes of alienation and failed community in urban America in the 1910s and 1920s. Solitary reveries are the central events of the inner streams of consciousness, and these emphasize the psychological theme of individual isolation. Clarifications of life and honest self-assessment come only in dreams and daydreams, and they are almost never shared. This theme gathers force in the last three volumes of the series, in which major characters die without having spoken their minds to anyone else. Against this choking tide, the young protagonist Danny O'Neill moves toward understanding of the social and psychological tragedies of his family's thwarted lives. His growth toward the resolution to use art as his weapon against these dual tragedies is the binding theme of the whole project. Through the first four books, Danny experiences the start of formal schooling, early adolescence, high school, and college. In the fifth novel, he comes around again to early childhood when home is the whole world. The slow and painful nature of his intellectual journey enforces another continuing motif—how hard we must work for enlightenment in this tough world. Here Farrell's love of the poetry of W. B. Yeats, from "Adam's Curse" to "The Circus Animals' Desertion," stood him in good stead. In the series overall, Farrell achieves a balance between the bump and flow of experience, both inner and outer, and a structural ordering into large thematic blocks and recurrent motifs. The mixture that results comes as close as fiction can to the rag and bone of reality. Most of the characters in these novels are caught in the flow and catch only brief glimpses of larger meanings. The Deweyan "poignancy of situations that evoke reflection" comes only to the reader, who is the one abiding witness to both confusing detail and clarifying pattern. The reader's perspective generates the sole, yet great and governing, irony that Farrell the author allows between his epigraphs and the last page of fictive text. And this whole consort makes for a powerful, compelling, and memorable reading experience.

The O'Neill-O'Flaherty series is autobiographical in obvious ways. Places and times often correlate with James T. Farrell's own facts of life. These include the ages and abodes of Danny O'Neill's grandparents and parents in the years covered in the novels, the number of his siblings and their approximate dates of birth (and death, in one case), and Danny's own formal markers of development: the start of elementary school (1911), graduation from high school (1923), and attendance at the University of Chicago (from 1925). But this is really neither here nor there for the novels. Here, once again, the example of Proust is useful. In the introduction to her translation of *Swann's Way*, Lydia Davis describes Proust's narrative in terms that also apply to Farrell's series: "The book is filled with events and characters closely resembling those of Proust's own life, yet this novel is not autobiography wearing a thin disguise of fiction but, rather, something more complex—fiction created out of real life, based on the experiences and beliefs of its author, and presented in the guise of autobiography."[51]

A World I Never Made takes place over five months, opening in August 1911 when Danny O'Neill is seven years old, and closing at Christmastime. *No Star Is Lost* covers two years, late 1914 (World War I is on in Europe) and 1915, when Danny is ten and eleven. *Father and Son* begins in 1918 with Danny fourteen and in eighth grade, and ends after his high school graduation in June 1923. *My Days of Anger* spans four years, 1924 through 1927, which include Danny's unfulfilling and abortive experiences of higher education at St. Vincent's night law school and the University of Chicago. The novel ends in the summer of 1927 when he is twenty-three. The fifth O'Neill-O'Flaherty book, *The Face of Time*, brings the series full circle, opening in the summer of 1909, when Danny O'Neill is five years old, and ending in December 1910.

In 1947, the World Publishing Company (Cleveland and New York) reprinted the four volumes of the O'Neill-O'Flaherty series that had appeared so far. The occasion prompted Farrell to write short introductions to the novels in which he outlines his aims with clarity and conciseness. He begins the first of these with a crucial distinction. Unlike *Studs Lonigan*, "which is mainly concerned with one central character," in this second series, "there are a number of major protagonists. . . . Each of them exists in his or her own right. Attention shifts from one to another of these characters. With this shift of attention the novel is unfolded in terms of a complicated series of contrasts. This story deals with two branches of one family, the O'Neills and the O'Flahertys. The former is a working class family; the latter is lower middle class. Three generations of this family appear in the work. There are contrasts in age, contrasts which have a class character and which are mirrored in different social attitudes, and, further, contrasts among the individual characters." And yet, Farrell continued, the lines from Housman that provide the first novel's epigraph and title—"I, a stranger and afraid, / In a world I never made"—indicate that "the central aim of this whole series has been that of portraying the emergence of Danny O'Neill." "An anxious little boy who has many fears," Danny "seen here first at the age of seven, is being prepared, educated in the day by day patterns of urban life." Thus, this bildungsroman begins.

In the World reprint introduction, Farrell stresses seven-year-old Danny's anxieties and alienation: "living with his grandmother, he is something of a stranger. . . . He is not in his own home." Furthermore, "it can equally be said that all of the characters here live in a world they never really made. All of them carry in their very consciousness the values of their past, of their *milieu*." Indeed, the "feeling of homelessness" experienced by Danny O'Neill and his two families is "noticeable in our whole modern period." Here, Farrell's deep reading of Dewey, Mead, and the pragmatists comes to bear. This vexed pervasive condition provoked Farrell's consideration of "one of the problems with which I was concerned in this novel. . . . What is the precise content of life of people in environments such as the environments described in this work? What does poverty mean in the intimate daily lives of those who must live in deprivation? Needless to say," he continues, "the novel does not seek to answer such questions in any formal and sociological manner. It seeks to describe, to recreate, to present in terms of immediate characterization." Not that these questions have no ramifications off the page. In the World reprint introduction, thirty-five years and one great international depression after 1911, the year in which *A World I Never Made* has its setting, Farrell declares that the "conditions of life under which the characters of this story live" and remain "strangers and afraid," still persist. Hence, the cultural relevance of the 1947 editions of the O'Neill-O'Flaherty series: "Before a world can be changed, it is necessary to know what the *nature of experience* [italics in text] is like in that world. This novel is one of the efforts I have made to go as deeply as possible into the nature of experience during the period of my own lifetime."[52] In my view, the stunning accomplishment in the O'Neill-O'Flaherty series of Farrell's dual purposes, aesthetic and cultural, justifies the present new editions from the University of Illinois Press. We are another sixty years down the road, and the value of such books is no less urgently evident. As William Carlos Williams so memorably said:

> It is difficult
> to get the news from poems
>   yet men die miserably every day
>   for lack
> of what is found there.

A World I Never Made begins in August 1911 with emphasis on the central characterization of seven-year-old Danny O'Neill as defined by his anxious, conflicted interactions with the other members of the two families between which he feels himself torn. In the first fifty pages Farrell introduces the essential dramatis personae of the entire series. First come the lower-middle-class O'Flahertys. Danny's grandmother, Mary O'Flaherty, is an aging immigrant matriarch. Recently widowed, she is devoted to her grandson but combative and cantankerous toward everyone else. Danny's Aunt Margaret O'Flaherty ("Peg") is twenty-four, a cashier in a Loop hotel, attractive but unstable. Resentful of the demands of her family and unhappy as the mistress of a married businessman whose promise of marriage she distrusts, Peg is drifting toward alcoholism. Danny's Uncle Al O'Flaherty, thirty-eight, is a fairly successful traveling shoe salesman and the main family breadwinner. Poignantly earnest, he reads Emerson and Lord Chesterfield for "self-improvement," and works hard to sustain a positive outlook in the face of the increased responsibilities and expenses of "two deaths in the family this year"—his father, Old Tom O'Flaherty, of stomach cancer, and his twenty-one-year-old sister Louise, of consumption. This is a household reeling from recently inflicted, deep dynastic wounds. In it, to young Danny's great confusion (and sometimes dread), brief periods of calm, often elicited by soothing music on the gramophone, alternate with fights that can escalate into vicious verbal and even physical pummeling, as when Mrs. O'Flaherty excoriates Peg for being an adulterous "chippy," who "goes out with the Devil," and Peg responds by accusing her mother ("you Irish whoremonger!") of nagging Old Tom into his grave.

Danny's "real" family, the impoverished O'Neills, live twenty-five blocks north in a much worse neighborhood. Lizz is an O'Flaherty, the hard-luck sister of Peg and Al. Now in her mid-thirties, she has already borne eight children. Three have died at birth, and the five surviving are Bill, eleven; Danny, seven; "Little Margaret," five; Dennis, four; and Bob, eighteen months. Small wonder, given what she has already endured, that Lizz is old-country superstitious, fiercely pious, and sometimes hysterical. She is, when the novel opens, suffering the throes of yet another pregnancy approaching term. This new baby will be born healthy and named Catherine. Lizz's husband, Jim O'Neill, is forty years old. An overworked teamster, he is trapped in a physically punishing job, ashamed of how poorly he provides for his family, and apprehensive about the future with another child on the way. It especially bothers him that he has been forced to send his second son away to be raised by his wife's parents, and that the boy is happy with the O'Flahertys: Danny calls his grandmother "Mother." Prone to violence when drinking, Jim is nonetheless a decent, thoughtful man who still loves his wife and kids and hopes against hope for better days. The O'Neills also fight, mostly when Jim's practicality clashes with his wife's escapist otherworldliness. For example, when they come into some money, he urges Lizz to get her teeth fixed, rather than buying "high masses for all your dead relations."

Farrell begins *A World I Never Made* by placing Danny O'Neill in the four milieus from which his character will emerge: at home (chapter 1, in his grandmother O'Flaherty's apartment), at play (chapter 3, at a White Sox game), and at school (in chapter 4, his first day at Corpus Christi school). Chapter 2 introduces the contrasting world from which Danny has been removed, that of his parents, Jim and Lizz O'Neill. Throughout this novel, Danny's mind swings between fear (of the consequences of missing Mass on Sunday morning, of the recent deaths of his grandfather and Aunt Louise, of the violent fights among the adults in his two households, of the strange new world of school) and escape into daydreams of mastery. Constant throughout this novel and those that follow, Danny's reveries also point, however tentatively, toward an artist's vocation. At the beginning of *A World I Never Made*, he sees himself as Buffalo Bill saving his Aunt Louise from the Indians, "Danny Dreamer in the funny papers," and the White Sox catcher, Billy Sullivan, warming up for a big game. Later, he pretends to be a laundryman, a butcher, and an artist selling his drawings. At the end of the novel, the boy has two related imaginative experiences at Christmas of 1911—a daydream of art and a nightmare of death. The first occurs on his way to the Loop with his Aunt Margaret to see Santa Claus: "He saw himself as two Danny O'Neills. One of him was sitting in the elevated train that was going along, swish, zish. The other of him was outside, running, going just as fast as the train was, jumping from roof to roof." Here is the artist's dream of doubleness and control—to step outside the self and walk easily through a recognizable world. The second experience occurs on Christmas Eve, when Danny dreams of hissing snakes and "a boy as big as Mother, with a beard like a dwarf and a black suit like the Devil," come to carry him off and kill him. These two daydreams connect in the fourth volume of the series, *My Days of Anger*, when the use of art to answer the finality of death becomes an article of faith at the start of Danny's life as a writer.

For the second O'Neill-O'Flaherty novel, *No Star Is Lost*, once again Farrell takes both title and epigraph from Housman. Here the second reverses the charge of the first. The title could be mistakenly read as supporting divine intentionality—until the epigraph provides the bleak context of philosophical naturalism (any man's death does *not* diminish the universe) combined with the irremediable human stain:

> Stars, I have seen them fall,
>   But when they drop and die
> No star is lost at all
>   From all the star-sown sky,
> The toil of all that be
>   Helps not the primal fault;
> It rains into the sea
>   And still the sea is salt.

In his introduction to the World reprint edition, Farrell indicates that "the note of Christmas quiet" at the end of *A World I Never Made* "carried, also, a note of foreboding," for "nothing truly tragic had happened to any of the characters." In this new novel, "the treatment of poverty" represented by the O'Neill family "is extended, further developed. The tragic consequences of poverty on the lives of the children are shown in what happens to the child, Little Arty, at the end of this novel." Overall, *No Star Is Lost* "deals more with the life of the children than did its predecessor. This is especially the case with the treatment of the boy, Danny O'Neill. Here we see Danny living more completely in the public world of a boy as well as in the private world of the home, the family." The clash and contrast thus evidenced, "creat[es] in Danny a tension and bewilderment which, I trust, suggests what will be the character of the problems and the resolution of these problems that he will face in the future, when he is seen at an older age."[53]

No Star Is Lost is a lacerating novel to read, especially in its advancement of two of Farrell's strongest themes with harrowing verisimilitude: the rendering of alcoholism and the use of children as witnesses to disaster. In its tracing of the O'Neill family's painful and failing struggle toward a decent life, the book focuses Farrell's central theme of social injustice. In 1914 and 1915, the O'Neills are living in a small, cramped cottage at Forty-fifth and Wells, and on cold days the children "take turns sticking their feet in the oven." Jim O'Neill is working a backbreaking six-day week as a poorly paid teamster for Continental Express. Again, Danny is spared the physical discomfort because he continues to live at the O'Flahertys. And yet, he experiences humiliation on the streets and playgrounds, where kids make fun of his grandmother's clay pipe and other Irish ways and his Aunt Margaret's drinking. Because he is more and more interested in baseball, Danny, now ten, is outside a lot, but he wishes he could move to a new neighborhood to escape the embarrassment of his family's worsening reputation. Farrell establishes the child's perspective by presenting the first seventy-five pages from Danny's point of view, the longest such stretch in the series. His dreams of guilt and dominance continue. In one, black and white angels vie for the boy's soul and he hears the latter ordered to "Go back and be a guardian angel to the White Sox." In another, he is grown up, "a man so big he could almost touch the ceiling," walking fearlessly through the neighborhood, past the convent of the Little Sisters of the Good Shepherd on Prairie Avenue and the Willard Theater on Fifty-first and Calumet.

Jilted by her married lover and frightened by the erosion of her good looks, Peg O'Flaherty goes on a terrifying, extended self-destructive binge of several weeks that nearly tears her family apart. All through this period, she and her mother engage in verbal and sometimes physical battles of epic ferocity, many of them observed by Danny. Night after night, Peg reels home comatose, incontinent, and hounded with delirium tremens so horrifying that she attempts suicide by turning on the gas. Her Hieronymus Bosch hallucinations feature snakes and devils, waiters pouring gin from bottles shaped like phalluses, hideous animals, mud, slime, and excrement. These nightmare visions stand in stark contrast to Danny's recurrent creative daydreaming.

There is a third type of vision here as well. An effective technique of Farrell's for revealing his characters, so many of whom have trouble expressing their deepest affections and motives aloud, is a kind of daydream-soliloquy, the first of which appears in *No Star Is Lost* when Mary O'Flaherty goes out to Calvary Cemetery and has a fine long chat with her husband Tom, who has been dead for five years. Recalling Ireland, the Mullingar Fair where they met, their first hard years in America, and the death of their first son, Mary realizes that this grave site is "the only plot of ground that they had ever owned in America." Suddenly, Tom O'Flaherty is standing there beside her, "a small old man in a white nightgown, with a slightly drooping gray mustache." Not fazed in the least, Mary reverts to her everyday self by administering a typical scolding to poor Tom, for whom even the grave is no protection. Having been annoyed several times by Lizz O'Neill's reports that her dead father has been speaking to her, Mary tells her husband to stop visiting Lizz: "If you have messages, you give them to me. It's me that should get them, and not her. . . . I'm a hard woman when I'm crossed, Tom, a hard woman, and I'll make you toe the mark, dead or alive."

The death of the youngest O'Neill child, two-year-old Arty, of diphtheria in 1915 is the climactic event of *No Star Is Lost.* All the O'Neill children come down with the disease, and Lizz is about to deliver another child as well. With his brothers and sisters falling down around him, Arty dies unattended by either the doctor or the priest. Neither will risk contagion by entering the O'Neill cottage. As the delirious Lizz attempts to feed her own mother's milk to Arty, it is five-year-old Bob who realizes that his brother is dead. "There's only one crime in this world, Lizz," says the heartsick Jim: "to be a poor man." Returning on a streetcar from his son's burial in Calvary Cemetery, Jim sees middle-class homes and says to himself: "In these homes the kids were happy and well-fed and had the care of a doctor when they were sick. And in these homes, the kids were alive." That same day, the rest of the O'Neill children are packed off to a public hospital in the police wagon and Lizz bears a stillborn son. This is not melodrama, but one of the places in the O'Neill-O'Flaherty series where Farrell's own family life matches that of his characters most closely. His baby brother Frankie had died of diphtheria, similarly unattended, in the Farrell cottage at Forty-fifth and Wells on June 21, 1918. That same afternoon, Mary Daly Farrell was delivered of a stillborn son. She was to have in all fifteen pregnancies, including eight stillbirths. So much, in this far from uncommon situation, for the "wages of whiteness," the heavily theorized and poorly evidenced idea that great numbers of Irish ethnics opted for the benefits of an improved quality of life by "becoming white" at the expense of people of color.

No Star Is Lost ends with a detailed example of neighborhood placement that is also a reminder that Danny O'Neill has been spared all this suffering. The boy gets his wish of a fresh start as the O'Flahertys move further south to a new apartment at Fifty-seventh and Indiana. This also means that Danny will attend a new school, St. Patrick's, at Sixty-first and Michigan. On his first day in the new neighborhood, he meets two older kids—Johnny O'Brien and Studs Lonigan.

Father and Son, the third novel, has a span of six years, the longest in the series. The two families have moved again, but most characters continue in established patterns. The marriage of Jim and Lizz O'Neill bumps along with fights, reconciliations, thwarted resolutions for change, and increasing anxieties related to Jim's health. Promoted to night dispatcher at the express company, Jim is able proudly to move his family south to Fifty-eighth and Calumet in Washington Park into an apartment with "a bathroom inside, running hot and cold water, steam heat, gas and electricity." The O'Flahertys have also moved further south—to 5816-1/2 South Park Avenue overlooking the park. Their home life is still a buzzing hive of contentious personalities: Peg drinks to excess, though less often; Al becomes more frustrated with his job and his autodidactic optimism takes on a willed, cast-iron aspect; and their mother continues to stir the pot of controversy. If anything, the tensions in this family are greater now, because second son Ned O'Flaherty has moved back home from Madison after the death of his wife. A preening narcissist and sometime soap-box speaker at the Washington Park "Bug Club," Ned has embraced the cockeyed spirituality of "New Thought," whose main tenet is the "power of the wish." He's no help to anyone.

The great theme of *Father and Son* is the struggle of Jim and Danny O'Neill to understand one another in the context of Jim's downward spiral to unemployment and helplessness because of three crippling strokes and Danny's painful stumbling through high school toward emotional and intellectual maturity. Theirs is the story of George and Gerry O'Dell writ large, and few readers will not recognize and be moved by the fully elaborated drama of this largely failed attempt at communication. In the World reprint introduction, Farrell explains that "the effect of the years of separation from [Danny's] father begin to tell. The misunderstanding between the father and the callow boy deepens. In difficult moments, Jim can only become angry with his son. Danny can only feel guilty towards his father, and, at the same time, sorry for him."

There is epiphany for both father and son, but, in keeping with Farrell's realist aesthetic, it is muted, inconclusive, and far from clearly revealed to the characters themselves. Heartbreakingly, Jim O'Neill in his last illness sees himself as having failed his family. And yet, in this novel he faces progressive debilitation and boredom with courage, dignity, and deepening compassion. Sitting alone by the apartment window, Jim meditates on the mystery of having children, the unreflective profligacy of youth, the solace of Catholicism (and its limits, for he rejects the view that contraception is sinful), the lack of justice in the world. Shakespeare is Jim's companion and consolation, as he often sits up at night reading *Julius Caesar* and *Hamlet*. His insights include a doubleness that, unbeknownst to either, echoes his son's artistic perspective: "Lying alone in bed, as he began coming back to himself, lying there so much alone, he had felt half in this world and half not in it, watching it. Yes, men tried and fought and raised hell and wanted all kinds of things, and yes, yes, *vanity, all is vanity.*" In his finest hour, Jim hears that the doctor who refused to attend his dying child Arty has himself died suddenly, and Jim forgives him his trespass. Farrell's depiction of Jim O'Neill's lonely struggle to understand his life and approaching death is one of the great achievements of modern fiction.

Jim's final weeks are filled with petty indignities. Another of his children is farmed out to the O'Flahertys, and Lizz suggests that he check into a public hospital. He is shamed by having to accept a Christmas basket from a Protestant charity. He has to make an X to get money at the bank, and he loses a five-dollar bill in the street. People on the El think he's drunk, kids mock and mimic his limp, and an apartment-house janitor accuses him of loitering. On Jim's last day, it is once again the children who register the tragic. Twelve-year-old Catherine sees that her father has wet his pants, and it is Bob, a year older, who discovers that his father has died. The social and economic dimension of this novel published in 1940 is also clear. Farrell declares in the World introduction that "the tragedy of the worker is the central social tragedy of our times. Jim's life is but one illustration of this tragedy." Furthermore, "it could well pose for the reader the question—is this a fair and open fight?"

As for Danny, "Now, on the threshold of manhood, he must find a place and a career in that world. He is still afraid, and he remains something of a stranger. But he has, among the other lessons he has learned, the example of his father's life. He gains the conviction that his father never had a chance. His father's death meant something, but he doesn't know exactly what."[54] Farrell describes Danny's abortive diary keeping and other failed writing projects, his clumsy attempts at male and female friendships, the superficial compensation of success in high school athletics, the persistent angst of his situation vis-à-vis his two families. And yet, despite the blunders and embarrassments of what Yeats called "the ig-nominy of boyhood; the distress / Of boyhood changing into man," *Father and Son* also contains an artistic breakthrough for Danny O'Neill. With a family fight raging around him, he is able to finish a story that he knows is good enough for the St. Stanislaus literary magazine. Here, life and art intersect again, because this turns out to be the same story, a romantic tale of a priest's martyrdom in Elizabethan Ireland, that Farrell wrote in 1922 for his high school magazine, the St. Cyril *Oriflamme*. In one sense, appropriating here his own adolescent version of sentimental Catholic fiction is Farrell's way of saying that, as a mature writer, he will not contribute to this genre of literature as propaganda. But in another sense, the story documents the milieu of the Catholic high school in the 1920s as an environment somewhat encouraging to the imagination.

Here again, Farrell's epigraphs speak volumes. For Jim O'Neill, he quotes Tolstoy: "Ivan Ilych's life had been most simple and most ordinary and therefore most terrible." For Danny, there is the Baudelaire of *Les Fleurs du Mal*: "—Ah! Seigneur! Donnez moi la force et le courage / De contempler mon coeur et mon corps sans dégoût!" And for himself, Farrell provides a credo of Bertrand Russell, who counters man's brief, powerless, suffering condition with an admonition "to cherish, ere yet the blow falls, the lofty thoughts that ennoble his little day; disdaining the coward terrors of the slave of Fate, to worship at the shrine that his own hands have built; undismayed by the empire of chance, to preserve a mind free from the wanton tyranny that rules his outward life."

As Farrell points out in his World introduction, *My Days of Anger* "differs in method of presentation from its three predecessors. . . . Here, the story is told with auctorial concentration on one central character, Danny O'Neill." Far-rell will do this by limiting twenty-eight of the twenty-nine arabic-numbered chapters of the book to the consciousness of this protagonist. The thoughts of everyone else are relegated to brief, italicized interchapters. His aim is "to pres-ent the way in which the disposition of an American artist is forged." This word naturally echoes Joyce's *Portrait of the Artist*, where Stephen Dedalus sets out for Paris "to forge the uncreated conscience of my race." Because of the challenges of his background and upbringing, Farrell explains, Danny's "disposition as an artist is forged in bewilderment and anxiety, in confusion and insecurity." However, along his difficult way, he makes "small decisions and resolutions [that] suggest a tension within him, a tension which is symptomatic of his need for change, for escape from the circumstances of his life." And when he prepares to leave for New York at the novel's end, "his mood is one of determination. He asks no quarter. He looks forward to struggle. In this sense, *My Days of Anger* is an optimistic book." Further, Danny "rejects the values of his past, but he does not completely destroy his sense of identification with his own people. He feels that he is going forth to fight not only war but their war. His conception of art, of writing, is a militant one." Again, as a realist, Farrell knows that anger is a limited and, ultimately, a distorting tool for the artist, and so this novel will end with Danny not quite launched into the concerted action of a life committed to writing. The novel's first epigraph, from Baudelaire's *Intimate Journals*, makes this proviso clear: "Nevertheless, I will let these pages stand—since I wish to record my days of anger."

In the World introduction, Farrell refutes the idea that his book is in any way a pastiche of Joyce by pointing out that his aspiring artist/protagonist "emerges from a background which is common rather than special; it is the background known to millions of Americans. Here, in short, I feel, is a detailed story of the American Way of Life."[55] At the same time, that *My Days of Anger* is Farrell's "common," "American" *Portrait* is clear from its second epigraph, an homage that takes the form of a poetic fragment by Joyce:

> Ah star of evil! star of pain!
> Highhearted youth comes not again
>
> Nor old heart's wisdom yet to know
> The signs that mock me as I go.

The poem is dated "*Bahnhofstrasse*, Zurich, 1918," when Joyce was thirty-six. Farrell had turned thirty-nine in February 1943, the year he completed and published *My Days of Anger*.

This novel's great emphasis on Danny is the capstone of Farrell's pioneering presentation of the growth of an American artist from working-class, urban, ethnic, and Catholic backgrounds. Again, scrupulous detail is all. In the outside world, Farrell continues to describe Danny's home life among the O'Flahertys and O'Neills, who appear in the counterpointing interchapters as stuck in familiar troubles. Peg steals at work, is fired, and gets drunk for a week. Al's shoe company fails and he has to go back out on the road in a lesser position. The aging Mary O'Flaherty becomes ill. Danny's brothers and sisters are growing up aware of their social and economic limits and restless for change. When *My*

Days of Anger opens, Danny is a year out of high school and still working at the Continental Express Company. He goes on to a South Side gas station, where he has more time to read and also learns about American capitalism firsthand. Farrell also breaks new ground for American fictional milieus by detailing Danny's "pre-legal" night-school classes at "St. Vincent's" in the Loop, and then taking us into his economics, history, and writing classes at the University of Chicago and the lunchroom dialectic among his fellow students. Emotionally, although he is now out of high school, Danny still suffers the tortures of the damned in his relationships with the opposite sex. He cannot find a steady girlfriend, he loses his virginity in a casual encounter on his twenty-first birthday in February 1925, and he picks up the habit of going to whorehouses with friends from the neighborhood. Intellectually, Danny's continuing fascination with words evolves at last into his first honest "Thought Diary" entries, and then into a torrent of fiction produced for his creative-writing teacher at the university, Professor Saxon. He loses his faith, at first in a dream, and wakes up a nonbeliever, "free of lies." (Studs Lonigan brings the news of Danny's atheism to the pool hall, diagnosing the cause as "too many books.") Other liberating rejections follow: of his pseudo-Nietzschean friend Ed Lanson, of the University of Chicago, and of Chicago as a place to live. At the same time, Danny's days of anger and confusion slowly give way to understanding of and sympathy for his family, friends, and other exploited Chicagoans, especially African Americans. In this process, the crucial experience is his grandmother's death in the spring of 1927.

A classic immigrant matriarch who has held her family together by sheer force of often vituperative will, Mary O'Flaherty, a self-described "hard woman from a hard country," has never been able to express love or compassion for her family—with the single exception of her grandson. As she nears death at eighty-six, a last extended daydream-soliloquy—the only full chapter in this novel from inside a mind other than Danny O'Neill's—provides a summary of her character and concerns. Farrell had been planning Mrs. O'Flaherty's reverie at least since 1938, when he traveled to Ireland for the first time to verify the immigrants' background. Upon completing *My Days of Anger* in 1943, he wrote a friend announcing the conclusion of this phase of his writing life, the "years of driving work, years of eight to fourteen hour days concentrating on these connected books." He was especially proud of the "long chapter, in Anglo-Irish, when Grandmother O'Flaherty sits by the window in a wheel chair, hip broken, slowly fading out of this life; it is a long reverie, more or less Joycean, in which past and present jumble, time loses significance, she dreams and she awakes." The writing here "is something fresh—the fading consciousness of an old woman, further, an old Irish immigrant woman, illiterate, who came out to America, raised her family here, [has] seen them grow up, and sits doing this while her grandson sits preparing to write, even about her own life."[56] As with

Jim O'Neill's lonely meditations, Farrell here solves the problem of speaking for those for whom self-expression comes hard with a restrained eloquence that is a hallmark of his achievement as a novelist.

When his grandmother dies, Danny finds his rejection of Catholicism tempered by understanding that "the sorrows of death remained, remained in the hearts of the living. . . . He understood now why people did what he could not do, what he could never do—pray." In an earlier conversation with friends at the university, Danny had agreed with Stephen Dedalus's refusing to pray at his dying mother's bedside in *Ulysses:* "What has kindness got to do with conviction? I won't bend my knees." And yet, on the morning of his grandmother's death, Danny kneels down, blesses himself, and pretends to pray with his family. A month later, as he prepares to leave Chicago for New York and a new life as a writer, Danny walks home down Fifty-eighth Street from the El, and feels the weight of the Washington Park neighborhood as "a world in itself . . . a world in which another Danny O'Neill had lived." Realizing that he has "finally taken off a way of life . . . as if it were a worn-out suit of clothes," he now has confidence in the "weapons" of his writer's trade: "now he was leaving and he was fully armed." In this, he echoes Stephen Dedalus leaving Dublin for Paris in 1902 with his own weapons of "silence, exile, and cunning." Danny also has a mature understanding of his position as an artist in relation to his family: "His people had not been fulfilled. He had not understood them all these years. He would do no penance now for these; he would do something surpassing penance. There was a loyalty to the dead, a loyalty beyond penance and regret. He would do battle so that others did not remain unfulfilled as he and his family had been." Rather than ending the novel here, Farrell goes on to create one final contrast between honest and false consciousness in the form of an overheard conversation back at the Continental Express Company, where the bosses who used to ridicule Danny look back with distorting nostalgia at his time with them, declaring that he was "a crackerjack clerk" and "one of the best kids I ever had."

Ten years after finishing *My Days of Anger*, Farrell published the fifth and final O'Neill-O'Flaherty novel. Although not part of his original plan, *The Face of Time* is an appropriate coda for the series. Opening in the summer of 1909, this book brings the design full circle to the final illnesses of Old Tom O'Flaherty and his youngest daughter Louise, the memory of which hangs over the first volume, *A World I Never Made*. Farrell also renders the elder O'Flahertys' memories of Ireland, the journey to America, and their early years in Brooklyn, Green Bay, and Chicago, thus returning his narrative to the beginning of this family's story. The result is one of the finest American fictional treatments of the felt experience of immigration.

For most of this novel, the focus alternates between the minds of the aging Irish immigrant, Old Tom O'Flaherty, and his five-year-old American grandson,

Danny O'Neill. Again, the child is witness to pain and conflict. The family fights among Mary O'Flaherty and her children are well under way, and Danny is also precociously aware that living with his grandparents has wounded his parents, especially his father. In addition, he is the terrified observer of his favorite aunt's worsening health and his beloved grandfather's decline and death. Old Tom lives out a restless retirement, bored or harassed within the family, and dies of a painful stomach cancer. In his characterization, Farrell's theme of thwarted communication of the heart's urgent concerns has a last statement here as well. Only in the unshared daydream-soliloquies of his final illness does Tom reveal his sad secrets: the "greenhorn" humiliations of his first displacements in the New World still disturb the old man; he has never felt at home in America; he is puzzled and embittered by having worked so hard and ended up with so little; and he wishes he could go back to die in Ireland. Tom's closest bond is not with his wife Mary, who tends to ignore him, but with his son-in-law, Jim O'Neill, representative of a new generation of hardworking, ill-rewarded laborers, people for whom the American dream remains unfulfilled. In turning over the insults and injustices to which the working man is prone and the compensating mysteries of marriage and children, these two share the closest moments in this novel.

The Face of Time is most moving in the variations—sometimes harsh, sometimes lyrical—that Farrell plays on the theme of elemental loneliness. In his fiction, immigration is but the prototype and metaphor for what he sees as an inevitable condition of humanity. The other most important voice here is the consciousness of Louise O'Flaherty, dying of consumption at twenty-one and holding terror at bay with dreams of the arrival of "Prince Charming," marriage, and children of her own. It is she who asks the big question, though only to herself: "And was this the end of love, one going, dying, the way her father was dying? Must you, in the end, always be alone?" Farrell's answer pervades this novel's conclusion. On his way to the hospital, Old Tom's voice breaks and he is unable to say good-bye to Danny. During the family's last visit to his bedside, Tom can hear his wife and daughter discussing his imminent death, but he cannot speak to them. When the hospital calls with the news of Tom's passing, Mary O'Flaherty shuts the bedroom door to grieve alone. Standing in front of his grandfather's casket, six-year-old Danny thinks, "There was Father. He couldn't talk. He was Father all right, and he wasn't Father." Underscored by the deaths of Old Tom and Louise, the inability of the O'Neill and O'Flaherty families to articulate the heart's speech of love and compassion brings *The Face of Time* around again to the initial provocations for Danny O'Neill's hard journey through the course of the other four novels of the series out of this stalemate and toward the solution of art.

In Farrell's materialist/pragmatist universe, time is the archenemy of all such solutions, a point underscored by this novel's title and epigraph from Yeats's

"Lamentation of the Old Pensioner." Relegated to "shelter from the rain / Under a broken tree," the speaker in the poem recalls his youthful participation in talk of love, politics, and revolution. Now, "My contemplations are of Time / That has transfigured me." And yet, he continues to affirm the storyteller's power of memory and to defy the changes rung by Time:

> There's not a woman turns her face
> Upon a broken tree,
> And yet the beauties that I loved
> Are in my memory;
> I spit into the face of Time
> That has transfigured me.

This is also the novel in which Farrell provides his most positive rendering of place. Grandfather and grandson walk abroad in their neighborhood world thoroughly at ease. Because they are absolved by age and youth from the crises and challenges faced by the other family members who are in the responsible middle way of their lives, Old Tom and Danny encounter fewer obstacles. Through them, Farrell presents Washington Park as home on a human scale. The two companions take great pleasure in the daily round: feeding the ducks on the pond in Washington Park, talking to the cop on the beat and the clerk at the corner grocery, checking in with a sympathetic priest who knows their story, watching Ty Cobb in town against the White Sox at Comiskey, and "rushing the can" for beer at the saloon. Given the fullness and fairness of his presentation throughout the series, Farrell is entitled to the lyrical backward glance at his native city in *The Face of Time*. In fact, it's part of the novel's overall elegiac tone. But he nonetheless avoids distorting nostalgia by keeping illness and isolation as the grounding bass notes.

Shortly after publishing the last O'Neill-O'Flaherty novel, Farrell wrote an essay, "How *The Face of Time* Was Written," that speaks tellingly of his method, themes, aims, and a crucial influence. He recalls the origin of this unplanned fifth volume on "a raw and sunless September afternoon in 1951" in the Chelsea Hotel in New York, just eight days after he had completed *Yet Other Waters*, the final volume of his Bernard Carr trilogy of novels: "Then suddenly . . . I had an impulse to write a short story which would tell of the death of Old Tom. I sat down and began it in longhand. Immediately, I thought of the old man and his grandson Danny. I began by putting them together on Forty-ninth Street in Chicago." Again, the imagination's catalyst is place. As he worked on, day by day, the conception blossomed into "a long story or novelette," and then into a novel. "When a story or book evolves in this manner," Farrell continues, "I know that I have a clear path from my unconscious. I have always believed that one must trust the unconscious and write out of it."

While completing the first draft in Paris in August 1952, "I thought of Proust, to me the greatest writer of the twentieth century. *Remembrance of Things Past* ended in that deeply tragic death mask scene and in Proust's mystical sense of time and existence in two times at once. I was living in two times at once. I had no mystical sense of time, but I felt, too, the dual sense of time." His working title, "to me very exact," was *A Legacy of Fear*, but to avoid mislabeling ("It could seem like a detective story"), he searched for another and found it in Yeats's poem. Farrell concludes this essay by generalizing from the completion of *The Face of Time* to the central goal that drove his working life: "In that novel I tried to achieve what is my constant and major aim as a writer—to write so that life may speak for itself. And life, speaking for itself, tells us again and again of the transfiguration of time. Joy and sadness, growth and decay, life and death are all part of the transfiguration of time. To look into the Face of Time, and to master its threat to us—this is one of the basic themes and purposes of art and literature."[57]

An appropriate gloss for James T. Farrell's commitment and career is the last poem, "Epilogue," in Robert Lowell's last book, *Day by Day*. What Lowell comes around to after his circus animals have deserted is what Farrell's life of unremitting literary labor represents and accomplishes:

> Yet why not say what happened?
> Pray for the grace of accuracy
> Vermeer gave to the sun's illumination
> stealing like the tide across a map
> to his girl solid with yearning.
> We are poor passing facts,
> warned by that to give
> each figure in the photograph
> his living name.

Notes

1. James T. Farrell, *Chicago Stories*, ed. Charles Fanning (Urbana and Chicago: University of Illinois Press, 1998), 106–15.

2. Letters to Clifton Fadiman, 24 June 1929; Ezra Pound, 14 February 1934; Ernest W. Burgess, 9 January 1937; James Henle, 12 February 1943; James T. Farrell Archives, University of Pennsylvania (hereafter, Farrell Archives).

3. Letter to Jack Kunitz, 7 August 1934, Farrell Archives.

4. "My Beginnings as a Writer," in *Reflections at Fifty and Other Essays* (New York: Vanguard Press, 1954), 157–63.

5. Farrell recalled that he made "the decision to write" on "a March morning in 1927." It was spring, and he was looking for a metaphor "to make new the miraculous unity of life. . . . I know that my sentimentalities were just that, and no more." Unpublished

manuscript, Box 495, Farrell Archives. See also "Beginnings," unpublished manuscript, 1961, Box 494, Farrell Archives.

6. "Beginnings," Box 494, Farrell Archives; "The World Is Today," *Park East* (New York), 8 May 1975.

7. Edgar M. Branch, *James T. Farrell* (New York: Twayne Publishers, 1971), 23. See also Branch's elegant short book, *A Paris Year, Dorothy and James T. Farrell, 1931–1932* (Athens: Ohio University Press, 1998), and Robert K. Landers, *An Honest Writer, the Life and Times of James T. Farrell* (San Francisco: Encounter Books, 2004). Wholly inadequate as criticism, Landers's biography is useful for details of Farrell's life.

8. Murray Kempton, *Part of Our Time: Some Ruins and Monuments of the Thirties* (New York: Simon and Schuster, 1955), 128–29.

9. Letter to James J. Geller, 16 February 1943, Farrell Archives.

10. Michael Denning, *The Cultural Front: The Laboring of American Culture in the Twentieth Century* (New York: Verso, 1997), xvii, xx.

11. Farrell preferred the term "bottom-dog literature," which he borrowed from the title of Edward Dahlberg's novel: "If we use 'proletarian' in the strictly Marxist sense, many of these works cannot be said to deal with the proletariat but rather with the lower middle class, the urban lumpen proletariat, the poor farmer." "Social Themes in American Realism," in *Literature and Morality* (New York: Vanguard Press, 1947), 21. See also Douglas Wixson, *Worker-Writer in America* (Urbana: University of Illinois Press, 1999), passim.

12. "The Short Story" [Speech before the First American Writers' Congress], in *The League of Frightened Philistines and Other Papers* (New York: Vanguard Press, 1945), 136–48.

13. Dempsey J. Travis, *An Autobiography of Black Jazz* (Chicago: Urban Research Institute, 1983), passim.

14. Michel Fabre, *The Unfinished Quest of Richard Wright*, 2nd ed. (Urbana: University of Illinois Press, 1993), 118–19.

15. *A Note on Literary Criticism* (1936; repr., New York: Columbia University Press, 1992).

16. Preface to *The Short Stories of James T. Farrell* (New York: Vanguard Press, 1937), l–li.

17. "James Farrell on James Farrell," *The New Republic*, 28 October 1940, 595–96. Murray Kempton recognized the class divide between Farrell and some, like Wilson, who opposed him: "Farrell once said that a writer's style is his childhood; in middle age, he chose to put on the title page of his *Bernard Carr* a terrible reflection of Anton Chekhov's: 'What writers belonging to the upper class have received from nature for nothing, plebeians acquire at the cost of their youth.' . . . Farrell's world, like Dreiser's, was one whose inhabitants understood the price the artist pays. They looked at the New York literary world and thought it commercial, supercilious, log-rolling, and absolutely alien." *Part of Our Time*, 128–29.

18. Carl Van Doren, "The City Culture," *Nation* 143 (24 October 1936): 483.

19. Carlos Baker, "Another Milestone in the Long Saga of Danny O'Neill," *New York Times Book Review*, 24 October 1943, BR 3; *New York Times*, 4 February 1937, 19; 12 February 1937, 21.

20. Peter Brooks, *Realist Vision* (New Haven and London: Yale University Press, 2005), 71–75.

21. Letters, Ezra Pound to James T. Farrell, 3 February 1932; James T. Farrell to Ezra Pound, 17 February 1932; Farrell Archives.

22. "Joyce's *A Portrait of the Artist as a Young Man*," in *League of Frightened Philistines*, 45–59.

23. "A Note on Ulysses" (1934); letter to Meyer Schapiro, 6 August 1938, both quoted in Dennis Flynn, ed., James T. Farrell, *On Irish Themes* (Philadelphia: University of Pennsylvania Press, 1982), 86, 169. Flynn's book is the invaluable guide to Farrell's engagement with all things Irish.

24. Flynn, introduction to Farrell, *On Irish Themes*, 4.

25. *Note on Literary Criticism*, 78, 83, 88.

26. *Note on Literary Criticism*, 118–23. Another writer who grasped fully and early on the importance of this concept in Proust was Samuel Beckett, whose brilliant little book, *Proust* (New York: New Directions), appeared in 1931. Here is Beckett:
Memory and Habit are attributes of the Time cancer. They control the most simple Proustian episode, and an understanding of their mechanism must precede any particular analysis of their application. . . .

The laws of memory are subject to the more general laws of habit. Habit is a compromise effected between the individual and his environment, or between the individual and his own organic eccentricities, the guarantee of a dull inviolability, the lightning-conductor of his existence. Habit is the ballast that chains the dog to his vomit. (7–8)

27. "The Writer and His Audience," Indiana, Pennsylvania, 12 June 1958, in Donald Phelps, ed., *Hearing Out James T. Farrell, Selected Lectures* (New York: The Smith, 1985), 108–10.

28. Here again, Beckett understood this fully in 1931: "Involuntary memory is explosive, 'an immediate, total and delicious deflagration.' It restores . . . the past object. . . . Because in its flame it has consumed Habit and all its works, and in its brightness revealed what the mock reality of experience never can and never will reveal—the real. But involuntary memory is an unruly magician and will not be importuned. It chooses its own time and place for the performance of its miracle." In all of Proust, Beckett counts "twelve or thirteen" of these miracle moments, "but the first—the famous episode of the madeleine steeped in tea—would justify the assertion that his entire book is a monument to involuntary memory and the epic of its action. The whole of Proust's world comes out of a teacup, and not merely Combray and his childhood. For Combray brings us to the two "ways" and to Swann, and to Swann may be related every element of the Proustian experience and consequently its climax in revelation" (19–23).

29. Marcel Proust, *Swann's Way*, trans. and ed. Lydia Davis (New York: Viking Press, 2003), 53, 68, 182, 184–85.

30. "Beginnings," unpublished manuscript, Box 494, Farrell Archives.

31. Walter Benjamin, *Illuminations* (New York: Knopf, 1969): 203–13.

32. "On the Letters of Anton Chekhov, in *League of Frightened Philistines*, 60–71. Farrell returned to this idea in judging John O'Hara to be a gifted short-story writer but a failure as a novelist, except for *Appointment in Samarra*: "In this novel, O'Hara attained

what Henry James called 'saturation.' I interpret this word to mean that the characters and their environment, including their cultural, social, and moral background, became a world, or a segment of a world, with a past and a present, and an assumable future, and with a play of meanings." "The Eternal Question of John O'Hara," in Jack Alan Robbins, ed., *Literary Essays 1954–1974* (Port Washington, N.Y.: Kennikat Press, 1976), 90–92.

33. "Nonsense and the Short Story," in *League of Frightened Philistines*, 81.

34. Unpublished manuscript, Box 495, Farrell Archives.

35. "How *Studs Lonigan* Was Written," in *League of Frightened Philistines*, 86.

36. Farrell quoted in the introduction to Ralph F. Bogardus and Fred Hobson, eds., *Literature at the Barricades: The American Writer in the 1930s* (Tuscaloosa: University of Alabama Press, 1982), 3–4; Donald Pizer, "James T. Farrell and the 1930s," in *Literature at the Barricades*, 75, 81.

37. Unpublished manuscript, "Memories of John Dewey by James T. Farrell," 5 November 1965, Newberry Library, Gift of Cleo Paturis. Farrell registered the excitement of first absorbing the pragmatists in a June 1930 essay published in *Earth*, a little magazine out of Wheaton, Illinois. The piece, "Half Way from the Cradle," is a concise anatomy of the serial engagement with and rejection of belief systems among adolescents and young adults in Jazz Age America: from athletics, sex, and rote education to the ideals of success, family life, and organized religion (for the less adventurous), and to Bohemianism, "art for art's sake," and engagement with "the twin [philosophical] problems of duality and certainty" (for the more thoughtful). His own resolution, a young man's bold declaration, is straight out of William James, Mead, and Dewey: "Only by eliminating certainties that are not referable to human experience can we be men—human beings—rather than parasites on an extra-experiential source of immutable Being." *Earth* (Wheaton, Illinois) 1, no. 3 (June 1930): 1–3, 14.

38. Harry Smith, "Defictionalizing Farrell," *The Smith* 22: 8.

39. "Topics: The Democratic Faith of John Dewey," *New York Times*, 22 October 1966, 25. See also James T. Farrell, "Reflections on John Dewey," *Thought* (New Delhi, India) 19 (27 May 1967): 14–16.

40. Robert James Butler, "Parks, Parties, and Pragmatism: Time and Setting in James T. Farrell's Major Novels," *Essays in Literature* 10, no. 2 (Fall 1983): 242.

41. Robert James Butler, "Christian and Pragmatic Visions of Time in the Lonigan Trilogy," *Thought* 55, no. 219 (December 1980): 465, 475. Butler points out that Farrell cogently reviewed G. H. Mead's *The Philosophy of the Present* in 1930 while he was working on the Lonigan material. The review demonstrates the importance for the beginning novelist's plan for fiction of the pragmatists' ideas on the consciousness of time as a three-part exercise in integration. Farrell explains that in Mead's thought, "the locus of both consciousness and value is the present, and it is in terms of this present that the past and the future are organized"; "Christian and Pragmatic Visions," 464.

42. "Continuity and Change" (2 July 1965, Austin, Tex.), in Phelps, *Hearing Out James T. Farrell*, 136–37.

43. Dennis Flynn, "James T. Farrell and His Catholics," *America*, 15 September 1975, 111–13.

44. Thomas F. Curley, "Catholic Novels and American Culture," *Commentary* 36 (July

1963): 34–42. Curley's essay remains one of the most insightful analyses of Catholic literary culture in the middle of the twentieth century.

45. "A Note on Sherwood Anderson," in *Reflections at Fifty*, 164–68.

46. Eudora Welty, "Place in Fiction," *South Atlantic Quarterly* 55 (January 1956): 57–72.

47. See also Charles Fanning and Ellen Skerrett, "James T. Farrell and Washington Park: The Novel as Social History," *Chicago History* 8, no. 2 (Summer 1979): 80–91.

48. Letters to Mary Farrell, 2 February 1934; 6 March 1934; 21 March 1935; 12 April 1935; 26 August 1935; 12 July 1937; Farrell Archives.

49. Farrell's example was followed by many Irish American writers of the 1940s, among them Thomas Sugrue, Leo R. Ward, Jack Dunphy, Harry Sylvester, Mary Deasy, Mary Doyle Curran, Betty Smith, Edward McSorley, and J. F. Powers. See Charles Fanning, *The Irish Voice in America, 250 Years of Irish-American Fiction*, 2nd ed. (Lexington: University Press of Kentucky, 2000), 292–312.

In an unpublished manuscript, "The Church in My Fiction," Farrell rejected the term "Catholic novelist" as inappropriate (given his unbelief) and limiting (given his wider aims). He continues: "However, my fiction is saturated with Catholicism. Many of my characters are Catholics. They are from cradle to the grave Catholics, and I bury a number of them in Calvary Cemetery, in Evanston, Illinois. The fundamental point to be made concerning my fiction is that being a Catholic in the world of my expressed imagination is a normal experience that need not be explained and defended. The Church is in their lives. It is part of their lives. Their reactions are those of persons who have lived in relationship with and to the Church. Their thoughts, emotions, actions are wound through the body of belief, ritual and practice of the Catholic Church"; Box 640, Farrell Archives.

50. "The Short Story," in *League of Frightened Philistines*, 137–38; "How *Studs Lonigan* Was Written," in *League of Frightened Philistines*, 87–88.

51. Lydia Davis, introduction to *Swann's Way* by Marcel Proust (New York: Viking Press, 2003), ix. Davis goes on to assert Proust's great theme—"how time will be transcended through art"—in terms that also describe Farrell's artistic faith: "For only in recollection does an experience become fully significant, as we arrange it in a meaningful pattern, and thus the crucial role of our intellect, our imagination, in our perception of the world and our re-creation of it to suit our desires; thus the importance of the role of the artist in transforming reality according to a particular inner vision: the artist escapes the tyranny of time through art"; *Swann's Way*, xi.

Interestingly, the French publisher of *Young Lonigan*, Nouvelle Revue Française, was the second of three houses to reject *Swann's Way*. André Gide was in charge at the time, and he later said this decision was one of the greatest mistakes of his life. With its name changed to Gallimard, the house did publish later editions of Proust. Gallimard has continued to publish Farrell as well.

52. Introduction to *A World I Never Made* (Cleveland and New York: World Publishing, 1947), ix–xii.

53. Introduction to *No Star Is Lost* (Cleveland and New York: World Publishing, 1947), ix–x.

54. Introduction to *Father and Son* (Cleveland and New York: World Publishing, 1947), xi–xii.

55. Introduction to *My Days of Anger* (Cleveland and New York: World Publishing, 1947), xi–xii.

56. Letter to Jim Putnam, 18 February 1943, Farrell Archives.

57. "How *The Face of Time* Was Written," in *Reflections at Fifty*, 35–41.

Selected
Bibliography

Works by James T. Farrell

Novels and Novellas

Studs Lonigan: A Trilogy. New York: Vanguard Press, 1935. Comprised of *Young Lonigan: A Boyhood in Chicago Streets* (New York: Vanguard Press, 1932); *The Young Manhood of Studs Lonigan* (New York: Vanguard Press, 1934); and *Judgment Day* (New York: Vanguard Press, 1935). There have been many reprints since, including in the Library of America in 2004.

Gas-House McGinty. New York: Vanguard Press, 1933; London: United Anglo-American Book Company, 1948; revised edition, New York: Avon, 1950.

Tommy Gallagher's Crusade. New York: Vanguard Press, 1939.

Ellen Rogers. New York: Vanguard Press, 1941; London: Routledge, 1942.

O'NEILL-O'FLAHERTY PENTALOGY

A World I Never Made. New York: Vanguard Press, 1936; London: Constable, 1938.

No Star is Lost. New York: Vanguard Press, 1938; London: Constable, 1939.

Father and Son. New York: Vanguard Press, 1940; [as *A Father and His Son* (London: Routledge, 1943)].

My Days of Anger. New York: Vanguard Press, 1943; London: Routledge, 1945.

The Face of Time. New York: Vanguard Press, 1953; London: Spearman and Calder, 1954.

BERNARD CARR TRILOGY

Bernard Clare. New York: Vanguard Press, 1946 [as *Bernard Clayre* (London: Routledge, 1948); as *Bernard Carr* (New York: New American Library, 1952)].

The Road Between. New York: Vanguard Press, and London: Routledge, 1949.

Yet Other Waters. New York: Vanguard Press, 1952; London: Panther, 1960.

This Man and This Woman. New York: Vanguard Press, 1951.
Boarding House Blues. New York: Paperback Library, 1961; London: Panther, 1962.

UNIVERSE OF TIME SEQUENCE

The Silence of History. New York: Doubleday, 1963; London: W. H. Allen, 1964.
What Time Collects. New York: Doubleday, 1964; London: W. H. Allen, 1965.
When Time Was Born. New York: The Smith-Horizon Press, 1966.
Lonely for the Future. New York: Doubleday, 1966; London: W. H. Allen, 1966.
New Year's Eve/1929. New York: Smith-Horizon Press, 1967.
A Brand New Life. New York: Doubleday, 1968.
Judith. Athens, Ohio: Duane Schneider Press, 1969.
Invisible Swords. New York: Doubleday, 1971.
The Dunne Family. New York: Doubleday, 1976.
The Death of Nora Ryan. New York: Doubleday, 1978.
Sam Holman. Buffalo, N.Y.: Prometheus Books, 1983.

Short Fiction Collections

Calico Shoes and Other Stories. New York: Vanguard Press, 1934 [as *Seventeen and Other Stories* (London: Panther, 1959)].
Guillotine Party and Other Stories. New York: Vanguard Press, 1935.
Can All This Grandeur Perish? and Other Stories. New York: Vanguard Press, 1937.
The Short Stories of James T. Farrell. New York: Vanguard Press, 1937 [as *Fellow Countrymen: Collected Stories* (London: Constable, 1937)]. Reprints the preceding three volumes.
$1,000 a Week and Other Stories. New York: Vanguard Press, 1942.
Fifteen Selected Stories. Avon Modern Short Story Monthly, No. 10. New York: Avon Book, 1943. Reprints stories from several volumes.
To Whom It May Concern and Other Stories. New York: Vanguard Press, 1944.
Twelve Great Stories. Avon Modern Short Story Monthly, No. 21. New York: Avon Book, 1945. Reprints stories from several volumes.
When Boyhood Dreams Come True. New York: Vanguard Press, 1946.
More Fellow Countrymen. London: Routledge, 1946. Reprints stories from several volumes.
The Life Adventurous and Other Stories. New York: Vanguard Press, 1947.
Yesterday's Love and Eleven Other Stories. New York: Avon Book, 1948. Reprints stories from several volumes.
A Misunderstanding. New York: House of Books, 1949. Small-press printing of a single story.
An American Dream Girl. New York: Vanguard Press, 1950.
French Girls Are Vicious and Other Stories. New York: Vanguard Press, 1955; London: Panther, 1958.
An Omnibus of Short Stories. New York: Vanguard Press, 1957. Reprints *$1,000 a Week and Other Stories*, *To Whom It May Concern and Other Stories*, and *The Life Adventurous and Other Stories*.

A Dangerous Woman and Other Stories. New York: New American Library, 1957; London: Panther, 1959.

Saturday Night and Other Stories. London: Panther, 1958. Reprints stories from several volumes.

The Girls at the Sphinx. London: Panther, 1959. Reprints stories from several volumes.

Looking 'Em Over. London: Panther, 1960. Reprints stories from several volumes.

Side Street and Other Stories. New York: Paperback Library, 1961.

Sound of a City. New York: Paperback Library, 1962.

Childhood Is Not Forever and Other Stories. New York: Doubleday, 1969.

Judith and Other Stories. New York: Doubleday, 1973.

Olive and Mary Anne. New York: Stonehill, 1977.

Eight Short Short Stories and Sketches. Ed. Marshall Brooks. Newton, Mass.: Arts End Books, 1981.

Chicago Stories of James T. Farrell. Ed. Charles Fanning. Urbana: University of Illinois Press, 1998.

Literary Criticism and Other Publications

A Note on Literary Criticism. New York: Vanguard Press, 1936; London: Constable, 1937.

The League of Frightened Philistines and Other Papers. New York: Vanguard Press, 1945; London: Routledge, 1947.

The Fate of Writing in America. New York: New Directions, 1946; London: Grey Walls Press, 1947.

Literature and Morality. New York: Vanguard Press, 1947.

[Jonathan Titulescu Fogarty, Esq., pseud.] *The Name Is Fogarty: Private Papers on Public Matters.* New York: Vanguard Press, 1950.

[with Jeannette Covert Nolan and Horace Gregory] *Poet of the People: An Evaluation of James Whitcomb Riley.* Bloomington: Indiana University Press, 1951.

Reflections at Fifty and Other Essays. New York: Vanguard Press, 1954; London: Spearman, 1956.

My Baseball Diary: A Famed Author Recalls the Wonderful World of Baseball, Yesterday and Today. New York: A. S. Barnes, 1957.

It Has Come to Pass. New York: Herzl Press, 1958.

[edited] *Prejudices,* by H. L. Mencken. New York: Knopf, 1958.

[edited] *A Dreiser Reader.* New York: Dell, 1962.

Selected Essays. New York: McGraw-Hill, 1964.

The Collected Poems of James T. Farrell. New York: Fleet, 1965.

Literary Essays 1954–74. Port Washington, N.Y.: Kennikat Press, 1976.

On Irish Themes. Ed. Dennis Flynn. Philadelphia: University of Pennsylvania Press, 1982.

Hearing Out James T. Farrell: Selected Lectures. New York: The Smith, 1985.

Secondary Sources

Our understanding of the writings of James T. Farrell springs from the work of Edgar M. Branch, whose essays, books, and bibliographies have created Farrell criticism and made further work possible. See his *James T. Farrell* (New York: Twayne Publishers, 1971), and *A Bibliography of James T. Farrell's Writings 1921–1957* (Philadelphia: University of Pennsylvania Press, 1959). Branch has published bibliographical supplements as follows: "A Supplement to the Bibliography of James T. Farrell's Writings," *American Book Collector* 11 (Summer 1961): 42–48; "Bibliography of James T. Farrell: A Supplement," *American Book Collector* 17 (May 1967): 9–19; "Bibliography of James T. Farrell: January 1967–August 1970," *American Book Collector* 21 (March–April 1971): 13–18; "Bibliography of James T. Farrell, September 1970–February 1975," *American Book Collector* 26, no 3: 17–22; and "Bibliography of James T. Farrell's Writings: Supplement Five, 1975–1981," *Bulletin of Bibliography* 39, no. 4 (December 1982): 201–6. Branch has also published the beautifully illustrated *Studs Lonigan's Neighborhood and the Making of James T. Farrell* (Newton, Mass.: Arts End Books, 1996), and an elegant short study of *A Paris Year: Dorothy and James T. Farrell, 1931–1932* (Athens: Ohio University Press, 1998).

Corroborating Branch, other critics have placed Farrell firmly in the context of American realism. See Horace Gregory, "James T. Farrell: Beyond the Provinces of Art," *New World Writing: Fifth Mentor Selection* (New York: New American Library, 1954), 52–64; Blanche Gelfant, *The American City Novel* (Norman: University of Oklahoma Press, 1954), 175–227; Charles C. Walcutt, *American Literary Naturalism, A Divided Stream* (Minneapolis: University of Minnesota Press, 1956), 240–57; Charles C. Walcutt, *Seven Novelists in the American Naturalist Tradition* (Minneapolis: University of Minnesota Press, 1974), 245–89; Nelson M. Blake, *Novelists' America, Fiction as History, 1910–1940* (Syracuse, N.Y.: Syracuse University Press, 1969), 195–225; Richard Mitchell, "*Studs Lonigan:* Research in Morality," *Centennial Review* 6 (Spring 1962): 202–14; Barbara Foley, *Telling the Truth: The Theory and Practice of Documentary Fiction* (Ithaca, N.Y.: Cornell University Press, 1986); and Barbara Foley, *Radical Representations: Politics and Form in U.S. Proletarian Fiction, 1929–1941* (Durham, N.C.: Duke University Press, 1993).

William V. Shannon began the consideration of Farrell's ethnic dimension with a section in *The American Irish: A Political and Social Portrait* (New York: Macmillan, 1966), 249–58. On Farrell and Irish America, see also Charles Fanning, *The Irish Voice in America: 250 Years of Irish-American Fiction*, 2nd ed. (Lexington: University Press of Kentucky, 2000), 257–91; Fanning, "Death and Revery in Farrell's O'Neill-O'Flaherty Novels," *MELUS* 13, nos. 1 and 2 (Spring–Summer 1986): 97–114; and Fanning and Ellen Skerrett, "James T. Farrell and Washington Park," *Chicago History* 7 (Summer 1979): 80–91; Ron Ebest, "The Irish Catholic Schooling of James T. Ferrell, 1914–23," *Eire-Ireland* 30, no. 4 (Winter 1996): 18–32; Patricia J. Fanning, "'Maybe They'd Call the Doctor': Illness Behavior in the Novels of James T. Farrell," *New Hibernia Review* I, no. 4 (Winter 1997): 81–92. A breakthrough book for placement of Farrell in the larger context of American ethnicity is Ron Ebest, *Private Histories: The Writings of Irish Americans, 1900–1935* (Notre Dame: University of Notre Dame Press, 2005).

Other useful criticism of many aspects of Farrell's work includes: Jack Salzman and

Dennis Flynn, eds., Special Issue: "Essays on James T. Farrell," *Twentieth Century Literature* 22, no. 1 (February 1976); Leonard Kriegel, "Homage to Mr. Farrell," *Nation* 223 (16 October 1976): 373–75; Celeste Loughman, "'Old Now, and Good to Her': J. T. Farrell's Last Novels," *Eire-Ireland* 20, no. 3 (Fall 1985): 43–55; Shaun O'Connell, "His Kind: James T. Farrell's Last Word on the Irish," *Recorder* 1, no. 1 (Winter 1985): 41–50; Bette Howland, "James T. Farrell's Studs Lonigan," *Literary Review* 27 (Fall 1983): 22–5; Blanche Gelfant, "*Studs Lonigan* and Popular Art," *Raritan* 8 (Spring 1989): 111–20; Donald Pizer, "James T. Farrell and the 1930s," in Ralph F. Bogardus and Fred Hobson, ed., *Literature at the Barricades: The American Writer in the 1930s* (Tuscaloosa: University of Alabama Press, 1982), 69–81; Marcus Klein, *Foreigners: The Making of American Literature 1900–1940* (Chicago: University of Chicago Press, 1981), 206–15; Lewis F. Fried, *Makers of the City* (Amherst: University of Massachusetts Press, 1990), 119–58; Arnold L. Goldsmith, *The Modern American Urban Novel* (Detroit: Wayne State University Press, 1991), 39–58; Charles Fanning, ed., Special Issue: "Irish-American Literature," *MELUS* 18, no. 1 (Spring 1993), which contains essays on "Farrell and Richard Wright" by Robert Butler (pp. 103–11) and "Farrell and Dostoevsky" by Dennis Flynn (pp. 113–25), as well as a recently discovered 1931 essay by Farrell on "The Dance Marathons," edited by Ellen Skerrett (pp. 127–43).

Explorations of Farrell's relevance as a social critic include: Ann Douglas, "Studs Lonigan and the Failure of History in Mass Society: A Study in Claustrophobia," *American Quarterly* 26 (Winter 1977): 487–505; Alan M. Wald, *James T. Farrell: The Revolutionary Socialist Years* (New York: New York University Press, 1978); Alan M. Wald, *The New York Intellectuals* (Chapel Hill: University of North Carolina Press, 1987): 83–5, 249–63; Douglas Wixson, *Worker-Writer in America: Jack Conroy and the Tradition of Midwestern Literary Radicalism, 1898–1990* (Urbana and Chicago: University of Illinois Press, 1994); Daniel Shiffman, "Ethnic Competitors in *Studs Lonigan*," *MELUS* 24, no. 3 (Fall 1999): 67–79; Kathleen Farrell, *Literary Integrity and Political Action: The Public Argument of James T. Farrell* (Boulder, Colo.: Westview Press, 2000); and Lauren Onkey, "James Farrell's *Studs Lonigan* Trilogy and the Anxieties of Race," *Eire-Ireland* 40, nos. 3 and 4 (Fall/Winter 2005): 104–18.

Robert James Butler has established both the philosophical underpinnings and the subtle architectonics of Farrell's fiction in these essays: "Christian and Pragmatic Visions of Time in the Lonigan Trilogy," *Thought* 55 (December 1980): 461–75; "The Christian Roots of Farrell's O'Neill and Carr Novels," *Renascence* 34 (1982): 81–97; "Parks, Parties, and Pragmatism: Time and Setting in James T. Farrell's Major Novels," *Essays in Literature* 10 (Fall 1983): 241–54; and "Scenic Structure in Farrell's *Studs Lonigan*," *Essays in Literature* 14 (Spring 1987): 93–103.

Dennis Flynn was the first to open the rich Farrell Archive at the University of Pennsylvania, a voluminous collection of letters, diaries, and manuscripts that constitutes one of the great personal records available to us of the social and intellectual history of America in the earlier twentieth century. See James T. Farrell, *On Irish Themes* (Philadelphia: University of Pennsylvania Press, 1982), edited by Dennis Flynn. Flynn's work in progress is an edition of Farrell's selected letters and diary notes, which will open up the possibilities of the collection for other scholars to follow. Much remains to be done to elucidate the full range and accomplishment of James T. Farrell as a writer. His work and influence in short fiction needs to be further explored. His last, unfinished sequence, *A Universe of Time*, has only just begun to be considered critically. In his later fiction he often left Chicago and the Irish to continue his explorations of time, death, and the possibilities in modern life for self-knowledge, growth, and creativity. Recent evidence of renewed interest in Farrell studies includes the completion since 1978 of at least twenty-five doctoral dissertations in which Farrell is a major figure.

Farrell's first posthumously published work, *Sam Holman* (Buffalo, N.Y.: Prometheus Books, 1983), is a novel of New York intellectual life in the 1930s, and there are other valuable works in manuscript form that have yet to be made generally available. One story published since Farrell's death is "Cigarette Card Baseball Pictures," in *Crab Orchard Review* 1, no. 2 (Spring/Summer 1996): 3–12. His novel of the 1919 Chicago "Black Sox" scandal, *Dreaming Baseball*, appears in 2007 in the Kent State University Press Writing Sports Series.

❀ ❀ ❀

In Farrell's centennial year of 2004, A new hardbound edition of *Studs Lonigan: A Trilogy* was published by the Library of America. This was followed by several new paperback editions of *Studs*. The publication of the five O'Neill-O'Flaherty novels by the University of Illinois Press guarantees that Farrell's grand design of the eight Washington Park novels will again be accessible to the American audience. Also in 2004, Robert K. Landers's biography of Farrell appeared. *An Honest Writer: The Life and Times of James T. Farrell* (San Francisco: Encounter Books) is useful for its collection and organization of the facts of Farrell's life, especially the early years. It is, however, inadequate as literary criticism. The integrated critical biography that Farrell deserves remains to be written.

From Rand McNally Atlas of Chicago for 1913

1. 4816 S. Indiana, Daly ("O'Flaherty") home, 1906-1910
2. 4953 S. Calumet, Daly ("O'Flaherty") home, 1910-1911
3. 5131 S. Prairie, Daly ("O'Flaherty") home, 1911-1915
4. 5704 S. Indiana, Daly ("O'Flaherty") home, 1915-1916
5. 5816 S. Park, Daly ("O'Flaherty") home, 1917-1928
6. 5939 S. Calumet, Farrell ("O'Neill") home, 1918-1923
7. 4831 S. Vincennes, Richard Wright home, 1929
8. 5730 S. Michigan, "Studs Lonigan" home
9. Corpus Christi ("Crucifixion") church and school, 49th and Grand
10. St. Anselm ("St.Patrick") church and school, 61st and Michigan
11. St. Cyril College ("St. Stanislaus High School"), 6410 S. Dante: one
    block south and five blocks east of this marker
12. University of Chicago

A WORLD
I NEVER MADE

James T. Farrell

To
Hortense Alden

I, a stranger and afraid,
In a world I never made.

— *"Last Poems" by A. E. Housman*

SECTION ONE

1911

1

I

They had all told him that it was a sin to miss mass on Sunday, and God didn't like it if you did, because when you missed mass on Sunday, you hurt God's feelings, and when you hurt God's feelings and He was disappointed in you, you didn't know what He mightn't do to you, almost anything. Yes, you had to watch your step about what you did, when-ever it was something that God didn't want you to do. But then if he should get sick this minute? That ought not to be the same, and God couldn't blame him for not being able to go to mass, because then it wouldn't be his fault. But if God was disappointed! He could send a kid even to Hell, and they had all told him that Hell was an awful place of fire where God sent people who were not good because they sinned. He didn't want to go there for sinning, and be burned and burned. If he just held his little finger in a fire for the littlest, shortest time, it hurt and blistered him so that he wanted to cry. And in Hell you would be in a fire for the longest time. He didn't want that to happen to him, so he had better watch what he was doing and not do anything to hurt God's feelings, or make God lose His temper.

Wearing his striped pyjamas, Danny O'Neill looked wistfully out of the parlor window. He saw the vacant lot at the corner of Fiftieth and Calumet Avenue, with the elevated tracks in the alley behind the lot and the advertising signboards running all around the front of the lot. He had to dress himself right away to go to church and be there on time, so as not to let God be disappointed. The lot across the street now, that was a place to play in! He would like to be in it right now, climbing signboards, where his aunt and grandmother couldn't see him and tell him not to climb, playing he was Buffalo Bill that Uncle Al had told him about, shooting Indians and saving a beautiful white girl, as beautiful as his Aunt Louise who had gone to Heaven only a little while ago, saving her from the savage Indians who wanted to tomahawk her. But, gee, he did have to be getting himself dressed and go to church.

An elevated train rumbled northward, and he watched it go out of sight. He rode on that train when Uncle Al took him to see the White Sox play. But gosh, he did have to get dressed, and he better hurry up about it, too. If there was something wrong with him, he wouldn't have to go to church. Now if he was sick, but not too sick, and just had maybe a cold so he would be kept in the house. Or maybe if he had a headache. He felt his curly head. Now if only he had a headache!

An electric passed, headed for Fifty-first Street, and looking down at the moving black roof, hearing squeaky, chainy sounds, he wished that he was riding in it.

"Son, get ready for church!" his grandmother called to him from the hall.

"Little Brother, dear, you better dress yourself now like a sweet little man. Or do you want your Aunty Margaret to dress you?" his aunt called to him.

"I can dress myself," he called back loudly, turning from the window, wishing that he didn't have to do it.

"Aren't you the big man, though?" his aunt lovingly said, watching him from the parlor entrance, and Danny looked up at her, his handsome, brown-haired, tall Aunty Margaret.

"Aunty Margaret, why do those electric things go?" he asked, thinking that if she started talking to him, and he had to listen while she talked, it might be too late, and then he couldn't go, and it wouldn't be his fault then, would it?

"What things, Brother?"

"The cars that Bill calls jewboxes, electrics?"

"They are run by electricity."

"And are electric lights run by electricity, too?"

"Yes, it causes light, too."

"Aunty Margaret, you know what I'm going to do?"

"What?"

"When I grow up to be a big man, I'm going to work and make lots of money, and I'm going to buy you a jewbox."

"You're such a sweet little darling, and you would do that for your poor aunty, wouldn't you?"

"I'll buy you two jewboxes, and you can go to the store in one, and ride to mass on Sundays in the other one."

"You're so cute. And will you take care of your aunt when she's old?"

"Aunty Margaret, who made electricity?"

"God made it."

"He made everything, didn't He?"

"Yes, Brother."

"Aunty Margaret?" he said, his expression becoming unexpectedly sad.

"What's the matter, Brother?"

"I think maybe I'm sick."

"You poor, dear little thing! Where?"

"I don't know. I just think I might be sick."

"You better go to church, Brother. Your Uncle Al will be mad if you don't."

"I want to go to church. I like to go to church. Aunty Margaret, I love to go to mass on Sunday, and I am going to get dressed right away and go, even if maybe I do think I might have something sick the matter with me."

"Uncle Al will be back soon, and he'll want you dressed and on your way to mass."

"And I'm going to dress myself right away. I am!"

"You're a little man, aren't you, Brother?"

"I am. I want to ask you something."

"What?"

"Aunty Margaret, before I get dressed, have I time to have you read me about Danny Dreamer in the funny papers?"

"Your aunt is busy now. After dinner she'll do it."

"You won't forget or not do it then?"

"No, you sweet little darling, I won't."

"And you'll read me the box scores, too?"

"Yes, you little schemer. But you get dressed now and go to mass," she said, smiling tenderly at him, turning, walking back to the rear of the apartment.

Danny sat down on the piano stool, cupping his chin in his hands. Now why, he wondered, did his Aunty Margaret almost never go to mass on Sunday? And why didn't Uncle Al make her go? And when she didn't, why didn't God never seem to do anything to her and punish her the way they all said that God would punish him if he sinned? There were all kinds of things like that about grown-ups that were a puzzle, all right.

He got off the stool and walked zigzag out of the parlor. He stood by the hall tree opposite the front door. It was a black piece of furniture, taller than his Uncle Al, but not as tall as his Papa, and it had hooks on each side, a round mirror between them, and a seat that opened up and was like a box inside. His baseball gloves were in it. Suddenly, before he had time to think about it and do it on purpose, he banged his forehead against the front door. He bit his lip in order to help himself not cry as a dull pain shot through his head. He walked slowly down the dark hallway, out past the dining room to the kitchen, holding his head where he had bumped it. Whimpering, he watched his grandmother, a small, vigorous, brown-haired woman in her sixties, with a beaklike, almost unwrinkled, face. She sang, washing dishes, unaware of his presence.

"Mudder . . ." he cried, suddenly breaking into sobs.

"What, Grandson?"

"Mudder," he said, and she turned to see him, holding his head, his sobs breaking out more loudly. "Mudder, I hurt myself."

"Oh, the baby! Margaret! Margaret! The baby," the grandmother excitedly called.

"I hit my head . . . I . . . bumped my head into the door, and oo, it hurts. I have an awful headache," he said in tears.

The grandmother quickly drew him to her, stroked his head.

"What's the matter with Brother?" Aunt Margaret asked, rushing to the kitchen.

Pleased by the attention given him, he yelled.

"Oh, the poor child!" Aunt Margaret exclaimed, touched, as he stood nervous, his head buried in his grandmother's gingham apron, his sobs now muffled.

"For the Lord's sake, Margaret, do something! The baby is hurt! Hurry! Hurry! Hurrish! The baby!" the grandmother said with great anxiety.

"All right. Be calm, Mother. I'll put a rag on his head," Aunt Margaret said, taking a towel from the rack over the kitchen sink and soaking it under the running cold-water faucet.

"Hurry, Peg! Hurrish!" the grandmother commanded as the aunt squeezed the wet towel. "The baby's hurt!"

"There! There, now! He's going to be a brave little man, isn't he?" Aunt Margaret said, holding the wet cloth to Danny's forehead, caressing his cheek.

Danny's sobs died. The dull ache was going away.

"Does it hurt now?" Aunt Margaret asked.

"Don't talk! Do something! Can't you see the little fellow is suffering!" the grandmother said. Danny sniffled. "Is it better now, son?" she asked, her tone of voice changing.

"It still hurts. OOH! Maybe I done something to myself," he said innocently, his voice simulating terror, his eyes wide as he looked up at her.

"He better lay down, and not go to church," Aunt Margaret said, bending down to kiss his tear-smeared cheek.

Now he couldn't help it, and God couldn't be disappointed in him if they told him to go to bed and not go to church. Aunt Margaret led him to his unmade cot in Uncle Al's and folded a sheet over him.

"Now, Brother, be quiet and rest. Try to sleep and your headache will go away," she said, kissing him.

Contented, he watched her leave the bedroom.

II

His headache gone, he squirmed and twisted, wanting to be up again. He sat up on the edge of the cot. He drew on his clean pair of white stockings, crumpling the pyjama legs over the knees, wishing he could roll them to look the same way that baseball suits looked on big-league ball players who got their pants and stockings rolled in together. He got out the cap to the blue baseball suit Uncle Al had bought him and put it on, with the peak turned backward. He walked quietly to the hall tree, found his twenty-five-cent catching glove, went into the parlor.

He was Billy Sullivan now, catching warm-up pitches from Big Ed Walsh while the White Sox regulars were out on the field waiting for the game with the Philadelphia Athletics to begin. Going through the motions of catching Walsh's fourth warm-up pitch, he pretended to fling the ball down to Amby McConnell, the second baseman. He took his glove off, stuck it between his closed legs, pretended to don and adjust his catcher's mask. He gave his imaginary chest protector a final tug, squatted, carefully held two fingers under his glove so that the Athletic coaches could not steal his signals. He stood up, with spread legs, and pounded his glove and encouraged Big Ed Walsh to strike out this fish, Danny Murphy, right fielder and lead-off man.

"Hey! Hey! Why aren't you dressed?"

Danny almost trembled at the sound of Uncle Al's voice. He turned and saw his uncle standing at the parlor entrance, a small man with a large, crooked, beaked nose. He seemed to see Uncle Al in a fog. Uncle Al's figure cleared before him, became distinct, a man wearing a single-breasted blue suit, high stiff collar, blue and gray dotted tie. Danny stood, still frightened, his eyes riveted on Uncle Al's clipped brown hair that was parted on the right side.

"Well, what have you got to say?" Uncle Al demanded, and Danny knew that his uncle was kind of sore.

"Mother and Aunty Margaret said I shouldn't go to mass because I bumped my head and got a headache. You can feel the bump on my head, right here," Danny said, touching his head.

"If you have a headache, why are you playing here like this? Fine way to cure a headache!"

"I was trying to do something to make myself forget about my headache."

"You better try and forget it at mass. And come on, hurry up and dress or you'll be late!" Uncle Al said, noticeably impatient.

"I am. It wasn't my fault. I was only doing what I was told, and they told me not to go because I bumped my head against the door and got an awful headache. If you don't believe me, you can feel the bump I got, right here."

"Come on, and hurry up! Dress yourself! You're going to mass!" Uncle Al snapped, his swarthy face flushing with anger.

"All right, but I was only doing what I was told to do."

Uncle Al rushed at him, grabbed his arm, and unceremoniously led him out of the parlor. Danny cried, afraid that his uncle was going to hit him.

"Come on, you, quit stalling! Get ready, and make it damn quick!" Uncle Al barked, dragging him into the bedroom.

Danny shrieked in fear.

"What's the matter, Al?" Margaret anxiously asked, coming to the front of the apartment.

"The damn little pup is lying in order to get out of going to mass," Uncle Al said heatedly.

"He bumped into the door and got a headache, and so we told him not to go. Don't hit him or scare him, Al. It's our doing, because Mother and I told him not to dress and go to church," Aunt Margaret said placatingly.

Sobbing, Danny started to draw off his pyjamas. He tried to stop crying, and he didn't want to be a bawl baby, and he could help himself. His body quivered, shook. Against his will, he let out a wailing, frightened yell.

"Do you want Aunty Margaret to help you dress, Little Brother?"

"He's big enough to dress himself. Let him start developing self-dependence. Come on, you, snap it up, snap into it!" the uncle said, beginning to breathe asthmatically.

"I am. I didn't ask her to ask me that," Danny bawled self-righteously, drawing a wistful smile from his aunt.

"Get ready and never mind the whimpering and beefing! If you continue stalling, I'll change your tactics for you!"

Danny struggled to untangle his B.V.D. underwear. Uncle Al, losing all patience, snatched the underwear out of his hands. Danny cowered as Al fumbled with the clothing, wheezing, his face flushed and contorted.

"You goddamn little fool! Here, learn to do things right!" Al belched at him.

"Al, please!" Margaret pleaded.

Danny took the underwear back. Helplessly unnerved, he couldn't get himself into it. He shook. Tears streamed down his face and his nose now. Putting his foot through the underwear, he received a sudden box on the side of his head. He cried hysterically.

"Come on! Come on!"

"Al, don't hit him. He's only a baby!"

"The goddamn dirty little lying fool! I'll teach him. Here, you little fathead, stick your arm through this!"

"Please, don't hit him, Al!"

"I won't. I'm not hurting him. But he's got to learn sometime. Here, you mutt, stick your legs through this! And quit sniffling. Blow your nose and stop crying like a baby. You're not hurt! Nobody's hurting him."

Danny tried. He continued shaking, his white face wet with tears. Uncle Al pushed and pulled him into his trousers, then handed him his white shirt. Trembling, crying, Danny was finally dressed, and his face wiped. He was pushed out of the door and sent off to mass, clutching the nickel he had been given for the collection box.

III

Now calmed, Al O'Flaherty picked up the front section of the *Record Herald* and, letting his eyes run over one of the headlines, he winced.

BUCK AND MECHANICIAN KILLED:
ELGIN STAND CRASH INJURING 88
NATIONAL AUTO RACE TO LEN ZENGEL

Auto racing was a great sport. But dangerous. Good money in it when you won a big race, but too damn risky. Too many were killed at it. Glad he sold shoes for a living instead of being a speed racer.

He glanced at the square-shaped Singer piano. He'd paid a hundred dollars for it for Louise. Poor Louise, she was resting peacefully in Heaven now. Such a beautiful, virginal girl, too, dying of consumption at twenty-one. And her going like that, only a couple of months after the old fellow had passed away with cancer of the stomach. Two deaths in the family this year! Besides the loss and the sorrow, it had cost a lot of money. And these days money was a worry. Both his father and his sister had passed away without insurance, and the old fellow's illness had been doubly expensive, because they had had to put him in a private room in the Mercy Hospital. Toward the end, he required a day and a night nurse. Plenty of expenses. But even so, he was proud that he, with some help from Peg, had been and still was able to meet these debts. And he would! By the end of the year they would all be cleared, doctors and all, even though it would leave his pocketbook a little bit pinched.

Well, they still had their mother. She would, he prayed to God, live a long while, and be a comfort in the home. And he would be able to care for her decently . . . and for the little fellow, too.

A wave of contrition rolled through him. Yes, yes, he was goddamn sorry for having lost his temper just now. And he had to watch his temper, not let himself go off the handle so easily, and not let himself be using so much profanity, particularly in the home. He hadn't meant to touch the little fellow. Even so, it had only been a little box on the ear that couldn't really have injured him. Only the stunt Danny had been trying to pull off! It was wrong to let him develop habits like that. And the boy's grandmother and Peg were fooled by him too simply and easily. Still, he did kind of wish that he could undo these actions and words of his this morning. Yes, he had to learn to control his temper. One of the greatest aids to a man in pursuing a successful career was self-control. He had to learn to develop more self-control.

And he hadn't meant anything but to discipline the little fellow and to teach him that stunts and lies wouldn't prove efficacious. He was proud, glad that he was able to raise the boy and give him a more refined home life than his father could give him. And the boy would get a good education, too, the college education which he himself had never been able to get.

Al stood in the center of the parlor, holding his Sunday newspaper in one hand, his other hand in his trouser pocket. He could hear his sister and mother talking somewhere in the back of the house. His face grew wistful, entranced. He envisioned the future, the boy Danny O'Neill, tall and straight and well-groomed, well-dressed but with nothing flashy or kike in his sartorial make-up. He would be just through college and entering the legal profession after having passed his bar examinations with an excellent average. Ah, that was what Al O'Flaherty had wanted. And by golly, that was what Al O'Flaherty was going to give to his nephew, Danny O'Neill.

Perhaps, too, Joe O'Reilley would help him get along. Joe had been doing very well now, ever since he had been given those brewery accounts to handle, and Tom Geraghty had been telling him not so long ago that Joe's star was on the rise in politics. He and Joe were, after all, in the same council of the Order of Christopher, and Joe was Jim O'Neill's first cousin. He'd have to try and cultivate Joe whenever he got the opportunity. Ah, he could see Danny as a grown and groomed man of the right sort, polite, a gentleman of the Lord Chesterfieldian order, and smart, too, smart as a whip. As a lawyer, Danny would even make such fellows as Joe O'Reilley look like bush leaguers. The boy, yes, he would get all that Al O'Flaherty had never been able to get, a college education. He and Dan would go together, be like pals. He could see them together at, say, an O. of C. fourth-degree banquet, or going to church on Sunday mornings, people pointing the boy out, saying that there was a smart young fellow who was beginning to amount to something. A deep regret crossed his mind. He wished that Danny was his son, his flesh-and-blood son. But then, in all but flesh and blood Danny was, was his son.

And in twenty years Danny would be launched, and he would have a neat sum of money in safe and sound investments. His face clouded in gloom. His heart! That murmur! But he was taking care of himself, and there was no reason why he shouldn't live a long life. He would. God would spare him. And perhaps twenty years from now he would have his own yacht, and they would all sail around the world on it, see the pyramids, and the Seven Wonders of the World, and the Blarney stone, the department stores in Berlin and Saint Peter's in Rome. Perhaps, too, he would be able to help all the O'Neill kids get a decent education and make something out of themselves in the world. But Jim O'Neill, poor devil, he was sorry for him, for Lizz and their other kids.

If Jim had had an education, he might have amounted to something. Jim did have some gray matter up there in his cranium. He had read Shakespeare even, and sometimes he quoted the Bard of Avon. But no, Jim was aggressive in the wrong way, pugnacious, always antagonizing the other fellow. And he drank, too. Jim would never do the right thing. His habits were . . . common, that was the word. No matter how you told him things, no matter how tactfully you put your suggestions to him, Jim wouldn't take them. Bull-headed! Stubborn as a mule! And a teamster with as big a family as Jim's couldn't afford to be like that. Well, he was at least glad that Danny was rescued from such a home atmosphere. Danny would have none of Jim's crudities and bad temper and his common habits.

He dropped the newspaper on the chair to his right, took a cigar out of his vest, smelled it, cut off the end with a pearl-handled pocket knife and lit it. He puffed in reflective contentment, standing in the center of the parlor, looking into the full-length mirror on the left wall. But still, Jim, poor devil, was a good fellow in many ways. And he had it hard. And now Lizz was having another kid. God, they ought to do something to quit having kids. Jim should not let that go on. Under the circumstances, it was being like beasts to go on like that, having more and more kids. He'd have to speak to Lizz about it the next time she came up. Poor devils! He thought that he better send ten dollars to Lizz. He could spare it, and it would come in handy now, with the new baby coming. And business might be good this fall when he went on the road. He hoped so. But then, he noticed that the New York, New Haven and Hartford Railroad had announced that business was of such a character that the strictest possible economy would have to be practiced and every un-needed man on the payroll would be laid off. That was a bad sign for the fall. He would have to pray and light a few holy candles for the special intention that he would have a good season. He'd have his mother and Lizz pray for that, too.

Even if times were hard, they would not always be that way. If things went down, they picked up again. And he knew that there was something good waiting for him on the distant horizon. He should not be too worried. All men had their cares and their responsibilities, but he was managing to get most of his met. And he was building solidly for the future, building by sane effort and hard work, and by careful investment in bonds with the little money that he could afford to put away.

But Christ, he wished that he hadn't lost his temper with the boy. Only the little fellow had to be trained, and trained right. When he grew older, he would

send him to Culver Military Academy down in Indiana. That was the best training and education a young fellow could get. And when Danny grew up, he would
more than thank his uncle for having trained and disciplined him in the proper
manner. Danny would, damn it, he would, have all the opportunities that he
had wanted himself. For, after all, he had only had a grammar-school education,
and then work, wrapping shoes, rising by himself and by hard work, until now
he was a high-class shoe salesman.

Yes, the future looked to him, and to Danny. God had already given the family its share of misfortunes and crosses for a while, and now they would have
easier sledding. He puffed at his cigar and then squashed it in an ash tray. He
decided to read the paper later, went to his bedroom off the front of the hall and
got out his mouth organ. He stood by his bedroom window, playing old songs,
feeling pretty good, and pretty hopeful. Carried away on his hopes and on soft
sentimental feelings, he stood by the window playing his mouth organ.

IV

Kneeling by the parlor window, Danny dreamily gazed down at the quiet Sunday
street that lay under a warm and muggy August afternoon. Mightn't he not ask
Uncle Al? He had on his Sunday clothes and the darn old white stockings, and
if he did go out, and they got dirty, he would get bawled out. His eyes centered
upon the picture of a sailor on one of the advertisements of the signboard. He
guessed that if he wasn't going to be a big-league baseball player he would be
a sailor and go far away on a ship. He turned, and watched his uncle who was
reading the newspaper in the rocking chair. He wished that Uncle Al would
go to the ball game today. He was afraid to ask him anything. This was one of
Uncle Al's cranky days.

He jumped up from the window. He hadn't known that his big brother, Bill,
was coming today, and there he was crossing the street. He would have Bill to
talk to and play with. He stood waiting, almost shaking with nervousness and joy.
The bell rang. He ran noisily across the parlor. Uncle Al looked up, frowned,
choked off a curse, called Danny back. Danny returned slowly.

"I didn't do nothing. I was just going to answer the door," he said defensively.

"Didn't I tell you enough times already to walk across the floor, and not to
run? Holy sailors! There are people living downstairs, and they don't want you
to be kicking the chandeliers down on them."

"Yes," Danny timidly answered.

"Yes, sir," Uncle Al said commandingly.

"Yes, sir," Danny parroted.

"And now walk across the floor!"

Danny walked across the parlor, but Aunt Margaret was already at the front door.

"Oh, my Billy boy! How are you? And how is your mother?" she said excitedly.

"Mama was in bed. She's sick," Bill said, an eleven-year-old boy, tall beside Danny, thin, bony, sallow.

"Hey, you, come here!" Al barked.

"Yes," Bill said, entering the parlor.

"Yes, sir! Holy Christmas, haven't you got any manners?" Uncle Al corrected.

"Yes, sir."

"How many times have I told you that when you come to see us, walk, don't run up the stairs. What kind of a place do you think we live in?"

"I didn't run."

"If you didn't run, how could you have arrived up here on the third floor so quickly after you rang the bell? Did you take an elevator upstairs?"

"I didn't run," Bill said doggedly.

"Goddamn you! I'll teach you not to lie!" Uncle Al said, springing up from his chair.

Aunt Margaret hastily sidled between Al and her nephew and told Al not to go losing his temper again.

"Well, holy Moses! He's coming to see us in our home, and he is going to be guided by the rules we lay down for conducting oneself in our home if he wants to keep coming here."

"Now, Al, the boy did nothing," Aunt Margaret wheedled.

"William," the grandmother said kindly and with enthusiasm as she entered the parlor, wearing a lace bedroom cap.

"Hello, Mother," Bill said.

"Better not let your own mother hearing you call your grandmother Mother. She won't like it," Aunt Margaret said, smiling.

"Nix, Peg, nix!" Al interposed.

"Mama is not Mother. She's Mama," said Danny, and the aunt smiled.

"When I was a wee one in the cradle, my Uncle William came to see my mother, and I remember it like the light of day. He picked me up in his arms this way, and he said to me mother, may the Lord have mercy on her soul, 'Here's a child that will nary a day know what bad luck is.' Ah, William, it's a fine name you have, and it will bring you nary a day's bad luck."

"What did you come for?" Al asked after Mrs. O'Flaherty had sat down primly on the piano bench.

"Why, he came to see us, didn't you, Billy boy?" said Aunt Margaret.

"It seems to me that there might have been plenty he could have done at home for his brothers and sister, with his mother sick," Al grouched.

"Pa told me I should come. And I wanted to. I came to ask you if I could take Danny to the ball game today?"

"No! He's been disobedient. This morning he tried to lie and stall from going to mass. He has to be punished for his conduct."

Danny was on the verge of tears.

"Where did you get the money to go?" Al asked, suspiciously eying his oldest nephew.

"I found a ticket," Bill answered with the air of a self-justified boy talking to his elders when he knew he was right and could not be refuted.

"Where?"

"I found a box-seat ticket at Twenty-sixth and Wentworth this morning on my way home from church. I asked Papa if he wanted it, and he said no, I should go and get Danny and the two of us go."

"See, you!" Al said, pointing to Danny. "If you hadn't tried to lie this morning, you wouldn't be kept in for punishment and you could go to the ball game now."

"I was only doing what they told me to do," Danny said, half-sobbing, pointing at his aunt and then at his grandmother. "See what you got me into, Aunty Margaret, by telling me not to go to mass. I told you I wanted to go." He turned back to his uncle with tears dripping down his face. "You told me to do what I am told . . ."

"Goddamn it, quit bawling!" Al snapped, interrupting him.

"I was only doing what I was told," Danny said, the tears coming more copiously.

"Oh, he's so sweet!" said Aunt Margaret, bending down, wiping his dribbling nose and his wet eyes.

"I'm not sweet," Danny sobbed in protest.

"No pampering, Peg!" Al said.

"Sure, Al, let the boy go," the grandmother said.

"Now, Al, don't be so strict. They have the ticket, and it's good only for the day. And I'd like them out of the house. I'm tired and want to take a nap, and I don't want the kids around here to wake me up. I'm tired. I worked late at the hotel last night and need my nap. Let them get out of the house. And this morning it was my fault, because I told him not to get dressed," Margaret said.

"Uncle Al, I will go to mass every Sunday, even if I am so sick I can't walk," Danny said, quivering with fear as he spoke, wiping his tears away with the back of his hand, smearing his face.

"If I let you go, see that I don't ever catch you pulling off another stunt like the one you attempted this morning," Al said, and Danny, his round face breaking into smiles, turned and started running out of the parlor. "Here!" Al barked.

Danny turned to face his uncle, again frightened.

"Al!" Margaret protested.

"I'm not going to hurt him," Al replied to his sister, and then he faced his nephew. "Remember, I said don't run like that in the house. And also, what do you say when somebody gives you something or does something for you?"

"Thank you, sir!"

"That's the sport," Al smiled.

"Here, Little Brother, let Aunty Margaret wash your face for you."

"I'm all right," Danny said.

Aunt Margaret led him to the bathroom to wash his face. He returned to the parlor, wearing his blue cap.

"Got any money?" Uncle Al asked without looking up from his newspaper.

"A dime," Bill said.

Al gave them each a quarter, and they thanked him.

"Don't spend it all on pop and red-hots," Al said.

"We won't," they both said.

The grandmother followed them to the door, and slipped them a half a dollar.

"God bless you," she said as they walked down the stairs.

2

Jim O'Neill went into the bedroom off the dining room where Lizz lay on the bed in a corner, her belly swollen under the soiled white sheet. Ah, his Lizz was now no longer a lass to send a lad's heart spinning at a picnic or a trolley party. He looked past her at the peeling wallpaper, and then at the window opening out upon the drab red bricks of the building next door. All the windows in the house were open, but still it smelled musty, and this room was the worst in the whole place. He glanced around, junk all over, the dresser in the corner piled with it, rags, clothes, junk, and the table on the left with a slab of grocery box in place of one leg, it, too, was piled and littered with every damn thing in the house. And Lizz, lying in all this, smiling weakly at him, her face round, full, unwashed, her mouth weak, her eyes dark, a soiled rag under her chin, her hair uncombed, looking at him almost like a cow.

Another pain came, and her expression became distorted as she moaned. Jim frowned with worry. He held her hand, and she almost dug her nails into his palm. Then she relaxed, smiled, told him that he shouldn't worry.

He stood by her bed. The very room made him feel suddenly hopeless. So thick and close, so disorganized. Broodingly, he told himself that it was one hell of a room into which a baby was to be born. Again he looked around, and noticing the kerosene lamp amid the litter on the small table, he silently cursed to himself. He wondered would he and his family ever have a decent home where they could live like human beings and bring the kids up right. He noticed the dust coating the floor under the bed and under the cradle, looking chewn and unpolished. He grimaced, shrugged his shoulders.

He came closer to the bed again while Lizz silently and lassitudinously watched him. He bent down and kissed her. Suddenly she moaned, a low moan. He asked should he get anybody yet, and she said that he should wait just a little while longer, because the pains were still pretty far apart. She asked him to get the small bottle of Easter holy water on the dresser and sprinkle some on her and around the room because when a child was born, the devils always came and tried to snatch the baby's soul before it was baptized. If the devils were not driven away, the child's soul might be possessed by them. And Easter holy water was especially good for chasing devils and making Satan hide his ugly head in fear. Jim dug through the litter on the top of the bureau until he found the bottle.

"Be gone, Satan!" Lizz repetitiously droned as Jim sprinkled holy water over the bed and around the room.

Jim then turned from her to replace the bottle on the bureau.

"Under the bed, too, Jim. Devils always hide under beds and in dark corners," she said weakly.

Jim frowned. He sprinkled the dusty floor, and Lizz imprecated Satan. She wearily stretched her puffy hand forward for the bottle and took it. She blessed herself, and invoked the protection of the Blessed Virgin Mary. With equal slowness she sprinkled the bed with wetted fingers, making the sign of the cross and intoning simultaneously.

"Out with you, Satan! You devil demon, spawn of Hell! Be gone, you cannot have the soul of the child I will bring forth into this world of toil from a bed of suffering! Be gone, Satan, foul spawn of the fire and brimstone of Hell!"

He replaced the bottle at the edge of the dresser.

"Jim?" Lizz sighed.

"Yes?" he replied, his rough voice suddenly gentle.

"When the baby comes, Jim, if it looks like it won't live, I want you to be sure to baptize it right away with Easter holy water. I got that Easter holy water from the Italian church, and it's powerful for chasing the Devil. The Pope is an Italian, and holy water, blessed at Easter time by an Italian priest, has a special and most powerful spell upon the Devil. If you do, the child's soul will be blessed, and it'll live to be a good and happy person, maybe a priest if it's a baby boy, or a nun if it's a girl."

"Yes, Lizz," he said.

He bent forward and brushed her damp forehead with a kiss. He mumbled that there would be no trouble.

"If anything happens to me, Jim, you must be sure that none of the children ever stray from the Church."

"No, Lizz, my rabbit, don't worry," he said in an effort to be calming.

"But, Jim, you must! I have a fear. I dreamt last night. In my dream, my father came to me, and he said, my father always said I was his favorite, and he said to me, Jim, 'Elizabeth, your time is come. Many are called but few are chosen. Your time is come. Tell Jim to guard my grandchildren.' That's what my father said to me when I saw him last night," she said, breaking into tears.

Jim winced. His face tightened with worry. He glanced away a moment, fighting to keep a grip upon himself. He turned back and smiled at his wife.

"You'll be kicking around and going to church in a week, Lizz," Jim said, his voice cracking.

"Promise me, Jim!"

"I do, Lizz!"

She smiled at him and squeezed his hand. He patted her, kissed her forehead, her lips. He said that she was just nervous and weak. There was a heavy silence between them, lasting about a minute.

"Anything I can get for you?" he asked.

"No, just . . ." A moan interrupted her words. When it subsided, and the pain had vanished from her face, she continued, "Just let me rest, and in a little while you call Mrs. Koffinger and the doctor."

He gripped her hand, turned, left the room, fear trembling within him as he struggled to convince himself that Lizz's dream or vision had meant nothing and that it had just been caused by nervousness and her condition.

He stood, indecisive, in the dining room, clenching and unclenching his fists, telling himself that goddamn it, there was nothing serious going to happen, and new kid or not, they were going to get along all right.

He looked around at the messy room, thinking that, perhaps, he ought to clean it. But he didn't feel like doing that, either. He felt like doing nothing. He glanced to his right, through the wide door that opened into the parlor, the largest room in the flat. He looked back around the dining room. It was darker than usual because of the day, and the wide dining-room window, set opposite the entrance to Jim and Lizz's bedroom, looked down on a small back yard of dirt and tin cans where kids yelled in play.

He walked to the round dining table which was covered with oilcloth. On it were the dishes and food from their Sunday dinner. And in its center stood a kerosene lamp, not cleaned from the previous night, its glass chimney blackened from smoke, its odors mingling with the many smells of the house. Behind was the sideboard, built into the wall, and he saw how it, too, was cluttered. Just looking at all this dirt and mess got on his nerves.

Goddamn it, he wanted the thing over with!

He felt himself imprisoned, cramped in a small hole full of dirt and food and kerosene smells. Yes, goddamn it, he wanted a clean home. But Lizz was sick with child, going through more than he was. There were the pains again. No place for anything in the goddamn five-room hole, and everything was in every place. And only two weeks ago he had spent a whole hot and lousy Sunday cleaning it when he could have been enjoying himself at the ball game. And for what? Look at it now!

Jesus Christ!

The ripped and unwashed curtain hanging over the parlor window fell to the floor. With a smothered oath on his lips, Jim went into the parlor to replace it. He noticed the old chairs out of place, the couch smothered with newspapers, the sooty lamp chimney, and through the door on the right the dark untidy bedroom where the three boys slept, their unmade bed revealed in shadows.

He stared down on La Salle Street, hearing the shouts of playing kids. Another moan from Lizz. Her moans seemed to cut through him like a knife. Off to the right he could see a slice of the corner of Twenty-fifth and La Salle Streets, and, beyond it, a few iron pickets in the playground fence and a slab of the railroad embankment to the east of the park. He glanced straight down at the narrow, cracked and dusty cement sidewalk, and across at the east side of the street, occupied by the loading platform and long, low red-brick structure of the Morgan and Hearst packing plant. The street, though, was so quiet compared with week days, when there was so much going on at the loading platform. Just the kids making noise today. He heard a train from the Rock Island tracks behind Morgan and Hearst, and soon it was gone with a diminishing echo and a tail of black smoke that drifted above the building. He watched some Italian kids as they wheeled about and cursed in a game of tag. He smiled as one of them pulled down the peaked cap of another over his face. And to his left, on the door step, that dago. Jim didn't know his name, but he was the one who always shouted at his wife and kids instead of talked, so that he could be heard almost all the way up the block to Twenty-fourth Street. There he was, sitting now, not talking, smoking his pipe, his fat wife silent beside him, a red bandanna strung over her oily black hair, black hair like Lizz's. Jim suddenly envied the fellow his seeming happiness. All the world, almost, was happy and quiet and resting today, and here he was, worrying.

Oh, goddamn it, he wished it was over!

Hell, he had been a father enough times not to be so worried. And here he was worrying, and afraid. Two women, one stout, the other thin, were walking below, both of them jabbering in foreign accents. That turkey, McGlone, who lived at the other end of the block and never worked, while his wife took in washing, there he was, staggering, with a newspaper under his arm. Jim smiled. A couple of wops passed. Jesus, he did wish that he could live in an American neighborhood. A boy carrying a foaming can of beer. Two of the kids who were playing tag almost collided with him, one of them sneering.

"Go fuck yourself!" the kid with the beer snarled.

"Yuh shit!" one of the other kids snapped back at him.

Jim frowned. He thought of his own kids. Little Margaret had taken her two younger brothers down the corner to the playground. He wondered if they were all right. He did want to get them out of this neighborhood so they could grow up decent. And until he could, he would have to see to it that his kids didn't play around the street with the dago and polack kids who talked like that. Damn it, he vowed to himself that he would break their backs before he let them get away with it. They weren't going to go through what he had, do what he'd done, learn the things he had learned at an early age. He didn't want them to have to do the same kind of work, the drinking and whoring around, either. By the living God, he would tan their asses six sides of Sunday first! Well, he still had a pretty strong back, and he was going to support them, and see that they got chances he'd never gotten.

The thought of educating his family caused remorse to flow within him because of the way he himself had balked at education. Joe O'Reilley had gone to night school, read books and law, while he had scorned doing that. Instead, he'd gone in for roughhouse hell-raising, bragging that none of that dude stuff went for him. Well, it wasn't dude stuff. Now, too late, he could see his mistake. Look where Joe was! He didn't want his kids to be dudes, but neither did he want them to break their backs and rupture themselves earning their miserable daily bread. He was going to make something out of them, something more than just drivers and poor workingmen.

Lizz moaned, longer and louder than before. Jim stirred to action. He replaced the curtain rods between the ledge, and, turning away, the noises and voices from the street drumming in his ears, he heard the chug and bells of another railroad engine. Again he envied the people below him on the street, because they were free of a thing that was such a load on his shoulders. He wished, he wished like everything, that on this Sunday in August, 1911, he were a free man. He went into Lizz. She said that soon now he had better be calling Mrs. Koffinger and Dr. Hart. Jim bent down and kissed her, patted her head, told her that she was brave and would come through the ordeal with flying colors.

Again the dirty house impressed itself heavily upon him, drove shame like a spike through him because it was into this house that he would have to bring their neighbor, that fat Mrs. Koffinger, and, also, Dr. Hart. He regretted now that he hadn't kept Bill at home. Bill would have to learn about these matters sooner or later.

He quickly snatched the dishes from the dining-room table and stacked them in the kitchen on top of a few other dishes that were clotted with the hardened leavings of food. He didn't want to wait until the water could be heated on the stove, so he began washing them in cold water under the faucet of the rusty tin sink, placing them on the board beside it.

Lizz moaned again. Suppose now that the young one should really die? He had already had three children die at birth, one of them still born. He knew how hard it would hit him, even if Lizz lived through it, and it did mean one less mouth to feed. Either way, whether it lived or died, it was bad for him. Jesus Christ, would he, would he ever get anywhere?

And would it be a boy or a girl, and what would he name it? He commenced singing *After the Ball Is Over*, because the song helped him not to worry, and made him remember things that used to be when he had courted Lizz and she was young and untouched, with black hair and those dark eyes of hers. And how he had resisted proposing to her until he had found himself getting more and more in love, his feelings and his love for her blasting the resistance out of his mind as if it were dynamite cracking rocks wide open. He had in a far-off kind of way figured out what would happen, how their lives would change and turn into something like just what they had turned into. But he had denied to himself what he had known in this vague way, and he had tried to steam himself up with hopes and pipe dreams that things would not turn out as he thought they would, and that Lizz would make a man of him of a different kind than what he was, and that she would bring him luck, and that marriage with her would be just what he needed to get himself the breaks. And the reason he had let himself in for thinking all these things was that he had wanted her more and more. And Jesus, those last days before he had gotten married, he not only loved her the way guys were supposed to love a decent girl. Christ, no! Christ, in those days, he had gone around with a constant bone on. Now, washing dishes, he laughed ironically. Well, this was the end of that perpetual hard on. This was what it had brought him. And how that one Sunday back around the end of the nineties, he remembered so clearly, when spring was coming and he had gone to see her with that new bowler hat and his wide-bottomed trousers, and he had lulled himself, thinking ahead into the future, how they would marry and be happy and prosperous, and have kids. And it had all come about, all but the prosperity. Yes, after the ball is over. . . . No, it wasn't that he was sorry. He loved Lizz, and he loved his kids. It was, Jesus, money. Goddamn it, that was what put a pair of hand cuffs on him.

He hastily dried the dishes and put them in the disordered cabinet opposite the unpolished rusty wood stove. Her next groan seemed to hit him in the back and run up and down his spine so that he almost dropped a plate. Yes, Lizz, too, she had her part to play, and he did not think that it was the part she dreamt of playing when she was that black-eyed shy girl he had known. And she was playing her part right now. But God, something, something should happen to make their lives better! And he would have to borrow money now from his brother-in-law, or from Joe O'Reilley. Go to them, just like a beggar! He wanted to be independent, goddamn it, and he had to go like a beggar, yes, just like a beggar, to Joe or to Lizz's goddamn brother, Al!

Again the groan, and she was calling him. He rushed to her, saw her pained, distorted face.

"I can't stand it, Jim! Oh! . . . OOOH! . . . They're breaking my back . . . OOOH . . . OOOH, Good Jesus Mary and Joseph . . . OOOH!"

"I'll get her now and Dr. Hart," he said, bending down to kiss her.

She shuddered at his touch. Abashed and worried, he hastened out of the bedroom and dashed down the front stairs, trailed by the echo of her cries.

3

I

I hope Ed Walsh pitches today. If he does, he'll skunk them, because he's the greatest pitcher there is," Danny said as they walked toward Fifty-first Street.

"How about Three-fingered Brown?" Bill said.

"Wait till you see Walsh pitch if he does today."

They paid the fare at the Fifty-first Street elevated station and waited in the center of the long boarded platform. Near them was a young fellow wearing a blue suit, high stiff collar and a plaid tie, and a girl in organdie with puffs of chestnut hair.

"Darling, it won't always be hard times," the fellow said.

"When things are better, we'll announce our engagement," she answered.

"They're in love," Bill said, smirking at Danny.

Danny wondered what it meant to be in love, and thought of how swell it was to be going to a ball game. He jumped about, twisted himself around, wished that he were already at the ball park.

"Jimmy Callahan is back in the game, Dan," Bill said.

"I like Pat Daugherty," Dan said.

"But Pat ain't the man he used to be. Pa was telling me something about how he helped win the world series of 1903 by hitting a home run with the bases full. Pa doesn't think, either, that Pat is the man he used to be. He's getting old," Bill said.

"I guess so," Danny said thoughtfully.

The train stopped alongside the platform. They got in and Bill took a seat next to the window. Danny wished he had it.

But the bigger guy always got what he wanted over a littler guy. At home they could tell him what to do, and they could tell Bill, too. And Bill, because he was four years older and bigger, could take what he wanted and give Danny the pickings. Just wait until he was a big man!

"If we were getting down earlier, we could stand by the players' gate and watch them come in in their street clothes, but it's too late now," Bill said, and Danny was even more disappointed than Bill. "Remember the game we saw with the Athletics, and we stood before it by the players' gate and when I said to you that there was Pat Daugherty, he cursed us?"

"Uh huh!" said Danny.

"Doc White and Roy Corhan are nicer. They paid our car-fare on the car after games this year. I guess Doc White, the pitching dentist, is a favorite of both of us, huh, Dan?" Bill said, and Danny nodded agreement.

They got off at the Indiana station. A kid of about ten kept staring at Danny and looking at his white stockings, and Danny would have been afraid if Bill wasn't along to stick up for him.

"Uncle Al makes you wear sissy stockings, doesn't he?" Bill said, noticing the kid staring at Danny's stockings.

"I don't want to. I got to. He makes me," Danny gloomily said.

"Papa calls Uncle Al the dude. Pa said to Ma that her two goddamn brothers were dudes, and Ma got sore, and they had a fight, yelling at each other, until Pa took a sock at Ma. Then he got sorry and sent me out for ice cream, and we had ice cream, and Pa started kissing Ma, and petting her, the same way she pets us kids."

They boarded another train, and stood on the platform where men were smoking. Danny overheard a fat man saying that the White Sox were no good, so he guessed that the fat man must be a Cub fan, just like Bill was. They got off with the crowd at Thirty-fifth Street. Crossing State Street, the sight of so many groups of Negroes lolling and talking on the corner made Danny afraid, because at home they always said that niggers would do things to him, and you never could trust a nigger because if you gave him an inch he always took a mile.

Bill took such long steps that Danny almost had to run to keep up with him as they pressed along Thirty-fifth Street in the steady parade of people who were hastening to the ball park a few blocks west. Suddenly, Bill pulled out a box of Melachrino cigarettes, paused to light one, proudly puffed and inhaled, letting the smoke come out of his nostrils.

"I copped these on Aunt Margaret the other night. But if you snitch on me, I'll lam your ears in," Bill said, placing his closed fist under Danny's nose.

"I won't. Honest!" Danny said, cowering.

They passed under the viaduct, and still Bill was walking too fast for his brother. A popcorn machine zizzed in front of the Greek ice-cream parlor at

Thirty-fifth and Wentworth. Danny kind of thought he wanted a soda, but Comiskey Park, Home of the White Sox, was just ahead, and they had to hurry. They could spend their money on popcorn and pop and red-hots inside the ball park. Drawing near the grand-stand entrance at Shields Avenue, they heard clapping and cheering from inside the stadium. Bill ran, and Danny tore after him on his little legs. Both of them were admitted through the turnstile on the single ticket. Bill galloped up the runway to the grandstand, and Danny, out of breath, tried courageously to keep pace with him.

II

Outfitted in gray uniforms with red trimmings, the Boston Red Sox went through their batting practice. One player after another took cuts at pitched balls while substitutes and pitchers trotted about the outfield catching and retrieving balls which traveled that distance.

"That's Tris Speaker batting, Dan," Bill said, pointing, both of them eating red-hots and sipping pop through straws.

They both watched the well-built left-handed batter take an even, graceful swing which seemed to have little force behind it, and yet the ball he hit bounced off the right-field bleachers fence, several hundred feet from the home plate.

"An easy double, maybe a triple in the game," Bill said, pleased with the blow Speaker had cracked.

"It's only practice and doesn't count," Danny said.

"Tris hits 'em the same in the game," Bill said.

"Gee, I wish it would start," Danny said, and he smiled, for just as he spoke he heard the bell signaling the end of the Boston team's period of batting practice.

He watched the White Sox, wearing white uniforms and white stockings, as they trotted out on the field. Hugh Duffy, the manager, slapped grounders to the infielders and they scooped them up and tossed the ball around. The outfielders shagged fly balls that were fungoed to them.

"Ed Walsh is pitching today, Dan," Bill said, and as he spoke he pointed to a pitcher warming up near the White Sox bench by third base, a husky man with a long-sleeved red flannel undershirt under his uniform shirt.

"The Sox are going to win," Danny said eagerly clapping his hands together, watching Ed Walsh toss pitches to a catcher.

"Don't count your chickens before they're hatched," Bill said.

Bill puffed on a cigarette. Danny watched the White Sox infielders practicing.

"Only fifteen more minutes and the game starts," Bill said after the bell had jingled again and the Boston Red Sox took the place of the White Sox on the field and went through their period of fielding practice in the same fashion as had the White Sox.

"A southpaw's warming up for the Red Sox, Bill," Danny said, pointing over toward the Boston bench, where a left-handed pitcher was throwing to a catcher.

"Dan, see that fellow on the third-base foul line hitting fungo flies out to right field?" Bill said, pointing.

"Who is it?"

"Buck O'Brien. He's one of the best fungo hitters in the big leagues," Bill said.

They watched Buck O'Brien toss a soiled ball into the air, grip the long light willow bat he held, swing, lift the ball, and it sailed out and out. Danny lost sight of it until he saw the bleacher's fans way out in right field scrambling.

"Knocked it clean out of the park," Bill said with admiration.

"They ought to hurry up and start the game," Danny said.

"Hold your horses," Bill said.

There was applause. Two blue-shined workmen appeared, carrying a white-boarded wooden rectangle. They laid it on each side of home plate, whitewashing in the batters' boxes, and at the same time another workman traced in the foul lines with a little whitewash cart.

A popcorn man came by, shouting in a peppy manner, selling freshly buttered Blue Ribbon popcorn, and they bought sacks. Eating it, they watched the captains gather by the home plate with the umpire, saw the White Sox trot into position, saw the announcer go with his megaphone directly behind the home plate, and call up the lineups to the press box. Then the announcer turned and began calling the batteries into the grandstands at various angles.

"THE BATTERIES FOR TODAY'S GAME! FOR CHICAGO, WALSH AND BLOCK! FOR BOSTON, W. COLLINS AND CARRIGAN!"

III

"It's good luck for a pitcher to strike out the first batter that faces him," Danny said to Bill with joyous hope, while the crowd still cheered, and Hendricksen, the Boston lead-off man, took a trip back to the bench with his bat in his hand.

"There's twenty-six more to get out before the ball game is over. But let's watch the game instead of jawing. There's Clyde Engle at bat now," Bill said, pointing, and just as he did the right-handed hitter at the plate swung, hitting a ground ball to second base and being retired at first.

Scattered handclapping greeted Tris Speaker as he stepped into the batter's box and stood waiting, measuring off his swings while Walsh cupped his hands over the ball and held it before his mouth.

"Put a lot of saliva on it for this boy, Ed!" a fan near Danny yelled in a booming voice.

"Come on, you Bull Moose! Oh, you Ed Walsh, strike him out!" Danny shrieked in a high-pitched voice, causing men around them to watch him with amusement.

"What do you think of that?" Danny breathlessly said to Bill amid his shrieks and cheers after Ed Walsh had retired the side by striking out Tris Speaker.

"It's just luck when any pitcher whiffs Tris," Bill said, but Danny did not listen to him, because he eyed Ed Walsh striding off the diamond, dropping his glove on the foul side of the third-base line, walking with lowered head to the White Sox bench.

"Come on, you White Sox, skunk them green!" he piped, while the White Sox lead-off man, Matty McIntyre, a left-handed hitter, faced the pitcher. He stepped into a pitch, the crack of the bat echoing, the ball sailing out into right field. The crowd was on its feet, cheering. Danny jumped up to his feet and clapped his hands with joy. Hendricksen was throwing the ball in, and Matty was rounding second and coming on. Safe on third!

A contagious animation permeated the spectators, and they sat cheering, calling, clapping, whistling, hoping that Harry Lord, another left-handed batter, would drive home the first run. There were groans. A pop-up, smothered easily by Yerkes, the Red Sox second baseman. Jimmy Callahan stepped into the right-hand batter's box, and he was applauded, entreated to bring in that run. And again Danny was on his feet. A bunt. The run in. A cheer. Callahan beat the throw to first base.

"The game's young yet. Lots can happen in eight more innings," Bill said, unheard by Danny.

The crowd broke loose as a burly ballplayer stepped into the right-hand batter's box, nervously pounded his bat on the white rubber home plate, half swung it in the air, faced the pitcher.

"Come on, Ping Bodie! Come on, Ping Bodie!" Danny cried.

"We'll see what the dago from the Pacific Coast League can do," Bill said.

"Give it the spaghet, Ping!" a mighty-voiced fan roared, drawing laughter from those who heard him.

"Oh, you fence-buster!" Danny shrilled as Ping Bodie stepped into a pitch, the ball traveling out into left field like a rifle shot.

Before the crowd had recovered its breath, Amby McConnell, the second baseman, had rifled a one-base hit to right field, and the second run was home. Danny clapped his hands, squirmed on his seat. The White Sox were winning, Ed Walsh was pitching, and he was seeing it all. The inning ended with a pop-up, and a foul fly which the catcher caught, and the teams changed positions. But he knew the White Sox were going to win. And he was again cheering, and clapping when the White Sox trotted off the field a second time, and Ed Walsh was again greeted like a hero for having retired the side in order, chalking up two more strike-outs.

The Sox up again. Block the catcher. Out. Walsh. Out.

"Come on. Matty, sock it green!" Danny called.

His expression dropped. McIntyre hit a slow bounder to Clyde Engle, the first baseman, and streaked it down the base line. A cheer went up, and Danny clapped his hands because he was safe. And now Harry Lord was up, and he ought to hit one because he was the captain of the team. The pitch, the swing, the crack of the bat, a sizzler over first base, both men running, McIntyre on third base, Lord on second, and everybody yelling. The White Sox were winning, and Ed Walsh was pitching. Wait till he got home to tell Uncle Al about it. Callahan batting amid cheers, swinging, the rising roar, Danny jumping on his feet, a groan of disappointment when the ball was caught way out against the bleachers.

"Nothing ever gets by Duffy Lewis in left field," Bill said proudly.

"Wait till next time, you wait!" Danny said.

"That boy Lewis isn't an outfielder, he's a well," a fan behind them said.

"It's raining, Dan. If the game doesn't go to four and a half innings it doesn't go in the record," Bill said.

"Gosh darn the luck," Danny said broken-heartedly.

They had pop and red-hots and Danny fretted while the game was delayed. He looked out with a pouting face on the green outfield and on the infield, which workmen covered with canvas. The rain continued. Gee, it was awful, the old rain cheating him and Ed Walsh. He asked God please to stop it from raining so the game could go on, and Ed Walsh not be cheated. Please, God, stop that rain!

He yelled when, after ten minutes, the canvas was drawn off the infield and the game went on. And with two men out in the third inning, Lee Tannehill, the rangy White Sox shortstop, swung a trifle late, and the ball soared out into right center field. He jumped on his seat, and saw Tannehill on third. Two Red Sox outfielders were lying on the ground, and players ran to them. There was a buzz of anxious conversation all around them, and Bill stood up, watching, and he wouldn't tell Danny what had happened. One of the players was walking in, helped by teammates. The other was not as badly hurt. The crowd cheered.

"Hendricksen is hurt worse than Speaker. I'm glad that Tris isn't too badly hurt," Bill said.

"What happened, Bill?" Danny asked.

"They ran into each other," said Bill.

"Gee, poor Speaker," said Danny, his voice sad.

Substitutes were sent in, a first baseman named Williams taking Engle's place,

Engle going out to center field and Riggert to right field. The announcer called out these changes, and the game continued.

The fourth inning. Engle getting a base on balls. Williams in Speaker's place on the batting order, out. Duffy Lewis, lofting a fly to right field, caught without effort. The Sox coming in, and Danny heard a man beside him saying that they hadn't gotten a hit off Walsh yet, and that was the first man to reach base.

"Bill! Bill! Maybe Walsh will pitch a no-hit game," Danny said.

"The game's young yet," Bill said.

In the fifth and sixth innings, both teams were set down in one-two-three order. Danny was clapping, twisting again. The White Sox were winning. And nobody was even getting a hit off the Bull Moose. He watched the big pitcher stride onto the field for the start of the seventh inning. God, please don't let it be the lucky seventh for Boston. Only three more innings to hold them. If Big Ed could do it. He would! God wasn't going to let Boston get any hits.

"I hope that he goes on and doesn't give them any hits. It would be tough luck to go this far and then get nicked," Bill said, making Danny so glad, because now Bill was for Ed Walsh, and not against him.

Two out already in this inning. God was helping Ed Walsh. Riggert up. Out. Oh, you Ed Walsh. God wouldn't let him hit Walsh now. He stood on his seat, yelled himself hoarse, clapped his small hands, and Walsh walked in to the bench receiving a thunderous ovation. And it increased when he walked out, bat in hand to start the White Sox half of the inning. He laced out a single, and the bat boy ran around to first base carrying a blue sweater for him to wear on the bases so that his arm didn't get cold. Danny watched Ed Walsh, his foot on first base, putting on his sweater. With eyes of adoration, he followed Walsh's fingers while the big fellow buttoned his sweater. And he clapped his hands when Ping Bodie, with two men out, smacked a single, and Walsh scored.

And the eighth inning. He couldn't stand it. Each time Walsh pitched, the ball might be hit safely. When he drew his hands to his mouth to spit on the ball, all the fans were quiet. They waited, just as Danny did, holding their breath, while Walsh pitched. They were so glad, as he was, when it wasn't hit. Three out. Another ear-splitting ovation. When he grew up, maybe the fans would cheer him like this. He wanted the White Sox to hurry up and get out. He couldn't wait. He wanted Walsh to strike them out, one, two, three, in the last inning. They were out now. The last inning. God was going to help Walsh. God was! God, please!

Yerkes, the second baseman up, come on, Ed, you got the end of the batting order, please, God, help him, and out, one gone. Now a pinch hitter for the pitcher. Who was it? Would he ruin things? The announcer. Nunamaker, the third-string catcher, a right-handed hitter. He couldn't be so hard. Strike one! Strike out. Danny cheered as loud as he could, his voice now feeble from hoarseness, his hands sore from clapping. Bill glanced up and down his score card, and said that that made eight strike-outs today for Walsh, and Danny was glad, but he couldn't talk. The last man. If God helped Ed Walsh get him out, he would never again try to miss mass, or not do what he was told at home. He would try every way he could to be as good as his guardian angel, and never hurt God's feelings. A bounder. He held his breath. Amby McConnell had it, the throw to first base. Out! Whee! He stood up on his seat and gave all of himself in a last yell, as the applause and cheering boomed. The players hurriedly scuttled off the field, Walsh chased by fans who wanted to get near him.

Just think of it, he had seen Ed Walsh pitch a no-hit game. And some day he was going to be like him.

"Come on, Dan, we'll go under the stands by the clubhouse and watch the players come out. We'll be able to see Ed Walsh."

4

I

His grandmother had taken him to school, and it had been sunny out, and he'd been so afraid because he didn't know what to make of it all. They had gone to see the Sister in black, and she and his grandmother had talked. Then Sister had smiled at him, and patted his head, and taken him to this lady who was going to be his teacher, and now, here he was, sitting in this seat with his hands on the desk, so afraid, with all these kids, boys and girls, around the room, and she was talking and he didn't know how many there were because he couldn't count so many kids as there were in the room, and his shoelaces were untied, and he didn't know how to tie his shoes, either, and maybe if it was seen, somebody would laugh at him and call him a baby who couldn't even tie his own shoes.

When they lived over on Indiana Avenue, the kids used to pick on him, and he would go home crying, and his grandmother would chase them all with a stick, cursing them good, and maybe these kids would do the same, and he couldn't run home for his grandmother to go chase them, and the room was full of kids his own size, boys and girls, and maybe yes, they would laugh at him, and what would he do? He didn't want to be here alone, all alone. He wanted to be home with Mother, or playing in the back yard, or with his brother Bill. Gee, he wished that Bill lived with them and was able to go to the same school, so that he could see Bill all the time, and then he would have Bill to stick up for him against any kids who would try to pick on him.

Yes, he wished he wasn't here. Darn it, he didn't like going to school like this. Wouldn't it ever get over? There was the woman teacher, and her nose was so big, and she was talking to them, saying something and looking at him, and what did she want? He looked at her, and gee, he hoped she wasn't going to say something to him, and he didn't see where he had done anything wrong.

"You, little boy, with the blue sailor suit, what is your name?"

He looked at her.

"Hey, don't fall asleep," a red-headed kid behind him contemptuously whispered.

He looked at her and jabbed a finger against his breast.

"Yes, son, you!"

"Me?"

A black-haired little girl in a white dress giggled. He didn't like girls anyway, except his cousin, Catherine Nolan. He liked to play with her.

"Yes, sonny, what is your name?"

"Daniel O'Neill," he said timidly, but she must have known it anyway, and what did she want to go asking him what his name was, when the Sister had told her, and she had said to him, patting his head when he didn't want to be touched and treated like a baby, she had said to him that, well, Daniel, we're going to get along as nice as pie. And she had a big nose, too, bigger than Uncle Al's nose.

"Would you like to come to the board and draw?"

"Me? What?"

"Come here now!" she said, gently.

She talked nice to him, as if she wasn't mad at him or anything, and her voice was kind, but he didn't want to draw, and he didn't want to sit here. He wanted to go home to Mother. He looked at her, begging with his eyes, and nearly all the boys wore black stockings, too.

"Come here, Daniel, I'm not going to harm you."

He sat, shaking his head, clenching his fists. She came toward him and he felt almost like he was dying or something, and he wanted to shrink way up inside of himself until he was so small that she couldn't see him, or he wished he had wings and could fly like a bird just right out of the room, and way, and away, and never come back. She was standing over him, and he felt all over again like crying like a little baby, just like he felt when they took him down to see his Mama and Papa, and left him alone with them, as if they were never coming back to take him home.

She touched his shoulder, and he felt like his heart was going to jump right out of his mouth. And now she was leading him by the hand, down the aisle to the front of the room, and they could all see his white stockings, and some of the girls were already laughing at him, and he didn't like girls, no, he didn't, he didn't like any of them except his cousin who was his girl, Catherine Nolan.

And now here he was in front of the room, standing before them, all these kids, faces and faces of them, and why did this woman have to do something like this to him? He didn't like her, and he didn't like school. He wanted to fly right out the window like a bird, and never, never, never come back. And they were looking at him, laughing.

"I want to go home to Mother," he bawled out, not able to help himself.

While he cried, the woman was talking, and her voice going and going. And she was patting his head just like Aunty Margaret sometimes did. He didn't want the woman to put her hands on him even.

He jerked away from her, and he was just ready to run, crying for help, when Father Hunt came in the room. Danny ran to him, looked up at him pleadingly, wanting his friend, Father Hunt, to take him home away from that woman with her big nose.

"Ah, here's the fine little Irishman. And how are you, Daniel? I'm glad to see you in our school," Father Hunt said, smiling, and his voice seemed so very, very kind.

"Hello . . . Father . . . Take me home to Mother," Danny said, while that woman was saying something to the kids. They all stood up, shuffling and scraping their feet, chorused good morning to the priest, and noisily sat down again.

Father Hunt was just going to say something, and here was that woman, smiling at him, and he didn't want his friend, Father Hunt, bothering about her a penny's worth. He only wanted Father Hunt to talk to him and take him home to Mother, and he didn't like that woman with her hair all up on her head like a puff, and her long nose. She was a skinny old bean pole. He didn't like her. But he liked Father Hunt.

"Daniel, you don't want to be afraid. What would your grandfather say if he should look down on you from Heaven this minute?" Father Hunt said kindly, stroking Danny's curly brown head.

A shy smile broke on Danny's face, a friendly but uncertain boy's smile. He was beginning to feel better now and not be afraid, he guessed. And Father Hunt was smiling at him, and so was the woman. And he didn't like that much, either, the way grown-ups always smiled at him. But he did like it, too, because he always liked them to pay some attention to him.

"Miss Devlin, Daniel here is an old friend of mine, and he is a fine lad. I knew his grandfather, Tom O'Flaherty, well, may his soul rest in peace."

Danny stood before the priest, awkward and straining. All the kids watched him, and he bet they wished they were in his boots.

"Daniel, you may go to your seat now," the woman said.

He didn't like her, and he wanted to stand up before them, and talk to his friend, Father Hunt. That woman, sending him back to his seat, the old telephone pole! Walking back down the aisle, he began to think that he would like school if Father Hunt would be teacher instead of that woman. Again at his desk, the seat seemed too big for him so that he could almost slide in it. He was lonesome all over again.

"Miss Devlin, Daniel there is the greatest baseball fan I ever saw," Father Hunt was saying.

"He is? How interesting! And well, Father, we'll also see if we can't teach him reading, and writing, and, of course, his catechism. Aren't we, Daniel?" she said.

He liked it, that woman and his friend, Father Hunt, talking about him, but instead of answering her question he looked at them, pointing his right index finger to his chest.

"Daniel, you should answer your teacher. Now say 'Yes, mam,'" the priest said.

"Yes, mam," Danny parroted, and then he suddenly smiled.

"Tell me, Danny, who's the greatest baseball player?" the priest asked.

"Ty Cobb."

"How does he bat?"

"Aw, gee, I showed you once, Father Hunt. Should I show you again?"

"Stand up in the aisle there, and show Miss Devlin," the priest said merrily.

Danny stared, uncertain, until he caught the smile in the priest's ruddy face. He grinned. If school would be like this, he would like it. He stood up, clapped his feet together, bent his shoulders forward, held his hands as if he were grasping a baseball bat, pretended he was swinging at a pitch like Ty Cobb. Some of the kids laughed. All of them looked at him. The woman was smiling at him. But he didn't like her. He did like Father Hunt.

And then Father Hunt left. Danny started to get afraid all over again. He wished they would let him go home to Mother.

II

"It's a sin to be seen in your pelt," Mrs. O'Flaherty said from her bedroom off the kitchen, where she sat in her rocking chair, sewing.

Naked, Margaret stood over the stove, waiting for the coffee in the white enameled coffee pot to heat. She was a well-built woman weighing about one hundred and thirty pounds, her hair brown and warm but not very thick, her eyes blue, her lips thin, her arms slender, her breasts small and upright, her pubic hair a large dark swab. The mother dropped her sewing, drew out her clay pipe, filled it, lit the pipe, stood in the doorway puffing, watching her daughter smoke a cigarette.

"My mother, may the Lord have mercy on her soul, would have skinned me alive if I went around in my pelt," the mother said.

Margaret went into the pantry by the sink, reappeared with a cup and saucer.

"Shame! For shame!" the mother said.

"What are you talking about?" Margaret asked, a rasp of anger in her voice.

"I wouldn't be seen showing myself in me pelt."

Margaret poured herself a cup of coffee, and sat down with it at the kitchen table, facing the door, looking through the glass upper half at a patch of sunny blue sky. The mother, holding her pipe, shrugged her shoulders.

"Can't you let me alone?" Margaret asked, her voice over-tragic.

"My mother would have cut the backside off me with a switch if I went around like you in my pelt."

"Oh, for God's sake, shut up!"

"Carrying on like a tinker in my son's house."

"Your son!" Margaret sneered. "This is my home, too! I've worked and given every cent I ever earned to you and your son's house. All right! I'll leave. I'll pack up and go, and say skidoo to the whole goddamn pack of O'Flahertys," Margaret said, huffing out of the kitchen.

"Humph!" the mother exclaimed, puffing again on her pipe.

"Oh, God, why must I bear this cross?" Margaret said self-pityingly as she nervously paced back and forth in her disordered bedroom off the hall, letting the ashes from her cigarette drop onto the rug and floor. "You should be dead!" she said in a high-pitched voice. "Dead alongside of your husband. He couldn't stand the sight of you in his last days. He used to come down to see me in the hotel, and he would say to me, 'Peg, that mother of yours is drivin' me crazy in my old age!' That's what Father thought of you. He knew you were an old witch!"

"Don't be talking so loud in my son's house," the mother curtly called from the dining room.

"It won't be long. I'm going to leave! I wanted to go two years ago when we lived over on Indiana Avenue, and Al wouldn't let me. Well, this time neither God or man can stop me. And when I go, it's for good. I'll never darken this door again, even if you are lying cold in your coffin. And when I go, then see if you can run your son's house without me. You hear me, you goddamn old hag! I'm leaving, bag and baggage!" Margaret yelled, growing more hysterical as she reached the end of her monologue.

"Burning his gas and electricity! Smoking cigarettes! Walking around in your pelt, carrying on like a streetwalker in a decent boy's home. The shame of God on you!" the mother replied.

"Goddamn your filthy soul!" Margaret screamed, pausing in the kitchen doorway. "Always men. You never liked girls. Not one of your daughters ever loved you, ever wanted to call you Mother!"

"Don't be disgracing my son before the neighbors by talking so loud in his house."

"Screw you and your sons! I'm going away. Roslyn Kiley always said to me, always advised me, 'Peg, don't stay with your family! Go! You'll never get anywhere as long as you do.' Fool that I was, I never took her advice. I should have left you long ago. But it isn't too late. There's still my life ahead of me. I'm going before you ruin my life, you leech!"

Margaret again lit the gas under the coffee pot. She took the filled cup she had previously poured and angrily dashed its contents into the sink. She waited by the stove, tears running down her unpowdered cheeks, hair straggling over her forehead, her breast heaving as she sobbed.

"Wasting my son's gas!" the mother nagged.

"Say, you goddamn hag! You toothless old witch! You needn't forget for one minute that I pay my way. I'm not dependent on you or your son. I give just as much as he does to this home."

"The curse of God on you that you would call your mother a hag! Chippy! Chippy!" Mrs. O'Flaherty said.

She went to her room, refilled her pipe, drew on it, sat rocking and singing.

> *You made your poor old mother cry,*
> *The day that you were born.*

"Abuse me! It won't be for long. I'm going, bag and baggage, and never again will an O'Flaherty set eyes on me. Not if I can help it. I'm going! And I'll never come back! Abuse me! Call me names that no self-respecting mother ever called her daughter. Anything I've ever done, it was your fault. You, you she-devil out of hell, you'd ruin my life if you could. But you can't. There's a just God in Heaven, and He won't let you. Thank God I found you out for what you are before it's too late. Thank God!"

"Go on, you chippy! Go and run with that Protestant married man," the mother said.

"Lorry Robinson is more a man than your son will ever be. There's more to him in his little finger than your precious son has in both of his balls," Margaret said.

"High! High! High!" the mother sing-songed, dancing a jig in derision and leering gnomishly.

"Curse me as you like! Your curses will all come to roost on your own head. When I was only a little girl, blind, without glasses, you cursed me, and you got drunk like a sow and fought with Father until the neighbors came. You never gave me a home. All you ever gave your husband and your family was nagging, and grief, and sorrow that spilled over the cup. Since the first day I worked, you've hounded me for money. And I got you money. Goddamn you, I got you money, more than I earned. I sold my body to men and got you money, and now you curse me. Call me a whore! The sin is on your soul. You'll answer for it! You'll answer for what you've done to blacken my poor soul and my poor life! You'll answer to God, you toothless hag!"

Ignoring her daughter, the mother sang, a deep and resigned melancholy creeping into her voice, as over and over again she sang.

> *You made your poor old mother cry,*
> *The day that you were born.*

"Oh, God! God, why must I bear this?" Margaret weepingly sighed, stretching her arms pitifully to the ceiling.

> *You made your poor old mother cry . . .*

"Sing! My poor old mother!" Margaret said in lip-curling sarcasm. "Witch! She-devil of a witch! All my life you've made me suffer and tortured me! Well, you won't any more. I'm going!"

Sobbing, Margaret drank lukewarm coffee. She went to her bedroom, and when she had cried herself out, she read the morning newspaper. Mrs. O'Flaherty sat sewing. In about half an hour she arose from her rocker and went to the door of Margaret's room.

"Peg, this is the boy's first day at school. We must cook a fine lunch for him. He'll be home soon!"

"All right, Mother. The little darling!" Margaret said.

III

Danny came home for lunch and told his grandmother and aunt about school, and Father Hunt, and the way he had shown them how Ty Cobb batted. He didn't have to go back after lunch because it was the first day of school and they had been dismissed for the day. He took his catcher's glove, and a grass-stained baseball autographed to him by Rube Waddell. His uncle had gotten it for him one day when he had seen Waddell pitch in the American Association, and Danny was proud of it. He thought that Rube Waddell must have been as great a pitcher as Ed Walsh. He went down to throw the ball against the brick wall at Fiftieth Street and the alley, and to make up a baseball game to play. He had the whole afternoon, and he could play a whole world series between the White Sox and the New York Giants.

About a half hour later, Danny came back to the house, pale, breathless.

"What happened, Son?" his grandmother asked, noticing the expression of terror in his blue eyes.

He couldn't even talk. He went into the dining room and sat in a chair by the radiator in a corner. He tried to breathe evenly. He might be whipped. They might come after him right away with a policeman and take him away to jail. And he had lost Rube Waddell's ball. He wanted to cry, but he couldn't, because only babies cried, not boys who went to school. Gee, but he was glad Uncle Al was on the road. What mightn't Uncle Al do to him if he knew?

"Margaret! Margaret!" Mrs. O'Flaherty called frantically.

"What's the matter, Mother?" Margaret asked, rushing into the dining room, her eyes still slightly swollen from the crying she had done because of her quarrel with her mother in the morning.

"He's pale as a ghost?"

"Are you sick, Little Brother?"

"No!" he whimpered.

"Did a dog bite you?" the grandmother asked.

He looked pleadingly at them, his nose running. He wiped away his tears with the back of his hands. Gee, if it only hadn't gone and happened!

"I'm all . . . right!" he finally choked out.

"Oh, the poor boy!" Margaret exclaimed sympathetically.

"Did a horse kick you? Tell us! Tell us! Peg, do something. He's white as a sheet," the grandmother said, her excitement mounting.

"Brother, tell Mother and Aunty Margaret what's the matter?" the aunt asked, kissing his forehead.

"Mother!" he called pitifully, reaching his arms out to his grandmother. "Mother, I . . . broke a window and I lost my new ball. I threw it, and it went through the window in the building at the corner of the alley. And the glass all broke."

"Bless me, that's nothing. We can pay for the window. Sure, I thought you were hurt," the grandmother said, while both of them laughed in relief.

Danny pouted at them. He didn't see anything to laugh at. But if they laughed, maybe it was all right. He broke into smiles.

IV

Danny sat at the dining-room table drawing baseball diamonds with crayons, making the base lines yellow, the foul lines red because he didn't have any white crayons, and the grandstands black and brown and green.

"Grandson?" his grandmother called to him from the kitchen, where she had been singing to herself while washing the supper dishes.

"Yes, Mother?"

"Are you all right?"

"Uh huh!"

He drew another diamond, and colored it. He looked at it. He pushed the crayons and paper aside. Gee, he wished that Aunty Margaret didn't have to go to work tonight at that old hotel. If she hadn't, he and Mother wouldn't be alone, and maybe Aunty Margaret might have read him more stories from *Grimm's*

Fairy Tales, like the one she had read him this afternoon about the three spinning fairies who spun the flax for the girl so she could marry the queen's son. But now that he was started at school, he would be learning how to read, and then he would read stories to himself. And maybe he would read them out loud to Mother, because she couldn't read, either.

If three good fairies would come to him like they did to the girl in the stories, maybe they would read him stories, or teach him so he could read them to himself. Or if fairies would come maybe they would make him be a big-league baseball player right away and not make him wait until he was a man. In a little while now, Mother would tell him to go to bed. Gee, now a man like his Papa, he wasn't afraid of nothing in the world, and he wasn't afraid to go to bed alone in the dark.

He went out to the kitchen.

"Mother?" he said, askingly.

"Yes, Son!"

"Mother, tell me something about Ireland."

"I'm not Irish. I'm English. My name was Fox before I married your grandfather."

"But I'm Irish, ain't I? My friend, Father Hunt, told me, 'Daniel you're a fine young Irishman!'"

"Oh, Son, Ireland is a poor country. They are so poor in the old country that it would make your hair stand up on end on the top of your little head."

"You mean that the people in Ireland are poor like my Mama and Papa and they don't have electric lights and radiators?"

"The people go hungry. The English and the landlords, ah, but they're swell people. They have all the money, and they go riding through the fields with their dogs on the hunt for the fox," she said, then she put the dishes away, filled her clay pipe and began to smoke.

"Your Mama and Papa, are they poor in Ireland, too, like my Papa and Mama?"

"They are in Heaven with your grandfather and your Aunt Louise, may their souls rest in peace. And sure, I'll be going there soon myself with me old bones."

"No! No, Mother! I don't want you to go away from me," Danny said with overseriousness.

"Grandson, you're not an O'Neill or an O'Flaherty, you're a Fox," she said, looking at him lovingly.

"Mother, do they have automobiles in Ireland?" he asked as she sat watching him by the enamel-topped table.

"We saw nary an automobile in Ireland."

"Why don't they have automobiles in Ireland?"

"Sure, they'd run behind the bushes and think it was the work of the Devil if they saw an automobile in the town of Athlone or at the Mulligan Fair."

"And did you go to school to the Sisters in Ireland when you were a little girl, like I'm doing now?"

"Sister, my sister, she was a scholar and went to school. I ran the fields and fed the pigs. I can see my mother sending me to school. If I asked her to do that, she would have skinned the hide right off of my backside."

"Gee!"

"And they have mean men in Ireland. Mean landlords. Me mother's landlord, Mr. Longacre, he was so mean that he would make you eat dirt off a shovel. And when the poor people had nothing to pay the landlords, they were put off the land, and they became tinkers, or they came out to America."

"Is that why John Boyle came to America and is a motor-man?"

"His mother was a little girl in the old country. They had nothing to eat but potatoes. I ran the brush with her, bare-footed."

His grandmother went to the ice box, and returned with a bottle of beer. She sat by the table, drinking.

"Mother, when I am a man I'm going to get some fairies and I'm going to go with them and fix those landlords in Ireland who are so mean," Danny said.

"Ah, the landlords would shave you without soap."

"I think the fairies that Aunty Margaret reads me about would do something to those mean landlords," Danny said.

"They're the hand of the Devil. Father McCarthy in the old country always said the fairies were a queer people and they were in league with the Devil himself."

"They are nice to boys and girls in the book. Did Aunty Margaret ever read you about the three spinning fairies?"

"Ah, I'll never be seein' the old country again," she said; she drained her glass of beer, poured the remainder of her bottle into the empty glass.

Danny went to the sink, filled a glass of water, sat at the opposite end of the table, watched his grandmother, and imitated her as she drank the rest of the beer. Looking at her closely, he saw a tear slide down her creased cheek.

"Mother, why are you crying?" he asked.

5

I

Mrs. Koffinger has just gone. She had come in to see how Lizz was, but Lizz knew that the fat German tub of butter had been snooping, looking at her house. Now she was gone, and Lizz, wearing a dirty apron-dress, lay in the soiled bed, her infant asleep in her arms. Her full bovine face was pale. She yawned. She looked dreamily at the girl baby in her arms. She smiled. She pursed her lips toward it in a kiss. Carefully placing it in the cradle, she got up and slow-footedly moved into the dining room.

Bob, the eighteen-month-old boy, was playing on the floor, talking to himself, half in words, half in gurgling baby syllables.

"Ah, my baby baby boy!" Lizz said happily, opening her arms to him.

Bob stared at her. He stood up. He faced in babyish indecision. He wavered toward her. He clutched at her dress. She picked him up, but he was too heavy, and she immediately set him down. She touched her spine where she had felt a strain. She would have to be careful, she decided, because she was still flowing, and she wasn't completely over the effects of this last birth.

"Mommy! Mommy! Mommy!" he said, staring up at her.

Bob pointed at the bed through the open door, and mumbled.

"Bed, Son! It's the bed, where you sleep at night," she said with patience, and the child smiled at her, nodded its head.

"Bed where baby dleep," Bob mumbled, and she smiled at him.

"Some day, oh, but isn't Mommy's boy going to grow up to be a big man like his Pa, and take care of his mother. He'll take her riding in a carriage so elegant that the O'Reilleys will turn green with envy."

"Mommy!" Bob repeated, a shy smile opening across his face.

He turned. He walked on unsure legs to the dining-room table. He stood in a corner. He looked askingly at her. She knew that he wanted her to watch him, and she watched. He pulled at a cloth amid the litter on a little stand. He tugged again. Everything on the stand was dragged down on the floor. He laughed. He clapped his hands. He stared at her for approbation.

"Oh, you bad boy! You little shyster, don't you ever do that again!"

Slowly and wearily, she picked up the litter, dumping it on the stand. She smiled again at Bob.

"You're a bad baby when you do that!"

Bob trailed after her into the kitchen. He studied her while she put a few sticks of wood into the stove and placed the kettle over the fire to boil. Noticing dirty breakfast dishes in the sink, she washed them. Some of the plates still had leavings of egg crusted on them when she set them on the board beside the sink. She hummed, drying the dishes, and Bob played and cooed on the floor.

"Jesus Mary and Joseph!" she exclaimed, seeing her son swinging the butcher's knife. "You little shyster!" she added, half angrily, snatching the knife away, and slapping him.

Bob bawled. He looked up at her through a mist of tears. He reached for the knife, imploring her with sad eyes.

"In the name of the Father, and of the Son, and of the Holy Ghost! Playing with the butcher knife!" she exclaimed.

She handed Bob a biscuit. Catherine, the infant, let out a frightened, angry cry. Lizz hastened to the bedroom and picked up the girl baby. She frowned. The diapers were wet again. But she felt that she hadn't the strength to change them. She got into bed, set a towel under the infant, opened up her apron, and let the infant suck on her breasts.

Bob waddled around the house. He chewed at his biscuit. He threw it on the floor. He laughed, and picked it up. He bit at it. He tossed it on the floor. He grabbed it again. He clutched it tightly. He bit at it. He moved into the parlor. He gurgled. He named and misnamed the objects in the room.

And in the bedroom, Lizz lay with the baby still suckling on her full and overhanging breasts, a lassitude and satisfaction filling her aching body. She dreamily closed her eyes. She sang.

Rockaby, baby, in the treetop . . .

Drowsy, she could hear noises from the sunny street, children playing, wagons, a passing train on the Rock Island tracks.

Bob crawled and waddled back to the kitchen. He dug gleefully into the garbage pail under the sink. He gurgled. He talked to the garbage and to the pail.

There were footsteps on the stairs. Cries. A scream. Dennis, the four-year-old boy, rushed yelling into the house, his face bleeding from having been scratched in a fight with kids on the street.

II

Lizz sat down in the parlor to say a decade of the Rosary for the repose of the soul of her departed father, and she was interrupted by a knock on the door.

"Hurrish! Lizz! Hurrish! Hurrish!" she heard her mother calling, as the old lady continued rapping nervously.

Dragging her feet, she went to the door, opened it, and flung her arms around Mrs. O'Flaherty.

Mrs. O'Flaherty burst into the parlor, wearing a black sealskin coat and a small flower-trimmed hat with a black veil. Lizz helped her off with her coat and laid it over a chair.

"Here, I brought some cakes. But where are the little ones?" she said, handing Lizz a bag.

"I let Little Margaret and Dennis go to the playground. I thought that I would get them out of the way and clean house today. But I am not able to. So I sat down to say the rosary for Pa, my father," Lizz said.

"Pa came to see me last night when I was asleep. Pa's in Heaven," Mrs. O'Flaherty said.

"I still cry over my poor father," Lizz said.

"We all are called to go," Mrs. O'Flaherty said.

"How is my son?" Lizz asked, her tone suggestively possessive.

"He's the cleanest-dressed boy in Crucifixion parish," Mrs. O'Flaherty loudly boasted, frowning at her daughter.

"You're so good to him, and he is such a cute child," Lizz said.

"The best is not too good for my grandson!"

"I've been wanting to come and see you and little Danny, but I'm still so weak from having little Catherine. Oh, Mother, I had a hard time, Mother, and I haven't been out since, except for the baptism and for mass last Sunday. As soon as I am stronger, I'll come up and see you. And my neuralgia is giving me so much pain, I have to keep this rag on my face," Lizz said, touching the filthy cloth tied around her head and under her chin.

"Make Jim take care of the little ones some night and come up," the mother said.

"Mother, look at my Robert. He's so sweet, like sugar. Come, child! Come and see your grandmother!"

"He is sweet. But, Lizz, none of your little ones are a match for my grandson, Daniel," Mrs. O'Flaherty said, studying her shy grandson.

"Say!" Lizz exclaimed, her face flushing with anger, but then she smiled sloppily. "I tell everyone I see what fine care you take of my son."

"Why shouldn't I? He takes after me mother," Mrs. O'Flaherty said.

"Is Al still on the road?" asked Lizz.

"The poor boy is away working to pay the bills, and, Lizz," Mrs. O'Flaherty leaned forward and lowered her voice, "Margaret is out nights gallivantin' with the tinkers and the high-lifers."

"Tell me about it, Mother! But come out in the kitchen and have a cup of tea."

"I will have a sip of tea, Lizz," Mrs. O'Flaherty said, following Lizz out to the kitchen.

Mrs. O'Flaherty dusted the chair, and sat down while Lizz fixed tea for both of them.

"Lizz, that man is in town. She's going out with him tonight."

"Jesus Mercy!" said Lizz.

"A black Protestant, and a married man with a wife and children. And she, like a streetwalker, seeing him. I never thought that I would live to see such a day."

"Does Al know?"

"How can the poor boy, away, carrying those heavy suitcases?"

"It's a shame!"

"If I ever get my hands on him, that black Protestant, that married man, I'll fist him!" said Mrs. O'Flaherty, shaking her fists wildly.

"No, don't do that, Mother. They'll put you in jail for disorderly conduct," Lizz said, and they drew near the table, put sugar and condensed milk in their tea, sipped it.

"I'll go the gallows yet for sticking a knife in him," said Mrs. O'Flaherty.

"I'll have Jim beat him up for you, Mother!" said Lizz.

"I'll give him ten dollars if he splits the head of Lorry Robinson. Ten dollars cash," Mrs. O'Flaherty said.

"Jim doesn't like such goings-on. Jim is a decent man, my Jim is," Lizz said.

"It's a shame against God. Her cutting-up with him, seeing him tonight. She with her cigarettes, and her drinking, and the parcel of high-lifers she is always taking up with, not one of them fit to walk the ground of the same earth that my son, Al, walks on. Him carrying heavy suitcases, and paying hard-earned money for rent and electricity so she can be running around with tinkers. Ah, my mother would have beaten my pelt black and blue if I did that in the old country. It's a shame against God, and no decent girl would do it. Doing God knows what with that black Protestant! But she won't carry on like that and live under my son's roof. You tell Jim I'll give him twenty dollars to break that Protestant's head."

"Say, Jim will do it. My Jim is a fighter," Lizz said.

"Twenty dollars to the man who brings me a pound of Lorry Robinson's flesh!"

"Mother, she's my own sister, but I know her and her ilk. The airs she puts on. She thinks she is somebody since she became cashier at the Union Hotel," Lizz said, her face becoming animated.

"It's against God. She's my own daughter, and she's the shame of the whole neighborhood," Mrs. O'Flaherty said.

"Mother, you mark my words! God will repay her! God says: *'Thou Shalt Not Commit Adultery.'* Her, Peg O'Flaherty, putting something over on God? Not on your tintype. Say, you can't go against the will of the Holy Man who made you, sinning, flouting His commandments, missing mass, you can't do that without paying for it in the fires of Hell. Woe to her who flouts Him! She might blow her cigarette smoke in our faces, but God will never let her blow it in His eyes."

"Lizz, you say the truth," Mrs. O'Flaherty said.

"But come, Mother, you must look at my precious, your brand-new baby granddaughter. She will never grow up to smoke cigarettes. Not her. She is going to be the nun her mother wanted to be," Lizz said, taking her mother's arm, leading her to the bedroom. "Mother, isn't she the cutest little thing? Oh, she's her mama's precious angel," Lizz added as they looked down at the puckered face of the infant.

"She's so pretty. A pity she's a girl," Mrs. O'Flaherty said.

They returned to the kitchen and Lizz poured more tea.

"With Al such a good brother, you would think Peg would be ashamed of herself doing what she does," Lizz said.

"She's a high-lifer! She leaves me alone every night she's not working, me and the little fellow, and for all she cares some burglar could come and hit us on the head," Mrs. O'Flaherty said.

"Mother, bolt your doors tight. Hang a Sacred Heart on the door. Put on the burglar lock. And pray to Saint Joseph, the father of Jesus. Saint Joseph was a father, and he will look over all decent households. Say three Hail Marys and three Our Fathers to him, and he'll keep burglars from hitting you on the head and robbing you," Lizz said.

"Sure, if a burglar came, I'd split his head with the coffee pot," the mother said.

"I'd come up and stay with you if I didn't have so much to do here," Lizz said, again sipping tea.

"You must take care of yourself, Lizz."

"It's hard on me, Mother," Lizz whined.

"The life is hardly in me these days with Peg and that nigger washwoman."

"Mother, you can never trust a nigger or a Jew. The Jews killed Christ, and the nigger is a Jew made black till the Day of Judgment as a punishment from God. The niggers are descended from Cain. Cain slew his brother Abel and God turned on Cain for killing his brother, and said that all the descendants of Cain would be black, and they would have to live in Africa where it is uncivilized. And to this day they are an outcast people, and their skins are black like monkeys. You can never trust them."

"This one eats too much of my son's food," Mrs. O'Flaherty said.

"The niggers living on the other side of the viaduct here at Twenty-fifth Street all carry razors and they would just as soon slit a white man's throat as look at him. They chased my Bill the other day," Lizz said.

"How is Jim?" Mrs. O'Flaherty asked.

"The poor man, his rupture troubles him, and he works so hard at the express company. He took the pledge right after little Catherine came, and he's kept it like a soldier. Mother, he brings his pay envelope home to me unopened every pay day."

"A finer man than your Jim, Lizz, never walked the earth, except for my son, and my uncle in the old country," said the mother.

"But, Mother, I want to move and get out of this dump, and this dirty neighborhood. It's full of Germans, and, Mother, never trust a German. I could spit in the eye of these Germans like Mrs. Ringel and Mrs. Koffinger, with their bellies so fat you would think they were carrying around twins. And they got nothing to do all day but gas and snoop around to see what kind of a house I have. They're sausage-eaters, Mother, that's what they are. When they come to see you, oh, you should just see them mince, and be sweet as sugar and nice as pie to me. But I know them! They can't fool me, the dirty sausage-eaters! They sniff around, and pump me about my Jim, and does he drink? Oh, but don't I know them! Just like an open book. Mother, the German is thick, and you can never trust him."

"Them that has to 'umble, must 'umble!"

"And there are Irish, and Polacks, and the dirty dagoes around, too, and, Mother, I am a white woman! I'm a white woman, and I come from a fine family. Your father and mother owned land in Ireland, and they were the descendants of kings of Ireland," Lizz said proudly.

"Ah, they were so poor in the old country!" Mrs. O'Flaherty said.

"I'm a white woman, descended from kings of Ireland," Lizz said, brandishing her arms, "and I have to live with niggers in back of me, using the same toilet with us. My children can't go out in the back yard and play without smelling pickaninnies. I'm going to move out of this dump!"

"Sure, you say the truth!" Mrs. O'Flaherty said, her head nodding in agreement.

"Oh, Mother, guess who came to see me the other day?" Lizz said, raising her voice.

"Who?"

"Mary O'Reilley."

"I never liked an O'Reilley. They are born of the Devil," said Mrs. O'Flaherty.

Lizz poured more tea.

"Her, with her O'Reilley airs. She comes here, and oh, she's so nice, bringing me old clothes for Jim and the kids that aren't fit to be worn. Just as sweet as angel cake with frosting!"

"What did she say?" the mother asked, leaning forward, her eyes gleaming with interest.

"If she means so well, and wants to help me, why doesn't she go to Joe and say 'Brother Joe, give me a hundred dollars for Lizz O'Neill. She's poor with all those children, and I want to help her.' But no, she's all sweetness with honey and words, and it doesn't mean a thing. I'm honorably poor, and Our Lord said: *'Blessed are the poor!'* The O'Reilleys with those airs they put on!"

"I knew an O'Reilley in the old country who didn't have a sheet for a shirt," the mother said.

"They're Jim's people, not mine, and you can't trust them!" Lizz bellowed.

"Lizz, you say the truth," the mother added.

"Those two old maids, Mary and Martha. They build an iron fence around their brother Joe, for fear Joe would give something away. They want it all for themselves. Mother, you mark my words, they'll die old maids. Mary used to go with Myles Rierdon, but he wouldn't have her. She wasn't good enough for him. And Martha, with her hatchet face. Mother, they couldn't get a man if Joe served them out to somebody on a platter of gold and silver, with diamonds shining in the platter. Not those two!"

"Lizz, wouldn't Myles Rierdon have Mary O'Reilley?"

"Say, he tied a tin can to her quick as a wink. She was trying to hook him at the same time that I was going with Jim. You know, Mother, I think she wanted to get Ned when Myles said one, two, three, skidoo with you to Mary. I think she did. She had her eyes on Ned then."

"You don't say? Why, that one is an old woman alongside of him. Why, if I caught her, I wouldn't have left a stitch on her back."

"Those two old maids can't get a man, and so they keep everybody away from Joe," Lizz said, and she leaned forward, her voice becoming secretive. "They want what Joe's got for themselves. That's what it is."

"Who would think it?" said the mother.

"They'll die old maids, and have white caskets," said Lizz.

"In the town of Meath, an O'Reilley wasn't good enough to lift a finger to a Fox," Mrs. O'Flaherty said.

"And now with their steam heat, and their lace curtains, and their home on Grand Boulevard, and living in Crucifixion parish, oh, are they swell! Mother, the O'Reilleys are just plain common Irish," Lizz said, getting up, forgetting her weakness, and hopping and jigging around, gesturing as she pantomimed.

"In the old country, me mother used to say, 'Never look at an O'Reilley. O'Reilleys are County Mayo tinkers.' And that's the very words she said," Mrs. O'Flaherty said.

"There's the baby. I've got to feed the little precious," Lizz said, hearing the baby suddenly begin to cry.

The mother waited while Lizz got the infant and returned to the kitchen, the baby suckling on her breast.

"She's her mother's little dumpling, Mother. I just know she'll grow up to be as beautiful as my beautiful sister Louise was," Lizz said, smiling, revealing her decayed teeth.

"If she looks like my Louise, she'll be as fine a girl as ever walked the street," said Mrs. O'Flaherty.

"I had a mass said for Pa and Louise last week," Lizz said.

"Oh, you're so good, Lizz. If my daughter Peg was only as good as you are . . .

"Don't cry, Mother! God wanted Louise to go to Him, and it was His will," Lizz said as the mother wiped her tearful eyes.

"It was that typewriting she learned and worked so hard at that gave her the consumption," the mother said, still crying.

"Louise was too pure a girl for this world. That was why God called her. She belonged with his angels in the heavenly choir. But, Mother, don't cry. She's happy."

"Sure, I'm getting to the latter end of me days, and I'll be seeing my Louise soon," Mrs. O'Flaherty dolorously said, almost in a chant.

"Why, Mother, you've hardly got a gray hair in your head. You'll bury most of us yet," said Lizz.

"Lizz, ah, there's little enough strength left in me old bones."

"I saw Sadie Powers not so long ago. And she said to me, 'Lizz, how is that mother of yours? She's so young.' Why, Mother, you're the talk of the town, without a gray hair in your head, so strong and active."

"Well do I know that me days are numbered, and that soon I'll be with Pa, and Louise, and the rest of me dead children."

"Maybe we'll both be better off, Mother, when we join Pa and Louise in Heaven. And, oh, Mother, how grand it will be to see your mother and father, my grandparents, in Heaven!" Lizz said.

"Good people they were, and hard-working."

"They were no more hard-working than you were, Mother."

"Ah, they had a hard life."

"When we go, Mother, it's because we are called by the Great Man above."

"You say the truth, Lizz."

"But, Mother, look at my little precious?" Lizz said, and the grandmother stood up to look tenderly at her infant granddaughter suckling intently.

III

Loaded with bundles, Jim let himself into the front room and kicked the door shut behind him. His face dropped as he glanced around the room in the last dim gleams of the fading day. It seemed dirtier than ever. He checked a curse. After all, Lizz was still too weak to keep it clean. But damn it, even so, a man hated to come home from work and always see the same damn disorder.

"Here's my Papa. My Papa is my money man," said Little Margaret, climbing around his legs.

"Papa! Papa! Papa!" Dennis said, almost stuttering, clutching at his father's left leg.

Ah, if he could make something out of all these little ones! And there was Bill, his favorite, reading a newspaper by the dining room lamp. But goddamn it, why didn't Bill do a little picking up? He could leave the baseball news wait a little while.

Jim dropped his bundles on the dining-room table. Placing his hands on his hips, he angrily glared at Bill. An oppression from his worries and his poverty suddenly came over him like a smothering blanket. He also recalled, how old Shaughnessy had bawled him out today. And he had to take it. He was in no position to climb down off his wagon and paste the old bastard's face in like he itched to.

"Hey, you, why are you sitting here on your can instead of doing something around the house, with your mother sick?"

"Ma told me not to bother to do anything except run down to Silverman's for groceries, and I did that," Bill said.

"She did, huh? And so that is excuse enough for you to sit here in all this dirt!" Jim said, taking a step nearer to Bill, his fists clenched.

"Jim, don't you hit my Billy-boy. I told him not to do anything," Lizz said, appearing from the kitchen at the same moment, the infant in her arms.

He swung around to face Lizz, relaxing. Women! They left a man so god-damn helpless. Sometimes he sure did wish that he'd never had anything to do with them.

"Oh, Jim, look at your little precious angel," Lizz said, her decaying teeth sticking out of her smile.

Jim perfunctorily kissed Lizz on the forehead. He smiled down at the red and shriveled infant face and at the few tufts of hair sticking out from the dirty swaddling clothes. His pride mounted. The cute little bugger! And his! He took the infant from Lizz, held it carefully but awkwardly. It commenced to squirm, and to cry. Lizz took it back, cooed and sang to it, and it ceased bawling.

Yes, he told himself, he was glad, glad that it had lived. And it would grow up to be a beautiful, dark-haired girl with blue eyes, looking as its mother had once looked. Ah! Yes, the little buggers were something for a man to work for! All he asked was that he be able to give them a decent chance to live, nothing else. But, Jesus, he hoped that he didn't have any more. And damn it, what could a man do? Being kept from it so long, because of the baby, it almost made him feel like a bull. And he couldn't use those damn rubbers all the time, crabbing some of the feeling. What else much was there for a man like himself?

"I didn't get a chance to start supper. As soon as I feed my little cherubim I'll start it, Jim. I got corn."

"I brought home some liver. I'll fix it. Don't worry," Jim said.

He gave Bill his cap and coat to hang up, and carried the bundles out to the kitchen. Dennis followed him with mute adoration. He called Bill to come out and get busy and wash some of the dishes in the sink. He put wood in the stove to get a better fire, set the kettle on for the water to boil, began frying the liver, and dumped the canned corn in a pot to heat. Opening one of his bundles, he washed some lettuce.

"My mother was down to see me today. She gave me two dollars," Lizz said, sitting down in the kitchen.

"The less I see of your people the better. Lizz, you mark my words!" Jim said, pointing with his left hand, the little finger missing. "You mark my words! They're going to make nothing but a goddamn dude out of our kid."

"They're so good to him, Mother has him wear a clean shirt every day. He's the cleanest-dressed boy in Crucifixion school."

"Soon he won't even know his own parents and his brothers and sisters. The way I think is that if our home is good enough for Bill and the rest of the kids, it's good enough for him."

"My mother loves Danny so much. She would scratch the eyes out of anybody who tried to take him away from her. And with Al away so much, and Peg working nights and running around like a high-lifer with that married man, Robinson, the way she does, my mother has no one with her at nights. She needs Danny for company," said Lizz.

"She had her own kids, didn't she? Well, it's too god-damn bad about her. I don't have kids to loan them out to keep old ladies company."

"Jim, if you and I are as good to our grandchildren as my mother is to my Danny, we can hold our heads mighty high in the air."

"I have nothing against her. I just don't want to be beholden to her, or to anyone. The old lady, she's all right. And so was Tom, the old gent. He was a regular fellow, and I liked to have a glass of beer with him whenever he came down. But all those dude brothers of yours can do is to sell shoes. After they've sold a pair of shoes they're helpless."

"Al is a good boy. He takes care of his mother, and he sends me something whenever he can spare it. I'll open the head of anyone with a milk bottle who talks about my brother, Al."

Jim was busy turning over the sizzling liver in the frying pan. He did not answer Lizz. The prospect of supper, Lizz and the baby, the sounds of his kids playing and talking, Bill coming in and going back to the dining room, setting the table, it made him feel good, not gloomy and pessimistic. He didn't feel so tired, either. Felt almost like singing, and he would, if he didn't have such a foghorn voice. His leathery face uncreased in smiles and good nature. He had his family, and the chance to help the kids make something out of themselves, and no man need ask for another thing from God. That and his health! He was a lucky man, he felt. And ah, when he and Lizz were old, when they pulled their oars evenly and together over the years, he would look back on all these days, and he would be grateful for them, grateful that they had had to fight through some days of worry and poverty.

And Lizz singing and cooing at the infant at her breast. It made him see how there was a kind of a wonderful mystery to all this life that the Lord had created out of nothing.

And now supper was ready. He led Lizz back into the dining room, carrying the food. He served Lizz and the kids, and then himself. He dumped catsup on his plate, looked up, smiled around the table.

"Well, Bill, how did it go in school today?" he asked.

"At the blackboard I got the problems in long division finished ahead of all the other kids. Miss Timins told me I was the fastest in the room in arithmetic," Bill said.

"Good, Bill!" Jim beamed. "Listen to the advice your old man gives you! Study hard! You're an O'Neill, Bill, and you want to make everybody know that the O'Neills are proud of their name, and they got as much stuff on the ball in the game of life as old Three-fingered Brown has when he toes the mound."

"Pa, Danny goes to school. When can I go?" Little Margaret said.

"You're all going to school. The O'Neills are going to be the smartest bunch of kids this side of Hades, aren't they, Lizz, old girl?"

"My Bobby is going to be a priest, and Denny is going to be a lawyer. Bill is going to be a doctor, and Danny a lawyer. And Little Margaret will teach school. This beautiful little infant will be a bride of Jesus. She is going to be a nun," Lizz said.

"They're all going to be better than their old man," boasted Jim.

"Oh, you little stinker!" Lizz suddenly said as Bob let corn juice dribble down his plump chin.

"Peggy, feed your little brother!" Jim said, reaching over and wiping Bob's chin with a towel.

"Jim, Mother was telling me that Margaret's friend, Robinson . . ."

"Not here with them around, Lizz," Jim interrupted.

"I know something about Aunt Margaret," Little Margaret brightly said.

"What?" Bill asked.

"She smokes cigarettes," Little Margaret said.

"Don't be talking like that, Peggy," Jim said.

"But she does, Papa. I saw her when I was at Mother's house."

"Talk about something else or I'll split your head!" Lizz said to her daughter.

"Don't talk like that to them. They're only babies."

"My sister is her godmother. She's good to her," Lizz said.

"I know I should never have let them have Danny," said Jim, and he turned toward Bill. "I don't want you hanging around the O'Flahertys so much. They'll try and make a dude out of you, and if I catch you trying to be a dude I'll tan that hide of yours with my razor strap."

"His brother Danny always cries for him and says, 'I want my Big Brother Bill,'" said Lizz.

Jim lapsed into silence. He ate. He looked at his ragged children. And that memory. It cut like a sharp pain to the base of his heart. That night! He would never forget it as long as he lived. He had gone to bring Danny home from the O'Flahertys. Ned had taken him there to stay when Lizz had had Little Margaret. And then that night he had gone to get Danny and take him back home. He couldn't ever forget it. It was burned right into him. Coming home on the street car, the boy had cried and screamed. Back with his mother, he had still screamed. Put to bed, he had screamed. He would never forget it. Getting up at two o'clock in the morning, dressing, while the boy screamed himself into convulsions. A man on the street car asking him, Jim O'Neill, who'd give his life for his family, asking him was he beating the child? Getting back to the O'Flahertys on Indiana Avenue. The boy stretching his arms out to his grandmother.

Mother, put me to bed!

He could never forget that denial of himself and Lizz by their own flesh and blood. He didn't blame little Danny. He was a baby. He blamed the O'Flahertys. They had done it. Caused a boy to deny his own father and mother, his father's house!

Silently, he cursed. He glanced around at his ragged children, from face to face, at his wife, at the gleaming kerosene lamp. He goddamned his poverty, the poverty that had robbed him of one son. God, would he ever break through it into something better?

6

I

"You're sure now, my Peg, that you weren't followed?" Lorry Robinson asked with some anxiety in his voice, a fretting expression clouding his dark, handsome face.

Margaret O'Flaherty nodded, and they embraced.

"Those eyes of yours. I dream of them. They're so much like the eyes of a little boy," she said, still in his arms, stroking his clipped brown hair.

They freed each other. Lorry sat on the bed of his hotel suite. She took a low chair opposite him. Her gaze became devouring.

"I'm worried," she said.

"Don't, Peg! Everything is going to be all right."

"Why are there private detectives sticking their nose in my life?"

"It doesn't surprise me. Brophy wants to get something on me. All he has been able to do is to try and lie, accusing me of blackmail."

"The cur!"

"He said that because I checkmated him in his crooked management of the Crown Point Lumber Company in which we're both big stockholders."

"Every time he passes me in the Floradora room I want to spit in his face," she hissed.

"Well, in Washington they couldn't shake my testimony. And if it weren't for our spineless board of directors I'd have driven him out of the Crown Point Lumber Company, too. But mark my words! The Senatorial Investigation is the finish of Brophy. He'll never get over the notoriety, and Graham is going to be unseated in the Senate in disgrace. Peg, the newspapers all over the country spread my testimony on the front pages. And they condemned Brophy." Lorry smiled enigmatically, patronizing his own words, "Peg, they condemned Brophy because of the unholy alliance between business and politics."

"Lorry, you're such a wonderful man," she said.

"I have Brophy's game perfectly ticketed. In the C.P. Lumber Company he became both a buyer and a seller in order to fatten the profits of his own lumber company here in Chicago. You know, I never trusted him. And that's why I brought him up on charges and exposed him at a directors' meeting." Lorry beamed. "But I put one over on him. I forced him to buy one hundred thousand shares of my C.P. stock at a dollar twenty-four a share. And just when I needed money most for one of my deals. And he's going to take thousands of more shares and pay me one thirty-eight a share. Because if he doesn't, I'll sell them to every little piker from here to Hell and back. I'll even sell it to niggers. If he doesn't take it at my price, he'll go to his next meeting to sit with more pikers and niggers than he ever saw before. If he wants to collect voting proxies, it'll take him a year to find them. There's no worry, Peg, because I have that turkey where I want him. He'll squirm plenty before he's finished with Lorry Robinson," Lorry said.

He paced the floor, growing noticeably nervous. She looked lovingly at him. He was a tall, evenly-built man, and oh, she told herself, he was so handsome, so noble, so fine. And he was hers. Tonight he was going to be hers only, body and soul, and she was going to love him, and pet him until there was no sign of worry left in those dark eyes of his, and she would stroke and love him into forgetfulness and sleep. She watched him as he lit a cigar. It made her sad. And afraid. When he was like this with his business cares, he wasn't hers. He seemed to be in a world locked out from her, a stranger. She was more jealous of his business than she was of his wife, that frozen, skinny little imitation of a woman. Oh, how in God's name had such a woman gotten a man like her Lorry? If only that woman would die. She should be afraid of God's wrath, wishing death on anyone. But she didn't care. She wished, yes, she wished that his toothpick wife would die from something as dreadful as cancer of the womb!

"I don't want Brophy dragging you into this, my dear. And if he does . . . I got detectives hired, too. I know lots more about Brophy, besides this Graham business and his management of the C.P. Lumber," Lorry said, talking to himself as much as to Margaret.

Suddenly he smiled, winked at her. Now he again seemed like her lover.

"I think that supper is what we need. It's too bad we'll have to have it here in the room. I'd wanted to go to De Jonghe's and then see a good lively play. But, well, Peg, there'll be other days."

He chucked her under the chin, bent down, kissed her. He phoned down to room service, and they ordered supper. He drew a bottle of bourbon out from a dresser drawer.

"Want one, Peg?"

She nodded. He poured out two drinks. They tipped glasses. After the drink, she smiled at him, hoping that he would not get to frowning again. She had been so excited all day, waiting for the time when she would come to him. And then to find him worried, thinking about business and politics, almost like a stranger to her. She wouldn't let him worry! She wouldn't! He took a second glass of bourbon, gulped it down.

"And, my Peg, how are you?" he asked, sinking down again on the bed.

"Oh, that family of mine! My sister had another baby in August, and she's so poor. I have to keep giving her money now. There's always the need of something in my family, and it falls on me."

"That brother-in-law of yours doesn't cause any rise in rubber stocks, does he?"

"Don't say that. It's vile," she protested.

"Be yourself, Peg."

"I am. I have so many burdens to bear, Lorry."

"I'll give you something to give your poor sister."

"Darling, you are so generous. But it's always the same. Money! Money! Money! And now times are bad. My brother Al is worried, and we're still paying the debts we made taking care of my father and sister, and burying them. Poor Louise. She liked you so much, Lorry."

"She was a fine girl. Almost as fine as her big sister. She had spirit, too, didn't she?"

"I loved Louise."

"Everybody did," Lorry said.

"She didn't want to be a burden. When she knew that she couldn't get well, Lorry, she wanted to die."

"We all go sometime."

"Oh, life is bad enough and times are hard enough without speaking of dying," Peg said impatiently.

"Well, Peg, things will pick up. The possibilities in this country are endless. America is going to be the richest nation in all history. Why, we've got everything here. Peg, you should see some of my lumber lands. Resources? They are beyond calculation. We're coming into an age that is bound to be the wealthiest the human race has ever known. Times are a little tight now. I know most of my money is tied up, and I've had to put up every cent I could raise as collateral for loans I needed to swing some of my deals out west. But that's only temporary. And Brophy is going to pay me for my C.P. stock. Hard times with money tight is only natural. It has to come now and then, just as it did a few years back in 1907. It is like a man who exercises a lot. After he does, he has to stop to catch his wind again. The business cycle is the same way. The business system is catching its wind again now. Don't you worry. When I get my affairs straightened out, and push through the deals I have on hand with my partners, Murphy and Sewall, you'll have nothing in the world to worry about," he said while she listened adoringly; then he came to her, kissed her again.

"Damn Brophy! I hate the sight of him! When I see him with his cocky little walk in the Union Hotel! Why, that little runt!"

"Come, Peg. I got him where I want him. And that handsome face of yours wasn't made for worry or hatred. Smile!" he said, and she forced a smile.

"Oh, darling, I love you so much. If you worry, how can I help it? And then I have all of my family on my poor shoulders."

"Peg, all this is only passing. When the right time comes, I'll be able to get a divorce. And then, we have the world. Mr. and Mrs. L. R. Robinson are going to be happy and travel then. Maybe they'll go to Europe, and buy up a few kings and princes just for the fun of it."

There was a knock on the door. Lorry opened it and a waiter carried in a table of food. Lorry signed the check and gave him a silver dollar for a tip. The waiter bowed himself out of the room.

"Lorry, dear, I hope all this publicity and trouble isn't going to worry you," Margaret said as they sat down to the meal.

"It's not. Except that I don't want Brophy dragging you into this."

"I can't understand it all."

"Let's eat anyway," he said, and they sat down to eat. "Didn't you read about my testimony before the Senate Committee?"

"You were so honest, and smart. I was so proud of you. I read it in all of the papers here."

"I told them. And it came straight from the shoulder."

"Why would Brophy spend so much of his money to get Graham elected senator?"

"It wasn't all his own money. He collected it from business men here. He was lobbying for a high tariff on lumber, and that's good for our business. We need protection from foreign competition. And Graham was a man he could rely on. He told me so in my room at the Union Hotel that day."

"What day?"

"When Brophy called up the governor. He came back from Washington, and came to my room from the train because we had some Crown Point business matters to discuss. He called up the state capitol long distance from my room and said that Graham was agreeable to Washington, and he was coming down on the next train with all the money needed to put Graham in," Lorry said.

"What did he do with the money?"

"Bought up enough votes to get Graham elected senator. Well, such things are no skin off mine. And we ought to have a good senator in Washington to get us the protection we need. But when I saw what Brophy was doing to our outfit in order to get bigger profits for Brophy Lumber Company here, well, I was not going to get double-crossed, Peg. When this thing broke, I was glad to spill out what I knew. And no one knew more than I, except Blaine, the thresh-ing-machine fellow here. Brophy tried to collect part of the jack pot from him. I've put a monkey wrench in Brophy's works now. And I'm getting out of this goddamn C.P. and I'm not losing a cent when I get out, either!"

"You're such a wonderful business man, Lorry," she said, both of them con-tinuing to eat slowly.

"I'll have to leave town. This whole affair with Brophy has taken up my time. I got to get back to my office. Lots of things are waiting for me in Minnesota. And do you know what else Brophy did to me?"

"What?"

"He has power in business and politics in Chicago. He went to the banks I usually get loans from here, and crabbed that. And just at a time when I found myself strapped for ready cash because of the deals I'm swinging with Murphy and Sewall out in Oregon."

"The gallows would be too good for that dirty runt!" she said, dropping her knife and fork.

"I got to get back to a lot of things, and I'll have to go down south to see about the pine market, and I might have to take trips up to Canada and way out to Oregon. You write me, care of my office, and sign your name J. S. Olson. You know what to say?"

"Yes, dear, but I'll miss you so much."

"Be careful, and a good girl."

"I have so much to do I won't have time to be anything else."

"I'll send you something."

"I'll need it, Lorry, honey."

"Don't fret yourself over money. I'm not going to be broke or anything like that. I have to draw in, and much of my money is tied up in deals, or frozen in stocks. But you need never worry. I'm going to take care of you the way you deserve to be taken care of."

"I love you, Lorry," she said, her eyes softening into an expression of adora-tion.

"Too bad we couldn't have gone out tonight, though! These goddamn dicks! Sometimes they are too damn good. I know it, because I had to use them a couple of years ago out West when I had labor troubles in some of my camps out there that we were logging. They were too damn good then—for the union," he said, smiling thinly.

"Honey, you need never worry about me. I wasn't born yesterday. And you know, Lorry, honey, that you can always rely on me."

"Peg, you don't know how much of a comfort you are to me, and how much I looked forward to my trips here, because I know that I'm going to be seeing you," he said, reaching across the table and patting her hand.

He must be tired, she thought, with all his business. After supper she was going to have him just lay that wonderful head of his against her breast, and stroke his hair, and kiss him, and with her lips and her fingers draw all the worry right out of him. Because when he was worried his mind was so far away, and she felt that then he wasn't hers, her Lorry. It was only when she could love him that he was hers. And then he got so much like a tired boy, putting his head close to her for protection and comfort.

"And, dear, times are going to get better, and you're going to have wonderful success," she said.

"I know it. Times got to pick up. The business cycle is a matter of ups and downs, action and reaction. I'm swinging these deals now, when things are down, and when the reaction comes, and they go up, I collect."

Peg nodded agreement. She was not sure that she completely understood the meaning behind his words. He was a brainy man, who knew all about business. And if he said times would be better, they would be. Look at all the money he was worth, and look what he some day was going to be worth. And he was hers. Yes, he was, and some day he was going to marry her, when he got things cleared up and could get divorced. But that wife of his, she was an icebox, not a woman for Lorry, not worthy of him. How could a man as fine as Lorry have ever seen anything in her. Why, she was just bones. But she had possessed Lorry. Peg would hate her for that to her dying day. She would hate every woman who ever had. But no, no, no woman had ever had Lorry as she had, and no other woman ever would. She had had him, body and soul, and she had given herself to him body and soul, and it had not been the same as it had been with other men that she had gone to bed with. And that child had sealed their lives and their love. That poor idiot child of theirs, now two years old, away in some institution being taken care of. Sometimes, all of her, her body, her mind, her heart screamed for that child. Hers and his. After they were married, they would have another, and it would be a normal child, just simply beautiful. And they would love it so, and take such care of it. It would look just like Lorry. But she hadn't better mention it. Every time she did, his brows knitted and he got surly.

"Well, that meal hit the spot," Lorry said, shoving aside his napkin, both of them finished with their supper.

She looked at him. He still seemed worried. And to think he was not always hers, not always with her. That she had to share any part of him with another, his goddamn wife! Let that creature die! Let her die the vilest death! Let him divorce his wife, place a settlement on her. Then she would have Lorry all to herself. Then she would leave the lousy O'Flahertys forever. She began to cry, fearing that she would never have this man that she wanted so much.

"Come, come, little woman, what is it?"

"Oh, Lorry! Lorry, you've got to get me away. I can't stand it, going on like this, seeing you so little, living with my people. They take every penny I earn. They drain me of every ounce of energy. Here I am almost twenty-five, and they still want me to answer to them. And when I finish working long hours at the hotel I got to go home and help with housework, cook. Everything, everything is placed on my shoulders."

"Peg, if you'll just be patient and bear with me until my affairs shape out better, we'll be able to make some plans. I promise!"

"I'll go mad. I haven't a nerve left."

Stretching his arm across the table, he patted her cheek.

"I bear all the burdens. Paying for burying a father and sister this very year. Oh!" she sighed.

"I think you've mentioned it to me," he said.

She cried. He poured drinks, and she lit a cigarette. They sat, holding their glasses.

"Lorry, I wish that you and I could just get away from it all," she said moodily.

"Some day," he muttered thoughtfully, and she drank after him.

She felt an unexpected terror which seemed to paralyze her entire body. Was she losing him? Didn't he love her? Again he seemed so far away. She felt that she was actually so little in his confidence and his trust. She wanted to know more of his troubles, to share them with him. She wanted his burdens to be placed on her shoulders, even though she had burdens of her own. And, oh, she just wanted to kiss and pet him like a baby when his brows knit this way in worry. God, God, if she lost him, she'd kill herself. There would be nothing to live for. She would just turn on the gas.

She reached across the table, grasped his hand, squeezed it almost frantically.

"I never want to lose you, darling!"

He smiled, his expression now mellow, his eyes tender. He poured more whiskey. They tipped glasses.

"To our future happiness," he said.

"I love you," she said, and they drank.

"You're fine, Peg."

"And we're going to get away from all this," she said.

"Peg, they can't stop me!" he said, pouring a drink, gulping it down. "They can't. I'm going to become one of the biggest men in this goddamn country. One of the men who runs it!"

"I know you are, Lorry, chicken. You're going to be a great man," she said, speaking slowly because she was getting drunk.

"That rat, Brophy! Here's what's going to happen to him," he said, clenching his fists in a crushing gesture, grimacing simultaneously, while she listened closely. "There's not going to be a man in the country big enough to stop me!"

They had another drink.

"And we'll be married, and oh, so happy. I know it. I knew it the minute I first laid eyes on you in the Union Hotel. I knew you were a man, not a little piker. Darling, you're going to be so big, so big, you'll be a tower they can't even look up to. You'll be like the Singer Building in New York."

She arose, swayed to him. He clutched her. They kissed, licking each other's tongues. He looked down into her drunken eyes. She curled against him, stroked his face.

"I'm the man behind the Graham scandal, behind the scenes. Brophy, he was double-crossing me, so I, Lawrence Robinson, Esquire, if you please, I turned the switch on. Now let his ass burn!"

"To hell with them! To hell with Graham! To hell with Brophy! Let their asses burn! Darling, I love you. They're not big, they're not honest like my darling! Kiss me, Lorry, kiss me hard!"

"Peg, a drink to the future!" he said, and pouring drinks, they tipped glasses.

"To the bigges' bigges' man in the worl'," she said.

"Maybe I'm only bragging. Maybe I'm a fool. But time will tell. Time will tell. You remember, darling kiddo, you remember ten, fifteen years from now, you'll see. You'll see whether Lawrence Robinson was a fool and a braggart or not, talking through his Stetson. I'm going to be big. I'm going to have power. Power!" he said, his face becoming hard, tense, the veins almost jutting out of it. "Power!"

"Lorry!" she said.

She staggered into his arms. He kissed her, and then he began roughly to disrobe her.

7

I

Reading a letter from Margaret, Al O'Flaherty sat in the large and glittering hotel dining room with its dominating crystal pendant chandeliers, its many ornamentations, its thick red velvet draperies, its carvings, scrolls and pillars. The waiter set his order before him, lifting the polished silver cover from a platter of juicy steak. Al glanced down at the food. But the letter had suddenly robbed him his appetite. He started eating mechanically. What Margaret had written was like a worm eating away in his mind. Complaints about the money she spent on the home. And gee, when he had left on this present trip, she had said that the ten dollars a week he sent to Mother was more than enough to take care of food and ordinary household expenses. Now she was complaining. And she said that Mother was nagging her. And Lizz needing money. And that goddamn Bill, always hanging around the house, getting on her nerves. And Danny would not mind her and Mother. She couldn't do her work at the hotel, she said. And, gee, when he had left, everything at home had seemed to be so satisfactory. And then this letter! Jesus Christ! Chewing a piece of steak, he asked himself would things ever run smoothly?

A string quartet at the other end of the room began playing *The Blue Danube*. His mind was easefully carried away from worry. His anxieties faded into vague, sad, wishful feelings. A wave of nostalgia flowed through him, and as he continued eating, he was as if transported back to the days of his young manhood. Then they had all been poorer. Margaret was working at Frascini's candy store, earning about five dollars a week. Ned was home, and out of work half of the time. He was only a shoe clerk on State Street, just promoted from his job of wrapping shoes. The old man was still driving a wagon and beginning to be troubled with those pains that turned out to have been cancer of the stomach.

Louise was just a pretty girl in pigtails. Lizz was working as a maid for that
Mrs. Lynn down on Drexel Boulevard. Ah, those days, olden days, gone now.
And now he was a man of thirty-eight, and he had come along somewhat in
life, come along on the power of his own ambition. And he was still climbing
up the ladder. It was a wonderful feeling, knowing that you were climbing up
the ladder. And yet . . . there was now a choke of sadness in him. It came from
the music, slow music, and waltz-time music, with each note seeming to trickle
through him, and each trickle to touch off these memories and these feelings.
Ah, olden, golden memories! Somehow he felt cheated now. He had a future.
He had ambition, and it had drawn the map of his life. And he was not the kind
to have ambition without faith in himself, hope in himself, and the energy to do
the things he had to do to win in the battle.

And still, he felt that life had not given him all of the things he wanted. It was
the music. It had given him the lonesome feeling he so often had when he was
on the road. He felt cheated. And the music seemed like a flow coming from
a beautiful world where there was no cheating. It seemed to emphasize in him
the feeling that despite everything good in life that he had won, and was winning, he was being cheated. For after each struggle was won, after each worry
was eased, there were new ones. He should not complain. Life was struggle, and
unless you struggled, you must resign yourself to plodding through your life
under the power of stronger wills than your own. You had to place your own
responsibilities squarely your own shoulders. You had to meet your worries
like a man sticking your chin up to life. No, he felt that he wasn't getting that real
something from life to make him a more happy man. That was what it was.

The music stirred, flowing through his head, touching off with melancholy that
feeling of having been defrauded. He mechanically ate his supper. He thought
of what had been blighted in his life, instead of what had been successful. He
remembered Norah Keogh, that black-eyed girl he had dreamed of marrying.
Fine girl, too, she was, rosy cheeks, and wonderful disposition, and she had
all the virtues that made womanhood shine like a jewel in the crown of God's
universe. How often, when waltzing with her, hadn't he dreamed, dreamed of
taking her to far-off, beautiful and gay Vienna, kissing her like a true lover in
the moonlight on the banks of the Beautiful Blue Danube. Everything he had
wanted, every yearning of those days, every ambition of betterment had seemed
pointing right into that gay, red-lipped, white-toothed smile of Norah's. And
she had lied to him. Jilted him? But then, maybe it had been for the better. In
the end everything was designed by God to happen for the best. Ours was not
to complain. Not to question why. Ours was to obey the designs of God, just as
the soldiers of the Light Brigade had obeyed. If he had married her, he couldn't
have been as good to Mother as he was able to be now. He couldn't be raising
Danny. And still. . . . He remembered Norah now. Ah, but wasn't she the wisp

of an Irish girl. It seemed to be only yesterday, and it was back near the beginning of the century. And here he was, many years later, eating alone in this hotel in Detroit after a discouraging day selling shoes. And there was a joy in being nostalgic for the past. To remember those olden days, to remember Norah, and how he had gone to Washington Park with her, taken her on picnics, hoped to marry her. And his hopes had been like a balloon, blown up so that the air could be let right out of it. Yes, it was a quiet joy to remember, and he liked it. Tags of emotion, tags of dreams, tags of wishes, tags of yearnings, all like a ragged patchwork in his mind, and he was lonesome here. He listened to the music that poured its sweet, sad stream through his ears.

And as he ate, his melancholy persisted. He thought that here he was doing his best to build a happy home for them all, and what was going on while he was away working? Trouble! Fighting! He forced these thoughts out of mind. He wanted to remember earlier days. And he had come into the dining room with the unopened letter, thinking it would contain joyful tidings from his home, and that reading it would be the best possible prelude to a fine meal. And instead it was this letter. And it came just on the day when business had been so disappointing. Just on the day when Shulman, buyer at Braddock's big department store, had bought ten cases less shoes than he had expected the kike to buy. And nobody else had bought a shoe off him. Not a shoe. Particularly in a bad season, it seemed to him that the firm should do some classier advertising, a series of ads like those about the girl of the Pingree Shoe. Ah, yes, sometimes a man certainly sank into the doldrums. That was where he was this very moment. *Doldrums!* That was a word he would have to spring on some of the boys. Not every salesman had words like that in his vocabulary.

Smoking a cigar after his coffee, he wished, holy Christmas, he wished that things would go differently. Home! He wanted to think of it as a beautiful sanctuary, the most sacred spot in his life, a place where he and Mother and Peg and the boy were all happy, enshrining their hearts in love. But always there was some disturbing note in it. His mother drinking. Fighting! His sister fighting, drinking, smoking cigarettes, going around with cheap people. Falling in love with that Robinson fellow, a married man who had almost dragged her name in the papers in the Graham scandal. He guessed that it was mainly because of Robinson that Peg was often so nervous that she would fly off the handle at any minute. Robinson was playing with her as if she were a bird in a gilded cage. Rich men did that. It made her nerves jumpy, and they had to pay at home for the way Robinson had her running around. And there was Lizz coming to their home without even washing her face, looking worse than a ragpicker or a washerwoman, and upsetting Peg and feeding Mother all that scandalmongering talk of hers. And Bill, who couldn't be trusted. He was too old for Danny. Why couldn't he stay at home and help his mother and keep out of trouble?

Goddamn it, he'd write and tell them to keep Bill out of the house. He was going to have smooth running at his home if he had to break every bone in Bill's body!

Al paid his bill and walked out of the dining room, his stride rapid and nervous. Frowning, he passed through the lobby, seeing traveling men seated about, some exuding boredom, others reading newspapers. There were some salesmen he didn't like, with their dirty jokes, their gambling, drinking, picking up with women in their indiscriminate way. Fellows like Dub Williams. Well, in the end they would pay. He would profit by the law of compensation. Emerson, ah, there was a great philosopher! When Dan was older, he would have him read Emerson's beautiful and inspired thoughts on self-reliance, love, friendship and compensation. But still, he envied some of the salesmen he knew. They seemed happy. They didn't seem to worry so much, or have troubles at home. The road didn't seem so lonesome to them as it sometimes seemed to him.

"Hello, there, Countess, how are you on this lovely autumnal evening?" he said to the well-built, healthy-looking dark-eyed girl at the cigar counter.

"Why, Mr. O'Flaherty, you're such a kidder."

"Nix, nix on that stuff!" he said, raising his left hand. "Nix on the slango. You want to be smart and refined and use refined language," he added, smiling genially as he spoke.

She looked at him queerly. He picked up a copy of *The Blue Book*, paid her.

"A lovely girl like you, you want to be refined," he said.

"Don't you think I'm refined, Mr. O'Flaherty?"

"Sure I do. Bet your boots you are. I was just dropping a little suggestion in your beautiful cranium."

"Oh!"

Some customers approached her.

"Good night, Countess. And don't forget, nix on that slango," he said, walking away, tossing his cigar in a spittoon.

Allowing her customers to wait, she looked after him, perplexed. He was a nice man. But he was so different from so many salesmen. Never really tried to get fresh with her. But still, he was a queer one. She shrugged her shoulders. A girl with a job like hers saw plenty of queer ones.

II

"Why, Al O'Flaherty! Gee, you're a welcome surprise. I was just thinking that here I was and I didn't see none of the boys I'd like to see. Well, it's certainly great to see you."

"Friend Jack Meeghan! How are you, Jack, old man?" Al asked, shaking hands with the broad, flashily dressed man who had addressed him, stopping him as he was walking to the elevator to go upstairs.

"Say, let's sit down and gab. I don't feel much like hoofing. Here I am, Al, a shoe man, and I get a pair of shoes that raises all holy Harry with my tender dogs."

"Always get 'em long enough, Jack. You can never go wrong if you're sure that your shoes are long enough. It's when they are too short or narrow," Al said as Jack led him by the arm to comfortable chairs in the lobby.

"They're big enough, Al. Christ, look at my gunboats," Jack said, elevating his right foot, and both of them looked at the broad, full-sized tan shoe, with its fancy perforated toe.

"Nice-looking pair, Jack."

"Sure, sure! Swell shoe. Best on the market. I sell it. But the damn counters are too stiff, and they're blistering my heels. But here, Al, have a cigar," he added, handing one to Al; they lit up. "Tell me, Al, how is business?"

"Not what I expected it to be. Not what I expected it to be, Jack. Golly, I'm going to get myself an Irish wishing ring and see if that makes it pick up for the remainder of the trip. All along my route, I've been selling less than I did this time a year ago."

"If you find any four-leaf clovers or horseshoes that you don't need, say, Al, do us a favor, slip 'em to us, will you?" Jack laughed.

"I'm afraid I'll need them myself this trip, Friend Jack."

"Al, when you talk like that you make me feel better. You make me think you're Old Man Optimism itself. I'm not alone. I was just about as deep in the dumps as a drummer can get."

"Wait a minute! Wait a minute! Where do you get that stuff! Drummer!"

"Why?"

"Nix on it, Jack. Jack, the wise guy doesn't call himself a drummer. He's a salesman. It's only these bush leaguers who use a word like that. You're not a drummer. You're a salesman."

"Nope, I'm nothing like it this trip, Al, my boy," Jack said, smiling.

"You get what I mean. The psychology of it. The days are gone, Jack, when a salesman was considered a pest. He's a business man now."

"Say, Al, you hit the nail on the head. We are business men. Only I'm one business man what ain't doing the business."

"Come on, Jack. You don't want to be using words like ain't. Jack, you're a wise guy, aren't you? Well, you want to show it."

"I think you're right. I never thought of it in that light," Jack said, his eyes lighting as if he had made a discovery. "To call ourselves drummers, that's like riding on horse cars."

"You said it, old man," Al said warmly, giving Jack a friendly poke in the ribs.

"But I'm glad I saw you. You cheered me up. When a cracker-jack salesman like you isn't selling too many shoes, I know it's no fault of mine that business is not coming in my window like a snowstorm."

"Hell, Jack, this is only passing. The biggest seasons we ever had are ahead of us. Say, Jack, this is an age for the salesman. Next season we'll be knocking them dead."

"Yes, you said it, Al. But say, when things are rotten, like now, the toughest prospects are the hebe buyers."

"Holy sailors, Jack, the long faces some of them have put on for me."

"Did you see Bromberg yet this trip?"

"Yes, I saw him," Al said knowingly.

"That hebe just promised me his whole store. I felt that I was going to be bringing a moving van up and take it right out with his good wishes. And then when I got down to brass tacks and tried to get his name across the dotted line on my order blank, well, sirs! Christ, I thought I'd have to get my suit pressed from the way his tears fell on my shoulders."

"That piker!" Al said contemptuously.

"Say, Al, tell me, how is the kid nephew?"

"He's going to school," Al said proudly.

"If he's not another Ty Cobb, I lose my guess. Say, one of the best times I ever had in my life was that day last summer when I went to the ball game with you and him. Only how in God's name can he know so much about the game at his age? Say, he's a prodigy."

"He's a dyed-in-the-wool fan, Jack."

"My kid is his age and doesn't know what a catcher's glove is. Mine started to school this year, too. His mother writes me that he doesn't take to it. But I guess he will. Takes time to break in a young steer. Your nephew is going to the Sisters' school, isn't he?"

"Of course. His grandmother would raise the roof if he wasn't."

"My wife's the same. But I guess it's the best place for a youngster."

"Of course it is," Al said with assurance.

"Say, that was something the Detroit Tigers pulled this season, wasn't it, striking the way they did when old Ty was suspended for socking a fan?"

"Ty Cobb did something that was not gentlemanly, but I guess some goddamn fathead in the bleachers brought it on himself. Some of these fatheaded fans, they have no sense of sportsmanship. The way they ride a player. I'm not sure that I blamed Ty at that," Al said.

"Some people, Al, don't know what sportsmanship means," Jack said.

"The thing I like about Ty is what makes him the greatest player the game ever knew. Ty plays with this," Al said, pointing to his head. "So many of those damn fatheads in the game, they don't."

"I don't suppose you'll get many men coming along in any line who got more gray matter than Ty," Jack said.

"And you know, Jack, it isn't just the gray matter. It's using it, and using it at the right time. I met a fellow who played with Ty in the minor leagues before Ty came up. He was selling hardware. I met him in Peoria. He was saying that back then, Ty used his head, thought about the game at night, and then put what he thought about into practice the next day on the diamond. And, Jack, that's what makes a man good in any game."

"You won't go wrong on that statement, Al. But say, I changed my mind. I think I'll run up and change my shoes, and maybe we can take in a show, see some girls kicking or something. Huh, Al?"

"All right. I was going to read, but I guess I won't."

"Sure, you'll come along. You'll get too highbrow if you read too many books. Come on, Al."

"The highbrow's a fellow with something upstairs, Jack," Al said.

"Well, anyway, let's go up to my room while I change my shoes," Jack said, rising.

Walking to the elevator with Jack, Al was glad that he wouldn't have to spend the evening alone. The closeness of the hotel room would seem like walls pressing against him.

"Yes, I think it's a good idea to take in a show. Come to think of it, Jack, I was almost letting myself fall into the doldrums."

"*Doldrums?* Where did you get that funny word?"

"No lowbrow stuff, Jack. Be a wise guy."

"I'm wise enough a guy in my way, I guess."

"Ever hear of Nicholas Algonquin Webster?"

"What league did he play in?"

"He pitched with a dictionary."

"Ha! Ha! Al, you got a sense of humor, all right. But here's the elevator."

III

He hoped anyway that Toledo would be better. But if sales had fallen off all along the route, why should he expect that they would be better in Toledo? No, that wasn't the right attitude. No business man should be a pessimist. Hard times were only a tougher obstacle. They could be gotten over. They would be surmounted! *Ye of little faith!* If he didn't make as much extra commissions this fall as he did last, well, he had winter, spring, next fall ahead of him. Sometimes you struck out. But you never stepped into the batter's box expecting to strike out. And still, he would be able to take care of them at home, and even give a little something now and then to Lizz.

He had not meant to do what he did with Jack last night. But then the flesh is weak in a man. He had taken the right precautions, too, and he wouldn't suffer any infections from it. And his was not a sin like Jack's. Jack, after all, had a wife, the loveliest little woman a man could want. And Jack said so. After he and Jack had left the brothel, Jack was saying just that to him. He remembered Jack walking beside him, towering head and shoulders over him, bending his head, and talking:

"Al, a little change now and then, it breaks your bad luck."

He had slept well after it, even if he had sinned. He had really needed to go and have a woman. And since he had taken the proper precautions, there was no danger of gonorrhea. *The flesh is weak.* And she had been a nice sweet girl, young, too fine a girl to be in such a life. He had talked to her, asked her how she got into it, and she had told him her life story. Poor girl! So poor! With a father out of work, a sick mother, little brothers and sisters to send to school, and a sick aunt, too, for her to help. Poor girl! She had plenty of crosses to carry, and she was a potentially finer flower of humanity, made by God, than many a good person who went to church on Sunday and then came home after mass and ripped everybody up the back with scandal and gossip and backbiting that gave you no fine thoughts or inspirations. Poor girl! Lovely little girl, too! Soft, and white, and she had been lovely to him. Yes, a man sometimes did have a nice experience with even girls like that. She had innate refinement, and when she did it with him, there was no coarseness about her. She had done it refined. And when he had left, she had said he was a gentleman, and well, he did try to be a gentleman. Ah, he'd bet that that poor unfortunate girl who had to live such a life because of poverty, that she did not get many men who treated her as gentlemanly as he had. Poor girl. Ah, yes, *the flesh is weak.*

He glanced out the window at fields and farm lands, with the colors turning, the trees and landscape slashed and brilliant with reds and purples and golds. The country was nice. If it was only sunny now. So much nicer with God's sunlight falling over the good earth. He hated to travel on such days, dull days. Life and the world seemed much more hostile, and, being alone, and traveling alone, and knowing that when he arrived at his destination he would have a lonely hotel room, yes, these sunless days made him feel these things all the more. His responsibilities seem so much heavier. He missed home so much the more.

He lit a cigar. He took the book beside him, *The Letters of Lord Chesterfield.* It was a happy thought he had had yesterday, buying this book. He was going to read every word of it. He lit a cigar and began reading through the introduction. Fine man, a gentleman Lord Chesterfield was, and he only wanted to be as poised and as educated a man. And he would make Danny into the kind of a poised and educated gentleman of the world that Lord Chesterfield had wanted to make of his son. He envisaged himself writing letters to Danny like the ones Lord Chesterfield had written. Only Danny would be everything that Lord Chesterfield's son hadn't been. *The Letters of Albert O'Flaherty to His Nephew.* After he was dead, if they were published, people would read them and say, now there was a poised and intelligent gentleman, why, he wrote as well as any college graduate. Gosh, if he only knew Latin so he could have Latin quotations in the letters. He would have to try and learn Latin some way, get a Latin grammar or something. As soon as Danny was able to read, he would write him letters and tell him how he should comport himself. Then, after he was dead, fathers would be reading his letters to their own sons. Ah! He stared wistfully out the window. He puffed at his cigar. He looked ahead where a group was noisily playing poker. He didn't care for that, gambling. Crooks rode on trains, just to get suckers. While those fellows, maybe they were salesmen, were wasting their time, he was reading a book that would cultivate his mind and give him suggestions for the way he could teach Danny to cultivate his mind.

One of the most important points in life is decency; which is to do what is proper and where it is proper; for many things are proper at one time, and in one place, that are extremely improper in another; for example, it is very proper and decent that you should play some part of the day; but you must see that it would be very improper and indecent, if you were to fly your kite, or play at nine pins, while you are with Mr. Maittaire.

Some day, if he made enough money, he could hire a private tutor for Danny. That would be wonderful. And the definition here of decency. Wonderful! He took a pencil from his vest pocket, underlined the words he had just read. He heard the gang up front playing poker. Lowbrows! Well, he was glad that he wasn't a lowbrow.

I hope, by these examples, you understand the meaning of the word Decency; which in French is Bienséance; and in Latin Decorum.

He repeated *Bienséance* and *Decorum* five times each to fasten them in his memory. He read on, thrilled by several letters. Then he set the book down, stretched, yawned, relit his cigar. Still quite a ways to go. But he would have the afternoon free to do some work in. Might have a run of excellent luck. Wished that he could do something with the colors this year. He had told Mr. Lovejoy that the firm was wrong in trying so many colors, and that they wouldn't take. Well, he would do what he could, sell as many as he could. They knew that about him. If he couldn't sell colors, well, Mr. Lovejoy and the firm would know that it was not through negligence or a lack of diligence. He wondered how Ned was making out. Hadn't heard from him in some time. He'd hoped to meet Ned in Detroit, but didn't. He'd like to talk to Ned, too, about home, and how to handle Peg. Ned had lots of sense.

He puffed at his cigar, and the train pounded through a sleepy hamlet. He looked at the crowd playing poker. He picked up his book again. He read. Suddenly, his head was nodding. His chin fell against his chest. He emitted a slight snore. The book slipped from his hand, fell to the floor of the train, and the cigar followed it.

IV

Just as he had expected. Less business everywhere. Crowder had given him such a glad hand, too. Crowder was always that way. Hello, Al, how are you, gee, I'm glad to see you back through this neck of the woods, and how have you been, Al, old man, how's tricks? He didn't like those insincere glad-hand types. They were all front. When it came to the showdown, they didn't come through. He doubted, too, if there was any game in the world where you could sink deeper in the dumps, in the doldrums, than the selling game on days when luck went against you, and on trips where your sales were down. There was nothing in the world to take everything out of a man like a road trip when nobody would buy shoes. At least, though, a happier letter from Peg had been waiting for him here, and she had forwarded his mail.

He combed his clipped hair, looked at his shoes, put on his derby and coat. He looked at himself in the dresser mirror. Nice crocheted tie he had, dull colors, dark red and blue. A man had to dress well, but not flashily. He did try to, too, dress well but not like a Polack. The way some of these fat-headed salesmen dressed. Take Cy Kane. He picked up the letter he had written home, with the note in it to Danny, smiled proudly, told himself that his little letter to the boy had just the right tone to it. He left the room and went downstairs, buying an evening newspaper in the lobby. Walking to a corner to get a street car, he reflected that the days were getting shorter now. It was the lonesome hour. He'd be lonesome, too, if he wasn't going out to see Mort and the missus for supper. On the car, he unfolded his paper and began reading the report of the testimony Brophy had given in Washington on being recalled before the Senate Committee in the Graham investigation. He smiled. Brophy had sure socked Robinson. Practically said that he was a blackmailer. He hoped that Peg would read this. He better use diplomacy, though, and not mail it to her. Perhaps when he got home, if he told her about it in just the right diplomatic manner, in just the right Lord Chesterfield diplomatic tone, it would sink in. But, golly, Brophy's testimony sure showed Robinson up as a sorehead. Trying to blackmail Brophy into paying high prices for stock he owned. The account made him think Brophy was smart, and maybe not so guilty as he had seemed. A man with as much money as Brophy had, he had to be smart. And Brophy was on the right side of the fence, an important Order of C. man, too.

He got off the street car and walked along a street of bungalows, thinking of how with the dusk of an autumn day settling over them, and the wind scraping leaves on the narrow sidewalk, it seemed like such a homey street, a street where people made their homes and were happy living in them. He was envious, seeing lighted windows, curtains clean against the panes, shadows of people moving within. A block down he spotted a boy riding a bicycle. Ah, boyhood days, and the thoughts of a boy are long, long thoughts. Plenty of these lowbrow sales-men, they didn't remember any poetry. He heard the distant sounds of a railroad train. He walked up a small sidewalk, rang the bell, waited.

"Well! Well! Well! So here you are. How are you, Al? Glad you came. We're almost ready and the little woman is fixing us up a real spread. Enter our domi-cile," Mort Goodwin said, shaking hands with Al.

He was a tall, fleshy, jolly man. He led Al into the conventional and prim little parlor with a picture, over the fireplace, of a knight and his lady sitting. He called to his wife that the visitor had come. He helped Al off with his coat, took it and his hat, hung them up. Al sat down in a rocker, feeling a glowing warmth within him, his feelings both happy and nostalgic. He wondered what Peg was doing now. And Mother. And the boy. Yes, Mort had a nice home, with a fine little woman to manage it, kids, his own little business, everything a man needed in life. Or at least almost everything. A home like this, with a fine little woman in it, Norah, and Danny as his son! And, of course, Mother, also. Well, a bigger one, so that they could have Peg, too. He saw a picture of Mort and his wife in bridal white set over a little desk in a corner. He wondered how a man felt when he married, had a beautiful girl with a sterling character at his side, vowing to be his helpmate for life.

"Hello, Al. I'm so glad that Mort got you out to see us. You know we always like to have you."

Al rose and shook hands with Mrs. Goodwin, a small, thin-faced woman who was wearing an apron over her black dress.

"Say, you're looking peacherinoes, quite *bienséance*," Al said, observing her gay eyes.

"What's that, Al? Gee, you're getting to sling some classy lingo at us plain folks here," Mort said.

"Never mind. It's between the lady here and myself," Al said, jokingly dismiss-ing Mort with a wave of his left hand.

"Al, I wish you could teach Mort to say such nice things. But sit down. I only came in to say hello to our honored guest. I have to go out and finish the sup-per."

"Yes, you better, before Al wins you away from me," said Mort with a smile.

"Look out, old man, or he will, he's a gentleman," she said, wagging her finger at him.

"So you call your breadwinner old man now?" Mort said.

"Well, look at you, how fat you're getting."

"It's your food. And if you would kindly go to the kitchen, which is woman's place, you would be preparing victuals for me to start getting a bigger corporation," Mort said, patting his paunch as she left the parlor.

"Great little lady, that wife of yours, Mort," Al said.

"None better. She can deal out cards and spades to most gals."

"Well, Mort, how's business?" Al asked after a pause.

"Al, if you know anybody who wants to buy a shoe store, send him around, will you?"

"Things could be better, all right."

"Say, some of these fellows I see at lunch, when they get to talking about business, I tell you, Al, you could cut the gloom with a knife."

"Things will shape up again, though, Mort. No excuse for pessimism."

"We just need a little retrenchment to get our wind again."

"Considering everything, I'm doing fair," Al said.

"You always do, Al. You're a crackerjack salesman."

"Say, Mort, do me a favor, will you?" Al said, smiling genially. "Tell the shoe man in town here that I'm a crackerjack salesman, will you?"

"Al, I always like to see you. You got a real sense of humor," Mort laughed. "But wait till I spring that one on Crowder. Ha! Ha!"

"Nothing you can say will make that piker buy shoes."

"I know it. And he's always crying about business. Every time I see him he weeps on my shoulder."

"Holy sailor, the glad hand he gave me this afternoon, and then, his pessimism."

"Like you was his long lost brother, huh, Al?"

"Supper," Mort's wife called, coming to the parlor entrance.

V

Sitting down, Al liked it, the cheeriness of the dining room, the food, the fresh linen tablecloth, the two well-behaved children.

"How you like the white hopes, Al?" Mort said.

"How are you, Sport? And little Mary there, a princess," Al said, and the two children smiled shyly. Al turned to Mrs. Goodwin, at the foot of the rectangular table, and said, "And supper spread out before us, it's fit for a king. I tell you the Duke and Duchess of Toledo have that *decorum* that gives the proper touch to every little thing."

"Al, you're so jolly," she said.

"Shouldn't he be? He's my pal, Alice, the Count of O'Flaherty is my pal," Mort said.

"I wish I could say that for all your friends, Mort," said she.

"And, Duke, the Duchess turns the most graceful compliments, just that right touch of *savoir faire*," Al said, mispronouncing the French phrase but hoping he had used it correctly.

"Duchess, the Count of O'Flaherty has lunch every day on a dictionary," Mort said.

"Let's eat," she said, and Mort began serving steak, peas and carrots, passing plates to Al, his wife and the children.

"And how hath the Count of O'Flaherty fared in his foreign travels?" said Mort, beginning to eat.

"Away with you, old man," Mrs. Goodwin said.

"The Duchess is, should I say, not concerned with highbrow talk tonight," Mort said while chewing steak.

"What do you think of it all, Sport?" Al asked.

"Me?" the nine-year-old boy said with a reticent smile, and Al thought that he was a well-bred youngster, but still, he wasn't going to be the well-bred lad that Danny would be. Mort was true emerald in every way, but he had something of the lowbrow in him, and he wouldn't be able to give his lad the air of refinement and polish that Danny would get. Like the letter he had just sent. But he better be talking to them. It wasn't gracious not to. Imagine Lord Chesterfield at a dinner and not keeping the conversation sparkling.

"An excellent supper, I must say," Al said, cutting off a small piece of steak, chewing, setting his knife across the edge of the plate instead of setting it on the table with the blade resting on the plate as Mort and Mrs. Goodwin did.

"I am so glad. I like people to eat heartily when they come to see us. My friend next door, Mrs. Brubaker, goodness gracious, you should see the pinched little meal she serves her guests. I don't like that. God gave us food to eat, and I believe we should eat it."

"Mort, the Duchess has just that right flair for everything," Al said.

"You go on with your joshing, Al," she blushed.

"Well, Al, if business picks up for us in the next year, when you come to Toledo we'll be taking you riding in an automobile. I'm thinking of getting me one and hitting these old streets up for twenty miles an hour just like that," Mort said, snapping his fingers in gesticulation.

"I'd rather ride on a grocery wagon than an automobile," Mary, the flaxenhaired seven-year-old girl, said.

"Mother, she's a tomboy," the boy said.

"Children!" the mother said in gentle cautioning.

"I'll bet Mary here is a real girl," Al said.

"She's too real when she gets to climbing fences all along the block," the mother said.

"Just like my nieces and nephews," said Al.

"That's right, Al, you're raising and educating one of your nephews, aren't you?"

"I got him in school now. He started this fall," said Al.

"Mary did, too, didn't you?" the mother said, looking at Mary.

"Uh huh!"

"That a part of the alphabet you learned today, Mary?" Mort asked.

"She don't know it," said the boy.

"Sport here is going to be a regular guy, isn't he?" said Al.

"In another year or so he'll be too tough for his old man," Mort said, receiving a reproving look from his wife.

"Aw, I can skin you now," the kid laughed, and Al, remembering Lord Chesterfield's letter on decency, that is, on *bienséance*, thought that Mort should read those letters.

"Say, Al, how is your brother Ned doing these days?"

"Pretty well, thank you, Mort," Al said, again nibbling at his steak.

"When he comes to Toledo we'll have to have him out here. Alice, Al's brother is another jolly O'Flaherty. And he's a good shoe man, too."

"I'll cook a nice supper for him. But here, Al, have some more," she said.

"No, thanks. I've had plenty," Al said, thinking that it was better manners not to take a second helping, but he was hungry, and it was a delicious supper.

"Give me his plate, Alice. When he comes to the Goodwins, he's got to eat," Mort said, and as she handed him the plate Mort filled it with a generous second portion. "Say, Al, I wanted to ask you how are the medium vamps going?"

"Not so well," said Al.

"I thought so. They aren't moving much in my store. The short vamps are doing much better," Mort said, his face full of steak.

"The round full toes are going better, too," said Al.

"Oh, you men! Can't you let business alone and see each other in the store tomorrow?" Mrs. Goodwin said.

"Anything that the Duchess' heart desires," Al said, pleased with his well-turned and gracious phrase.

"Alice, the Duke of O'Flaherty knows the right gab for the ladies," Mort said, laughing.

"I don't think that that is the proper *decorum* and eloquence for a discussion of the knightly practices of chivalry, do you, Duchess?" Al said.

"Say, what is that word you always use, *decorum?*" Mort asked.

"Latin. It means proper and fitting, everything in its proper place," Al said with pride.

"Say, Al, did you go to college? You know such a lot," said Mort.

"Al, you do. You talk like an educated man," she said.

"No, I never went to college."

"Neither did I. But say, you must be a whiz to educate yourself and learn all them words you know without getting it in college," Mort said.

Mrs. Goodwin went to the kitchen for tea and dessert, and she returned bringing glasses of milk for the children. She went out, and as she came back with a freshly baked cake, she said:

"I'm afraid the cake's sunk a little."

"These kids of mine don't at all like their mother's cakes," Mort said.

"Aw, go on, Dad," the boy said.

"I do so, Daddy," the girl said, with the adults laughing; the girl eyed them curiously for a moment, but then she laughed, too.

"It'll melt in your mouth," Mort said.

"Countess, it is a cake fit for royalty," Al said.

"Al, when I got me a little woman, I told myself I was going to get me one that can cook, and I wasn't fooling myself none, either."

"Al, I don't think the cake deserves such praise. It sunk in the oven," Mrs. Goodwin said.

"Don't kid yourself, Alice. You're the best cake-baker this side of Hades," Mort boasted.

"That cake is art," Al graciously said.

"Wait till you taste it first," she said, handing Al a piece on a small plate.

"A most fetching delicacy from the royal oven," Al said after his first bite.

"Melts in your mouth," Mort mumbled, his words choked off because he had put so much cake in his mouth.

"Such joshers! Goodness gracious!"

"I like it, Mumsy," the girl said.

"You got a sweet tooth," Mort said with imitation gruffness.

"I do so like it, Daddy."

"Arthur there, he doesn't. He's just going to eat a second piece so he doesn't hurt his mother's feelings," Mort said.

"I'll clear the dishes and get the children set for study in their room. You men go and talk in the parlor," Mrs. Goodwin said when the meal was finished.

"You ought to let us try our wings on the dishes," Al said.

"I wouldn't think of it. Al, you're our guest. And if I let that hulk there do it, he'd break every dish and cause a leak in the faucet," she said.

"Is that so?" Mort joshed, arising, and he and Al went to the parlor.

VI

"Say, Mort, what's Joe Goddard doing now?" Al asked as both of them were comfortable in the parlor with their cigars.

"Nothing," Mort said.

"He's not a bad scout," Al said.

"You know, Al, he's too happy-go-lucky. Business is business, and when a man's got a responsible job, he has got to take his responsibilities seriously. He didn't. He was always drinking, running around after women like one of these Bohemian artists you read about in the papers, the ones that live in Paris. Well, you can't be the buyer in a first-class department store and waste your time hitting the bottle and chasing skirts."

"Too bad. If he watched his business like the real wise guy does, he could have been a good shoe man."

"Didn't have the will power. You know will power isn't all that you got to have in the game of life, but if you ain't got it, well, you are as bad off as a guy trying to hit Walter Johnson's smoke-ball pitches in the dark. He got let out, and I don't blame 'em for letting him go, either. He had a good job, too. And his wife, as dandy a girl as you'll ever find. Joe treated her like a dog. I feel sorry, not for his sake, but for hers. He had every chance a man can expect to get in the world, and well, when Old Man Opportunity knocked on his door, he was out in the alley horsing around. I feel sorry for that lovely little woman. He treated her like a dog," Mort said with intensified self-righteousness.

"That's bad. *Bad!* That stuff doesn't mix with business," Al said, thinking proudly that he had never let opportunity find him out of the house when it knocked; and he never would. And he would never mistreat a lovely woman, either.

"You got to play the game according to the rules to get anywhere, Mort."

"No exaggeration in that pearl of wisdom, Al," Mort said, ensconcing himself more comfortably, blowing smoke rings, watching them drift to the ceiling.

"Anyway, business ought to be better in the spring," Al said.

"Sure it will. This is a great country, and a great age. In an age like this there is absolutely no excuse for the quitter, the loafer, and the Joe Goddard. Things are happening every day, marvels, wonders of the world. Why, look at that airplane race from coast to coast they got on now," Mort said.

"Before long in America, Mort, we're going to have a luxury age," Al said philosophically.

"When we do, you and I are going to sell more shoes. It'll be good for you, handling a high-class expensive line of shoes like you do."

"My shoes are not expensive, if you consider the cost of production, the material, the workmanship that goes into them. Now one number we got . . ."

"I know that, Al. I meant expensive for the average pocket-book. Like most of my customers. They don't want to pay five, ten, twelve dollars for shoes. Well, when the luxury age comes, they will. And then Mort Goodwin's Classy Shoe Store will spread all over the block downtown, Al."

"I suppose that you boys are selling shoes again," Mrs. Goodwin laughed, coming into the parlor.

"We was only waiting for you to come in, Alice. Say, how about tickling a few keys for us?" Mort said, pointing to the piano.

"Sure, let's have some fine old-time songs," Al said.

"Mort, you know I don't play well enough to exhibit myself in company," she said demurely.

"Say, I'll wager that you're an exquisite pianist," Al said.

"Al, you can bet your boots on it, and you won't go wrong. There isn't a little lady on this whole block that can tickle more heartache out of those keys than my little lady there can."

"Al, I know you won't agree with him if you hear me," she said.

"She's just bashful, Al."

"We'll be charmed to hear you," Al said.

"If you insist. But it's your asking," she said, sitting down at the piano.

She began with *The Rosary*. Al hummed, and Mort nodded his head to the tune. Soon they were standing over her, reading the words over her shoulder, singing. Mort's voice booming off key. Their faces softened with sentiment, became dreamy, their eyes misty, faraway. They sang old-time songs yearningly.

About nine-thirty Al left. Walking back to the car line, he thought of home, wondered how they were there, wished his trip were over, hoped some day to have as happy a home as Mort, with his own little kids in it. He looked at the bungalows, lights cracking through drawn shades. In every one of these houses, perhaps, there was a home. People happy with their families, the home a shrine. Perhaps in these homes love shot its arrows of bliss into every heart. Now, if Norah? . . . He wondered about Mother, and Peg, and the lad. From far away he heard the melancholy notes of a train whistle. He walked along humming to himself.

8

I

"Now, Brother, you make an A this way," Aunt Margaret said, sitting with him before sheets of paper on the dining-room table and slowly writing out a large and legible capital A.

Danny stuck the sharp point of the pencil in his mouth, studied his aunt's writing, seriously and slowly attempted to copy it.

"Peg, you shouldn't have bought all those things for me and the home. Sure, I didn't need such grand lace caps you bought me," the grandmother said, rocking away, darning Danny's socks, looking over the five-and-ten-cent-store glasses which were pushed down toward the top of her beaked nose.

"Mother dear, I love to do things for you, and buy things for you and the home. And Al works so hard, I love to help him out with the expenses when I can. Al deserves a good home. He works so hard," Peg said.

"The likes of my Al never walked the face of the earth," Mrs. O'Flaherty said.

"And Lizz needed money so bad. I gave her twenty-five dollars and bought things for her kids. They are such dears," Peg said.

"Look, Aunty Margaret!"

"You're so smart, Brother. And now what comes next after an A?"

"B," he said proudly.

"Now, Brother, how do you make a B?"

"Like this," he said, scrawling out an awkward suggestion of a capital B.

"Fine! Try it again and see if you can make it a little nicer and neater," she said while Danny looked up at her with blue eyes that begged praise.

He stuck the pencil in his mouth and earnestly tried again.

"That's much better," she said, bending down, kissing his light brown curly hair.

"Isn't it wonderful, Peg, the things that people can do nowadays, with their schooling and their automobiles, and with steam heat and electricity, and nearly everybody being able to read what's in the newspapers?"

"I'll read you the papers when I finish with the little one," Peg said.

"My poor mother, may the Lord have mercy on her beloved soul, what wouldn't she be saying if she could see the things that they do nowadays? Indeed, she wouldn't believe her own eyes. Ah, God is a wonderful Man to be giving such things to people, letting them read what's going on in the newspapers."

"I'll read them to you right away," said Peg.

"No hurry, Peg, I have to be darning the holes in my grandson's stockings."

"It's little schooling that I had, damn little. Anything I know I learned and earned for myself," Margaret said dreamily, but with bitterness underscoring her words.

"I know what comes after B, Aunty Margaret," Danny said, gazing innocently at her, causing her to return his look with a self-weary smile.

"What, Brother?"

"This!" Danny said, showing her a line of scrawled-out C's.

"And now what is after C?"

Danny frowned importantly, trying to imitate Uncle Al's frown when his uncle seemed to be thinking about something that was very important.

"E," he said uncertainly, taking the pencil out of his mouth.

"No, Brother, it's D."

"That was what I meant to say," Danny said as his grandmother looked at him with adoration, still peering over her glasses.

"How do you make it?"

Danny looked up at his aunt. He watched her write out a large and clear letter D. He studiously copied it, and then waited for praise.

"Good, Brother," she yawned.

"Aunty Margaret, how do I write my name?"

"Like this," she said, and he watched her intently.

His attempts to copy resulted in illegible scrawls, so his aunt guided his hand as he wrote out his name.

"Now, you show Mother what you did, and how neatly you wrote your name."

"Mother, look! That's my name. Aunty Margaret showed me how to write it," Danny said, handing her the sheet of paper with all the scrawlings on it.

"Glory be! You'll be a scholar some day, Son! Now isn't it grand!" she said in awe of the writing he held up to her.

"He's going to learn faster, all right, now that I am helping him, Mother."

"Mother, when I learn more, I'll write your name for you, and show you how to write it. Then when you get money orders from Uncle Al, you can sign them yourself instead of having to have Aunty Margaret do it for you."

"Indeed, you won't. I can write my own name on my son's money," she said haughtily.

"Brother, when you grow up to be a man, what are you going to do?"

"Gee, maybe be a baseball pitcher like Ed Walsh and pitch no-hit games."

"And are you going to be rich?"

"I'll make lots and lots of money. This whole room full of money, Aunty Margaret."

"And who are you going to take care of and buy presents for?"

"You and Mother."

"Ah, I'll be rotted in my grave then," the grandmother soliloquized.

"You won't, Mother, because I'm going to buy you a great big shiny automobile."

"Brother, Aunty Margaret is tired now and she has things to do. She'll help you another time," the aunt said.

"Aunty Margaret?" Danny said as she got up from her chair.

"What, Brother?"

"Read me my letter from Uncle Al again."

"Some other time. Your aunt is tired."

"No! Now!" he said imperiously, pulling out the crumpled letter from his pocket and handing it to her.

"Read it, Peg. I want to hear it meself," Mrs. O'Flaherty said.

"Brother, you're so sweet. But you're a trial to your tired aunt," she said, taking the letter from him and sitting down.

Dear Sport

I hope you are being an obedient boy and doing what your aunt and grandmother tell you to at home and what your teacher and the Sisters tell you to do in school. You want to be a real sport and a real sport obeys his superiors. When you study you must think of your studies and, when you play you should think of play. And in school, and at home, listen to how those older than you speak and try to speak like them and develop a better diction. And don't forget to say yes mam to your teacher. Be good now.

Sport.

Your uncle,

AOF

"My uncle sent that to me and it's all for me," said Danny.

"He thinks so much of you. You must be good now as he says," Peg said.

"Indeed, Al does think of his nephew. Al thinks that nothing is too good for him," the grandmother said, raising her voice in pride.

"I'll be so good. And when you help me to learn my ABC's, I can write letters to Uncle Al when he's away on the road, can't I, Aunty Margaret?"

"Yes, Brother. And Al will be so proud of you then."

"He will, won't he?"

"Peg?" the grandmother said.

"Yes, Mother?"

"Any murders in the paper tonight?" the mother asked, her eyes alight.

"I have to do some things in my room, and then I'll read them to you."

She left the room. Talking to himself, Danny scrawled on the paper, copying from the alphabet at the beginning of his first-grade reader. The grandmother resumed her darning, still looking over her glasses as she worked.

Puffing on a cork-tipped Egyptian cigarette, Peg strode thoughtfully and nervously back and forth in her room. She suddenly wrung her hands. She paused before the mirror and studied her handsome, worried face. She tried to look tragic. Ah, it was the sad face of a great tragic actress in life looking at her out of the dusty mirror. Her cigarette was almost burning her lips. She went to the chamber pot under her bed, took off the lid, dropped the butt in, and there was a sizz as it was extinguished. She quickly put the lid back on, and made a face. Filled, too. She would have to be emptying it in the bathroom. But she wanted to get that letter written first.

She sat down at her small and disorderly desk in the corner, brushed things aside, began writing, destroying sheets of paper, rewriting, destroying more sheets, and then writing out a short letter quickly, and in a graceful handwriting.

Dear Mr. Robinson

Business conditions are not very favorable at present, and it seems as if they will get worse unless something is done. I thought I better write to you to give you this information. It will be imperative that something be done to cause a turn for the better immediately

Sincerely yours

J. S. Olson

She addressed the envelope and sealed the letter, thinking that this ought to get her some money from Lorry. She had spent so much buying things for the house, and helping Lizz, and she hadn't even spent a penny on her own poor self. And she had taken a hundred dollars from her petty cashbox, too. She had to put it back before there was any audit. Here she was, bonded, risking her bond. If she got caught, she could never get another job. She was risking the blacklist for her family. And did they appreciate it? Did Jim O'Neill, that long-legged, bucktoothed teamster show gratitude? Well, she had learned something from hard and bitter experience in life. She had learned that there was no gratitude, *no gratitude*, in the human heart. None whatever!

And money! Oh, God, the very idea of it would some day drive her crazy. She looked over the envelope. She kissed the name she had written on it. If she could only see him tonight, be with him, kiss him, have him hold her in those strong arms of his, have him undress her, spill himself into her, oh, God.

She smiled suddenly, sadly, hearing her nephew talk to his grandmother. Such sweet sounds. If only she and Lorry had a beautiful child of their own like Little Brother! Instead, that poor thing, born a bastard, put in an institution for the feeble-minded. Oh, God, oh, God, oh, God, was there no justice in the world!

She walked back to the dining room.

"Peg, any murders in the paper tonight?"

"I haven't looked. I have to go down to the corner to mail a letter. I'll get the latest edition and come back right away and read it to you."

"Aunty Margaret, can I go with you?"

"No, Brother, it's cold out, and you must study."

"I want to go with you!"

"What did Uncle Al write, Brother? He said you must be obedient, didn't he?"

"Gee. . . . Will you bring me back some candy?"

"Yes, you little darling!" she said, kissing him.

II

Peg walked rapidly along Calumet Avenue toward Fifty-first Street. It was a cold and frosty night, and a mist hung over the apartment buildings along the street. A carriage crunched past her. She heard the rumbling elevated trains. Ahead of her, she could see the not-too-brightly-lighted window of O'Callahan's saloon at the northwest corner of Fifty-first and Calumet. Suddenly a westbound street car flashed in front of her. It was an Indiana Avenue car, and it would turn on to Indiana, and go downtown. It made her remember how once when she and poor Louise had been going downtown in the afternoon, Little Brother had followed them, dirty-faced and crying. He had climbed on the car with them, and they had had to take the little darling along, just as he was. Danny had loved Louise so. He used to call her his Beautiful Aunt Louise. And she had loved him, the little darling angel. It was so sad when she was dying. The little angel did not know it, and he was shouting and making noise, and Louise was in the side bedroom—dying. Poor Louise, she had been so pale and beautiful on her deathbed, her lovely long brown hair, and her blue eyes that men liked so much, and her lovely face, like glass, and so colorless. Lorry had once said Louise was a fine girl. It had made her so jealous of Louise. Ah, had she known, had she known what sad fate was bound to overtake poor Louise, she would never, never, never have been jealous.

Walking more slowly, she began to think of how much she loved Lorry, and how she wanted only to be with him forever. Two boys passed, shouting and swearing at one another. Her lips curled. Nasty little runts! Not like her darling nephew. A man, wearing an overcoat with a velvet collar, gave her an inviting stare. It pleased her. She knew, as she walked on, that he had turned to look after her, Well, if he wanted to look at her ass moving when she walked, let him, the poor goddamn fish. Yes, she was glowingly pleased to be a handsome woman, handsome enough to have little pikers oogle after her. They would come with their tongues hanging out, too, if she gave them the chance. But why should she? She who knew men, gentlemen, men who were rich, Lorry. Lorry, what was he doing at this minute? Might he, right now, be thinking of her, wanting her, wishing that he was with her here in Chicago? Or would he be thinking of that creature? The mere thought of that goddamn wife of his made her want to puke. Think of it, Lorry, her lovely Lorry, in bed with that skinny bitch of a wife! Think of it! Oh, God! Yes, yes, yes, yes, yes, why, why, why didn't that bitch die? She was no good, no good on earth.

"Peg O'Flaherty! How are you, darling? I'm so glad to see you."

"As I live and die, Martha Morton," Peg answered, and the two women kissed.

They faced each other, smiling. Martha was a frowsy, blown woman, with a large and flowery hat, a fur coat, a wrinkled, painted face, thick crass lips, circles under her stupid blue eyes, and piles and layers of red hair.

"Peg, my dear, let's go some place where we can sit down and talk," Martha said.

"Just as soon as I get a stamp and drop an important letter in the box," Peg said, and she left Martha to enter the drug store on the corner.

She came out immediately, and dropped the letter in the mailbox. They crossed the car tracks, walked down the side of O'Callahan's saloon, and entered the door marked *Family Entrance*. They took a corner table in the small, dimly lit room, with its damp smell, its scattered tables with oilcloth coverings, its pictures of hefty actresses on the walls. It was connected with the saloon proper by swinging doors, through which they could hear echoes of male talk, sudden bursts of masculine laughter.

"How have you been, Martha?" Peg asked when they were comfortably seated.

"Peg, it's a terribly long story. Peg, my dear, my heart has just been eaten out. But how have you been, dear heart? Tell me what has been happening to you? Do you ever see that little runt, Older, any more?"

"That! That! That!" Peg sneered.

They smiled at each other, a mutual feminine contempt for a male. They laughed. A waiter appeared, and they ordered beer.

"Oh, Martha, I can't go on tolerating it much longer. All the weight of responsibility that I carry on these poor shoulders of mine."

"Oh, you poor dear thing! Peg, I always said that you had too kind a heart. I always told you that."

"I won't much longer. Martha, I am thinking of clearing out, bag and baggage. I love my family, and my lovely darling mother, but Martha, oh, a family is such a burden on a poor girl's shoulders."

"Peg, you can love your family. But I don't love mine. Jesus Christ, I most certainly don't. I would be a different woman today, a different woman, if it wasn't for the family I had. My father, he screwed me when I was thirteen. Can you imagine that? I was only a little girl who hardly knew how to pee and that's what my father did to me."

"My family is such a burden. My poor brother, Al, he means well, but he is such a mollycoddle. With a man like that in the house, I can't have any life of my own."

"I know how bad he is. Didn't he have that nasty little nephew of yours tell me that he didn't want me in your house when I lived over you on Indiana? I know what he is. But he isn't as bad, he can't be as bad, as a father who screwed his own thirteen-year-old daughter."

"My poor father. He was such a good man, such a hard-working man, so badgered and nagged. And he was so sick, dying from cancer. Well, poor dead Dad, he has gone to his reward with God at last. And he is better off, better off, maybe, than his poor daughter who loved him so much."

"Well, he was not like that rat I had for an old man. Peg, did you ever hear of a father doing to his thirteen-year-old daughter what mine did to me?"

"It's just that my family is too big a burden to be laid on my poor shoulders. And my brother, Al, I wish that he would just go and clear out and get married. He's such a mollycoddle," Peg said.

"I'll bet he's just like Mr. Morton. Well, Mr. Morton learned some things. He learned that Martha Morton couldn't be dictated to."

"That's been my trouble. I let them dictate to me. But they won't continue to! They won't! They won't!"

"Don't let them, honey," Martha said, frowning harshly and reaching across the table to touch Peg's arm.

"Why, Martha, do you know that I can't even have a friend without them asking me questions in that goddamn snooping way of theirs? Where have you been? What have you been doing? Who were you with? Martha, I'm of age, and it's none of their goddamn business!"

"Peg, you're right. You're of age, and it's none of their goddamn business!" Martha said.

"I almost have to ask that brother of mine if I can take a piss," Peg said.

"Do what I did, Peg! Leave 'em! My husband, Mr. Morton, tried that kind of a game on me. Well, it didn't ring the way he wanted it to. I wouldn't stand it. And so today you see Martha Morton, a free woman answerable only to her God. I don't have any little snooping male who can't even get into bed with a woman and give a man's slug, I don't have no runts like that snooping around about what I do. Not on your funny old tintype!" Martha said.

They rang for more beer, and the waiter brought in foaming steins.

"That little bastard, Mr. Morton! Peg, when I was with him, I was always asking myself: Martha, what did you ever see in him? Just what, Martha, just what, in the name of Jesus Christ Himself, did you ever see in him?" Martha said, her high-pitched voice cracking as she spoke; and then after laughing she lifted her stein to drink, spilling beer on her chin.

"That snooping brother of mine is just an imitation of a man who's always trying to jam that hawk nose of his into my affairs."

"Him! Peg, it's because of that five-and-ten-cent edition of a man you call your brother that you'll never see me in your house as long as there is breath in my body. He insulted me as no man ever did. He didn't want me in his home. Well, I tell you I never went in it because of him."

"I'm so wearied of it. I tell you, Martha, I can't have a friend. The way they insulted you, well, every friend I ever had and brought into the house was insulted that way. I have no privacy whatsoever with them," Peg said. She heroically wiped her tears away. "And, Martha, I knew men better than him. I still do. I know men who could buy and sell that brother of mine just as if he was a cheap cigar."

"I could buy Mr. Morton with a peanut shell."

"Martha, oh, Martha, I got to get away from it all. I can't stand it any more. I can't!" Peg said histrionically, and they ordered more beer.

"Don't put up with it, Peg! Dearie, girls like you and me, we got to be free and live our own lives. Don't put up with it!"

"Martha, I'm so glad I saw you. You have given me heart. I will do it, dearie! I will! I will be free, by God! You made me see things before it's too late. I'm going away, far, far away from all the goddamn O'Flahertys in the world. And once I go, they'll never see me as long as there is breath in my body."

"We'll drink on that, dearie," Martha said, and they touched steins and drank.

"Never, never will any man, let alone Mr. Morton, dictate to Martha Morton," Martha said, and they looked into each other's eyes, Peg suddenly smiling sadly, Martha leering lewdly.

The waiter came in and they ordered more beer.

"I have been a fool! A fool! A fool!" Margaret said in a voice loaded with weariness.

"Peg, my dear, you are still young. You don't need to be a fool. You are young. Look at me, a woman of thirty-five . . . even if I don't look it."

"You don't look a day older than twenty-five. . . . But, Martha dear, you have opened my eyes. I won't go on like this any longer," Margaret said, and the waiter returned with more beer.

"Never be a man's slave," Martha proclaimed, and she paused to drink. "A man, what is he? A fool. And he's got something hard. He wants you to make it weak and soft for him. Well, do it for him, do it and have your fun out of it. But always, then, see that he pays. If a woman isn't smart and quick, she pays, and she pays. Peggy, dearie, us women, we pay."

"Yes, Martha, the woman pays," Margaret began as Martha drank slobberishly, getting beer on her chin and staining her stein with cheap lipstick. "Yes, dear, the woman pays and pays," Peg continued, and then she took a long drink.

"Dearie, that's the reason why we got to be smart. Then we make the men pay," Martha said as if she were telling a dark secret, and they drank in agreement on Martha's sentiment.

"Martha, I got to get away. I got to get away with my Lorry."

"Who is he? Another clown?"

"He isn't a clown!" Peg glared.

"Peg, dearie," Martha said quickly in a soft and persuasive voice, reaching over to pet Margaret's hand as she spoke. "Peg, darling, I'm sorry. I didn't know. I just didn't know."

"I understand, Martha. But my Lorry is different. He's my sweetheart. He is going to be a great man some day."

"Has he got plenty of onions in the bank?"

"He's a millionaire. A millionaire! A *millionaire!* And he's going to marry me as soon as he gets his divorce."

"Peggy!" Martha shouted, arising, running around the table to embrace Margaret. "Darling!" she said, her arms still enfolding Margaret, her beery breath whiffing into Margaret's nostrils. They kissed. Breathless, Martha again sat down. They drank. "I'm so glad," Martha added, a sudden cutting glare coming into her eyes, and Margaret, catching this look, smiled sweetly back, reached over, squeezed her friend's hand, and they finished off their steins, ordering new ones.

"Lorry is so kind and so gentle. He is such a wonderful man. He's too good for this world," Peg said sentimentally, her eyes dreamy and far-off, so that she did not catch the cynical curl of Martha's lips.

"I wish I had a man like that," Martha said as the waiter set new steins before them. "I wish I did," Martha said, drinking. "If I had the right man, I would settle down. I would keep home. I would slave for him. But I never met a man who was worth the tiniest part of a woman's toenail. Now take that runt, Mr.

Morton. What good was he? He wasn't worth a fart in bed. And do you know what his salary was? A measly one hundred and thirty-five dollars a month."

"Most men are little pikers like that hawk-nosed brother of mine," Peg said bitterly, drinking after her remark.

"Peg, I speak the truest words ever said when I tell you that most men aren't worth the tiniest part of a woman's toenail."

"Pikers!" Peg said, and they finished their beer and ordered still more which the waiter brought promptly.

"Oh, Peg darling, don't cry, don't!" Martha said, beginning to sway in her chair and to see Margaret in tears through bleary eyes. Her voice became thickly sweet. "I'm unhappy, too, my Peg."

"My family will ruin my life," Peg said while Martha drew a handkerchief from her hefty pocketbook, wiped her eyes, and then loudly blew her nose.

"That's what Mr. Morton did to my life," Martha said in a contemptuous tone, and, drooling, they drank from their steins. "I was such a sweet and innocent thing, such a lovely flower of a girl when I met Mr. Morton. Mr. Morton and those fine promises of his, kneeling before me, saying he loves me, calling me his tootsie-wootsie. And what did he do when I, innocent thing that I was, when I believed him? Why, I didn't even get one decent night in bed from him." Her face became hard, firm. "Well, I tied a can to that funny little ass of his, god-damn it if I didn't!"

"Sometimes, Martha, I get so nervous, and everything seems dark, and goes black before me. And I think of ending it all," Margaret said after they had more beer.

"Peg, so do I."

"Martha, if I hadn't met you tonight, oh, I might have done it. Martha, you're such an understanding friend."

"Girls like us, Peg, should be understanding to each other. Walking along tonight, I was thinking. Now there are the street cars. Suppose I just fling myself under one of them. Who will care? Who will miss poor Martha Morton? Nobody! *Nobody!* But then, the world would know of the perfidy of Mr. Morton. I almost did it, dearie."

They drank more beer. They cried. They decided to leave. Martha made no effort to pay. Peg paid the bill. Arm in arm, they left the saloon and staggered to the corner of Fifty-first and Calumet. A carriage with two men in top hats stopped by the curb. They entered the carriage. The elevated driver lightly applied the whip. As the horse broke into a trot, Martha and Peg were heard singing drunkenly,

> *Come on and hear, come on and hear, Alexander's ragtime band.*
> *Come on and hear, it's the best band in the land.*

9

I

"What did she do?" Bill asked as he and Danny sat on the lower ledge of the back stairway, looking out onto the back yard which was cut into two squares of withered grass by the narrow sidewalk that ran to the few steps at the alley gate.

"Oh, she came home awful late, and she hollered so loud that the people on the second floor below us hammered on the radiator for her to shut up. And Mother woke up, and tried to get her to go to bed and not yell so much, and she and Mother had a fight, and she cursed Mother," Danny said, spitting through the stair railing.

"She was drunk," Bill said knowingly.

"When I came home from school for dinner today she was crying and walking around the house, saying she was awful nervous," Danny said, trying to seem as knowing as Bill.

"Pa doesn't yell so much as Aunt Margaret when he comes home drunk. But after little Catherine was born, Ma made him go see the Italian priest and take the pledge again," Bill said.

"Mother says it's a sin against God to drink. But she drinks beer herself, and she cries and makes noise, too, when she drinks too much of it," Danny said, again trying to spit through the stair railing, his saliva missing, striking against the wood and slipping slowly downward.

"Mama says the same thing to Papa, and she says that Uncle Al never drinks, and then Papa gets sore and tells her he doesn't give a damn what her dude brother does," Bill said, pulling a long cigarette butt from his pocket, squeezing off the used edge and lighting it. "I hope Mother doesn't catch me smoking," he added mysteriously.

"She's upstairs working. But gee, Bill, I wish you could stay for supper," Danny said.

"It's starting to get dark and I got to go. Pa said I got to be home for supper."

"Gee, I wish you could stay. We could talk about baseball."

"Pa said for me to be home when he left for work, and if I ain't, he'll maybe get sore, and I might get a whaling with his razor strap, and it hurts a hell of a lot," Bill said.

"Gee whiskers!"

A grocery wagon clattered down the alley toward Fiftieth Street.

"Danny!" the grandmother called shrilly from the porch up on the third landing. "Daniel! Daniel!"

"Here I am, Mother," Danny said, running out from under the stairs so she could see him. "I'm with Bill."

"Daniel! Daniel!"

"Here I am, Mother," he shrieked.

"Don't get your little self cold, Son."

That woman living under them looked down at Danny, then up at the grandmother. From one of the yards down the alley a dog was heard barking.

"Bill, Aunty Margaret saw that awful woman who lived under us on Indiana that Uncle Al said couldn't come in the house," Danny said ingratiatingly, because he felt Bill would like him to talk about this thing, and he wanted Bill to like him, and praise him.

"Mama was telling Papa that Mrs. Morton is getting divorced from her husband, and Mama said it was awful. Pa said he didn't want to hear what such people were doing," Bill said, inhaling, letting the smoke out his nostrils.

"What is that, to get divorced? Aunty Margaret talks about people getting that, too," Danny said with added interest.

"It means a man won't live with his wife any more."

"Why?"

"Jesus, Dan, you don't know your rump from a hole in the ground, do you?" Bill said contemptuously, shooting his butt several yards as he spoke. "It means a man won't live with his wife any more, and he won't make babies with her."

"God makes babies, doesn't He, and gives them to their father and mother, like He just did when he gave Mama and Papa my little sister Catherine."

"That's all you know!"

"That's so. Aunty Margaret told me."

"Daniel! Daniel! Daniel!"

"Yes, Mother," Danny said, again running out from under the stairs.

"Don't go 'way, Son! It's getting late."

"Yes, Mother. I'm talking to Bill right here," he yelled, his voice rising above the sounds of another wagon passing in the alley.

94

"That's all you know about babies!" Bill said, almost sneering.

"Aunty Margaret told me that when I asked her."

"You're too young a punk to know any better."

"Why?" Danny said, pained by Bill's scorn.

"When you get older, I'll tell you how babies are made."

"Please tell me, Bill."

"You're too young, and you'd snitch on me if I did."

"Why? Is there something bad about knowing it?"

"Mama and Papa don't know that I know what I do," Bill boasted.

"Tell me, please, Bill."

"You're too young."

"Here, Bill, I'll give you this if you tell me. It's all I got. Mother gave it to me today," Danny said, handing Bill a nickel he had just dug out of his trouser pocket.

"You're too young to know, but I'll tell you," Bill said, taking the nickel. "But if you ever say I told you, I'll lam the shit out of you."

"I won't, Bill."

"When Pa and Ma want a baby, they go to bed. And there is a hole in all women where they pee, and Pa puts his dick into Ma's hole."

"And does he pee into her, and does that make a baby? That's funny. I don't believe it. You're teasing me. God makes babies."

"All right, you dumb little prick, call me a liar. I'll never tell you anything else. Here, take your lousy nickel back."

"I don't want it."

"You're just dumb, Danny. Anybody ever tell you you were dumb?"

"Bill, if you say it's so, I'll believe you," Danny whimpered. "But, Bill, how can peeing in the hole make a baby?"

"White stuff called jism comes out, and that makes the baby inside of Mama."

"Gee!"

"It hurts a woman, too."

"What hurts?"

"Having the baby. The baby is inside of Mama, and Mama's belly swells up like a balloon, and after the baby comes out of her hole she has to stay in bed for a while, and when little Catherine came out of her that way, gee, there were a lot of bloody rags that Papa threw in the garbage pail."

"Why does Mama have a baby then, and why don't God make it another way?"

"I heard Mama talking to Pa about it, and they didn't know I was listening. Mama said it is a punishment of God. When Adam and Eve were made by God, God said to them that they can't do that, and they did, so God said to them they had sinned, and women would always have to have babies in pain and suffering that way."

"Aunty Margaret and Miss Devlin at school said they ate an apple."

"They did, and they did this thing, too. Only they don't tell kids about this, because kids aren't supposed to know it."

"Daniel! Daniel! Daniel!"

"Here I am, Mother."

"Don't let your little feet get cold!"

"I won't, Mother. Honest I won't. I'm all right."

"The hurt only happens, Danny, when the baby comes out of the hole. It doesn't hurt when Papa puts his pecker in Mama. Women are supposed to like a man to do that with them. I heard that from the kids older than me at school."

"Do all women like it? Do they all do it?"

"I guess so. But it's a sin, unless the man and woman are married."

"Is that why Ma and Pa are married?"

"Uh huh!"

"Gee, I never knew that," Danny said, and another wagon passed in the darkening alley. "Can't they do it together if they ain't married?"

"It's a sin. If a woman lets a man put his pecker in her, and she ain't his wife, it's a sin."

"Gee!" Danny exclaimed, quizzically scratching his head.

"It's supposed to be a lot of fun," Bill said.

"Can I do it, too?"

"You got to get big down here first," said Bill, pointing.

"Some day I'll have hair like Uncle Al has?"

"Everybody does. I'm starting to already. Sometimes kids like it with girls. Down on La Salle Street, a cop caught some kids doing it with a girl. They were all naked in a barn. There was hell to pay, and I heard Mama telling Papa that they might be put away in reform school."

"That's funny. And God made it, too, didn't he?"

"You saphead, God made everything."

"I know it. It's in my catechism lesson. It says, *Why did God make you?* And I know the answer. *God made me to know Him, to love Him, and to serve Him in this world, and be happy with Him in the next.*"

"You belong in the first seat at the head of the class," Bill sneered.

"Gee, I never knew about that thing."

"It's what makes men and women different from each other."

They sat in silence. Danny wondered, should he tell Bill how he and Little Margaret had played doctor that day over in the house on Forty-eighth and Indiana, and he had played that Little Margaret had been kidnaped, and tied up so tight with ropes by the kidnapers that every part of her was hurt, and he was the doctor coming to examine her, and he had lifted up her dress first thing and touched her with a card from a deck of cards, but he'd been afraid to touch her with his fingers. And Aunty Margaret had come in the bedroom, and she had seemed worried, and asked them had they done anything else, and she was less worried when they told her no they hadn't. Now he knew what it was. Aunty Margaret had been afraid he had peed in Little Margaret. Gee, the next time that Little Margaret was up to see them, and they were alone, he wanted to play some more doctor with her.

They sat. Danny felt lonesome. Bill seemed like he didn't want to talk to him any more. Gee, he wished he was as big as Bill.

"I got to grab a street car and get home," Bill said, getting up.

Danny sadly watched Bill walk in the growing darkness to the alley gate. He heard Bill whistling after Bill was out of sight. He felt afraid now, with the darkness. He might be kidnaped or something.

"Daniel! Daniel! Daniel!"

"I'm coming, Mother," he said, starting to run up the stairs.

"Daniel! DANIEL! DANIEL!"

II

Usually when his grandmother went out like this at night, he was terribly afraid of burglars and Blackhands, or that somebody might hurt Mother and he would never see her again. And he loved Mother, he guessed, even more than he did his Mama.

But he wasn't so afraid now, because he wanted to think about what Bill told him, and he wanted to think about himself peeing babies in girls, and in Little Margaret's hole, and his cousin, Catherine Nolan, and girls in school, and Hortense Audrey, the girl he liked so much. When he grew up he would like to marry her, only she wasn't a Catholic, and Mother and all of them said that you shouldn't marry anyone who was a Protestant. But Bill had said that doing it without being married was a sin, but gosh, he couldn't help it, because he had just this wish in him that he could go around doing it to one girl, and then to another girl, and he wished that God would make it so that he could do it without it being a sin, even if it was a sin for everybody else. He wished that God would make him just as God made Himself, and then, like God, he couldn't do anything that was a sin.

He unbuttoned his pants, and looked at himself in the parlor mirror, hearing the rumble of an elevated train as if from a distance. He fingered himself, thinking that it was really funny that God made boys and girls different. Now why, he wondered, did God give this thing to boys, and something else to girls? And why had God had to fix it that babies were born the way Bill said they were? Gee, that was funny, he told himself, scratching his head. He went closer to the mirror to study himself, because he could see so much better if he was up closer to it. He wanted God to give him right away a pecker as big as Uncle Al's. He fingered himself with self-indulgent pleasure. He looked from the mirror to himself, and back again. He wished that he could go around everywhere like this, without his pants having to be buttoned up, so that everybody could see him just like he saw himself in the mirror.

He turned thoughtfully away from the mirror and pretended that of all the people in the world he only was allowed by God to walk around with his pants not buttoned. He was like a king in a fairy story, and everybody stood to watch him like he was a king and a whole parade by himself. He walked around the edges of the reddish patterned carpet, telling himself that he was the king of everybody, and he walked around like he was a whole parade by himself, and every time he felt like it, he stopped and peed a baby into some girl who was one of his subjects. Leaving the parlor, he stopped at the hall tree, and imagined that he was peeing a baby into his cousin, Catherine Nolan. He moved down the dim hallway, stopping again to imagine that he was peeing a baby into Hortense Audrey. He halted at the entrance to the dining room. He started back, playing that he was the king of everybody, with a purple crown on his head and a purple robe over his shoulder, and no clothes where his pants should be buttoned up. He held out his hands as if he were holding a trumpet, and he filled his cheeks with air until they swelled and then let out the air as if he were blowing a trumpet because the king was parading with his pecker out. And on both sides of the street girls lined up to watch the king, waiting for him to pee babies into them. And it would not be a sin, either, when he did it, because God let him do it without calling it a sin on him. But God wouldn't let anybody else do it without it being a sin.

The bell rang. He quickly buttoned his pants and, disappointed, he pressed the buzzer to open the downstairs door. He opened the door and waited, hearing his grandmother ascending.

"Son?" she called.

"Yes, Mother," he said innocently.

"Are you all right?"

"Yes, Mother."

He watched her coming up the final flights, wearing her knitted black shawl and carrying a can of beer.

"I hurried back so you would be all right. And I got this to wet me whistle," she said, holding up the can as she reached the top flight. She bent down and kissed him, but he didn't like the kiss because of her beery breath.

"Your uncle will be coming home soon and I won't be able to be getting out like this again, so I thought I would get this and wet me whistle," she added, entering the apartment, Danny slamming the door behind her.

III

"Hurry, now, and get your breakfast eaten so you won't be late for the Sisters, Son," the grandmother said, setting soft-boiled eggs before Danny as he sat down to his breakfast, rubbing his sleepy eyes with his knuckles.

"Aunty Margaret thought that she would get up early and have a cup of coffee with Brother," the aunt said, seated opposite him in a pink kimono.

"Peg, you don't work today?" the mother asked.

"I'm off because I worked Sunday. I'm going to give the house a good cleaning to have it all spick and span for Al. It's a shame that his train doesn't come in earlier. If he was going to be here in time for supper, I'd cook the most delicious meal for him."

"I'm going to bake some fresh bread for my son," the mother said.

"Now eat your eggs there, Brother, dear," Aunt Margaret said.

"Mother, are you my mother, or is my Mama my mother?" Danny suddenly asked, his lips stained with egg.

"Why, what do you mean, Brother?"

"I'm his mother," the grandmother said.

"If you are, then I came out of your hole instead of my Mama's?" he asked.

"Why, Danny, what are you saying?" the aunt said, so puzzled that she held her cup of coffee suspended in mid-air.

"Peg, Peg, what's the little fellow saying?"

"Well, Bill said to me that everybody is born that way, and if Mother is my mother, then I came out of her, and not out of my Mama."

"Glory be!" the grandmother said, blessing herself.

"Brother, what are you talking about?"

"I was only saying what Bill said to me," Danny said naively.

"He did. Only let me get my hands on him! He did!" the grandmother shouted in blind anger.

"Brother, that is a bad thing to say. You must not talk like that," the aunt said.

"Ooh, let me get these hands on him. I'll cut his eyes out with a butcher knife," the grandmother said.

"Well, Bill, he told me that men pee into women, and that makes babies, and down on La Salle Street a policeman found a lot of boys doing that to a little girl in a barn, and they were all naked," Danny said.

"Jesus Mary and Joseph, may all your curses cripple him for saying such things to my grandson!" the grandmother shrieked dramatically.

"Brother, that's bad talk and a sin, and a sweet little fellow like you must never again say that, or your aunty and grandmother will have to wash your mouth out with soap," the aunt said, and while she spoke the grandmother rushed into her room, grabbed the holy-water fount from her wall, returned, and sprinkled holy water around.

"Is it a sin, Aunty Margaret?"

"It's an awful sin, and it would make you burn in Hell. Promise your aunty you'll never again think or talk like that."

"I will. I wasn't saying it myself. I was only telling you what Bill told me, and asking you," he said.

"God bless my soul, but I'll never rest in a night's peace until I can lay these hands on him," the grandmother said slowly, seriously, her beaked face intense with passion.

"What did Bill say to you, Brother?"

"What I told you," Danny said, petulant, afraid now that they were going to worm things out of him the way grownups always did.

"Peg, I'll rip the tongue out of his mouth! Telling such things to an innocent baby. If his father don't beat him, I'll slit his father's ears with the butcher knife!" the grandmother said, nervously dancing and hopping around the kitchen.

"Just what was it?"

"Peg, call Lizz! I'll scratch his eyes out. I'll tear the flesh off him and feed it to dogs in the alley!"

"Go ahead, Brother, you tell Aunty Margaret everything."

"I didn't do nothing," Danny pouted.

"We know, Brother. We won't hurt you. But tell us what else Bill said to you."

"That's all. He said that's how babies were made."

"Brother, promise me you'll never think or speak of this again."

"I won't, Aunty Margaret, because it's a sin, isn't it?"

"Yes, Brother . . ."

"Peg," the grandmother interrupted, "we got to get the boy off to school."

"Yes, because we have catechism first, and Miss Devlin says none of us should be late and miss anything from the catechism lesson. She said if we do, our guardian angel puts a black mark against us in his book."

"Hurry up and finish your breakfast, Danny," the aunt said.

"Oh, Blessed Virgin Mary, give strength to these arms that I might chop that one with a hatchet, him saying things not meant for the ears of a baby," the grandmother said, as if in prayer.

IV

Danny marched out of school in his regular place in line, thinking how at home they would blame Bill and tell Uncle Al. And Uncle Al would sock Bill, and Bill would be sore at him then. And gee, he hadn't meant to tell them what he did. The words had just slipped out of his mouth, when he hadn't meant them to at all, and now, gosh, how would he be able to make Bill believe that he hadn't been a snitcher.

The children marched out of the small, fenced-in schoolyard, and the line dispersed at the gate leading onto Fiftieth Street at the alley. As Danny crossed the alley beside the schoolyard, there were kids all around him, walking, running, talking, shouting, wrestling. Artie Lenehan, a plump boy of seven, who always threw spitballs and made trouble in the schoolroom, came up to him.

"Sissy!" Artie said.

"You go 'way, and let me 'lone. I'm not doing nothing to you," Danny said.

"Sissy! Wears white stockings. Sissy!"

"I ain't a sissy."

"Wears white stockings on Sunday! Wears white stockings on Sunday! Wears white stockings on Sunday! You're worse than a sissy."

"What am I?"

"You're a sonofabitch."

Danny knew that he shouldn't let awful things like this be said about his mother.

"You're worse than a sissy, because a sonofabitch is worse than a sissy," Artie said, standing in the center of a gang of kids who laughed at Danny.

Danny got mad. He closed his eyes and blindly ripped into Artie, punching, kicking, scratching. He fell forward with his eyes closed. When he opened them, he was on top of Artie, screaming, scratching, shouting for Artie to take back what he had said, and Artie was yelling murder, and shouting that he never would. Danny was dragged off Artie by a bigger kid he didn't know.

"I'm going to tell my mother on you," Artie screamed, his face scratched and bleeding.

"You can't talk about my mother bad," Danny sobbed, quivering and nervous as Artie ran away, still shouting.

Danny walked home alone, his body shaken with sobs, not knowing even if he was walking the right way. He rang the bell in the front entrance way, as if he was doing it in his sleep. Walking up three flights of stairway, he tried not to cry. His grandmother was at the door, and she kissed him as he stepped across the threshhold.

"Son! My Son! Your dinner is ready. Where were you?"

He walked ahead of her to the kitchen, and when she followed him into it she saw that his eyes were red from crying, and that his clothes were mussed.

"Son, are you hurt? Are you sick? Who hit you?"

"No, Mudder. A boy called me a sissy."

"The little devil, who is he? Tell me, and I'll tear his mother's hair out of her head."

"Artie Lenehan, who always makes trouble and does this all the time," Danny said, lip-farting to show his grandmother what Artie always did.

"Lead me to him, and I'll flay the hide off him! I'll go see the Sister this afternoon. Did he hit you?"

"No. I hit him."

"Did you scratch the little devil's eyes out?" the grandmother said, and as she spoke the bathroom toilet was heard flushing; she folded her arms around him, kissed him, muttered proudly, "Son!" Peg entered the kitchen. "My grandson tore his eyes out of his head."

"What's this? What happened, Brother?"

"Artie Lenehan called me names, and I hit him good."

"Are you hurt, you poor little thing?"

"No. But I hurt him. I tried to scratch some of his flesh, and bring it home to mother, but it wouldn't come off of him," Danny said, and the aunt laughed loudly.

"Brother, it isn't nice or gentlemanly to fight like that."

"Tear their eyes out!" the grandmother said.

"Why, Mother!" exclaimed Margaret.

"Come, Son, sit down and have a warm dinner."

"Yes, but I don't have to wash my hands, do I? I'll be late for school," Danny said.

"Here, Aunty will do it for you," the aunt said, taking him to the sink and quickly washing his hands while the grandmother nervously bustled about the table.

"If any of those little devils touches a hair on your head, you tell them you'll get your grandmother after them," she said.

"I beat him up."

"Come, drink your soup while it's hot," the grandmother said.

V

Sitting in the classroom, he thought of how, gee, he was always a little bit afraid when Uncle Al came home, and always a little bit glad when he went away. Because when Uncle Al was around, Danny did not know when Uncle Al would go losing his temper, and bawling him out or socking him.

He looked around the room, and he thought of how when he was marching up in line, some of the kids had said to him it was good the way he went and socked Artie Lenehan. He didn't care, Artie had no right to call his mother an awful name.

There was a knock on the door. The eyes of nearly every child in the room were turned toward the door. They saw Sister Marguerita's head, framed in the stiff white headpiece and black-hooded veiling of her order. She and Miss Devlin talked.

"Daniel O'Neill," Miss Devlin called, turning from the opened door, the nun still standing there.

He looked toward his teacher, afraid. They were now nearly all looking at him.

"Daniel, I am calling you," Miss Devlin said.

"Yes, mam," he replied timidly.

"Sister Marguerita wants you."

He knew that something was wrong, and it must be because of Artie Lenehan. It hadn't been his fault, either. He looked hesitantly at his teacher, while she motioned for him to come forward. *That woman!*

"Come here, Daniel!" Sister Marguerita said, a squat wrinkled-face nun, and her voice was not as angry as Miss Devlin's had been. "I want to speak with you in the office," Sister Marguerita added as he walked down the aisle of desks, toward the nun.

"Yes, Sister," he said spiritlessly as he followed her out of the room and down the corridor, hearing the heavy rattle of the long beads she wore and the swish of her clothing.

They passed into Sister Marguerita's small office which was overcrowded with furniture, statues of saints, and holy pictures. Danny looked down at the green carpet. He knew all right that something was up because there were two fat women sitting on each side of the desk, looking as if they were really sore. The nun sat down, faced him. He halted about eight feet away, pale and breathing a little hard.

"Daniel, were you fighting?" Sister Marguerita asked in a surprisingly stern voice.

Gee, he liked Sister Marguerita all right, but he hoped that she wasn't going to do anything to him. He squirmed. He couldn't talk.

"Daniel, answer me! Were you fighting?"

"Yes, Sister," he replied in a half-whisper.

"Come closer to me," the nun commanded, and he took a careful step forward, muttering inarticulately. "Closer!" He took a few more steps. "Here, come right up before the desk. . . . Now answer me! Why were you fighting?"

Maybe he could talk if the two fat women were not there, with their mean faces. They seemed to look at him like they didn't like him, all right. He guessed that one of them must be Artie's mother, and the other something like his aunt. Well, if they put a hand on him, he would tell Mother, and she would come and tear their darn old eyes out, she would.

"Answer me, Daniel! Speak! I won't swallow you," the Sister said.

"Yes, Sister."

"Why did you scratch and beat up Arthur Lenehan? He wasn't able to come to school this afternoon."

"He . . . called me a name."

"Sister," said the fat woman on the right, "Sister, I don't think he's telling the truth. He's lying. My Arthur told me that he just hit and scratched him with absolutely no provocation, and my little Arthur never lies. He's just the best-behaved and the most mannerly child. He wouldn't even call a flea a name. My neighbor here, Mrs. Stone, she'll vouch for every word I am saying."

"He called me a sissy because I wear white stockings," Danny said while Mrs. Stone continued nodding her head in affirmation of Mrs. Lenehan's statement.

"Daniel, aren't you a little man? You are in school now, and you shouldn't be fighting over such little things."

"Sister, he called me something else, too."

"What was it?"

"I can't tell you."

"Why can't you, Daniel?"

"It's too bad and awful."

"Daniel, surely you can tell me."

"No, I can't, Sister," Danny said, nodding intently.

"Why?"

"I can't say it. It would be a sin."

"It won't be a sin to say it now to me. Tell me."

"No, Sister. I'm afraid. I'm afraid to say it. It was an awful word about my mother."

"Sister, it's not so. My little Arthur, coming from the home we give him, he couldn't say anything like that. Why, he doesn't even know such words because he never hears them at home," Mrs. Lenehan said.

"Sister, I didn't want to fight. He called me names."

"Daniel, you must listen to me. I don't want to hear of you fighting any more, and if I do, I'll send for your grandmother. She's one who might be able to take care of you if you carry on as you did this noon."

"Yes, Sister," Danny said, hoping that she would let him go so he wouldn't have to have the two fat women looking at him as if maybe they even wanted to chew him up or something.

He felt funny, as if there were two Danny O'Neills, one of them on the outside of something like a box, and the other Danny O'Neill on the inside. And the inside one of himself seemed to be getting smaller and shrinking, and getting smaller, and still smaller, and he was just awful afraid, and he wanted to get away from here, with these two mean old fat women. He didn't like them, he didn't, and he wanted Sister Marguerita to let him go.

"Daniel, you must promise me something," Sister Marguerita said.

He knew the sister was talking to him, and he didn't know what she was saying, and all he knew was that he was afraid, and there she was, and she seemed to be very far away from him behind her big desk.

"Daniel, don't you hear me?" Sister Marguerita said, her voice sharper, so that her words cut through his confusion like a light knifing a fog. "Answer me!" she said sternly while he feebly nodded his head.

"Yes, Sister."

"I want you to promise me that you won't fight any more, and that if you have any trouble with any of the other boys you will come and tell me about it instead of fighting. I cannot let you boys be fighting. You must act like little gentlemen. Do you understand me?"

"Yes . . . I mean, yes, Sister," he said awkwardly.

"Sister, he scratched my little Arthur up so badly that I couldn't let him go to school this afternoon. I never heard of such a thing happening before in a Catholic school," Mrs. Lenehan said, her fat face bloating with contorted indignation.

"I'm . . . sorry," Danny meekly said.

"After acting the way you did, Daniel, if you were not sorry, it would be very wrong and bad. It would not be Christian, and, Daniel, you must be a little Christian who conducts himself after the example of our Good Lord. When He was called names and the Jews gave Him vinegar and gall to drink, and hit Him and threw stones at Him, He turned the other cheek. And even when the Jews crucified Him, He said that He forgave them. You must be like that, Daniel."

"Yes, Sister, I will. Honest I will."

"Tell Mrs. Lenehan that you are sorry, and that you want her to tell Arthur you're sorry, and that you will never do it again," she said.

"I do."

"Well, go ahead and say it!" Sister Marguerita said, her cracked face suddenly breaking into a whimsical smile so that she turned aside lest Danny notice it.

"I will, Sister, but I forgot it."

Again the nun turned her face aside to smile, but the two fat women glared, and Danny was still afraid of them.

"Well, Sister, I am sorry, and I want Artie's mother to tell him I'm sorry, and won't do it again."

"Daniel, if you do this again you will be punished. I shan't punish you this time, but I will place you on your own responsibility not to do it again. I'm going to let you prove to me that you can be a sturdy little Christian. This noon, you acted the same way that the Jews did when they crucified our Good Lord. You don't want to act like that, do you?"

"No, Sister," Danny said, nodding weakly, only wanting to be let go so that he wouldn't have these old fat women watching him.

"Daniel, what would your grandmother say if she knew that her grandson was fighting like a tough?"

"I donno."

"Yes, you do. You know that she wouldn't at all like it. She would punish you, because she wants you to grow up to be a fine gentleman, not a little rowdy like boys from public schools."

"I guess so."

"Your grandmother is too fine a woman to want you doing such bad things. Now I never want to hear such stories about you again, Daniel. Mind me, now! Never again!" she said, and he shook his head negatively. "You may go back to your classroom but don't forget my warning."

"Yes, Sister," he mumbled leaving the office hastily, quite relieved.

VI

Danny sat very quietly in his seat, the first one in the third row in a classroom with five rows of desks, each one consisting of ten seats. Most of the other children had their heads bent in their first-grade readers while dark-haired Helen Smith read the day's lesson. Danny followed her unsurely as she pieced out the words about how a good cat caught the bad rat that had been chewing up a little girl's rag doll, only he could not read all the words yet. All around him were boys, many of them twisting and squirming in their uncomfortable seats. He tried not to twist like that because he was afraid after being in Sister Marguerita's office, and he wanted to try and be a little Christian like she had said he should be. He must not go fighting again. But he didn't want kids picking on him, calling him a sissy, and he didn't want to fight, and he didn't like school and wished that he was home right now with Mother, or that he was playing with his big brother Bill. He didn't like any of these kids. He only liked Hortense Audrey. When his uncle and aunt tried to tease him, and asked him if he had a girl, he would like to say to them yes, he did have a girl, the nicest girl in the first grade, and he was afraid to tell them that because then they might tease him even more. Gee, he wished that he had a seat near her, but she sat in the next row to him and way in the back of the room. He liked to look at her with her short black hair, and he would like school if he could just sit here all day and look at her. But he couldn't unless he kept turning his head. The boys almost all seemed to like to look at the girls, and now, all around him, they were looking, and there was Albert Throckwaite, two rows away, the boy with white hair and a funny voice. Albert was looking at some of the girls, too. Were these other kids thinking that all these girls had holes that you could pee babies in? Gee, he wondered.

"Children!" Miss Devlin said in that voice she used when she seemed to mean what she was saying.

Danny stared at her in awe. She was looking around the room, angry, fingering her brown puffs of hair.

"If you don't stop looking all around the room, and gazing at things instead of following the lesson in your readers, I shall have to punish some of you. I'm going to make every boy I catch turning around sit with a girl, and every girl will be made to sit with a boy if she tries any star-gazing while we continue with this lesson. Now, Helen, go on and read," she said, and some of the kids laughed, but Danny didn't, and, gee, he figured that he better watch himself. "If you boys want to be punished now, you just go ahead and look around."

Gosh, maybe if he looked around he would be made to sit with Hortense Audrey, and then, well, anybody that wanted to could laugh at him and tease him all they wanted to and see if he would care. He would just wait a little minute, and then he would look around and be made to sit with her by *that woman*. There would be nothing in the world as nice as sitting with Hortense Audrey, because he liked her. Maybe, too, he would go walking with her, and they could play together. He wished she didn't live on the other side of Grand Boulevard, because then he could walk home from school with her every day and carry her books. He would like it, too, if he could say that Hortense Audrey was his girl. He wouldn't care, he wouldn't, no, he wouldn't, if they went and laughed at him then.

He gazed dreamily around the classroom, and then up at Miss Devlin. He could never know what that woman was thinking about, and when she would bawl them out and tell them to pay attention to the lesson. He turned back to his reader, but when he tried too hard to read and spell out the words, his eyes got watery, and sore, and sometimes it almost looked like he was crying. He glanced around again. Hortense was paying attention to the lesson and right in back of her was that girl he didn't like at all, Margaret Grady. All the kids teased her by calling her Maggie. She was looking all around the room, and she was a goofy, and she was not at all nice or pretty like Hortense Audrey was, and, yes, he liked Hortense Audrey, and he didn't like Maggie Grady and he wouldn't like to have to sit with her. He wondered now would there be any boy who would want to pee a baby into her hole? He wouldn't. From the corner of his eye, he could see that Miss Devlin was not watching him. He wished that Hortense would look up from her book and see him looking at her, and that Miss Devlin would catch him. He wouldn't care if he was the only boy in the class made to sit with a girl. Only if he was, and Sister Marguerita came in, and Miss Devlin told her, it would be bad, and he didn't at all want that, either.

Now Adam Morrison was reading. Hortense Audrey was still looking into her reader, because she was the smartest girl in the room. Darn it, why couldn't that woman catch him? Maggie Grady was still looking around. He didn't want her to think he was looking at her, the old thing. He would tell her some day that she wasn't a nice girl like Hortense Audrey was a nice girl. He turned back to his reader, disappointed.

"I see, Daniel O'Neill, that you didn't believe me, and for ten minutes now I have watched you turning around and looking at Margaret Grady. Perhaps you better sit with her."

He stared at Miss Devlin, shaking his head negatively, feeling all over again as if he was shrinking up inside of himself.

"I won't do it again," he pleaded, blushing, with the room thrown into excitement and many laughing at him.

"Daniel, you go down and sit with Margaret for the rest of the afternoon."

"Aw, gee!"

"Daniel, go ahead! You've already done enough harm in one day by fighting with Arthur Lenehan."

"Teacher, I'm afraid he'll beat me up," Margaret Grady said, waving her hand in the air.

"I'll tend to that," Miss Devlin smiled.

"Gee!" Danny exclaimed as other children joined in laughing at him.

"Yes, Margaret?" Miss Devlin said after the girl had waved her hand nervously to attract attention.

"Miss Devlin, I wasn't looking at Daniel O'Neill," Margaret Grady said.

Descending from her dais, Miss Devlin led Danny to Margaret Grady's desk.

And he didn't even like the way Margaret Grady smelled. She smelled like boiled eggs or something. And the seat was hardly big enough for the two of them. He had to look in her reader with her while the class went on, and Hortense Audrey in front of him wouldn't even turn around.

"Now, if any other children want the same treatment, you can just do what Daniel O'Neill did," Miss Devlin said.

"Were you looking at me?" Margaret whispered, spitting in his face as she spoke.

"No!" he answered, wiping his cheek with his hand.

"Were, too. I didn't ask you to."

"I was not."

"I want no whispering back there," Miss Devlin called out.

"She's talking to you," Margaret whispered.

"She is not."

"Is, too."

"Is not."

"Anyone I catch talking will have to stay after school and beat out erasers," Miss Devlin said.

"Don't talk to me," Margaret Grady said.

"I'm not."

"Don't!"

"I won't"

"Don't!"

"All right!"

He wished school was out, and he could go home and never have to come back here. But, gee, Uncle Al was coming home. Gee, if he was only a man now. He could do what he wanted to do, and he wouldn't then sit here and be laughed at, and he wouldn't go home and be afraid of Uncle Al. He would be a motorman, that's what he'd be. He'd wear a motorman's cap and have buttons on his coat, and he'd stand in front of the car, turning the switches on and off and ding-ding-dinging the bell to make horses and wagons get off the track.

"Why did you look at me? I don't want to sit with you," Margaret Grady said.

"Miss Devlin made me," Danny said.

"Go sit with Miss Devlin."

Danny caught Adam Morrison and Hilda Wilson crossing their fingers T-wise in shame at him. If he only had wings and could fly right out of the room, away, away, away off across the sky and never come back. He felt worse than he did when he was called a sissy. He was always being laughed at by them. And here he was, so near to Hortense Audrey that he could smell her, and she wouldn't even turn her head to look at him. Gee, why did this have to happen to him and not to other kids? And, gee whiz, he wished, yes, he wished very awful much, that he could fly away, or run away, and never come back to school, and here he was with this old Maggie Grady who couldn't even sit still in her seat.

"You can look in my book with me," she said.

He wouldn't answer her, he wouldn't. He wanted the bell to ring so he could run right home to Mother and ask her never never to let him come back here.

"Oh, all right, smarty. You don't have to look in my book. I don't care."

He wouldn't, he wouldn't! Oh, God, please make the bell ring quick, please make the bell ring!

10

I

"Ma, I promised Dan that I'd be up today," Bill said.

"William, you get up to Mother's all the time and I never get out. I want you to stay here and watch the house while I run down to the Italian church to pay a visit to the Blessed Sacrament."

Lizz noticed the sulky expression on Bill's face. She went to her bedroom, and dug into the shapeless, overladen black pocketbook that lay amid the litter on the top of the bureau.

"Jesus Christ, you little pisspot!" she yelled, almost falling over Robert who was crawling around the dining-room floor, making choo-choo sounds.

"Margaret, why don't you watch Robert here?" Bill yelled, receiving no answer from Little Margaret who was out in the kitchen, playing house and talking to two rag dolls which she pretended were her children.

"Here, William," Lizz said, handing him a nickel. "Now you watch the house. I'll be back in a jiffy."

"Ma, I guess maybe I don't want to go up to Mother's anyway," Bill said, pocketing the coin. "Uncle Al is coming home, and sometimes when he comes in off the road he's as cranky as the deuce."

"I'm your mother. He has nothing to say over you. But you mark my words, William! Don't trust the O'Flahertys! Don't do a thing for them, unless they put something in there first," Lizz said, holding out her left palm and pointing her right index finger into it in added emphasis of her meaning.

"Ma, Mother said that Aunt Margaret has been seeing Mrs. Morton. Mother said that Mrs. Morton is a high-lifer," Bill said.

"Oh, my poor mother and my poor son Daniel. What they must put up with living under the same roof with that aunt of yours," Lizz sighed.

"Ma, Dan and I, we don't like Mrs. Morton."

"Don't you dare even mention her name in my house! And if she is ever at Mother's when you're there, don't you go running to the store for cigarettes for her. If you do, I'll lambast you. Your father works too hard for you to be wearing out your shoe leather running errands for a hussy who never even thinks of the word of God."

"Ma, it'll be getting dark soon. You better be hurrying, maybe, if you want to pay a visit to church."

"Yes, Son. You watch things, and I'll only be gone a jiffy," Lizz said, going into her room and putting on a stained black dress.

Bill sat at the dining-room table, arranging pictures of major-league ballplayers which came as premiums with packages of cigarettes. As soon as his mother slammed the door and left, he went to her room and looked to see if she had gone without her pocketbook. He couldn't find it. He quickly looked under covers and in drawers to see if he could spot any hidden money. Failing, he returned to his baseball pictures. Robert crawled about, gurgling. Dennis marched back and forth from the dining room to the parlor, making ding-dong sounds and playing that he was a street car. Little Margaret was still out in the kitchen, playing house, talking to her rag dolls. A train from the Rock Island tracks was heard chugging by behind the Morgan and Hearst plant.

II

Wearing a shabby brown man's coat, high shoes with knotted laces, and an unclean rag tied under her chin, Lizz walked westward along Twenty-fifth Street just as the sun was beginning to fade. A new Mitchell passed her, sputtering, traveling on eastward under the viaduct behind her. She was afraid of automobiles. But Al ought to buy one for Mother. Her Jim could learn to run it easy. Couldn't he drive a team of horses? Al could hire Jim as a chauffeur, and that would be easier work than staying at the express company and having to do hard work when he was ruptured. Wouldn't she lord it over the Germans and the shanty Irish around here when Al bought Mother an automobile? And, yes, over the O'Reilleys and all of Jim's relatives, too. Al was a good boy, and he would get an automobile for Mother, and then Jim wouldn't have to do such hard work.

A drunken Slav staggered by her, mumbling to himself. She was proud as a peacock that her Jim had taken the pledge and kept it. Her Jim was a fine man, he was. At the corner of Twenty-fifth and Wentworth three men leaned against the side wall of the saloon. Loafers, out-of-works, she sneered to herself. Not like Jim or her brothers. Her brothers were as swell and as well off as Joe O'Reilley. And some day Jim would be, too. And when her boys grew up, they would be rich and have automobiles, and buy their mother a house on Grand Boulevard that would make the O'Reilleys spit with jealousy.

She scuttled across Wentworth Avenue. Continuing, she slackened her pace, because her feet were starting to ache and her neuralgia bothered her. She thought that she loved her Jim, all right. Only if they didn't have so many kids! That worry each month, asking herself would her woman's curse come again. Tonight Jim would be like a bull, because she had just gotten over it. Ah, the sad life of a mother with a large family and a poor man for a husband. If she had only entered the convent. God had called her to it, and she had denied God for the flesh. Ah, Jesus, Mary, and Joseph, why had she scorned the call to be a nun? That was why she was so poor. It was the cross she must carry for not answering her call. But her own people, why didn't they help her more when she was so poor? Ned could do something for her, having a good job and a wife who owned a millinery store. And here was Al, going to buy an automobile. If Al bought an automobile, he certainly could give her and her little ones something. Blood wasn't thicker than water when it was O'Flaherty blood.

She walked along a street of dull red-brick buildings and shabby frame houses, and she went into a quiet brown-stoned Catholic church. A few old men and shabbily dressed women were scattered about the pews and before the altars, praying. She liked it here where it was so quiet. She could be with God, her true Father Who would always watch over her and protect her. She knelt in a rear pew, bowed her head humbly, prayed to God for herself and her family and her relatives. She arose, genuflected histrionically, moved slowly to the front of the church, dragging her feet as she walked. She dropped seven pennies into the slot before the altar of the Blessed Virgin and lit seven candles in the rack, thinking that since she was poor, God would permit her to make an offering of only one cent for each candle. She bowed her head before the cold, blue-robed statue of Mary and prayed. She moved back from the altar railing and prostrated herself in adoration, hoping that her piety would be observed. Arising, with her clothes gray from collected dust, she knelt in the first pew and gazed devoutly and obliviously, and then vacantly, at the perpetually burning red altar light. She said the Rosary. With closed eyes, she lowered her head.

Oh, God, oh, pure and holy Virgin Mary, Tower of Ivory, Comfortress of the Afflicted, Mary, Mother of all Mothers, she, Lizz O'Neill, she wanted guidance, she wanted Mary's intercession at the Throne of the Great and Powerful Almighty God. She did not want to be so poor, unless it was the will of God. She wanted it, God willing, that her man would have a better job. She wanted health for herself, and all of hers. Oh, Mary!

And it was so quiet in the church. She was able to be so alone with God, with Mary, with all of the angels and saints, with her father, her sister, Louise, all her own dead children. Here was where she belonged, she who had ignored the call to take the veil, she who should be bound to God by oaths of poverty, chastity, obedience. *Hail, Mary, full of grace.* . . . Outside, there was a muffled rumble of a passing wagon. *The Lord is with Thee.* . . . At home was the dirty house full of kids. Her man was out working hard, maybe straining himself, with his rupture. And here it was so peaceful, so like Heaven must be. She was alone with her soul and her God. She flung herself mercifully into His arms and His care. He would give everything to her and hers, He would.

Her eyes became transfixed upon the blushed marble cheeks of the statue of Mary, on the chiseled, darkish Italian face. There was Mary, a holy woman chosen by God to be the Mother of His Son. Mary, whom God had taken as a Virgin Mother. Lizz's mind dwelled on the life of Mary. The Archangel Gabriel had gone to her with trumpets and told her that she was anointed of the Lord and chosen to carry the Precious Holy Burden in her womb. Good Saint Joseph had taken Mary to Bethlehem, and Mary's time had come in a little stable, warmed only by the breath and bodies of the little lambs. Mary had lain with the pains coming, and Jesus had been born of woman. Ah, how pretty a thing Mary was. Lizz's eyes were still glued in fascination on the Italian features of the statue, the large red lips, the eyes, the lovely reddish blush of the cheeks. And she thought that Mary had raised little Jesus, just as she, Lizz, was now raising hers. God had chosen Mary to be the Mother of Jesus! God had chosen her, Lizz O'Neill, to be a mother!

Lizz sat in the church for over a half hour. She blessed herself, genuflected, dragged her feet down the aisle, blessed herself wetly with holy water, genuflected a second time, went out into the gathering dusk. She walked home, not seeing the buildings, vehicles, people about her. Turning the corner of Twenty-fifth and La Salle, she realized suddenly, painfully, that she was going back home to stinking diapers.

III

Jim sighed, expressing a sense of relief. He walked toward the corner of Twenty-fifth and La Salle, seeing the iron picket fence and the unstirring trees of Harding Square ahead of him. There was a thin, faint moon, and an overhanging haze falling from the sky.

Hell, a glass of beer wasn't breaking his pledge. And he wanted a glass tonight. And of course a man loved his family and wanted to be with them, but once in a while, too, he liked to spend a little time with some of the boys in a saloon, not getting drunk, just having a glass of beer or two. Turning on Twenty-fifth, he heard a train behind him. He stepped along, the street seeming deserted, almost shedding a spirit of lonesomeness. It was just the time of the night and just the period of the year when he got this kind of a lonesome feeling walking down a street by himself.

He pushed through the swinging doors of the saloon at Twenty-fifth and Wentworth, waving as some of the fellows lined along the bar nodded to him. He stood at the end of the row of fellows, his foot on the rail.

"How's tricks, Jim?" asked a mild-faced, gray-haired fellow with pronounced Irish features.

"The world goes on," Jim said with a shrug of his shoulders, and then he turned to the plump, sandy-haired bartender. "A beer, Pat."

A thin, peaked-faced fellow came in with a can and set it down on the bar.

"Here you are, Jim, as good a swig of beer as you'll get this side of Hell," the bartender said, shoving the glass over to Jim.

"Fill the bucket, Pat," the peaked-faced fellow said, nervously shifting his weight from foot to foot.

"How's business, Mr. Underhill?" asked a hefty, leathery-skinned chap as the bartender filled the can.

"It's just business."

"Stay and have one with us, Mr. Underhill?" the leathery-skinned fellow asked.

"I can't tonight, Henehan, but thanks," Underhill said, laying down the price of his beer, taking the full can and leaving.

"Am I imagining things, or is that lad off his nut?" asked Jim.

"He's a nice fellow, but he falls on the batty side of the ledger," Pat said.

"I can't dope him out. I guess he just isn't a sociable guy," Henehan said.

"Not like you, huh? Imagine Larry Henehan turning down a drink anybody offered to buy him," the kindly-faced Irishman said.

"Not on your old lady's petticoats," Larry said.

"I guess they got your number, huh, Henehan?" laughed Jim.

"A hell of a lot they can talk. None of these guys around here ever broke their arms buying me drinks," Larry said.

"It's because we're your friends," a thin gangling fellow said.

"Sure you're my friend, Schmaltz. You always break your arm digging down in your jeans to buy me drinks because you're my friend," Henehan said, laughing in loud enjoyment of his remarks. "Sure, you're a friend of mine, but me, poor turkey, I'm deficient in comprehension."

"Still chewing up dictionaries, aren't you, Larry?" said Jim.

"Say, I know what that Underhill needs. If you ask me he needs a woman," a stout ruddy fellow said.

"Mike, don't we all now and then?" said Pat.

"He needs one steady with him for twenty-three hours or so."

"If he could stand that much, Mike, he's a better man than I am," Larry Henehan said while they were nearly all still rocking with gusty male laughter.

"How about you, Jim?" asked Pat.

"He's a better man than I am, Gunga Din."

"Who the hell is Gunga Din, some Turk with a harem?" asked Mike.

"You dumb face, don't you know? That's poetry," Larry said.

"Jesus, Jim, you read poetry?"

"Listen, Jim and I haven't got bone in our heads like you got, you obtuse son-ofabitch," said Henehan.

"You know, gettin' back to what I was thinkin' about before we all started re-citin' poems, there's things to be said for a woman, and things to be said against her," Schmaltz began.

"Well, I'll be damned if this isn't Wagner. How goes it, you German?" said Henehan, interrupting Schmaltz.

"Boys, I'm a slave without a master," Wagner said glumly.

"Lost your job?" Larry asked, waxing sympathetic.

"Yeh," Wagner said dourly, and then he ordered a whiskey straight.

"I tell you, boys, we're living in an age when there is an unholy confraternity of business and politics, and the poor man hasn't got a chance to be anything but a sucker," Larry orated.

"That's because Teddy Roosevelt stepped out of the White House and gave the job over to a fat man who likes to laugh all the time," Schmaltz said.

"What the hell could he do? He's a Republican," Pat said.

"Any workingman who votes for a Republican is a damn fool," Jim said.

"Say, Henehan, you sound like you're trying to become a Haymarket anarchist," said Mike.

"Sorry to hear about losing your job, Wagner," Jim said, but Wagner's only answer was a grimace before he downed his whiskey.

"Some day we got to do something about this unholy confraternity of business and politics," said Larry, looking at Jim. "I'm a union man and always will be one," Jim said.

"I don't like finks, either," said Larry.

"Goddamn it, a man ought to have a right to a job when he has a wife and kids," Jim said.

"Say, Jim, put that sentiment in a letter, will you, and send it to my ex-fore-man," said Wagner.

"Here, Wagner, have one on the house."

"Thanks, Pat, I will."

"Hell, don't take it so hard. Every man loses his job sooner or later, and gets another one. Maybe it's for the best," said Pat.

"Goddamn it, fellows, you know I'm still puzzled about this guy Underhill. I guess maybe he does need a woman," said Schmaltz as Jim signaled for another beer.

"What does the lad do for a living?" Larry Henehan asked.

"He's a watchmaker," said Schmaltz.

"And he ain't married. That's why he ain't got gray in his head like this gazook here," Larry said, pointing to the kindly-faced Irishman.

"These gray hairs are the products of the course of nature. Whether you are married or not, my lad, you'll get them yourself, if you don't lose all your hair beforehand," the kindly-faced Irishman philosophized.

"Another one," Wagner said to the bartender.

"Getting married and having kids gives you something to look forward to in your old age," Jim said.

"When they grow up, they run and get married just as they should," Wagner said.

"Mine won't," Jim said, his voice intense.

"I hope you're right. You deserve a break from your kids, Jim, because you're a hard-working guy," Larry said.

"And sometimes a hard-drinking man, too," Pat said, winking.

"I took the pledge before my last kid was born. That's why I'm sticking to beer. I don't count a couple of glasses of beer," Jim said, and some of them knowingly laughed at him.

"How many times is it that you took the pledge?" asked Mike.

"It's sticking this time," Jim said.

"Have a shot on me, Jim," said Larry.

"No, have one on the house," Pat said.

"No thanks, boys," Jim said in humorless earnest.

"When you break the pledge, Jim, remember these offers and collect on them," Mike said.

"Say now, this lad, Underhill?" said Schmaltz quizzically.

"Don't get such a brainstorm over him," said Henehan.

"Another," Wagner said.

"Say, boy, you won't only be a slave without a master, but you'll also be a slave without a penny," said Larry.

"What difference does it make, a few goddamn pennies, when I'm out of work? If my family doesn't starve this week, well, it'll starve next week," Wagner said, taking his drink, gulping.

"Don't take it so hard, fellow. When life seems the darkest, there's sometimes a ray of light behind the fog," said Larry.

"Another," Wagner said in answer to Henehan.

"You know, I'm still wondering about this guy, Underhill."

"We hung Underdrawers on the line. He's washed now," Pat said, and they laughed.

"He's just a little bit cracked up here, and that's the thing in a nutshell," said Larry.

"Yes, I guess maybe it is a woman that he needs," said Schmaltz thoughtfully.

"When a guy gets a woman, what the hell does he do with her?" queried Baron, a tall thin young lad.

"Learning the answer to that question, lad, is what is called getting experience," said Mike.

"I just got that, fellow. I knocked up a chicken, and, Jesus, she came around to see me acting like she was the city water-works, saying I ruined her. She wanted me to put the ring on her finger. I had to talk myself blue in the puss before I got her to agree to get fixed up with a midwife."

"You keep your sailor out of the rain, or you pay, sonny," said Larry.

Jim looked around the dim saloon. He had a warm feeling for these fellows, good fellows, fellows like himself, poor but decent, who liked a drink now and then, and a little talk in a saloon. Hell, a saloon and talk like this and a few shots or a few swigs of beer, that was almost the only fun a working-man got.

"Say, goddamn it, I'll be damned if I don't puzzle this lad Underhill out. Now he's a watchmaker, isn't he?"

"No, Schmaltz, he's a Chinese puzzle," Jim said.

"I'm serious. You know, you come across a fellow you can't dope out, and so you try to figure out, now just what the hell is it that makes him tick different from what makes you and me and the rest of us tick."

"Wind him up and take him apart. But don't ask me," the kindly-faced Irishman suddenly said.

"He's probably just like all of us, trying to get along, only he's just not sociable," said Jim.

"Yes, trying to get along, as best we can. Best as we can. Some of us, slaves with a master. Some of us, slaves without a master. You're a slave. I'm a slave. All slaves. Another drink," Wagner said, reeling as he spoke.

"Better brace up, Wagner, and go home to the old lady so you can be out looking for a job in the mornin'," Pat said.

"What? When? Oh, yes, look for a job tomorrow. That's right. Look for a job tomorrow. I got it now. Put myself on the block in the slave market," said Wagner.

"Say, this is a free country, only there's a unholy confraternity . . ."

"Hire a hall, Henehan," said Pat.

"Tough, all right," Jim exclaimed with a slow nod of his head.

"Well, maybe it's so. I mean what was just said about Underhill, and maybe it isn't," said Schmaltz.

"And maybe . . ." said Wagner, reeling more noticeably.

"Schmaltz, why don't you go home and sleep over this Underdrawers?" said Pat.

"Come on, Wagner, brace up. The world might look like sunshine in the morning," Henehan said.

"Yeah, we'll eat the sunshine for breakfast in a week," said Wagner, sneering drunkenly.

"Well, Dutch, now, everybody gets a tough jolt now and then. And when it comes, you got to say this is life, and take it," said Henehan.

"Take it on shrinking guts," said Wagner, staggering out of the saloon, followed by sympathetic eyes.

"I know how the poor devil feels. Sooner or later we all get the same thing," said Jim.

"But we get new jobs. Now, when I lost mine with that trucking outfit, well, I felt low. But then I got on the cars, didn't I? Well, I'm better off on the street cars than I was then. Well, it's the same all around," said Larry.

"Tough just the same."

"Rotten."

"Well, boys, I got to be running along," said Jim.

He paid up, and left, waving.

He walked back home, liking the boys, thinking that it was nice getting around to having a drink and talking with them, and—well, no, a glass of beer wasn't breaking his pledge. And Lizz was at home. Ah, he wanted to get back and into bed with Lizz, Lizz who would be so warm. A little chat with the boys, and then your woman, warm beside you in bed, it made you forget a lot of things. But that poor Dutchman, tough luck, all right. Yes, Wagner was right. Most of them were slaves with or without a master. Hell with it! He could forget it for the night. He had had a nice time with the fellows, and now he could go home to bed with Lizz.

11

As the train pulled into the Englewood station, Al was nervously glad, keyed in anticipation. He told himself that there was nothing in the world like home. All things considered, he had pride in his home. And Peg's last letter gave him the feeling that now everything was bright on Calumet Avenue. Yes, after the trip, with its worry and with the disappointing volume of his sales, it was a wonderful feeling to be coming home.

He stepped down off the train, identified his baggage in the heap on the platform, and followed a red-capped Negro who lugged his thick suitcase and his burdensome sample case. Yes, he was glad to be coming home, with Mother and Peg and the Sport. Now, Mother, she was a great character, witty, a wonderful woman even if she couldn't read and write. And she was his mother, his! What a fine thing it was to know that he would be able to give her a comfortable home as long as she lived, to give her the things she had never had in her younger days. Peg was a wonderful girl, too, if she would only settle down and use that fine sense and acumen which she displayed on occasions when she wanted to. But she would now, judging from the bright rays of sunshine that had been spread over that last letter of hers.

Following the porter through the station waiting room, he noticed the people collected about, many of them folks like himself, bound for home. That was something wonderful, just the thought of people going home. That big-shouldered fellow on his right, maybe he was headed home to see his little lady and his kids. Maybe Chicago was as good to many of these people as it was to him at this very minute. It was all the home that he knew in the world, and even if it was disturbing now and then, well, after all, he guessed that no home ever ran smoothly all the time. But perhaps his would from now on. It would. He wished that he had a wishing ring and a four-leaf clover, and if he had, he would wish for just that boon from the grace and bounty of God. And, yes, it was something of greater importance than even his sales record. But then, all things considered, he hadn't had such a bad trip.

"Just a minute, Sport," he called to the porter in an authoritative tone.

While the porter waited, he stepped into a telephone booth, called his own number, spoke cheerily and briefly, saying that he was coming right on from the station. Stepping out of the phone booth, he saw a woman rushing into a man's arms, kissing him. Ah, a sight of joy, wonderful to behold. A man and his wife meeting after absence. Often, now, didn't he wish that he had a wife, a tall woman, stately, like a queen, with inward and outward grace, beautiful, refined, dark, handsome, a woman like Marie Menard! The man and woman meeting here, they seemed so happy in their reunion. Ah, the wonder of love! If he were coming home to a wife now! Some salesmen talked of how, after being on the road, they got their wives right into bed. He wouldn't. That was unrefined, making the bestial part of man the uppermost part of his love. Well, even if he didn't have a wife, it was still wonderful to be coming home. And he did have Mother, Peg, Danny. And sometime, maybe, there would be more. Perhaps!

"Here, Sport!" Al said, giving the porter a fifteen-cent tip after the Negro had shunted his luggage into a black-and-white-painted Shaw taxi. He guessed, this time, he would afford the luxury of a cab.

He was driven along Sixty-third Street, dim, dusty, dismally lit. But he was eager, and he imagined his happy homecoming. The street became warm to him as an exuding reflection of his own mood and spirits. It was warm with people whom he saw for the snap of a second or so as they walked along. A boy, running with a bag. A policeman twirling his club. A horse hitched to a lamppost, looking like the very life picture of Old Dobbin himself. A man in overalls, singing.

Yes, even so, yes, even if his trip had not been as successful as he had hoped, well, he'd have better luck next time. The taxi lurched past White City, curved onto South Park Avenue. Getting along. Danny would be home. He was going to educate the boy, make him a smarter and more successful man than Joe O'Reilley, the lawyer. The park. Trees shedding their leaves. God was putting the trees to sleep until He gave the world a wonderful new spring once again. The buildings along South Park. Might be nice to be moving out here. Nice people lived here. Mother's cousins, the Nolans, owned a nice new building at Fifty-seventh. Tennis courts along the edge of the park. Tennis wasn't the game that baseball was. Fun, too, it was, taking the boy to the games where he cheered like an old-timer. Garfield Boulevard. More automobiles on the streets every year now. The day of the horse was doomed. The duck pond. Fifty-third Street. Father and Louise used to take the boy to the duck pond. He used to say, *Pader, take me to the da-duck pond!* Al smiled over this memory. There was where Jean

Menard and his sister Marie lived. Old sights. Good to see them. Good to be home. He remembered how he felt the night he had supper with good old Mort, in Toledo. Fifty-first Street. The cab turning. Almost there. Calumet Avenue. Al dug into his pockets for the fare. The cab stopped before his house. The driver was dragging out his cases. Another trip over with. Upstairs, the faces of his loved ones. Yes, home was the most wonderful place in the world.

Noisy and gay, Peg and Mrs. O'Flaherty welcomed Al with hugs and kisses. Then Al bent down and brushed a kiss on Danny's flushing cheeks.

"Well! Well! Well! It's certainly a treaterino, all right, all right, to be home," Al said joyfully.

"Al, take off your coat and have a cup of tea," Mrs. O'Flaherty said, hopping around Al energetically.

Al went to his room, removed his topcoat and his jacket coat, hanging them up, and placed his black derby hat on a closet shelf. Danny watched his grandmother pushing Aunty Margaret out to the kitchen, telling her to fix the tea. He stood alone in the hall, his arms folded, not knowing for sure if he was or if he wasn't glad that Uncle Al was home again. He followed his uncle out to the kitchen, sat down opposite him at the table.

"Al, did you have a good trip?" asked the mother.

"Oh, it was fair. Fair!"

"Isn't it terrible that hard times should come? You know, they laid off some of the chambermaids at our hotel, and poor Miss Gluck, the one with the paralyzed mother who used to relieve me, the poor thing was let go, and she spoke to me the other day with tears in her eyes. The poor thing!" Margaret said, standing over the kitchen stove.

"But tell me, Peg, how is the slim countess faring these fine days?" Al asked jollily.

"Oh, Al, my nerves have been bothering me. I have to work so hard at the hotel," she said with oozing self-pity; Al frowned, then he quickly forced a smile.

"You don't want to let your nerves get you, Peg. You got to say to yourself every day, 'I'll be happy, and my nerves won't get me down,'" Al said; he paused to light a cigar. "And, Peg, if you want to take a rest, I think we can manage it."

"I couldn't. I'm a business woman, not a housemaid."

"Peg, I didn't mean that you stay home. I meant go away."

"I went to New York on my vacation last year, and it cost me too much money. I haven't a penny to my name to go away with, and I won't be a burden to you, Al. You work too hard for your money," Margaret said.

"Peg, if you need a change, I think we can try to manage it."

"I wouldn't think of it. But, Al, I do wish that you would write to Ned. It seems to me that he could do something. What's he ever done for our home? What's he ever given us? A few damn presents at Christmas. And that's the total of his generosity to us," Margaret said.

"Don't be saying anything against my Ned. He's Daniel's godfather. When my Lizz was sick, having the little girl, it was my Ned who brought my grandson here to stay with me," Mrs. O'Flaherty said.

"That's all well and good, Mother. But what has he ever done? When he was home, he wasn't working half of the time. He would lay in bed until all hours of the day. And he even went out in the street and picked up some cur dog and brought him home to stay with us. I was never done scratching the fleas off me from that damn dog of his, Rex. He'd lay in bed, and if I went near him to wake him up, there would be that damn dog, and he'd nearly snap my leg off me," Margaret said.

"Well, Peg, Ned is all right," Al said, pained at this turn in the conversation.

"All right, be damned! I'm going to have my say. He runs off and marries a woman older than himself and leaves all the burden of the house on our poor shoulders," Margaret said bitterly.

"Oh, but Ned's wife Mildred is a lovely woman," Mrs. O'Flaherty said.

"I don't say that she isn't. I like Mildred. But I don't like the way Ned ran off on us the way he did. And then what happened when he came to Father's funeral? He takes out his handkerchief, and goes snooping in corners, wiping it on window sills, and he comes to me, and he says, 'Peg, look at all this dust.' Now wasn't that a fine thing to say when our poor father was lying dead in his casket, and you and I not knowing where we could turn to get money to pay the bills? Oh, yes, that was a fine how-do-you-do, it was. I tell you, Al, as long as I live I'll never forget those words of his. And no, neither will I forget the way he ran off and married, leaving a sick father on our hands. I won't, Al. I hold nothing against Ned, but I can't forget these things."

"Peg, you don't understand Ned. He's all right, and he's very good-hearted. He's doing well now, and I think he's settled down. Mildred has steadied him. Before, he was hotheaded, and he always knew more than the boss did, and so he kept quitting his jobs. If something wouldn't be run his way, he'd walk out. But he's settled down and steadied now. Ned's going to be a good shoe man," Al said.

"Well, I'd like to see some of the results of it in some cold hard cash that he might send us."

"We're getting along, aren't we?" Al asked.

"Yes, but he could help us," she snapped.

"I won't say a word against my Ned. He's as fine a son as any mother would ever want. And he loved Pa. When Pa was dying, Pa said to me, 'Mary, before the Lord takes me, you bring our Ned here. Mary, I'll never rest easy if I go without a last word to our Ned.' Them's the very words that Pa said," Mrs. O'Flaherty said.

"I never knew of a brother before who brought a cur dog into the house and trained the dog to bite anybody who would wake him at twelve o'clock noon, to ask him to get up and go out and get a job to pay for his own damn keep."

"Well, Peg, I just came home and let's discuss it later," Al said, still pained.

"Al, I got a letter from my sister," the mother said.

"How is Sister?" Al asked.

"The holy nun, she's sending clothes to Lizz for Bill from her orphan asylum in Brooklyn," the mother said.

"Good!" Al said, liking the cozy feeling he got in the kitchen, dwelling upon the wonders of home, hoping that Peg wouldn't explode again and go spoiling his homecoming.

"Al, will you be home long?" asked the mother.

"About a week."

"I'll have to cook a lovely supper with a pot roast for you one night," Peg said.

"Anything you cook, Peg, is grapes for me," Al said, drawing comfortably upon his cigar.

Watching his uncle closely, Danny suddenly began to worry. They might tell Uncle Al about something he did, and he might get bawled out. Aunty Margaret told on him more than Mother did. She might tell Uncle Al what he told her Bill had told him about how babies were made. Gee, he wished that Uncle Al hadn't come home. He was afraid, all right.

"Here's your tea, Al," Peg said, setting a cup before him.

"Drink it, Al, while it's hot," the mother said solicitously.

"Can I have some?" Danny meekly asked.

"Of course you can, Brother," said Aunty Margaret. "He can get it himself. It's time he was instructed in self-dependence," Al said curtly.

"He'll learn self-dependence some place else besides fooling around the stove here. You sit there, you little dumpling, and your aunt will give you a cup of tea."

"I was talking with poor Lizz on the phone yesterday. The poor thing, she needs so much for herself and her kids, and Jim makes so little. I gave her twenty-five dollars that I could ill afford," Margaret said.

"She wrote me, and I sent her five," Al said, puzzled. "What does she do with her money?"

"With all those little ones, putting food in their mouths, and clothes on their back, and shoes on their feet, sure, whatever is given to her comes back to him who gives. She is one of God's own poor," the mother said.

"I told her again and again she has too many kids!"

"Al!" Margaret warned, and Danny thought he knew why, and it was because they were going to talk about babies except that he was here.

"Uncle Al," he said hastily, trying to think of something to say to get them talking about something else, because if they talked about babies, Aunty Margaret might remember his telling her what Bill said, and she might go and tell Uncle Al about it.

"Yes, I don't see why she and Jim don't stop having kids, goddamn it, when they can't afford to raise them," Al said.

"Al," Margaret repeated, and, catching her brother's eye, she nodded toward Danny.

"The stork, by golly, likes her too well," Al exclaimed with a self-conscious smile, but Danny had caught the nod, and it made him feel that Bill had told him what was what about babies, and they just didn't want a kid to know because he was a kid. But maybe Aunty Margaret wouldn't tell after all, just as she had never told Uncle Al about how she had caught him and Little Margaret playing doctor.

"Al, have some more tea," the mother urged.

"No, thanks, Mother. This is enough."

"Here, it'll warm you up," she said, taking his cup.

She placed a fresh cup before him. He sat stirring it, and Danny thought that, yes, they had no right to get sore about Bill telling him about babies when they talked about it themselves. If Bill was right, why couldn't he know? They were just treating him the way grown-ups always treated a kid.

II

"But, Al, you're just home, and we ought to let him stay up a little longer in celebration," Margaret said.

"If he wants to be a regular fellow, he better get his proper quota of sleep. He has school tomorrow, hasn't he?"

"I'm going. I didn't say I wasn't, did I?"

"Well, come on, then, you better be getting to bed, Sport."

"Does Little Brother want Aunty Margaret to help him get undressed?" asked Aunty Margaret.

"He's old enough to help himself, aren't you, Sport?"

"Yes. . . . Yes, sir!" Danny said, and he felt that Uncle Al wasn't so grouchy after all, and now maybe everything would be all right, if they didn't tell. He got up from his chair and walked out of the kitchen. They all said good night to him.

"Good night, everybody," he yawned.

"He's so sweet. And Al, he's been such a good boy, such a comfort to us."

"Al! Al! He's the cock of the walk at Crucifixion school."

"Will somebody turn on the light for me, please?" he called, thinking that if they were talking that way about him, it was going to be all right.

"Peg, go turn on the light for my grandson!" the grandmother imperiously commanded.

"I'll do it," Al said, going after Danny, turning on the light in the front bedroom. "Now, Sport, get yourself in bed so you'll be fresh for school in the morning."

"Uncle Al, I'm learning to read and write, and Aunty Margaret is helping teach me," he said proudly and, also, ingratiatingly.

"Fine. If you learn better, and can show me how well you can read and write, I'll give you a reward of a quarter."

"I'll try," Danny said, thinking that if he made Uncle Al pleased with what he learned, Uncle Al wouldn't be too grouchy with him.

"And, Sport, when you kneel down to say your prayers tonight, say a prayer for your uncle's business getting better," Uncle Al said, patting Danny's light brown curly head.

Danny undressed as his uncle went back, and now he hoped, he hoped awful much, that they just wouldn't go telling Uncle Al. He stepped into his pyjamas, and he could hear them talking away in the kitchen, but he couldn't make out all of what they were saying.

"And Martha Morton is getting a divorce decree," he suddenly heard Aunty Margaret saying, and that was good, he guessed, because so far she hadn't told him.

"Peg, you're too smart a girl to be seeing a person like her. She can't do you any good. You can't learn a thing from her that'll get you a nickel."

"Why, of course not, Al. I haven't the time. I just met her by accident, and talked to her on the street, that's all," his aunt was saying.

"That one has the Devil in her," the grandmother said.

Danny knelt by his cot, closed his eyes, lowered his head, palmed his hands together. *Hail, Mary, full of grace, the Lord is with thee. . . .* He was praying to ask God to keep his aunt from telling Uncle Al what he told her that Bill said about making babies. *Our Father, Who art in Heaven. . . .* He was praying, too, to ask God to make business better for his Uncle Al like Uncle Al just asked him to. . . . *Our Father, Who art in Heaven, hallowed be Thy name. . . .* He was praying to God to bless his Aunty Margaret, and Mother, and Uncle Al, and Uncle Ned who was his godfather. . . . *Our Father, Who art in Heaven, hallowed be Thy name, Thy kingdom come. . . .* He was praying to God for Mama and Papa and his brothers and sisters and his brand new little sister, Catherine, and for God to never let them get sick, and be good to them. . . . *Thy will be done on earth as it is in Heaven, and give us this day our daily bread. . . .* He was praying to God to forgive him for sinning just like Miss Devlin in school had said they all should pray and ask God to forgive them all for their sins every night when they went to sleep and he wanted God to know he was sorry. . . . *Give us this day our daily bread, and forgive us . . . forgive us our sins now and at the hour of our death. Amen.* He blessed himself, thinking that it was pretty good the way he had learned to say his prayers all by himself like this.

He stood up, looked around at the roses on the wallpaper, and still he could hear the murmur of their talk in the kitchen. He got into bed, turned his face away from the light, thought that it was good that Uncle Al was home, because now he wouldn't be afraid at night, afraid of kidnapers and Blackhands, or of the old Devil coming after him the way Mother said the Devil was always coming after you. Mother was laughing at something. He wished they would talk louder so he could hear them.

"Peg! Peg! Go turn the light out so it doesn't shine in my grandson's little eyes," he heard his grandmother saying very loudly.

Gee, he wanted the light on. He would tell Aunty Margaret he did. Footsteps in the hall. It was Uncle Al. He was afraid to ask Uncle Al, and he pretended he was asleep. Al came into the room on tiptoe, smiled gently down at his nephew, turned, pulled the chain on the lighting fixture, and Danny felt himself smothered in this awful darkness as he heard Uncle Al's retreating footsteps. But if anybody came after him, he would run out to Uncle Al in the kitchen. And they were talking. He wished he could hear them. He sat up in bed, trying to listen. But they were talking too low. He yawned. God, please keep Aunty Margaret from telling. He yawned. He lay back. He looked around him at the darkened room. He was glad Uncle Al left the door open. He drowsed. Their voices were just a murmur. If they told, Bill would sock him good, and call him a dirty little snitcher. God, please keep them from telling. Well, if Aunty Margaret snitched, he would go to Uncle Al and say that she got drunk with that old Mrs. Morton. Still talking. Why didn't they talk louder? He heard the murmur of voices like receding sounds. His head sunk against the pillow. He fell asleep.

12

"Here's my girl," Jim said, folding Lizz in his arms, kissing her until her lips were wet with his saliva. Cold to his beery-breathed kisses, she freed herself from him. She petrified him with a hurt and wronged expression, and he faced her like a guilty boy trapped red-handed in disobedience.

And why, Jesus, why, he thought to himself, did a woman act this way? Why that accusing look, as if he had stabbed her in the back? Here she was, facing him as if she was going to keel over and faint or else start chewing the rag at him.

Well, the hell with it all! There was his side to it. But, gee, now, he wished that Lizz wouldn't go on acting like this.

"A fine man, a fine husband you are, taking bread out of the mouths of your little ones to drink it up in a saloon," she stormed at him.

"Gee, Lizz, I only had a few glasses of beer. Christ, haven't I even got the right to spend a few goddamn pennies on myself?"

"I don't."

"You give it all to the church."

"Blessed Mother of God, did you hear what he said?" Lizz shrieked.

"Good night, Mama," Little Margaret called.

"And he took the pledge, too. No wonder he broke it, begrudging the minister of God the few pennies I scrimp for holy candles and the collection box. The Holy Father in Rome says that you must contribute to the support of your pastor. Ah, no wonder he broke his pledge, no wonder," Lizz said, brandishing her fat arms as she spoke.

"There's nothing wrong in a man having a couple of glasses of beer. You wouldn't call that breaking the pledge, would you?"

"So he took the pledge! And he stays in with his family, and he helps his sick overworked wife put his kids to bed. Oh, he is such a good husband, such a fine man! Shit!"

"Aw, Lizz!"

"And he has the crust to come home, after breaking his pledge, and to stain these pure lips of mine with a kiss of poisonous alcohol. Oh, such a fine man I married!"

"I tell you, Lizz, I only had a few glasses of beer."

"And here I was, alone with this dirty regiment of kids, sick, when I should be in bed and be taken care of. And where is he? Out drinking in a saloon with dirty bums and loafers. Oh, good Mother of God, why did I ever marry him? Oh, Blessed Mary, why didn't you save me from him, me that should have been a holy virgin inside of convent walls, me that belonged with the sacred nuns working in the vineyard of Jesus? Oh, Mother of God!" Lizz said in a moaning singsong, lifting beseeching hands and a pleading face to the cracked calcimine of the ceiling.

She stood hurt and sorrowing before him, until his face shed pain and bewilderment and his long arms hung awkwardly at his sides. Clumsily, he put his arms around her. She huffed out of his reach, glared at him, her thickish lips compressed in anger.

"I give up. I'm going home to my mother," she sighed.

"Listen, she has her little nip whenever she wants it. And that sister of yours, I suppose she's Carrie Nation," Jim said.

"Praise be to God that he should speak scandal against my poor old mother. Him whose mother and father deserted him and left him in an orphan asylum."

"My mother died. That's why I was put in an orphanage."

"Well, I want you to know that no matter what you say, my mother, and my father, they gave me a decent home, and they brought me up to be a lady. Fool that I was, leaving them for a man who comes home drunk."

"But I'm not drunk," Jim said, twisting up his face in the effort to convey to her that he was sober.

"Good night, Papa!" Dennis called from the crowded bedroom off the parlor.

"Shut up!" Jim snarled, angered by the disturbing sound of his son's voice.

"Don't you dare talk to my children that way! If they haven't a father who gives two shakes for them, they at least have a mother. They have a mother!" Lizz said, gesticulating melodramatically.

"Oh, please, Lizz."

"That the shame of God might soften your hardened soul!"

"What the hell do you want a man to do? Why, I could crawl on my knees through broken glass and it wouldn't please you."

"It doesn't matter what I'd ask you to do."

"For Christ's sake, Lizz, let's cut out the comedy!"

"Don't talk to me!"

"Don't worry, I won't!"

She walked out of the room. Jim clenched his fists, started after her, halted, relaxed, sighed. He blew out the parlor lamp, and went into the dining room, dogged by the smell of kerosene. He thought, God, how a man got himself tied up. Hell, it would serve her right if he just walked out on her the way many men did on their wives. If he didn't find himself saddled with the responsibility of her and the kids, what mightn't he do? Hell, here he was, doing the best he could, and . . . Jesus, she wouldn't even wash her face.

As he stared around the dining room, the house seemed to crowd in upon him. The torn papered walls appeared as if charging upon him to crush and compress him, to choke and smother the very breath of life within him. He looked at the table, with its dirty oilcloth covering, the papers and rags on it, the lamp burning with its funnel-shaped chimney smoked almost black. He wondered, as he was so often wondering these days, when, when would it change? When would he escape from this kind of life? When would he and his family be able to live decently? Here he was, strapped with all these cares. He saw himself as he had once been, young, decked out in stylish peg-top pants, wearing a derby and a stiff collar, faring forth on a Saturday night with his pay in his jeans, as foot-loose as the winds. Ah, those carefree days when he was so unafraid! And now! He looked at Lizz, hoping that she would relent. Ignoring him, she stood in a corner muttering prayers half aloud. All he wanted was to go to bed with her now, and then, after it, to sleep so that he would get up for work tomorrow feeling better than he did now.

"Aw, Lizz what the hell," he said.

She frowned, and then continued muttering prayers half aloud. He stood by the table, feeling that his arms were out of place as they dropped by his side. He gulped.

"Move over. Don't take up the whole bed. And be still. I want to sleep," he heard Bill yelling.

"I-I-I-am. I'll call p-p-papa," he heard Dennis answering in a stuttering whine.

And the kids making so damn much noise that a man couldn't hear himself think. He went and looked at the boys' darkened bedroom.

"Shut up and go to sleep!" he barked ferociously.

He sat in the darkened parlor. He heard a wailing train whistle, and he thought that trains went to other places, and that if he took one he wouldn't be here, and then he wouldn't be sitting in the midst of all this dirt, fighting, worry, poverty. All that he had to do to get away from it was to hop on a train that would carry him to another place. But he knew that he'd never do that. Deserting his family would make him more unhappy than he'd be staying to face the music.

He heard Lizz's slipper dragging on the slivery floor as she went out to the kitchen. From the street, he heard some drunk singing a song in a foreign language, and he thought it was probably a stewed hunky. He asked himself now was that guy, that poor bastard, going home? Lizz rattling pans and he knew she was doing it on purpose because she was sore at him. And, Jesus Christ, he hadn't done anything, had he? He'd only gone out for a little while, drunk a few glasses of beer, made himself feel good and forget a few worries for a little while, talked with fellows, all of them decent hard-working men like himself, except for Larry Henehan who was a walking and talking showcase, all front and nothing behind. He became very lonely, alone in all the world, with no one whom he could even talk to and explain how he felt. And he guessed that there must be, right now in Chicago, right now in all the cities of the country, other poor bastards who must feel like he did when he had handcuffs on him.

"Jesus Christ!" he said, half aloud and in self-disgust.

Dragging her feet, Lizz came back into the dining room.

"Want a cup of tea, Jim?" she asked.

"No, thanks. I don't feel like tea, Lizz."

"We got to get up early. We better be going to bed, Jim."

She went back to the kitchen, and he could hear her urinating into a pot. The image of her doing this became fixed in his mind, and it seemed to destroy his wanting her. It made him feel that everything in life was just one goddamn ugly mess. But anyway, at least she had gotten over her crabby fit. He'd be able to sleep, and for a few hours the world would all be closed out, away from him. And again, a whistle from the Rock Island tracks, a passing train, gone. Where to? To go to wherever that train was going? To start his life all over again from scratch? She was finished. He went out to the kitchen.

"You can use this, Jim," she said, wiping herself as Jim placed his hand on the kitchen doorknob.

"I'll be right back."

"Watch yourself so you don't fall in the dark," she said tenderly.

He walked down the rickety steps and into the blackened yard. He saw lights through curtained windows of the house at the back end of the yard. He heard a sudden explosion of Negro laughter. He cursed. Even had to have niggers for neighbors.

He stood in the center of the yard, near the wooden shack of an outdoor toilet, and he looked up at the removed and frosty blue sky, and he saw the stars like so many new and undiscovered jewels. He thought of a line from Shakespeare's play, *Julius Caesar*, which he had seen a couple of times on the stage.

130

I would rather be a dog, and bay the moon. . . .

The moon, silver and frosty, nice up there, and the sky so far away, so clean and clear, so cut off from all the troubles of a man like himself. Looking up, awed, he felt so small and unimportant in the world. He heard more rocking Negro laughter. Even the goddamn niggers could be happy. And he couldn't. He even had to use the same goddamn crapper they used, had to go into it and smell nigger shit. Oh, Jesus Christ!

I would rather be a dog, and bay the moon. . . .

So many times in his life he was being made to feel like he was worse than a dog, lower, less important than a she-bitch baying the moon.

He pushed through the crumbling privy door, and the retching stench of human defecation almost smothered him, filling his nose, seeming to cake in his nostrils. He thought of how this was what came out of all men. Ugh! He quickly performed his natural function, got out for air, went back to the house, wanting only to sleep.

He blew out the kitchen lamp, carried the alarm clock into the dining room, wound and set it. When it rang in the morning . . . work.

Lizz stood in the bedroom, clad in a soiled flannel nightgown. In the dim light, he saw his two little girls, soundly sleeping, one in the bed, the infant in the cradle. He took Lizz in his arms, kissed her, and she accepted his kisses, lifelessly, but without hostility. He began to undress.

"I'm sorry, Jim," she said as he stood in his long dirt-grayed underwear, the truss he wore for his rupture almost jutting out of it.

"I know, Lizz old girl," he said, his voice cracking because of a sudden welling of emotion and of sorrow.

He blew out the lamp and climbed into bed beside Lizz, smelling the heavy odor of her sweat, sensing her beside him as a warming presence.

13

I

Lugging his bulky sample case, Al walked along Calumet Avenue as briskly as he could. There was a snap in the air, but that was because it was still pretty early. It was going to be a balmy early October day. And man should be thankful to God for lovely days. Yes, man should be grateful to God for very many things. Al was! Some fellows, like Charlie Granger, the village atheist who ran the Fox Shoe Store in Des Moines, they said that they didn't believe in God. The lobsters! The sapheads! Reminded him of what Thomas Edison said in one of the Sunday papers a few months ago. Edison had said that he wasn't a non-believer in God, and that science was only imagination that came from the eternal mind. God was the eternal mind.

His left arm and shoulder tired from the dead weight of the black case. The muscles of his back and left shoulder ached. He transferred his burden to his right arm, slowed down his gait, breathed noisily. He thought that it was good for a man to be up early instead of sleeping late, lying around the house, creating lazy habits. Watching people go to work, he could pick out the real ones just like the snap of a finger. If a man slouched along without any pep like that fellow across the street wearing a black derby, you'd be risking nothing in betting that he wasn't a live wire. Different from that fellow in the gray suit and dark coat who was gingery like a go-getter just ahead of him. If he didn't have this heavy case, he would walk that way. Seeing him going downtown in the morning, nobody would mistake him for a slouch. Not on your life! When a man dragged himself to work in the morning, you could be pretty certain that he had no zest, no *élan vital* for work, and that he'd never get anywhere in life. Like he had read in some newspaper editorial, or somewhere, a fellow said that at the present time we hate quitters more than they were ever hated before because in this age there was less excuse for a quitter than there had ever been. His case was getting to be an increasingly heavy and dead weight, dragging the strength out of him. He was tempted to rest a moment, but he didn't, because he believed that he shouldn't quit in little things any more than he would quit in the big ones. But *élan vital!* That was a corking phrase to spring sometime. It was the idea of Bergson, the new French philosopher he'd read about last summer in one of the Sunday papers.

Turning onto Fifty-first Street, he shifted the case to the left side, forced himself along, thinking of the feeling of relief he would have after he had toted it up the steps to the elevated platform. He stopped at the newspaper stand by the station and bought a morning newspaper. Puffing, he lugged it on upstairs to get his downtown train. He sighed, waiting for it.

The train came along. Ignoring the pressure behind him, he waited for the women to enter before he shoved and was shoved in. He pushed along uncomfortably with his case until he set it down near the center of the car, against the back of a double seat. He sagged. The pain in his shoulders caused a sudden wave of gloom to pass through him. He saw himself as forever dragging big sample cases around from place to place. But that was no way to think. No place for the quitter in this great age, no place at all. He clung to a strap and began reading his paper, noticing that Andrew Aiken Fletcher, owner of the Chicago *Questioner* and newspapers all over the country, had just made a speech saying that Italy's present war with Turkey was a war for humanity, civilization, progress, and righteousness. Fletcher was a yellow journalist, but a smart man, too. And maybe he was right. Of course, the golden rule and live and let live should apply all over the world, but the Turk, he was against Christianity and he should be driven out of Europe and the Holy Land. The Turk had conquered by the sword, and whoever conquers by the sword shall perish by the sword.

"Forty-seventh Street. All aboard!"

He felt the pressure of oncoming people, and he was squeezed and pressed almost into the lap of the old woman seated before him. The train again swayed, and the conductor barked into the car, "Forty-third next!"

And there was more about the Senate investigation of Graham's election. And here was a speech by Graham, saying that all progressivism was Socialistic. If that was so, something ought to be done to stop the Progressives, but then, Teddy Roosevelt was a good man, and not like most Republican presidents. Teddy wasn't for the big fellow. Taft was. If the Democrats didn't put up a good man, Teddy would be elected. But Teddy wasn't a Socialist. He was just against the big fellow. A priest he once talked with, going to Peoria, had told him about Socialism and the way it was against the home and the family and religion. Pope Leo's encyclical had spoken against Socialism. That was a great treatise of thought. He would have to read it sometime. And not so long ago he had read where Cardinal

Gibbons had spoken about some of these things. The great churchman had said that the Constitution had to be preserved because it was the palladium of our liberties. He remembered the speech because the word palladium was one he had never heard before, and he'd looked it up in the dictionary. A good word, too. Swell one to spring on some of these fathead salesmen. Cardinal Gibbons had said that the direct election of senators and the referendum and the recall of judges was an attack upon the Constitution. Brainy man, and a good Churchman, Cardinal Gibbons. But wait a minute! He wondered would this Graham scandal have happened if senators were elected direct, like Congressmen were, instead of being chosen by the state legislature? No, he guessed that it wasn't the system and the way it was done. It was an abuse of the system and a betrayal of the people by certain state representatives that had caused the scandal. He guessed that a man as great as Cardinal Gibbons must be right on these points, and on the Constitution.

Rattling and grunting, the train stopped at the Indiana station. Al heard the conductor calling out that it was the last stop until Twelfth, and change for local trains, Kenwood, the Stockyards. He was glad. This was the last crushing until then. He figured that the elevated company ought to put more trains on during the rush hours and give the public better service. Maybe former Mayor Dunne had been right when he campaigned for municipal ownership. Only some said that that was Socialistic. The present mayor some day wanted municipal ownership. Well, it didn't seem bad, whether or not it was Socialistic, and certainly the service couldn't be any worse. He felt like writing a letter to the elevated company or the newspapers about it.

More pressure and squeezing. The slamming sound of the gates. The train moving, making the passengers lurch as it curved onto the express tracks and turned northward, and then the steady, speedy, disturbing rocking movement as it went ahead. He thumbed to the editorial page. It was the best part of the paper. He'd see what it had to say. Here was something constructive, ought to be acted upon by the mayor and the alderman. Maybe he would write a letter to Mother's cousin, Paddy Slattery, the alderman from a ward back of the yards, and suggest it to Paddy. If he did, Paddy would see that he was a smart fellow. The city was growing and something would have to be done about the traffic problem, because the Loop was getting more and more congested all the time, and automobiles were now safe so that people were buying them and there were more and more automobiles on the streets every year. Yes, steps should be taken to have something done about the traffic problem. And, yes, he liked the editorial page when it was constructive like this. The fellow who wrote this editorial, now he had some good Caucasian brain lobes in his head. There should be more of such constructive thought expressed in the newspapers.

And the train rushed on. He heard conversation buzzing around him, and there was some loud-mouth lobster behind his back going on with silly, non-constructive talk about hard times. He shouldn't be doing that, spreading gloom. He should talk about optimistic things. There he was, off again.

"Tony, if there wasn't so much goddamn graft, and so many crooks, we'd all be better off. But what the hell, the trusts, the octopus controls everything."

He'd just like to tell that thickhead a thing or two. And the fellows shouldn't be using profanity out loud in a public conveyance with girls and women hearing him. He thumbed on to the sports' page, and noticed that Harry Haggin Jackson, the football coach over at the University, was gloomy about the chances of the University this season. And another fight manager chasing for white hopes to return Jack Johnson's title to the white race. It was a shame, the nigger being world's champion. And married to a white woman, too. He wanted to know what kind of a white woman was it who would marry a nigger? She must have no shame, no pride. What a betrayal of her lovely sex!

"Twelfth Street. Congress next!"

He was squeezed, and then he had more room. He winced from the sudden image of a white woman in bed with a nigger, of Jack Johnson's wife with the fighter. She ought to be ostracized by all decent Caucasians. But he had heard that niggers had a charm over white women. Suppose some nigger should charm Peg like a snake? No, no, Peg had better sense than that. But suppose! His genital organs became troubled because of this vision which seemed to stick like glue in his mind. It made him hope that Johnson would get knocked out by a good clean young white fighter, an Irish lad who could fight like Terrible Terry McGovern in his prime.

Congress. The train emptied. He dropped into a seat and waited, nervously folding his paper. It seemed to be taking unduly long to go a couple of blocks from Congress to Adams. He sat forward on the edge of his seat. The motorman must be a fathead, creeping along this way. People on the train had to get to work. Why have it creep along like a snail?

He lugged his case to the platform as the train was drawing into Adams Street. The conductor called out the stop.

"Say, Sport, tell that motorman that it takes a long time to get a couple of blocks from Congress to Adams," he told the conductor.

"He doesn't need help runnin' the train."

"Say, that's no way to talk, Sport. Why don't you be a regular fellow and take good suggestions when they are given to you?"

"Out in front!" someone called, and he got out, with the conductor laughing at him.

The fatheaded conductor! He didn't like people who were discourteous and who were not open to constructive suggestion. He dragged his case down the station steps and stood on the east side of Adams Street, waiting while the traffic clattered by, creating a din of horses hooves, wagon wheels, automobiles, while overhead the elevated trains roared. Sunlight slanted weakly in a few streaks through steel rafters of the elevated structure.

"And so I told him that I didn't let anyone get fresh with me, even for bracelets," a young blonde girl in a blue suit and white shirtwaist said to her chum, both of them waiting beside him, and he thought now there was a decent girl, and he would like to tell her that, but she might think that he was cheeky or a masher.

The traffic halted at the traffic policeman's whistle. The girls stepped in front of him and hastened across the street, their dresses sweeping the paving. Young girls made him feel a bit old, old enough to be forever removed from the life they lived and from that joyous innocence which he sensed in them. It made him think, too, of Louise. Lord have mercy on her soul!

He walked as rapidly as his burden permitted, and as he entered the lobby of the Potter Hotel a bellboy took his case. He walked to the desk.

"Hello, Mr. O'Flaherty! Glad to see you back," the plump middle-aged desk clerk said, smiling as he spoke, and Al thought how good it was to be known and greeted this way.

"Hello, there, Mr. Du Bois. I'm glad to be back. How is business in your nonpareil hostelry?" he cheerily replied.

"Oh, Mr. O'Flaherty, it's much the same as usual. We have as many guests as we generally always have, but some of them are spending a little less, perhaps. Times are a little hard, but everything like that passes."

"That's just the kind of a hopeful note I like to hear you stressing, Mr. Du Bois."

"Yes, Mr. O'Flaherty, I don't believe in looking just at the dark side of the clouds. If you want to know what I think, I think that hard times are as much here," the clerk pointed to his head, "as they are in the pocketbook."

"You adumbrated that right in a nutshell. They are as much psychological as they are anything."

"Well, thank you. I am so glad you agree with me, Mr. O'Flaherty, because you are a smart business man."

"Well, I try to be. I don't think that there are any laws forcing a man to be dumb, do you?"

"No, Mr. O'Flaherty, I don't. Now, let's see, about your sample room. Good, I can give you the same room you had before," the clerk said, looking at a list before him.

He handed a key to the bellboy, and pushed the register forward for Al to sign it. Following the bellboy to the elevator, Al thought that Du Bois was much smarter than a lot of these wise-aleck hotel clerks. He thought that he'd go upstairs, get his samples spread out in the room so that buyers could come up and see them, and then he'd look around town.

II

"Believe me when I say that in all my life I never had as sweet a little chicken as that little waitress in Kokomo," Jack Doyle said, one of a group sitting around a table for lunch in the Grillroom of the Potter Hotel.

Al frowned. Of course, it was natural for a man to do it, but still the way fellows like Jack boasted was bad taste. You'd never find Lord Chesterfield or any other gentleman boasting this way.

"Jack, where have I heard you say that before?" grinned Syd Cohen, and they laughed.

"Syd, this time I think I'm right."

"The Jew here must be jealous of you, Jack," said Ken Smith.

"Oh, no, the Jew is a master craftsman himself. With a face like his you wouldn't know how he could do it. But he does. I know it, too, because I seen him working on the girlies," Jack said.

"Al, here, doesn't seem to like the talk of you lowbrows," Ken Smith said, noticing Al frown a second time.

"He never thinks of anything but business," said Syd while the others were still laughing over Ken's remark.

"After my last trip, I say, that's one thing I don't want to think of," Jack Doyle said.

"Me, too, with the luck I'm having this time out," Dud Morgan said.

"Say, Al, how's your kid brother, Ned?" asked Doyle.

"He's doing well. He's selling for Fisher and Mostil now," Al said.

"They're a good outfit," Dud Morgan said.

"Both of these O'Flaherty brothers are as good shoe men as you'll find in the game. You mark my words, some day the two of them will be thriving in their own business," Doyle said.

"Well, thanks for the boost, Jack. I'll give you as much some day," Al said.

"Ned O'Flaherty's a swell, jolly fellow, and lots of fun," Dud said.

"Both of the O'Flaherty boys got that Irish twinkle in their eyes," said Jack Doyle.

"Doyle, lay off the fight for Irish independence during this lunch, will you?" laughed Morgan.

"If you don't, why Syd here will have to take up the cudgels for Jerusalem, and where'll we be. After all, this is America," kidded Ken Smith.

"I'd only fight for shoe orders, or for the dimples on the knees of a sweet yama-yama girl," laughed Syd.

"Syd, that's not a bad idea," said Dud, smiling.

"You fellows are all cockeyed, with this talk of fighting. You don't want to count so much on fighting. The smart fellow relies on the touch delicate and the retort adroit," Al said, proud of his ability to say such things.

"Jesus, that's a hot one," laughed Jack Doyle.

"Al, you're gettin' highbrow on us," said Dud.

"That was a good one, wasn't it, Jack? Jack, what's wrong with these fellows is that they haven't schooled themselves in subtlety, like we have," Al said, laughing with Jack, who nodded agreement.

"What's all that got to do with how you see a dimple on a chicken's knees when she doesn't want to let the lights be put on it?" asked Syd.

"No! No! No! No, Syd! That's not wise-guy stuff. Take a tip, Syd, school yourself in the retort adroit and the approach indirect," Al said, again splitting them with laughter.

"Al, with that hot line, say, you should be a lady-killer. How did you keep single this long?" asked Dud.

"You fellows better get more adeptly developed comprehensions in those Caucasian brain lobes of yours if you want to play ball in the same league with Jack and I," Al said.

"They sure do, old man," said Jack.

"Yes, and watch out there, Friend O'Flaherty, or they'll be coming after you in a wagon and taking you away," said Syd.

"Nix, Syd! Nix on that kike humor! That's not the right way. It's not kidding. It's insult, and insult isn't kidding. If you want to be a real smart fellow, kid but don't insult. Don't pull kike stuff," Al said constrainedly.

Syd colored. He continued eating. Al nibbled at the remains of his pork chops. No one talked for over a minute. They sat uncomfortably as the waiter began removing their plates and serving them with coffee and dessert.

"Say, you know what kind of shoes we're going to sell a lot of next year? Rocket shoes," Jack said, breaking the tense quiet.

"Not on your life! Not on your life! Tell those hams in your factory, Jack, to come again, and with a different number."

"You're dead wrong, Friend Dudley. I've talked with plenty of buyers and retail people. You wait and see if you don't have to eat your words," Jack answered.

"I got an appointment, and I'm going to sell any kind of shoes that the traffic will bear," Syd said, arising, leaving a dime under his cup, nodding around the table.

"So long, old man, and no hard feelings," Al said.

"Well, sell shoes, and don't get nearsighted trying to see any dimples," said Ken Smith, and they laughed.

"Good luck, old man," Al said.

"Thanks, and see you all later," Syd said.

"Say, I didn't want to hurt his feelings. But you know, the kike side always comes out," Al said.

"He's all right. Al, I frankly think you can't take too much kidding yourself," Dud said.

"Sure I can. Nobody likes kidding better than I do. But there's a difference between kidding and getting personal," Al said.

"Anyway, boys, Al was right. Syd is all right, I guess, but he is a kike. He has no sense of fair play. He undersells, and he does anything and everything to get a sale. I know, because I watched him sellin'. He is a kike, and he has no sense of fair play," Jack Doyle said.

"He ain't any sweat off my balls," Dud said.

"Pulling kike stuff, you know, Jack, that doesn't go," Al said.

"The way I figure it out is that I guess a Jew doesn't know any better than to be a Jew," Jack Doyle said.

"What I would like to know is this. What kind of a decent show or amusement is there in town that a man can see?" asked Ken.

"They don't have shows on Friday afternoons in Chicago for lazy and tired salesmen," Dud jibed.

"How about a chicken?" said Doyle.

"If I only knew one," said Ken.

"Don't tell me, Ken Smith, that a man of your parts and talents, now . . ." Doyle insinuated.

"Say, that reminds me of one I heard in Muncie the other day. A fellow selling hardware, he told it to me," Ken said.

"Tell it. But I bet I know it already," Jack said.

"Just a minute, Al. Wait till you hear this one," said Ken as Al arose and dropped a dime under his cup.

"Sorry, old man, but I got to go. Got a buyer coming up to see me," Al said.

He walked rapidly away from the table. He knew that when they started on stories, they were good for the whole afternoon. There were too many things for a man to do besides sitting around listening to a bunch of lowbrows tell smutty stories like a gang of truck drivers. That kind of stuff, it didn't cast any credit on the profession of salesmanship, either.

"Well! Well! Well! If you aren't getting to look more like a Princess of Graustark every day," Al said, smiling at the slightly corpulent cashier behind the desk.

"Hello, Mr. O'Flaherty. I'm glad to see you back with us again after your trip. Did you have a good one?"

"Fair! Not so bad. But let me tell you, Miss Malloy, every time I come in off the road and see you, why those cheeks of yours get to looking like rosier and rosier red apples," Al said, paying his bill.

"Mr. O'Flaherty, you and your brother are such kidders. I have never seen the likes of you two."

"We're the Counts of O'Flaherty," Al said, and she laughed, showing fine teeth.

"Yes, I never met the beat of you two boys."

"Well, goodbye and good luck. Take care of those apple cheeks," Al said, leaving, thinking that you should kid 'em all the time, and they liked it; kid 'em with a little sauce and spice.

In the lobby he paused, wondering what he would really do today.

III

Walking in the crowds along State Street, Al thought how it had turned out to be a fine sunny day. He stared at the dressed-up windows, thinking that from the looks of things you'd never guess that times were hard. Lots of people out, many of them well-dressed, numbers of them pushing in and out of the store entrances. Look at this window, full of fur coats, minks and sables. Only, Jesus Christ! This was a window of one of the biggest and swellest department stores in America, handling the finest in goods and material, and look at those wax models with the fur coats draped on them! Hell, the faces on the models were Jewish. That one with the gray squirrel on it. If it was a real girl, and you met her on the street, you'd call her Rebecca. That wasn't sound business methods, either, using models that looked so Hebrew. Whoever the fathead was who had charge of this department, well, he didn't know his p's and q's. Not by a damn sight! He guessed that it was the kikes who had charge of the window dressing, and they were using their position to further Jewish interests.

A window full of shoes, arranged in crowded rising rows against a background of white ledges and steps, the men's shoes on the left, the boots for milady on the right. Plenty of styles were arrayed, too, high-laced and buttoned women's shoes, oxfords, calfskins, plain, ornamented, buckled shoes, nice patent leathers, colors, plenty of tans and black, lots of styles. He noticed, too, a whole row of bulldog-toed men's oxfords with perforations over the surface. He scrutinized the women's shoes more attentively. Olson, that goddamn pig-headed Swede! What the hell was he doing? Not one of his own numbers in the whole window. That thickheaded Scandinavian! He had stuffing and straw where he should have Caucasian brain lobes.

Al swept into the store, bustled along the crowded aisles, took the elevator up to the sixth floor, almost chewing his fingernails as the car rose from floor to floor with the delays for entrances and exits.

"How do you do, sir?" said the mushy-faced floorwalker in a blue suit, with a blue-bordered handkerchief in his pocket, bowing stiffly to Al as he spoke.

"Where's Mr. Olson?" Al curtly asked, casting darting glances about the shoe department, with clerks and salesmen bending down and waiting on customers.

"He's out for the day. Is there anything that I can do for you, sir?"

"No, I wanted to see Olson."

"Won't his assistant do?"

"No!"

"His assistant is on the floor, sir."

"Listen, don't be a fathead! I told you I didn't *care* to see his assistant."

"Yes, sir! Only he usually refers most calls to his assistant, Mr. Wilson. And if you were desirous of seeing some of our latest styles, I can see that you are properly taken care of, sir."

"Listen, don't be such a fathead!" Al snapped, thinking to himself that it was no wonder that this dumbbell was only a floorwalker.

"What do you mean . . . sir?" the floorwalker asked, nettled.

"Listen, get this into your nut! Don't try to treat people like suckers when they aren't suckers."

"Why, sir, you misinterpret me. I was only trying to be helpful. Our motto here is courtesy to everyone."

"You can be courteous without being peripatetic," Al said, causing the floorwalker to screw up his brows quizzically. "A man's time is money. When you talk to me, come to the point. Tell me that Mr. Olson is not in, and don't try to act like an English lord when you tell it to me! You don't know who I might be, and how busy I am, do you?" The floorwalker opened his mouth to speak, but Al prevented him by rushing on. "All right, in this age you got to be quick, snappy, businesslike, you got to come to the point. Don't be a kike and try salving me with a kike line of talk!"

"But, sir, I don't understand you. I was only trying to explain . . ."

"All right. I got you. Tell Mr. Olson that Al O'Flaherty was in, and will he please telephone me at the Potter Hotel after nine in the morning."

"Yes, Mr. O'Flaherty."

The floorwalker sneered as Al cut back to the elevator. Riding down, Al thought of how that floorwalker was a first-class, A-number-one brand of unadulterated fathead. All that he deserved to be was a floorwalker.

He pushed out of the store, thinking that times couldn't be so hard when the place was this crowded, doing as much business as it seemed to be doing. By spring times would surely be better and there would be more buying. America was too great and too rich a country to suffer from panics and hard times. It came back after the panic of 1907. It would always come back bigger and stronger.

He again joined the crowd moving along the sidewalk on State Street. He thought that Chicago was a fine city, all right. He was always glad to get back to it. Getting better and more prosperous all the time. Getting big buildings, too. Look at the Masonic Temple. Say, the Flatiron Building in New York wasn't worth a nickel as a building compared to the Masonic Temple. But that was put up by the Masons, and they were against the Church. Now, wouldn't it have been wonderful if the Order of Christopher had put up a building like that!

He noticed the name lettered on the window of a red-fronted shoe store . . . Feinberg and O'Shaughnessy. He looked at the shoes priced in the window. Cheap shoes. Must be a new idea that Nat Feinberg was developing here. But such damn shoes, bum leather, soles like paper, would wear out in a couple of weeks. He started walking on, but he noticed a familiar face in the doorway.

"Why, hello, Al! Glad to see you. How are you?" Albert Dorian, a medium-sized, sandy-haired, full-faced man in his middle thirties said, giving Al a warm hand.

"And how are you, Albert? I didn't know you were with this outfit here," Al said.

"The firm I was selling for up in Milwaukee went bankrupt."

"That's too bad. Sorry to hear it."

"I've been here a month, managing the store," Albert said as Al glanced quickly about, noticing the salesmen bustling for shoes among the boxes lining both walls, bending down, measuring feet, trying on shoes.

He remembered when he had done that at O'Toole and Ginzburg. He remembered how he had dreamed of getting ahead, going on the road. Now he had achieved what he had dreamed of in those days. Would these fellows here make the grade?

"Looks like you're busy here. Like it better than being on the road, Albert?"

"There's no comparison. I had my share of tank towns, dumpy hotels, all the inconvenience of the road. Here, this way, I put my feet under my own table every night, and I'm with the little lady and my kids. And we had a splendid sale last month, with our sales constantly rising. You know, I hear a lot of sour talk about hard times, but I have seen no signs of it here."

"How's Nat Feinberg?"

"Nat's in tip-top shape. He's just bustling with plans for development. I think he's got a great idea in these stores. You watch, Al, my boy, and before you know it, there'll be Feinberg and O'Shaughnessy stores all over the city, all over the Middle West, all over the country. It's a live-wire organization here, and it is based on a sound idea, high-class shoes sold at reasonable prices."

"Yes, it is. Nat always was a live wire," Al said.

"They don't come in this league with any more electricity than Nat has. Al, old man, Nat's one of the liveliest shoe men in the country," Albert touched Al's arm, a friendly and emphasizing gesture, "and he's proving it every day."

"He has something in his noodle, all right. But here, Albert, have a cigar," Al said, handing Albert one.

"No, thanks, Al," Albert said.

Acting like the lord of all he surveyed, Albert drew Al back to a corner in the rear of the store, Al again taking in the store in hasty, nervous glances, noting the salesmen at work, the cashier taking in money, ringing it up, wrapping shoes in neat packages. He thought, too, that Dorian was acting a little swell-headed about his job. Well, Al O'Flaherty didn't have to feel humble before Dorian. He had his job, his prospects, his reputation, and so what the hell! There weren't many men in the shoe game who would place the name of Albert Dorian alongside of that of Al O'Flaherty. Hell, Dorian wasn't even playing in the same league with him.

"Yes, Al, this is something that looks like a good thing?"

"Yes, it's a pretty nifty idea, and Nat and the Commodore of the Irish Navy should cash in on it."

"It was Nat's idea, and Nat organized it. Commodore O'Shaughnessy put up most of the jack. Also because of his name, a Jew and a mick, it made a good partnership. Like O'Toole and Ginzburg down the street. I wish I had all the money that the good will of their name is worth. Well, Feinberg and O'Shaughnessy are going to make their name the same. Nat has plans. I tell you, old man, that boy has vision. Why, he is already talking about starting up a factory to manufacture our own shoes."

"He'll never miss a trick," Al said.

"And that makes my prospects first rate. I'm getting in here pretty much on the ground floor."

"Well, good luck, old man."

"Going, Al?"

"Yes. I have to see a fellow down the street."

"Stop in again. And, say, we got to get together for lunch some day. Too bad, too, you sell such tony shoes. We could use them if they had a lower price tag on 'em."

"Nix! Nix on that. We handle only the best."

"I was only joshing, Al. But wait and let me show you some of our numbers?"

"The next time I stop in. I got to hustle along now. And tell Nat and the Commodore I was asking for them. Say I wish them luck, and that they should forge ahead with the old sockerino," Al said, waving as he walked out of the store.

Good idea, but then he'd rather have a store like O'Toole and Ginzburg's and not sell piker shoes. From those he'd seen in the window, he could tell the poor quality of their goods. That's why he hadn't waited to look at some of their numbers when Dorian asked him to. No use making hard feelings by telling Albert what he really thought of Feinburg and O'Shaughnessy shoes. And he could lie and say that the paper their shoes were made of was good leather. Doing such a thing went against his grain. But, well, some day when he had a nest egg, and felt like retiring from the road, he would have his own store. It would be great to see his name on the window of the classiest shoe store on State Street.

Al O'Flaherty High Class Shoes

Or maybe he and Ned would run it together. Have a joint that would knock the whole trade dead. Ah, he could see the store, the refined gentlemanly atmosphere, the aroma of the best, the best people coming to trade with them, their own names on the window. He could see.

O'Flaherty Brothers
The Best Is Not Too Good At O'Flahertys'

Something like that!

"Say, fellow, couldn't you help me to get a cup of coffee? Brother, I'm just on my uppers," a shabby and shivering bum asked, holding out a hoary dirty hand.

Al brushed on.

"Thank you!" he heard the bum sarcastically barking after him.

It wasn't the money but the principle of the thing. He could spare the dime, but these fellows wanted money, not for food, but for booze. All they wanted was to soak themselves in it and never work. They could get something to do if they tried, and really wanted it. He walked jerkily on. If he and Ned did have a store it wouldn't be a cheap one, selling piker shoes like Nat and the Commodore were doing. The best would not be too good at O'Flahertys'.

14

I

Danny stood on the southeast corner of Fiftieth and Calumet Avenue, looking across the street at the large half block of dirt-patched and weedless vacant lot which extended all the way to the alley over which the elevated structure towered.

Usually when it was like this, still not dark, kids were playing in the prairie, and sometimes they had bonfires. He always wanted to go near when they had fires, but at home they had told him that he couldn't. But now there was nobody in the prairie. In summer, kids played ball here, too, big kids, some of them bigger kids than his brother, Bill. When he got bigger, maybe he would play ball here. He would be such a good player that he would always be taken first when sides were picked for a game. And maybe Hortense Audrey would come around sometimes when he was playing, and she would see him hit a lot of home runs.

This noon, Aunty Margaret had been saying that soon, in a couple of months before anybody knew it, Christmas would be here. And she had told him that he would have to be a very good and obedient boy, because if he was, he would get anything he wanted from Santa Claus, but if he wasn't Santa Claus would know all about it, just like God knew all about everything bad that a person ever did, and when a boy was bad and not obedient, then Santa Claus didn't give him any good toys at Christmas. That was Santa Claus' way of punishing a kid who was a bad boy. He wasn't going to give Santa Claus a chance to do that to him, because he wasn't going to do even one little thing that was bad, from now until Christmas. And he was going to hurry up and learn all about reading and writing, so he could write a good letter to Santa Claus, telling Santa Claus all the toys he wanted for Christmas.

Danny spat at a crack in the sidewalk. He walked on a few feet, paused before a gray brick three-story apartment building. He walked slowly, pigeon-toed, and, gee, he wished that Bill had come up today to play with him. He had run home a little while ago to see if Bill had come, but Bill hadn't. He heard the rumbling of an elevated train. He hopped, skipped, and jumped over five sidewalk squares. He stood still and looked wistfully up at the blue autumn sky. He thought, gee, now, it was the sky. What would it be like to walk upside down on the sky, and have everybody down on the earth looking up to watch him walking upside down on the sky? But he guessed they couldn't see him if he was walking upside down on the sky, because Miss Devlin in school had told them all that the sky was so many many miles away that everything in the sky looked very small, when it was really very very big, and the sky was way bigger than the earth, and the stars, and the sun, and the moon, they were very very big, too. So if he walked on the sky upside down, how could people see him when he would be so far away that he would seem smaller even than a pinhead? But suppose they could see him walking? They would look up and they would say, now, who is that, walking up there on the sky upside down? And they wouldn't know. That would be so funny it would make him laugh, because he would be fooling them. He would laugh at all the people asking everybody who he was, walking upside down way up there on the sky. It would be a real hot one, all right.

He watched a laundry wagon go by, the driver loosely holding the reins and smoking a cigarette. He'd like to drive a laundry wagon and smoke a cigarette. When he would grow up, maybe he would be a laundry-wagon driver, and he would drive along, holding the reins and smoking a cigarette just like the man in that wagon had done. He sat down on a wooden railing in front of a red brick building, stuck a pencil stub in his mouth, yelled giddyap, and he was a laundry-man. He took the pencil out of his mouth, and blew as if he were blowing out smoke just like Bill and Aunty Margaret did when they smoked cigarettes. He pulled like he was driving a horse, and his horse went now, cloppety clop, cloppety clop, and he was driving his laundry wagon.

"Whoa!" he yelled loudly, and a lady wearing a long blue coat stopped to smile at him.

"Hello, little boy. What is your name?" she said in a very nice voice.

"My name is Danny O'Neill. I'm a laundryman," he said proudly.

"But, Daniel, when you grow up, you want to be something better than a laundryman, don't you?" she asked, still smiling.

"I'm a laundryman."

"Do laundrymen chew their pencils?"

"That ain't a pencil. It's a cigarette," Danny said, pulling the pencil stub out of his mouth and pretending to blow out smoke. "Well, I got to go in here and get the lady's laundry."

She watched him with twinkling amusement in her eyes as he ran up the steps, pushed, opened the door to the building entrance hall, and stood inside it.

"Hello, Mrs. O'Flaherty, have you any laundry for me today?" he asked, standing inside the hallway.

He imagined that she said that she had, and that she wanted it back quick. And she was telling him that she was giving it to him because she was firing the nigger washwoman who came to do her washing, because the nigger washwoman ate too much of her son's food.

"We ain't got nigger washwomen in our laundry, Mrs. O'Flaherty," he said, pretending to pick up a bundle of laundry.

He pretended to carry it out to his wagon and dump it in the back. He looked around, and saw that the nice lady in the long blue coat was gone. He sat again on the wooden railing, seeing himself driving his horse, going along cloppety cloppety clop, and puffing on his pencil stub as if it were a cigarette.

He suddenly jumped off the railing and walked on, biting his fingernails. He wanted to grow up and be a man right away and drive a laundry wagon. But when he grew up it would be better to be a baseball player and pitch no-hit games like Ed Walsh and have the fans yell for him.

Look at the funny fat man walking across the street! A fat man was always funny, because he was a fat man. Danny watched the fat man lumber along, and he thought, gee, now look how big the fat man was, and look how little he was. When he was a man, he wanted to be like his Papa, but he didn't want to be a fat man. Now, what was the fat man's name? It wouldn't be Danny O'Neill, because Danny O'Neill was himself. But the fat man would have a name. Everybody had a name. When you knew them you knew them by their name. Everybody who knew him knew him by his name, and his name was Danny O'Neill. And everybody who knew that fat man knew him by his name. He didn't know the fat man, so he didn't know his name. But the fat man had a name, because everybody had a name, and if you didn't have a name you wouldn't be anybody.

It was getting darker now, and soon it would be dark, and then the day would be over, and it would be night instead of day. He would have supper with Mother and Uncle Al, and he hoped Uncle Al wouldn't be sore about something. He wondered, now, was God like Uncle Al, always flying off the handle. If God was that way, he didn't see how anybody was ever going to get to Heaven and be able to stay there. Gee, he wished Bill had come up. And here was an automobile, with lights on, coming, making noises, put-put-put. Automobiles made more noises than horse-and-wagons or jewboxes. Horses went cloppety clop, and jewboxes sort of just squeaked, and automobiles went put-put-put. Gee, he wished Bill was with him. And he wished he was big enough to be in fourth grade in school, instead of in first. If he was in fourth grade, he would be nearer to being in eighth grade, and when he was a big kid in eighth grade he would be nearer to being a man.

Gee, suppose that right now he didn't know where he lived, and he was lost far far away from Mother and home, with it getting dark. He would be afraid. Gee! What would he do? He stood still, stiffened in terror. A kidnaper might pick him up and drag him away and he would never again see Mother. That man across the street was a kidnaper who stole little boys like himself. He was lost and he had to be careful. He took a stealthy step forward. There was the man, like a thief in the night as Mama always said. The man had a black mustache. Danny dug into his pocket, pulled his hand out, pointed his finger as if it were a gun.

"Bang! Bang! Bang!" he yelled, the man looked at him and went on, but he had shot the man, and the man really was dead.

Danny walked along. If he was lost somewhere in the dark, and he had his gun, he could shoot kidnapers like he just shot that one with the mustache. He tried to step on sidewalk squares with his right foot. It was getting too dark to be alone on the streets where it was dangerous. And, gee, he had to watch the way he walked. He almost stepped on that last square with his left foot. He couldn't do that or something bad would happen to him. He wove a spell around himself by stepping on squares with his right foot, and if he touched one with the wrong foot the spell would be broken. Then a kidnaper with a black mustache, like Desperate Desmond in the funny papers, could take him away. Almost again with his left foot! He checked his stride, touched the next square with his right sole, walked on, landed correctly again, changed his stride to get the next square. With this spell no kidnaper like Desperate Desmond could touch him and take him away so that he would never see Mother and them all any more. His left foot! Right on the square before he knew what he was doing. The spell was broken. He had to get home right away, before something happened to him. He ran so that he wouldn't be kidnaped. He fell. He got up, crying, his knee hurting him, his left stocking ripped. Had to hurry, hurry, hurry. He rang the hallway bell, pushed in the inner hall door when the buzzer sounded. Safely inside the inner door, he leaned against the glass breathless. He saw a man pass. That was the kidnaper who would have taken him away if he hadn't gotten in just in the nick of time. He should have not broken his spell by stepping on that crack with his left foot. But he was safe now. He looked at his knee. It wasn't cut, and it didn't hurt any more. He brushed his pants where he had fallen, and bounded upstairs.

II

"Where were you? I was waiting for you," Bill surlily said to Danny, meeting Danny at the door.

"I was playing. I didn't know you were coming up today," Danny replied apologetically, feeling both happy and surprised at seeing Bill.

"I'm just leaving now. It's late."

"Gee, can't you stay here for supper?"

"Nobody asked me to. You ask Mother if I can."

"Is that my grandson?"

"Yes, Mother, it's me," Danny yelled back to the kitchen.

"Come here, Son!" she yelled loudly, and he saw her scurrying along the hall to greet him.

"Ask her while she's feeling good," Bill said, nudging Danny.

"Come and have a glass of milk, Son. Were you out running in the prairie?" she asked, smothering him against her apron.

"Can Bill have some, too, Mother?" Danny asked as he and Bill trailed after her to the rear of the house.

"Anybody of the name of William will never have a day's bad luck. That was the name of me uncle in the old country. Come on, children!" she said, and in the kitchen she set graham crackers on a plate and put glasses of milk before them.

"Thanks, Mother," Bill said as she returned to the board by the sink, took up a pot of peeled potatoes, carried them to the stove, lit the gas under them.

"Danny!" Bill said, signaling toward her with an incline of his head.

"Mother, ain't Bill going to stay for supper?"

"I don't think that I can," Bill said, causing Danny to dart a surprised, shocked glance at him.

"Whenever there's food in my kitchen, my grandson William is welcome to it."

"Goody!" Danny exclaimed, clapping his hands together.

"Let's go in the front," Bill said, standing up.

Danny galloped toward the front of the house, making loud noises, his feet banging heavily.

"Aunt Margaret at work?" Bill asked, plunking down in a chair in the parlor.

"Yes. She went to work late today."

"Come here!" Bill commanded.

"What do you want?" Danny asked, absent-minded.

"Come here! If I didn't want you, I wouldn't be calling you," Bill said bullyingly.

"Is something the matter?" Danny asked, approaching Bill.

"No, but there will be if you don't wake up and quit being such a damn fool. Say, how did you ever get so smart?"

"I don't know," Danny said foggily.

"Well, if you ever find out, let me know. Listen! Drop your dumbness down a sewer, and listen. Are you listening?"

"Yes! Yes . . . I'm listening."

"Listen!" Bill said, farting, and Danny looked at Bill with an innocent hurt on his face, and he wished that Bill wouldn't go doing things like that that weren't at all nice.

"Come on. You stick in the dining room and give me jiggers if Mother comes. I want to see if I can find a cigarette in Aunt Peg's room. I need a fag. And if you let me get caught, or snitch on me, see this!" Bill said, holding a closed fist under Danny's nose.

Danny shook his head up and down, his eyes blank.

"You're not a dummy, are you? Answer me!"

"Uh huh!" Danny responded, perplexed.

"Somebody ought to hang a dumbbell like you in the Harding Square gymnasium. You go and give me jiggers. And don't forget! If I get caught, I'll kill you!" Bill said, again planting a fist in Danny's face.

"Yes."

"I want to get some cigarettes," Bill said, going out of the parlor after Danny.

Standing in the dining room, Danny worried, because it was not right to steal, or for Bill to smoke, and he didn't want Mother to catch Bill in Aunty Margaret's room. And if Uncle Al ever found out about it, he'd hit and kick Bill, and never let Bill come up here any more. He trembled. He could hear Bill in her room. And Mother seemed to be busy in the kitchen. His face became inordinately pale from fear. He tiptoed to his aunt's bedroom off the hall and saw Bill rummaging through a dresser drawer.

"She coming?" Bill said, quickly but quietly closing the drawers and rushing to him.

"Can't you find them?"

"Get out of here, you little sleeping Jesus, and watch, or I'll bust your nose!" Bill said, shoving Danny back toward the dining room.

Danny sat on a chair by the entrance to the hall. He was too nervous to sit still. He tiptoed to the swinging kitchen door. He heard his grandmother singing, moving about. He guessed it was safe for Bill. But he wanted Bill to hurry up. And if he let Bill get caught, Bill would sock him and call him a snitcher. Oh, God, please help Bill to hurry up and find the cigarettes. He put his ear to the door. Footsteps sounded behind him. He swung around, frightened. Seeing Bill, he gasped a sigh of relief.

"Listen, don't you ever tell anybody about this. Do you hear me?" Danny shook his head. "If anybody asks you was I in Aunt Margaret's room, you say

no, and you saw me every minute. Get that!" Again Danny shook his head. "If
you snitch on me, you won't live to snitch on anybody else!"

"I won't, Bill. I promise, honest, I won't!" Danny said with ringing sincerity.

"See that you don't!"

"Bill, who do you think will be the world's champions next season?" Danny
asked, gazing at his brother with frank admiration.

"I got to go and crap," Bill said.

"Can I come in with you and talk?" Danny asked.

"Sure! I might even let you hold my head."

"Is that what you took?" Danny asked, as Bill flashed a box of Melachrinoes
in the bathroom with the door locked.

"I found them in a drawer. But don't forget! If you snitch, I'll kill you!"

"Honest, I won't, Bill."

Smoking, Bill let down his pants and squatted on the seat. Danny plopped
down on the edge of the bathtub. He heard the noise from the movement of
Bill's bowels, and quickly the bathroom was filled with a bad odor. He wanted
to get out because of the smell, but also he wanted to stay and talk with Bill.

"Bill, do you think the Sox will win the pennant next year?" he asked as Bill
sighed loudly and a splash was heard.

"Ah, I feel better now," Bill said after another sigh.

"Do you think they will, Bill?"

"I like it, crapping in a joint like this instead of in the shithouse we got in the
back yard at home. Boy, that place smells! And when you go there in winter,
your ass freezes. Pa don't like it none, neither. He's always complaining because
the niggers living in back of us use it, too. He asks why he should have to use
the same crapper with niggers, when his grandfather fought with the Confederate Army in the battle of Shiloh. Pa says he's glad that the North won the Civil
War and preserved the Union, but he wishes Lincoln did something with the
niggers."

"Do niggers ever get to play in the big leagues?"

"You bet your boots they don't. If they did, there are plenty of fans like me and
Pa who wouldn't go to the games. But, say, Aunt Peg smokes good cigarettes,"
Bill said, inhaling, letting the smoke out through his nose.

"Isn't it bad for a kid to smoke? I heard Aunty Margaret saying to Uncle Al
that it was."

"They say lots of things. They say that the storks bring babies," said Bill, and
Danny grew tense with fright for fear that Aunty Margaret did, or would, tell
Uncle Al what he said Bill told him about babies, and that Uncle Al would beat
Bill up, and then Bill would sock him and be mad at him.

"Are you through, Bill?"

"Hold your horses. It isn't every day that I get a chance to have a smoke and take a crap in comfort like this. One of the reasons I like to come up here is that I can get a good cigarette and sit down here and take a crap like a king. That's a swell feeling, too. Crapping in a real bathroom, with a cork tip in your mouth."

"Gee!" Danny exclaimed because he didn't know what to say, and he was thinking that when Bill went to the toilet, sometimes there was an awful smell in the bathroom. After a pause, he added, "But, Bill, if Mother finds me in here with you on the toilet, she'll put up a great big holler. She doesn't like me to be in here with you when you're doing number two. And then when Uncle Al gets home for supper, she might tell him, and maybe he'll get sore at us."

"She hasn't found us yet. And this cigarette is too good to throw away before the last drag."

"Does Pa know you smoke cigarettes?"

"He'd kick my tail all the way up and down La Salle Street if he found out."

"I want to grow up and be big so they can't tell me what I got to do and make me wear white stockings."

"They want to make a sissy out of you. And Pa doesn't like it at all. He says to Ma, 'Jesus Christ, putting white stockings on the kid, and when I was his age I didn't have any stockings at all on my long legs!' Pa would never make any of us wear white stockings," Bill said, dropping his butt under him in the toilet bowl.

"Well, some day I'm going to be a man. You see if I don't."

"It'll be fun when we're both men, won't it?" Bill said, starting to wipe himself.

"I wish it would hurry up and come."

"It's a long time off. But I'll be a man before you," Bill said.

"I wish it wasn't so long a ways off," Danny said wistfully.

"Say, this is the nuts. Real toilet paper. At home, we always got to use old newspapers. Mama don't buy toilet paper because she says that if she did, and left it outside in the crapper, the niggers would use it, and she ain't going to be spending Pa's hard-earned dough buying toilet paper for niggers."

"I wonder how many games Ed Walsh will win next year," Danny said.

Bill buttoned up his pants and opened the small window to let out the smoke. He pulled the chain, and there was a gurgling rush of water. Danny was glad Bill was finished. Now they could get out of here, and Mother wouldn't know the difference. She didn't holler about lots of things like Aunty Margaret and Uncle Al did, but she always yelled at him and said it was a sin for him to stay in here with Bill like this.

"Say, Bill, let's play the battle of Bunker Hill," Danny said, as they left the bathroom.

"I'm not a baby any more," Bill said, leading the way to the parlor.

III

"It's Uncle Al," Danny said as a key turned in the front door, and they stopped talking to wait nervously.

"Hello, Uncle Al!" they chorused.

"Hello, Sport!" Uncle Al said genially, but stepping into the parlor he saw Bill, and his mood changed, his face became pale and he glared at his oldest nephew.

"Mother is getting supper in the kitchen," Danny quickly said to be saying something when he sensed that Uncle Al had it in for Bill again.

"Doesn't your mother need you to help her at home?" Uncle Al asked.

"She sent me up to see Danny," Bill said.

"Hadn't you better hurry if you're going to get home for supper?"

"I was all ready to go and Mother told me I shouldn't, I should stay here for supper," Bill innocently said while Danny twitched on the edge of the piano stool.

"Yes, Mother said she wanted Bill to stay with us," Danny timidly said.

"You better go. I think your mother might need you."

"All right," Bill said, getting up from a rocking chair.

"And don't get surly with me, either!"

"I wasn't," Bill said.

"Don't talk back to me! And sit down. I got something to tell you. It's good you are here. I want to talk to you!" Uncle Al said, his face lighting up sadistically with the recollection of the bone he had to pick with Bill.

"I better go or I'll be late at home for supper."

"I got something to say. Goddamn you, sit down," Uncle Al said, and Bill, pale, almost trembling, fell into a rocker as Uncle Al turned to Danny who quivered on the piano stool. "You go out and tell your grandmother I said you should help her!"

"She said she didn't want me."

"Get out of here! Do what you're told to do!" Uncle Al said, and Danny left, his hands shaking. "Now you, your Aunt Margaret told me that you . . ."

"Mother, Uncle Al said I should help you get supper ready," Danny said to his grandmother who was setting knives and forks around the dining-room table.

"Sure, the Lord love you, you'd only be in the way. Go play with William," she said, and he followed her into the kitchen, hearing Uncle Al's angry voice, but not making out what was being said.

"Are you sure I can't help you, Mother?"

"Go play with William, you angel."

Standing in the hallway, his knees quaking, struggling to keep from crying, Danny heard Uncle Al going after Bill.

"You sit there and have the nerve to deny that! You dare to say that you didn't tell those things to your brother! You call your aunt a liar!"

"I didn't," Danny heard Bill answer, almost in tears, and he knew now that he was the cause of it all, and he was only a dirty old snitcher, and because he was, Uncle Al would beat Bill up.

"Why, you dirty little liar! If you say that again, I'll punch some truth into you! By God, I will!"

"I didn't. Danny must have made it all up."

"Danny!" Uncle Al belched, and as Danny was trying to reply that he was coming, Uncle Al rushed out, grabbed him in the hall, dragged him roughly into the parlor. "Sit down! And look me in the eye! When I was away, did your brother tell you anything about children on La Salle Street in a barn?"

"What things?" Danny sobbed.

"Answer me! Did he?"

"I don't remember."

"Think a minute! And damn you, don't lie to me!"

"I didn't!" Bill said, trying to catch Danny's eye and signal to him.

"You shut up! You're to be seen and not heard around here!" Uncle Al flared at Bill, and then he turned again to look piercingly at Danny. "You remember the things that you told your aunt that he told you?"

As Danny slowly shook his head negatively, Uncle Al leaped forward, towered menacingly over him.

"You do remember! Look me in the eye and answer me! . . . Jesus Christ, stop crying!"

Bill slunk toward the hall.

"I'm not crying!" Danny said, tears rolling down his red cheeks.

"Do you remember . . ."

"I . . ." Danny couldn't talk; he convulsed in sobs.

"I'm not going to hurt you. Stop crying like a baby!" Uncle Al said, breathing asthmatically.

"William, where are you going?" Mrs. O'Flaherty called from the hallway.

Uncle Al heard the front door slam. His face went white, and he stood in momentary surprise.

"What's the matter? Did you send William to the store?" the grandmother asked, coming to the parlor.

"Why, that dirty little lying dog!" Uncle Al shouted, running to the door, opening it, calling down the hall. "Come back here, you!"

He heard the downstairs inner door slamming shut. He stood with clenched fists, shaking with anger. He closed the door, and returned to the parlor to see his mother bending over Danny.

"Al, did you scare the baby? Did you hit him?"

"Nobody touched him, Mother."

"The poor baby is white as a sheet, and look at him crying."

"He wouldn't tell the truth. And that brother of his, he never is to be allowed inside of this door again. Tell his mother to keep him home. Jesus Christ, just wait till I get my hands on him, the degenerate little lying cur!"

"Al! Al! What did the children do?"

"They wouldn't tell me the truth. And for punishment, he doesn't have any supper."

"But the poor little one . . ."

"He goes to bed this minute, without supper!"

"He's so weak. He's got to have a bite in his little stomach."

"You hear me, you! Get to bed!" Uncle Al said as Danny sat with a sunken head, tears rolling off his face.

"I didn't do a thing," he wailed.

"I'll teach you to tell the truth! Come on!" Uncle Al said, grabbing Danny's sleeve, dragging him to his cot, ignoring his mother who followed them, protesting and confused. "Now, shut up! Quit crying and go to bed! Then the next time you'll know enough to tell the truth!"

Al ordered his mother out of the room and closed the door on Danny, who lay screaming on his cot.

IV

Bill heard Uncle Al calling him back as he ran down the first landing. He bolted through the inner hall door, plunged down the few tiled steps in the outer hallway, opened the outer door, jumped down the stone steps in front of the building, tore down to the corner at Forty-ninth, rounded it, and hit on toward Grand Boulevard. He stopped by the alley between Grand Boulevard and Calumet, his side stitching on him. He watched, but he didn't see Uncle Al shagging him. There was a man coming along, walking very fast, but he was much bigger than Uncle Al. He lit a cigarette. Regaining his breath, he thought of what a little stinker his snitching brother was. If Danny told about what he did today! Jesus God! Well, the next time he saw Danny he'd pound every ounce of snitching out of the dumb little punk. He liked Danny, liked to be with him and go to ball games with him. But if Danny was going to snitch, and be so dumb! Oh, he couldn't wait until he got his hands on the goddamn little fool. He gritted his teeth, clenched and raised his fists in frustration because he didn't have Danny before him so that he could sock the talking little mutt.

The man came closer, and Bill could see that he had a rough hard face. He was afraid of the man, and something inside of himself told him to run. But he hadn't done anything, and this man wasn't Uncle Al, Pa, or a truant officer. The man was closer. He was afraid. Why hadn't he run? He made a start.

"Just a minute, Son!" the man said, firmly clasping Bill's coat sleeve.

"I didn't do nothing," Bill self-righteously protested, sensing that the man was a dick and worrying over what might happen if he was searched and the ring was found on him. "Let me go, I done nothin'!"

"You just ran out of a building around the corner there. What made you run so fast? Snitch something?"

"No. I just came from my aunt's house."

"You did? What's your aunt's name?"

"Mrs. Smith," Bill said, sure that he was in the hands of a dick and wondering what story he could tell if he was frisked and the ring was found on him.

"What's your name?"

"I don't have to answer you. I didn't do nothing," Bill said, figuring he would bluff his way out.

"See this!" the man said, bending down, opening his coat, flashing a star. "Now tell me, what's your name?"

"Daniel Jones," Bill said, wondering about the star, because it was a star, all right, but it wasn't like a copper's star, or like the star Pa's cousin, Pat Dennison, the dick, wore.

"Come clean, you punk, your name is O'Neill."

"What did I do?"

"Answer me! Your name is O'Neill, isn't it? I was waiting for you to come from your grandmother's."

"But I ain't done nothin' but smoke a cigarette. You ain't gonna haul me for that, are you?" Bill said, shooting away his cigarette with a shaking hand.

"You answer my questions, and I'll decide what to do with you."

"Yes, sir!"

"What's your aunt's name?"

"What did I do that you're holding me like this?"

"For Christ's sake, answer my questions, or I might belt you one! What's your aunt's name?"

"Margaret."

"Margaret what? Jesus, I never thought an Irish punk could be as dumb as you. Come on, snap up, Margaret what? It isn't Levy, is it?"

"Margaret O'Flaherty."

"Is your aunt at home now?"

"No, sir!"

"Where is she?"

"I think she's at work."

"And she's a cashier at the Union Hotel. So you see, lad, I know something. Now don't try to lie when I ask you something!" the dick said, and Bill looked at him in awe, wondering how the dick got all this dope, still trying to figure out a good story if the ring was found on him. "Listen, now, your aunt knows a guy named Robinson, doesn't she?"

"I don't know," Bill said, suddenly relieved, because now he got it all, and he knew that the dick was a private gum-shoe trailing Aunt Margaret about this man, Mr. Robinson, whose name had been in the newspapers in a political scandal. He heard Mama telling Papa how Aunt Margaret had been followed home a couple of times by gumshoes after she was out with Mr. Robinson.

"You ain't tongue-tied, are you? Did you ever hear your aunt say anything about a guy named Robinson?"

"No, sir!"

"Listen, about a week ago, you called up the Shrifton Hotel and asked the clerk if Mr. Robinson was stayin' there," the dick said, and Bill again looked at him in awe, wondering how that had been found out. "You did, didn't you?" the dick added, and Bill got it all now. The wire had been tapped, like he had read about in dime novels, and he was excited. He suddenly saw himself as a real crook, and a figure in things happening the way they did in dime novels, and he was going to show how Bill O'Neill, the dippy-fingered one, was smarter than a real dick. "Talk, punk, and come clean! How about that telephone call?"

"It must have been my brother."

"You ain't comin' clean."

"I don't live with my aunt, and I don't know everything about her."

"You know she knows a guy named Robinson!"

"No, sir!"

"Now, tell me the truth. Do you know anything about this guy, Robinson?" the dick asked, pulling out a five-dollar bill, holding it carelessly before Bill's eyes. "Does she ever say anything about seeing him?"

"I don't know," Bill said, watching the five-dollar bill, figuring that he could say something maybe to get the money, and still not give anything away on his aunt, because if he did that it would be snitching.

"Ever see anything like this paper I got in my hand?" the dick asked.

"It's a five-dollar bill."

"How would you like to stick it in your pocket?"

Bill smiled, thinking of the cigarettes, sodas, things that the dough could buy.

"Well, if you tell me the truth, you might get it."

"I am telling you the truth."

"Well, tell me, now, what have you ever heard your aunt say about this guy, Robinson?"

"Well, all I know is that she knows him."

"When she gets you to call up the hotel and ask if he's there, what does she say to you?"

"Just that. She asks me to call up," Bill answered, guessing that this wasn't giving Aunt Margaret away, because the dick already knew that much.

"Tell me the exact words she uses."

"I don't know. She just tells me to call up."

"Ever hear anybody else, your mother or grandmother talking about him?"

"No."

"Does she ever say she goes out with him, or that she loves him?"

"I don't know."

"Did you ever hear her say that he gives her money?"

"No," Bill said, still freezing his eyes on the five-dollar bill, tempted to tell more so that he would get it, telling himself, like a martyr, that he couldn't be a snitcher.

"Well, why did she have you call up a hotel to find out if he was there?"

"I guess she wanted to talk to him."

"Is there nothing else she ever says about him?"

"No!" Bill said, trying to figure out how many nickel shows he could go to with that money.

The gumshoe studied him closely. Was he, or wasn't he going to get the money? If the dick gave it to him he'd be rich. And he'd sell the ring and have enough money for nickel shows, and cigarettes, and penny arcades downtown for longer than he could imagine.

"I guess that's all," the gumshoe said.

Bill watched his face, wondering, should he ask for the money, reach for it, or what?

"Listen close, kid! If I give you this money, I know what you'll do. You'll go right back to your aunt, won't you?"

"No, I wouldn't! If I did, and took the money, maybe I wouldn't get my pants whaled hot as cinders!" Bill said, shaking his head negatively, still eyeing the money.

"If I give it to you, will you listen, remember what you hear, and tell me whatever she says about this guy, Robinson?"

"But if I do, maybe I'll get in trouble."

"Don't worry about that. We won't let on. Your aunt doesn't know who I am, and she won't, unless you tell her. And if you do, I'll ring your goddamn neck off your head! Get me, punk?"

"Yes, sir!"

"All right, here it is. Don't forget! You don't say boo about this. If you do, you won't get another chance. I'll see you again. Remember everything she says. And whenever you come here to see your brother, look and see if she has any letters from him. I'll give you five bucks for every letter of his to her you get me. Watch the mailbox and see if he sends her any money in the mail, too, and tell me. Will you do that?"

"Yes, sir!"

"All right, now. Here's the dough. But if you squeal, goddamn you!" the gum-shoe said, jamming his fist under Bill's nose.

"Yes, sir!" Bill said, taking the money.

He watched the burly fellow walk off. He fingered the money. It was too good to believe. The money was his. He took out the ring he had swiped from his aunt's drawer, studied its shiny stone under the lamplight. He'd sell it, too. But if Danny ever gave him away! What the dick threatened to do to him was nothing at all, nothing at all, to what he'd do to Danny!

He lit another cigarette, walked proudly over to Grand Boulevard and down toward Fifty-first Street. He was living a life like they lived in stories, with stolen rings, private detectives, money. He couldn't wait until he grew up, because when he did, he was going to be the greatest crook there ever was, greater than Jesse James or Alias Jimmy Valentine. He puffed at his cigarette. He felt the five-dollar bill and the ring in his pocket. He wouldn't go home now. He'd buy supper in a Greek restaurant on Fifty-first Street, and he would eat three chunks of apple pie. And tomorrow he'd bum from school, go downtown, have a swell time. He had done a pretty smart day's work today, all right. Ah, just wait till he grew up. Wouldn't he make the crooks in dime novels look sick! Just to show himself what he was, he pulled out a cork-tipped cigarette, lit it, took one puff, threw it away like a butt, lit another one. He walked down to Fifty-first Street, whistling a gay tune. And from now on at Mother's he'd have to watch the mailbox, because if the gumshoe was right, and Mr. Robinson did send Aunt Margaret dough, well, he might pinch some of it.

V

Lying on his cot in the darkness, Danny's eyes stung from crying. And he was hungry. Uncle Al was just mean. He never wanted to see Uncle Al again, or speak to him. He would go home with Papa and Mama, and even if they didn't have a bathroom in the house, and steam heat, and electric lights, he would go home, or he would run away. He would run away and not come back until he was a man as big as Papa, and then he would come back and beat Uncle Al up, good and plenty.

Turning around to lie on his belly, he saw the blue sky and the dark night. And if he hadn't been a snitcher and told on Bill, this would never have happened, and Bill would be here, talking to him about ballplayers, right this minute. Bill told him that a snitcher was the worse thing a kid could be. And he was a snitcher.

He let out a wail. He waited to see if anyone came in after his scream, No one did. He looked out at the night, and it was so dark it made him afraid. It would serve Uncle Al right, too, if some kidnaper or Black-hand came in the window, took him, killed him in a dark black woods, let a bear eat him up, or gave him to some Indians who would tomahawk him and kill and eat him the way they did to the soldiers, just like Aunty Margaret had said they had done in Custer's last battle. And, yes, he was sore at Aunty Margaret, too, and it was her fault. When he saw her in the morning, he wouldn't even speak to her. And if she could tell Uncle Al on Bill and him, he could tell Uncle Al that she came home drunk, and cursed, and didn't go to church on Sunday, and told Mother that she was with that Morton woman that Uncle Al didn't want her to see and said never could come in his house.

It was so dark. He curled his head under the covers. He might smother, though, this way. And if he did, it would be their fault. And then it would cost them money for his funeral, because funerals cost money, and Aunty Margaret was always saying how it cost her so much to have a funeral for Father and for Aunty Louise. He wanted Aunty Louise to be here so he could tell her what they did to him. She would stick up for him if she was here. When he went to church next Sunday, he was going to pray and ask God to send Aunty Louise back to him from Heaven where she was. She wouldn't let them starve him until he was so hungry that he had pains in his tummy. No, she wouldn't.

He heard a noise. It was the door, opening. It was Uncle Al, or a kidnaper! OOO!

"Whist! Son!"

He pulled the covers aside and saw his grandmother carrying something in the dark. Suddenly, the light was on and she was beside his bed, holding a tray of food.

"Ssh! Don't let your uncle hear you! You poor child. Here, eat this quick!" she said, putting the tray on his lap, kissing him tenderly.

15

I

Bill told his mother that he had to go out the back way to go to the toilet. He glanced furtively up from the bottom of the rickety steps to see if she was looking after him. He smiled with gratification when he saw that she wasn't. He ducked under the steps where he had hid his money and the ring last night, using match light to see. The treasures were undisturbed and he stuck them in his pocket, thinking that he had to have a flashlight. He'd get one downtown. How could he work without one? He darted across the small back yard, a patch of hardened dirt strewn with broken glass, tin cans, sticks, and assorted rubbish. He skipped along the passageway to the alley which ran by the side of the tumble-down clapboard house in the back where the Negro family lived. He dumped into a garbage can the lunch his mother had prepared and wrapped for him. Hell, he was rich today and he could buy himself anything that he wanted to eat.

With a feeling of freedom and hope, he stepped out onto Twenty-fifth Street. The bare trees of the deserted playground across the street glistened in the morning sunlight. Two foreigners in smeared overalls passed in front of him, carrying lunch boxes and jabbering away in their native tongues. He tossed a look of contempt after them. They couldn't speak English like his father could. A troop of Italian kids, none of them older or bigger than Danny, dragged in front of him, yelling, pushing one another, cursing. He watched them, thinking that they were only dirty dago brats, and he didn't like wop kids. Sometimes they'd even use a knife on you. Down on Wentworth Avenue street cars rumbled, and then their echo was momentarily smothered by the noise of a swiftly rushing train which clattered behind him on the Rock Island tracks. A teamster bawled at his horses, driving a Morgan and Hearst wagon to La Salle Street, and Bill sneered after the wagon because he knew that that man couldn't drive a horse as good as Pa could. He guessed that Pa could drive a horse better than anybody in the city, and when his grandfather was living, his grandfather must have been pretty good, too, driving horses. He started stepping on sidewalk cracks.

"Hey, O'Neill! O'Neill! Hey, Skinny O'Neill!"

Bill swung around and saw Big Ears Delaney running toward him, yelling his name as he tore forward.

"Jesus, stranger! Hello!" Big Ears said, short of wind when he reached Bill; he was Bill's size and age, but huskier, olive-skinned, and with ears that suggested his nickname.

"How are you, Big Ears?"

"Going to school today to pay Miss Harris a visit?"

"I'm gonna buy an apple and put it on her desk," Bill said.

"Hell! We ain't seen you in school this week. And Mr. Morgan in manual training was asking for you. You got a drag with him like you got one with Miss Timmins in arithmetic, because you're so good in both things."

"I was sick."

"You was sick two weeks ago. Is it the same thing that's the matter with you this week?"

"You don't have to believe me. But I was, I was awful sick."

"Say, what the hell you think I am, teacher's pet? I'm not going up to Miss Timmins and say you been bummin' from school and I seen yuh," Big Ears said, drooping along at a slow pace beside Bill.

"I got to go downtown on an errand for my old lady so I can't come today," Bill said.

"Horse! Say, listen, I ain't wishin' you bad luck, but I want to warn you. I hope you don't get what I got. I was caught bummin' from school by Cockeye Colman, the new truant officer. He seen my old man about me. So the old man thrun me up for grabs, and beat my ass black and blue. You better watch yourself, boy, because we ain't never had a sonofobitchin' truant officer around here as tough as this bastard, Cockeye Colman, is."

"He won't get me," Bill bragged, thinking how he would certainly be smart enough to fool a truant officer if he was going to grow up to be the world's greatest crook.

"That's what they all say, Skinny! But he nabbed me. And Miss Harris went to the old hen herself about me. That old hen we got for a principal, she and Cockeye Colman said if I didn't want to go to school, they would put me in a joint where I'd have to go. And my old man tol' me that if I didn't want to go to school and get myself smartened up, he didn't give a damn if I was jugged in a reform school. But, say, Skinny, got an extra butt?" Big Ears said, as they stopped at the corner of Twenty-fifth and Wentworth, in front of the saloon.

Big Ears Delaney's eyes popped in awe when Bill pulled out a box of Mela-chrinoes and handed him one. Bill took one, and they lit up.

"Cork tips! Say, where'd you snitch 'em?"

"My uncle's. I was at his house yesterday."

"He must have dough to smoke fags as classy as these. My old man, he rolls his own."

"My uncle is rich. He travels all around sellin' shoes, and he's got lots in his kick," Bill said, ashamed to say that he'd stolen the cigarettes from his aunt, rather than his uncle, because he didn't want kids in the neighborhood to know that he had an aunt who smoked.

"Boy, I never drew on anything like this before. Say, you got a box of 'em, how about another for me for afterwhile?" Delaney asked, and Bill magnanimously handed him a second cigarette. "Thanks! You're a regular kid, O'Neill. Any time you get in trouble, you call on me. Me and my gang, we'll stand by you. But, say, you shoulda been around yesterday. We went down under the viaduct there after the nigger kids on the other side of Twenty-fifth."

"Did you clean 'em out of house and home?"

"Did we! Did we! We had a fight! The cops had to come to break it up. One of the black stinkers damn near cut the arm off of Tony Scarsella with a razor."

"You shoulda gone after them with brass knuckles and a couple of twenty-twos. All the shines carry razors."

"Yeah, they don't fight fair! But when you get close to 'em, all you got to do is kick 'em in the shins, and they'll yell for their pickaninnies. One swipe in the shins with your boots, and you got 'em licked. But we got 'em plenty. You know what we did. We went around to back yards and copped some clothes poles. And Tony snatched some spikes in the Jew's hardware store on Wentworth. We druve the nails in the poles, and went over after 'em with the poles. They didn't expect that. Hell, Mickey Galligan damn near druve a spike through one black bastard's eye. I wished he did get the eye instead of the cheek. Anything you do to a nig-ger is all right. Even my old man doesn't whale me when he knows I was fightin' with the blacks. I tell you, you shoulda been around, Skinny. It was a swell fight. The cops had to come and break it up. They took two shines away with them in the paddy wagon. And we're goin' back tonight. We know the nigger that cut Tony. His name is Abraham Lincoln Grant, and we're gonna get 'im tonight. Say, come around, and don't miss the fight. It's gonna be a humdinger."

"I'll be there. Maybe I can get up and cop my uncle's twenty-two to use," Bill said.

"Jesus, that's swell. Say, do it, and meet us down at the corner there around four o'clock. We need all the guys we can get. When you go down under the viaduct, the niggers keep flocking out from all sides, and we need all the guys we can get for 'em."

"I'll be there, But, say, Delaney, ditch school, and come along downtown with me. I'll pay your carfare."

"No, sir. With the school term only about a month old, I've been in enough dutch, as it is. I'm gettin' my last chance. I don't want the old man poundin' lumps all over me. He's swillin' again now, broke his pledge the old lady made him take, and he always lams me when he's drunk. And I might get myself shoved in reform school, too, if I get caught bummin' from school any more."

"Aw, come on, you can get away with it."

"No, not for me. I learned my lesson, Skinny."

"Well, I'll hop this car that's comin'. I'll see you this afternoon."

"Say, Skinny, you couldn't spare a jit, could you? I got some bottles saved up that I'm gonna sell Saturday, and I'll pay you back then. Cross my heart on it."

"Here," Bill said, lavishing a nickel on Delaney.

"Thanks! Say, you're a prince, Skinny!"

"Well, here's my car, Big Ears," Bill said, running across the street while Delaney waved after him.

II

Bill waited until the Wentworth Avenue car started up, and then he flipped it. He stood on the jammed smoky back platform, hardly able to wait until he could get downtown. Next to him there was a blond guy talking with a young fellow who looked like he might be a dago or a hunyock.

"I'm quittin'. It ain't safe to drive a newspaper delivery wagon for my paper any more and belong to the union. I'm shaking the dust off myself. I like this Swedish head that I got on my shoulders," the blond fellow was saying, and Bill didn't get what he was talking about.

"We should all stick together and fight," the other one said.

"We don't stand a chance fighting the hooligans the paper hired," the blond one said.

"We got to fight for our union," the other was saying, and Bill wasn't interested in what they said, but he would be if they talked about baseball, or burglars and robbing, or girls.

The car rumbled on, more passengers crowding onto the platform, and Bill was pushed away from the two he had heard talking. There was a lot of talk now, but he couldn't make out much of it because of the noise the car made in running, and the many voices. He felt the ring and the money in his pocket. It was great to be rich, all right, rich and not at school on a day like this, on any day. And if Danny hadn't been a snitcher, he'd go out to Mother this afternoon and buy Danny a soda. Now, he wouldn't. All he was going to do to Danny was sock the daylights out of him. The car clattered on, and many of the men on the platform got off. Bill turned and looked through the window, seeing Saint Peter's church. It was where Mama had gone to school. He wondered about Pa when he was a kid. He'd bet Pa bummed from school. But he guessed Uncle Al never did. He bet Uncle Al was a teacher's pet in school.

"Van Buren Street!" the conductor called, and Bill hopped off the car, dodged in front of a horse-and-wagon, and landed on the sidewalk. Elevated trains thundered overhead while he stood on the corner of Clark and Van Buren. He asked himself where could he sell the ring. He might try a pawnshop. Only he was kind of leary of trying to hock the ring, because he had on short pants, and the Jews in the pawnshops might be suspicious. They might even call the cops on him. He didn't know what to do about the ring. He ran across the street. A restaurant window containing apples and bottles of catsup caught his eye. He liked restaurants, the smell of them, the pies and sandwiches they sold, and when he grew up he was always going to eat in restaurants, and never at home. He went in and sat at the counter, looking at slices of pie, cake and cookies, bottles of catsup, sauces, oranges and apples which were directly in front of him. A fat Greek flat-footed to him and set a glass of water by his right elbow as he leaned on the counter.

"Apple pie and coffee," he ordered as if he might have been a man ordering.

He carefully watched the counterman slide a cut of pie onto a plate, draw coffee, pour cream into it. The order was pushed across the counter to him, the coffee slopping over the rim of the cup, almost filling the saucer. He gobbled up the pie in chunks, and gulped down his coffee, thinking that this was swell, this was the life. But still he was wondering, somewhere in the back of his head, what he was going to do with the ring. He was afraid of being caught, and he told himself that he wasn't afraid of being caught, and he wasn't afraid of nothing at all. He noticed two men, several seats to his left. They were eating ham and eggs and talking, their voices a little low so that he couldn't get their words. Would they buy it off him? Might he take a chance on them, and say that he found the ring? He tried to make up his mind, and he let his gaze drift out the window. He saw an express wagon shoot past, the horse galloping. Was it Pa's by any chance? Wouldn't that be good! Himself to be walking around downtown, and Pa to see him and ask him why wasn't he in school? Wouldn't Pa be sore, and wouldn't he get it on his ass with the razor strap tonight? He'd watch the express wagons carefully today. Pa drove his some place downtown, but he didn't know where. Tonight he'd have to just ask Pa and find out, and then, after this, he would know what streets to keep off of when he was downtown bumming from school. He hadn't told Pa and Ma about Uncle Al last night. Well, if they said anything to Pa and Ma, he would say Uncle Al just got sore. Pa would stick up for him. Pa always said that if anybody was going to hit and punish his kids, he would do it himself, but just let anybody else try and lay a hand on a kid of his! And Pa meant it, Pa was a real fighter, and he was proud of Pa for it. But that ring? He had to sell it to make some money. The men were still talking. He wished he had just happened to sit nearer them so he could hear what they were saying. He saw one of them bending over, scooping fried egg into his mouth, wiping his chin with a napkin when some of the egg yellow dribbled down it. Now, why didn't he get ham and eggs? Well, he could. He was rich enough to eat as much ham and eggs as he could get into his belly.

"An order of ham and eggs," he called to the waiter.

He thought of how swell it was going to be when he was a man and could eat all that he wanted to in restaurants like this one. And then he wouldn't be afraid of Uncle Al, or even of Pa. And when he was a man, he was going to be rich like Uncle Al, and not poor like Pa. He wasn't going to drive an express wagon and make hardly enough money to take care of his kids. Bill O'Neill would be the smartest crook in the world. Well, he wasn't such a dumb one at eleven.

But suppose that he tried to sell the ring to those two men, and they were dicks. But they weren't. You could always spot a dick, because the dicks seemed to have their own way of looking and talking. He wished they would hurry up with his ham and eggs. He was going to eat them like a man, and pay for them like a man. The men were finished with theirs, but they were still talking, ordering more coffee. He heard the cook calling from the slide in the wall that opened into the kitchen, and he saw the counterman get the plate, come forward with it. He pitched into the ham and eggs as if he had been starving. He ate with his eyes set on the men. He would catch them when they were paying their checks. Seeing that they were still taking their time, he ate more slowly. He had a hunch it would work, and they'd buy the ring. If he didn't sell it to them, he would try a hock shop. He was a daredevil, and he would take his chances.

He ate, waiting, feeling himself grow tight inside. But no, he told himself, he wasn't afraid. He just wanted to get it over with. When they swung off their stools, he felt like shouting hurray. He got off his, and got to the case in front at the same time that they did.

"Hey, mister, want to buy this ring?" he said, speaking rapidly to one of the men, a fellow with a hard face and a black derby shoved back on his head.

"Where'd you get it? I'll bet you found it," the man sarcastically answered, talking out of the side of his mouth, and the other one, a pimply thin guy with a felt hat, looked Bill in the eye until Bill had to turn away.

"I did. Right outside on the sidewalk," Bill said, trying to be very innocent.

"Well, I don't want it. And better watch the way you find things, Bud," the man said, causing Bill almost to gulp with disappointment.

"Kids like you always find things. Why ain't you in school?" the pimply one in the felt hat said.

"My mother sent me downtown to the store."

"Here, let's take a look at it," the pimply one said, smiling at Bill, causing Bill to return the smile, but still, he was wary, and he edged himself to the right of the men so that if it looked too hot, he could take a chance on snatching at the ring and beating it out the door.

"How much you want for it?" the man with the derby asked.

"Five bucks."

"I'll give you two bucks and pay your check," the pimply one said, and Bill reached his hand out suspiciously, while he anxiously and enviously, watched the fellow peel off two one-dollar bills from a thick roll.

"It ain't worth that much," the one with the derby said.

"I know it, but we'll give the kid a break," the pimply one said, handing Bill two dollars and taking his check.

Bill hurried out of the restaurant, watched by the two smiling men and the frowning Greek. Crossing Van Buren Street, he congratulated himself on his luck. He had over six bucks now and the whole day in which to spend it. He looked behind him. They might follow him. No, he couldn't see them. He ran down Clark Street anyway, just not to take any chances.

III

Bill felt unsteady for a moment after he came out of the show on South State Street. He felt funny. The man next to him grabbing at his pants that way. He knew that kids at school tried to stick their hands up under a girl's dress, and he tried it on Polack Mary once, and she had nearly scratched him for doing it. But she let Big Ears Delaney put his hand under her dress, and the other kids said that she and Big Ears had taken off all their clothes together in the cellar of an empty house at Twenty-fourth Street. But he couldn't see why a man should try and do that to a kid. It had sent shivers running up and down his back. He stood at the curb edge, watching the traffic pass. He turned away from the curb. If he stood there, it would be just his luck for Pa to drive past. He stuck his hands in his pockets and ambled slowly along. He thought of the women he had seen in the show without a lot of clothes on. He had seen their legs, and he could tell that their boobies were bouncing when they danced. He wanted to see all the women in all the world without a stitch on, just as he was sometimes lucky enough to see Aunt Margaret at Mother's. He wanted to see their tits, and the hair under the bellies, and their belly buttons. He saw Mama's tits, but they were big, and she fed the baby with them, and he was not interested in seeing them the way he was in seeing Aunt Margaret's. And when Mama gave Little Margaret a bath in the washtub out in the kitchen, he saw Little Margaret, but she was too little to have anything to see. Gee, too, didn't he wish that he was able to! He had tried to find out if he was, and his arms had just gotten tired, and nothing had happened, the way some of the kids said something happened when you tried that stunt. But he would be able to. He was getting a little bit of hair now. And there were places called whorehouses where men went and paid money, and women let them, and the men saw and did everything. If he was only able and could find a place like that to go to today when he had money.

Another express wagon. He guessed he better hug the inside of the sidewalk.

But when he was able to, he'd cop some money off Aunt Margaret or Mother and go to one of those places they called whorehouses and find out. He looked at a woman coming toward him. Her titties did not shake as much as those of the girls who danced in the show. But on the street women wore corsets. Aunt Margaret had corsets, and sometimes she had her corset on, but no dress, only that, and stockings, and he could see her legs. Mama didn't wear corsets.

He noticed a penny arcade, and stepped in, because he could see slides and moving pictures of girls taking their clothes off, and diving, and swimming. He stopped at the counter in front and bought hot dogs and root beer. He got a bellyache, and went back to change a dollar and look at everything he could see. He noticed the shooting gallery in the back. He walked to it first. Since he was going to be the greatest crook that ever lived, he had to know how to shoot. He picked up a revolver, fondled it, wanted to own it, thought that it was the most beautiful thing in the world, and thought that he wanted a gun like this one more than he wanted anything else in the world. He wondered, could he get away with stealing the silver twenty-two that Uncle Al kept in his closet?

IV

It was getting on toward four o'clock and there was a slightly chilly wind when Bill came out of the store, carrying the flashlight. And since he hadn't been able to cop it, well, it was worth the buck he had spent for it. Now if he only had a pearl-handled pistol, then his tools would be nearly complete, unless he wanted to go in for safe-cracking. He touched the flashlight as if it were a delicate object. He looked at its black frame. He lit it, but it wouldn't show any light until it was lit in the dark. He unscrewed the top, and the small bulb, looked at them, put them back in place. He opened the bottom, and took the batteries out for examination, then put them back. He couldn't wait until it was dark, so he could play with it and the light would be bright. But when Pa and Ma asked him how he got it, what story could he tell them? Better not say he found it. Not with Pa. Pa wasn't easy to fool like Mama and Mother were. He'd say he won it in manual training at school for his work. That would make Pa proud of him.

He shoved the flashlight in his back pocket, and it bulged, bulged as much as if it were a gun. He walked along State Street, trying to make up his mind whether to stay down a little longer or else go out around home and get in the fight with the niggers. He looked at his money, only a dollar left. He had spent a lot of money today, and he had eaten too much. But he wasn't sorry. Only, he had to figure a way of getting some more money now. He took out a box of Murad cigarettes. The clerk in the cigar store had been dumb, and when he had said you got to have a note to get cigarettes when you're a minor, he told the clerk they were for his boss, and the clerk believed him. He opened the box, took out a cigarette, lit it. Ah, he felt like a king. There wasn't many kids who had his luck. None of the kids around La Salle Street did. They didn't smoke the cigarettes he smoked. They had to snipe butts on the street. He inhaled, thinking how much smarter, how much better off he was than kids like Big Ears Delaney. Maybe tomorrow if he saw Big Ears he'd give him a Murad. He could see Big Ears' eyes popping, and he could hear Big Ears asking did he get these off his uncle. He would be mysterious and not tell Big Ears where they came from. Let him guess. Hell, if time would only hurry up, so he would be a man and have all the money he wanted to spend on everything he wanted. But, gee . . . Uncle Al was coming his way, across the street. He turned, ran across State Street. A horse-and-wagon burst through the line of waiting traffic. Bill did not see it. He was knocked down, and run over, but when the wheel passed over his leg he gritted his teeth, closed his fists, dug his fingernails into his palms, so as not to yell. He lay, feeling as if his leg were crushed, numbed from the pain in it. But he wouldn't cry. Uncle Al might hear, and recognize his voice. Weak, his consciousness almost fading, he hid his head as the crowd gathered around. Uncle Al might be one of these people. A man was bending over him, asking him was he hurt, and what was his name? He weakly turned his head from the man. He moaned slightly.

"I'm hurt!" he sobbed.

He started to tell himself to be careful and hide his head so Uncle Al didn't see him if Uncle Al was in the crowd. He fainted.

V

Walking briskly down State Street, Al saw the crowd gathering in the street, heard a woman scream, and knew that it was an accident. Men scurried by him. He heard one man say that a kid had been run over by a wagon, and he heard another say that the driver was a foreigner and didn't stop with the traffic cop's whistle. A kid being run over made him think of Danny. It could happen to Danny. Perspiration broke on his brow at the thought of this possibility. He stopped in his tracks, frightened into a trance, seeing Danny in his mind, run over, killed. He shook himself. It hadn't happened yet. He would tell Mother and Peg to not let him play in the street. He would talk to Danny. And God would protect the little fellow. He was again aware of the crowd, the noise, the excitement in the street where the accident had occurred. He took a step to see for himself. He turned, kept on his way. He had an appointment with a buyer and he would just make it. It was wrong to be late for business engagements, even a minute late. A man should let nothing interfere with business. He walked briskly on to his appointment. Even if it would have wasted only a minute, a minute was time, and time was money. No one with whom he did business could say he was ever even a minute late, if he could help it.

16

I

"He was mad as a bull. And, Peg, your heart would have bled for the little fellow if you saw him crying in bed when I carried his supper into him. He was just like a frightened little rabbit," Mrs. O'Flaherty said as she and Margaret sat in the kitchen, vegetables on the stove filling the room with the odor of cooking food.

"Al has his nerve. Of course, he should have given Bill a talking-to, after the things Bill said to little Danny. But Willie-boy isn't to blame. It's his home environment. That place on La Salle Street is not a fit place to raise a dog in," Margaret said, puffing away at a cigarette.

"Praise be to God, my grandson Daniel doesn't have to live in it with the O'Neills, Peg. He's not an O'Neill. He's a Fox, and he takes after me own people. Sometimes when I do look at him, I think that he's the spittin' image of me own father."

"It's certainly grand, Mother, that we can give the little darling a decent home."

"Yes, but poor Lizz, she has a hard time of it, the poor thing."

"She doesn't have any harder a life than I do, working the way I have to at the hotel. Sometimes I think that my head is going to split wide open, I have such a headache. Those foreigners, the waiters, they keep coming at me with checks, and every one of them will cheat me if he gets a chance. They aren't even honest. And I have to balance, watch every penny, and keep making change like a machine. I have a job that is made for a machine, not for a young girl like me," Margaret said self-pityingly.

"And don't I know that you work hard, Peg," the mother said, filling her clay pipe, as Peg strode over to the stove and lifted the lid on the pot of boiling potatoes.

"This is going to be a wonderful supper, Mother," Peg exclaimed, turning from the stove, and then she added, thoughtfully, "No, Mother, I don't blame the boy. I accuse the mother. The only time that that poor consumptive Willie-boy ever sees what a decent home is like, and ever knows what it means to eat good healthy food, is when he comes up here. Lizz isn't a fit person to raise pigs, and I say that, Mother, even if she is my own flesh and blood," Margaret said, again sitting down.

"Ah, Peg, you say the truth," Mrs. O'Flaherty said after lighting her pipe.

"Many a woman is as poor as our Lizz. Because she is poor, that's no reason why she can't at least keep herself clean. Water costs nothing, and she could buy all the soap she needs, with the money she spends filling those poor little babes she has with that awful doughy cake and those indigestible sweet rolls she's always stuffing them with. When they grow up, they won't have a good tooth in their poor little heads, and their stomachs will be ruined, ruined. And she always has rags and papers all over the house. No, Mother, there is no earthly excuse for her, none whatsoever. She is just lazy and she's always gossiping with those dirty neighbor women in that old Irish, back-fence, old-fashioned way," Margaret said with mounting contempt.

"Sure, I couldn't be bothered listening to her like that. It's common, and it always makes me think of what me mother said, 'Don't show me bread in another man's window.' What she says to me goes in one ear and out the other."

"And that poor ruptured hard-working husband of hers. She gives him no home. She gives him no peace. What kind of a life can poor Jim have with her? I tell you, Mother, it's no wonder that the poor man takes a drink now and then. Any man would under such circumstances. What surprises me is that he isn't drunk all the time, having to put up with a woman like Lizz. And I say that, even if she is my own sister. She was always common. Remember when she was home with us, and she was working out as a servant with Mrs. Lynn on Drexel Boulevard? She came home every night filling us full of servant talk. Mother, I don't know how you and Father could have had children like Al and me, and a daughter like Lizz. My heart sometimes aches for those poor little ones she has. I wish I could take Little Margaret and keep her here, raise her like a girl should be raised." Again Margaret became self-pitying. "Raise her like I never was raised."

"A girl is too hard to raise," Mrs. O'Flaherty said curtly.

"How can that lovely innocent little child ever be anything, living under such a roof?" Margaret said in disgust.

"My Lizz means well. The poor thing!"

"I wonder what time that man is coming home. I wish that he would call up if he's going to be late. I don't know when to put on the meat," Margaret said with sudden petulance, getting up to pace back and forth across the kitchen.

"He'll be home soon. He's out working hard to keep a roof over his mother's head," Mrs. O'Flaherty said, a gleam in her eyes.

"Mother, Al is a wonderful boy, and I don't deny it. And he does work hard. He has get-up and go to him. He doesn't sleep all day like Ned used to when Ned was home. But he has the ugliest temper. When he loses it, I am sometimes afraid of him. Some day Mother, with that temper of his, Al is liable to kill some one."

"My Al, he wouldn't hurt a lamb. He just works hard, and he does worry about business. He has so many things on his mind, the poor boy."

"As far back as I can remember, he had his temper. He must have gotten it from Father. Father had a temper, too. Al was always dictatorial. When I was a poor little girl, half blind and needing glasses, and hardly able to walk after coming out of the County Hospital from diphtheria, he beat me. He beat me because of Lizz. I'll never forget that beating as long as I live. Not that I hold it against Al."

"Last night, he was so mad I was afraid he was going to hit the little fellow."

"If I ever catch him touching a hair of the boy's head! If I ever catch him! He'll never do it a second time. I'll have him put behind bars. I won't let him do to Daniel what he and Lizz did to me when I was a thin, half-starved little thing, half dead on my feet from diphtheria. I won't, Mother!"

"Peg, sure he loves the little fellow like a father. He would give his right arm for my grandson," Mrs. O'Flaherty said, contentedly puffing on her corncob.

II

"Peg, here he is. Put the meat on!" Mrs. O'Flaherty commanded as they heard Al coming in the front door.

"Hello, Al! We were waiting for you before we fried the steak," Peg called in to her brother as she arose and went to the stove and Al yelled a cheery hello out to them.

"Where's Dan?" he asked, coming into the kitchen coatless, smiling, and carrying a small bundle.

"Son! Son! Your uncle wants you," the grandmother shouted.

"Al, you shouldn't have been so mean to him last night. The poor child has been so sad all day. He didn't go out to play after school, and he just went about the house like he was heartbroken," Margaret said reprimandingly.

"I didn't want to, and I didn't do it for pleasure," Al replied apologetically. "It's just that he has to learn certain things, and if he doesn't learn them now, he never will. We want to bring the boy up like a gentleman is raised, not like Lizz and Jim are bringing up his brothers and sisters."

"I was just telling Mother that Lizz is the last person in the world that I would allow to raise a child," Peg said.

"Peg, between you and me and the lamppost, she and Jim better start doing something about Bill. If he grows up with the nature he has now, it's going to be Joliet or worse for him. And everybody get this straight. You too, Mother! He doesn't get inside of our door again. He's a bad influence on Danny. And he abused our hospitality and our courtesy by lying to us. Why, Peg, he stood before me last night and lied like a trooper. And, listen, wait until I see him! I'm going to put some sense into that head of his, even if I got to pound it in. Why, Peg, do you know that he denied ever telling any such thing to the little fellow," Al said, spelling out his last words because Danny had come into the kitchen. "But, hello there, Sport, how are you, and what did you do today?"

"I was studying my reader," Danny said, his ingenuousness impelling them all to smile tenderly upon him.

"Al! Al! My grandson is going to be the best scholar in the Sisters' school," the grandmother said.

"Here, I bought this for you. But brighten up, smile! . . . That's the way," Al said, rubbing Danny's curly brown hair with feigned roughness, handing him the package he had been holding.

"Let me open it for you and see what Uncle Al brought you, Brother," Peg said, reaching for the package.

"Nix, nix on the rush act!" Al said to Peg with mock gruffness, arresting her hand in mid-air. "It's for Sport here, and he's a little man and can open his own presents," Al said, not hearing Danny thanking him.

"Daniel, your uncle is so good to you. If you grow up to be as good a man as he is, you'll never break your poor old grandmother's heart," Mrs. O'Flaherty said while Al beamingly watched Danny open the package and pull out a red-and-white stocking cap and a pair of mittens which matched it.

"Oh, they're so cute, so sweet, Al. Try them on, Brother!" Margaret said.

"He'll be the most beautiful boy in school, wearing all the fine clothes his uncle buys him," the grandmother said while Danny put on the cap and mittens and stood to be looked at in the way that he knew he should. "He's such a pretty boy, Peg, isn't he, Al?"

"He looks so adorable," Peg said.

"He's a real Sport now, aren't you, Dan?" Al said, giving his nephew a light and playful touch on the chin with his left fist.

"Goodness, I have to turn the steak," Margaret said, going to the stove, turning over the sizzling meat.

"Uh huh! . . . Yes, sir!" Danny said to his uncle.

"Say, Dan, do you play in the street much?" Al asked gravely.

"I wasn't out today," Danny said guardedly.

"Al, he was such a darling good boy," Peg said sweetly.

"Well, don't play on the street. Play all you want to on the sidewalk, or in the back yard or the vacant lots. But don't play and run in the street. Stay off it. And when you cross the street, be sure and look carefully in all directions, and if anything is coming, wait, let it pass. Never run in front of an automobile or a wagon."

"Little Brother is so careful, Al," Peg said.

"A kid was run over by a wagon downtown on State Street. It made me think of Danny. We better train him to be cautious in crossing the streets. These days, there are more and more automobiles in use every day."

"Al, was the boy hurt? The poor child! What will the poor mother do?" exclaimed the grandmother.

"I don't know. I didn't see him, or the accident. I had to rush to keep a business appointment. But I heard people saying the kid's leg was broken, and that it was a foreigner driving the wagon that hit him."

"Oh, how terrible! Brother," Aunt Margaret said, wrapping her own hands over Danny's mittened ones. "Brother, before you cross the street, you must always watch to see that the road is clear."

"And if a policeman is on the street, have him take you across," Al said.

"And, Brother, promise your aunt that you'll never go across Grand Boulevard alone. There are too many automobiles on it now," Aunt Margaret said, and Danny promised with a nod of his head. She turned toward Al. "I always did believe that any mother worthy of the name wouldn't let her child go downtown alone with the streets so crowded. God, some of the mothers of this world should be put behind bars, behind bars!"

"Yes, Peg, a lot of parents are just plain fatheads. You know, it would be just like Lizz to have her kids hurt that way. But here, Sport, you run and put your presents away and wear them when it gets cold enough," Al said, and Danny instantly obeyed.

"Better be washing for supper. It's almost ready," Peg said.

"Right away, Peg! But, say, that food smells delicious," Al said, going to the bathroom.

III

"Peg, that was a lovely supper," Al said, leaning back in his chair, rubbing his hand across his belly.

"We worked hard cooking it, we did," the mother said, receiving an indulgent smile from her daughter.

"Sport, you get me a cigar. You'll find one in the outside pocket of my suit coat," Al said, and Danny slid off the chair and ran down the hall.

"I hate to think of him ever growing up. He's at such a lovely age now," Margaret said, smiling wanly.

"There's some that run away and forget all you ever done for them after they're raised. But if my grandson does that, I'll tan his backside inside out," Mrs. O'Flaherty said.

"Nobody's ever putting anything over on a wise doll like you, are they, Mother?" Al said affectionately.

"Al, for Mother, the sun never sets on you and Danny," Peg said.

"Maybe I never went to school, but I met the scholars," the mother said.

"Thanks, Sport," Al said, taking the cigar from Danny, cutting off the edge with his pearl-handled penknife, putting a match to it, puffing, while Danny watched him, wishing that he owned a knife with a pearl handle like Uncle Al's, and if he did, he would be very careful so that he wouldn't cut his finger.

"Peg, let's do the dishes. I want you to read me what they been doing in the newspapers," Mrs. O'Flaherty said, starting to stack the dishes.

"Mother just loves me to read her the murder stories in the papers. She eats it up," Peg said.

"Indeed I don't. What do I care about people that's killin' one another like pigs? Ah, if they had the fear of God in them, the way me mother in the old country put the fear of God in me, they wouldn't be killin' one another like pigs, and sinnin' like the animals that run in the bush. Indeed, I don't. I want you to read me the death notices to see if anyone I know from the old country has passed on," the mother said, and as she spoke the telephone rang.

"I'll answer it," Peg said, jumping up so fast that she nearly upset her chair, thinking to herself with unexpected hope that it might be Lorry phoning for her.

IV

"Mama! Mama! Here's my money man!" Little Margaret gleefully shouted, dropping her paper cut-outs and rushing to her father as he came in the house from work.

"And what are you?" Jim asked, lifting the girl up, kissing her, swinging her high over his head until she ooed and shrieked with delight.

"Papa's girl," she giggled, and Jim continued to hold her aloft.

Feeling Dennis and Little Robert clambering and clutching at his feet and legs, Jim proudly reflected that these children were his. He was their father. He was a man, and here was his family. And some day he was going to give his family a decent home. He set Little Margaret down and swung his two boys on his shoulders in succession, causing them likewise to shriek and giggle with joy. He went to the bedroom and, noticing his sleeping infant, he looked at it with awe and reverence as he dropped his coat and cap on a chair.

"Hello, Pa! OOH! Our Pa has come home! Our Pa has come home! Our Pa has come home! Our money man is back! Our money man is back! Our money man is back!" Lizz singsonged before him in the dining room, jigging with slopping old slippers, her decayed teeth sticking out of her smile like sores, the dirty rag under her chin almost falling off.

"How's the girl today?" Jim asked after he had perfunctorily kissed his wife.

"Oh, Jim, my bones ache, and I have so much to do around here. I hardly have time to sit down and drink a cup of tea. And I'm almost never free to pay a visit to the Blessed Sacrament as every Catholic woman should do. I tell you, Jim, I'll be glad when we have this regiment raised. And my teeth ache so! It seems to me that with all the money the O'Flahertys got, they could help us some more than they do."

"They haven't got any money. And even if they did, I wouldn't be beholden to them, or to any man. I tell you, Lizz, old girl, we've gone this far. We'll manage somehow to go the rest of the way," Jim said, his voice softening as he concluded his remarks.

"Supper will be ready very soon. The baby was crying and I had to change her diapers, and I couldn't start on it early enough," Lizz said.

"No hurry. But say, where's Bill?"

"He didn't come home from school. He must have gone to the O'Flahertys."

"Why did you let him?" Jim asked, nettled.

"I didn't. He didn't come home. He must have gone there straight from school."

"Goddamn it, I told you I don't want him going up to the O'Flahertys all the time! If his family and his own home ain't good enough for him, well, by the living Christ, I'll soon make it so!"

"Jim, his brother Danny loves to see him and cries for him."

"And you say he didn't come home from school to find out if you wanted him to do anything for you?"

"Maybe my mother had something she wanted him to do, and he forgot to tell me when he went to school this morning."

"She did? Well, let me say that she had her goddamn nerve. Having things for my kid to do. Well, tell her to hire a nigger to do them! I'm going to call them up and give them a piece of my mind, and tell them to send Bill straight home. If it's the last thing I do on earth, I'll see to it that he stays out of that house! They're spoiling one of my kids. Well, they ain't going to spoil another!"

"Jim, please don't! Al's home, and I don't want you fighting with my relations.

I don't fight with yours. And I'll have supper ready in a second. It'll get cold if you go out to telephone. Please, Jim!"

He pushed her entreating arm aside and rushed to the bedroom for his coat and cap. He bolted out of the house and went snarling over to Wentworth Avenue. A fellow passing him said hello, but he didn't even hear the greeting. Goddamn the O'Flahertys! Goddamn all aunts, and uncles, and brothers-in-law, and sisters-in-law, and mothers-in-law! Goddamn all relations! And he was through just telling Bill to stay away from them. When Bill got home, he'd blister some obedience and respect for his home on Bill's ass! He crashed into Green's drugstore at Twenty-fifth and Wentworth, and he jammed into the telephone booth as if he wanted to knock it to smithereens.

V

"Hello!" Margaret called into the mouthpiece, her body as taut as a strung wire.

"This is Jim."

"What? Who? What number do you want?" she replied in a sinking voice when she recognized that it wasn't Lorry.

"Jim O'Neill! Who is this? Margaret?"

"Oh, hello, Jim! How are you? And how is Lizz? Is there anything wrong?"

"Is that Jim O'Neill? Tell him I want to speak to him," Al called from the dining room.

"Why, no, Jim, he isn't. He hasn't been here all day," she said.

"You say he wasn't?" Jim bellowed into the phone.

"Let me speak to him," Al said, standing tense by his sister's side.

"He didn't come home from school, and his mother thought that he'd gone up to your place."

"He must just be out playing, then. We haven't seen him since yesterday," Peg said.

"Well, I wonder where he can be?" Jim said, his anger evaporating into concern and confusion.

"Don't hang up on him," Al said, standing on tiptoes, scarcely able to contain himself while Margaret went on telling Jim again and again that Bill wasn't here, and that he must be out playing somewheres.

"Well, Jim, no news is good news," Margaret said.

"Let me speak to him!"

"And another thing I want to say is this! Don't be asking Bill up there to run errands, and be keeping him there. His mother needs him to help her around the house."

"But, Jim, we never ask him to raise a hand. And, of course, we're always glad to see him, but we don't force him to come here. And, of course, Jim, if you don't want him coming here, we won't have him. You're his father."

"We are, like hell, glad to see him," Al said under his breath.

"And I'm going to be his father," Jim said in a strained voice.

"Al!" Peg exclaimed, shocked and indignant as her brother grabbed the phone out of her hands.

"Hello, Jim! How are you?"

"Pretty good, Al, all things considered. I just called to see if Bill was there, but Margaret tells me he isn't."

"I wanted to talk to you about him, Jim."

"Five cents, please," the operator said, and Al heard Jim telling the operator just a minute, and then he faintly heard the click of a coin.

"Jim, aren't there things he can do to help Lizz around your house instead of coming up here so much?" Al said.

"I told him not to, and I told his mother not to let him, and not to be giving him carfare to go on."

"You know, Jim, it isn't that we begrudge anything that we can do for you and Lizz and the children. That's the last thought that would enter our heads. But he isn't good for Danny."

"What do you mean?" Jim asked, partially controlling his anger and at the same time thinking how he would like to have his hands around the neck of that sawed-off dude salesman this very minute.

"It's hard to speak about over the telephone," Al said, striving to keep his temper under control.

"Bill's his own brother. He ought to be better company for the boy than a lot of kids that come from dude homes," Jim said heatedly.

"Just a minute, Jim! Just a minute! Don't lose your temper."

"I'm not. But it's a funny thing for an uncle to say to a father about his two kids."

"Don't fight with him, Al! Please! He's got an awful disposition, and he's beneath you."

"Now, Jim, if you'll hold your horses a minute, I'll tell you, though it's a little bit of a ticklish subject to bring up over the telephone."

"I'm holding them!" Jim said, choking with resentment and humiliation, realizing that if he wasn't a miserable pauper Danny would not be with them, and he wouldn't be having to have this shoved down his throat.

"Well, you see, Jim, it seems that Bill told things to Danny that he oughtn't to know, things about . . . babies . . . how you and Lizz have them."

"When? What do you mean?"

"The Facts of Life. He told the boy about the Facts of Life, and Danny went to Mother and Peg and asked them questions. You know, the kid here, Jim, is too young to have his head filled with . . . with the Facts of Life," Al said, embarrassed.

"Why, I'll break his neck!" Jim said, turning pale in the telephone booth, suffering suddenly from a complex of shame and humiliation, the realization that his kids were aware of him and Lizz, and the realization that Al had indirectly referred to him and Lizz in bed, coupled with self-disgust because he was a man, with a man's desires for his woman.

"He ought to be taken in hand, Jim," Al said after a pause.

"Listen, Al," Jim sputtered. "I don't mean no hard feelings, and I ain't got nothing against you. But I'm the boy's father. And I don't need to be told how to raise him. I'm the only one who is ever going to take him in hand. And I'm able to do it!"

"Jim, please, please don't misunderstand me. I'm not trying to tell you how to raise your kids. All I'm saying is that we don't want Bill coming up here so much."

"You won't be bothered with him any more. If I learn of his going up there, I'll break his neck!"

"It isn't that we don't like him. We do. We give him spending money, and we treat him fine. It's just that he feeds Danny the wrong kind of talk. And when he has to go to the bathroom, he takes Danny in with him and locks the door."

"What do you mean?"

"I don't mean that there's anything in it, except that it just isn't right for the little fellow."

"Lots of things aren't right for him. I'll say that much."

"And yesterday, when I came home, Bill was here, and I tried to talk with him about what he had told Danny, and he lied right to my face and ran out of the house."

"When was this?"

"Yesterday, just before supper."

"Didn't he have supper at your house?"

"No. He ran out after lying to my face."

Jim was too ashamed to say more. He blamed Lizz with her goddamn O'Flaherty blood. Once an O'Flaherty, always an O'Flaherty, he guessed.

"You can understand, Jim, it isn't that we don't want him, or . ."

"I know. Thanks, Al," Jim curtly interrupted.

"And Jim, old man, I don't want you to have any hard feelings about this."

"I won't!" Jim said, almost swallowing his own words.

"We'd like to see you and Lizz soon."

"I'm busy. I'm a workingman."

"Well, give our love to Lizz."

"Say, let me speak to Danny a minute before I hang up!"

He waited while they called Danny. He heard them talking to him, heard Danny asking what would he say.

"Hello, Papa?"

"Hello, Boy! How are you, and when are you going to see your Papa?"

"Papa, I'm learning to read and write."

"That's good," Jim said, tears almost welling up in his eyes.

"And Uncle Al bought me a new cap and pair of mittens today."

Jim could still hear the O'Flahertys coaching his son on what to say. He couldn't talk to the boy now.

"You be a good boy, and your father and mother will see you soon."

"Yes, Papa."

"Goodbye, Boy!"

"Goodbye, Papa."

Jim walked slowly out of the drugstore. He stopped in front of the saloon opposite it. He stood there, hesitant. He walked on, still slowly. He didn't care what they said, Bill was a decent kid, and he would turn out better than Danny if his goddamn mother didn't ruin him. But why should Bill have lied and said he had eaten supper there last night? Where did he eat? Hell, he didn't give a good goddamn! Wait till he came home! He was going to pound some truth into Bill. He took out a plug of tobacco, bit on it, started chewing, spat it out.

VI

"Al, did something happen to Willie-boy?" Peg asked as they went back to the dining room.

"If I could get my hands on your Willie-boy, something would happen to him," Al said.

"What did Jim say?" she asked with increasing curiosity.

"He didn't like what I told him, and he went on saying that he was Bill's father, and he would take care of Bill. Well, Jesus Christ, then why doesn't he? All that I wanted to tell him was to keep Bill away from here, and to watch Bill for Bill's own good. And he gets sore. You know, Peg, Jim is crude. You have to be exceedingly diplomatic with him. He flies off the handle at the least provocation," Al said.

"Al, it's no skin off your backside. Let the O'Neills stew in their own juice," the mother said.

"Who's he that he has any right to get on a high horse?" Margaret haughtily asked.

"Them what has to 'umble must 'umble," the mother said.

"A common ordinary teamster who can't even support the kids he brought into this world with his own pleasure!"

"Be careful, Peg!" Al said, touching her wrist, winking in Danny's direction.

"Him with his pride, when he is only an ordinary teamster, and he has his kids in rags, and we often got to scrape and sacrifice ourselves so they don't go hungry," Margaret sneered.

"He can't help that, I guess. He had no education," Al said.

"What education did I have? Or you? We both went to work at an age when other kids were in school. But are we like Jim?"

"You know, Peg, Jim has no innate refinement," Al said.

"Them what has to 'umble must 'umble," the mother repeated.

"Jesus! The day that I saw Lizz bringing that lanky, buck-toothed gawk home, I asked myself, was *this* the best she could get?" Margaret said contemptuously.

"He doesn't have an innate refinement. You have to be very diplomatic with him or else he flies off the handle. I don't like people who are that way," Al said.

"Don't fight with him, Al. He's beneath you," Peg said.

"Al, when you see him, fist him! Fist him good! If you can't, I'll hire the butcher to. I'll give him five dollars to blacken both Jim O'Neill's eyes," the grandmother said.

"But, Al, what happened to Bill? What do you think?"

"Sure, he's runnin' the prairie somewheres," said the mother.

"Do you think the police locked him up for stealing or something?" Peg asked.

"If they didn't this time, they will sooner or later unless Jim takes him in hand pretty damn quick."

"You know, Al, I don't trust that boy. And I think he has consumption, too. He looks consumptive. That's why I don't want him coming up here and playing with Danny so much," Peg said.

"All he's got is too damn much nerve for one his age," Al said.

VII

"He hasn't been there all day. Where is he?" Jim asked Lizz, pointing his finger accusingly at her.

"Jesus, Mary, and Joseph, how should I know?"

"You're his mother!"

"Yes, I'm his mother. I suffered in the valley of the shadow of death bringing him into the world, bringing all your kids into this shitpot of a home you give them. And you are the boy's father. You owe a responsibility to God for the boy. If anything happens to him, the finger of God's guilt will point at you, not at his poor sick mother," Lizz said in semi-hysteria.

"I work damn hard, and damn long hours every day to put some food into their mouths. The least you could do is to know where your kids are!"

"Mama, I'm hungry. I want to eat," Little Margaret said, pulling at her mother's skirt.

"Look what time it is! And the babies have to come crying for their supper."

"Supper would have been on the table if you didn't go running out of here to insult my people, my people who are raising a child you can't support. They go without themselves to keep one of your offspring," Lizz said sarcastically, jigging as she spoke.

"Well, the little boy isn't staying with your family any longer. He's coming here to take the same pot luck that his brothers and sisters take."

"You pauper, you can't feed him! And if you take him, my mother'll stick a knife in your back."

"I'll spit on every goddamn relation you got . . . Yes, and I'll make them like it, too!"

"I'm hungry," Dennis moaned.

"Give them their supper!" Jim said.

"You ain't a cripple!"

"And if you were a mother, and had raised Bill right, we wouldn't be wondering where in God's name he was this very minute," Jim said, his voice strained.

"If you'll stay home and change stinking diapers, I'll go out and work. I'll scrub floors for my babies! Oh, good Jesus, Mary, and Joseph, why, why didn't I go into the convent?"

"I wish to Christ I knew why," Jim said, slumping into a chair.

"I didn't, because I listened to all the honeyed words you fed me. You and your promises! Look at them all around here now, in all this shit! You telling me what we would have, what we would do, and how you couldn't live without me. And me, innocent virgin that I was, I believed you. Oh, why was I such a fool?"

"Well, Lizz, you ain't the only fool there's been in this world. Don't you know that poem?

> *A fool there was, and he made his prayer,*
> *To a rag, a bone, and a hank of hair."*

"Say, what the hell do you think you are, a gold brick?"

"Oh, for Christ sake, shut up! You give me a headache!" Jim said, stepping toward her with clenched fists.

"Hit me! Hit me. And I'll leave you. I have a mother to go to."

Jim winced, turned aside. He saw the children huddled together, sobbing. He couldn't realize that these poor little beggars were his, that they had come out of his groins, and they were his flesh and blood. Suddenly, they seemed like another man's, like orphans. And Bill? Where was he? He went to the kitchen, took the supper off the stove, started bringing it into the dining room. The children watched him with tearful, frightened gazes.

"And so this, this is the payment I get for taking care of your home and your stinking kids," Lizz sneered.

"I suppose they ain't yours?"

"I didn't want them. I was a virgin."

"I wish to Jesus I knew what you ever do want."

"All I wanted was to serve and honor the Man Above. I would have been a Poor Clare doing God's work for the poor, only for you."

"You couldn't have gotten into a convent. They make the nuns wash their faces," Jim said, returning to the kitchen for plates. "Come on, for Christ sake, turn off the faucet," he said, seeing her in tears as he came back to the dining room.

"In the name of the Father, and of the Son, and of the Holy Ghost!" she exclaimed, blessing herself and dropping to her knees.

"Go ahead and pray like a hypocrite. A hell of a lot of good such prayers do."

"How dare you blaspheme!" she yelled, jumping to her feet.

"Why in hell don't you stop neighing like a goddamn horse?"

"Ah, God will punish you! God will punish you!"

"If I could afford it, I'd buy a phonograph. I'd rather hear it than you."

"Hail, Mary, full of grace, the Lord is with Thee," Lizz began intoning.

"Come on, you kids, here's your supper. Your mother is too busy praying to eat hers," Jim said, and the cowed children came slowly to the table.

Dishing out food for them, Jim cast a look of disgust at his wife. Just then there was a rap on the door. He rushed to answer it, opened the door without asking who it was.

"Mr. O'Neill?" a huge policeman asked.

"Why, yes, Officer! Come in!" Jim said, a lump rising in his throat.

"Oh, Officer, what is the matter?" Lizz asked, rushing forward.

"What's the trouble, Officer?" Jim asked.

"Officer, do you know my mother's first cousin, Sergeant O'Leary at Grand Crossing station? He's my mother's first cousin, and his people come from Mullingar in County Westmeath?"

"Why, no, mam, I don't. Mr. O'Neill, have you a son named William O'Neill?"

"Yes," Jim gasped.

"Officer, he's such a good boy. He never did a bad thing in his life. Why, he wouldn't even steal a pin," Lizz said.

"He hasn't done anything wrong," the policeman said.

"What happened, Officer?" Jim asked, almost dizzy with suspense.

"He had a little accident. He was run over by a wagon in the Loop, and his leg is broken . . ."

"Jesus Mary and Joseph!" Lizz exclaimed, flinging her arms in the air, fainting in a heap on the floor.

They lifted her onto the couch. Jim ran to the kitchen for water. Bill! His favorite son! And where would the money come from? Wouldn't it ever let up on him? Jesus, what had he done to merit this calamity on top of everything else? He turned the faucet off, walked back to the parlor with a glass of water. The policeman was fanning her with a handkerchief.

SECTION TWO

1911

17

I

Margaret walked across the lobby of the Union Hotel, her day's work done. She was not so tired today, and she knew that she looked well in her new blue serge suit and her wide hat with the birds on it. She hadn't really been able to afford these, but she couldn't go around in rags. And all the other cashiers here, they had clothes, and so did all her girl friends. She couldn't let herself look like a pauper. But, God, she was getting nervous. When was she going to get some money from Lorry? When would he be back in town? She hadn't seen him in months. Oh, God, she ached for him. But he ought to be here soon. Even if she was worried about her cashbox, well, everything would happen for the best. Last night she had sent a dollar to the Poor Clares in a letter asking them to pray for her special intention. God would heed the prayers of the good nuns, and He would not have the auditor check on her until she put back that money she'd borrowed from her cashbox. She was sure that God would not let her down, after all the good she did for her family, for Lizz and the kids, for everybody.

But just think of it! Who, seeing the skinny child that she was ten or twelve years ago, who would think that that skinny child would have grown up into this well-dressed, handsome, worldly girl that she now was as she walked across the hotel lobby, leaving a good job after her day's work? Who? Ah, strange were the ways of life! Who then would have said that while all the girls she knew would love and marry motormen, and teamsters, and piker salesmen and clerks, she would get a millionaire as her lover, a man as fine, as brainy, as handsome as her Lorry Robinson was? Ah, yes, strange were the ways of life!

But she did hope that God would answer the prayers the Poor Clares would say for her. She did hope that He would see to it that Lorry would be in Chicago soon, and that he would give her the money she needed.

She stopped. There was Brophy, sitting comfortably in a chair by the door near the edge of the lobby. Should she go out the other entrance? No, she wouldn't! She wasn't afraid of him, she told herself, while her hatred for the man flared like a hot fire inside of her. She would walk right past him. The little rat! The little teacup imitation of a man! Oh, there was no word contemptible enough to describe him! Oh, that she were a man for five minutes that she might hit him! She would walk right by him, her head flung high, wearing her new hat and suit that were so becoming. She would walk right by him, a handsome woman that he could never have, and yes, after she passed, she would shove her ass out at him to let the runt know what she thought of him.

She could tell, too, that he had seen her. His eyes were on her. Good! Now she would walk right by him as if he were such an insignificant little thing that she did not even know that he existed. He was getting up. It was gratifying to her to realize that he was not as tall, not as handsome a man as her Lorry. He was just a little runt that Lorry could break with one hand. Why, he even looked a little bit dried up, and she wouldn't be surprised if there was nothing at all in his pants. Oh, wouldn't it be wonderful to have Lorry ruin him, destroy him, take away every penny he owned. Why, this little crooked lying runt saying on the witness stand in Washington that her Lorry was a blackmailer! Oh, wouldn't she love to spit in his eye! Oh, wouldn't she love to cut the nuts right off him! Wouldn't she!

He was standing up. She was passing him. He was in back of her, and she would bet that those rat eyes of his were just trying to ferret holes in her back. She brushed through the doorway, smiling to Alex, the doorman.

"You seem to be in a very great hurry, my young lady," Brophy said to her outside the hotel.

She stopped, pretending surprise, but she felt that she had really expected this to happen, even though the thought of it had not dawned upon her. It was something that she had known was going to happen without knowing it.

"I have things to do," she said decisively, meeting his gaze unflinchingly.

"I imagined you did from the way you went out of the hotel. Miss O'Flaherty, if you only knew how very charming you looked walking through the lobby as if you had a grudge against all the world! The only thing that I could compare you to was to a fine racehorse. It occurred to me that I could well understand why, say, a man I would know in my business, I'm in the lumber business, you know, but as I say, a man I know in my business would find you to be a deucedly interesting young woman."

"What do you mean? I'm not accustomed to being insulted on the street by strange men."

"I'm complimenting you, my dear and flighty girl. And really, are we strangers after all the checks of mine that you have o.k'd?"

"Mr. Brophy, what do you want?"

"Well, if you're in such a hurry, it might be meaningless for me to want anything."

"I am in a hurry."

"But on the contrary, if you were not in such a hurry, why, you might be very interested in what I want. Of course, if you are in too great a hurry, you might just dash away from something that might be to our mutual advantage."

"Mr. Brophy, I don't like beating around the bush. What are you talking about?"

"Now, Miss O'Flaherty, you are talking like the sensible girl that I've always believed you to be. Only we can't very well talk here. You know we might be disrupting the, ah, pedestrian traffic. As you know, we in Chicago are having a deuce of a time with our traffic problem. In fact, I'm on a committee to study it."

"I know what you want to talk about. I don't know a thing about it."

"But, Miss O'Flaherty, let's be logical. Now if you know what I want to talk about, why do you say that you know nothing about it?"

"Because you think you can get something out of me."

"Please! Please, my dear girl! I don't want to get something out of you. I pay for anything I get. And perhaps I might be giving you something, so that it might even develop that you are doing more of the getting than I am. You never can tell, particularly when one is dealing with a young woman as smart and as handsome as you are, if you will permit me to talk in such terms of . . . of familiarity."

"Well, what is it? Spit it out!"

"Now, Miss O'Flaherty, if you have the time, we can stop some place for a cup of tea, and we can talk. You know, since my last trip to England, I find myself sometimes liking tea in the afternoon."

"I haven't much time."

"Perhaps we could stop at the Shrifton for a moment."

"Come on!"

She strode along, and the few inches of added height she had over Brophy showed more plainly as they walked. Several men were walking together side by side, blocking the sidewalk, and since they did not split to let Margaret and Brophy through, Brophy took her arm to lead her around them. She drew in. He looked at her, annoyed. He shrugged his shoulders, smiled at some inward thought. She was thinking that she would let him talk, and then she would tell everything to Lorry. It would show Lorry how much she loved him, how much she was ready to do for him. And she knew that this little runt would offer her money. She would throw it in his face. She would tell him to stick his tainted money up his ass-hole! She wouldn't betray her Lorry!

But she did need the money. Why, at work she trembled every time her boss, Mr. Harding, came up to her desk for fear that he was going to tell her that the auditor was around. And still with no word and not one cent from Lorry. If he was going to ignore her that way, she had a right to fend for herself and get money somehow. He ought to know that if she wrote him for money, she needed it. If he ignored her, it would serve him right if she dealt with Brophy. But no, no, never! She would go to jail first! She would lose her bond and be blacklisted from every hotel in the city before she would betray him. And then after that sacrifice, after she was disgraced, she would find peace, peace from all the troubles of this unhappy world in the cold waters of Lake Michigan. But even then Lorry might never never know what she had done for him, how much she had loved him, how much of her heart, and her soul, and her body she had given to him.

A smile supplanted the look of a tragic heroine which had accompanied these thoughts. All was not yet lost! She had not been audited yet. And she might worm some money out of Brophy without telling him a thing. But God was witness to her vow that she would starve, die in gutters, go in rags before she would ever be a Judas and betray the man she loved.

II

"Are you sure that you don't want to change your mind, Miss O'Flaherty, and have a drink?" Brophy graciously asked as they sat at a table in a corner of the Blue Room of the Shrifton Hotel, while a string orchestra gently played *The Rosary*.

"I never drink, Mr. Brophy," she said, cockily telling herself that she was up to his game, that she knew he wanted to try and get her drunk and then worm things out of her. Well, she would show this funny little fox a thing or two. She smiled genially and said, "Maybe you would like a drink. I don't object to your drinking."

"No, thanks, I never touch it. Not during the day, at least. Once in a while I take a cocktail in the evening. But, Miss O'Flaherty, it occurs to me that I have known you for several years."

"Well, I should think you would. You've been coming into the hotel ever since I started working there, and I have handled a number of your checks and vouchers."

"I use the hotel a great deal."

"I know it. Sometimes you telephone from there," she said.

"Yes, but never on the kind of business that I have been publically accused of. But that's neither here or there. I have lots of business engagements at your hotel, and I have to take a number of men to lunch. Sometimes, of course, I have to see lumber men there. In fact, I have sometimes heard associates of mine in the lumber business speak of you," he said, purringly soft and overly gracious.

"Of course, lumber men often stop at the hotel, and I handle their checks and vouchers the same as I do yours."

"One of my associates who has sometimes mentioned you is Lorry Robinson."

"He stays at the hotel often. He is a very nice man."

"He and I are stockholders in the same company out in Minnesota."

"A lot of his checks are drawn on Minnesota banks."

"I don't see Lorry as much as I used to, even though we are partners in the same company. But there was a time when I saw a great deal more of him, and he used to tell me, if I remember correctly, that you were rather interested in him, and that you called him up a lot. Now you must forgive me, Miss O'Flaherty, if I am wrong, because I am not expressing my own opinion, but I remember him giving me the impression that he felt you were chasing him."

"He did not! He absolutely did not!"

"Well, perhaps I was wrong. Maybe, Miss O'Flaherty, you know Lorry Robinson better than I know him," Brophy said, smiling and suavely lifting a teacup as he spoke.

Margaret suppressed the contempt for Brophy that welled within her. She felt her body growing tight. She wanted to scream, to scratch Brophy's eyes out, to run away. And through her mind a sentence ran like a refrain.

Play the game! Play the game!

"Let's be frank with each other, Miss O'Flaherty," Brophy said, leaning across the table, becoming crisp and businesslike.

"Yes, Mr. Brophy!" she answered with false cordiality.

"You have been reading the papers. You know about the Graham senatorial investigation. I have been given some notoriety in it. I am perfectly innocent. I am being blackmailed by my enemies."

"Oh, are you? I read things in the papers. In fact, my hotel has been mentioned in them. A telephone call or something you were supposed to have made from Mr. Robinson's room."

"Do you know the testimony I presented in Washington proving that I am being blackmailed by Lorry Robinson?"

"Why, I didn't know that," she said innocently.

The sonofabitch! The sonofabitch! she kept thinking to herself.

"I might tell you, Miss O'Flaherty, that Lorry Robinson is not big enough, not smart enough, not powerful enough really to whip me by blackmail and perjury. He can't do it. And when he learns that he can't do it, he is going to pay dearly for that lesson," Brophy continued, causing fright and worry to streak through

Margaret's mind, but she only revealed her emotions by a slight wrinkling of her brows.

"Of course, Mr. Brophy, I've always known that you were a very rich and influential man of affairs."

"I'm going to talk point-blank to you, Miss O'Flaherty. If you string along with Lorry, you'll be riding a dead horse. He is already the loser in this unfortunate affair, and he has failed to do what he set out to do. Far from driving me off the board of directors of the Crown Point Lumber Company, he is off the board and discredited among most of the stockholders. And he hasn't unloaded his stock on me at his price, either. And his testimony in Washington has been successfully refuted by my own, and by that of others. He overplayed his hand, and he is not, decidedly not, going to be the power in the lumber world that he thought he would be. I assure you that if you stick with him, you are sticking with a dead horse."

"I don't understand you. I'm only a hotel cashier."

"Yes, you do, Miss O'Flaherty. We understand each other quite clearly," he said incisively, and she grinned back at him.

"How are you going to do all this to Mr. Robinson?" she asked naively.

Brophy smiled at her, reached across the table, chucked her chin.

"You better be careful. If a private detective saw you doing that, it might be a scandal," she said, her words intended to cut like a knife.

"You're a very clever girl, Miss O'Flaherty," he said, unperturbed by her sharpness.

"Come on, Mr. Brophy, put your cards on the table!" she said with apparently sudden recklessness.

"I will if you will put yours down. Now, what would you like in the way of gifts and money?"

"I can't be bribed."

"Now, please don't speak of bribes."

"I'm sorry, Mr. Brophy. I didn't mean to touch a sore spot."

"Let's put the curtains aside and speak frankly. There is no use beating around the bush the fact that you and Lorry Robinson have been very . . . friendly."

"I won't admit anything."

"You know Mr. Robinson is married. You possibly have learned by now that he is the same treacherous person in personal relationships as he is in business. You are experienced enough in the ways of the world, I take it, to know something of the ways of a man with a maid," he said, and she listened, controlling herself when she wanted to scream, wanted to pound and kick and scratch him, because he was low, because he was taking advantage of her, because he could sit and say such things about her, about Lorry, as coldly as if he were saying that it was a nice day.

"Oh, yes! Oh, yes, I know something about men," she said, clenching her fists under the tablecloth, looking directly in his eyes as she spoke.

"Well, then, you should sense what fate awaits your friendship with Lorry Robinson. You don't think that some day you are going to be Mrs. Robinson, do you?"

"I don't think that that deals with what you and I came here to talk about," she said.

"Well, it does. Because, after all, what I want to talk to you about is to suggest something that is going to be to your own best interest."

"Oh, it is! Well, it is good for a girl to look out for her own interest. If I had all along in life, I would be much better off than I am now," Margaret said, lapsing into self-pity.

"That's the way I like to hear you talk!"

"Yes, Mr. Brophy, if you don't look after your own p's and q's, you are never going to get anywheres in this world."

"Right you are, my girl. And we can make some things out to our own interest."

"How?" Margaret said, anxiously thinking to herself how she might worm something out of this cold fish.

"Now, you probably know certain facts about Mr. Robinson, and you could tell me things which, in the possession of my lawyers, would be of great assistance to me in this case that is going on, this unfortunate investigation which my enemies are causing in the effort to blackmail and ruin me."

"Could I? What facts?"

"Well, facts about his personal life, and things that he might have told you about his business dealings and relationships. And when you see him, you could discover other things, his plans and the like."

"I don't even know where he is. Do you?" she said.

"No. I guess he is out west somewhere."

"What would you do with what I told you?" she quickly asked, thinking that Lorry mustn't have gotten her letter, because he was out in Oregon, and if he had, he would have sent her the money. He would be getting it any day, sending her the money. Oh, God, make it come, bring him back, before it was too late!

"It would be added to a great burden of proof which has already been accumulated by me, my associates and my lawyers as a necessity for clearing my name of charges against me that are totally unfounded."

"Who are your associates? I want to know what I am doing."

"My partners. Lorry knows them. And, my dear girl, I might as well tell you now, I can't be pumped."

"Your game is to pump me. You don't care what you would do, drag a decent girl's name into the mire, anything. I suppose that that is business," she said with heavy sarcasm.

"Please, please, Miss O'Flaherty! This isn't a game. This is a serious effort on my part to clear my name and my reputation of unproved accusations against me."

"I see. And you want me to become involved in muck as a betrayer."

"No, it isn't that. It is just that it might be to your interest, to your future, and to your profit to tell me things that you may know, and to find out further things that I may want to know."

"And?"

"You know, or if not, I shall tell you, Miss O'Flaherty, that this investigation is not going to drive me out of business. I may be of great use to you. I have watched you in your work, and I have spoken to Mr. Shevlin, the manager of the Union Hotel, and I know that you are a clever girl of extreme competence and ability. Now I might find something for you to do in one of my organizations that would provide you with a greater future than you have at the hotel where you cannot give full scope to your abilities as a young business woman," he said, and Margaret resented the intonation of his voice when he used the word *business*.

"And how much money do I get?"

"Well, that depends. You might get five hundred dollars and a better job than the one you now have."

"And that for spying on Mr. Robinson."

"Please, please, Miss O'Flaherty, don't allow yourself the luxury of using such unfortunate words."

"Well, I like to call a spade a spade. When do I get the money? Do I get it down now?"

"You would have to see my lawyers first."

"Mr. Brophy, you have had private detectives prying and sticking their nose into my private affairs, and you have done things to me that no decent self-respecting man would do to a girl. Having them following me around. Why, the very idea of it makes my stomach turn! What kind of a man are you? Have you no manhood in you to stoop to such depths?"

"Just a moment, girl! Don't be so rash; I have not had any private detectives following you. I may or may not have certain agencies acquiring certain information about my enemies, and they may or may not have found out that my enemies are men who lead double lives. But wherever there is smoke, my girl, there is fire."

"I wouldn't stoop so low! Not if it meant my life."

"Of course, that is a matter for you to decide at your own discretion. But I want to assure you again that you are going to be very unwise, very foolish, indeed, by being loyal to someone who can't win, and who, even if he does win, is not going to mean much to you."

"So you know a lot! Well, there is one thing I will tell you. I'll tell you something that Mr. Robinson did say. He said that you're a crook, and a lowdown dirty rat. I feel contaminated even sitting with you. You couldn't bribe me! You couldn't buy me, not with all your dirty money, all your banks, not with every dollar you own! So stick that in your pipe and smoke it. And what's further, if you drag my name through any mud, well, I will tell what you said to me today."

"Walls have no ears," he said, grinning as she arose and stamped out of the room in dudgeon. He shrugged his shoulders and followed her. Hastening out of the hotel, he saw a private detective picking up her trail. He smiled slyly.

18

I

"Well, strike me dead if it isn't my beautiful darling sister, Peg! I didn't know you were coming. I'm so glad to see you," Lizz said, pouncing on Peg as she let her in.

"How are you, Lizz darling?" Margaret said, submitting to an embrace and kiss from her unkempt sister.

"And you look like such a beautiful lady. Say, I wish the neighbors could see you. It would just kill them. Can I run out and get Mrs. Koffinger and Mrs. Bodenheimer? Why, they'll never get over the sight of you."

"Please don't. I'm nervous, and I don't want to see them," Peg said coldly.

"I just wanted to show you off. I want them to see what kind of a family I have," Lizz said, disappointed.

"Some other time. I'm nervous," Margaret said while Lizz dusted off the upholstered parlor chair for her to sit in.

"I'm glad to see you, Peg. I've been so sick, with my back aching me, and my neuralgia!" Lizz said.

"I know, you poor thing. I brought you this," Margaret said, handing a five-dollar bill to her sister.

"Oh, thanks, Peg, dear. I need it so badly. Dennis needs shoes, and I'll have a mass said for Father out of it."

"Don't be having masses said out of it. Use it on yourself and the children. The church and God don't expect those that haven't got to give," Margaret said impatiently.

"You're right. And the insurance man was here today. I have policies for Mother, and for all the children, and Jim and me. I just took one out for Catherine. They don't cost much, only about ten cents a week for each policy. But

I couldn't pay the man last week. I can now. It's so hard making ends meet. Jim does the best he can. He works long hard hours, the poor man, but he never makes over sixteen dollars a week, and by the time we buy food for the house, and pay the rent, and the insurance, and Jim pays his carfare to work, why, there isn't a penny left."

"How is Jim? He isn't drinking again, is he? He seemed very mean on the phone the other night, and I was afraid he and Al were going to fight."

"No, he took the pledge right after the little one was born, and he hasn't broken it. The poor man was just worried about Bill. Bill is his favorite. Peg, my Jim, he thinks the world of Al and Mother. And you! Why, Peg, he says to me, 'Lizz, nothing in the world is too good for your sister, Peg!' Oh, Peg, Jim just thinks the world of you," Lizz said, getting up from her chair, gesturing and hopping around gaily as she talked.

"How is Willie-boy? I was so sad to hear he had been hurt. And you know, Al was walking right down the street when he was run over, but he had an appointment and he hurried on and didn't look. If Al had seen Willie-boy just a few seconds before the accident, it might not have happened. And Mother, she's so broken up about it. She loves the ground that Willie-boy walks on. Next to Danny, he is her favorite."

"The poor boy, lying there alone in the hospital with his leg broken, and without his mother to take care of him," Lizz sighed.

"Doesn't he get good attention?"

"Yes, but there's no one to a child like his mother, no one in the whole wide world. And that will set him back a whole year in school. The sooner he graduates the sooner he can go to work and give his father a helping hand."

"I'm going to try and bring Mother and Brother to see him Sunday."

"Oh, my William will be so happy. Last night, he said to me, almost with tears in his eyes, 'Mama, Mama, I want you to bring my brother Dan to see me.' Oh, Peg, my William, he likes his brother Danny so much. But come and see your little niece, Catherine. She's asleep, but we can peek at her. I just got her to sleep. She has a cold and she was crying all morning. But she went to sleep like a lamb. I got the other children in the kitchen, and I told them to be quiet so they don't wake her up."

Lizz led Margaret to the bedroom, and they gazed down at the infant girl who slept, swaddled in old rags and blankets, her reddish face screwed up.

"Isn't she her mother's precious?" Lizz whispered, a coo in her voice.

"Lizz, all your children are such darlings!" Margaret said when they went to the kitchen.

"Hey, you kids, come and say hello to your beautiful auntie!" Lizz said.

"Oh, they are so sweet. You little dears," Margaret exclaimed, looking at them, bending down to kiss each child in succession.

"Look at your namesake! You never would have thought, when you stood up for her in baptism, that she would grow into such a fine girl as she is, would you, Peg?" Lizz said loudly, pointing at Little Margaret.

"She's a doll. And she's almost as big as Daniel," Margaret said.

"How is my son, Daniel?" Lizz asked, pronouncing the name possessively.

"He's such a sweet boy, Lizz. And Al adores him so! He brought him home the cutest little pair of mittens and the darlingest stocking cap the other night," Margaret said.

"Here now, you kids, run in the parlor and let your aunt and mother talk. But don't make any noise and wake your little sister up. She has a cold, and she has to sleep," Lizz said.

"Mama, can we have some cakes? We're hungry," Little Margaret coaxed, giving her mother a dirty-faced grin.

"Mother's precious, they'll make all of you sick."

"Gee!" Little Margaret exclaimed sadly; she sniffled.

"All right, here," Lizz said resignedly, taking three chocolate cupcakes from the breadbox, and handing them to the children while Margaret looked on in disgust.

"Peg, I just want to call Mrs. Bodenheimer over for a minute to have a cup of tea with us. I'd give my right arm to see the expression of envy on her face when she sees my sister, dressed like a lady," Lizz said.

"I'll have to be going right away," Margaret said icily.

"It'll just be a minute," Lizz said, ignoring her sister's lack of enthusiasm.

Lizz went out the kitchen door and stood on the ledge at the top of the steps.

"Mrs. Bodenheimer! Mrs. Bodenheimer! Mrs. Bodenheimer!" she yelled at the top of her lungs, and when there was no answer, she repeated this shout while scraggly children playing in the yards and alley looked up at her.

"My mother isn't in, Mrs. O'Neill," a seven-year-old child whose pants were falling down from under her dress yelled back from the back porch of a house five doors away.

"Where is she?" Lizz shrieked while Margaret disgustedly and nervously paced the kitchen.

"My mother isn't in," the little girl yelled a second time.

"When she comes in, honey, you tell her that she should come right over for a cup of tea. Tell her my sister is here. She has a new suit and hat on I wanted your mother to see. Tell her it's very stylish!" Lizz shrieked.

"Hey, don't maka so mucha noise. My wife she'sa sick," a grizzly-faced Italian cried up at Lizz from two doors distance.

"Tell her to come over as soon as she gets back," Lizz again shrieked.

"She's not in, Mrs. O'Neill," the little girl yelled, and the Negro woman who lived behind the O'Neills looked out the window at Lizz, grinning ironically.

"Hey, don't maka the noise. My wife, she'sa sick," the Italian cried,

"Go on, you foreigner! Go make a noise like a hoop and roll away, or I'll have my man put his fist through your nose," Lizz flung at him, returning to Margaret in the kitchen.

"She's not in. We'll have a cup of tea ourselves, Peg. But I would have given anything just to see her eyes when they lit on you," Lizz said as soon as she had recovered her breath.

"I don't want to see your neighbors," Margaret said.

"Oh, Peg, you would like Mrs. Bodenheimer. She's the loveliest woman. She is so nice. But her husband, he's a German. She tells me that he begrudges her a pinch of salt. He is always beating the children. Saving, miserly! If I had him for a husband, I'd break the sugar bowl over his head. But how is my mother? I have been wanting so much to go up and see her, and I just can't. And now with my oldest laying all alone in the hospital with his limb broken, I don't know how I'll be able to get out of the house. Jim or I go and see him almost every night."

"As soon as I get my hands on some money, I'll help you out, you poor thing. I'm expecting some."

"I'll light a holy candle, and I'll send a nickel to the Poor Clares in a letter and ask them to pray that you get it," Lizz said, throwing some sticks of wood in the stove and setting a kettle of water to boil.

"Lorry has some money tied up. As soon as he gets it free, he'll give me some, and I'll help you out."

"He must be a good man. It's a shame you couldn't bring him into the church."

"He's a wonderful man. He's better than many that are in it."

"I read in the papers that Jim brings home that they are picking on him. They're Republicans, Graham and Brophy. And my Jim says that a working man is a fool who votes for the Republicans. You never can trust them. Show me a man that's a Republican, and I'll show you a man that's as crooked as a corkscrew. Say, if you asked my Jim to vote for a Republican like that Graham, he'd blacken your eyes. Why, Jim says that he knew that Graham when he was only a streetcar conductor. And Brophy picking on a wonderful man like Mr. Robinson. Say, Peg, I knew Brophy when he was only a stinking little shyster on the West Side and he didn't have a shirt. He had to wear a sheet for a shirt," Lizz said while Peg sat, bored.

"He's crooked. He just waylaid me leaving work, and he tried to bribe me to tell him things on Lorry," Peg said.

"That pisspot stinker! Say, you let me see him. I'll tell him a thing or two, and when I get through with him, he'll not try to bribe you, and he'll never say boo again against a wonderful man like Mr. Robinson. Oh, I tell you, Peg, I know a thing or two about the shanty Irish like Brophy. His people ran a little lumber yard on Blue Island Avenue in Saint Ignatius parish when I was a girl. And he, the little pisspot, he used to go out in the alleys and pick up box wood to sell. Oh, you just let me see him, and I'll tell him! I'll say, 'Mr. Brophy, I know you. I knew you when you wore a sheet for a shirt and went around alleys picking up box wood that your father sold in his lumber yard. And your grandfather was a boozer, and he couldn't walk home on his own feet on Saturday night. He used to fall down in the gutters, and your mother used to give kids a penny for bring- ing him home. He was a boozer, and one Saturday night when he got drunk, he fell down and broke his leg, and he never walked again, and I used to see you rushing the can to Pete McCoy's saloon for him.' Oh, I know the Brophys," Lizz said, gesturing with her fat arms, grimacing, acting out her words, while Peg watched without interest. She bent down and touched Peg's hand. "Peg, I never knew a Brophy yet who was any good."

"That wasn't the same Brophy family," Margaret said.

"Oh, yes, it was. I know them well. So does Mother. You ask her about the time on Blue Island Avenue when our father had a fight with Brophy's grandfather. Pa nearly knocked Brophy's grandfather through a basement window. Pa said to him, 'You sonofabitch! You sonofabitch! Your people came from paupers in the old country, and you ought to go back! You sonofabitch! You greenhorn! If I ever lay sight of you again, I'll spread the nose on your face from one ear to the other.' And you ask Mother about the goat they kept in their back yard, and it used to eat all the clothes off Mother's washline. Say, I knew the Brophys, Peg, before you were born," Lizz said, having a good time, continuing to gesture, smiling with her decayed teeth sticking out, poking and nudging her sister as she spoke.

"No, Lizz, that's a different family. Brophy, the lumber man, comes from Minnesota."

"Well, these Brophys on Blue Island Avenue were cousins then. Yes, they were. They come from Cork, and the grandfather was driven out of Ireland for stealing a pig. But gracious, the water is boiling over," Lizz said, rushing to the stove.

She poured water on top of tea leaves that lay in an old enameled pot.

"As soon as it steeps, I'll give you a nice cup of tea to warm you after riding here on the cold street cars," Lizz said.

"Is Jim going to be able to get anything on Willie-boy's accident?" Margaret asked, getting up and beginning to pace the floor nervously.

"If we don't, my Jim will punch the dirty dago that run Bill over until he hasn't got a leg to stand on. I'll go down to his house on the West Side and move the furnishings right out. And if a copper stops me, I'll say, 'Officer, I'm a poor woman, and my husband is a hard-working man. This dirty dago ran my oldest boy over in the street and broke his leg, and he won't pay!' That's what I'll do. And I'll say, 'Officer, I'm a cousin of Sergeant O'Leary of the Grand Crossing station, and if you arrest me for taking what's my due, I'll have Sergeant O'Leary take that star off your coat.'" Lizz said, again enacting a role as she spoke.

She poured out tea in two thick cups, and set one before Margaret and the other before her own place. She shoved an opened can of thick condensed milk before Margaret, went to the bread box, and drew out stale sweet rolls. She sat down and bit into a roll.

"You should have Jim get a good lawyer to handle it," Margaret said, stirring her tea.

"Jim's cousin, Joe O'Reilley, is the best lawyer in the city, and he'll take care of it for Jim," Lizz boasted.

"I guess he is. Al thinks a lot of him. Joe O'Reilley isn't like that piker, Dinny."

"Oh, say, Margaret, Dinny is getting swell. They moved down around Garfield Boulevard and Indiana," Lizz said.

"Say, I wouldn't walk across the street to see that cheap cigar, Dinny Gorman," Margaret said disdainfully.

"Mae was down to see me. She came in sashaying around, her with her swell ways," Lizz said, making faces as she talked. "So I told her how swell my sister and my brother are, and how rich Al is, and how Ned has a good job and married a woman who owns the swellest millinery shop in Madison, Wisconsin."

"Lizz, Al isn't rich. He hasn't got a nickel in the world other than what he earns, and he can hardly make ends meet. Why, if I didn't help with every cent I earn, we wouldn't be able to keep our heads above water," Margaret said petulantly.

"But, Peg, I wouldn't for a minute let the Gormans think they were getting ahead of the O'Flahertys," Lizz said. "And you know, she was talking about her Dinny's law practice. Why, I felt like saying, 'Say, you, you with your dude husband! He's only an ambulance chaser. But my brothers, they're business men! Business men!' I tell you, Peg, the day'll never come when any of those steam-heat Irish can put anything over on me."

Margaret stood up, disgusted.

"Going, Sister darling?" Lizz asked.

"Yes, I want to go home and help Mother cook supper. Everything falls on my poor shoulders," Margaret said.

"Mrs. Bodenheimer will be chewing her fingernails that she missed you," Lizz said.

"Goodbye, Lizz. And as soon as I get some money, I'll help you and Jim out," Margaret said.

"Just a minute! Just a minute!" Lizz exclaimed.

She ran into her bedroom and returned quickly.

"Here's a medal of Saint Anthony," Lizz said, handing a small silvery medal to Margaret. "It's blessed. If Mother keeps this in her pocketbook, she'll never lose any money or anything. You tell her to take it with her wherever she goes, and every morning when she gets up, to say a prayer to Saint Anthony, and he'll guard her property. He's a powerful saint. I'll get Saint Anthony medals for you and Al, too, Peg."

Margaret dropped the medal in her pocketbook, said goodbye, and left.

II

Margaret had not gone five minutes before there was a knock on the door. Lizz, with the infant in her arms, dragged her feet to answer it. All of the children gathered around her. A burly, rough-faced man stood in the door. She screamed, and pushed to close the door, but he put a foot against it, preventing her.

"Mrs. O'Neill?"

The lady of the house isn't home. I'm just the nurse here. I'm minding the children for her. I don't know anything," Lizz said.

"If I could come in a moment, I could explain what I wanted," the man genially said.

"I'm alone with my children, a poor helpless woman. If you don't go away, I'll call the police. My man's cousin, Pat Dennison, is a plain clothes man, and he'll run you in. And my sister went to school with Judge Mahoney, and he'll send you up to Joliet if you harm an innocent woman like me."

"I have no intention of doing you any harm, Mrs. O'Neill."

"I'm not Mrs. O'Neill . . ."

The man flashed a star.

"Jesus Mary and Joseph, what's wrong now? Oh, my God, what's happened to my husband? Is he dead?" Lizz said. She turned to Little Margaret. "Sister, hold the baby, your mother is fainting."

"There's nothing wrong," the man said, catching Mrs. O'Neill before she fell. "I just want to ask you some questions."

"Come in. Officer, do you know my cousin, Sergeant . . ."

"I'm a private detective," the man interrupted.

"What do you want?"

"I'm working on a case, and I want to ask you some questions, Mrs. O'Neill."

"I'm the mother of six children, and my oldest boy is in the hospital with a broken leg. I never get out of the house. I can't answer your questions. I don't know the answers," Lizz said.

"I want to ask you some questions about your sister. If you can answer them it might be to your advantage."

"My sister is a handsome girl. She is a wonderful girl, and she's good to my mother. She is as pure and innocent as these little ones here," Lizz said, pointing to her children, who eyed the man with silent, half-frightened curiosity.

"Yes, I know that. She works in a hotel, doesn't she?"

"I never ask her where she works. I mind my own business."

"She's a cashier in the Union Hotel, isn't she?"

"When I die and go before the Throne of God Almighty, one sin that will never be black on my soul is the sin of not minding my own business," Lizz said histrionically.

"It might be to your interest and profit to answer my questions, Mrs. O'Neill."

"The minute I saw your face in the door, I knew that you came from the Devil. Go on back to him. That's where you belong."

"Please, now, Mrs. O'Neill. I want to ask you if you know anything, or ever heard your sister say anything, about a man she knows named Mr. L. R. Robinson."

"I never heard of him. I don't know him. The Republicans are trying to blackmail him because he's a Democrat. If you came from Brophy you go back to him, and tell him that his grandfather in the old country was a pauper and a dirty boozer, and that I knew him when he was a little stinking brat rushing the can along Blue Island Avenue for his boozing grandfather."

"Please, be sensible about this, Mrs. O'Neill," the man said when Lizz paused for breath. "If you know something about her friend and tell me, you won't go without a reward, and I am sure that what money you earn by simply answering my questions would be very useful to you," the detective said, glancing about the dirty house.

"Say, you, this is a decent home! And I got a ring to put on my finger, too! Don't you go hinting about my home. It's honorable, even if I am poor. And all the gold in the world wouldn't make me tell you things about my beautiful sister. Why, I haven't even seen her in months. I don't know anything about her, except that she is the finest girl that walks in this city."

"I know all about that," the man said, shrugging his shoulders and turning toward the door.

"Say, you devil, get out of my house or I'll split your head with the stove poker!" She turned to Dennis. "Dennis, go get your mother the stove poker!" She turned back toward the man. "Go on, get out, or I'll break your neck! If my man was home you wouldn't come here insulting the mother of six children and casting insults at my beautiful sister. My man will wring the neck off him who touches my sister's little finger. If he was here, you dirty gumshoe, he'd send you rolling down those stairs like a broken barrel!"

"Yes, mam!" the detective said, leaving.

Lizz slammed the door after him.

"In the name of the Father, and of the Son, and of the Holy Ghost!" she exclaimed, blessing herself.

She ran to the window, opened it, leaned out, and when she saw the detective coming out of the building, she shrieked, "You sonofabitch! You skunk! Go on, beat it before my man comes home and sweeps the street with you!"

The man walked on without looking up at her. Little Dennis pulled at his mother's skirts to hand her the stove poker, while she knelt with her head out the window, still screaming after the private detective.

19

I

The October Sunday afternoon was mild, almost balmy. Many people strolled slowly, draggingly, along Calumet Avenue, men with wives and families, parents pushing baby carriages, young blades and their girls. Margaret and Mrs. O'Flaherty walked toward the Fifty-first Street car line, with Danny between them, clutching their hands, dragging, straining almost like a dog on leash.

"Mother, now don't forget to watch for the mail while I am at work tomorrow. As soon as you hear the mailman ring, you go down and get the mail. I am expecting a very important letter," Margaret said.

"Never fear, Peg, never fear! I will."

"Mother, you look so elegant in Louise's black sealskin coat. And it fits you. You almost look like a chicken, and I'll have to watch you or mashers will be bothering you," Margaret said.

"I'll spit in their eye!" Mrs. O'Flaherty said, her small brown eyes flashing through her veil.

"I'll bet you were a belle in your day. You must have given Father plenty of cause for worry," Margaret said.

"We shouldn't be seen talking on the street this way on the Lord's Day. Only servants and common folk make free when they are out," Mrs. O'Flaherty said crisply, and Margaret looked over at her mother with twinkling eyes.

"Mother, why couldn't we get my Aunt Louise to come down from Heaven this afternoon and go see Bill with us? You ask God to let her come," Danny said, causing Margaret to smile sadly at him.

"Ah, the little fellow was the apple of my Louise's eye," Mrs. O'Flaherty said, the words sighing out of her mouth almost like a keening song.

"You liked your Aunt Louise, didn't you, Brother?" Margaret said.

"Uh huh!" Danny mumbled with a child's abstractedness.

"Bless my soul, but the boy is a care and a worry. Here I am raising grand-children after I raised all me own, and worked me hands to the bones for them and for Father," Mrs. O'Flaherty said.

"Oh, look at the man," Danny said, freeing his right hand from his grand-mother's grasp and pointing.

"He's just a man, Brother."

"Look at him. He's a funny man,"

"Peg, it's your fault that the boy is acting so common. He gets this from you."

"Why, Mother, you must have gotten out of the wrong side of the bed this morning."

"With such goings-on, the people will take us for greenhorns," the grand-mother said.

"If I saw a Blackhand now, I would be afraid. And I would run and hide. Mother, are you afraid of the black hands?" Danny asked.

"I'd tear them limb from limb!" the grandmother said.

"When I grow up to be a man, I'm going to make lots and lots of money, and I'm going to buy jewboxes for you, Mother, and one for you, Aunty Margaret," Danny said.

"I'll only ride in a carriage like the one me Uncle William had in the old country. It was drawn by a dozen horses, and when me Uncle William went to church in it with his coachman driving, all the men stood by the side of the road and took their hats off. I won't ride in anything else," Mrs. O'Flaherty said curtly while Margaret looked at her with open-mouthed wonder, and then broke into a knowing smile.

"Aunty Margaret, why are legs broken?" Danny asked.

"Because they are."

"But why?"

"It's the same as when you throw a ball through a window, the glass breaks. Well, if you twist the bones in your body, they break. The horse-and-wagon ran over your brother's leg and broke it."

"Why did God let the horse-and-wagon run over Bill's leg?"

"God didn't."

"Well, then, who did?"

"He didn't see where he was going, and he was knocked down by the horse and the wheels went over his leg. That's what you get for not being careful when you cross the street."

They stopped at Fifty-first Street and waited for a street car.

II

Danny sat between the two of them on a side seat at the front of the jangling Indiana Avenue street car. He looked at the picture up above on the other side of the car, where the man held a bottle in one hand and fed a little girl something black in a spoon with the other hand. The man didn't look like any man he ever saw, and the girl didn't look like Hortense Audrey.

"Aunty Margaret, what's that picture?" he asked, pointing.

"Sit still, Son!" the grandmother said.

"Indiana Avenue!" the conductor called through the car as it stopped.

"That's an advertisement, Brother."

"What's that?"

"When you have something you want to sell, and you are in business, you tell what you want to sell by putting an advertisement in the newspapers and the street cars."

"Is the man with the spoon selling something to the little girl?"

"No, it's just a picture to interest people in the advertisement," Aunt Margaret said as the street car swung around the curving tracks onto Indiana and proceeded northward.

"Be still, Son!" the grandmother said.

"Who is selling, then?" asked Danny.

"A company."

"What is the company selling?"

"Castoria, that you take when your tummy aches."

"I don't like Castoria. Why is the little girl being made to take it?"

"She must have got a tummy-ache from eating too much candy."

"Look at the man!" Danny yelled, drawing attention as he pointed at a tall man coming up the car aisle toward the front platform.

"Brother, I told you not to point," Aunt Margaret said, blushing as other passengers laughed and the man passed them, smiling, and pushing out to the front platform.

"Brother, it's not nice to point at people in public. They don't like you to," Aunt Margaret said.

"Why?"

"They think you're making fun of them."

"I wasn't making fun of the man."

"Maybe he thought you were."

"Gee! That's funny!" Danny said, laughing.

"Don't do it again, Brother."

"Forty-third, Root Street!" the conductor bawled into the car.

"When I grow up to be a man, can I point at anybody I want to in the street car?"

"Brother, it's never polite to point in public. A gentleman never does that."

"And am I a gentleman?"

"Yes, brother, you're a little gentleman."

"Mother, do they have gentlemen in Ireland?"

"Don't bother me. I'm English. I'm not Irish. I don't know that woman you are with," the grandmother said, and Margaret flashed anger at her mother; then she relaxed and smiled patiently.

Danny twisted about to look out through the window. He glued his nose to the glass. The car was going fast. There were houses, and people, and a boy, and girls jumping rope, three kids running around a lamppost, a policeman, a man as big as Papa, a nigger baby.

"Turn around and sit still, and don't get your face dirty against that window," Aunt Margaret said.

"I don't want to," Danny pouted.

"Do what you're told, or I'll never take you out in public again."

"I want to look out the window," Danny whined as his aunt gently pulled him around.

"Peg, watch the streets. We'll be gettin' off soon," Mrs. O'Flaherty commanded.

"I will, Mother," Aunt Margaret said wearily but with patience.

III

Margaret and Mrs. O'Flaherty greeted Bill effusively, kissed him, and set the basket of fruit, which they had bought near the hospital, on the stand beside his bed. Danny glanced curiously around the room, at the bed, the stand, the bedpan. He became fascinated with the bricks hanging from the foot of the bed.

"When I was in my cradle, me Uncle William, my father's brother, picked me up, and he said to me father and mother, 'This one will never have to live on dry potatoes like we had to.' I remember his words to this day, and I know the name of William is blessed. Anyone with the name of me father's brother, William, will never know a day's bad luck. Me Uncle William was the finest man that walked the face of this earth," Mrs. O'Flaherty said ebulliently.

Danny studied the bricks, his eyes still full of overweening curiosity. Funny, having bricks there. He took a step toward them.

"You poor boy, did it hurt? Did you cry when you were run over?"

"Naw," Bill said.

"You're such a brave boy. You darling, you must have suffered so," Margaret said, moved by the sight of his thin-cheeked, sallow face.

Danny couldn't see why they had bricks like that by Bill's bed. He took another step nearer them.

"He's not hurt, Peg. Sure, didn't me Uncle William break his leg in the old country when a tree fell on it in the Year of the Big Wind. And he was back in the fields with the men in a week. William, if you're like me Uncle William, you'll be runnin' in the bush with your brother again before you know it," the grandmother said.

"Willie-boy, your brother has been so lonesome for you. Haven't you, Brother?" Aunt Margaret said.

"Yes," Danny muttered vacantly, stepping closer to the bricks, his eyes glued to them.

"I guess I got to stay in this old bed a little while. But I didn't cry when I was run over, or when they set the leg. Catch me crying," Bill said with bravado.

Danny snatched at the bricks. Bill let out a loud, wild shriek. Margaret looked at Bill, frightened, and Mrs. O'Flaherty blessed herself and ran to his side. Margaret saw what had happened.

"Stop that!" she yelled at Danny, but Danny had already retreated to a corner, and as Bill yelled again, he guiltily dropped his eyes.

"What did you do that for?" she said sternly to Danny as Bill moaned and whimpered and his grandmother stroked his forehead, striving to comfort him.

A nurse came frantically into the room and asked what was the matter.

"His brother started playing with the bricks," Margaret said.

The nurse went to Bill, looked at his leg under the cover, turned to Danny and frowned.

"If you do that again, I'm going to bring a boogey man after you," she said, leaving the room.

"I'm sorry. I was only trying to find out why the bricks were there," Danny shyly said.

"You should know better than to put your hands where they don't belong," the grandmother said.

"You hurt your brother. Those bricks are there as weights to hold his leg in place in the cast," Aunt Margaret said.

"I didn't know," Danny said, almost in a whine.

"You're dumb. If you do that again, even if I can't walk, I'll get up, and I'll fix you. You hurt me. If you had a broken leg, I wouldn't do that to you," Bill said in an injured tone.

"If he ever does a thing like that again, I'll put him to bed on bread and water and tan his little behind," the grandmother said.

"Tell your brother you're sorry," Aunt Margaret said.

"I'm sorry, Bill," Danny said timidly.

"All right! Don't do it again," Bill said, putting on an adult manner.

"William, if they don't give you good care here, you tell me, and I'll come down here and drag the teeth right out of their heads. You tell them that here," the grandmother said.

"Mother, you're so cute," Margaret said.

"Cute, be damned. I'll scratch the eyes out of them that's not doing what's right," the grandmother said.

"They treat me nice here, Mother," Bill said.

"Do they give you good food, Willie-boy?" asked Margaret.

"Oh, Aunt Margaret, it's swell," Bill said enthusiastically.

"Poor thing, Mother. I'll bet he gets better food here than he ever got in his life," Margaret said to her mother under her breath.

"Willie-boy, don't you want a banana from the basket we brought you?" Aunt Margaret asked him, and when he shook his head yes, she handed him one.

"Can I have a banana?" Danny asked while Bill peeled his.

"Brother, where are your manners? Your brother is hurt, and we brought these to him. You should show consideration for him," Aunt Margaret reprimanded.

"But, gee, if I had a broken leg, and you gave me bananas, and he asked for one, I'd give it to him," Danny said.

"Give him one of my bananas, Aunt Margaret. But he doesn't deserve it after what he did to me," Bill said.

"Here. After this, now, Danny, you show consideration," she said.

"Oh, I will!" he said, shaking his head to emphasize the sincerity of his intention.

"Bill, I brought these for you," Danny said, handing Bill a small stack of baseball pictures.

"Gee, Dan, thanks!" Bill said.

"Where did you get them, Brother?" asked Aunt Margaret.

"I stood outside the cigar store yesterday at Fifty-first and Calumet and when the men came out, I asked them for the pictures of ballplayers that came in their packages of cigarettes."

"That was so sweet of you."

"Gee, here's one of Topsy Hartzell. I didn't have one of him in my collection," Bill said.

"And, Bill, there's pictures there of Joe Tinker and Johnny Kling," Danny said.

"Johnny Kling? I didn't know they had him in this series," said Bill.

"He is," Danny said.

"Let's pick teams from the players here, huh, Dan?" Bill said.

Margaret began to look bored, and she started pacing about the room.

IV

"Here's my son-in-law. I was just saying that no finer man has ever walked the face of the earth than Jim O'Neill," Mrs. O'Flaherty said spiritedly as Jim and Lizz entered the room, Jim carrying a small basket of fruit.

Seeing her mother, Lizz flew into the old lady's arms, talked loudly, spoke gaily all around. Jim greeted Mrs. O'Flaherty cordially, and Margaret with restraint.

"And here is my little precious," Lizz cried, bending down and holding her arms wide for Danny, who went to her shyly while Mrs. O'Flaherty watched with distinct displeasure.

Jim was wearing a black suit, white shirt, stiff collar, but his Sunday clothes gave him an awkward, uneasy appearance. Lizz wore an out-of-style black dress that had a few stains on it, her face was washed, and when she removed her crushed shapeless black hat, she revealed nicely combed, silken black hair.

"Why, Lizz, you look nice," said Margaret in surprise as Jim spoke with Bill, affectionately running his fist across Bill's hair.

"Of course I do. Why, any daughter of my mother is a lady," said Lizz.

"Jim, look at your son. He's fit for a king," Mrs. O'Flaherty said, poking at Jim.

"Hello, Dan," Jim said.

"Hello, Papa," Danny said awkwardly, a bit in fright.

"Jim, we were so sorry to hear about Willie-boy. And I hope you have no hard feelings because of what Al said over the phone the other night. Al is quick-tempered, you know, and he really doesn't mean what he says. He really likes Willie-boy very much, and would do anything in the world for him," Margaret said, her voice oozing so much sweetness that Jim showed marked discomfort.

"Let's forget it, Peg. I have more important things to worry about," said Jim.

"Oh, my poor hurt son, William. Give your mother a kiss," Lizz said, bending down, planting a wet kiss on Bill's nose.

"Jim, I was just this very minute saying that anybody having the name of me Uncle William will never go in want for a bite to eat as long as he lives," Mrs. O'Flaherty said.

"He won't as long as he has a father, Mary," Jim said to the old lady.

"Peg, you should have seen me when that man came up the other day! You should have seen what I said to him," Lizz said to Peg in a corner.

"Yes, you told me over the phone, Lizz," Margaret said, obviously not wanting to talk about it.

"Why didn't you split his head with the poker, Lizz?" Mrs. O'Flaherty said.

"I was going to, Mother. I sent my Dennis to get me the poker, but he ran. He was afraid of me, Mother," Lizz said.

"How they treating you, Bill?" Jim asked.

"Fine, Pa. I had roast beef for dinner."

"Swell. You're going to be all right. You're a brave lad, and your old man's proud of you," Jim said.

"Gee, Pa, I wish I could get up and walk. How long they gonna keep me like this?"

"The bone has to set and knit, lad. You'll be up on crutches in a few weeks."

"Lizz, will the boy be crippled?" Mrs. O'Flaherty whispered.

"No, the doctor said no. It's a clean fracture. And I went down to the German priests at Saint Peter's and I asked them to pray that he wouldn't be. They are praying. God wouldn't inflict that upon us, Mother."

"Sure, God is good," Mrs. O'Flaherty said.

"And, say, Mother, the night before it happened, Father came to me in a dream. He stood before me just as plain as the nose on your face, and he said, 'Elizabeth, watch that oldest of yours!' Mother, if Father wasn't watching over my Bill from Heaven, he would have been killed," Lizz said.

"Lizz, why do you believe all that old Irish superstition?" Margaret said, impatient.

"Lizz, where was the saint who takes care of roofs last night when our roof leaked during the rain?" Jim asked, smiling at the talk between his wife and mother-in-law.

"Lizz, I saw Pa the other night," Mrs. O'Flaherty said to Lizz.

"Come here by your father. He won't bite you," Jim said to Danny.

"Jim, Danny loves his father. He talks to us about you all the time, and he says that when he grows up he wants to be as tall a man as his father," Margaret said as Danny drew close to his father with hesitant steps.

"Pa, look what Dan gave me," Bill said, proudly revealing the baseball pictures.

"That was nice," Jim said to Bill, at the same time patting Danny, noticeably touched.

"Look, Pa. Here's a picture of Johnny Kling. I didn't have any of him in my collection," Bill said.

"And, Mother, you mark my words! That O'Rourke hussy is possessed by the Devil," Lizz said to her mother.

"She's a child of Satan. If I was her mother, I'd put a strap to her behind, and get the priest to rid her of demons," Mrs. O'Flaherty said to Lizz.

"Jim, ever since Danny heard that his brother was hurt, he kept saying to me, 'Aunty Margaret, when are you going to take me to see my brother Bill?'" Margaret said.

"I'm glad the boy remembers that he has a family," Jim said ironically, and Margaret turned her head aside as she bit her lip.

"My grandson isn't an O'Neill. He's a Fox," Mrs. O'Flaherty said.

"Why, Mother!" Margaret said as Jim glared.

"Sometimes I think you're right," Jim said to his mother-in-law cuttingly.

"Jim, our Daniel does take after his grandmother. Why, look at him! He's the spittin' image of my mother," Lizz said.

"Jim, how are the other children? I was down to see Lizz the other day and I saw them. Oh, they're such little darlings," Margaret quickly said.

"We left them with Mrs. Bodenheimer," Lizz said before Jim had a chance to reply to Margaret.

"That was nice of her to take care of them," said Margaret.

"It was not. It was the least that German washtub could do to help out a poor sick woman, when she and her hard-working man want to go to see their oldest son who's laying in a hospital with a broken leg," Lizz said.

"Pa, did you ever see Hit-'Em-Where-They-Ain't Willie Keeler play?" Bill asked.

"Sure, Bill," Jim said.

"Was he better than Ty Cobb?" Bill asked.

"Nobody can be better than Ty Cobb because Ty Cobb is the greatest player that ever lived. That's what I think. And that's what Uncle Al says, too," Danny said.

"Well, wait and let Pa tell us. You never saw Willie Keeler play," Bill said.

"I think Cobb is very good. But I guess that Willie Keeler was the master batter of them all," Jim said.

"See!" Bill said to Danny, self-justified.

"Jim, your son is the neatest boy and the best scholar in Crucifixion school. I make the Sisters give him first place in everything," Mrs. O'Flaherty said.

"Mother, you're so good to my son," Lizz said.

"I was just thinking we might take him home with us to see his brothers and sisters," Jim said.

"Oh, he couldn't," Mrs. O'Flaherty said.

"Couldn't come to the house of his father and mother?" said Jim.

"He has to go to school tomorrow. I couldn't let him miss a day," said Mrs. O'Flaherty.

"Well, I won't keep him from school," Jim said.

"It will be so nice when my son grows older, and he can come all alone on the street car to see his mother and his brothers and sisters," Lizz gushed.

"I'll have you know I'm mighty careful where I let my grandson go," Mrs. O'Flaherty said.

"He's your grandson! But he's my son!" Jim said.

"Jim. Mother doesn't mean anything by what she says. You know that," Margaret said apologetically.

"I just want to remind everybody! This lad here is my son!"

"Bill, why don't you give your father and mother one of the bananas we brought you?" Margaret hastily said.

"Yes, look, Pa, at what Aunt Margaret and Mother brought me," Bill said, pointing to the basket of fruit on the bed stand.

"Well, we stayed long enough. I got to be going. Come on, Son! Come on, Peg!" Mrs. O'Flaherty said haughtily.

"Mother, come and see me soon," Lizz said.

"I'm a busy woman. I have to cook food every day for my grandson's little stomach," Mrs. O'Flaherty said.

"Well, goodbye, Jim! Goodbye, Lizz. And goodbye, Willie-boy, you little angel. When you get well, you got to come to see us and let your auntie cook you a lovely supper," Margaret said; she went to the bed and kissed Bill goodbye.

"Danny, aren't you going to kiss your mama goodbye?" Lizz said.

"Yes. I was just going to," Danny said, not liking it that he had to go, because he wanted to stay and talk about baseball with Bill and his Papa. But he was afraid to say anything because he didn't want them all fighting.

"You're my son, not my stepson," Lizz said after she had kissed him and he had pecked at her cheek.

"Goodbye, William, and don't forget. As long as you have the name of me Uncle William, a day's harm can't come to you," Mrs. O'Flaherty said, bending down and kissing Bill.

She slipped a quarter into his hand. "Don't tell them," she whispered.

"Goodbye, Mother," Lizz said, flinging her arms around her mother.

"Don't make so free with me," Mrs. O'Flaherty said.

"Goodbye, everybody," Danny said as his grandmother grabbed his hand and moved toward the door.

"Goodbye, Jim. William, if you grow up to be as fine a man as your father, you'll never regret the day. Come on, Son!" Mrs. O'Flaherty said, leaving with Danny and followed by Margaret.

"Jesus Christ! Maybe she wants to charge me an admission price to see my own flesh and blood!" Jim said, surprised, hurt, angry, looking fiercely at the door through which they had just passed.

"You know Mother, Jim. She doesn't mean a thing. She's just proud. Say, she's the best there is up in that house," Lizz said.

"I knew I never should have let them have him. And that whore of a sister you got!"

"Jim!"

"Pa, look at this picture of Joe Tinker that Danny brought me," Bill said.

20

I

"Oh, Lorry, it's so wonderful to be with you again. And just last night I had the most awful dream about you. I dreamed that you were dead. It made me so sad. I woke up in a cold sweat. I just sat up in bed in the middle of the night and I cried. I was so lonesome for you!" Margaret said, snuggling herself against him as the carriage they were riding in clopped out to the West Side, crossing a bridge which spanned the scummy waters of the Chicago River.

"Peg, for God's sake, please don't do this in the carriage!"

"You don't love me any more. You've found someone else!" she said in an injured voice.

"Peg, it's just this goddamn situation. If Brophy tried to bribe you, and one of his lowdown private detectives terrorized your sister as you said he did, well, you can see to what lengths the man will go. We just have to be very careful. Suppose one of his lousy gumshoes should hop in on us with a camera before we knew what was happening."

"I'm sorry, darling. You'll forgive me," she said humbly, and when he shook his head, granting her request, she added, "Blow me a kiss of forgiveness."

Lorry pursed his lips in a kiss.

"Lorry, Brophy didn't get anything out of me!"

"I wish you could have pumped him when he said that he had me check-mated."

"I tried to."

"I know that he's a sly one, all right. But, my Peg, you haven't told that sister of yours anything that she might inadvertently blurt out, have you?"

"Why, Lorry, how could you ask me such a question?" she said accusingly.

"Forgive me, Peg! You are my Old Faithful, and I know that your mouth is as tight as a clam's," he said, squeezing her gloved hands, and at the mere pressure of his touch her eyes poured gratitude upon him. He continued, "I didn't call you because I was afraid. I was trailed all the time. I only shook them yesterday, after I registered at two hotels. I hope that one of the lice trailing me is still getting his tail-end warmed sitting in the lobby of the Shrifton."

"It was lucky I bumped into you on the street," she said while he grinned and lit a cigar.

"Lucky, and dangerous. But you know I was just going to take a chance and write you."

"Lorry, you know any letters of yours would be safe with me."

"Peg, we've gone into that. Letters get lost and stolen."

"Yes, Lorry darling! But honey, you are so smart, so brainy. Only a man with brains like yours could have thought of such a clever idea, having me get in a closed carriage and ride two miles before I picked you up," she said, beaming adoration on him.

"Well, we're taking a risk. It's for you I worry, more than myself. I don't want to let them drag you into it."

"I don't care what happens to me as long as Brophy doesn't do anything to you."

"He won't! But say, I did pull a sneaker on them this time, didn't I?" he said, chuckling to himself, his face lighting up.

"Lorry, you're simply wonderful."

"I'll say this much for myself. A man will have to get up a little earlier in the morning than Brophy does if he wants to put something over on me. And, Peg, if he tries to drag you through this, and give you notoriety, well, maybe I might find out something about his life. That fine Catholic Brophy, well, we might manage to scandalize a couple of bishops, and parish priests with his history, too. I'll fight fire with fire, if he tries that line."

"Oh, Lorry, I'm so proud of you. Tell me about Brophy's double life. Has he got women on the side?"

Lorry smiled.

"Tell me about it," she asked, keenly interested.

"What's there to tell? You know everything that can happen. You know, Peg, man has wonderful ingenuity about many things. But it is pretty damn hard for him to invent anything new in that line. The most original man in this world will be the man who can invent a new sin."

"You're getting horrible," she jibed gaily.

"Peg, you know about my testimony in Washington. They tried to trip me up with questions in cross-examination, but they didn't get very far on that tack. Every last word of what I said about Brophy was the truth. He did make that call from my hotel room at the Union Hotel and speak of a jack pot he had to pay in getting Hogan elected. Blaine, the harvester man, was asked to put up ten thousand of the jack pot. He's going to testify. He hates Brophy's guts, and he's fighting with Brophy over getting in on the control of some banks here. I don't care about the Graham angle. They'll kick him out of the Senate. The man I want to get is Brophy. All the reform people are yelping like chickens with their heads cut off about this thing. Say, Peg, they make me laugh."

"They are the ones who like blue laws. If they got their way in this country, we'd all do nothing on Sunday but go to church and twiddle our thumbs. But if we work in a hotel, they won't kick about that. We can work on Sunday. Not that I mind working. I love to work and be independent. But all these reformers and suffragettes want is to have us work and go to church on Sunday. The way I look at it is I want to be independent. But I'm not a suffragette," Peg said, determining to impress him with how smart and how informed she was about politics and the big questions of the day.

Lorry patted Margaret's leg. He turned, looked out through the back of the carriage, gazing closely and intently for about a minute.

"We're not being followed?" she said in sudden fear.

"It doesn't look like we are. I was just trying to make certain. This is the third time he's followed my instructions to drive around a block and back, and there's no sign. I guess it's all right."

"Brophy!" she said, oozing hatred. "But I told him a few things! I told him how low he is."

"I certainly would have loved to have heard you. You must have been a real tiger cat!"

"I told him! If I didn't make him ashamed of himself, well, it's because he's incapable of shame. I told him that no one with an ounce of manhood would stoop as low as he was stooping!" she said, showing pleasure under the glow of his compliments.

"They don't come very often like you, Peg."

"Oh, Lorry darling, let's get away from it all," Peg said.

"Why, Peg!" he said in surprise.

"I just don't want everything going on this way."

"How could a man like me leave his affairs? Peg, I hardly have a free moment. I have this fight with Brophy, and I have my affairs in Minnesota, and my deals that I'm swinging out in Oregon, and some of these damn anarchists with bombs got the men in a couple of my lumber camps all stirred up in a strike when I had to get some big rush orders out."

"I know it, Lorry, you have so much to think of. But you have such a wonderful brain to think of it with. If I was a man, I would ask God for nothing more than a brain like yours," she said.

"Well, brains never hurt."

"Lorry, you are such a brainy man! Oh, Lorry, I hate to ask you about this, but I simply have to mention it. You know, I need money so badly," she said, a note of nervous desperation coming into her voice.

"Peg, when some of this frozen money of mine gets loose again, you can have anything your little heart desires. You've more than earned it," he said understandingly.

"I need it so. My sister's oldest boy, and oh, he's such a lovely boy, he was run over by a wagon. He's in the hospital with a broken leg. His poor father can't pay the expense, and neither can my brother. It's going to fall on my shoulders. Everything does. My family would be in the poorhouse, only for me."

"Well, Peg. I can probably help you. If you just have a little patience, there's nothing that you need worry about."

"But sometimes it's so hard. Didn't you get the letter I wrote you? I signed it Olson."

"Why, no! When did you send it?"

"Weeks ago," she said, wondering suspiciously whether or not his surprise was genuine.

"It must be waiting for me at my office. I hardly even ran through all of my mail that hadn't been forwarded to me."

"Lorry, you promised to watch out about my letters. And you know my handwriting," she said, her manner both injured and reproving.

"It's that damn secretary I got."

"You ought to fire her. Lorry, you know I have often thought, wouldn't it be grand if I went to business college and learned typewriting and short hand, and then became a secretary. I would make a wonderful business woman, and I could help you so," she said.

"Yes, and then wouldn't that be a nice hello to my wife!"

"I hate your wife."

"Yes, but that doesn't put the law on your side. The law hates no man's wife if she drags him into court."

"I don't want to talk about her."

"I don't like to think about her."

"But, Lorry, I was nearly out of my mind with worry. And I waited and watched the mail day after day, day after day," she said melodramatically.

"I wish I'd gotten it. I would do anything and everything to help my Peg," he said, and her suspicions of him melted like butter; she thought that no, her Lorry wouldn't lie to her, and yes, he was her Lorry, and it must have been just as he said it was about the letter. "You see, Peg, I have so much on my mind these days that I overlook lots of things. You must forgive me."

"I do. Darling, it was just that things went so bad. Oh, Lorry, you must, you simply must help me. If you don't, I don't know what I'll do. I have so much at home to bear. You could just never imagine all the expenses there are to keeping up a home. And all the girls at the hotel are better dressed than I am. I bought this outfit, even though I couldn't afford it. I had to. I was in rags."

"We'll have to attend to such a pressing matter."

"Oh, Lorry, you're so dear. I don't know what I'd do without you."

"Nothing is too good for a girl like you, Peg," he said, again patting her leg, eliciting a grateful smile for her.

He puffed on his cigar contentedly.

"Why, Peg, what's the matter?" he asked as she began to cry. "We've just decided that we'll fix you up with a wardrobe that will make you an envy to women. I'll be worried for fear that some fellow will be hopping along to take you away from me."

"No man could take me from you!" she said with a seriousness so heavy as to be painful. "I'd marry you tomorrow, even if you didn't have a nickel. Oh, Lorry, kiss me, hug me!"

"Please, Peg, not here," he said as she edged toward him.

"That lowdown sonofabitch Brophy! Oh, wouldn't I love to stick a knife in him!"

"He's not in too soft a spot, Peg. This investigation isn't doing him an ounce of good. A wedge has been driven in on him, and I'm going to drive it right on through. When he told you he had me, he was bluffing, whistling to keep up his courage."

"Oh, you're so wonderful!" she said; then, her mood changed suddenly and she again began to cry.

"Peg, don't worry about me! Don't cry. Tell me now, what is troubling you?" he asked, concerned.

"I can't see straight, with worry."

"About what?"

"Money."

"But we're going to do something to settle that."

"Oh, you don't know what it is, even."

"Well, tell me!"

"I borrowed money from my cashbox. Any day I might be audited. If they do, oh, I just tremble for fear of it! I'll lose my bond. I'll be disgraced, disgraced, blacklisted. And I didn't do it for myself. I did it for my poor sister, my dear mother."

"Peg, I asked you never to do that again! For your own sake!" he said impatiently.

"Oh, you just can't understand."

"Peg, that's bad business. Why, it amounts to . . . stealing."

"I didn't do it for myself," she sobbed.

"Now, come, come! Don't cry!"

"Oh, you'll never understand! No one will ever understand!"

"I can understand, Peg, only . . ." he said, stopping his remark, gazing at her, confused and embarrassed, as she sobbed.

"No one will ever understand!" she sighed.

"Peg, give me a chance to," he said, and as he spoke she looked dolorously past him, at three-story apartments, and houses with withering hedges. She thought that happy people lived in them, not miserable creatures like herself. She saw a child running, and she thought despairingly of how she would like them to have a child, a beautiful healthy child that looked like him. The carriage jogged on, and he said cautiously, "Peg, listen to me!"

"Yes, Lorry, darling. But it's all right! Don't worry! I'll go on, and if I am blacklisted as a common thief, the world will never know!"

"Peg, stop cutting up like that! You know you can depend on me. We'll get this business settled for you, and your worry will be ended."

"But I hate to be coming to you with things like this when you have so much on your mind. I wouldn't . . . if I didn't have my family."

"It's a trifling matter. How much is it?"

"A hundred and fifty dollars," she said, and immediately she caught the puzzled expression which crossed his face. "I'm sorry, darling. Lorry, you needn't do it. I'll be branded. I'll go down in the gutter. I'll sink down in the mire. Maybe I'll end up as a whore!"

"Peg, stop that!" he said with sudden but unangry firmness.

"I love you, Lorry!" she whimpered, adoring him for his firmness, her eyes softly upon him, her hand clutching for his.

"Well, if you do, you got to promise me something."

"I do! I won't ever again touch the cashbox. Not as long as I live! On my word, I promise!"

"And something else!" he said, his firmness now seeming fatuous.

"Yes, darling. I am yours, body and soul!"

"You've got to promise me never to talk again like you've just talked!"

"I won't. I was a weak thing, wasn't I? Forgive me."

"As soon as we get inside, I'll give it to you. And if I give you something for clothes, you've got to promise me that you will buy things for yourself and not your family."

"I will. Oh, you're such a wonderful man, so generous!"

"I want to be," he said, tossing his cigar out the window.

She fell toward him, flung her arms around him, kissed him hungrily, and he returned her kisses.

"But this is dangerous," he said, recovering himself.

"I'm sorry! I couldn't help it. I love you so that sometimes, I don't care. I want to shout to the housetops that I love you. But I won't. I won't be weak like this again," she said, edging meekly into the opposite corner of the carriage from him.

"I don't see any signs of those gumshoes trailing us," he said, relieved.

"Oh, how I hate that rat, Brophy!" she hissed.

II

After Lorry had again looked back to determine whether or not they were being followed, the carriage drew into the courtyard of a large gray over-ornamented building outside the city line.

"You wait, Sport, and you'll be taken care of. And go into the bar and have a glass of beer, and I'll settle for it."

"Thank you, sir!" the ruddy-faced carriage driver said, jumping down from his lofty seat, leaving a whip upstanding behind him.

"Ah, Mistah Johnson. How do you do? Good day, Madame," a small Italian greeted them at the entrance way.

"Hello, Tony! A private room," Lorry said with the air of a man used to giving orders.

Talking volubly, and not listened to by Lorry and Margaret, the Italian ushered them up a dully red-carpeted stairway and into a large room with a table and chairs in the center, a couch in the corner over which a red and blue covering was spread, and blue curtains shutting out the light from French windows. The wallpaper was of an elaborate rose pattern, and on it were hung two pictures of formal rose gardens.

"I senda the man up, Mistah Johnson," Tony finally said, bowing himself out.

"I feel so funny," Margaret said while Lorry removed her coat and hung it on a hook beside the door, alongside of his topcoat and derby.

"We've been here before. And those damn gumshoes didn't pick up our trail."

"Lorry, kiss me!" she said yearningly.

Their embrace was interrupted by a rap on the door, and Lorry opened it, admitting a tall dark waiter. They sat at the table, and Lorry studied a card with liquor lists and prices on it.

"I don't want any food, only a drink," she said.

"Whiskey?" he asked her, and she nodded.

"A bottle of Gold Star, some ice, and ginger ale," he ordered, and the waiter bowed himself out, yes-sirring Lorry.

"I'm so glad to be with you," Margaret said after the door had closed them in alone.

"And so am I, Peg, my girl," he said, smiling wistfully across the table at her.

She went to him, pressed his head tightly against her stomach, caressed him, kissed his hair.

"Peg, wait until he comes back with our order and leaves us alone," Lorry said when she began licking his left ear.

"Oh, Lorry, can't you take me away?" she begged, again seated before him.

He leaned forward, grasped her hands. Their eyes met and were locked in an intense mutual gaze.

"Peg, I only wish I could. I long for the day when I can," he said, speaking slowly, his voice scarcely above a whisper.

"If so many things, so many goddamn people weren't in our way. It makes me hate them! It makes me hate the world!"

"Whether we hate the world or not, my dear, it's right here, pressing all around us," he said, squeezing her hand.

"Why didn't God make the world decent, Lorry?" she asked, her manner beseeching, as if he could answer her questions.

"We can make the world something ourselves. I'm getting my hands tight on the one thing that enables you to make the world anything you want to make it. Money!" he said, his face intense when he uttered the last word.

"Things are such that they make me hate! They make me hate everyone and everything but you, Lorry. Ever since I was a little girl, I had things against me. Lorry, I hate the world! I hate people! I hate!" she said, spitting out her words.

"Peg, a girl like you, so handsome, so smart, so clever—say, you should wear the world around your little finger like a ring. You can tie it to your toes and swing it like a trinket."

"I can't. You're just trying to make me feel good. What did I ever have? Nothing! I was a weak, sickly little thing. I almost died in the County Hospital with diphtheria. I was almost blind as a child, and I couldn't even see the blackboard in school. I went to work in a candy store before I ever got out of the eighth grade. I've had nothing but work, and fighting at home. My brother was always beating me, and my sister, poor thing, she egged him on. Why shouldn't I hate the world? I earned everything I ever got, by hard work. I had to learn everything for myself. I didn't have any mother to guide me. My mother, poor thing, she can't even read or write. She's just a greenhorn, like my father was. Why shouldn't I hate?"

"Because your face is too handsome, with those brown eyes of yours. Hatred does not sit well on such a handsome face."

"I hate every woman in the world who is happy! I hate everybody who's happy! What right have they got to be happy? Oh, my darling, if you only knew how I miss you, what I go through when you're away!"

The waiter interrupted them, carrying their order in. Lorry gave him a fifty-cent-piece for a tip, and he went out, smiling. Lorry lifted his glass to hers; they drank. She smiled wearily at him, blew him a kiss.

"Peg, I've had to fight, too. I never went to eighth grade. My father could read, but the only thing he ever read was the Bible. He read it all day Sunday. I ran away from home at the age of thirteen. I fought for everything I ever earned, too. Say, the things I stood! I've nearly frozen to death in prairies without a thing to cover me at night. I've starved. Many a time I've been without a nickel. But I don't hate the world. I use it. I fought it, and I won. So now it fights for me."

"But you're such a wonderful man. There's no man on earth like you."

"Peg, you must know I miss you. When I have to be traveling about, with so many business worries on my mind, I often think to myself, now if I was only in Chicago and able to see Peg."

"Do you think such things, Lorry, my precious?"

"Of course I do."

"You are so fine, so noble, and I love you. I was watching you, too, darling, with the waiter. You were so democratic with him."

"Peg, let's drink to when we are together," he said, extending his glass to clink it against hers.

"Oh, I am afraid it will never be," she said, her words dripping with misery.

"We're together now. Let's hang no crepe outside our meeting," he said, his smile infecting her, making her think of how her Lorry was so boyish.

"I was a bad girl, and I'm sorry, darling. It isn't that I want to be sad. I don't. Only I see so little of you, and I don't even have you to talk to with all my troubles. Oh, Lorry, I can't live without you. Honestly, I can't."

"Let's drink again to when you won't have to," he said, fixing new drinks for each of them.

They drank. She tossed him a smile.

"Well, that's warming," he said.

"Yes," she said, her voice seeming distant.

"It's almost as warming as a certain Peg that I know."

"Lorry, when you say you love me, and want me, do you really mean it?"

"You know that I do."

"I'd die if you didn't. I'd commit suicide. I'd kill myself with gas and let them bury me in potter's field, where I'd be forgotten and the world would never know how much I loved you."

"Peg, you needn't talk like that. You mustn't."

"I won't. I won't have to, when I have such a wonderful man as my Lorry."

"Who's going to come and sit on my lap?" he asked.

She went to him, plumped in his lap, kissed him, petted him, kissed him, moaning as their tongues touched.

III

Feeling giddy, Margaret got out of the carriage at the elevated station, and paid the man. No necessity of spending all that money riding downtown, particularly when the elevated was quicker. Lorry had been so generous, giving her the money to ride back in a carriage, but she could save it, buy something, a pair of stockings, something for Danny that he would look sweet in, a lace nightcap for Mother. Lorry wouldn't know the difference, and a penny saved was a penny earned, as poor dear Mother always said. Now if she was with a man who was a piker, he wouldn't have done what Lorry had. To think of it. He had given her a hundred and seventy-five dollars. And next week, he was going to send her more. She could put the hundred dollars she had borrowed back in the cashbox, and then let the auditor come. And never again, as long as she lived, would she do such a thing. Ah, fool that she had been!

She stood on the station, her cheeks almost blushing red, and she looked around at the people, an odd assortment of men and women. Poor things! Poor women, like that thin one who looked like she had consumption. Ah, life was not as good to many people as it was to Margaret O'Flaherty. God would forgive her for the white lies she told him, saying it was a hundred and fifty she needed instead of a hundred. She could buy clothes to put on her own back, things for the family. And Lizz needed so much, now that Willie-boy was hurt.

That poor consumptive-looking woman. She was probably married to some cheap cigar of a man who made twenty or twenty-five dollars a week. If she only knew the man that Margaret O'Flaherty had. Just think of it, there was no woman in a book who would ever have a life as interesting as hers. No woman in a book would ever know more sorrow than she had known, more poverty, more heartache, ruination almost, sadness and death and sickness in her home. But no woman in a book would ever be as happy as she was, with a lover like Lorry Robinson. No man on earth, let alone a lover in a book could be like Lorry. So fine! So noble! So generous! So like a little boy! Such wonderful lips! She dreamed of them. Such a fine body, without fat on it, like many men had! He was so strong, and when he put his arms tight around her, why he seemed to have muscles made of iron. What woman in a book, what woman on earth, had a Lorry Robinson to put his arms around her, squeeze her until it hurt with love, lay on top of her naked, pour his love into her oh, so, so wonderfully? And through Lorry, look at the role she was playing. Private detectives following her. Being bribed by one of the most influential men of affairs in Chicago. Why, tomorrow she could go to him, and couldn't she just smoke him up like he was a cheap cigarette? She would like to. She would like to ruin his life, disgrace him before his wife, whoever the goddamned hypocrite of a thing was. Ah, no, she thought, smiling. She would like to pretend to go to bed with him, and then squeeze his balls off, kick him there until he rolled off the bed and moaned on the floor. And while he lay moaning, dress, spit in his face, fart at him, walk out of the room, slamming the door. Ah, her life was a wonderful life, with its terrible sorrow, its wonderful joy, its mystery. It was just like a book. Why, it was more dramatic than a book. And just like a book ended in such happiness, so would hers, with her Lorry. Some day, she would walk down the street and people would look at her and say, why there goes the handsome Mrs. Lorry Robinson.

Her train came along. She got in, and sat thinking, her face wreathed in smiles. But she didn't want to go home now. She wanted fun, excitement. Oh, if she only had a girl friend to talk to. She hadn't one, not one in this wide world except Mildred Lewis who was in Europe for a year. But then, Lorry made up for everything. But if she only had a girl friend now to go and talk to. Mother, what did Mother understand? She was so old-fashioned, so ignorant, poor thing. And she told everything to Lizz, and Lizz was such an ignorant thing, and God knows what Lizz didn't tell her neighbor women, and the Gormans, and the O'Reilleys, and the O'Learys, and God knows who else.

Ah, yes, she wanted fun. She wanted to talk to some girl friend. She felt her pocketbook. She smiled. Ah, Martha Morton. Martha was a dear. She was so understanding. She might be a little bit coarse, but men had made her so. She had never been refined by the love of a man like Lorry. She would call dear, understanding Martha up and go see her. She would just talk to her. But she wouldn't touch one more drop. She was through with that. And now, why, Margaret O'Flaherty was the happiest, the most fortunate, girl in the world! She could hardly wait for the train to reach the Loop so that she could get to a telephone booth and call dear, understanding Martha Morton.

21

I

"When I was getting Jim's breakfast this morning, I said to him, 'Jim, I had a dream last night. My baby brother, Ned, is coming to see us,'" Lizz said to Ned with a gush of energy.

Ned sat opposite her on the parlor couch. He was twenty-seven, an attractive man with an almost baby-face type of handsomeness. His face was soft, weak, with blue eyes and pinkish cheeks. His light, nearly taffy-colored hair was parted on the left. He was wearing a stylish, well-made, tight-fitting black suit, a pink pleated shirt, a knitted gray tie with a pearl stickpin in it, and pearl cuff links.

"Tell me, Lizz, are you going to be able to sue the fellow who ran over Bill?" Ned asked.

"I should hope so! How are we going to pay the doctor and the hospital bills if we don't?"

"Well, have you a good case?" Ned asked, drawing a cigarette from a silver case, tapping it lightly, putting a match to it.

"Have we? The traffic policeman blew his whistle for all wagons to stop, and this guinea drove right on, and knocked my son down. The policeman's name is McGrady, I knew his mother down on Wabash Avenue. He knows Jim's cousin, Pat Dennison, who's now a plain clothes man. He said to me, when he found this out, 'Why, Mrs. O'Neill, if I had known your boy is a cousin of Pat Dennison's, say, I would have given that wop such a third degree that he would have been carted home on a stretcher.'"

"I'm glad you have a good case," Ned said.

"Say, was I born yesterday that I'm going to let a dago walk all over me? When I go before the judge, I'll say to him, 'Judge, I was born in this country, and I'm an American. My mother came over here before Lincoln was shot. Judge, are you going to let a dago run over an American child in broad daylight and get away with it?'"

"But what's that got to do with it?" Ned asked, puzzled.

"We Americans make laws for Americans, not for the wops. Say, when I speak in court I'll say," Lizz jumped to her feet, bristled, gestured extravagantly, while Ned smiled his weak smile, a veil for annoyance, boredom, and mild torture, "Ned, I'll say, 'Judge, when Christopher Columbus went to the wops and asked them for money so he could discover this country, they wouldn't give him a cent. They said skidoo to him, and kicked him out of Italy. Judge, are we going to let the wops run our country when they wouldn't lift a finger to help Columbus discover it?'"

"Has Jim a good lawyer?"

"We gave the case to Joe O'Reilley. But, say, if you go to Joe and ask him to handle a case for you, he'll tell you to go get somebody you can sue for a hundred thousand dollars. You just try and catch a lawyer like Joe suing any Tom, Dick, and Harry! Just try!"

"Well, Lizz, who is your lawyer?"

"Joe told my Jim to let Dinny Gorman handle it."

"How is Dinny?"

"Dinny's going to make that wop put something right there for Jim and me," Lizz said, holding out her left hand and slapping the palm of it with her right paw.

"He's a pretty good lawyer and ought to win for you. He studied and worked hard to get where he is."

"Say, but is he high-toned and classy! He wears spats." A gleam came into her dark eyes. "The last time I saw him, I said to him, 'Dinny, I suppose you don't want me to call you Dinny. But I knew you when there was hardly a soul who would even call you that.' And, Ned, you'd have died laughing if you saw his face. But, Ned, just throw the cigarette butt on the floor. It's all right."

"No, I won't," Ned said, getting up, looking around, finally squashing his cigarette butt in a saucer on the dining-room table.

He came back and again sat on the parlor couch.

"Ned, you should see what a dude Dinny has become. I said to him . . .'"

"Lizz, I haven't a lot of time. I don't want to hear all this talk."

"But, Ned, wait till you hear this! I said to him, 'Well, Dinny, my brother Ned now carries a different cane every day in the week.' Say, he didn't have any comeback to me. He's afraid of you, Ned. He knows you used to go with his Mae before he married her, and he's jealous."

"Why, Lizz, you have no right to talk like that. I took her out to a dance now and then in the old days, but that was all. She never particularly cared for me," Ned said with muffled indignation.

"Oh, Ned, when you were home you were the catch of the neighborhood. All the girls were sweet on you, and their mothers were always telling them, 'Why doesn't that handsome Ned O'Flaherty take you out?' Why, there wasn't a better catch than you to be found in those days, Ned."

"It seems to me that you were trying to get Dinny to lose your case for you," Ned said.

"Let him try! If he does, I'll have Jim's cousin, Joe O'Reilley, get him disbarred."

"Lizz, why don't you see the good side of people, and talk constructively about them? There's good in every one of God's creatures, and the Lord wants us to see the good in those He created," Ned said, annoyed.

"You say the truth, Ned. And, say, let me make you a cup of tea?"

"No, thanks. I couldn't touch it. I just had lunch downtown a little while before I came out here."

"Ned, how is my beautiful sister-in-law, Mildred. She's an angel. She's the cream of God's creatures," Lizz said.

"Yes, Mildred is a wonderful woman, and she has a sweet disposition. She never backbites, and she always sees the good in people," Ned said, looking directly at Lizz.

"I know it, Ned. She's so wonderful," Lizz said without batting an eye.

Ned clucked his lips in amazement.

"She's much stronger now. These last months, she's gained over five pounds," he said.

"I know she did. I lit five holy candles for her, and that's what did it," Lizz said.

"That was very nice of you, and I know that she'll appreciate it, Lizz. That brings me to why I came here. Now, Lizz, with Mildred so much improved, she and I talked this proposition over. I'm away a lot, and she's alone, and she likes company. We decided that we would love to take your Little Margaret with us to keep Mildred company. We'd raise and educate her, and see that she gets a good schooling."

"But, Ned, wouldn't it be so much trouble? Girls are so much harder to raise than boys. They need so much more time and attention."

"No, Little Margaret is her aunt's favorite among your children," Ned said.

"I'll have to ask Jim," Lizz said.

"We want you and Jim to talk it over, and if you decide to let us do it, well, we'll give her a lovely home. We have plenty of room in our place in Madison, and she will have the best food, plenty of air, and room to play in, and we'll watch her just as if she was our own child."

"Oh, Ned, you're so good. And it would be just grand for the little tot, even though Jim and I would miss her. Every night when he comes home from work, she runs to him, and he lifts her up and kisses her. She calls Jim her money man. But it would be so good for her, and what kind of parents would Jim and I be if we stood in the way of betterment for one of our little ones?"

"You and Jim think it over, and let us know. I expect to be down this way for the shoe convention late in January, and I think that Mildred will be well enough to come along. We could take her back with us then," Ned said.

"Oh, Ned, it will be so grand. Just a minute, and I'll call her in to see you," Lizz said.

Lizz went out to the back. Ned walked around the room, sniffing, looking at the dust on the floor, the papers, the rags, the debris cluttered about. His face showed disgust. He heard Lizz yell from the back steps to Little Margaret and heard the girl answer. Lizz shouted a second time. He sat down, slowly shaking his head.

"God!" he muttered, half aloud.

Lizz led Little Margaret back to Ned. The child was mussed from playing, and there was a rip on the left side of her spotted dark-blue dress. She smiled shyly at her uncle.

"Sweetheart, go to your Uncle Ned. He's going to be your foster papa."

Margaret started to run to her uncle. She stopped. She looked at him with dirty-faced uncertainty. She smiled, walked to him. He lifted her onto his knee.

"Like your Uncle Ned, sweetness?" Lizz asked.

"Umm hmm!"

"Would you like to go away and live with your Uncle Ned and your beautiful Aunt Mildred in a great big house with steam heat?"

"Uh huh!" Little Margaret said.

"Oh, but I'll miss her so, Ned. She's like a little mother to the other little ones. And you know, she talks with me just like a little woman," Lizz said.

"I imagine so," Ned said pointedly.

"But it will be such a help to me and Jim. The poor man works so hard, him with his rupture, and the little finger he lost in a machine after my Bill was born and just before the twins that died came."

"Well, you and Jim talk it over. Of course, we'll bring her back to see you whenever we can, and maybe some time, when things get better for all of us, you and Jim could come to see her and us in Madison," Ned said.

"Well, Little Mother, do you want to go and live with your uncle and aunt in Madison?"

"I like my uncle," Little Margaret said, giggling while Ned bounced her on his knee.

"He'll give you dresses fit for a little queen. Like dresses?" Lizz asked.

"I want a new doll," the child answered.

"Just a minute, Ned. I have something for Mildred," Lizz said, going to her bedroom.

"You'll get dolls, too. Your aunt thinks you're a doll," Ned said, and the child smiled up at him.

He kissed her forehead.

"You're a lovely little thing, Margaret," he said.

"Here, Ned!" Lizz said, returning. "This is a scapular blessed by the Pope. I got it the last time I went down to Saint Peter's church. You give it to Mildred. Anyone who wears the scapular of the Blessed Virgin will never die without the last sacraments. The Blessed Virgin promises to all who wear her scapular that they will pass away in a state of grace."

"Why, thanks, Lizz, but can't we talk of something happier than death?" Ned said, his face completely changing into a mask of gloom and sadness at this turn of the conversation.

"Oh, Ned, the Blessed Virgin has a great power at the Throne of Almighty God," Lizz said with great conviction.

"I know it, Lizz. And thanks for this."

"Mary is the greatest comfort to me in my life with all its afflictions and its poverty. Without the comfort of the Blessed Virgin, I don't know what I'd do," Lizz said, her face shining, her eyes enflamed with devotion.

"Well, Lizz, the thing for everybody to do is to have faith. Jesus said: *Ye of little faith*. What everybody should do is to fix in their minds that things are going to get better for them, and to have faith. Faith can move mountains. With faith, things will get better," Ned said.

"Oh, Ned, I do so wish that my Jim could get a better job," Lizz said.

"He will. With faith, we can have anything we want. God made the world for us so that we could be happy and have the good things of life," Ned said.

"Oh, no, Ned! It is the will of God that some of us are poor. Jesus said: *Blessed are the poor*. He told us that it is easier for a camel to go through the eye of a needle than it is for a rich man to enter His Kingdom. It is His will that I am so poor. And if I am poor now, well, I know that He will reward me and make me rich up above when I see my father and my sister in Heaven," Lizz said.

"Lizz, we don't know what awaits us in the next world. We should get good things in this, and not have to cut anybody's throat to get them."

"It is blessed, Ned, to be poor. Jesus was poor. He didn't have a place to lay his head," Lizz said.

Ned sighed. He looked at his niece as she watched him with studied intensity. He smiled at her, stroked her thinnish light hair.

"Well, Lizz, I have to keep a business appointment downtown. You and Jim talk it over and make up your minds. But you can feel absolutely confident that we'll give her the best and the kindest of care," Ned said.

"Oh, Jim will be so glad. My Jim, he thinks the world of my brothers. He looks up to both of you," Lizz said.

"All right," Ned said, setting his niece down, arising. He straightened out his trousers, stretched his arms, pulled his shirt cuffs out from under his coat sleeves.

"Just a minute, Ned, I have something else for you," Lizz said; she again rushed to her bedroom.

"Will you like going to school in Madison, and living with your aunt and uncle?" he asked Little Margaret.

"I will if I get a new doll," Little Margaret said.

"Ah, you coaxing little beggar," Ned said, putting a brand-new nickel in her hand.

"This is Easter holy water, blessed at the Italian church. There is a great power against evil in it. Bless yourself with it, Ned, before you go," Lizz said, carrying a small holy water fount with a statue of Jesus carved above the receptacle for water.

Ned blessed himself while Little Margaret proudly examined her brand-new nickel, and showed it to her mother. Ned gave Lizz five dollars, and left. After he had gone, Lizz stood in her tracks for a moment. Her bovine face clouded, saddened. She set the holy-water fount on a table. She bent down, and fiercely swept Little Margaret to her. She held the girl with a fierce tightness.

"My baby mine!" she muttered.

She sobbed.

"Why didn't he marry a woman who could have children of her own?" she asked bitterly.

She kissed her daughter.

II

"For the last time, I'm saying this, and I won't say it again! I don't want to be beholden to any damn dude O'Flahertys!" Jim said in controlled anger, his face blanched.

He got up from the table.

"Jim, they have been so good to us," Lizz pleaded.

"I'll take care of mine. Let them mind their own business. If they would blow their own noses, instead of mine, they would find that they could be plenty busy. If anybody needs caring for, it's that drunken sister you got."

"Jim, don't you dare talk like that about my people!"

"All I ask of them is to leave me alone and tend their own furnace."

"Your cousins, the O'Reilleys, have never offered to do as much for us."

"The hell with the O'Reilleys," Jim snapped.

He looked at Little Margaret as she sat on the floor, scolding her rag doll.

"I'm goddamn sick and tired of being helped. Let them stick their help up where I'd like to see them jam it," Jim said, striding back and forth across the dining room.

"Fine words to hear from you! Fine words!" Lizz said, her voice like a drone in his ears.

"Oh, will you drop it!" he said, enunciating each syllable with undue slowness.

"Forget it! Forget what you say about my people! Where would you be without the money they give me? Oh, but you should talk! You should talk! With the pay envelopes you bring me home. Why, there is so much money in your pay envelopes that the greenbacks just bust the envelope open. You should talk! And who fed you and yours when you were out striking and fighting like a hooligan in that teamsters' strike right after my Daniel was born? You, out fighting with cops, and coming home with your head nearly split open. Who fed you then? My brother and sister did."

"Yes, and I'd go out and fight again to defend my union against scabs. And listen! I don't need advice on what to do. See these. They're pants. And I'm wearing them. And I'm doing the best I can! No man can do any better than that!"

"And I don't do anything but gad about like a lady. I'm never sick. I don't wash pots. I don't cook and scrub. I don't empty pots full of shit. I don't wash stinking diapers. Oh, no, I don't do that! I live like a lady!" Lizz said, mincing, ironically sweetening her voice, grinning idiotically with her decayed teeth caught in a gleam from the kerosene lamp.

"Lizz, I know you work hard, too," Jim said, placing his hands on her shoulders.

"Don't come near me or I'll get the butcher knife! Oh, that I ever married the likes of you!" she said, drawing away from him.

"Maybe I didn't get such a bargain either."

"My brother Ned comes here today, out of the goodness of his heart, and he offers to help us by taking a little one off of our hands and giving her the upbringing she deserves. And this is the thanks he gets from you."

"What in the name of God is there wrong when a father wants to keep his own little girl in his own home with her father and mother? Isn't it bad enough that we had to let Danny go?"

"I'll tell you what's wrong. The father can't make enough money to put bread in their mouths and decent clothes on their back so that I won't be ashamed to have the neighbors see them on the streets."

"The other kids in this neighborhood are no better off. They're all poor people around here."

"But they aren't poor people where my brother Ned and Mildred live. They'll make a lady out of Little Margaret there."

"Jesus Christ, you'd think it was my fault."

"What kind of a father are you? Standing in the way of your own daughter?"

"Oh, Lizz, for Christ sake, cut it out!"

"And isn't that a fine how-do-you-do! Isn't it! Well, yes, cut it out. I'm through. I'm going back to my mother and leave you with all this shit and stink. Then see how you like it! Then we'll see you smile like sunshine when the shoes start pinching your feet," Lizz said, lifting her dress and jigging.

"Jesus Christ, go ahead! Do any goddamn thing you like. But remember this! These kids stay right here!"

"Jesus, Mary, and Joseph!" Lizz tearfully exclaimed.

"That's it! Go ahead and pray!" Jim said.

He walked away from her and sat alone in the parlor, chewing tobacco. He heard someone singing on the street. Singing? Well, he'd like to sing, too. A few minutes passed.

"Jim, if we get the money in time, we'll have to buy a couple of new dresses for Margaret to go to Madison in, when her uncle and aunt come to take her after the New Year."

"She doesn't leave this house! Not if I have to get the police and the courts to stop it!"

"Why, you sonofabitch!" Lizz shrieked at him in fury.

"I've taken enough from you! Woman, get the hell out of here before I lose my temper and paste you!" Jim said, half crying with anger.

Lizz fainted.

<h1 style="text-align:center">III</h1>

Ned was staying at the O'Flahertys' for the night. About nine o'clock he answered a ring at the doorbell. Lizz stood before him, red-eyed, disheveled, dirty-faced.

"My God, Lizz, is there anything wrong? What's happened?" he asked.

"Where's Mother?" Lizz asked in a heavy voice as she stepped past her brother.

She strode heavily to the rear of the house. Ned followed her in utter bewilderment.

"Oh, Mother! Mother! Your daughter has come home to you! Take her!" Lizz said, falling into her mother's arms.

"What's the matter, Lizz?" Mrs. O'Flaherty asked, trying to free herself from Lizz's weight.

"Is Jim drunk again?" Margaret asked after rushing into the kitchen in a state of anxiety.

"Oh, Mother, never again let me fly away from your nest! Mother, always keep me here under your wing!" Lizz said.

"Calm yourself, Lizz! Tell us what's the matter. Is there anything we can do to help? Is Jim drinking again?" Ned asked.

"I want my mother. I'll only talk to my mother!" Lizz said, pouting baby-ishly.

"Have a cup of tea and warm yourself," Mrs. O'Flaherty said, finally freeing herself from Lizz's clinging.

"Mother, your wandering daughter has come home!" Lizz sighed, dropping into a chair.

"So you came home to roost, did you?" Mrs. O'Flaherty said.

"Jim ought to be ashamed of himself. Coming home drunk, spending what little money he earns on liquor when he has all his babies to feed. Why, I never heard of a man doing such a thing. And what does it all mean? It means that the responsibility for feeding his brood falls upon us," Margaret complained.

"For God's sake, Lizz, tell us what's happened, and what we can do for you," Ned said.

"Oh, Mother, why did you ever let me go away from you?" Lizz asked.

"It's your own fault. You should make your man toe the mark! Ah, but I made my Tom toe the mark! I made him afraid of me!" Mrs. O'Flaherty said.

"Oh, Peg, you should have stopped me when I did it," Lizz said.

"I tried to, Lizz," Margaret said, and then she paused in sudden thoughtful-ness.

"I left Jim!" Lizz said in a throbbing voice.

"Hello, Mama," Danny said, coming in just as she made this statement.

"Come here, my son!" Lizz said, opening her arms widely for him.

"Danny, haven't you any lessons you have to study?" Ned said.

"Can't the baby see his own mother?" said Lizz.

"Here, Danny, I want you to do something for me," Ned said, taking Danny's arm.

"He's doing no harm," Mrs. O'Flaherty said.

"I want my son. Can't I even see the only child that I have left in the world?" Lizz said.

"Why, Lizz, has something happened to the others?" Margaret asked in fright, but Ned caught her eye, winked to her, and she nodded back knowingly to him.

"You can see him in a minute. He has something to do for me," Ned said.

Ned led Danny out of the kitchen and told him to go in the parlor and stay there until he was called for. He gave him a nickel.

"These aren't matters for the ears of a little boy," Ned said, returning to the kitchen.

"Oh, Mother, if I had taken the veil, I wouldn't be here now, throwing myself on my knees at your mercy," Lizz said, and she flung herself on her knees before her mother.

"Peg, give the poor thing a cup of tea," Mrs. O'Flaherty said while Lizz knelt before her with bowed head.

"Lizz, be calm! Sit down and be sensible and tell us what's the matter," Ned said, annoyed.

Ned and Margaret lifted her up, and sat her back in a chair.

"I came home, because I know that my mother will always find a place for her poor erring daughter," Lizz said.

"But we haven't any room," protested Margaret from the stove.

"I'll sleep on a sack in the corner, and I'll do the washing and scrub the floors for my keep," said Lizz.

"Yes, Peg, let her stay and do the washing. She won't eat as much of my son's food as the lazy nigger washwoman does," Mrs. O'Flaherty said.

"Everyone else in the world may desert you. But your mother, never! There's always a place in a mother's heart for an erring child," Lizz said.

"Lizz, what did Jim do to you? Did he sock you?" Mrs. O'Flaherty asked.

"Say, Mud, where do you learn all this gutter language?" Ned asked.

"Did he?" Mrs. O'Flaherty asked, ignoring Ned's remark.

"I can't stand it any more, cleaning stinking diapers full of shit," Lizz said.

"And listen to that elegant language!" Ned said.

"You should have split his head with the hammer," Mrs. O'Flaherty said.

"Make Mud stop feeding her," Ned whispered to Margaret.

"Mother, now don't you go worrying our sister here. And here, Lizz, here's your tea. Drink it while it's hot. It'll make you feel better," Margaret cooingly said, setting tea before Lizz and putting milk and sugar in it for her.

"Jim won't do it, Ned."

"Won't do what?" Ned asked.

"He won't give you Little Margaret," Lizz said.

"Well, even so, that doesn't call for this display of fireworks. Cripes, this isn't the Fourth of July," Ned said.

"The beggar, without a stitch on his back," Mrs. O'Flaherty said.

"He said no, and cursed me. He blamed me for everything," Lizz said.

"What's gotten into him?" asked Ned.

"Maybe you didn't talk to him the right way. You didn't use what Al calls psychology on him," Margaret said, winking at Ned.

"He drove me out of the house. I thought he was going to kill me," Lizz said.

"Why, the goddamn fathead!" Ned exclaimed, and then he stopped himself.

"And tell me, who is Jim O'Neill? What's his name? What's he got in his pocketbook? Why, he doesn't have a pocketbook. All he has is a hole in his ass. The beggar!" Mrs. O'Flaherty said.

"Here, Mother, don't go getting so excited," Ned said.

"I can't stand him any more. I can't!" Lizz tragically said.

"Is he drunk, Lizz?" Margaret said.

"I am a mother. A mother is sacred. Oh, if my boys were grown up, their father wouldn't do these things to me. Oh, when Danny grows up, if Jim touches me Danny will protect me," said Lizz.

"Here, Lizz, take this milk bottle home with you, and if he opens his mouth, give it to him. Split his head open and bring me his brains, and I'll give you five dollars," Mrs. O'Flaherty said, setting an empty milk bottle before her daughter.

"Say, goddamn it, Peg, where does Mother learn that talk?" Ned asked, annoyed.

"I don't know," Margaret said hopelessly.

"She oughtn't to talk like that. Don't read her any more of the murder stories in the paper. Only give her constructive news," Ned said.

"Say, you, don't be picking on my mother! I won't let you. I have no one to stick up for me! I have no brother to protect me. But my mother has me. I'll die before I let anyone pick on my mother," Lizz said.

"In the old country, if me father didn't like a man, he'd rip his guts out and bring them home to show to me mother," Mrs. O'Flaherty said.

"Nobody's picking on Mud, Lizz. Be calm! I'm just trying to give her an idea of the way civilized people should converse," Ned said.

"Whatever my mother says is all right," Lizz said.

"Here, Lizz, drink your tea," Margaret said.

"Lizz, where did he hit you?" asked Mrs. O'Flaherty.

"Oh, Mother, I only wish that I had been a man for five minutes tonight," Lizz said.

"All right, go ahead! Turn the kitchen into the Stockyards and spill everybody's guts all over the floor. Drink all the blood you want. I'm going in the front and see if I can find some constructive things to read in the newspaper," Ned said, walking out in disgust.

IV

Lizz looked toward the front to see if Margaret or Ned were coming back. Then she leaned toward her mother and spoke in a lowered voice.

"And, Mother, another thing, Peg is always after me to use a douche bag."

"Bless my body and soul, don't, Lizz. It's a thing of the Devil. Why, we never heard of such contraptions in the old country. If me mother saw one, she would have crawled to the church on her hands and knees," Mrs. O'Flaherty said.

"Mother, I'm a decent woman like you are, and the Lord made me. I'm good enough as I am, just as the Lord made me. Mother, I won't touch a douche bag. The Devil made them. She says I should to be clean. Mother, this marriage ring on my finger makes me clean, clean in the sight of God."

"Lizz, I swear the Devil made them things," Mrs. O'Flaherty whispered.

"She uses it so she won't have children. I know her. And, Mother, we were made to have children, When God threw Adam and Eve out of the Garden of Eden, he said that man must work by the sweat of his brow, and that woman must bear children. Well, Mother, I won't do it. I resign myself to the will of my God," Lizz said proudly.

"Don't, Lizz! Don't go against the will of the Great Man. But hsst, here comes Ned and Peg," Mrs. O'Flaherty said.

"Lizz, Jim will be waiting for you. Don't you think that you better be going?" Ned said, coming into the kitchen with Margaret.

"Just as soon as I have this cup of tea," Lizz said.

"It's cold. You better get a fresh one," Mrs. O'Flaherty said.

"Jim will be waiting for you. He might be worried. You told him you were going right home a half hour ago when he called on the phone," said Ned.

"He knows where I am. I want to talk to my mother. I don't see my mother every day in the week," Lizz said.

"It's late, you know, and the streets are dangerous at this time of the night," Ned said.

"What have I got that a burglar would be wanting, a poor woman like me? And I'm not afraid. I am protected from up above," Lizz said, pointing to the ceiling.

"Lizz, don't you think you better be going? It's such a long ride home, and you have to change street cars, too. There aren't many cars running at this time of the night."

"I'm going right now. I was just going to tell Mother about the Murphys. You remember them, Ned, on Wabash Avenue, before you married Mildred? Why, the Murphys all thought that the O'Flahertys were the salt of the earth," Lizz said.

"They were good people. Dick Murphy worked hard like Pa did," Mrs. O'Flaherty said.

"Yes, they were," Margaret said.

"Mother, Dick Murphy drove a team of horses, remember, and once the poor man was crossing a railroad track, and a train came along, and cut his wagon clean in two, taking the back half off of it. I tell you, it was a miracle that he wasn't killed," Lizz said.

"Yes, he worked as hard as Pa. Don't I remember how I used to get up at four in the morning down on Blue Island Avenue in Saint Ignatius parish? It would be so cold that your hair would stand up like icicles. I used to have to get feed for the horses and breakfast for Pa and the men," Mrs. O'Flaherty said.

"Look, Lizz, it's after ten," Ned said.

"And, Mother, wait till I tell you this one," Lizz said.

Ned walked out of the kitchen. Lizz left at twenty minutes after eleven.

"Mother, why do you listen to all that gab? What good does it do you? You can't get a nickel for it. Why, you'd be better off saying the Rosary or just sitting and meditating and having good fine thoughts," Ned said.

"Ah, Ned, the poor thing, she likes to talk. What she says to me, it goes in one ear and out the other. But, well, I have to be getting to me rest so I can be up early in the morning to fix my grandson's breakfast," Mrs. O'Flaherty said.

22

I

Margaret opened the mailbox with trembling hands. She grabbed the letters. All for Al. She crumbled them back into the box and pushed it shut. She walked slowly upstairs.

Goddamn Lorry! It was already Thursday. If he loved her, he would have sent her the money by now, just as he had promised to last week.

She went to her bedroom. She sat on the edge of the bed, her head sunken in her hands. She got up and paced back and forth across the room. She sat down on her bed again. She lit a cigarette, and walked around in a circle. She stood in the center of the room, her hands shaking.

"Peg?" her mother called, eying Margaret curiously from the dining room.

Continuing to pace, Margaret did not answer.

"Peg?" she said.

"Yes," Margaret answered, half dazed.

"Is something the matter with you? Are you sick?"

"I'm just nervous."

"You'll be wearing out my son's rug walking on it that much. Why don't you go and wear out the rugs of him you was out drunk with last week?"

"The hell with your son's rugs," Margaret said, turning her back on her mother.

"The day will come when you won't be sayin' to hell with my son's rug."

Walking to the parlor, Margaret did not hear her mother. She sat down on the piano bench, looking in a blur at the songs on the piano, not reading the words that stood before her eyes. She swung around, and her glance lighted upon the framed picture of Louise to the right of the mirror. She went to it. She looked at it closely, the image of a thin-faced, beautiful girl with a wide hat and a veil

240

covering the eyes. Louise had such beautiful brown eyes, too! Oh, why hadn't God taken her instead of Louise? Louise had been the lucky one, she, the poor unlucky devil. Louise had only suffered a little while, that last year or so, when she lay thin, yellow, wasting away like a beautiful flower, dying in the spring. But she, the living, she must go on.

Oh, Louise! Oh, Louise, in Heaven, help your suffering sister, Margaret, pray for her, help her through all these miseries of life!

Why, why hadn't Lorry sent the money as he had promised that he would?

She paced around the parlor, repeatedly opening and closing her hands. She heard the rumble of an elevated train. She gazed out of the window, down at the gray day that squatted over the corner, closing the sky down tightly upon the street. She felt as if it were closing in on her. What would she do? A man walking along. Was he married and in love with another woman? Did he see his sweetheart, write to her? Ah, no, men were all the same. And the woman always paid, always paid. A woman crossing the street. Did she have her man? Was he good to her? Oh, crap!

She cried before the picture of Louise. The image of Louise seemed to rise mysteriously before her, a tall, thin girl, with lovely tresses of brown hair. When she and Louise walked down the street together, ah, no wonder many a man spoke of those lovely O'Flaherty girls. She sneered. The family, the whole caboodle of them, had talked of Louise as if she was a sacred virgin. She remembered the white satin burial dress that had been spread out on the poor yellowed corpse of her beautiful sister. The white coffin in which she had been buried, too! Ah, little they knew! Little they knew!

Oh, why had God taken Louise away when she was so young, so pretty, when she had so much in life waiting for her? She remembered the way Louise would sing when she dressed to go out on a date. She remembered the sparkle in her eyes when she came home and told of a man who had taken her out. The fun there was in Louise! The way that Louise could have such a good time! It was so terrible to die. And it was so terrible to live. Oh, she wished she were dead, lying out in Calvary Cemetery beside poor Louise.

She again paced the hall. Oh, what a fool she had been. Oh, if she had only come home after seeing Lorry last week. She would have had her money. She could have put it back in her cashbox. She would not be trembling now with the fear of disgrace. Fool that she was! Seeing that dirty bitch Martha Morton. What had ever possessed her to call on Martha? Why, Martha Morton was just a washed-up bitch who couldn't even get a job in a whorehouse. And she had loaned Martha seventy-five dollars. Oh, fool that she was. Letting herself be an easy mark for Martha Morton. And they had gone out, and she had spent twenty-five dollars, God knows where. She would bet that Martha had stolen some of it. She had not wanted to get drunk that day. She had just been happy and gone with Martha. She could just kill herself for having been such a fool. And she didn't know where she could turn now to get that money. Just think. She had had a hundred and seventy-five dollars. And she had pissed nearly all of it away.

Oh, God, she was sick of life. She wanted to vomit it up like puke. She wanted to spit it out of her mouth like poison. She never wanted to see another man. She wanted to die.

Why hadn't Lorry sent her that money? God, what would she do? She had racked her brain and she didn't know where she could borrow it.

She could hear her mother singing out in the kitchen.

> *A shantyman's life is a wearisome one.*
> *Some call it free from care,*
> *The swinging of an axe from morn to night*
> *In the midst of a forest clear.*

What right had Mother to be happy and to sing? She squatted in her home, smoked her pipe, drank her beer, chewed the rag about her hawk-nosed son's flat and his electricity. She had the nicest life of any mother on the face of this earth. There wasn't a mother alive with a more considerate daughter. And what did she do for her daughter? What did she care if her daughter was unhappy? What did she even know of her daughter's troubles and sorrows? Well she might sit out there with her pipe stuck in her toothless mouth and sing.

II

Peg ransacked the dresser drawer, flinging its contents out pell-mell. She was sure that she had left the ring in this drawer. And it was a present from Lorry. She hated to pawn it, but she had to, and she would redeem it with the first money she got her hands on. But where was it? She was sure she had left it in this drawer, just as sure as she was that her name was Margaret O'Flaherty. She frantically ripped through the pile of underclothes and handkerchiefs she had flung about the floor.

Jesus Christ, where could it be? She clenched her fists. She walked back and forth across the room, wringing her hands. Had she worn it of late? No, she hadn't. It couldn't be lost. She must just be calm now, and look. She piled through the other drawers, and did not find it. She pitched into the clothes closet, and did not find it. That this should happen to her! Lorry's ring, gone. She looked again. Still failing to find it, she let out a shrill scream.

"Peg? Peg? For the Lord's sake, are you sick?" the mother asked, worried as she stood in the doorway.

Margaret gazed at her mother like an insane woman. She let out another shriek.

"Peg, what ails you?" the mother asked.

"Who took my ring?"

"What ails you, Peg?"

"Who took my ring?"

"Are you possessed of the Devil to be carrying on like this? I was out in the kitchen, fixing some warm victuals for my grandson's lunch, and I heard you yelling like you was being killed."

"The hell with your grandson! Who took my ring?"

"The way you're yelling, the neighbors will think someone is being killed here."

"It's gone!"

"What? What? What?"

"The ring that Lorry gave me with the beautiful emerald in it."

"Where is it?"

"It was in that dresser drawer. It's gone."

"I ain't seen sight or light of it. And it can't walk."

Peg began flinging clothes about the room madly.

"In the name of the Lord, what's gotten into you that you let yourself be cuttin' up like a crazy woman? Is it them that you was out drunk with last week that did this to you?"

"Goddamn it, can't you understand English, you toothless greenhorn? It's stolen! Stolen!"

"Don't be calling me no greenhorn in my son's house!"

"Well, where's my ring, then?"

"I ain't seen nary a sight of it."

"The only thing in the world that I prized. The beautiful emerald stone that Lorry gave me."

"I told you there was never a day's luck that was to be had out of anything that a married man gave you."

"Shut up! When I brought you home money he gave me, when I bought you lace caps last week out of his money, you didn't say that. Shut up, you old crone, and tell me where my ring is."

"Ah, I tell you, the Devil will take anything that you get from the likes of him."

"Get out of my sight before I scream!"

"My son pays the rent for a roof over my head. Don't be ordering me around in my son's fat!"

"Oh, God, how can I go on!" Margaret sobbed as she viciously kicked at the corset that lay before her.

"God will punish anyone that speaks against me."

"Who comes into this room? Does the nigger washwoman?"

"I should like to get these hands around her throat if she ever takes a step past the kitchen in my son's home. Sure, it takes her all day in the basement to do the washing, the lazy devil."

"I have looked everywhere for it," Margaret said hopelessly.

"Maybe it fell under the dresser," the mother said, bending down, looking under the dresser.

"It's gone. The only thing in the world that I owned. I'm a marked woman. Everything I have, my whole life, it's smoke. Smoke! I'm a marked woman!"

"Maybe it will turn up when you're least looking for it."

"No, it's gone."

"Maybe if you pray to Saint Anthony you'll find it."

"Oh, shut up with that goddamn piety you learn from Lizz!"

"Don't you be blaspheming."

"I don't like hypocrites like you!"

"Calling her own mother a hypocrite! The day that you were born, it was a sorry day for me. A sorry day, indeed!"

"The sorriest day of my life was when I was born out of that belly of yours."

"It's only one that has the Devil in her heart that would speak like you do."

"Keep quiet! I'm tired of your nagging voice."

"Well you might be! And well you might be! She's tired of my nagging. Well, I'll be nagging anybody who lives under my son's roof and does not toe the mark!"

"Kiss my ass!"

"That I should live to hear those words come out of the mouth of my own daughter in the latter end of my old age."

Margaret ironically laughed at her mother.

"You bellyaching about your old age. You're as strong as a horse, without one gray hair of sorrow in your head, without a care in the world, with your children supporting you in luxury, waiting on you, hand and foot. You'll outlive all your children, and you'll not give a damn when they go. You were born under an evil star with a devil in you, and the life of everyone you know is fated to be miserable. You're a witch! Phooey on your old age!"

"God will punish you for plaguin' your poor old mother."

"Shut up and find my ring!"

"I can't be bothered. I got to get a warm lunch for my grandson's little stomach," Mrs. O'Flaherty said, starting out of the room.

"Mother!" Margaret called, her face lighting up, her voice introducing a note of concern.

"What's the Devil putting into you now?" the mother asked, swinging around to face her daughter.

"I know who got my ring. I'll swear to it on the Bible."

"Who?"

"Bill. When was he last up here?"

"Sure I don't know. The day before the poor boy got his leg broken."

"Was he in this room stealing cigarettes and poking around?"

"I didn't see him. Sure he's a good boy."

"When he was run over he had a brand-new flashlight on him and a dollar in his pocket. He told his mother and father that he won the flashlight in school, and then the truant officer was around to their house looking for him. He stole my ring, and sold it. It isn't the first time he has stolen up here, either. He stole five dollars out of my pocketbook over on Indiana Avenue just before we moved out of that house. I'll lay my life on it that he stole my ring."

"If he did, in my son's house, may the curse of God be on him, and may his broken limb never mend!"

"That little rat! After all I've done for him. That ungrateful little cur! Ah, I tell you, he'll swing on the gallows yet. After all my kindness to him, all the money I gave him for candy, all the times that I saved him from a whipping by Al. That he should do a thing like this to me!" Margaret said, her voice rising hysterically, she talked.

She snatched a handkerchief from her dresser and wiped her tearful eyes. She studied herself in the mirror, thinking that she was a picture of pity and sadness. The tears coming out of her eyes, they were the blood of her poor soul. Oh! She blew her nose loudly, folded her arms, turned to face her mother.

"That he should have done such a black ungrateful thing to me who has always befriended him! I tell you, that boy will go to the gallows yet! And when he does, not one word of sympathy will he ever get from me. Not one word!"

"I was in the kitchen."

"What do you mean?"

"I was in the kitchen that day, and he was in the front before Daniel came home. That was the day that Al was mad as a bull, and when I was out there, I don't know hide nor hair of what he was doing."

"And you didn't watch him? You know what he is. He's taken things from your pocketbook, too."

"And how could I be watching him and cooking supper for my son after he was out on the street all day, working hard to keep the roof over my head?"

"I know it! I knew it long ago. If I only left you, left all my stinking relatives to fend for themselves. Not even my property is safe in this goddamn house!"

"If you don't like my son's house, there's always a door without any key for you in it," Mrs. O'Flaherty haughtily said.

"You dirty old hag, I'll get out! I'll never come back. I'll never darken your door again. Not as long as I live. You can keep your son's flat, and, yes, keep your son's ten cents' worth of electricity, too. Stick them up your withered old Irish ass!" Margaret shrieked with reddening fury.

"In the name of the Holy Ghost!"

"Get out of my sight before I scream," Margaret screamed.

"God will curse you for your words," the mother said.

There was a tapping on the radiator.

"The neighbors are knocking for you to keep still. What will they think, with you the disgrace of the building cutting up like the tinkers?"

"This is my room! Get out!" Margaret belched.

"My son pays the rent for it."

"Fuck you! Fuck your son!" Margaret shrieked.

"May the Blessed Virgin tear the guts of you for saying that to me!"

"She'll do it to you! Every curse you've ever put on my poor head, it'll come back to roost on you! Curse me again! You're only cursing yourself. There's a God Who sees you. He knows the kind of a mother you've been to me. You're no mother. You're a wolf! You'd be better off dead than alive!"

Mrs. O'Flaherty looked fearlessly into her daughter's eyes. She spat. Her spittle landed on Margaret's nose. Margaret shoved her mother out of the room, and the old lady landed against the wall.

"Hittin' your old mother. May you never know a day's good luck as long as you live for sayin' that!"

"It's your fault. You nagged me until I haven't a nerve in my body. It's your fault! It's the dirty old Irish in you that makes you spit in my face!"

Margaret shrieked hysterically. Mrs. O'Flaherty solemnly knelt in the hallway, palmed her hands together prayerfully.

"Holy Virgin, Mother of God, may the blackest curses of the Devil fall upon my sinful chippy of a daughter that came ass-end out of my backside on the day that she was born! May she live in want, die like a pig, and be buried in potter's field! Blessed Jesus, may all your curses and evils be poured on her head like dirty water used to feed the pigs! Blessed Jesus, may her teeth fall out, and may she die blind!"

"Go ahead, curse me, curse me! It'll all come back on you, you she-devil! You she-wolf! You filthy hag!"

"May the curse of God be upon her head! May you never see the sight of God! In the name of the Father, and of the Son, and of the Holy Ghost! Amen!" Mrs. O'Flaherty said, blessing herself, getting off her knees.

"You've never been a mother to me!" Margaret wailed.

"Now, don't bother me. I have to make me grandson a warm lunch for his little stomach after he comes in from school out of the cold," Mrs. O'Flaherty said calmly to her daughter.

She went out to the kitchen.

Margaret fell face forward across her bed, her body shaking with sobs.

And he hadn't sent the money!

Oh, Lorry!

23

I

Margaret moodily sat in a corner of the back room of O'Callahan's saloon. She had to have it. She had to have something to quiet her nerves or else she would simply go crazy. It wasn't her fault. She worked too hard. She had too many worries on her poor head. She had too many burdens laid upon her poor shoulders. She was too unhappy. Discovering that Bill had taken her ring, that had been the last straw. It had left her the completely broken woman that she now was.

This one drink of gin would pull her together. Then, she would take a walk. It was a bracing day. And, yes, it was good that today was her off day. The sun and the chilly little snap in the wind would do her good. She would walk until she tired herself, and then she could go home and get the sleep and the rest that she needed.

I am so tired! So tired! she told herself silently, heavily.

The slovenly waiter set a tumbler of gin and a small glass of water before her. She vacantly glanced after him as he pushed out through the swinging doors. She stared dismally into her gin. She snatched up the tumbler, gulped. The gin made her cough and sneeze. She hastily drank water.

Now she would just sit here a minute to compose herself. But just think of it, her beautiful emerald ring had been stolen. God knows what he had done with it. That he should steal it from her, the one thing in all the world that she treasured! That he should be such a dirty little ingrate! If he had only come to her and said, Aunt Margaret, I need five dollars, ten dollars. She would have given him the money. She would have gotten it for him, even if she had had to go out to steal for it. But, no, he hadn't done that. He hadn't been that honorable. He had stolen her ring. She could understand now why a wagon had run over him and broken his leg. It was a punishment of God visited upon him for what he had done to his kind aunt. As long as he lived, the punishments of God would be visited upon him for what he had done to his best friend in the world. Only, the little brat's neck should have been broken. And when she saw him, just as sure as she was sitting here this very minute, she would break his neck!

She looked vacantly into her gin glass. She was so upset that her poor hands were shaking. She lifted the glass and sighed for herself as she saw that she could not even hold it steady. And look at her hands! They were not soft and beautiful like the hands of most of the girls she knew. Most girls would not walk into a kitchen for fear of soiling their beautiful hands. And look at her poor hands! Burned from cooking! Rough from housework! She was a nervous wreck from all the things that were done to her.

She just had to have one more drink. She wasn't going to get drunk. She wasn't going on a spree. She wasn't a drunkard like Jim O'Neill was. But she did have to have one more drink so that she could get a firm hold on herself. Oh, God, why, oh, why did she have to be born with nerves such as she had? Other girls didn't have her nerves. They were never tied up in knots like she was right now. Oh, God, what a misfortune it was to be Margaret O'Flaherty!

She rang for the waiter, and when he answered, she ordered another gin. She had to have it because there was nothing else that would help her in a state like the one she was now in. Mother had upset her so much! Mother had been so cruel to her just when she was suffering from the blow of discovering that Bill had stolen her priceless ring. Oh, God, God, would people ever stop betraying her? What had she ever done to earn such unhappiness? Always, even as a little girl, she had been unhappy, beaten, mistreated. Once she could remember when Lizz was going out with lanky Jim, and she couldn't find a clean pair of stockings. Lizz had blamed her and put up a yowl. Al had lost his head, and when he heard Lizz blaming her about the stockings, he had believed Lizz. He beat her unmercifully. She, poor innocent little thing, she had never seen the stockings. Always such things had been happening to her. Oh, God! God! God!

The waiter quietly set a second tumbler of gin and a chaser before her. She watched him push out through the swinging doors. She looked at the painting of a buxom woman on the moldy wall. Ah, the woman in the picture was just a big fatass. She stared vacantly at her gin. She really needed this drink. At times in this unhappy veil of tears that was the world, a woman had to do something to hold herself together. She took out a cigarette, lit it, inhaled. She stared into her gin. She heard the echo of rattling wagon wheels outside. She stared into her gin. Oh, God, why did she have to live such an unhappy life? Oh, God, why did she have to be a nervous woman, so alone in the world, carrying such heavy crosses on her own weak shoulders?

She snatched up the gin, poured it down, and followed it with her chaser.

She sighed. She was so sorry that she had fought with Mother. But it was Mother's fault. Mother knew she was nervous. Mother knew that she was nearly out of her mind with worries over the money she had to return to her cashbox. Mother shouldn't have provoked her at a time when her nerves were jumping and twitching. And the way Mother had cursed her. She forgave Mother. She wished Mother no harm. But never, never, never, never, never, as long as her heart beat in her breast, never would she forget those curses. That was what had upset her. Her own mother wishing such evils upon the kindest daughter that any mother on the face of this earth had ever had. Those curses were what had upset her, driven her out, and into this saloon.

But she was pulling together now. She would just sit and finish her cigarette, and then she would be all right. She would be able to leave. She would take a lonely walk in Washington Park. She would recover. And, oh, if only she got her cashbox straightened out, she would go on, and she would make the best of life. If not? Oh, what a fool she was! Loaning her money to Martha Morton. Spending money on Martha Morton. Well, she had learned her lesson. God, get her safely out of this! God, help her get the money to pay back, and she would never again get into such a scrape. And she would send five dollars to the Poor Clares as soon as she could. And, yes, Ned could have loaned her the money the other night when she'd asked him. His saying he didn't have it, it was a black lie!

And, God, God, where was her Lorry at this very minute? What was he doing? If he was only here with her now! If she could only lay her tired head on his shoulder and forget, forget! If she could only tell him now to take care of her, to make her happy! Where was he? Why hadn't he sent her the money this week? Had something happened to him? Had his enemies done something to him? Oh, if they did, if anything happened to Lorry, no, she couldn't bear it. She would throw her body into the lake. The cold waters would close over her and all her sorrow would be over. She couldn't live without him, and she was going to tell him so. She was not going to go on like this because she simply could not stand it! She clamped her lips together grimly and vowed that she would have a showdown with Lorry. She would make him do something so that they could always be together. If he wouldn't, if they couldn't always be together, there was no use in her living. Then, the cold waters of Lake Michigan!

She must watch herself, because she didn't want to get drunk now. But she simply had to have another drink. Then she would take her walk. She rang, and the waiter again appeared.

"I'm so nervous, I have to have just one more," she said apologetically.

"That sometimes happens, mam."

"I don't do this habitually. But I have had such troubles. There have been deaths in my family. My poor father died of cancer and I lost my beautiful lovely younger sister by consumption. I'm just so nervous and unhappy that I got to pull myself together."

"Oh, yes, you were in here before and told me about such sorrows. Yes, I know how it is, mam. Indeed I do," the waiter said, wagging his head.

"I just have to have a few drinks to pull myself together," she said dolorously.

"Gin sometimes does that, mam," he said, leaving.

He wouldn't think she was a drunkard, a woman bum, a whore. He was an understanding sort of a waiter. And if she sometimes needed a drink and didn't have the money on her, he would probably give her trust. He was sweet. He could see that she was driven to taking a few drinks because of her sorrow.

She took out a small mirror and powder puff. She slowly powdered her face. She studied her puffed eyes. Just think of it! That such a girl as she should have been driven to the point of nervous collapse. That her eyes should be so swollen from the tears of misery. Oh, God! But, yes, she would now take hold of herself. She would drink this last shot, and go. She would be all right. But her being all right would be the result of her own fighting with her nerves, with herself.

Oh, God!

The waiter brought her gin, went out. She stared at it glumly. She heard a street car outside. She heard some men talking in the front. They were not unhappy like she was. Men never were. They did not pay. Women paid. She stared at her glass of gin. She gripped it firmly. She swallowed it quickly. She hastily drank her chaser. She sat. She didn't care. She didn't care what happened to her. She didn't care what became of her. She gave up. She just didn't care. She didn't. She rang the bell.

"More!" she told the waiter.

<h1 style="text-align:center">II</h1>

"Peg, my beautiful sister, Peg," Lizz said, almost childishly ecstatic as Margaret lumbered up the stairs.

"'Ullo," Margaret mumbled, feeling the chunky plaster along the walls, teetering on up from step to step.

Lizz opened the door wide. Margaret walked in and stood in the center of the parlor. Her hat was askew. Her veil was ripped and it hung over her face crookedly. She looked about her, bleary-eyed. Lizz stared at Margaret, silenced from her shock of surprise. She straightened the unclean rag tied under her chin. She wiped her hands on her dirty apron.

"I don't like those goddamn stairs. Dark! Too high! Move your goddamn flat downstairs the next time I come. I won't climb 'em any more," Margaret said, speaking slowly.

"Why, Peg, how are you? Sit down, and let me make you a cup of tea," Lizz said.

"Don't like tea. Like gin. Got any gin?" Margaret said, swaying, her eyes fastened upon a strip of torn wallpaper in the corner.

The children, who had been playing house in the dining room, rushed to their aunt.

"My aunty is here. She likes me better than she likes anybody else in all the world," Little Margaret said, pulling at her aunt's skirt.

"You little darling, I'll miss you so when you go to Madison," Margaret cooed.

Robert sat at her feet, gazing at her. He stuck his thumb in his mouth, looked up at her, his nose dripping.

"Nobody loves Peg O'Flaherty. Nothing but the cold waters of Lake Michigan love Peg O'Flaherty," Margaret said, a tear dribbling down her left cheek.

"Peg, don't talk like that. It's a sin to talk of suicide. What's happened? What's the matter," Lizz said, moving closer to her sister.

"Go way! Go way! Scat! She's my aunt. She's not your aunt!" Little Margaret said impertinently to Dennis.

"If . . . If . . . If . . . If. . ." Dennis began to stutter, and then he stopped in helpless silence.

"She's not your aunt," Little Margaret said, giving him a shove.

"If . . . If . . . If . . . If . . ." Dennis again stuttered.

"Go way! You're making her cry," Little Margaret said.

"Oh, my lovely sister, Elizabeth," Margaret mumbled to the accompaniment of tears.

"Are you sick?" Lizz asked, but catching the stinking alcoholic whiff of Margaret's breath, she turned her face aside as Margaret tried to kiss her.

"Mommy!" Dennis whined just as Margaret succeeded in planting her slobbering lips on Lizz's neck just below the ear.

"Go way, you little shysters, and let your mother talk to your aunt," Lizz said.

"Mama, she is my aunt, and she likes me better than she likes Dennis. He makes her cry. Now, you tell him to go way," Little Margaret said, putting on the airs of a scolding adult as she spoke.

"I give up," Margaret sighed, flopping into a chair.

"Go on, Mama said I should chase you away," Little Margaret said.

"She . . . she . . . she . . . dddddid not," Dennis indignantly protested.

Little Margaret shoved him. She clouted him in the face. He stumbled. He fell over Robert. Both boys let out a howl.

"Shut up, you crybaby! It's your fault. I told you to go way. You wouldn't. You

252

made me chase you. It's your fault. Shut up and keep quiet, you crybaby!" Little Margaret scolded.

"Shut up, you little shysters!" Lizz barked while they continued howling.

"Keep your goddamn brats quiet! Don't you know I got nerves," Margaret said.

"See, now! You're making my aunt get nerves! You get out of here or I'll sock you! And you take that dirty face there with you!" Little Margaret said to Dennis, pointing at Robert.

Catherine awakened and began to bawl. Lizz rushed to her, saw her screaming in the crib, her bare feet kicking.

"What's the matter with Mama's little angel precious?" Lizz cooed, lifting the infant.

She saw that the child was dry, and was pleased. She washed enough stinking diapers. She kissed the infant's fuzzy head, cooed to it, while from the parlor came the sounds of Little Margaret raging at her brothers. Lizz opened her left breast. The infant, with an intense animal hunger and concentration, poked and fought to the nipple, sucked. A benign expression spread over Lizz's face. She hummed, walked back to the parlor, saw Margaret sitting helplessly in tears.

"You have a family. I have nothing, nothing left in God's world," Margaret drooled.

"Don't say that. You're talking against the will of God, Sister," Lizz said.

"Is it the will of God for me to sit before you with my eyes red like this, sore from weeping the tears of sorrow?" Margaret said.

"Don't cry, Aunty Margaret. I love you," Little Margaret shyly said, standing before her aunt.

"Look, Peg, the way the little ones love you," Lizz said.

"Nobody loves me," said Margaret, ignoring her niece.

"I do, honest, I do, Aunty Margaret," said Little Margaret.

"I don't care! Shit on the world! Piss on the world!" Margaret said, standing up, raising her voice.

"Don't be talking like that in front of my innocent little ones," Lizz said.

"They'll have to hear it sooner or later. When I was a babe, I heard it from my mother, and, yes, from you."

"You certainly did not. You won't say that against me or against my mother. We are both honorable married women. If my Jim heard you talking like that against me in his house, he'd throw you out before you even knew what was happening to you."

"Just let him try it!" Margaret sneered, enunciating with drunken carefulness.

"This is Jim's home."

"And I gave him and you plenty of money to keep it up," said Margaret.

"Yes, and you're an Indian giver. You take the good out of everything you ever do for me by backbiting me after you do it. Oh, I know your kind, Peg O'Flaherty. Gives with the right hand, and snatches it back with the left."

"Mama," Little Margaret sobbed, standing before her mother, looking from her mother's face to the suckling babe at Lizz's breast.

"So that's the gratitude I get from you, Lizz O'Neill," Margaret said, swaying.

"Mama, I don't like you to talk mean to my Aunt Margaret and make her cry," Little Margaret impertinently said.

"Go way, you little shit, and stop giving orders to your mother," Lizz said without looking at her daughter.

"Jesus Christ, look at the filth! Why don't you clean your house? Why don't you be tidy? Why don't you be a woman, instead of an old-fashioned Irish biddy?"

"Say, I'm a decent mother! Don't you call me names, you!" Lizz said.

"That's all you know. That old Irish talk! Why don't you call the neighbors in to hear you?"

"I'd be ashamed to let them see a sister of mine in your condition. I'd be humiliated," Lizz said.

Lizz almost tripped over Robert. He squealed. She stumbled, firmly grasping the baby with both arms.

"Go ahead, break your neck!" Margaret sneered.

"Little Margaret, watch that pissing little brother of yours, and don't have me falling over him when I'm nursing your hungry little sister," Lizz commanded.

"You're an O'Flaherty from the word go," Margaret said, laughing ironically.

"Say, you go sit on a tack!" Lizz rejoindered.

"Get out of Mama's way. Go and sit over there in the corner, you bad boy!" Little Margaret said to Robert, speaking to him like a little mother.

She led him to a corner.

"You'll never have any luck, talking against a poor woman like me. You mark my words, you'll never have luck. I'm under the protection of Saint Joseph, the foster father of Jesus. Saint Joseph was a father. He guarded Jesus and Mary. He'll guard me and my little ones," Lizz said, sitting down again.

"You're just like your old witch of a mother. Cursing and abusing me, just like she did," Margaret said, drunkenly striving to be tragic.

"Dennis, I'm ashamed of you. Why don't you take care of your stinking little shyster of a brother? Why do I have to be always taking care of you and him? I'm busy. I got lots of things to do beside watching him and picking your nose for you," Little Margaret snapped at Dennis.

"WWhat dddid I I I I I dddddo to you?" Dennis replied, looking at Margaret with an uncomprehending face. Lizz shifted her infant to her other breast.

"You llllllet me 'llllllone!" Dennis said, putting up his hands to protect himself lest his sister slap him.

"LLLLet you 'llllllone," she mimicked. "I'll let you alone when you show some manners and upbringing like my brother Daniel does."

"All you're good for is to be a cow. Why don't you go into the dairy business?" Margaret said, watching the infant milking.

"The Blessed Virgin was a mother, and I'm a mother. But you're not a mother. You're not a mother," Lizz yelled.

"If I was a mother, I'd be a better one than you. And I'd never be the mother to buck-toothed Jim O'Neill's brats."

"I'll have you know that Jim is an honest, hard-working man. I don't read anything in the paper about Jim O'Neill being a blackmailer. And no detectives go to anybody's door because of me or Jim."

"Fart on you!" said Margaret.

"And, yes, a great big fart out of my ass for you, you drunken streetwalker," Lizz shrieked.

"Yes, abuse me! Call me names! I'm not a whore, though, when I give you money. You're just like all the rest of the family. You abuse me and call me names just like Mother does."

"I've never walked into your house drunk. I've never walked into any house drunk."

"A good drunk would do you good, you sanctimonious hypocrite."

"If I wasn't a sick mother, nursing one of my little ones, I'd break your face in. I'd pull that dirty tongue of yours right out of your mouth. And if I tell my Jim what you said to me, he'll slap your face for you."

"Yes, and you and your lanky Jim would do better by making something out of your brats."

"You should talk! You should say anything about my children! Here they are! Look at them! Not one of them is an idiot. Not one of them is a bastard!"

"You would say that to me! Oh, God! Oh, Jesus Christ!" Margaret said, turning away from Lizz and sitting down to sob.

"It's about time that you cried. It's about time that some sorrow should enter your hard and sinful heart. It's about time that the fear of God should strike your dirty soul. It's about time!"

"Yes! Well, say, you let me tell you!" Margaret shouted, springing to her feet. "Well, let me tell you that if you were a mother who knew how to take care of your children, that dirty little thief of yours wouldn't be in the hospital now with a broken leg that is the punishment of God."

"Say, don't you call my son a thief!"

"He's a thief! A dirty little thief!"

"He never stole anything from you. All he ever did for you was run to the store to get you cigarettes and booze."

"He stole my beautiful emerald ring that Lorry gave me."

"He did not."

"Give me back my ring!"

"Take care how you talk, Peg O'Flaherty. God is listening to you. Take care what you say!"

"Hypocrite, get me the ring your son stole out of my house!"

"Wait till Jim hears what you say! Jim says to me, 'Lizz, keep our Bill out of the house where your sister is. I don't want my son around a whore.'"

"He does, does he! Well, you tell him to give me back the ring his son stole, and then he can kiss my ass."

"If I didn't have this baby in my arms, I'd tear that foul tongue of yours out of your mouth."

"Give me back my ring!"

"See this hand," Lizz said, holding up her left hand. "The only ring I have was put on this hand by an honorable man. The only ring I got is one you couldn't wear. It's a decent married woman's ring!"

"Tell your buck-toothed husband I want my ring."

"Tell him yourself, and he'll hit you between the eyes. Wait till he sees you. He'll make you see stars for what you said to his sick wife."

"I want my ring!"

"Hold the baby, Little Margaret," Lizz said commandingly.

<h1 style="text-align:center">III</h1>

She was holding little Catherine. Little Catherine was like a doll, only she was heavy, and a doll never wet her diapers like little Catherine did. You could hold a doll forever, and never be wet from number one.

Mama was talking loud, shaking her fists, and acting like she was going to beat up Aunty Margaret. She hoped that Mama wouldn't beat her Aunty Margaret up and hurt her, because she loved her Aunty Margaret. Aunty Margaret was crying, and she was standing up before Mama, only she couldn't stand straight, and she was see-sawing like a see-saw before Mama.

She knew what was the matter with Aunty Margaret. Aunty Margaret was drunk. Sometimes Papa came home drunk. When he did, he cursed and talked loud, and then Mama talked loud, and they fought, and sometimes Papa hit Mama. Then she cried, and fainted, and Papa had to give her water to wake her up. Papa hit Mama, but he almost never hit her, or Dennis, or Robert. He sometimes hit Bill if Bill was a bad boy. And sometimes, when she was up to

Mother's, Mother got drunk. When Mother got drunk, she cried. Aunty Margaret was drunk, and crying, and she wasn't able to stand up straight. She was making Mama get madder and madder. Mama was yelling, and crying, and shaking her hands at Aunty Margaret. She was afraid that Mama was going to hit Aunty Margaret. And then maybe Aunty Margaret would hit Mama. They would fight, and hurt each other.

"Lizz O'Neill, don't you call me a whore!"

She knew what that was. Mama had called Aunty Margaret a whore. Aunty Margaret did not like to be called a whore. Whore was an awful bad word, as bad as shit and sonofabitch. Whore, shit, sonofabitch, shit, whore, sonofabitch, sonofabitch, whore, shit. They were bad words. Mama used them when she was mad. But if she or any of the kids used them, Mama would get mad. She would bawl them out and hit them, and take them out to the kitchen and wash their mouths out with soap, for using bad words. Only when you said these bad words, it didn't make any different taste in your mouth than if you said words that weren't bad, like God and Blessed Virgin Mary.

"Whore."

There she had gone and said it, only Mama and Aunty Margaret didn't hear it because they were too busy yelling at each other and fighting. They looked like they were going to fight and hit each other, and that would be awful. But she had said the bad word, and there was no bad taste in her mouth, and nothing awful had happened to her, and Mama couldn't wash the badness out of her mouth with soap because Mama was fighting with Aunty Margaret. She was glad, too, that Mama hadn't heard, because she didn't like the taste of soap.

"Whore."

"God."

Now she had said both words, and still there was no different taste in her mouth, and she didn't see why Mama had to wash her mouth out for using bad words. Mama was using an awful lot of bad words right now, fighting with Aunty Margaret. But she never saw Mama washing her own mouth out with soap to get the badness off her own tongue.

"You're not fit to be a mother!"

"Peg O'Flaherty, you couldn't even get a man to marry you and make you the legitimate mother of his children."

They were talking louder and saying such mean things to each other that she was afraid they were going to hurt each other. She wished they wouldn't fight this way. But being drunk made Aunty Margaret and Papa and Mother all say and do mean things. Only sometimes being drunk made Papa happy, and he laughed and gave them all pennies.

"What kind of a mother are you to be raising a son a thief?"

Aunty Margaret was yelling over and over again that her big brother, Bill, stole a ring. Mama said that to take anything that belongs to somebody else and not to you is stealing. That's what it meant to be a thief. And Dennis had taken her doll yesterday.

Mama was shouting at Aunty Margaret now. And Dennis had taken her doll yesterday.

Carrying little Catherine, she walked over to Dennis. She didn't like little Catherine so much when she had to hold and carry her, because she got heavier and heavier. She would rather have a little sister who got lighter and lighter when you carried her.

"This is the gratitude I get after all that I've done for you and that buck-tooth of yours."

"Keep your money! Use it for the Devil the way you do. Give it to Martha Morton and your other Protestant sinful friends. Keep your tainted money."

"Dennis O'Neill, you are a thief!" Little Margaret said sternly.

"You lllllet me 'lllllone," Dennis stuttered, drawing back from her.

"Dennis O'Neill, don't you dare run away from me! You stay right here!" she said in her best grown-up manner. He edged further away from her. "You come right here and stand before me while I talk to you, Dennis O'Neill!"

"I wwwwon't."

"Don't you dare talk back to me, you little brat!"

"If you hit me, I'll tttttttelll PPPPPPPapa."

"Go ahead, hit me!" Margaret wailed. "You hit me when I was a poor little sick girl, the weakest and the most innocent little thing in the world. You told Al that Louise and I went and walked with boys, when there was not one bit of harm in it. And he beat us, us the most innocent little things in the world. Pick on me now! Hit me! You always did. I'm used to your abuse."

"Dennis O'Neill, you listen to me or I'll hit you hard."

"I dddddon't wwwwant to tttttalk to you."

"Give me back my ring!" Margaret shouted.

"I haven't got your ring. It's cursed by Satan," Lizz yelled.

"You are a thief, Dennis O'Neill! Yesterday you stole my doll? Why are you a thief? Why did you steal my doll?"

"Say, don't you talk about stealing. What about that Easter Sunday when I was going to a picnic with Jim and you stole my only clean pair of stockings? You call anybody a thief!" Lizz bellowed.

"That you, and your stockings, and your Jim may have been drowned at that Easter Sunday picnic!"

"Dennis O'Neill, you thief, you get out of my sight! You go and stay out of my sight in the kitchen this very minute or I'll kill you!"

He ran. He fell, face forward. He got up, crying, holding his knee.

"It serves you right, you thief!" Little Margaret said, turning on her heels, struggling back to the couch with the heavy baby in her arms. She sat down, and held the infant beside her.

"Get out of my sight, you buck-tooth!" Little Margaret said as Dennis whimpered in the dining room.

The infant cried.

"Keep still!" she said, looking at it sternly.

It reached its tiny hands for her face.

"You be quiet while your mother minds you. I'm your mother," Little Margaret said to the infant.

"Get out of my house before I call the neighbors!" Lizz cried.

"Give me my ring and I'll get out! I want my ring!"

"Get out before I call the police."

Margaret and Lizz closed in on one another. Margaret pushed Lizz's face back with her left hand. They grappled.

"Take your hands off me, chippy! Help! Murder! Police! She's killing me! Take your hands off me! Stop beating a mother! Help! Call the Fire Department! Police!" Lizz shrieked, pushing, batting at Margaret, slapping her face until Margaret's left cheek reddened.

They were hitting each other. She didn't want them to do that. She didn't want Mama to hurt her Aunty Margaret. And she didn't want her Aunty Margaret to hurt Mama. Aunty Margaret was crying, and she couldn't stand up straight. Ooh, Mama hit Aunty Margaret again. Aunty Margaret was falling. She fell in the rocking chair. Mama was shouting at her to get out. She didn't want them to fight like that. Aunty Margaret was getting up, crying, and she didn't have a handkerchief to wipe her eyes. And ooh, she needed to blow her nose. The snot was coming out of it, just like it came out of Robert's dirty little nose. Aunty Margaret was cursing Mama, and saying she would never come back and darken this door again. She loved her Aunty. Aunty Margaret was good to her and gave her nice things. Aunty Margaret was going to the door. She couldn't walk straight. She bumped into the wall. Mama was calling her bad names, using that bad word, whore. Aunty Margaret was crying. She was going. She was gone. Mama was cursing her. Mama was slamming the door. Aunty Margaret was gone. OOOOH!

Little Margaret sobbed. The infant bawled. Lizz stood by the door, struggling to regain her breath. Googooing, Robert crawled toward Little Margaret.

"Go way, Robert, you little thief! You stole my doll!" Little Margaret said.

And here was Dennis, the bad little thief. And she could see that he had done number two in his pants. Nasty! And Mama was gone to the bedroom. Mama had hit her lovely Aunty Margaret. Naughty little Dennis, doing number two in his pants.

"Shut up, you little brat. Don't cry, you shyster!" Little Margaret said to the bawling infant, the tears running down her own cheeks.

Mama was back. She was throwing holy water around the parlor.

"Be gone, Satan!" Lizz commanded.

"Mama, Dennis is bad. He did number two in his pants."

"Be gone, spawn of Hell!" Lizz exhorted, spraying holy water about, and a drop of it struck Little Margaret's tearful right eye.

IV

A raw wind blew through the October dusk. Yellow lights fell about the corner of Twenty-fifth and La Salle. Down on Wentworth the store lights were on. Margaret staggered about the lamppost. Her eyes were puffed. Her face was scratched, with clotted streaks of blood on the left cheek. Her hat was on crooked. Her coat was opened, and her long black dress was covered with cigarette ashes. She staggered.

"Don't fall down, sister!" a teamster yelled at her, riding by on his wagon.

A black-shawled old woman passed her, stopped, watched her with criticizingly curious eyes, turned up her nose, walked on. A band of kids followed her, laughing, talking at a respectful distance.

"Gee, look at the dame. She can't walk straight."

"She's drunk. My old lady walks like that when she gets drunk. And then the old man socks her in the kisser. The cops came last week when he socked her."

"And what else happens?"

"The cops took her away. But the old man always goes and gets her out."

"Go on, you alley rats!" Margaret yelled back at the kids.

They laughed. Two of them began staggering, imitating her. An old man in rumpled clothes stopped, drew the pipe out of his mouth, watched her, a smile twisting the lips of his almost corduroy face.

She zigzagged on slowly toward Wentworth Avenue, still followed by the hooting kids. She paused. She listed toward the curb edge. She wavered over it, and a ten-year-old girl, whose pants were hanging down, imitated her to the delight of the other kids. Margaret retched. Her vomit hit the lower portions of her dress. The kids followed, making noises with their mouths, pretending that they were regurgitating.

She told herself that she needed a glass of gin, and then she was going to see Martha Morton and get the money Martha owed her.

24

I

Mother was keeping him in the house because he had a cold. He didn't want to go out anyway, because these days, the older kids, like Bull Young and Cross-Eyed Bucky Haight, who played in the prairie out in back, they were picking on him. They told him he was tied to his grandmother's apron strings. Well, he wasn't. But, gee, he wished Hortense Audrey lived near him instead of way over on the other side of Grand Boulevard. If she did, they could play together every day in the back yard or on Calumet Avenue. He would rather play with her than with Bull Young and Bull's brother. He wished, too, that Bill · was out of the hospital and could come up and play with him every day.

He went out to the kitchen. He sniffled, then coughed. He stood by the opened door to Mother's small bedroom, and she sat in her rocking chair.

"Mother, why are you crying? I don't want you to be crying!"

"That I should have ever lived to see the day!"

"Mother, where is Aunty Margaret? She promised me she would be home and help me learn to read today."

"She's out somewhere with the Devil."

"She's not out with the real Devil, is she?"

"Indeed, she is!"

"But, Mother, I learned in my catechism lesson that when the Devil gets you, it's bad for you. He gets your soul, and takes it away from God, and then you won't never be able to go to Heaven and see God."

"She was born for Hell, even if she is me own daughter," Mrs. O'Flaherty bitterly said.

"But, Mother, Miss Devlin said that no one was born for Hell, and that if we go there, it's because we sin. She told us that we can sin as soon as we reach the age of reason and make our first Holy Communion. She said we would all in my class reach the age of reason next spring and make our first Holy Communion then."

"Ah, had I only known how I would rue the day that she was born!"

"And Aunty Margaret really went out with the Devil?"

"She's with him this very minute."

"Maybe we ought to go and find her and take her away from the Devil. I'll do it. I'll go and get her, and I'll say to the Devil, I will, 'You go away, you Devil, and you keep your dirty old self away from my aunt. And if I catch you trying to steal her soul again, I'll make you sopping wet with holy water. I will!'"

"Son, you're the only comfort that a poor old woman like me has left in this world," she said, smiling through her tears.

"Mother, don't cry! And, Mother, I'll never go out with the Devil."

"If you do, I'll scalp you!"

"And I'll tell Aunty Margaret not to, either."

"Ah, she's good riddance. She's gone like the garbage, and I don't want her back. But, Son, you run along and play. Your grandmother wants to say her rosary beads."

II

Danny went thoughtfully to the parlor, carrying an apple and a paring knife. He sneezed, and blew his nose. It was chafed and red, and it hurt when he wiped it. He asked God please to take the soul of Aunty Margaret back from the Devil, and please to fix it so that Aunty Margaret and Mother would never fight any more. If God would do that, he would promise God he would do his best never to let himself think of anything but God and Heaven and holy things on Sunday mornings when he was at mass.

He knelt by the parlor window, dreamily eying the darkening day. He watched an elevated train crawl on the tracks like a great big animal. It was like a great big snail. There was a picture of a little snail in his first-grade reader. The elevated train was a great big snail. Gee, he hoped that Aunty Margaret came home all right for supper and stayed in tonight. If she didn't, what with Uncle Al away on the road, he and Mother would be all alone with it dark outside. He would be afraid. And if the Devil had come and taken Aunty Margaret, who was grown up, what was going to stop the Devil from coming and taking him away? And he didn't want the old Devil taking him. There was a man on the other side of Calumet. It wasn't his Aunty Margaret. He wished it was his Aunty Margaret instead of a man.

He cut a slice of apple. He would play butcher, and that would help him forget about being afraid. He was a big butcher man, wearing an apron and standing behind a butcher counter in a store on Fifty-first Street. This apple was all his meat, steak, and pork chops, and lamb chops, and ham, all his meat. He made various-sized cuts of the apple and spread them out before him on the window sill. He was a butcher now.

And here was a nice lady coming to buy some steak off him.

Good day, lady.

Good day, Mr. Butcher.

I have all kinds of good meat to sell, lady.

I want a pound of tenderloin steak for my husband's supper. He likes steak.

Yes, lady.

Paring off a piece of apple, Danny pretended that he was cutting steak, and then that he was wrapping it up and handing it to his customer. He ate the piece of apple he had cut. He guessed that next Christmas when he was taken to see Santa Claus, he was going to ask for a toy butcher shop, with scales, and shelves, and a little counter, and a cash register with toy money. Then it would be more fun playing that he was a butcher. He would call himself Mr. Castle, the butcher man.

Good day, sir! Would you like some meat?

Give me six pork chops.

He selected another slice of apple. He hit at it as if he were chopping it. Then he pretended that he was sawing with a real butcher's saw. Next he had to cut off little bits of fat. Then it had to be wrapped and given to the man.

Thank you, sir! Call again!

He munched the pieces of apple he had cut up. He sneezed. Outside it was getting darker. Soon it would be all dark. Aunty Margaret ought to come home. There was a policeman. He would like to go downstairs and ask the policeman to go out and try to find Aunty Margaret and bring her home safe. She was out all alone with it getting dark, and the Devil had her. He would never never sin again, not even if he lived to be a hundred years old, if God would only send Aunty Margaret back home again right now and not ever let the Devil get her again.

Darker out, almost black now. If he turned around from the window, he could hardly see in the parlor. A man on the sidewalk. He looked like he might be an awful dangerous man. An elevated train with the lights in it lit up. An automobile. Dark, with the lamppost at the corner lit. His Aunty Margaret was out with the Devil. He did want God to please send her home safe, and never to let her and Mother fight again.

He coughed. His nose ran.

He was crying.

III

After supper, Danny sat at the dining-room table drawing pictures of cats, dogs, houses, and baseball diamonds with his crayons. Every time he thought of how dark it was outside, he would try harder to keep his mind on his drawings. He took a sheet of paper with scrawlings and colorings on it and went to his grandmother, who was rocking in a corner by the sewing machine.

"Mother, look at the picture I drew," he said, handing his picture to her.

She gazed at it over the glasses which were set low on her nose.

"Isn't it beautiful, Son! Your teacher should be giving you the best marks in drawing when you can make pictures like this," she said in amazement as she continued to look at his crude drawing.

"No, Mother! Miss Devlin said I should draw much better than I do. She says I'm not very good at drawing."

"If I ever hear her saying that about my grandson, I'll tear her scalp off."

"That's funny," Danny said, laughing.

"Son, what are you sayin'?"

"I was thinking, Mother, that you would be a very good Indian. Aunty Margaret told me that Indians are always scalping people."

"I'll scalp anyone who's in league with the Devil."

"I'll scalp people for you, Mother, if you want me to."

"Is this a cat you drew, Son?"

"It's a puppy dog."

"Isn't it pretty! Now, Son, you draw some more pictures."

"I'll draw one for you, and you buy it off me."

"You make me a fine picture, Son, and I'll give you a penny."

"Oh, no, Mrs. O'Flaherty! I can't sell my drawings for a penny. Times are hard, Mrs. O'Flaherty. I got to charge you more than a penny."

"I'll give you two pennies," she said, smiling.

"Oh, no, that's not enough, either. I have to take care of my grandmother, and she needs nice things, and good food and milk, and I can't get things for her unless I charge you a nickel for my drawing."

"Here, here's five cents. You do me a fine drawing, Son," she said, chuckling, digging down into her apron pocket, fishing for a nickel, handing it to him.

"I'll give you a good drawing, and you'll not be sorry you put your trade with me," he said, going back to the table while she beamed upon him, her eyes filling with tears of affection.

IV

"Son, I'm going to whist down to the corner to get tobacco for me pipe," the grandmother said while Danny labored over his picture of a green house with red windows, talking and humming to himself as he worked.

He gaped at her, so fearful, surprised, that he could say nothing. He forced himself not to cry.

"I won't be gone but a jiffy."

He meekly and silently dogged her steps back to her bedroom. He stood by the door while she flung her knitted black shawl over her head. He followed her to the front door. He stood while she opened it and turned to him with her hand grasping the outer doorknob.

"Don't open the door for anyone. I'll be back before you can count ten. I have me key, but I'll ring the bell a long time so you'll know it's me. I'll be back before you can say boo. You be careful, and don't let man nor beast in while I'm gone."

He stood alone, looking emptily at the closed door. Tears grew in his eyes. He might be kidnaped, hurt, killed. Anything might be done to him before she got back. And he knew why she went. There was a package of Tip Top Tobacco on her dresser that she had never even opened. She had left him all alone like this to go and drink beer. Uncle Al didn't like her to drink beer, either. If he knew she was doing this, Uncle Al would bawl her out. She was mean, leaving him all alone like this when anything could happen to him. It would just serve her right if he told Uncle Al about it, and Uncle Al got good and mad at her. And he had a good mind to tell, too, when Uncle Al came home again off the road.

He cowered against the door, transfixed, afraid to move. The house seemed chained in an awful quiet. He felt that it was just the kind of quiet that ghosts liked before they came to haunt a house. If they came now, while Mother was gone, could they do anything to him? He wished that Aunty Margaret was not out with the Devil. He wished that Uncle Al was home, and that Uncle Ned was in from Madison, and both of them were sitting in the parlor talking about baseball, with him listening to what they said.

He was sure that he heard some mysterious sound behind him, a creaking board, a noise like maybe someone was sneaking on tiptoe behind his back. For all he knew, it could be a robber who would stab him in the back with a dagger. And then when Mother got back, she would find the house robbed, and there he would be fallen and killed by the door with his blood all over the carpet. Wouldn't she be sorry she left him like this! And wouldn't Aunty Margaret be sorry she had gone out with the Devil! Still that creaky, creepy noise. He dared not move. He didn't even know how he was able to breathe, or how his heart was

able to go on beating. Whoever it was or whatever it was, the noise was getting
nearer. Oh, if Mother would only come back! Nearer!

Danny frantically swung around on his heels. He saw only the dim and empty
hallway, and at its end the lighted dining room. There was nobody. But maybe
there was. Maybe the ghost or the robber knew that he was going to turn around
and had ducked into Aunty Margaret's bedroom. He took a cautious step toward
the dining room. He halted, his face twisting with hideous fear. If he prayed,
maybe God would not let the house be robbed and anything happen to him.

Oh, God, please save him and the house from robbers, kidnapers, ghosts,
Blackhands, and the boogey man!

He scurried into the unlit parlor and knelt by the center window. He could
see the lighted lamplights and parts of the street where the moonlight was on
it. And there were awful black shadows on the streets and across the street in
the prairie. They were like haunting ghosts turned into shadows. And there
were people walking, an automobile, a horse and buggy, another automobile, a
policeman. He wanted to call the policeman up to come and stay with him until
Mother got back. Why was it taking her so long? Didn't she care about what
happened to him? An automobile coming from under the elevated, going over
to Grand Boulevard. Why was it taking her so long?

Another elevated train. The wind was making noises against the window. He
coughed, and his eyes watered. There was a big kid who was probably already in
sixth grade at school. He wanted to be bigger, as big as Jimmy Hanlon who was
in third grade at Crucifixion, as big as Bill who was in fourth grade in the public
school down around Twenty-fifth Street, as big as that kid across the street who
was maybe in the sixth or seventh grade. When he was big, he wasn't going to
be afraid of anything. He wanted to be a brave man who was not afraid to stay
alone in the house at night. If burglars came, he wanted to be able to beat them
up and chase them away. His nose was running, and he wiped it smearingly with
the back of his hand.

Oh, where was Mother?

He could have gone for her tobacco and come back six times over already.
He was good and mad at her. When she came back, he wasn't going to speak to
her. He was going to show her. And when Aunty Margaret came home, he was
going to be mad at her, too. If they thought that they could leave him all alone
like this where he might be hurt or killed, well, he was going to show them a
thing or two!

A train whistle from far away. It was like a ghost crying from somewheres way
off. Maybe it wasn't an engine whistle at all. Maybe it was a ghost. Maybe all
ghosts spoke like engine whistles and that was why engine whistles made you
afraid when you heard them at night. Maybe what he had just heard was the

ghosts of Father and Aunty Louise calling to Mother. It might have been Aunty Louise bawling Mother out because she had left him all alone like this.

A man on the street. Was he a burglar? And there was a policeman. A horse-and-wagon going cloppety clop. He coughed, raspingly. This horse-and-wagon was maybe driven by a kidnaper. The boogey man might even be hidden in it, and maybe he had just stolen a little boy who was left all alone, and he was going to do something awful to the boy, like kill him.

Gee, he was afraid, all right, alone on a dark night like this, when you could almost see the wind blowing and you could hear engine whistles that sounded like ghosts coming to haunt you, or ghosts talking and sounding like engine whistles. Oh, please, Mother, come home! Please, God, send Mother home safe and soon, right away quick, please, God!

Another elevated train. If he was riding on an elevated train he wouldn't feel so afraid, because burglars and kidnapers and the boogey man would be afraid to harm him in front of all the people that there would be riding on the train. Oh, why didn't Mother come home? Leaving him alone like this, when he was sick with a cough. Tomorrow he would have to go to school unless his cough was too bad. He hoped it was. He didn't like school. The kids crossed their fingers shame at him and said he liked Maggie Grady when he didn't like Maggie Grady at all. He didn't like any girl in the whole first grade except Hortense Audrey.

He coughed. Maybe he was getting sick, too.

Was that Mother? It looked like her, a woman with a shawl, coming along almost at a run. Mother! Oh, Mother! It was her.

He ran to the door. He waited by it in shaking anxiety, not knowing what to do with his hands, sticking his fingers in his mouth, taking them out, clapping them together. The bell rang, long and sharply. He ran to the buzzer down the hall a little ways, stretched up on tiptoes to press it. He ran back to the door, stood waiting, his heart pounding, his breath gushing rapidly. He waited, and again it was so quiet. A creak in the floor. He was sure it was somebody, and he might be grabbed before she got upstairs. That noise. A ghost tiptoeing behind him, coming, coming, coming. . . . He opened the door.

"Mudder?" he called in fear.

"Are you all right, Son?"

"Yes, Mudder!" he said, hearing her come up, seeing her trudge forward toward the top, her head bent, carrying a bag in which there were rattling bottles of beer.

"Were you afraid, Son?"

"No, I wasn't afraid."

"I whisted down and back as fast as my old legs would carry me. I wasn't gone long," she said, bending down to kiss his forehead.

She closed the front door, and again kissed him, this time on the lips, and he smelled the beer on her breath. He hoped that she wasn't going to carry on, crying and yelling like she sometimes did when she drank beer. And sometimes when she was drunk, she was sad. Other times she was mad, and she cursed him, and he was afraid of her. When he was a man, he was going to be like Uncle Al and never get drunk.

"I just got some tobacco and a swallow of beer to quench me thirst," she said, going back toward the kitchen.

"I was watching for you by the window."

"Here's for you, because you was a good boy," she said, fishing a stick of peppermint candy from her apron pocket and handing it to him.

He sucked it, and suddenly he sneezed.

"I got to watch your cold or you'll get sick. Come and I'll give you some cough medicine," she said, setting the bag of beer bottles on the kitchen table and flinging her shawl over a chair.

V

She was starting to talk loud and make noise like she did when she was drunk. And her voice was sounding funny when she talked. He wished he could fall asleep and so not hear her if she got awfully drunk.

"Mother, I'm tired," he said, yawning drowsily.

"You poor child, and you have a cold. Your grandmother will put you to bed."

"No, maybe I'm not tired," he said, thinking that maybe he should stay up and watch her, because if she got too drunk she might hurt herself.

"Son, you're not an O'Neill or an O'Flaherty. The next time you see your parents, you tell them you're a Fox, and turn your face to the wall on them."

"Mother, honest, do you want me to turn my face to the wall when I see my Papa and Mama?" he asked.

"You're too good for the likes of them," she said.

She took a swig of beer, and then wiped her lips and chin with her gingham apron.

"Mother, maybe you're tired and want to go to bed?" Danny said, thinking that if she went to bed she couldn't get too drunk.

"I'll be putting my old bones to rest soon, Son."

"I just thought that maybe you were tired," Danny said.

She took another drink from her glass of beer. He coughed.

"All the children who I washed diapers for and nursed at me breast, they left me," she said melancholily.

"Gee!"

"My Ned, running off and marrying that woman in Madison. He should have his behind flayed until it burns him. And she so sick that she has hardly a leg to stand on. Lizz marrying a pauper who can't put bread in the mouths of his own offspring. Al getting himself work where he is never home. Margaret out with the Devil himself. Oh, little I thought that I would come to this with my children in the latter end of me days. Ah, here I am, with me poor man dead and alone out in Calvary, and my lawful children leaving me alone night after night. Little I thought that I would come to this when I was a wisp of a girl running the bush in the old country, barefooted and with me backside showing through my dress."

She seemed so sad, and she talked so sad in a funny way like this, that he hardly knew what she was talking about. He wanted to tell her not to be sad. He looked at her, large-eyed.

"Sure, my children are no comfort to me. Out married, high-lifing, taking jobs at the four corners of the world so that they are never home of a night with their mother," she said, drinking beer.

"Mudder, you got me to take care of you and not let anybody hurt you," Danny said, his nose dribbling.

She smiled at him. She drew him close, wiped his nose with her apron, kissed his forehead. He wished she wouldn't be sad like this. But it was the way beer made her.

"Ah, and if I had known, I never would have worked the skin off me hands for them, indeed, I wouldn't have!"

"Mother, I'll never leave you," Danny said.

"You're all that your poor old grandmother has left in the world," she said with inebriated tenderness.

"Mother, I like you better than I like my Mama."

"If you didn't, I'd rip the skin off your face," she said, emptying her last bottle of beer into her glass.

"Mother, why does beer foam?" he asked, suddenly fascinated by the beer as it foamed in the glass.

"Come here, Son!" she called, her eyes large with tears. She crushed him to her. "You are my son!"

Her kisses were wet and they smelled awful of beer. And she didn't have her teeth in, so when she talked, he could see her gums. She looked nicer when she had her teeth in. She relaxed her embrace of him. He stepped back several feet.

"Mother, why are you so sad?"

"I've lived too long in this world, Son. There's no place for me in it now," she said, drinking.

"Mother, please, don't cry," he said, seeing the tears roll down her cheeks, wondering what he could do to make her stop crying.

"I'm crying because you make me happy," she said, finishing the glass of beer.

"I never cry when I'm glad. I cry when I'm hurt," Danny said.

"That mother of yours, she, too, makes me rue the day that she was born. Leaving a decent home and a good job in service to marry a long-jawed pauper smelling of manure. Ah, but then, when everything is said and done, he's a decent hard-working man and he lost a finger in the machine at the factory. Son, your father is a decent hard-working man just like Tom, your grandfather, was."

"I like Papa, Mother. But I like Uncle Al more."

"If you're as good a man as your Uncle Al is, Son, you'll walk the earth with the blessing of God on your head."

"I want to be like Uncle Al when I'm a man, and buy you electricity."

"You're a fine boy," she said, patting his head.

She went to her bedroom. And she couldn't walk straight. She came out with her shawl over her head. He started to cry, and was interrupted by a fit of sneezing. He looked at her, his face twisted with apprehensiveness and horror.

"Son, you sit right here and be good. Your grandmother has to run down to the corner again. This tobacco I got doesn't draw right, and I got to get another pack of it."

"Please, take me with you, Mudder?"

"You have a cold. You just wait right here. I'll not be gone more than a jiffy."

Betrayed, he silently followed her to the front door. He watched it close behind her. He stood facing it, sniffling. He ran into the darkened bedroom off the front. He flung himself on his cot, his body shaking with sobs. He moaned himself to sleep.

VI

Out of a world full of pain and noise and fear, a world of awful figures, and terrible shapes and boogey men and devils, he awoke, coughing, sweating, surrounded by darkness. He heard shouting in the house. He gasped. He began to yell, and his cries were interrupted by a fit of coughing. Beads of perspiration stuck out on his head. He sat up. He discovered that he was in his own cot. He heard them yelling. He didn't know how he got to bed. Mother must have taken his clothes off and put him to bed while he was asleep.

"Mother! Mother! Mother!" he plaintively called.

Mother and Aunty Margaret were fighting, and they didn't hear him. He could tell they were both drunk from the way they were yelling. Being drunk was an awful sin. When he was a man he would never get himself drunk. He wished that Mama, Uncle Al, somebody was here now.

270

"Mother!" he tearfully called.

"The curse of God on your soul!" Mrs. O'Flaherty cried at her daughter.

"Why, you goddamn toothless old hag!" the daughter screamed.

He lay in bed, shivering with cold, too terrified even to wipe his running nose. The way they were shouting made him feel certain that something terrible awful was going to happen. He drew his knees up under his chin and hid his head under the covers.

God, please, make them stop! Please, don't let Aunty Margaret hit Mother and hurt her! Please, don't let anything awful happen! God, please, make Mother and Aunty Margaret sober right away, this very minute! God, please!

He pulled the cover off his head. He sniffled. He lay quiet.

"Don't shout so the neighbors can hear you, you chippy!" the mother screamed.

"You drove my father into an early grave with your tongue!"

"May God burn the tongue out of your mouth with red-hot irons!" the mother shouted.

Oh, why did they talk so loud, and say awful things, and fight? And wasn't God going to make them stop? And now the people downstairs were hitting on the radiator to make them stop keeping everybody in the building awake. And there was Mother right outside the door. He wanted to tell her, please, don't cry like that, Mother.

"A plague on the day that my womb bore such rotten fruit as you! Curse the day!"

"I tremble with shame before the world that I should have a mother like you. But there is justice in the world. There will be a day of reckoning, and you'll pay! You'll pay, you Irish whoremonger!"

He could see Mother in the hallway still, but she didn't look like Mother. She was leaning against the hall tree, and her hair was falling down. She looked like maybe she was a witch. And there was Aunt Margaret coming toward her, leaning against the wall. And now the people downstairs were hitting the radiator awful hard.

"Don't shout in my son's house!" the mother said.

"Shit on your son!" Margaret belched at the top of her voice.

"Merciful God!" the mother exclaimed with upraised hands.

He wished that Aunty Margaret wouldn't use bad words like that, because it was a sin to do it.

"Go get a broom and ride on it howling through the night and you'll look like a witch," Margaret yelled.

"Blessed Saint Joseph, that I should have to see such a day," Mrs. O'Flaherty exclaimed.

"Ah, the world would crucify you if it knew what you were! I'll tell the world, I'll tell the world, and I'll have you crucified for all the evil you've done. You nagged my father out of his mind. You put him in his grave. And don't think I don't know how you nagged him into a fit of insanity so that he threw your baby, Martin, on the floor and killed it from a broken neck. Don't think I don't know that! Don't think I don't know what you are. Murderer! Murderer!" Margaret yelled until her voice broke from the strain.

"That God might strike you blind this very minute!" the mother yelled.

The people were still hitting the radiator. And there was an engine whistle from far away. And an elevated train. He cried, almost hysterically, his tears and his running nose dripping onto the blanket. He looked out the window and saw the face of the Man in the Moon, as if the man in the moon was just right above Calumet Avenue. Oh, Man in the Moon, make them stop, make them go to bed!

He could see them. Aunt Margaret was beating Mother up. Mother was sitting on the floor, crying. Aunty Margaret stood over her, shouting. And the people downstairs were pounding the radiator. And it was so cold and so dark. He was afraid to move. He gave way to uncontrolled sobbing. He folded his small hands and he prayed slowly, trying not to hear the way they were yelling and screaming.

25

I

Jim lay in bed listening to the last feeble tinklings of the alarm clock. He felt the presence of Lizz beside him, large, warm, and sweaty.

"I'll get up and make your breakfast," Lizz said, yawning.

"Don't bother. I'll fix it myself," Jim said.

"Catherine will have to be fed anyway," Lizz said.

"Yes, Lizz, this is what we call another day," Jim said, reluctantly getting out of bed.

He stretched his long arms out to their full length and yawned. He stood for a moment, a tall, rawboned man in long and soiled heavy underwear. He picked his truss off the chair where his clothes were flung, and put it on carefully. He sat on the edge of the bed, drawing on his socks and smelling the odor of his own feet. He guessed that he'd have to bathe himself tonight. The goddamn business of making your living as a driver! It always gave him the feeling that he smelled of manure.

"Jim, I'm worried," Lizz said.

"I tell you, Lizz, forget worrying about that drunken sister of yours. The best thing in the world that you could have done yesterday was beat her up the way you did. If I was here, and she around drunk and looking for a fight like she did, I would have just picked her bodily and pitched her down the stairs without any to-do about it," Jim said.

"It's not that hussy, Jim, who worries me."

"Lizz, we have other things to worry about besides the O'Flahertys. If you'd have taken my advice long ago, and kept Bill away from them, she wouldn't be coming down drunk like she did yesterday, accusing the poor kid of taking her damn ring. She probably got stewed somewhere and lost it."

"Jim, it's something else. You know, the curse should have come to me yesterday."

"Well, isn't it sometimes not regular and you, Lizz, you're always getting your count mixed up, too."

"Yes, but yesterday I felt sick to my stomach. Oh, Jim, what are we going to do? I told you not to do it, and you made me. Now we might have another mouth to feed, as if we didn't have enough already."

"Lizz, let's not cross our bridges before we come to them. It seems to me it shouldn't be due for a week or two yet," Jim said.

"I don't see how it could be. Mother told me that you can't be caught with a new baby as long as you are still nursing a baby at your breasts. And Little Catherine is far, far from being weaned yet."

"Lizz, I say again, let's just not try crossing our bridges before we come to them. It may be as I just said, that you got your count mixed up."

"But, Jim, I'm so afraid. What are we going to do if I am caught?"

"When we got so much to worry about, and so much weight on our shoulders already, we better just try and not let ourselves worry and not start crossing bridges before we come to them," Jim said.

"I'll get up now and make your breakfast, Jim."

"Let me get the fire going first," Jim said, buttoning his blue work shirt as he left the room.

II

In the chilly kitchen, he rubbed his hands together and wriggled himself to get his blood circulating. He lit the kerosene lamp. He cleaned out the ashes from the stove, put in old papers and sticks of box wood. He stood watching the fire leap, hearing its crackle as the wood caught on. He put in a few more sticks, and smiled in fascination at the roar and leap of the golden bright flames, and at the louder crackling of the burning wood. He dropped in a thick chunk of dirty wood with rusty nails sticking out of it, and put the lid over the fire. He filled the kettle with water and set it on the stove to heat. He washed his hands and face in cold water from the running faucet, thinking how some day it would be swell if he could afford a flat with running hot and cold water. Then he would get up in the morning and wash and shave in warm water that ran out of the faucet. He dried himself with a soiled towel. On cold mornings the radiator would already be sizzling. Breakfast would be made by lighting the gas range. Well! Wouldn't that be nice! It seemed like a nice pipe-dream, anyway, particularly if Lizz was knocked up again. But he was pretty sure she was miscounting, as she often did. He rubbed his hands across his smooth chin. He was glad he'd shaved last night. He glanced around the dim kitchen. Yes, he'd sure let himself in for something. The worst thing in the world for a poor workingman to do was to get married. It seemed so.

Well!

He shrugged his shoulders.

His belly was empty, just one big noisy hole. He wished breakfast was ready right this minute.

Lizz appeared in her dirty flannel nightgown, her unwashed face smeared with sleep, her black hair loosely tangled in a knot.

"Better put a robe on, Lizz, or you'll catch cold."

"Yes, I think I will. It is chilly. I only hoped that I would get breakfast going before the little one woke up crying for her milk," Lizz said, turning around and dragging her slippered feet out of the kitchen.

He looked toward the covered pot in the corner. Hated goddamn pisspots! But it was chilly, and his kidneys were damn near floating. As he was urinating into the pot, Lizz came back, wearing an old brown skirt over her nightgown and a rag was tied under her chin.

"You got the fire going good and quick," Lizz said, going to the stove.

"Yes, I'm experienced at making fires by now," Jim said.

Lizz looked at him affectionately. Meeting her gaze, he thought of the Lizz that once was, the thin, beautiful shy girl with the beautiful black hair, the trim, neat white body, the lovely complexion, the dark eyes. Her dark eyes were about all that carried over from the Lizz who once was. He looked into those eyes. They closed as he clutched her in his arms and planted a long wet kiss on her lips. He held her tightly. Her body was warm. She clung to him. He released her. He smiled weakly, then grimly. He patted her head.

"Don't worry, Lizz! You and I are going to stick together and come down the home stretch like greased lightning with the banners waving for us."

"My Jim!" she said with emotion.

III

Lizz set the larded frying pan over the stove. It sizzled, sputtered off grease. She dropped strips of bacon into it and stepped back lest she be burned by a flying speck of grease.

"Well, it looks like it's going to be a raw day," Jim said.

Lizz took the bacon off and set it on a plate which she put on the top ledge of the stove.

"How many eggs you want, Jim?"

"Two."

"You better take three. A man needs his belly full when he's doing outside work like you are."

"We can't afford it, me eating three eggs a day. That'll be taking food out of the mouths of you and the kids."

"Our Papa is our money man. We got to do well by him. And Jim, the Lord always provides for His own," Lizz said, dropping three eggs into the frying pan.

"Lizz, on the way home tonight, I better stop in the drugstore and get you some medicine, just to make certain," he said.

"No, Jim, I can't take any! That would be flying in the face of God. If God wants me to have another child, He has His own good purposes, and He'll take care of it."

"All right," Jim said helplessly, his hands dropping to his sides in a despairing gesture. He began to set the table for breakfast.

"You sit down, Jim. I'll do that. You'll have enough work to do on the wagon today."

"It's nothing," Jim said, continuing to set the table.

Lizz set eggs, bacon and coffee before him. He spooned sugar and thick canned condensed milk into the coffee. He took a sweet bun from a bag and spread oleomargarine on it. He began eating like a famished man.

"I was hungry all right, Lizz," he said, his mouth stuffed.

Lizz sat down with a cup of coffee. She snatched a sweet roll from the bag. She bit into it. She made a face, and her hand went to her jaw.

"Your teeth?" Jim asked sympathetically.

"Yes," Lizz said; she quickly drank coffee, rolling the warm liquid around her aching tooth. "I can't eat sweets. The sugar gets in my teeth."

"We'll have to try and see that you get to a dentist real soon and get your teeth fixed. Doctors' bills and everything else but necessities can wait for that."

She smiled at him. Jim could see the vacancies in her mouth.

"I should have chewn on the other side. Having so many children seems to have made them soft, and they get cavities easy because of it."

"Well, old woman, one thing we're going to see to is that they get fixed."

"They're all right, Jim. It's nothing to worry about," she said, picking the frosting off her bun.

"We're going to collect from the fellow who ran over Bill. Dinny is after him, hot and heavy. The poor wop hasn't got so much, but he has more than we have. He owns his own horse and wagon, and his own little fruit business. And he was clear wrong. We'll make him pay, and get your teeth fixed first thing as soon as it's settled. Bill will be home by then, and he can stay in and watch the kids on afternoons when you go to the dentist. We'll do lots of things we need to do with the money. We'll move and try and get a better place to live in, with more sunlight, and a bigger back yard for the kids to play in," Jim said.

"Yes, and if I am caught again, we'll have some money for it, too," Lizz said.

"Yes," Jim said glumly.

He silently finished his breakfast. The infant squawled. Lizz went to it, and came back with the baby suckling. Jim poured himself another cup of coffee. He sipped it, and watched the baby at its mother's breast. Wonderful, the way kids were born, fed at their mother's breasts, and grew up. He was sure proud of his. But another! Well, he'd postpone worry until it was certain.

"Ah, isn't she the little sugar dumpling that knows when to call her mother if she's hungry! Isn't she? Look at her, Jim! Isn't she her Mama's little sugar cake! And she has a hole in her little tummy that makes her all the time cry for Mama's milk, hasn't she? She thinks her mother is a dairy farm, doesn't her Mama's little apple pie?"

Jim grinned weakly. He watched with softening mellow eyes, and an intent face. He was glad that he had kids. Damn glad, even if they were so much trouble.

"The little bugger is cute," he said.

"She's her Mama's darling," Lizz said.

Jim's eyes drifted away from Lizz and the infant. He looked out the window. The sky above the Negroes' shack was gray with the first touches of the dawn. Soon it would be pink, and then the sun would bust through it. It was nice to watch the dawn coming, the sun busting right square into a new day. It was nice, too, to wake up and know that it was another day. You felt better waking up fresh at the beginning of the day than you did when you tumbled into bed at the end of it.

The morning of a new day made you feel that something might happen to you, for you. He could see red now beginning to spread through the grayness. Soon the sun would be big above the shack. Yes, it was nice to see another day coming. But what could happen to him? . . . Still, it was nice.

Jack and Jill went up the hill,
To fetch a pail of water.

He turned back and listened while Lizz sang, and he watched the infant, its lips firmly clasped over its mother's nipple.

"I'll be glad when our family is raised, Jim."

"Then the boys will be able to work and bring some money in. We'll have a big home, a decent place, with electricity and steam heat, everything that the O'Flahertys have. The old man and the old woman will have a few comforts for themselves then," Jim said.

"Yes, if they don't leave us when they grow up, the way my brother, Ned, ran off with Mildred. She's so sick, and she's older than he is. I never knew why he did it. Not, of course, that she isn't one of the finest women you would ever expect to meet."

"Well, that's Ned's business, not ours."

"But just let me catch one of mine turning stinker and running off to marry some girl when their mother and father need their pay envelope! Let me catch them!"

"We won't have to worry about our kids, Lizz . . . unless the O'Flahertys spoil Danny. And anyway, that's a bridge that needs no crossing for a long time to come."

"Oh, Jim, look at Mama's little cherubim!" Lizz said, turning her eyes down on the feeding infant.

"She's getting to know us, too, isn't she?" Jim grinned.

"Know us? Say, she's the smartest little thing! Smart as a whip. Ah, yes, she knows her Mama who feeds her and takes care of her, and she knows her great big Papa, and she knows all her big brothers and her sister, too. Ah, she's the smartest little thing, and when she grows up to be a great big bootiful girl, she's going to be a schoolteacher," Lizz said.

"Ah, they're cute little buggers," Jim said.

> *Jack and Jill went up the hill,*
> *To fetch a pail of water.*

IV

Jim held the infant while Lizz made the sandwiches for his lunch.

"I want to hurry with this, before that herd in there wakes up and comes out here for breakfast," Lizz said.

"Yes," Jim said abstractedly, his eyes shifting from Lizz to the baby that slept in his arms.

"I'm glad I got the little sweetheart fed before they're up," Lizz said, spreading oleomargarine lavishly on the unduly thick slices of bread that she had cut.

"Lizz, just this minute I was looking at the little bugger's face while it's asleep. It looks like the face of an old man," Jim said.

"They're cute. But they are a heap of trouble to take care of."

"You know, Lizz, it's interesting, the way they slowly begin to know us and to understand. You know, they are like little animals, and then they gradually become human, don't they?"

"Say!" Lizz said, swinging around and holding aloft the saw-bladed bread knife. "Don't you say that a child of mine is an animal."

"Lizz, you didn't catch what I was driving at. I didn't seem to make myself clear, and you didn't catch what I was driving at," Jim said with a struggling persuasiveness in his voice, seeking by his tone to convey to Lizz what his words had failed to convey.

"A child comes from God," Lizz said belligerently.

"I know it. I didn't mean that it didn't, Lizz."

"God gave my little one a soul. He didn't give a soul to animals," Lizz said.

"I know it, Lizz. You didn't see what I mean."

"God created us because He needed souls for Heaven. When God made the angels, the archangel, Lucifer, was too proud. He wanted to be like God. So God banished him, and all the fallen angels who sided with him, and said that they must live in Hell for all eternity. They became devils, and the Devil, and all his other devils, they're all fallen angels. And there was room in Heaven for souls. And God created Adam and Eve, the first man and woman, and every offspring from Adam and Eve on down through all the ages, they have souls. There is a place in Heaven waiting for them if they obey the laws of God and the Church, because of the room left in Heaven by Lucifer and all the fallen angels who were guilty of the sin of pride. Animals don't have souls, though."

"But, Lizz, you'll wake the little one here."

"But don't say my precious little sugar cube is like an animal. She has a soul, a soul washed white as the cleanest sheet by the holy waters of baptism. She's not mine and yours. We're only her caretakers. She's God's."

"I didn't mean it that way."

"And, Jim, she's so smart. Ah, she's a little wise one, she is," Lizz said.

"She should be. She's an O'Neill. And when she grows up to be a big girl, she's going to be as pretty as you, when you were a girl. Isn't she, Lizz?"

"Oh, Jim, I was never pretty."

"You were, too. You were the prettiest little trick. God, Lizz, I'll never forget you in the days when we used to go to dances and do the cake walk."

"Well, here's your lunch, Jim, four sandwiches. That ought to do you, with an apple and a piece of cake. You can get yourself a cup of hot coffee," Lizz said, embarrassed.

"It's too much, Lizz," Jim said.

He studied the sleeping infant in his arms, its tiny face that looked so sour. He remembered his other children when they had been at this stage of infancy. He recollected how they had grown smart, and learned to cry and bawl when they wanted food, their diapers changed or to be played with. He recalled how they had all fought with almost bitter animal intensity to get their lips around their mother's nipple, and how they all cooed when their little bellies were full. God, what a funny thing it was to have kids! He would be hot for Lizz, and his old john would stand up for her, and he'd go at her. And out of it a kid would form and grow inside of Lizz. She would carry it like some troublesome burden, and as it grew within her, her face would become soft and beautiful in a way that a woman's face never was beautiful except when she was having a kid. And her time would come. She would holler from the pains, as if she couldn't stand them. And then, in a lot of pain, and blood, and mess, the kid would come. And here it was, and it fed at her breast, and slowly grew, laughed, cried, learned to walk and talk, and got to know its father and mother, and its brothers and sisters. It became a person not like any other person in all the world. It grew up, went to school, learned to read, became a man, or a woman, and then. . . . He had been a kid like this, a sleeping little bugger without a care in the world except his mother's tits. And from all this beautiful innocence he had grown up, walked through muck and, Christ, what else, and . . .

"Well, Lizz, when the little bugger grows up, she won't have it as hard as her old man and her old lady," he said reflectively.

"She'll live off the fat of the land. She'll have rings on her fingers and bells on her toes," Lizz said.

Jim's eyes traveled to the kitchen window. Outside, over the shacks, above the alley beyond Wentworth Avenue, the sky was lighting. An ink of colors was dripping through the mist, and clouds, and receding darkness. There were irregular red streaks, deep-dyed reds, and rich, darkish pinks coming out. The break of day, now that, too, like kids, that was something wonderful. God has certainly made a wonderful world for man, if man could only take a decent advantage of it, and bring some justice into it.

"Old man O'Neill, you better be hustling if you don't want to be docked," Lizz said.

"Yes, I guess so," Jim said.

"Here, let me take my little precious angel back now," Lizz said, and Jim carefully but awkwardly handed the infant back to his wife.

"Mama, is breakfast ready?" Little Margaret called.

"Now, here comes the regiment," Lizz said.

Jim kissed Lizz.

"Take care of yourself, Jim."

"Yes and you, too, rabbit," Jim said, picking up his lunch bundle.

"We'll be here waiting with supper on the table when Daddy comes marching home," Lizz said.

"Mama!" Little Margaret called.

"Hello, there. How's the man this morning?" Jim said to Dennis, who stood barefooted and sleepy in the kitchen doorway.

"Hello, Papa!" Dennis said.

"Go put your shoes on before you catch pneumonia," Lizz said.

"Come on, and your old man will carry you back to get dressed," said Jim.

He put Dennis on his shoulders.

"Papa's my horse," Dennis giggled as Jim jogged him back to the front bedroom.

"Kiss me, Papa!" Little Margaret called from the dark and airless bedroom, where she was sleeping in Bill's place.

Jim dumped Dennis on the bed. He picked Little Margaret up and took her breath from her by swinging her up high over his head. He kissed her.

"Whose princess are you?" he asked as he set her back on the bed.

"Papa's," she said breathlessly.

"Who do you love best in all the world?"

"My Papa! And he's going to swing me again. Isn't he?"

"Papa has to go to work now."

"Aw, gee, just once more?"

He swung her, and she giggled.

"Stop crying, you bawl baby!" Little Margaret said as Robert cried, watching his father and sister hopefully, in the darkness.

Jim swung Robert, kissed him, tossed him gently back onto the bed.

"You kids mind your mother, now," he said.

"I will. But, Papa, I have a most awful time with these bad boys," Little Margaret said.

"You be their little mother," Jim said.

"See, Dennis, Papa said you got to mind me, and you, too, Robert, you little stinker," Little Margaret said as Jim left the bedroom.

"Lizz, you better write Ned and Mildred today and tell them the little girl will be all dolled up for them when they come after her. It's best for her, and we shouldn't stand in her way. We'll be able to do better by the rest of them then," Jim said, standing in the kitchen doorway.

"I wrote them already. I knew you wanted me to, Jim," Lizz said.

She went to him, lifted her face, and he kissed her goodbye a second time.

He went to his room, got his coat, put on his thick, square-topped teamster's cap, and slowly walked out of the house to go to work.

26

<hr>

I

Jim dropped the weight from his wagon and hopped off the seat.

"Hi, Express!" a passing teamster yelled from the top of a wagon, owned by a local delivery outfit, that passed down the alley.

Jim waved. Those boys had worse working conditions than he had. Didn't make as much dough, worked longer hours, worked more Sundays, too, than any of the boys on the express wagons. Some of them probably had to support families on less than he got. Oh, well, here was a load packed into his wagon. Had to get it off.

He pulled down the tail gate and carried several packages to a loading platform on his left. He got onto the platform and entered a small, disorderly office where a fat man in shirt sleeves yawned beside a cluttered desk.

"Mr. Express, can't you guys leave a man sleep peacefully after his morning coffee?" the fellow said dryly.

"I'd just as soon. Some damn fool, let's see," Jim read the waybill on the package, "yes, some pest out in Idaho decided that you'd have to be woke up after your morning coffee, so he sent these packages on."

Jim dropped the packages on the floor and handed the fellow a form to be signed.

"Well, if you see that nosey bastard out in Wyoming who woke me, you tell him to quit playing these pranks on me so early in the morning. I don't like my peace disturbed after my morning coffee," the fat fellow said, signing the form and giving it back to Jim.

"I'm dropping over to have my dinner with him at twelve o'clock," Jim said, sticking the bill in his coat pocket.

"O.K., Charlie. Ha! Ha! Going over to Idaho to put on the feed bag for your lunch. Ha! Ha! Say, Mr. Express, you know what I wish?"

"What?"

"I wish to hell I could go over to Idaho for breakfast, dinner, and supper, and lots of them. I'd like to be a cowboy or some goddamn thing besides being a shipping clerk sitting here every damn day of my life, watching my ass get too fat for this here chair."

"I guess we all wish we were something that we aren't," Jim said.

"Why, damn me, but you're smarter than most of those goddamn wiseacres from the express companies who come in here early in the morning, waking me up when I'm snoozing over my morning coffee."

"Sure, thanks," said Jim, leaving.

"So long, pal. My regards to all the chickens in Idaho."

Christ, yes, he did hope that Lizz wasn't, Jim thought as he stepped off the platform.

He tossed the weight back on by his seat and led the horse along the alley for a few paces. He dropped the weight again and rang a bell by a freight elevator that opened into the alley. He spat tobacco juice. A Harrison Express Company wagon passed him, and he waved to the driver on it, Big Boy Corhan. Big Boy was a nice lad.

"Express?" said the elevator man, a deformed little dwarf with an enormous head.

"I think that's it," Jim said.

"Got much for this buildin'?" asked the dwarf.

"Just a few packages for Wayfare's."

"Let's see now. . . . Yes, that's the fourth floor," the dwarf said.

Jim took three packages off the back of his wagon and entered the elevator. The car slowly clogged upward. He and the elevator man were silent. The dwarf banged open the door at the fourth floor, and Jim stepped into a large light freight room. Young punks were rushing backward and forward, toting bulky packages to a counter, where a thin, sallow, gray-haired man barked numbers to a fellow at a desk who wore a green eyeshade and black arm-bands over a white shirt. Other kids then took the packages off the counter and piled them to the right of the elevator. Jim walked to a weazened little fellow who sat at a corner desk, his face obscured by his eyeshade.

"These are for you."

"Which company?" the fellow asked without looking up from his desk.

"Continental."

"I just phoned to try and find out about 'em. They are waiting for 'em up-stairs."

Jim set the packages beside the desk, and the fellow signed for them, handed Jim back the receipt.

"You're welcome, my boy," the weazened fellow said.

"I always like to be welcome," Jim said.

Walking back to the elevator, he noticed a kid of about seventeen scuttle past him with a bulky package. He wanted Bill and the rest of his kids to have better jobs than this lad. That's why he had to let Little Margaret go to Madison where she would be given things. They could get an education, get up in the world. Well, it looked like he would have enough kids so that some of them would get somewhere. A few of his kids ought to amount to something because of the sheer law of averages, if for no other reason. He pressed the elevator bell, and waited. He heard them working behind him, calling out names of towns and states. Wondered would that be a Continental load, or would one of the other express companies get it? At the stables this morning, he'd gotten a bulletin for all the wagonmen from Patsy's office. They should impress upon shippers the advantages of Continental Express service over all its competitors. What should he do? Go to the little fellow back there and give him a speech? Better to walk upstairs and see the president and the board of directors of the company, sit down, smoke a two-bit cigar with them, and say, see here, now, Mr. President, now look at me, I'm a representative of the Continental Express Company. We ship from coast to coast. We ship on the same trains as other companies, but when we ship, our shipments go faster. Now I drink the same booze that the boys do on the Harrison wagons, and on the wagons of all the other companies. But I am more courteous than they are because I work for the Continental Express Company. So you give us your shipments. It means that we'll make more money, and I'll get the same wages, so you give us all your business. And thanks for the cigar, I'll take another, Mr. President, just for a remembrance. . . It looked as if the poor little runt running the elevator wouldn't get it up here until dinner time. Nope, here it was. The door swung open and Jim entered.

"Going down?" the dwarf asked.

Jim nodded.

"Whenever you go up, you go down, don't you?" the dwarf said expressionlessly.

"Yes, Pop, you do," Jim said, thinking that now, that was a bright idea, all right.

"Yes, sir, going up and down here all day in my little Katy, I call the car Katy, well, I keep sayin' to Katy, 'Now, Katy, whenever I take you up, you can always be sure that I'll take you down again.' But Katy, here, she gets cranky. Some days she doesn't go up as well as she might. She seems to get sore on me, and doesn't seem to want to go up at all. By golly!" the dwarf said, turning a toothless grin upon Jim.

"That's the way it goes," Jim said.

"Say, isn't it, though! Even an elevator doesn't work the same every day, let alone a man. Well, sir, that's what life is like. Different every day. Better some days, and worse on others," the dwarf said, shaking his head as he spoke.

"That's just about it, Pop," Jim said reflectively.

"Well, such is life," the dwarf said, halting the car at the alley landing and swinging the wide door open with his powerful hands.

Jim left the elevator with a grin and a wave of his hand, and led his horse further along the alley. He thought of Little Margaret and he immediately pushed her out of his mind.

II

The horse jogged out of the alley. Jim pulled on the reins before the freight entrance of an office building.

"Whoa!"

"Got much?" a shipping clerk yelled to Jim as he backed his tail gate into the loading platform.

"Lot of my load goes in the buildin' here," Jim said, jumping down from his wagon.

"I'll get a couple of these fellows to help you then. . . . Hey, you guys!" he said, and two fellows in aprons on the platform came up.

Jim handed out packages which they carried inside and piled by the freight elevator. Then, carrying a stack of papers he went inside.

"Well, it seems that whether or not times are good or bad, there's enough freight moving around to keep guys like us up off our tails, doesn't there?" the shipping clerk said.

"I guess there is," Jim said, bending down to arrange his pile by the elevator.

"That's what puts the bread on our table every night," the shipping clerk said.

"Yes, I guess so," Jim said.

"Well, and when times are good or bad, we handle the stuff, and we don't have a hell of a lot more bread on our table when times are good, either," the shipping clerk said.

"The big fellows are never satisfied. The more they get, the more they want. Just the same as the buildin's downtown here keep gettin' bigger—well, their greed seems to grow the same way. So a few get too much, and as you say, a hell of a lot more bread isn't put on your table and my table. But—well, I got to get this stuff delivered. So you hold down the fort while I get rid of this."

"I will. And, yeah I guess I'll hold my ass down on a chair. I don't have much to do until a little later."

Jim piled the packages into the elevator.

"That guy could talk a leg off you," the elevator starter said.

"Uh huh," Jim said, sorting out his papers.

"He's one of these guys what's never satisfied. He's always complainin' about something. Now me, I keep tellin' him, 'Joe, why don't you let well enough alone?' Oh, I guess he's a born complainer."

The elevator stopped at the second floor. Jim left packages outside it.

"Yes, every mornin' when I see him, I say, 'Well, Joe, what you grouchin' about today?'" the starter said.

He stopped at the third floor, for Jim to leave more packages.

"And so he starts in. If it isn't the weather, why, it's the boss, or it's business is too good, or else it isn't too good. So I say to him, 'You'd talk a leg off me if I let you, wouldn't you, Joe?'"

They went on up, and Jim left packages at other floors.

"So I say, don't pay no attention to Joe. He means well, but if he was born with a silver spoon in his mouth like some is, he'd still be complainin' of the quality of the silver and asking why didn't the Almighty make it gold," the starter said as Jim stepped out with his last packages at the top floor.

Jim started down the corridor with an armful of packages. He pushed through a door marked with the name of the Marquard Corrugated Box Company, entering a large room piled with boxes. Several young girls and lads were behind a counter, wrapping packages. It would be better for Little Margaret to go to Madison and get a good education than it would for her to take a job like these girls did. No future in such work. He didn't want his girls to have to work, except maybe be school teachers. And then, too, if she went, there would be more room in bed. It wasn't right that a man and wife had to have their little daughter sleeping at the foot of their bed.

"Continental?" a shipping clerk asked.

"Yes. Four for you," Jim said, handing him a receipt to be signed.

The shipping clerk dodderingly put on a pair of glasses, read the receipt, and examined the shipment. He nodded. He gazed at Jim dubiously.

"All right," he said, signing the receipt and returning it to Jim.

Jim stuffed it in his pocket and went out. He got more packages by the elevator, and carried them through a door marked Nogel Educational Publishing House. A handsome switchboard girl, wearing a white shirtwaist, stared coldly at him. Jim was struck by her looks. He hadn't seen such a fine-looking girl in a hell of a long time. She was a beauty, all right, with such fine golden hair. But what the hell? What did girls like that care about a driver who was fifteen or twenty years older than they were? They wanted younger, better game. He laid his packages beside her and handed her the receipt. He took the signed paper and went out. He stopped in the hall. That girl was sure a sight to be seen. She was something for a fellow to get, all right. Lizz had been young once. She had never been as beautiful as that girl at the switchboard, but she had held her own with most girls. Jesus Christ, what was it like to have a handsome young girl of eighteen or nineteen? It had been so long now that he couldn't remember just what it was like. With Lizz, it was warm and all right, but. . . . When he took Lizz he seemed to know just what it was like, and just what it was going to be. Christ, and there had once been a time when it was something so sweet and warm and wet, and each time seemed as if he had never had it before. And now, he couldn't help himself about half of the time. He felt like he was just a pig. He glutted himself and got it over with, and he wasn't sure whether or not Lizz liked it. Christ, yes, what would it be like with that young girl in there by the switchboard?

He picked up more packages by the elevator, again swung down the corridor. At its end, he looked out a window upon the jagged and irregular line of roof tops of downtown Chicago. The sky was blue and clear, dotted with puffy white clouds. The sun was brilliant over the clouds and the roofs. Trailing smoke drifted westward in dark gray and blackish clusters. And below, the roof tops were knifed with the hollows of streets upon which the traffic moved like so many toy automobiles and wagons. Nice day! Nice sight. He went on with his packages.

He galloped down the steps to the next floor. He again arranged his deliveries, picking up an armful.

III

"Now, here's another working man who loves his chains too much to lose them," said Levinsky, shipping clerk of the Hennessey-McGee Company as Jim entered with a package.

"I'm not buying today," Jim said.

"Buying? I'm not a salesman. I'm not even selling you the keys to unlock your chains. I'm giving them to you."

"It sounds to me more like a free ticket to the lunatic asylum. Here's a package for you," Jim said.

"It's not for me. It's for the company and the boss. I only sign for it."

"I'll be obliged for your signature," said Jim.

"And that I'll gladly give. If you know anybody who'll lend me money on it, I'll gladly give him my signature twice," Levinsky said, taking the receipt from Jim and signing it.

"Here's your package, anyway."

"You mean my boss' package. Some day you'll kick your boss out, and I'll tie a can to mine, and other fellows like us will do the same thing. Then we'll own the world. How'd you like that?"

"Do me a favor, will you?" said Jim.

"Sure, always, comrade," smiled Levinsky.

"When you lunatic Socialists and we Irish own the world, throw in this building for good measure. It's got too many stairs for me to climb deliverin'. I want to chop off a couple of floors," Jim said.

"I'll gladly oblige. Why, that'll be as easy as giving you my signature. Say, you go right out and chop the top floors off. Cut them all down to, and including, this one. Then I won't have to sign for any more packages," said Levinsky.

"O.K. Got a hatchet?" said Jim.

"No, but seriously, you Irishman, as sure as the sun comes out, we'll own the world with all the means of production and the buildings, too, even this goddamn rat-trap," said Levinsky.

"When that happens, I'll divvy up with you. You take half of the floors here, and I'll take the other half."

"Comrade Irishman, you don't understand. You're politically backward," said Levinsky.

"I'll always be just another sonofabitch, I suppose. You know, Levinsky, the ones they call the people. I'll make my kids something better, though," Jim said.

"You ought to organize," said Levinsky.

"I got my union card in this pocket. And every month I pay my dues. And I believe in the eight-hour day, and in every other advantage a workingman can get."

"How you going to get it?"

"Maybe if we get the Democrats in Washington next year they'll give the people some things. For others, I suppose some day we just got to pull a strike, wreck the wagons, and punch the living Jesus out of every damn scab who tries to drive one. That's the way it was before. But they brought out the law guarding the scabs."

"What did you do then?"

"Hit the scabs anyway."

"And I suppose you won? Did you?"

"No, we didn't."

"Sabotage and violence will never get you anywhere. The bosses like that. They can put the cops on you then, and the newspapers say that you're anarchists."

"Well, maybe you're right. I got nothing against you Socialists. But I'm not voting for Debs. He's a good man, and he's for the workingman, but you Socialists will never get anywhere."

"In the elections for mayor last spring, our man, Rodriguez, got 24,825 votes. If you had voted for him, we would have gotten 24,826. And if all the guys there are like you had voted for him, he would have gotten thousands upon thousands more."

"I damn near," Jim said.

"Why didn't you?"

"Well, the Republicans had a dude professor in, and the way I look at it is this. Any workingman who votes for the Republicans is a damn fool. I was for Dunne in the primaries. But he lost. The guy that won, I don't like him. I fought with his cops in the drivers' strike. But then it's throwing your vote away for the Socialists, and the Democrats are the party that the workingman belongs to. My cousin, Joe Reilley, he's a Democrat. He's an honest man, he is."

"Some day you'll learn better," Levinsky said.

"And I got lots of work to do. You're all right, but you Socialists are lunatics. You mean well, but I don't think you'll ever get anywhere."

"Well, come back, and let me sign some more papers for you."

"I will. And don't get any brainstorms from those ideas you got up there in your noodle."

"Brainstorms, ha! I should have a brainstorm! Workingmen like you, you should have brainstorms! You and the workers all over the world, you should have brainstorms! I should give you the brainstorms, and then I'd be happy. Come back and see me," said Levinsky.

"Well, so long," Jim said.

IV

It grew wearisome, going through corridors, from office to office, tramping down from floor to floor. He supposed that since buildings were getting bigger, it was going to get worse and worse, too, shagging your ass down from the top of buildings. Well! And Levinsky, nice guy! But crazy. Socialism? Where was it going to get you? The country was Republican, and what did the Republicans care for the workingman? Levinsky always said the Democrats were the same, but. . . . Well, Socialism was all right, the same idea as that of Christ. How were you going to practice it? Hell, he didn't have time to be cracking his brains about it. And he had learned that a man just about had to depend upon himself and do his own fighting. In this world nobody else cared a lot for you, and you fought for yourself. It would be all right, too, if you could just stand up and fight everything out with your fists. But you couldn't. And . . . he had a lot more work to get off. He bent down, picked up more bundles, trudged down another corridor.

He pushed through the door of the Hope Filter Company. He saw a white-haired man in a freshly pressed gray suit nervously and jerkily striding back and forth across the box-ridden package room.

"You from the Continental?" the man asked abruptly, standing in the center of the floor and glaring at him.

"That's me," Jim said, setting his packages on the counter opposite the door.

"I've called up five different offices in your concern, and I must have conversed with three regiments of flunkies and officials about some shipments I have been expecting. They should have been here at nine o'clock this morning."

"I don't know nothing about that."

"Does anybody in your goddamn concern know anything? You've delayed my whole business routine this morning."

"I'm sorry. I don't get the drift of your complaint. I'm just a wagonman, and I've got these deliveries for your company. If somebody will sign this receipt, I'll leave them here now."

"Why didn't you get them here earlier?"

"I came as early as I could. The freight was falling off my wagon, and I had to take you in turn. Here are these packages."

"What do you mean talking to me like that? Who do you think you are?"

"Who signs for this stuff here? I got work to do, and I can't stand here giving you an argument about things that aren't my business. Here are packages for you."

"You haven't time! Who are you?"

"Here, will you sign for these, or should I take them back?"

The fellow went to a door on his left and opened it.

"Jackson, come here and sign for some packages," he commanded.

"Yes, sir!" a fellow in shirt sleeves said obsequiously as he entered the room. He examined the packages and signed the receipt.

"Say, you, what's your name?" the gray-haired man said authoritatively to Jim as he turned to leave.

"I'm not used to being talked to like that," Jim said, striving to keep his temper in control.

"You aren't! You, a teamster!"

"We're all born free in this country. This is America, the land of liberty," Jim said.

"Yes . . . you . . . you . . ."

Jim sneered at the fellow.

"I'll report you!"

"You've got nothing to report! Go ahead," Jim said, his eyes flashing contempt.

He walked out of the office. Goddamn dried-up old dude! Despite his age, he didn't know how close he'd come to a mash in the puss.

He bent over more packages by the elevator.

V

A quarter to eleven. He'd gotten the deliveries cleaned up in pretty good time. But he did feel a little pooped. Climbing so many stairs had done it. He could stall time until feeding. But then, what the hell? It was his job. He had it to do. And Jack Muldoon was a nice guy. Might as well play ball with Jack. Jack deserved it. He'd just snatch a shot of whiskey, and then buzz Jack on the phone and tell him he was empty.

He left the wagon and crossed the street to a rickety saloon. He strode confidently up to a bar where there were a few straggling men.

"Shot of whiskey!" he ordered.

The bartender shoved it across the counter. Jim paid. He gulped it down and stood liking the warming feeling in his guts. Nothing in the world to pick a man up like a good shot of whiskey. And think of it, a lot of these damn fool Protestant ministers and lunatic women without a man were trying to get Prohibition and close up the saloons. Why, there was no place in the world for a man like a saloon where he met a few decent lads, had a drink or two, and talked of an evening, maybe sang a song or two. What the hell did they want him to do, work all the time, and sleep, and, for fun, sit and twiddle his thumbs? All these ministers and reformers who wanted to close the saloons, they must have been sissies, when they were kids, who brought an apple a day to their teacher.

He glanced down the bar. Didn't like the looks of some of these birds. That ratty-eyed fellow who was staring at him looked like a louse. Why was he looking that way?

"See anything green?" the fellow sneered, coming toward Jim.

He was about an inch smaller than Jim, who was over six feet, but he was broader. He was wearing a shiny, loud-striped blue suit.

"What do you mean?" Jim asked calmly.

"You walked into this joint looking for trouble, didn't you?"

"What do you mean?" Jim repeated and the bar flies collected around them.

"What did you come in here for?"

"To get a chocolate ice-cream sundae with whipped cream and walnuts on it," Jim said.

"You're a wisealeck, aren't you? I tagged you for a wise guy the minute you walked in here, actin' like you owned shares around here."

"Listen, stranger, what do you want to go around inviting trouble for?" Jim said.

"Say, who do you think you're . . ."

The fellow never finished his sentence. He looked up glassy-eyed from the sawdust-strewn floor. He struggled to arise and pulled out a knife. It fell out of his feeble hand. He fell backward, and passed out.

"I didn't come in here looking for trouble, but he wanted it. Anybody else?" Jim challenged, his eye traveling from face to face.

"He got what he had coming to him. Come on, fellow, and have a drink on me," a fellow said.

"No, thanks. I got to get to work. But I don't like rats, and when he gets up, tell him so."

Jim walked out of the saloon and back to his wagon. He drove around the corner to telephone Jack. He felt swell. There was a satisfaction in punching some sonofabitch square in the jaw like that, calling curtains on him in one punch. Hell, if all life was only as simple as a fight! He jumped down in front of a drugstore to make his phone call. Entering the store, he realized that he had broken his pledge with that drink. He hadn't even realized it. Well, that didn't count, when it hadn't even occurred to him. And it hadn't hurt him any, either.

VI

Jim walked past empty freight bins on the platform of the New Jersey depot.

"I'll be damned if it ain't Jim O'Neill, the Irish wonder," Joe Peters, the dispatcher, said.

"Hello, Joe. Jack Muldoon sent me to pick up a few values you got going back to him. And how's business? I see you're cleaned up."

"Yes, but life's all grief."

"What's happened now?"

"Oh, that goddamn Irishman, McGoorty. I don't know why Patsy McLaughlin had to sick him onto me. I would rather have the dumbest Polack from South Chicago than that stewed idiot."

"What's he done now?"

"He got drunk again."

"That's not unusual."

"But he was so pie-eyed that somebody stole his whole goddamn wagon off of him."

"Anything in it?"

"No, just a load of deliveries. There's going to be hell to pay, too. But what I wonder about is this. Why in hell didn't they leave the horse, and hitch McGoorty to the wagon and drive McGoorty away, too."

"They can sell the horse. What can they do with McGoorty?" said Jim.

"Yes, that's so."

"I had him figured out for these values. Anyway, Jack gave me you. At least, though, I won't be getting any more gray hairs from him."

"Well, I better get those values! I got to get them over to Jack, and get my feed bag out. Got a heavy pickup route these days.

"All right. They're right down here. And, Jim, any time your boss doesn't want you, tell him to trade you to me. You can work for me any day in the week, Jim," said Joe.

"Well, Joe, the way I look at it is that I got to do my work to butter my bread. So I just go along and do it the best I can," Jim said.

"I know it, Jim," Joe Peters said.

27

"Are you sick, Peg?" Mrs. O'Flaherty asked, looking up from the stove where she was making vegetable soup for Danny.

"I'm just nervous, Mother, and I have such a headache," Margaret said, pacing back and forth across the kitchen, wringing her hands as she walked.

She looked out through the kitchen door.

"It's a miserable day. It's a good thing you kept Little Brother home from school and in bed today with his cold," Margaret said, fingering the scratch on her left cheek.

"The soup I'm making will give the little fellow strength. Will you have a bowl of it, Peg? There's a world of good in vegetables that come out of the ground," the old lady said.

"Maybe I will."

It was good of Miss Kelly to work in your place at the hotel today and give you a chance to rest and take it easy. You'll be well again tomorrow," Mrs. O'Flaherty said.

"I'd do as much for her, and I'll have to work her shift for her tomorrow. Mother, I know that I was drunk yesterday and didn't know what I was doing. And I'm paying for it today with remorse, with my head splitting me, and with my nerves like wires. But don't think that that Kelly one is an angel. Listen, do you remember how last year I worked a whole week while she was off sick? Do you remember, Mother?"

"Indeed, I do, Peg. You were up and out almost at the crack of dawn, and you were late at night getting home from the hotel."

"Well, she was knocked up and being taken care of. She's no angel," Margaret said vindictively.

"What do you mean, Peg?"

"She was with some fellow, and going to have a baby if she didn't have it taken care of. She had to go to a midwife. No, Mother, Kelly is no walking saint herself."

"You don't say?"

"Plenty of them I know aren't. They'll run with men for a hat and a dress. They make extra money by whoring, and they wear it all on their backs. Mother, you won't find many girls giving everything they make into the home like I do. Not many. Kelly doesn't. She pays five dollars a week board to her family, and she keeps the rest of it. Why, when she heard how much money I give home, and what I do for my family, do you know what she said to me? She said, 'Peg, you're a walking fool.' That's what Kelly said to me."

"Peg, you're a good girl. The soup will be done soon, and it will put some strength into my little grandson's ailin' bones. The little fellow has a cough."

"We'll keep him in the house until he gets better. We can't afford hospital bills and such things for any more of Lizz's children. But he isn't so sick. He has no fever."

"'Pon my soul, Peg, I never would have thought that that Kelly girl is a chippy," the old lady said, turning away from the stove.

"She isn't. She just looks out for A-Number-One in every way that she can. The young girl who doesn't look out for herself, Mother, is just a fool. She's just a fool, and she has no one to blame but herself."

"You say the truth, Peg."

"But come to think of it, Kelly's pretty rotten, Mother. She'll sleep with anything in pants for money so she can put some more glad rags on her skinny back. And every time I see her, she's wearing a new dress. She isn't in rags like me. Not that one! No, sirree! You should see all the fine clothes she wears. I tell you, she couldn't buy them out of what she gets. She only earns eighty dollars a month, not as much as I make. But she dresses like a queen. All the young girls I know dress better than I do."

"That one's mother should put a switch to her behind," Mrs. O'Flaherty said.

"She's rotten. But then it's no skin off my backside. I've got my own worries," Margaret said.

"If she had the mother I had, Lord have mercy on me mother's soul, she wouldn't be gallivantin' herself to Hell. Why, in the old country, if my sister and me even looked at ourselves in our pelts, me mother would have beat the blazes out of us. Indeed, she would have. Ah, me mother was a one to make you toe the mark."

"Mother, you're not mad at me for yesterday and last night, are you?"

"Bless me soul, I'm not."

"I didn't hurt you, did I?"

"I'll place a five-dollar bill in the hand of the one that can hurt me. A five-dollar bill. Why, I'm me Uncle William's niece, and me Uncle William is a strong man. He could lift a tree with his right arm. Show me the one that can hurt me!" Mrs. O'Flaherty said, gesturing extravagantly with her thin arms as she spoke.

"Mother, you do forgive me?"

"It was nothing, Peg."

"I just lost control of myself when I found out about the ring. And the things Lizz said to me. Mother, I swear before God that all I did was to go down to her as meek as a lamb, and ask her if she knew anything about the ring. And, Mother, she sprang at me like a wild woman. Why, she was fit to be chained. I thought she was out of her head, the way she pounced on me."

"You don't say?" Mrs. O'Flaherty said slyly.

"The last thing in the world that I wanted to do was to fight with Lizz. I never said a word to her. I'm always helping her, going without things for myself to give her money for her children. And look at the way she beat and scratched me. I tell you, Mother, I'll hold nothing against her. I'll help her whenever I can spare it on account of her children. But as long as I live, I never want to see her. The way she beat me up, it was disgraceful. I know that I had taken a few drinks because of my nerves and my despondency. But I wasn't making any trouble. Why, I acted like a lady in her house. She was just like a she-wolf. She would have scratched my eyes out if she could."

"Oh, she just talks to be talking, Peg. Her bark is worse than her bite," the mother said, while down from the alley they heard the sing-songed echoes of an Italian peddler.

"Mother, if I don't get that money, I don't know what I'll do. If they audit me and my cashbox is short, I don't know what I'll do. I simply can't afford to lose my job and have my bond forfeited."

"The Lord will provide."

"Mother, I was a fool, loaning money to Martha Morton, treating her."

"I swear before my God that if that one ever comes to my door, I'll get a shotgun for her," the grandmother said histrionically in the center of the kitchen.

"When I went to see her yesterday to collect the money she promised to pay me back, to collect, mind you, my own money, she was entertaining some little fart of a man in her kimono. Why, I wouldn't give two cents for any man that sees something in a faded old bitch like Martha. And, Mother, do you know that she just about threw me out of her house, and she did it in the condition I was in? She was suspicious. She was afraid that I was going to steal her little fart from her. Why, Mother, to the men I know that little penny she was with yesterday is just counterfeit money."

"There's little to a man that would go traipsin' after the likes of her."

"Oh, Mother, you're so cute. You're such a darling. And you do forgive me, don't you, you little dollie? I didn't know what I was doing. I was simply out of my mind from nerves and worry."

"Peg, they won't find out about the money you owe while you're off today, will they?"

"No. Each of us cashiers has a separate cashbox, which we take care of ourselves. They check on us only when they have the auditor around. But I know they will have the auditor around soon."

"Maybe the Lord will find a way," the mother said, returning to the stove. "It's ready, Peg. Will you drink a bowl of it?"

"I couldn't touch it. I haven't any appetite," Margaret said semi-tragically.

"I got to bring some hot soup in to the little fellow."

"I'll take it in to Little Brother."

"You sit there. I can feed my own grandson when he has a cold."

She poured soup into a bowl, and put it, with crackers, on a tray. She carried it in to Danny, who was sitting up in bed in the front.

Peg sat at the table, her chin moodily supported by her hands. She could hit herself for the fool she had been. But she had learned her lesson. From now on she wasn't going to be anybody's easy mark. And never again, never, would a drop of liquor cross her lips. Only, it hadn't been her fault yesterday. She had been driven nearly out of her mind. But Lizz needn't have hit her, scratched her. She touched the scab on her cheek. It would heal. It wouldn't leave any scars. If it did! If it did? She'd choke Lizz O'Neill blue in the face.

Margaret jumped up and went to her mother's bedroom. She looked at her scratched cheek in the dresser mirror which was next to a picture of the Sacred Heart. No, it was a simple little scratch, and it would heal without leaving a mark. But it wasn't with any thanks to Lizz that she wasn't disfigured for life. Lizz would have liked that.

She paced the kitchen. And still Lorry hadn't sent her that extra money. Oh, God, what a heavy cross she had to bear! Well, she would bear it! While other girls were gay, and did not have a care in the world, here she was loaded with them. Well, she had learned her lesson. She knew now that there was not one soul on earth on whom she could depend. From this day on, she would place all her trust in herself. From this minute forth, Peg O'Flaherty was going to look out first and foremost for Peg O'Flaherty.

But, goodness, why hadn't she thought of it before? She could go to a loan bank and raise the money. She had a steady job. They charged high interest, but it was better to pay the interest than it was to lose her cash bond. Gee, where had her brains been all this time! It only went to show how worry could blind one, how troubles could impair one from seeing what was before one's nose. That's what she would do.

"Mother, I know what I can do," she said eagerly as the mother returned to the kitchen with the tray and the empty bowl.

"My grandson is getting well. The soup did him a world of good."

"Mother, I have it now."

"What's that you're saying, Peg?"

"I can go to the Watson Loan Bank. They'll give me a loan if I can get two signatures. I'll go down this afternoon and see about it."

"Will they give you the money?"

"Yes. I'm sure. That will save me."

"I knew the Lord would provide. But, Peg, if you're borrowing, get a little more than you need and buy the little fellow a suit."

"I will, and I'll buy you something. You're so sweet, so good. I don't know what I'd do without you."

"Sure what do I be needing? Get something for yourself and the little fellow."

"If I hadn't been so worried, I would have thought of it sooner," Margaret said, going to the stove and pouring herself a cup of coffee.

Margaret sat down to drink her coffee. She took a slice of bread and reached for the butter.

"Here, not that butter," the mother said firmly.

"It's good, isn't it?"

"That's for my grandson. Just a minute, I'll get you the help's butter," the mother said.

She went outside to the icebox, returned with a dish of butter, and set it before her daughter. Margaret smiled on the old lady. Mrs. O'Flaherty went to the stove and got herself a cup of coffee. She sat down opposite her daughter.

"Peg, get the paper and see who's dead," the mother said, sipping coffee.

Margaret went to the front and returned with a morning paper. She put on her glasses to read with.

"Ah, many of the old people are gone. When the Great Man calls us, we got to go. If you are His own, He takes you up above. If you aren't, and have been gallivantin' with tinkers, He sends you down below. There's nobody but what has got to toe the mark for Him. Peg, God's a good man, but, I tell you, He's a hard man. It won't be long before He'll be calling me, and my old bones will be laying out in the graveyard with Pa. But it's a good thing that Pa and me bought our lot out in Calvary and paid for it. I'll at least get a decent burial."

"Don't talk like that. Mother, I couldn't bear to think of you dying," Peg said, tears almost coming to her eyes.

"When our time comes, there can be no dallying. But go ahead, Peg, read me the death notices."

Margaret read.

Aherne, Patrick, fond father of . . .

"And well he may be dead! When I was in Green Bay, Wisconsin, with Pa and his people, before you were born, there was an Aherne there from Wicklow, and he cheated Pa out of fifty cents of his hard-earned money. He stole fifty cents of Pa's money. Why, today that would buy ten cakes of soap. Pa said to me after that, 'Mary, when you see a Wicklow Aherne, don't pass the time of day with him. Just split his head with a rail!' Ah, well may a Wicklow Aherne be dead, I say."

"I never saw people fight like you Irish, Mother. You fight just for the love of it, don't you?" Margaret said, glancing up from the newspaper.

"I'll fight the Devil himself! But I'm not Irish. I'm English. My name is Fox."

"You're such a cute thing, Mother. I'm so sorry I fought with you and was mean yesterday and last night. But I was so nervous and upset. You do forgive me, don't you, Mother?"

"You were just worried, you poor thing! Read on!"

"You love to hear about the deaths and murders in the papers, don't you, Mother?"

"Indeed, I don't. But sure, how else could I be hearing what's happening to the people I knew from the old country, and them that I knew as neighbors on Blue Island Avenue and on Twelfth Street when all of you were just out of the cradle?"

"Mother, you must get around more to see your old friends. I must take you. We'll go to see Mame O'Leary, maybe next week."

"Not me! Take yourself or Lizz. She likes to be gadding about. I haven't the time to be wasting. When I came out from the old country I worked for Mrs. Janz in Brooklyn. And do you think she would go visiting? She was a lady. She had a carriage and her own coachman. And besides, I have to be taking care of my grandson."

"Oh, you're so cute, Mother. I love you."

"Who else is dead, Peg?" she said, and Margaret turned back to her newspaper.

Nora Garrity, seventy-four, fond mother of . . .

"Why, Mother, that's Bridget Garrity's mother. Poor thing! That's a shame," Margaret said.

"A pity it is. What did the poor thing die from?"

"Pneumonia."

"Wait till my Lizz hears it. She'll be broken-hearted."

"If I know Lizz, she knows it already. As soon as she can get a neighbor woman in to watch the kids, she'll be down to the drugstore telephoning to let you know."

"I'll have to go to the funeral."

"I'll get you a seat in a carriage."

"No, you won't. I'll go to the church, and they'll see me, and then I'll whist out to the cemetery on the train, and they'll be none the wiser. I won't be spendin' your hard-earned money for a seat in a carriage."

"She was such a sweet old woman, too," Margaret said.

"I'll wear me new black dress. Poor Nora! Who would have thought it? Why, she came over five weeks after I did, and Pa stood up for her first son, Padney, the one that got a nail in his foot and died of blood poisoning the year before you were born. Well do I remember her when she came out from the old country. She was the prettiest little thing, and all the fellows in Brooklyn were running after her like dogs with their tongues hanging out. So, Nora Garrity is dead! May her soul rest in peace! She was a good woman, and she worked hard."

"I sometimes think that maybe we'd all be better off dead," Margaret said almost in a tone of self-reprimand.

"Life and death is a power beyond us, and we never know but what we'll be the next to go. Who would have thought that my Louise would be dying so young of the consumption?"

"Mother, you know, when Louise had that fistula when we lived down at Forty-seventh and Indiana, I knew it then. I did."

"No, that wasn't what gave it to my Louise. It was the learning to typewrite. She didn't have the strength in her to learn the typewriter. That's what did it. Ah, if I had the doing of it over again, I would have thrown that typewriter in the furnace when she brought it home to be giving her health to it. But go ahead, Peg, who else is dead?"

Margaret again looked at the list of death notices. The telephone rang. She rushed to it, suddenly expectant. She answered it and her voice dropped. Mrs. O'Flaherty followed her, heard her talking to Lizz. As soon as Margaret could edge in a word, she said she would give Mother to Lizz.

"I'm busy. I can't be letting her talk my leg off. Tell her the lady of the house ain't home," Mrs. O'Flaherty said.

She took the telephone.

"Hello, Lizz. I couldn't hardly believe my ears when Peg read it to me out of the morning's paper . . ."

"Don't let her talk too long, Mother. I don't want the line tied up. I might be getting an important call," Margaret said.

28

"I was so glad that you called up. I've been nervous, and I didn't feel well. I had to take the day off from the hotel. I was just going out on business, because I had to, even though I felt badly, and I got your call," Margaret said ingratiatingly, smiling at Dick Smith, who had packed his girth into a rocking chair on the far side of the O'Flaherty parlor.

"I tried to get you earlier, but your phone was busy. You must have had plenty of knights in arms wooing you by long distance today."

"I did not. My mother and married sister were talking to each other. An old friend of my mother's died, and she and Lizz, that is, my married sister, they buried the poor thing on the phone today," Margaret said, causing Dick to smile.

"Must have been a long funeral."

"It was. And do you know, Dick, if it had been anybody else but you who called me today, I wouldn't have seen him."

"Well, you look like you were brawling or something, Peg, with that scratch on your cheek."

"It's awfully embarrassing, isn't it? I was at the house of a girl friend, and she has the most vile cat. It scratched me. I hate cats!"

"So do I. And that scratch you got looks like the work of a cat, a human cat, if not the other kind."

"It was a cat. I was bending down to pick up a handkerchief I'd dropped, and the cat just came up and scratched me with its front paw. I was lucky it didn't scratch my eyes out."

"That's the funniest accident I ever heard of."

"It wouldn't seem funny, Dick, if it had happened to you."

"I guess you're right. But anyway, Peg, old kid, I'm sure glad to see you. And how about sneaking us a little kiss?"

She crossed the room, and sat on his knees. She kissed him sweetly, unpassionately.

"Please, Dick!" She protested mildly as he strained to kiss her more sensuously.

"Oh, kid, be a sport. I've been away months."

"And while you were, I suppose you were a monk," she teased.

"Peg, when a man loves life as much as Dick Smith does, well, he's only human."

"That's why you're such a darling, Dick. Because you're so human."

"When a lady like you says that about me, well, maybe there must be some truth in it. A lady like Marge O'Flaherty couldn't tell a lie," he said, and she winked at him lasciviously. "But come on, sneak over another little osculation on us. I'm hungry for a little osculation from the gayest and cutest little lady in all Chicago, Marge O'Flaherty."

"You say such nice things, Dick," she said, bending forward and brushing a kiss on his puffed, ruddy cheek.

"Come on, Peg, make it a real one, a kiss that comes right up from the heart."

"You want a kiss that comes from some place lower than my heart, don't you, Dick?"

"Dirty mind! Dirty mind! Dirty mind! Dirty mind!" he sing-songed.

"Oh, well, if that's the way you feel," she said, flouncing off his lap, walking several feet from him, flinging a mock pout back at him.

"I love you, dirty mind and all," he said.

"It isn't a dirty mind," she said, continuing the game.

"Ah, you women are all the same," he beamed, stretching his pudgy legs, the fat on his thighs threatening to burst through his gray trousers. "But still, I like the ladies, God bless 'em, one and all. And God especially bless my little Maggie O'Flaherty."

"Don't call me Maggie. That's the awfullest name you could call me. It sounds as if I was a washerwoman."

"Well, then, the Princess O'Flahertyesquenola."

"Better . . . if you really meant it."

"I do. I mean it. I'll make my princess the Princess Smithovitch."

"You're such a dear, Dick. And you have such a sense of humor. It's fun to be with you."

"What other things could I say to a lady? What the heck you think I am, girlie, a sailor?"

"No, except sometimes you act like a sailor in port after being six months at sea," she twitted.

"Margaret, my Duchess, a sailor is usually younger than I am. A young buck is a young buck. When he's a young buck, and a sailor, well, that's something the fair hearts like more than they pretend they do in polite society. Now, if you take me, with my avoirdupois and all, well, I'm a sailor with a pretty good sailor and I sail just about as well as I can be expected to sail," Dick said, talking loudly and getting enormous enjoyment out of his own wit.

"If you keep using fancy words like that on me, Dick, I'm going to have you make love to my brother, Al, instead of to me. He speaks out of the dictionary, too."

"Say, if you're writing a trick like that for me up your sleeve, better dash out a new sales order. I don't make that kind of love. But all kiddin' aside, Margie, I get the impression from you that that brother of yours is pretty smart."

"Is he smart? Say, Dick, Al is smarter than many a man who's gone to college. You should hear some of the words he uses. Big ones like you use."

"I'd like to meet him sometime."

"Yes, I must bring you two boys together, Dick."

"We'll sling dictionaries at each other like these guys are beginning to sling pies around in the nickel shows nowadays, huh?"

"Dick, you're such a nice thing. And you're so funny."

"Finish the sentence. Margie. Tell me that all the world loves a fat man."

"It does . . . if he is lovable and his name is Dick Smith . . ."

"Know what I'm on the verge of doing? I'm threatening, threatening, mind you, to go regularly to a gymnasium and take up volley ball to see if it'll take some of this gut off me."

"I don't like such an awful word."

"It means avoirdupois. Now, that's as good a tongue walloper as your brother would be using on week days, isn't it?"

"It would be nice to hear you and him talk. You would both use the most scholarly words."

"How does he say the shoe business is these days?"

"Oh, he complains of hard times."

"Well, he's not a damn sight wrong. Things aren't good with me. Why, I had to lay off half the men working in my factory down in Toledo."

"That puts burdens on me, too. Not that I would complain. I'm glad to be able to do what I can. We help my married sister out, too, and the boy we keep for her, he's so lovely. He has the loveliest hair. I only wish I had hair like his."

"Margie, I wouldn't change you for a fortune."

"Now, don't you go soft-soaping me, Dick. But as I was saying, we have it pretty hard, helping my poor married sister out. Her oldest boy is in the hospital with a broken leg, and I suppose I'll have to pay the hospital bill. Poor thing! But then, I always say that when we do things like that, acts of mercy, it'll come back to us some day."

"Margie, some day I might be able to help you out in a really sizable way. You deserve it, you're such a wonderful sport, and you're so good to your people. Some day I'll be able to do a lot for you, not just twenties and fifties, but a lot. You be nice to Dick Smith, and when that ship of his comes sailing down the harbor laden with its gold, Dick Smith will be nice to the Princess Margaret O'Flaherty Smithovitchesquenola, from the Imperial Court of the Grand Muckety Muck of Smithonia."

"Dick, you're so funny. And you're so kind with such a great big generous heart."

"Well, Margie, I believe in helping the other fellow when the other fellow is as pretty and as deserving as you. And I don't believe in walking around all day with my map looking like that of an undertaker. I believe in fun and good times. You know me well enough to know that. That's why I've taken a real shine to you. You're fun, you're a real good time to me."

"Dick, you know, I like you."

"Well, sweetheart, drop over here and prove it instead of waiting to call me up some rainy afternoon when the sky is blue."

"I have, haven't I?"

"Do it again. Little sweetheart, we're now talking about a kind of proof that I never can get enough of."

"But, Dick, not here. The little fellow is in bed with a cough in the next room, and my mother is liable to come in on us. She's such a doll. But she's terribly old-fashioned. She thinks that a girl shouldn't even kiss a man unless he's engaged to her."

He waddled to her, quickly wrapped her in his chubby arms, kissed her long. There was a sound of feet padding in the hallway. She quickly escaped from him.

"I don't want Mother to catch us."

"She shouldn't object. We're only doing something that's natural to do. And listen, hon, don't tell me that a spirited old gal like your maw didn't act natural, plenty natural, too, in her day."

"Dick, you shouldn't speak like that."

"Oh, heck, Margie, I was only kidding. I was just floating a few slow balls over the pan on you."

"What's that mean?"

"Don't worry, it's nothing dirty. You don't get it, because you're a gal, and few gals know anything about baseball."

"I'm learning a lot. Little Danny, oh, he's so sweet and cute, he pesters the life out of me to read him the baseball news. And the other night, when I came home late from the hotel, I heard him talking to himself about baseball in his sleep. He was just as lovely as a picture, sitting up in bed, asleep, in the dark, saying to himself, 'Schulte left, Tinker center, Hoffman right,'" she said.

"That's a scream. Only, the positions aren't right," Dick said, laughing heartily.

"Then it's my mistake. You can't fool the little fellow about baseball."

"He ought to be another Ty Cobb when he's a man."

"I hope he's something better than a shoe salesman."

"The shoe game isn't so bad in better times."

"Oh, I wish it was good now. I have so many worries on my head."

"Say, Margy, kiddo, you're a sweet one. I think maybe I ought to help you out a little."

"Well, Dick, if you could spare it, it would be a godsend. But I wouldn't expect it of you if times are bad."

"It's just like I said, Margie. I'm not making as much money as I used to, and there are some knots tied around my bank roll. But I can help some, not a whole lot, but some."

"I certainly need money."

"Well, kiddo, would a hundred be of any use to you?"

"It would. Of course it would, Dick, you darling. But, Dick, you couldn't possibly make it two hundred, could you?" she coaxed.

"Well!" Dick exclaimed, his fatty face grown ponderously thoughtful. "Well, now, two hundred is a lot. It would leave me short. I'll tell you what I'll do. I'll give you a hundred and twenty-five, and maybe later I'll be better fixed to help you out a little more."

"Dick, I don't know how I can thank you," she said gooily.

"Well, sneak over a fast little kiss on us, first."

She embraced him, kissing him long, and planting her body tightly against his. He pulled out a wallet and counted off the sum, handing her the small stock of bills. She folded the money, and stuck it down her bosom. She kissed him again, forcing his face to redden. He puffed with desire.

"Now, let's get going and have our good time, Marge, kiddo."

"Yes, Dick, I need a little fun. I've been so nervous, and feeling so badly. I had to take the day off from work, and I feel like I need a little fun. I'm so glad you called. It's so lovely to see you, because you're such fun, you're so jolly, and, Dick, you have such a warm, generous heart. And just when you called me, I was almost out of my head with worry. I was racking my brains about money worries. I was just going to go out to try and borrow something, but God knows where."

"Margie, any time I can help you out, I'm only too glad to do it. You know that. And what about our getting started on the fun trail?"

"I know it, Dick. If more men in this world were like you, it would certainly be a finer world. You don't know how much I appreciate your kindness. And you don't know how nervous I've been."

"Well, that's settled. And, Margie, I know just what the prescription is for nerves when the patient is as handsome and healthy a girl as you are."

"Now, there you go, Dickie-dear, getting insinuating and dirty again," she teased, wagging an index finger at him.

"Who said I was getting dirty?" he retorted, feigning indignation.

"Nobody had to say it. You were, Dickie-dear."

"Now, all I said was that I knew what would be good for your nerves. All right, then, if you're going to convict me on such flimsy circumstantial evidence, all right!" he said, pretending to sulk.

"Knowing my little Dickie-dear as I do, I say he was getting dirty," she joshed.

"How did you know but what I was going to recommend some iron or a nerve tonic? Are you a mind reader or a fortune teller?"

"No, but sometimes I can read the mind of Dickie-dear Smith. Oh, you're such a wonderful and darling man."

"Finish it off now, Margie. Say you love me."

"You know I do, Dick."

"You see, Margie, I'm low tonight and I need a little love."

"And if you don't get too fresh and insinuating, my Dickie-dear, you might get it," she cooed at him.

"Now, don't go bawling me out, Margie. Maybe my nerves are strung like wires and I shouldn't be bawled out," he said boyishly.

"I'm sure of that! A man as healthy and as comfortable as you."

"But how do you know I haven't got business worries?"

"Oh, Dickie, I know! I know," Margaret said, lapsing into the semi-tragic manner. "I know how it is. I'm meeting business men all the time at the hotel. They worry more than most of us. They worry infinitely more than a man like my brother-in-law who's only a teamster, because they have so much more to worry about."

"Margie, you're a smart girl. You're quick as a whip to get things. You see how it only stands to reason that we business men should worry more. We got so much more to worry about. Now, I guess I got enough to make me hop around and worry a little. And you know, some of these people, these reformers, they want to slap income taxes on us, and they want to have laws about the kind of machinery we got to install. I tell you, they are a worry all by themselves. Golly, I hope that they keep the man in the White House they got now. I don't want Roosevelt back. He's too unstable. And I don't want any Democrats. I hear some people talking about some professor who is Governor of New Jersey named Wilson, and they say there are some that want him to get in. But then, why should I be bothering your beautiful head with politics? That's a man's lookout."

"Oh, no, Dickie, I'm interested in politics and the topics of the day. But then,

I ain't a suffragette. And, yes, I heard of this Wilson. He's like the man they ran for mayor here, Merriam. He's a professor. And do you know, business men who come in my hotel, they were laughing at him. But Dickie-dear, I am interested, very much, too, in the topics of the day. I read all about this scandal, you know, the Graham case, and some of the men in it who have testified, they stop at my hotel."

"But come on, let's get started. I want some fun. You and me, Margie, we're going out tonight, and we'll paint the town red. And we're going to drink champagne. You go and fix your pretty face up prettier."

She kissed him, and then skipped out of the parlor. She went out to her mother who sat in her back bedroom darning stockings for Danny.

"Mother, you hide this money away for me. I'm not going to be a fool again. I got too much at stake. I'll take it down with me to work in the morning and fix my cashbox," Margaret said gaily, drawing the money out from her bosom and handing it to Mrs. O'Flaherty.

"Glory be, I knew the Lord would provide, Peg."

"He did. It was God who sent Dick Smith to me today. But Dick is so nice, Mother. God sent him. You remind me tomorrow to send five dollars to the Poor Clares and to write them a letter and thank them, and tell them that God answered the prayers I had them say for my special intention."

"God is good, Peg."

"Mother, why don't you go in and say hello to Dick? He's in a jolly mood, and he likes you. He might slip you a five, too."

"Sure, I'm not dressed up. I wouldn't go in and see him unless I was dressed up in a new red dress."

"Go ahead, Mother."

"Indeed, I won't. And Peg, when you go, be sure to turn off my son's electricity."

Peg swept back. She hastened to the front, took Danny out of bed, where he was sitting playing with his collection of baseball pictures, helped him on with his bathrobe, and led him to see Dick.

"Brother, you entertain Mr. Smith. I'll be ready in two shakes of a lamb's tail, Dick," Margaret said, and over Danny's head she blew him a kiss.

"I'm sick. I got a cold," Danny said shyly to Dick Smith.

"A tough guy like you ought to need more than a cold to put him down," Dick said with genial gruffness.

"My nose runs, and my aunty and grandmother say I shouldn't go to school until it stops and I get better."

"I'll bet that will cure you by tomorrow. I'm sure a guy like you is crazy to be in school."

"Oh, no, I don't like school," Danny seriously said, causing Dick Smith to roar.

"Who's going to win the pennant next year?" Dick said when his laughter had subsided.

"The White Sox."

"I think the St. Louis Browns are. I'm for them."

Danny looked at Dick Smith. He suddenly laughed at him.

"What's the joke?" Dick asked, pretending to be offended.

Danny answered him by laughing again.

"Can't a man root for the Browns?"

"Oh, they're a punk team," Danny said, gesturing in disdain.

"Look up!" Dick said, digging his hand in his pocket.

"I don't see nothing," Danny said, fastening his eyes on the ceiling.

"Ever see anything like this?" Dick asked, waving a two-dollar bill before him.

"Yes. It's money."

"What would you do with it, if I gave it to you?"

Danny looked at Dick, too hopefully surprised to speak.

"Will you tell anybody?"

"No," Danny said, grinning widely, shaking his head from side to side, holding out his hand and taking a step closer to Dick.

"All right, here. And when you grow up and become a star pitcher on the White Sox, I'll come and see you play," Dick said, handing the money to Danny.

Danny put it in his bathrobe pocket and grinned.

"All right, Dick," Margaret called.

"Why, Margie, you look like a million dollars interest."

"Now, Dick, don't be feeding me sugar. It's bad for my teeth," she said.

Margaret kissed Danny good-bye, and told him to be a good boy. He waved them farewell as they went out. He ran to the parlor window and watched them crossing the street, with Mr. Smith holding Aunty Margaret by the arm. They were gone. Gee, he wished they would have stayed. He liked Mr. Smith.

He felt his money. He was rich. He was going down to the drugstore at Fifty-first and Grand Boulevard as soon as he was well, and he was going to buy a Ty Cobb Louisville Slugger bat with Ty Cobb's picture on it. He wasn't going to tell them beforehand, either, because they might make him save his money instead of buying the bat. They would say he was too small and couldn't swing it, and that he had bats enough, and all kinds of things. He just wouldn't tell them. He was going to buy the bat. He would be able to swing it by next summer, because he would grow bigger by then. And, gee, wouldn't all the kids in the prairie wish they were him when he came out to play with his Ty Cobb Louisville Slugger bat! But they couldn't use it. Nobody could but him and Bill.

"Son, you better get back to bed," his grandmother said, coming into the parlor and turning off the electric light.

SECTION THREE

1911

29

"Want me to come in and talk to you?" Little Margaret asked, standing at the bedroom door in a thin nightgown.

"Yes," Danny said, sitting up in his uncle's bed.

"Nobody is here. Mother is gone to mass because it's Sunday, and Aunty Margaret went to work early. I was alone in her bed. Nobody is home but you and me," Little Margaret said.

"I'm not afraid," Danny said with bravado.

"Neither am I. But wouldn't you be afraid if it was dark outside now?"

"No!"

"Why do you look at me so funny?"

"I wasn't looking at you. I was looking out into the hall, and you're in the way of the hall."

"You looked like you was looking at me because I'm a girl and I only got my nightgown on."

"I don't care what you got on. I don't care about girls," Danny said.

"Aunty Margaret bought me this new nightgown and said she wanted me to stay up here awhile because she loves me and she's going to miss me when I go 'way to live with my Aunt Mildred next month."

"You can stay with us if you're good."

"I don't have to ask you if I can stay here. You don't own the house."

"You got to be good if you want to stay with us," Danny said.

"Say, puff on you, you're not so much. Aunty Margaret is my aunt, and she likes me better than she likes you. So there! And Mama says I'm Aunt Mildred's favorite."

"Well, I'm Uncle Ned's godson and anybody that lives here has got to toe the mark. We just don't let any old O'Neill that we pick up in the alley stay here with us."

"Quit looking at me that way, Daniel O'Neill!"

"I'm not looking at you. Can't I even look at the wall in my own bedroom? Why did you come in here? You make me get nerves," Danny said.

"You said I should come in here."

"I didn't. You can get right out of my room. You're good riddance," Danny said.

"I will then, smarty!"

"Go ahead."

"I will when I get good and ready."

"Well, stay here then. Only, don't say I'm looking at you."

"You can look at me in my nightgown if you want to."

"What do I want to look at you for?" Danny scornfully asked.

"Lots of boys like to look at girls."

"They do not!"

"They do so!"

"Oh say, they don't care two cents about girls."

"They do so, because girls are girls."

"Is that so!"

"Do you like my new nightgown? It's better than your pyjamas. You can see through my nightgown, but I can't see through your pyjamas."

"Ho! Ho! Ho! Ho!" Danny laughed.

"Don't you laugh at me. Daniel O'Neill, you're the meanest thing. You're a stinker!"

"Ho! Ho!"

"Go ahead, then, laugh! Little boys like you are nasty, and all you know how to do is laugh and do mean things."

"What are you shivering for?"

"I'm cold."

"Why don't you go back to bed if you're cold?"

"I'm lonesome, and the bed is cold alone. At home I never go to bed alone."

"You're afraid to! You're afraid of the dark."

"I'm not. I'd sleep in a bed all by myself in a jiffy, only there isn't any bed for me to sleep in alone. I sleep with Mama and Papa. And then when Bill got run over, I slept in his place with Dennis and Robert. But now, he's home and he doesn't need crutches any more, so I sleep again with Mama and Papa and my baby sister. Mama and Papa sleep at the head of the bed, and I sleep at the foot. And Mama says when I go with Aunt Mildred I can have my own bed all to myself."

"Go on, if you're alone in the dark you cry like a bawl baby."

"Don't you dare say that or I'll wash your mouth out with soap, Daniel O'Neill. I'm cold and shivering, and you talk to me like I was maybe a nigger or something."

"Oh, well, if you're cold, why don't you get in bed with me?" Danny said.

"You didn't ask me to."

"I'm asking you now, ain't I?"

"It's about time. You would have just as soon let me stand here all day and freeze and get pneumonia and my death of cold, for all you would care. That's because you're so mean."

"Well, hurry up and get in bed! We can't afford to be paying for doctor's bills and funeral expenses for every Tom, Dick, and Harry like you. We haven't got the money, and we got other things to worry about besides paying for your funeral after we buried my grandfather and my Aunt Louise and had expenses."

"Daniel O'Neill, you're just saying those things because you heard Aunty Margaret say them. Why, you're just a copy cat."

"I'm not! I'm just telling you we can't afford to be burying our poor relations all the time. Stop shivering and get in bed with me."

"I will. But I wouldn't if Aunty Margaret was still here, because I would stay in bed with her."

"I wouldn't care two fingers if you did," Danny said as Margaret crawled in beside him.

II

"What'll we play?" Little Margaret asked.

"What do you want to play?" Danny said, hoping that she would say let's play doctor. He was afraid to say so himself, because he knew that it was a bad sin to play doctor and if he said it and she snitched on him, they would all know, and they'd tell Uncle Al when he came in off the road next week for Christmas, and who knows but if they were mad enough, they might even tell Santa Claus.

"What kind of an old cat are you? You don't know anything to play," Little Margaret said.

"I do know things to play."

"What?" Little Margaret asked derisively.

"Lots of things."

"Name them!"

"Think I'm going to tell you," Danny said haughtily.

"You're not, because you can't. Can't tell! Don't know!"

"I know more than you. I'm older than you, and I go to school, and know lots more than you do."

"Prove it!" Little Margaret challenged.

"I can't be bothered."

"Let's play asking questions. You ask me a question, and then you show me if you know anything or if you are just a dumbbell."

"What kind of questions?"

"Any kind of questions. Questions."

"All right. What's the first letter of the alphabet?" Danny asked.

"Why don't you ask me something hard?" Little Margaret said, laughing at him.

"Why don't you answer? Because you don't know, that's why."

"I do so know, smarty, the first letter of the alphabet is A."

"I asked you an easy one, because you don't know many things. What's the next letter?" Danny asked.

"I answered your question. Now you got to let me ask you one."

"All right, go ahead," Danny said flauntingly.

"Why do Mama and Papa sleep in the same bed every night?"

"Because they want to sleep."

"That ain't it," Little Margaret said.

If he let on that he didn't know, she might tell him. And she would maybe want to do it with him. Only he hoped that he didn't pee a baby in her, because if he did, they'd all find out, and that would mean that there would be all kinds of mischief to pay. But he guessed that he couldn't give her a baby, because Bill had said that he wasn't old enough to be able to do that yet. He wanted her to tell him about it, and then to say, come on, Danny, let's us do it together. If he asked, she could go to Aunty Margaret or some of them and snitch on him. But if she asked him, instead of him asking her, then she couldn't very well go snitching. And if she asked him, and Mother or somebody caught them doing it, he could say that he didn't want to do it, and she begged him and almost made him do it. As long as he didn't let on like this, he could get out of any trouble.

"If that ain't it, what is it?" he asked.

"I don't know if I should tell you or not."

"You don't know nothing to tell. That's why you say that. Ho! Ho! Ho!" Danny said, hoping that he could egg her on this way, waiting for her to, and, gee, getting awfully excited.

"I can't," Little Margaret said.

"You can't because there's nothing to tell," he said, hoping that she would want him to do it with her.

"Oh, yes, there is. There's lots that I could tell you, but if I did, how do I know but what you'll snitch on me?"

"What is there to snitch?"

"Lots. And anyway, you are just a child, and a child like you shouldn't know such things."

"I'm older than you are."

"But you don't know as much as I know."

"You don't know anything. You're just pretending to know about secrets because you don't know any, and you want to buffalo me."

"Just for that, I won't tell you. I was going to, but when you talk to me like that, just to fix you, Daniel O'Neill, I won't tell you anything."

"Dare you to tell!"

"If I do, promise you'll never let on that I told you?"

"Why?"

"Because it's something bad, and you and me shouldn't know it."

"What is it?" Danny asked with growing anxiety.

"Mama would have cat fits if she knew I know and told you. So promise you'll never breathe a word of what I say to a soul."

"All right. Promise."

"Cross your heart!" Little Margaret said.

"Cross my heart."

"Do it!"

He crossed his heart.

"That don't count. You got to say, while you cross your heart, 'Cross my heart and hope to die!'"

"I cross my heart and hope to die," Danny said, crossing his chest as he spoke.

"Goofy, you still didn't say it all just right. I don't know if I ought to tell you because you're trying to get out of having to keep your promise by not saying what you should say."

"I am not. Don't tell me!" Danny said, very fearful that she wasn't going to, and then, maybe, he wouldn't get her around to saying let's do it and find out what it's like.

"You say this. 'I cross my heart and hope to die if I ever tell any living soul what Margaret tells me about why Mama and Papa sleep in the same bed at night.' And while you say that, you cross your heart with the first three fingers of your right hand, or otherwise it don't count."

"I cross my heart," Danny began, obeying her instructions simultaneously, "and hope to die if I ever say to any living soul what Margaret tells me about why Mama and Papa sleep in the same bed at night."

"Now if you ever snitch, you'll be cursed, and you'll die an awful death, worse than a dog. So don't you snitch! You hear me!"

"I won't," he said, hardly able to wait for her to tell him.

"Well, they do something together."

"What do they do?" Danny asked, pretending to be in the dark about what she was saying.

"Something that's bad."

"What?"

"Papa has got something like you got to make number one with and he puts it in Mama."

"Why does he do that?"

"See, Smarty, I told you I knew something you didn't know."

"I don't believe you. You're just making it all up."

"If you don't believe me, you're calling me a liar, and any boy who calls his sister that isn't nice."

"I didn't call you nothing. I only said I don't believe you. How do you know Papa and Mama do that?"

"I saw them in bed when they thought I was sleeping."

"That's awful funny. Why would he be doing that?"

"Because that's what every man does with his wife when he gets married. That's the way babies are born. Papa puts that thing he goes to the bathroom with in Mama, and then the baby grows in Mama's stomach and it comes out of her."

"Who lets that happen?"

"Why, Daniel, you're an awful silly. God does."

"Would God let everybody do that, or just Papa and Mama?" Danny asked, hoping she would catch on to what he wanted from this talk, and say let's us two do it.

"God only wants people who are married to do it."

"Gee, that's funny."

"It is not funny."

"It is so funny," Danny said, laughing.

"It is not, because Papa and Mama do it, and my Papa and my Mama are not a bit funny."

"When you and me grow up, will we get married and do it, too?"

"Yes, only we can't marry each other."

"I don't want to marry you."

"Why, Daniel O'Neill, I wouldn't marry you if you was brought to me like a dish of bananas and cream."

"You wouldn't have to."

"Even if I wanted to, I couldn't, because I heard Mama saying to Mrs. Bodenheimer that relations can't ever marry."

"I'm never going to get married, because I don't ever want to have to do that," Danny said, hoping that would lead her to ask him to do it with her.

"Why don't you want to do it? Papa does, and you aren't better than Papa."

"I just don't want to do it ever. How could anything like that ever be any fun?"

"Well, I'll just bet it is fun."

"I bet it ain't."

"I bet it is, even if when you do, it's bad. I'll bet it's still fun."

Gee, she was going to say let's do it now, and they could, with nobody home to catch them. And if she didn't ask him, he was going to say kind of like he didn't mean it, that he would do it to her just to show her it was bad and it wasn't any fun. If he said it that way, and they were caught, he ought to be able to get out of trouble.

"Why do you lay here with me like a mummy? Why don't you talk? You're not tongue-tied. You don't stutter like my brother, Dennis, does," Little Margaret said.

"I wasn't quiet."

"You were so. You weren't saying one word. And you're so mean that you didn't even thank me for telling you things. I'll never tell you one more thing, Daniel O'Neill. You wait and see if I do."

"I was thinking. I wasn't quiet," Danny said, and he wanted to say let's do it, and he was afraid, because he might be caught, and because it was bad, and maybe if he did it, Santa Claus wouldn't give him any toys for Christmas.

"Well, if you're not going to talk to me, I won't stay in bed with you and tell you things."

"I don't care."

"All right, I'm going back to stay alone in Aunty Margaret's bed."

"Stay here. We can play something," Danny said, worried.

"I'll give you just one more chance to treat me nice like a boy should treat a girl. But mark my words, I'm giving you your last chance, Daniel O'Neill."

"What will we play?" he asked, still not able to come right out and say let's do it.

"You make up the game. But you understand, Daniel O'Neill, I won't play anything that's bad."

"I wasn't asking you to, was I?"

"Well. . . . No! Only I won't play any games or do anything if it's bad."

"And I won't play any game, either, if it's bad. I got to be good because I want toys from Santa Claus. But don't you know a game we can play that isn't bad?" he said, feeling his hopes sink because she said she didn't want to do anything bad, and now he guessed she wouldn't do it with him.

"You say what, and I'll do it, unless it's bad."

"Leap frog," he said, his eyes lighting because she would have to bend over and stoop down to play it, and she only had on a nightgown, so when she did, he would see what little girls had, just like he saw it that time she had played doctor with him.

"We got to get out of bed to play leap frog," she said.

"Let's," he said, hoping she would say no, let's find out what happens when we do what Mama and Papa do in bed.

"I have no clothes on, except my nightgown, and you can see me if I play. If I play, you got to promise me you won't look at me."

"I promise. I don't care if I look or not."

"Maybe you don't know what there is I got, but I know what you and all boys got. I know because Mama has me put Robert on the pot, and then I see."

"I don't care," Danny said, thinking how he was going to see, and hoping still she might say let's come on and do it.

"Come on, lazybones, get out of bed," she said, and they jumped up.

"You be down," he said.

"I'll bet you can't stand on your head as good as I can stand on my head," she said.

"If you're so good, do it," he said eagerly.

"All right. But you got to hold my legs out for me for a minute while I get balanced."

He was glad. He was having swell luck. She got down on the floor, sinking her head on the carpet.

"You take my legs and pull them up and hold them out. But don't you dare look at me," she said, giggling.

Danny bent down and grabbed her ankles. He heard a key in the lock.

"Here's Mother," he said, frightened.

"Darn it," she said.

As the door opened, they ran to meet their grandmother.

"We were waiting for you, Mother," he said with a sense of guilt.

"Yes, we were watching at the window for you to come back from church," Little Margaret said.

"Come on, you little ones, and your grandmother will give you a warm breakfast to put in your little stomachs," Mrs. O'Flaherty said, leading them out to the kitchen.

"Mother, will you take me and Daniel to the nickel show this afternoon?" Little Margaret said.

"When your aunt comes home from the hotel early today, we're going to visit the Poor Clares convent on Lafayette Street and take you two with us," Mrs. O'Flaherty said.

They skipped down the hall after her.

30

I

"Why, hello, Jim! How are you? Glad you were able to come up and see me," Joe O'Reilley said, shaking hands with Jim and leading him into the stuffy parlor of the O'Reilley home on Grand Boulevard.

"You're looking good, Joe," Jim said, sitting down opposite Joe, who was a tall, well-set-up handsome man with wavy brown hair.

"I'm feeling tip-top, Jim. How about the family?"

"Pretty well, thanks! Lizz had neuralgia, and one of the small boys had bronchitis, but they're getting over that now. And Bill, my oldest, is off his crutches now, too."

"That's fine. And oh, say, the girls were saying something about some things they have for Lizz. They went to Benediction this afternoon. They might be back before you go. If they aren't, I guess they'll be going down to see Lizz one of these days before Christmas," Joe said.

"Thanks, Joe. And how are Mary and Martha?"

"They're in the best of health. They've been busy this last week or so. They are helping the Daughters of Isabella fix up some Christmas packages for the poor. But say, Jim, what about a drink?"

"That wouldn't hurt my feelings, Joe."

"Let's go out in the kitchen, and I'll fix one up. Remember, Jim, when we were lads? We had many a good drink together, didn't we?" Joe said fondly.

"So we did," Jim said nostalgically.

"Come on. It'll be just like old times, Jim."

"Joe, I fear we'll never get days like that back again," Jim said, following Joe out of the parlor.

Looking about at the furniture, the pictures, the swell beds he noticed passing down the hallway, Jim thought that Joe had a nice home, all right. How he'd like as nice a place for his own family! Well, yes, he should have studied and plugged away just as Joe had done. He could have tried to study law, or engineering, bookkeeping—something. No use crying over spilled milk, though. His kids would profit by their old man's example. He'd see to that. They'd be as big and as smart as Joe. Bigger! Finer! Smarter!

"Have a chair there, Jim. I like to sit in the kitchen and drink when I'm here alone like this. If the girls were home, though, they wouldn't think of it. You know, Jim, the women always have fancier notions than we men do. That's the women all over, God bless them!" Joe said.

"Yep, you feel more at home drinking in the kitchen, Joe," Jim said.

He sat by an enamel-topped table. It was a big kitchen. Fine new stove, must have cost a couple of hundred bucks. All kinds of gee-gaws, too, for cooking. And he could see into the pantry. It was stuffed with food and dishes. Enough food and dishes to feed a regiment of hungry soldiers in there, he guessed. Well, Joe had earned it, too. He had studied law hard.

Joe produced a bottle of good bourbon and emphatically laid two small glasses on the table.

"We can take our liquor straight and hard, can't we, Jim?"

"I should hope so," Jim smiled.

Joe poured out two drinks and pushed one over to Jim.

"Here's spitting in your eye, Jim!" Joe said, holding out his glass.

They tipped glasses and drank.

"Like this bourbon, Jim?" Joe asked.

"Yes. It slides down just like velvet," Jim said, thinking how it was so much better than the booze he got in bars for a nickel a shot.

Joe smiled pleasantly. They sat silently for a few minutes.

"Well, Jim, things look pretty good for me politically," Joe said, a gleam of pride coming into his brown eyes.

"That's fine. I didn't think they were so good since your man, Dunne, lost in the last primary," Jim said.

"Well, Jim, our forces are lining up with Bart Gallivan in the spring. We're going to whip this aristocratic mayor we got in. He thinks that he can run the Cook County Democracy, but he's riding for a fall."

"Bart Gallivan?"

"Bart has a pretty powerful machine lined up. If we join forces with him, why, we ought to sweep in to victory in the primaries. And I think that the Democrats are going to make a lot of big gains next year. You know, the people want more than a fat man smiling in the White House. And then Teddy Roosevelt is sure to split their ranks. They're going to be split by all this progressivism that's in the air. Then, locally here, the Graham scandal isn't going to do them an ounce of good.

"What about that investigation?"

"Well, Graham will be unseated in the Senate. The evidence against him is too strong. No question of the way he got his votes."

"How about the Brophy angle to the case?"

"Well, I don't know so much there. I read about the testimony of Blaine, the Harvester man. They were fighting in town here for business control of some banks and the like. Blaine's testimony was predicted as the last coffin nail for Brophy. But I guess they must have made a deal. I was down to the City Hall the other day, and a reporter I overheard was saying that Brophy bought off Blaine and they came to terms. So Blaine denied that Brophy had gone to him and asked for ten thousand dollars for the jack pot to put Jack Graham in. That helped to clear up Brophy pretty much. So Graham is going to be unseated, and it'll rest there. That's about the thing in a nutshell."

"One of the fellows in it used to stop at the hotel where my sister-in-law works. Robinson's his name. He seemed to be against Brophy in it."

"I don't know much about him. I guess he and Brophy were having some business scrap. He's probably small fry alongside of Brophy, and I guess he doesn't count. What interests me about it is that Graham had a strong following over on the West Side, and we're going to capture some of it. Our forces are counting on bringing them into the Democratic column and swelling our own primary vote."

"But say, Joe, I always felt that Bart Gallivan was a crook. He got a lot of money from the gas people, according to some of the newspapers."

"Here, let's have another drink," Joe said, pouring out two more drinks.

They drank.

"You know how paper talk goes, Jim. Bart's an honest man, honest as a man can be in politics. Bart's a smart politician, too, Jim. Now, here's what he did. He pretended to swing along with the Graham forces. He wasn't doing that for money. He wanted to show Graham up. You see, by showing Graham up before the people, showing that he was a grafter—well, that pushes them over to our side. Now, that's not dishonest. In doing that, Jim, Bart rendered the people a service."

"Of course, Joe, I don't know much about it all, and I take your word on it," Jim said.

"I'm going to be put up for State's Attorney, and from the looks of things, a Democratic nomination in the next primary is tantamount to victory," Joe said, after another silence between.

"Let's drink to it, Joe," Jim said.

Joe poured drinks.

"To the next State's Attorney of Cook County," said Jim, and they drank.

"And, Jim, of course if I do win, I'm going to see that you get a decent job, and that you don't have to go on working on a wagon."

"Well, Joe, you know, I go along and do my work. I'm pretty sure of keeping my job as long as Patsy is the superintendent. And politics is an uncertain business. You're in one day, and out the next. Now, you can afford to go into politics, because you have your law practice to fall back on. But then if I go in, and I'm out in a few years, what have I got to fall back on?"

"But, Jim, while you're in, you're in, and you'd make more money. If we get in, it's at least four years."

"I'm a workingman, Joe, and I don't trust myself much getting a political job."

"If we whip them, I'll have something to say about jobs, and I ought to be able to fix you up, maybe as a bailiff or something like that."

"Well, Joe, I'm not a man to be crossing bridges before I come to them," Jim said.

There was another silence between them.

"It's going to be a real fight with every vote counting," Joe said.

"Too bad that it's not about twenty years from now, Joe, because then, from the looks of things, there ought to be enough O'Neill votes alone to put you in," Jim said, grinning.

"You're not having another already, are you, Jim?"

"No. We were worried, but it was a false alarm," Jim said.

"You might help a little in my campaign down in your neck of the woods. There's a lot of Democratic votes around there," Joe said.

"Gee, Joe, I'd like to! But I don't get around much and I don't know so many people in the neighborhood, except some that I see when I stop in at the saloon on the corner to have a glass of beer now and then."

"You don't know Jack McGuire, do you?"

"I don't think I do. What's he look like?"

"He's a big fellow, and he's got the map of Ireland printed right on his face. He's going to run things for our forces in your ward. You can look him up and talk to him. If you can help him in any little things—well, I'd appreciate it, Jim."

"Sure. Give me his address."

"He's going to organize a Joe O'Reilley Club. He's got a little store at Twenty-fourth and Wentworth, right on the corner, and he'll be setting it in order soon, now. He'll make it a headquarters. You'll be able to find him there. But, Jim, you might do a lot of good with the boys on the express wagons. Patsy is going to help me, naturally, and so could you. Whenever you get to talking with them, steer the subject around to politics, and plant the seeds. Word-of-mouth approbation like that is the best advertisement a candidate can have. You're a popular fellow with the boys, I'm sure, because you always were popular with men. Between now and next April, you might be able to swing a lot of votes over to me. And, Jim, every vote is going to count like hell."

"Naturally I will, Joe."

"Let's drink on it, Jim. And you know you needn't be sorry for doing it, Jim."

They drank.

"How's Dinny making out on your case, Jim?"

"He's managing to get a settlement out of court. He'll get me a thousand dollars, and he says that he expects to have some of it before Christmas."

"That's good. You can use it, too, I imagine. I knew that Dinny Gorman would do right by you."

"Dinny's been pretty decent, and he's managed it smart. And he won't take his regular fee, but only a small one for a matter of form. I appreciate that in him, Joe."

"Dinny's all right. He's going into politics, too, and I think he's going to get somewheres. But speaking of you, Jim, maybe your worst times are over, and from now on you're going to be sailing on in clearer waters right into the sunshine," Joe said.

"I hope so," Jim said earnestly.

"Often, Jim, a stroke of what seems to be bad fortune turns out to be a blessing in disguise. It must have been hard on you and Lizz to have your oldest boy run over, but then, you're getting a good nest egg out of it."

"Only I wish I'd gotten it some other way. You know, Joe, when you are a father, the least thing that happens to one of your kids, it breaks you up pretty damn terribly."

"I know how it is, Jim. I understand. But I also always say this, and I think it's the truth. The ways of God do not submit themselves to man's scrutiny and understanding. As Shakespeare says:

> *There are more things on heaven and earth, Horatio . . .*

"Yes, Joe. I've seen some fine actors playing in Shakespeare, and I've read some of his plays. I once bought a set of them, but I don't know what's happened to it now."

"Good. I was just going to say, Jim, that reading is a fine thing to improve the mind, and you ought to read. When you do, you ought to read Shakespeare. He comes in doubly handy to me, because I give a lot of talks, and it's impressive when you can quote from him or from a poet like Longfellow. Ah, Jim, Shakespeare was a great genius," Joe said.

"Yes, Joe, he understood the human heart. He says many fine things. When you read him, you stop, and you tell yourself, now I understand this and that, and now life is like that. Take *Macbeth*. You read it, and when you come to think about it, you tell yourself now when a man gets ambitious like Macbeth did, and his hunger for power chokes him so that he keeps stepping on the other fellow to get it—well, he's likely to get what Macbeth got. When I read that play, I thought just that, Joe."

"And in *Hamlet* now, Jim, there is a speech by one of the characters, Polonius. Fine philosophy, fine moral philosophy there. It begins like this:

These few precepts in thy memory keep . . .

"Yes, I say, fine moral philosophy there. But let's have another drink, huh, Jim?"

"Why not? Sure!" said Jim.

They drank.

"Jim, another thing I want to say as long as you're here is this. When one of your kids grows up, the older one, or the one that stays with your brother-in-law, O'Flaherty, maybe they can study law, and work in with me. I'll be pretty well along in years then and I'll be able to afford taking things easy. A couple of bright young lads, one of your kids, and one of my brother's—well, they can be a help to me and get their own start. They can go on as O'Reilley and O'Neill. That's a wonderful pair of names, too, isn't it, Jim? And take it from me, if I was giving advice to bright and ambitious young fellows, I'd say, go in for law!'"

"I guess you're right. There's a real future there."

"I'm set on making a lawyer out of my brother's oldest boy. And his girl who stays with us here now, Gertrude, she'll be a school teacher."

"I want all my kids, Joe, to be better men than their old man," Jim said.

"I'd wish the same for mine, if I had any."

"Well, it's getting late, Joe, and I guess I better be going," Jim said.

"I'd ask you to stay, but I got an important appointment. But one more thing before you go. Jim, you're not a Christy, are you?"

"No, Joe, I never joined the Order of Christopher."

"You ought to. It's a fine order for Catholic laymen. You know the Masons are together, and we all ought to stick together in the Christys."

"I never thought much about it, to tell the truth, Joe."

"Well, I wish you would, Jim. You belong with the Christys."

"I will. And I had a good time talking with you, Joe."

"Glad you came. And here, before you go, let's have one last drink."

They drank. Joe walked to the front door with Jim.

"Here, Jim, you can use this to buy something for the kids," Joe said, offering Jim a ten-dollar bill.

"I don't need it, Joe. But thanks just the same."

"It isn't whether you need it or not. Take it!"

"Joe, I don't need it, but thanks just the same."

"Oh, come on, Jim. I won't see you again before Christmas. Call it a Christmas present," Joe said, dropping it in Jim's coat pocket.

"Well, all right, then. Thanks, Joe. And Merry Christmas to everybody."

"Same to you, Jim. So long, old man."

II

He felt pretty good. Life was picking up and promising, all right. He walked down to Fiftieth and Grand Boulevard, a broad smile on his face. A suffusing warmth seemed to flow through him.

The December afternoon was fading. Automobiles, electrics, carriages, all passed down the Boulevard in a seemingly endless succession. He waited to cross. He wished he hadn't taken the money from Joe. Joe had the best of intentions in the world in giving it, but still, he wished he hadn't accepted. Joe was a regular fellow. He hoped Joe became State's Attorney.

He bit off a chunk of tobacco. He crossed Grand Boulevard and walked west on Fiftieth Street. Kids living in this neighborhood were getting a better chance than any of his kids were except Danny. And now, Little Margaret. And what those two got was not with any thanks to their father. Well, some got things in this world and some didn't. It wasn't a perfect world.

He saw the back porch of the O'Flahertys ahead of him, off the alley beyond the vacant lot that ran along Fiftieth Street. He'd see his two lucky kids now, since Little Margaret was staying with her aunt for a few weeks. He hoped that his sister-in-law wasn't home. The old lady wasn't so bad. And the old man Tom had been a real good scout. He missed Tom. Tom used to like to come down to La Salle Street, and the two of them would go out and drink beer. Tom was fun. And he would say, Tom would:

Jim, I niver thought that I'd be comin' to this in the latter end of me days. Here I am, a retired taimster, and I want to be sittin' home readin' me newspaper, and ah, Jim, it's a dog's life that I do be ladin'. The tongue on that woman I married, ah, Jim, it would make a serpent stand up on its ear with envy! It's always Tom, do this, and Tom, do that. Tom, take the baby out, or Tom, put up the line for the nigger washwoman . . .

Good old Tom O'Flaherty! The funny part of it was that Tom couldn't read, and you'd often find him holding the paper before him upside down. Tom had been a comical turkey, but his heart had been pure gold. God have mercy on his soul.

He walked faster, getting more anxious to see his kids. But that night he had

had to take Danny home bawling for his grandmother! It was burned in his memory. He'd never forget it. But, hell, he felt too good now to be stewing over anything. And the old lady was a good sort. Yes, Mary O'Flaherty was. She had the kind of fight in her that he liked and respected. He hoped that she'd be home alone with Danny and Little Margaret.

He rang the O'Flaherty bell, thinking that some day he would have his name on a bell in a building like this one. He hopped up the few steps to the inner hall door and waited for the buzzer. There was no buzzing. Gee, he hoped they were home. He rang the bell again, and waited. No buzzing. He pressed the bell hard. Still no buzzing. They weren't in. Just his luck. He held his thumb on the bell for about forty-five seconds. Nope, not in!

He left the hall. He stood on the stone steps in front of the building, looking across the street at the unlit signboards. It was getting dark now, and they ought to be home soon. He dully watched an elevated train crawl out of sight. He looked down toward Fifty-first Street where he could see lights in store windows. All there was to do now was go home, unless he wanted to take his chances and wait. Hell, being so near and missing them! If he could manage to see enough of Danny, maybe the boy wouldn't act so much like a stranger toward his own father. And Little Margaret would go away, and her father would become a stranger to her, too, in a year, two, three years.

There were times in a man's life when anger boiled up within him, and he couldn't get rid of it. He stood cursing, with his fists clenched, and his heart clenched, and, yes, his soul clenched, too. All he could do was curse.

Jesus Christ!

He took a couple of steps. Down the street, kids running, shouting. Another elevated. Muffled sounds from the street cars on Fifty-first Street. He took a few more steps. He turned around, went back again to the front of the building. He gazed across the street at the two-story brick building next to the vacant lot. To own a house like that with plenty of room inside, and all that prairie for the kids to play in. Then Danny wouldn't have to live with his grandmother and Little Margaret wouldn't be going away to Madison. The only trouble with being in that house was that it was too near the O'Flahertys.

He started toward Fifty-first Street to get a drink. In back of him, a kid's voice. Made him think of Danny. Hell, now, didn't he want to give his kids a chance. And wasn't Danny being taken care of, fed, educated? Why should he be ungrateful? A father should never, not even in his thoughts, stand in the way of his kids getting somewhere. What kind of a world would it be if kids didn't turn out better than their old man? But where would the kid get to? What kind of an education would he get? If Danny started acting like a dude when he was eighteen or nineteen, he'd step in and go a couple of rounds with him. It was going to be a long way off before any of his kids would be able to take their old man into camp with their dukes. And, yes, if Danny grew up to be a dude he would knock such fancy notions right out of his noodle.

He crossed the Fifty-first Street car tracks. Another drink would just fix him up.

III

Jim staggered out of the entranceway to the building. Still nobody in. Now why, oh, why in the name of Jupiter X. Columbus didn't they come home? Oh, why, oh, why in the name of Christ didn't they come home with his kids? Sunday, when their old man could see them because he had two brand-new silver nickels that he wanted to give them to buy candy with, and the O'Flahertys take the kids out. Oh, why, oh, why, oh, why?

He swayed on the sidewalk. A woman turned the corner, saw him listing, and immediately changed her course, crossing over to avoid him.

"All right, lady, just a harmless father waitin' for his kids to come home," Jim said in a low, thick voice.

He watched the lady, swayed. Well, wasn't that something to put in your pipe and smoke! What in hell was he, a blue-beard, or a Blackhand? Why, goddamn her! She was probably the wife of some rich dude and she named her kids Percy. It made him kind of wish that some guy would grab her, drag her across the street in the prairie and give her five or six inches of what her dude husband probably didn't have to give her.

He swayed. He walked unevenly toward the corner. Now, why didn't the O'Flahertys come home with his kids? Oh, why, oh, why, oh, why in the name of all the saints that Lizz prayed to, why weren't the kids brought home?

Whoops!

Anyway, he felt swell, better than he had in a long time. And right across the street, next to those lighted signboards, there was the house he was going to buy some day for all his family.

Whoops!

"How's it going, fellow?" a lad smiled, passing Jim.

"Fine, Charlie! Fine!" Jim said genially, waving a long arm.

Now, was that the right thing to do? To take the kids out on a Sunday afternoon when Jim O'Neill wanted to see them and give them brand-new nickels to buy any kind of candy their little hearts desired! Now, was it? No, it wasn't. It was no way to run this man's world.

He felt so good that he was going to sing.

> *Has anybody here seen Kelly? K-E double L-Y.*
> *Sure his hair is red, his eyes are blue, and he's Irish*
> *thro' and thro' . . .*

Why, he hadn't thought he was ever going to feel so good, or that the world was going to seem so swell! Hurray! All these buildings with lights in them. They were the homes of guys who were a little better off than he was. Homes of guys who were putting their shoulders to the wheel, and the wheels of industry were turning, oh, the wheels were turning, oh, the wheels were turning. And so he just took the reins in hands, and told the horse of Life to go giddyap, giddyap, giddyap! And so they did. And so they were raising families, just like he was. And they all tried to do something for their kids. He stopped in the middle of the block, listed, pointed an unsteady finger at a lighted parlor window.

"You, there, you, go ahead and do everything for your kids that you can. And the day will come when no matter what you did, they'll look up the ladder and there will be Jim O'Neill's kids ahead of them. By Christ, they will! And how'll you like that, Charlie!"

He swayed and zigzagged on, again bursting into song.

> *She was happy till she met you,*
> *And the fault is all your own.*
> *If she chooses to forget you,*
> *You will please leave her alone!*

It began to snow. He staggered on to O'Callahan's saloon for another drink.

31

Al O'Flaherty dipped the silver spoon into his chicken soup, pushed it away from him, delicately skated it off the rim of his soup plate so that there would be no drippings, lifted it to his mouth, drew the soup noiselessly off the spoon, swallowed it. The real wise guy always displayed correct table manners without making any show of it. Ned wasn't using his soup spoon in the right way. He pulled the spoon toward him when he dipped it in. That was the way to do it if you wanted to decorate your vest with stains, although Ned wasn't spilling any. Even though he wasn't he still wasn't doing it the right way. There was a right way and a wrong way to do everything. Well, he wouldn't say anything to Ned, because Ned had an argumentative tendency in him, and he often got sore when he was corrected. Al finished his soup, unostentatiously proper in his technique.

They sat in a corner of the main dining room of the new Chandler Hotel in Indianapolis. It was a medium-sized room divided up with ornate pillars. The ceiling was white with a golden pattern traced through it. Soft black velvet drapes hid the windows. A string quartet played *Till the Sands of the Desert Grow Cold*. The waiter took their soup plates away and served them their steaks.

"Yes, Ned, this is a classy job, all right," Al said.

"I only wish that we had as classy a hotel in Madison. It would do a lot of good for the town," Ned said.

They were silent for several minutes.

"But say, Ned, I'm glad to hear that Mildred's feeling so much better. Too bad you and she can't spend the Christmas holidays with us."

"Al, I'd like to, but I couldn't. Mildred has to spend Christmas and New Year's with her people, and I won't be able to get away. I'll be taking a train out of here for Chicago tomorrow morning after breakfast. I'll see Mud and Peg, wish them

330

a Merry Christmas and a Happy New Year, and then catch a train right out for Madison. But Mildred's coming along when I come down for the shoe convention next month."

"Is that when you're going to take Little Margaret back with you?" Al asked.

"Yes. It'll be a great thing for Mildred. She's always wanted to have a child of her own, you know, Al," Ned said.

"I'm very glad that you're able to do it. The little girl will have a much superior home environment than the one on La Salle Street," Al said.

"Yes, Al, you don't have to tell me about Lizz. I saw her. Cripes, the way she talks! I never heard the beat of it. Say, Al, where in the hell does she get such a line of talk?"

"She's a bird, Ned, isn't she?" Al said.

"Can't you have a serious talk with her and get her to change?" asked Ned.

"Ned, for over three years I've been trying to get her to wash her face and comb her hair when she comes to see us," Al said.

"Well, you failed. That night I stayed at Mud's, when she came she busted in looking like a hurricane. No, Al, you haven't succeeded."

"But, Ned, Peg's been writing me cheerful letters these last few weeks. It seems like all's well at Calumet," Al said, his eyes becoming soft, expressive of his happiness as he said this.

"When I was there, she was trying to borrow a hundred and twenty-five dollars off me. Hell, Al, I didn't have it to spare. But I couldn't seem to make her believe me," Ned said.

"She did?" Al said, almost jumping out of his chair.

"Yes. She said that she spent so much on the house and on Lizz. Oh, she told me a long story that was all mixed up. But, gee, Al, I'm sorry. I didn't mean to upset you," Ned said, noticing his brother.

"Damn it, Ned, I tell Peg time and time again to keep every cent she makes and spend it on herself. I really don't know what she does with her money. Of course, she's always buying little things for the home, and that's nice."

"Well, she ought to. Everybody should do things about their home," Ned said, and the orchestra played *Mother Machree*.

"I tell you, Ned, a lot of worthless people like that Morton dame just see Peg coming. Peg's such a good-hearted girl that, well, she just lets her salary dribble away and people walk all over her," Al said.

"She seems to think that I'm a millionaire, Al. You know that if you get hard-pressed, and need anything, why, I'd give anything I got. But, hell, we don't have any fortune. We've had so much expense because of Mildred's health. And then she had to get an electric to go around in, because she hasn't the strength to be walking and taking street cars. No, Al, we're not millionaires, but from the way Peg talks, you'd think that we were."

"I understand, Ned."

"Al, I really think that it would be a very good thing if Peg met some decent, self-respecting chap who's well-off and married him."

"She's got plenty of time for that. I don't know why she ever let herself get mixed up with this fellow, Robinson," Al said.

"He's a cur! A cur! He ought to be tarred and feathered and run out of town on a rail," Ned said, his face reddening.

"I really don't understand how he could do what he does, taking a decent girl and ruining her life, teaching her to smoke and drink. God, Ned, hasn't the man got any conscience, any chivalry?"

"Can't you do anything about it, Al?" Ned asked.

"I'd like to know what I could do. Peg's such a high-strung girl. She's got to be handled with kid gloves."

"God, I'd like to get my hands on him, the cur! . . . Say, Al, let's find out if he's in town during the shoe convention next month. If he is, we'll see him. And then just let me talk to him!"

"Say, that's a promising plan of strategy. Only we can't let Peg know that we're doing it. She'd say we're interfering with her life, and she'd raise a big rumpus at home. She always has to be handled with tact, Ned."

"Tact, my eye! Tact in a pig's ass-hole! There's right and wrong. There's decency and indecency! And I tell you, Al, this whole business isn't right! It isn't decent! Say, doesn't he know that Peg has a decent mother and a decent family? What does he think we are? Well, Al, it's up to us to do something about this situation," Ned said.

"Yes, I guess so. Only I do think now that it's going to blow over. They made a sucker out of him in Washington in the Graham investigation. When he went after Brophy, he bit off more than he can chew. I think that they'll break him now, and he'll go back to the bush-leagues in Minnesota. He's only a piker alongside of fellows like Brophy."

"I hope so. But, say, I haven't had a chance to ask you how this trip went," Ned asked.

"Fair, Ned. Fair! Early in the month I sold a lot of shoes. But now, of course, the season is over until after the New Year. But then, all things considered, I've had a fair year."

"How did the medium vamps move this fall?"

"Slow. Not much there," Al said.

"The same with me," Ned said.

"But to get back to what I was saying, I hope next year is better than this one was," Al said.

The waiter removed their plates and served them with coffee and dessert. The orchestra played *Holy Night*.

"But I don't know about next year. It's an election year. If the Democrats put up a man who's for the people against the interests, I'm afraid that the interests will draw in their money and sit tight on it, and that might mean bad business."

"Al, I thought that you were a real live wire," Ned said in disappointment.

"Well, I am! But, say, what the hell are you trying to do? Tell me something I don't know when I know what I'm talking about? I said that presidential years are never too good for business. I can show it to you in figures. Now, last week I was reading a copy of *The New York Times* that I picked up on a train. There was a financial article that proved in black and white that presidential years are bad business years."

"Now, just a minute there, Al! Just a minute! Always remember this. Be snappy but not snappish! Discuss but don't argue! Now, if you want me to discuss this angle with you I'll do it. But if you're going to start jumping down my throat and arguing in a loud voice, I'm not going to talk about it. I don't believe in wasting my energy arguing," Ned said.

"I'm not snappish, and I don't argue. I discuss," Al said, relaxing.

"All right. Now, let's get down to brass tacks on this angle. Now, just what does this stuff about a presidential year amount to?"

"What?" Al interrupted.

"Well, give me a chance, will you? I listened to you. Now let me finish," Ned said.

"Pardon me! Go ahead!"

"What does it amount to? It amounts to this. Some of these birds put on long faces and predict calamities. My God, to hear them talk, you'd think they were Socialists. Now, here's the way you want to handle such birds. When a prospect hedges out of buying from you on this excuse, here's the line to give you. You say to him, 'Mr. So-and-So, you know what you are?' He'll ask you what. And you tell him this: 'Mr. So-and-So, you remind me of a healthy man trying to prove that he's sick. Do you stop eating because of politics, unless you're a defeated candidate? No, you don't. Well, then, Mr. So-and-So, why do you stop buying?'"

"Say, Ned, that's a corker of a sales argument to use in combating these birds who are professional pessimists. I'm going to spring it," Al said, enthusiastically slapping the table.

"Go ahead! You're welcome to it. But don't give it out to anyone else," Ned said.

"Of course I won't, Ned," Al said.

"Al, cooperation is the life and soul of trade. I believe in applying that principle, too. But there's too many damn shoe men on the road now who won't play the game fair and square. They're all for themselves. That's why I won't give my secrets away. Goddamn 'em, let 'em learn for themselves! If they can't, let them quit and go out and dig ditches where they'd have to use their backs instead of their brains."

"And, Ned, a lot of these birds selling shoes these days think that selling is just talk. It doesn't matter what they say as long as they keep bulling all the time. Why, the damn fat-heads! They're no better than kikes," Al said.

"Al, don't I know 'em! They're sputtering gas engines, and they give off nothing but fumes. But, Al, such bush-leaguers aren't worth counting. In ten years they won't even see the dust of fellows like you and me," Ned said.

Al wondered how much farther up the ladder would he and Ned be in ten years. He almost wished that it was ten years ahead, just to see where he would get to. But in ten years he would be ten years nearer to death. In ten years Mother would be over seventy. Would she live that long? Lord spare her to them. Ah, time was swift, and fast, and fleeting.

"Al, you and I can't lose. The power of wishing and concentration is a mighty force that no man can beat. Jesus said that faith can move mountains. And it can! Al, if you wish for something, and concentrate on it wholly and completely with strong faith in your wish, there is nothing on God's earth that can stop you! Absolutely nothing! The power of the wish is the mightiest of powers. It is the true kernel of wisdom in the teaching of Jesus. That's what he meant by faith."

"Of course, he meant also that you should have faith in the hereafter, and God and the Holy Trinity," Al said.

"That's all well and good, Al. But I'm here now, on this beautiful earth of flowers and fruits and sunshine that God made. And God didn't put me here to be poor and unhappy. And God gave me the power not to be unhappy. That is the power of faith, the wish," Ned said.

"There's true wisdom to what you say, Ned. But faith, too, has to be supplemented by deeds," Al said.

"I know whereof I speak, Al. Because I've tried it out, and it's been proven true. It's worked for me. Now, just last week, I was in Kokomo. I've never before sold as much as a shoelace to old Guggins of the High Class Shoe Emporium there. So I said to myself that this time I was going to sell him. I sent out a wish that old Guggins would buy some shoes off me. I told myself over and over again that he'd buy. Before I called on him, I sent out a thought-wish that would go through the cosmos and connect up with his psyche. Then I walked in on him, and I said, 'Well, well, well, if it isn't Mr. Guggins himself. And, say, you're looking fine, young and peppy, just like a college boy. How's business, Mr. Guggins? Is it as bright as the sunshine we have this morning spread like happiness through every nook and cranny and corner of this up-and-coming city of yours?' Well, Al, to make a long story short, he bought three cases of shoes off me. And you know, he still doesn't know how he was sold," Ned said.

"Yes, Ned, there's a lot to what you say," Al said, liking it that Ned used a word like *psyche*; it was a pippin of a word, and he often used it himself.

"But say, Al, I see they want to close up here. These poor devils around here want to get home. They work hard, so let's not keep them. We can talk just as well in the lobby," Ned said, noticing that the waiters were doing chores for closing, and that the musicians were getting ready to leave.

"Sure! Sure. But no, Ned, this is mine. Let me have it!" Al said, taking the bill which Ned had already picked up.

Al paid the bill and tipped the waiter. They went out to the lobby, found comfortable chairs, sat down. Al smoked a cigar. Ned puffed on a cigarette.

"Say, Ned, are your people going to put out much in the way of colors for next season?"

"You know, Al, those goddamn fatheads in the home office! I told them that colors are not going to move fast this spring. But I tell you, Al, when a man has a top story that seems more like a warehouse for lard than it does a head, what can you tell them? Fisher and Mostil are lard-heads. You can't tell them a damn thing, not even for their own good," Ned said.

"Next spring is not going to be a color season," Al said.

"This year I told them that we would clean up if we came out with some classy new broad-toe lasts. So they had too many staple styles two lasts narrower than they should have been. They shouldn't be running a shoe factory. They should be laying brick," Ned said.

"We're coming out with some fine quality shoes. Wait till you see the numbers we have on display at the convention next month," Al said.

"Yes, you're with one of the best outfits in the shoe game," Ned said.

"I was talking with Matt Lovejoy in Cleveland last month. He had to come out west. I think that I'm going to be able to put aside a little of my earnings each year, and buy into the factory. It's a good investment, too. It will be a little each year, but it'll add up in time, and it's worth it," Al said.

"Fine, Al, fine!" Ned said.

But don't tell Peg. You know how she is," Al said.

"Of course I won't, Al. But, say, there's a nickel show down the street. Let's take it in, huh?" Ned said.

They went up for their coats and met in the lobby.

"Yes, Ned, I'm looking to the future with confidence. And I think that this ought to be a happy Christmas for all of us," Al said as they walked out of the hotel.

32

I

Danny pasted his nose against the window, and the elevated train ran along, zush, so fast that you could hardly see anything. Before you got a good look at something, it was past, and there was something else in its place. Everything he saw seemed to move as fast as the train, and in the other direction, telephone poles, buildings, roofs with snow on them, streets, barns, back yards full of dirty snow, stations where the train did not stop. They all just jumped past him, that's what they did.

"Aunty Margaret, how can Santa Claus come down a chimney if he's fatter than the chimney?" asked Little Margaret, who sat by the window opposite Danny, facing forward.

"He makes himself small so he can squeeze down," the aunt said, patting her niece, who was sitting on her right.

"Well, why doesn't he fall down and hurt himself? I tried to walk on air by stepping off your bed, and I fell down and bumped my nose," Little Margaret said.

"He has the power to go down a chimney like a man walking on air," the aunt said.

"Aunty Margaret, can Santa Claus do as many things as God can do?" Danny asked, swinging away from the window to face her.

"No, Brother. He hasn't the power that God has. God made Santa Claus, just the same as He made everybody and everything else in the world."

"Then he doesn't know as much as God does?" Danny reasoned.

"Nobody knows as much or is as powerful as God, Brother."

"You're sure of that?" Danny asked.

"Yes, but why did you ask?" the aunt said.

"I just wanted to know and make sure," Danny said, turning his attention back to the window.

He was glad to know it. If Santa Claus didn't have as much power as God, Santa Claus couldn't know the things that God could know. If Santa Claus was God now, Santa might know about the thoughts he had and the things he wanted to do with Little Margaret when she came into bed with him last Sunday. But Santa Claus wasn't God. Nobody but God could know his thoughts. And then, he had not done anything. So he didn't see why he should be punished for those thoughts. But he was certainly glad, anyway, that Santa Claus wasn't able to do everything that God could do.

"Aunty Margaret, will Santa Claus give me a doll that will close its eyes and sleep?" Little Margaret asked.

"If you ask him, and you are a good enough girl, he will," the aunt said, smiling tolerantly.

He didn't want an old doll. He wanted a baseball glove, toy soldiers, and an electric-train set. And he would be asking Santa Claus for a Ty Cobb Louisville Slugger bat, too, if he hadn't bought one with the money that Mr. Smith had given him.

All these dirty back yards with snow rushing by him were in the nigger neighborhood. He was glad, though, that he was on the train instead of walking, because Bill had told him about nigger kids. Bill said that none of the white kids around Twenty-fifth and La Salle would go under the viaduct alone for fear of being caught by nigger kids on the nigger side of the railroad tracks. Gee, if nigger kids did such things to white kids, would Santa Claus give them toys at Christmas?

"Aunty Margaret?" he asked, turning.

"Yes, Little Brother?"

"Does Santa Claus bring toys to nigger children and nigger babies?" he asked, and passengers overhearing him laughed.

"Brother, never say that in public. Say colored," she said, relieved at noting that there were no Negroes within hearing distance.

"Well, does he give things to colored boys and girls?"

"If they are good and obey their fathers and mothers, he does."

"I just wanted to know," Danny said, turning back to the window.

He guessed it was the same as with white kids. The good nigger kids got things from Santa, and the bad ones didn't. The telephone poles and buildings passed him like sixty. He saw himself as two Danny O'Neills. One of him was sitting in the elevated train that was going along, swish, zish. The other of him was outside, running, going just as fast as the train was, jumping from roof to roof, leaping all the way across the streets that the train passed, going on jumping and leaping and keeping right up with the train. Now, then, if he could really do that, wouldn't he be able to do things that nobody else could do, not even Santa Claus? There was a street with car tracks, and an elevated station, and the one of himself inside the train could see the one of himself outside the train, jumping, swish, right across the street to the roof of a big red building that was higher than the elevated tracks. He ran along the roof of the building, keeping ahead of the train, jumped way down like he was diving, landed on an old barn three back yards away from the red building. Without stopping, almost with the same motion, he jumped up high onto the roof of the building right beside the tracks, off it without falling in the snow on a house next door that was lower than the tracks, up again, down, over, up, up, down, over the street, up, down over one two three four five back yards, up over one two three back yards, along even roofs, all the way over another street. . . . Gee, this was fun.

"Aunty Margaret, is my brother, Daniel, a gentleman?" Little Margaret thoughtfully asked.

"Of course, he is. He is the sweetest little gentleman," the aunt said.

"Well, I'm glad. I was jus' thinking, if he isn't a gentleman, maybe Santa won't like it. Then he won't give me so much, if I was to go see him and drag along a brother who isn't a gentleman," she explained.

"Why, whoever put such thoughts in your head? Santa Claus will give you just as much as he gives your brother."

"I want him to give me more," Little Margaret said.

"But, Little Margaret, darling, that isn't fair to your brother. You shouldn't want that."

"But I don't care! I do, because I'm a little girl, and a little girl should get more than a boy. Girls are always nicer than boys."

"Why, Little Margaret! The way you talk!"

Away, right over another street, and wasn't that a jump, down over a street and over one two three four back yards onto a barn, and then, without stopping or falling, or getting wet by snow, springing right up onto the roof of a building bigger than the tracks, then down again about four stories onto a back fence. Boy, didn't he wish he could really make jumps like that, instead of just pretending that he was making them!

"If Santa hears of you being so selfish, he mightn't give you a thing," said the aunt.

"Then, Aunty Margaret, you got to promise me that you won't tell him on me."

"I won't tell him if you don't say such a selfish thing again."

"I should think that Danny would let me have more. If I was a boy, and Danny was a girl like me, I'd let him have more toys than I would be getting."

"Santa tries to give equally to all boys and girls, except that he gives more toys to those who obey their fathers and mothers and their elders than he does to disobedient little children," the aunt said.

"Then he's got to give me more. Mama says I'm a very good girl. And I help Mama by taking care of my baby sister and my two little brothers."

"You cute little darling, you tell that to Santa Claus and he'll give you more toys."

"I will. He likes me to take care of my little brothers and sister, doesn't he?"

"He wants all boys and girls to do good things, and to do what they are told to."

It was fun riding on the elevated and playing he was making jumps like this. He could feel himself being two Danny O'Neills, and he could feel the one of himself on the outside, jumping high up, way down, moving just as fast as the train. And the train was going fast, swish, zish, fast. Yes, it was fun seeing himself running through the air and over roofs, going just as fast as the train. It was more fun than listening to Little Margaret chew the rag.

II

"Now, you children stay close to me so that you don't get lost in the crowds. Take my hands, you little dears," Aunt Margaret said, guiding them downstairs from the elevated station at Madison and Wabash.

"Will we see Santa Claus right away?" Danny asked, clinging to her hand while they waited beside piled-up snow for the traffic to stop, and the elevated trains dinned overhead.

"We'll see him right away if he isn't busy, Brother."

"If he's busy, what will he be doing? Making toys?"

"No, he'll be seeing other children like you and your sister."

"I want to see Santa Claus making toys," Little Margaret said.

"He makes them up by the North Pole before he comes down at Christmas time," Aunt Margaret said.

"There's the traffic policeman's whistle now. Come on, children," she said, tightening her grip on their hands and leading them across Wabash Avenue after the traffic policeman's whistle had blown, loudly and puncturingly.

"I want to be a traffic policeman like that and blow a whistle to tell wagons and automobiles when to go and when to stop," Danny said, tagging along beside his aunt.

"Children, don't be pulling at me this way," the aunt said, walking along Madison Street as both of them tugged and strained almost like puppies on a leash.

"Aunty Margaret, there's Santa Claus!" Danny excitedly yelled, breaking away from his aunt and rushing up to a Salvation Army Santa who stood by a basket and a sign, ringing a cowbell.

"Hello, Santa Claus!" Danny said, looking up enrapt at the grizzled painted face, the false whiskers, and the bleary eyes.

"Hello, Son!" the Santa Claus said, whiskey-voiced and smiling.

"I came downtown to see you. Only they told me I would see you in a store," Danny burst out.

"In the store," the Santa Claus said, stamping his feet, ringing his cowbell.

"Hello, Santa Claus. I'm here to see you!" Little Margaret said.

"Come on, Brother. We have to hurry," Aunt Margaret said, annoyed, taking his hand to lead him away.

"I want to talk to Santa Claus and tell him what I want," Danny whiningly protested.

"Me, too. I want to speak to him. Daniel O'Neill, you wait and let me tell Santa what I want. Girls always come before boys," Little Margaret said after escaping from her aunt and standing before the man with upturned eyes.

Margaret dropped a dime in the basket and winked at the man.

"You little tots go along now with your mother because she wants you to go with her," the Santa Claus said, again dingling his cowbell.

They were led away. Disappointment was scribbled on their faces. Pulled by his aunt, Danny glanced wistfully back at the Santa Claus who stamped his feet and rang his cowbell. Little Margaret sulked, then cried. Danny felt like crying, too, because he had come to see Santa Claus, and here, when he had only said hello to him, Aunty Margaret had meanly pulled him off.

"What's the matter?" Aunt Margaret asked solicitously, bending down to her niece.

"You wouldn't let me see Santa Claus and tell him what I wanted."

"We're going to see Santa Claus, you little doll," Aunt Margaret said patiently, even with amusement.

"There's Santa Claus, back there."

"No, it isn't," Aunt Margaret said.

"Oh, yes, it is, Aunty Margaret," Danny said, determined that he wasn't going to be fooled.

"I want to see Santa Claus," Little Margaret bawled, while pedestrians paused to look and to smile at the little group.

"That man is just dressed like Santa Claus to collect money to give the poor people baskets of food and turkeys on Christmas. The real Santa Claus is in the store where I'm taking you."

"Aunty Margaret, you're not fooling us, are you?" Danny said so overseriously that his aunt burst out laughing.

"You little darlings, no, your aunt isn't fooling you. You trust her and you'll see the real Santa Claus," she said, leading them on; and suddenly she recalled that the Salvation Army Santa Claus had referred to her as their mother; she wished that she was their mother, and that Lorry was their father.

"Are there lots of men like that, dressed up like Santa Claus?"

"Yes, Little Brother."

"And they aren't the real Santa Claus?"

"No! I'm taking you to the real one," Aunt Margaret said, guiding them across Madison Street to go north on State Street.

"My goodness, where do all these people come from?" Danny said, talking like an adult, but unheard by his aunt.

III

"You two stay close to me," Aunt Margaret said as they stepped away from the revolving doors at the entrance to Sheriff and Forest's department store.

"Aunty Margaret, I'm afraid!" Danny said, clutching her dress, seeing the crowds of people flowing by him.

"Daniel, you are a little baby! If you are older than me, you shouldn't be afraid when I'm not afraid," Little Margaret pertly said.

"Aunty Margaret, don't you lose us here with all these people," Danny said, frightened.

"I won't, if you stay close. Now each of you take one of my hands and we'll go right up to see Santa Claus."

They proceeded along a jammed aisle. Directly in front of him, there was the funniest fat woman, and she seemed to be having the awfullest time walking on her big feet.

"Aunty Margaret, look at the big feet on the fat woman!" Danny exclaimed loudly.

"Brother!" the aunt remarked quickly and reprimandingly, while the corpulent female turned to glare at Danny and to drive a fierce look into Margaret.

"Excuse him," Margaret said feebly.

"Some there is that don't know how to teach manners to their brats," the fat woman said noisily to a feminine companion.

"If you say any more things like that, Danny, I'll tell Santa Claus on you and I'll never take you out again," Aunt Margaret said, slinking back to allow others to get in between her and the fat woman.

"I want to go on the walking stairs," Little Margaret yelled, pointing to a crowded escalator.

"You might get hurt on it."

"All those people on the walking stairs aren't getting hurt," Little Margaret said.

"They're grown up, and they can take care of themselves."

"So can I. If I can take care of my little brothers and sister, I ought to be able to take care of myself, oughtn't I?" Little Margaret said.

"This way, darlings!" Margaret said sternly, dragging them toward the crowd collected about the store elevators.

People pushed and squeezed to enter and leave the elevator with their bundles and their children. Margaret managed to crush forward and to lodge them both beside her in a corner of the car without incurring any damage more serious than having her toes stepped on.

It was funny, Danny thought, riding up in an elevator like this one, and not falling. Nobody near him seemed afraid, so why should he be? And he wasn't. Only it was awful crowded, and there was some funny kind of feeling inside of him, just as if part of him inside, like his stomach, was falling downward while he was being taken upward. He wished he was out of it. It was stopped. He was glad.

"This isn't our floor, Brother," his aunt said, grabbing him as he tried to get out.

More people jammed in. A woman stepped on his toe. Darn her, why didn't she keep her feet to herself? Had to be very careful now, or he'd lose Aunty Margaret and his sister.

"Here I am, Aunty Margaret," he called so she would be sure to know where he was.

Going up. He had the feeling again that part of him inside, something around his stomach, was going down as he was carried higher. He wanted to get off.

"Ain't this our floor?" he asked his aunt, at the next start.

She held him tightly during the exodus and entrance of the passengers. Going up again. He was afraid he was going to get sick before he got out of this. He didn't ever want to ride on an elevator like this again. Ooh, it made him feel worse than being tickled all over would make him feel.

IV

"Take your time, children. Santa Claus will be here all day, and he has enough toys for everybody. You won't miss a thing by not pulling your poor old aunt along like this when she's tired," Aunt Margaret said with a sigh, trying to check the two of them as they pulled and dragged her along faster, through a section of Oriental rugs to the toy department that was beyond it.

"Aunty Margaret, does Santa Claus make more toys for boys or dolls for girls?" Little Margaret asked, looking innocently up at her aunt.

"He makes enough of both," the aunt said curtly.

"I'm going to talk to him about the toys I want for next Christmas as well as for this one. Maybe I can get him to make me toys to order, just the same as Mother says Uncle Al has suits made to order for him," Danny said.

"Aunty Margaret, do people buy these rugs here?" asked Little Margaret.

"Aunty Margaret! The toys! The toys!" Danny gleefully cried, pulling her forward.

"Don't run!" she said, halting them.

"Hurry up!" Danny yelled, ignoring her, still pulling as he saw the crowded toy department ahead, with boys, girls, and grownups all milling around the counters.

"Now, you children be careful not to touch things that you shouldn't touch," Aunt Margaret said as they reached the toy department.

"Where is Santa Claus?" Danny asked, not having listened to what his aunt had just said.

All around them there was happy talk, gay laughter, expectant cries from children. Margaret stood, indecisive as to which way to turn.

"Don't you darlings want to look around at the toys first, before you see Santa Claus? Then you will have a better idea of what you want him to bring you for Christmas," she said.

"I want everything," Danny said.

"No you don't," corrected Little Margaret.

"How do you know if I do or don't? Who made you teacher?" Danny retorted to his sister.

"Well, you don't want a doll, do you?"

"No!" he said, glaring defensively at Little Margaret.

"Santa Claus doesn't like to hear of brothers and sisters fighting with each other," Aunt Margaret said.

"Aunty Margaret, I didn't come downtown with you so that I would be plagued by him," Little Margaret said, trying to act grownup and pointing a stern finger at Danny.

"This way, children!" Aunt Margaret said wearily, holding their hands tightly as she guided them along another jammed aisle, and Danny gazed absently from left to right, thinking, gee, now, wouldn't it be nice if he could live in a toy store all the time, or at least if he could come down to a toy store to look at toys every day in the week.

"Aunty Margaret, will Santa Claus give me any kind of a doll I want?" asked Little Margaret.

"You'll have to ask him and find out," the aunt in a dreary voice answered, as she edged them close toward a doll counter.

"Would you like a doll like this, madam?" a saleslady quickly said, holding a large and expensive blue-eyed, brown-haired doll before Margaret.

"I'm just looking around now, and I don't know," Aunt Margaret said, while Little Margaret tried to chin herself to get up to see the dolls.

Gee, that doll was almost as nice to look at as Hortense Audrey was, Danny told himself as he waited, looking at the doll.

"I want to see all the dolls," Little Margaret said impetuously.

Danny guessed she might shake a leg about doing it. Didn't she think he had things to look at, trains and things, and then there was Santa Claus. She and her fool dolls made him a little bit sick.

Margaret lifted Little Margaret up, and the girl bounced about in her aunt's arms, pointing, squirming, making herself a heavy burden.

"Oh, what kind of a doll is that, Aunty Margaret?"

"It's a lovely Dutch doll."

"I want that big doll in the blue dress," Little Margaret said imperiously, as the aunt, with aching arms, put her down again on the floor. "I want to see the dolls again!" Little Margaret whined.

"You're such a big girl, your aunt can't lift you for long."

"I want to look again!"

Grimacing, Margaret again lifted her niece. Why couldn't that slob of a mother take the kids downtown to see Santa Claus? Why did this, like everything in the family, have to fall on her poor shoulders?

"I like the doll in the case with the lace cap. Will you buy it for me, Aunty Margaret?" Little Margaret said, twisting in her aunt's arms.

"Miss, I'll take that doll," Margaret said, thinking that she could afford to buy something out of the twenty-five dollars Lorry had sent her for Christmas.

V

"How soon can I speak to Santa Claus?" said Little Margaret, lugging the package containing the doll her aunt had bought her.

"I showed you the dolls. Now you must come while your brother has a chance to look at some toys. Then you can both see Santa Claus," Aunt Margaret said.

Danny looked at the toy trains. Some of them ran by being wound up, and the better ones ran by electricity. A salesman just concluded demonstrating a train set as they got to the counter.

"I want to see the trains run!" he said demandingly.

"Brother, the man just ran it."

"I want to see it run again!"

"The man's busy. Maybe Santa Claus will give you a train set for Christmas, and you can run it yourself all you want to. But now the man there is busy."

"Mister, are you busy?" Danny asked.

"Not at all, what is it?" said a sleek young man who was behind the counter on which train tracks, engines, and cars were piled.

"I want to see the train run again!"

"Why, surely you can," the salesperson said.

"See, Aunty Margaret, he isn't busy," Danny said as if conveying a point of information to her.

"Why, it's no trouble at all to demonstrate," the man said while Margaret blushed. "This is one of the best sets we have. It's electric, runs smoothly, causes no trouble, and it is more convenient and more serviceable and durable than the non-electric engines. Besides the engine, four cars, a good-sized track and this rather attractive little tunnel go with it. The cost is only twelve-fifty. It's one of the best bargains to be found in our entire toy department."

He started the train running over tracks that made a figure eight. Danny watched, fascinated, listening to the echoing noise as the cars rolled on. He looked closely when it went through the tunnel and emerged on the other side. He wished it would run and run the longest time, just like a real train, stopping at stations where people who wanted rides would be picked up. And now it was slowing down. He didn't want it to. That was the trouble with so many things. They didn't last long enough.

"Would you like this set for the little fellow?"

"It's too expensive."

"It's not expensive considering the things you get in it. But, of course, we have cheaper sets. Now here's one, non-electric."

"I want an electric-train set," Danny said.

"I want a train set that runs, too," Little Margaret said.

"Sister, I just bought you a doll," Aunt Margaret said.

"I don't care. I want a train."

Margaret bought Danny a two-dollar train set, and then she took them on to see Santa Claus.

VI

Little Margaret was just ahead of him, and there were a lot of kids in front of her in the line waiting to see Santa Claus. Just inside of the railing before the line-up, he could see Santa, too. He had a big white beard, and red and white clothes on. There was a sack of toys by his side, and behind him Danny could see the painting of Santa Claus in his sleigh, driven over snow by reindeer.

Heck, these other kids could hurry up and get done with telling him what they wanted. It took them an awful long time. Slowpokes!

"They're slow as molasses in January. If I was their mother, I would fix them good and plenty, I would, for taking so long to see Santa Claus," Little Margaret said, turning to Danny.

"Just be patient, you little dears," Aunt Margaret said, smiling down at them from beside the line.

Danny looked around, and he was sure that he had never in all his life seen so many toys, and so many kids. Now, if it took Santa Claus so long to be here and see kids, how could he see kids in other places, too? He looked up at his aunt.

"What is it, Brother?"

"Does Santa see all the children in the whole world, just before Christmas?"

"Yes."

"How can he do it? If he is here seeing us, can he be somewheres else at the same time, seeing other kids?"

"He can do that, just the same as God can do it," the aunt said.

"Did you hear that, Little Margaret?" he asked, poking her.

"What? Don't bother me. In all my born days, I never saw a one who talked like you do. I'm out of sorts today with my neuralgia," Little Margaret said.

"Aunty Margaret says that Santa Claus is just like God, and he can be all over at the same time."

"Don't pester me! You're dumb!"

It certainly took them time. They ought to get a move on. It was only children who had bad manners, just like Aunty Margaret would say, who didn't get a move on when they should, and kept other people waiting and standing in line. And now, would he be able to get a baseball glove, and toy soldiers, and an electric train, or wouldn't Santa give him all these things? Now, suppose Santa Claus would give him all kinds of tracks and engines and cars. He could put the tracks all over the house and have a regular toy railroad running from one end of it to the other, just as Uncle Al said there were railroads running everywheres in America. It would go into every room in the house, with toy tunnels, and stations, and toy cities, and signals, and switches, and all kinds of trains, big ones and little ones. He would let Bill and Little Margaret run the trains with him, and they would keep trains running all the time, out into the kitchen, back to the parlor, into all the bedrooms. Under the bed in his own room, he would have the train sheds that were the same as the carbarns for the street cars, and there, the extra cars and engines would be kept, and when they'd pretend that an engine needed fixing, they would run it in there. He didn't know of anything that could be more fun than playing railroad with so many tracks, and all kinds of engines and cars.

But, gee, could he ask Santa Claus for so much? If he asked Aunty Margaret could he, she would say no, he shouldn't hog it all, and he should leave something for other children. But if Santa Claus was something like God, and could make all the toys he wanted to, then he didn't see why Santa Claus couldn't give him that many toy engines and pieces of toy track and the other things he would need to have a toy railroad all over the house. Santa wouldn't be taking it away from any other boy. It would just be extra toys that he had made and given to Danny O'Neill. God could do that, because God could do anything He wanted to. If Santa was like God, he could do things, too.

"Little Margaret?"

"'Pon my soul, Daniel O'Neill, I never in all my born days saw such a troublesome boy. Now what do you want?" Little Margaret said.

"I wanted to ask you a question, but if that's the way you feel about it, all right, I won't."

"Since you started it, go ahead, ask me."

"What are you going to ask Santa Claus for?"

"That's my business, and if you mind your own business, Daniel O'Neill, you will never get into any kind of a fix."

"Are you going to ask him for more than one thing?"

"Maybe I am, and maybe I'm not! See!"

"Well, I was just thinking," Danny said seriously.

"Danny!" Little Margaret said, her tone suddenly changing. "Do you think we could ask him for more than one thing?"

"I can."

"What will he say?"

"He'll maybe say all right, because he knows I have been a good boy."

"I've been a gooder girl."

"Maybe you have, and maybe you haven't."

"What are you going to ask him for?" asked Little Margaret.

"I'm thinking."

"I know what I want."

"What?"

"I'm thinking."

"If you'll tell me, I'll tell you," Danny said.

"All right! You tell me first."

"No, you tell me first."

"If I do, how do I know you'll tell me?"

"Yes, I will. What are you asking Santa for?" Danny said.

"I'm gonna ask him for a great big Dutch doll, with real hair, and blue eyes, and a different dress to put on her every day in the week. And I'm gonna ask for a rag doll, and a doll's house with, oh, all kinds of doll furniture and everything in it that you will find in a real house, dishes, and chairs, and a table, and bedrooms, and a parlor with curtains, and a mother doll, and a father doll, and a sister doll, and a brother doll, and an aunty doll, and an uncle doll, and a grandmother doll."

"There aren't boy dolls, only girl dolls."

"How do you know there aren't?"

"Because there aren't."

"There are."

"Not!"

"Are!"

"Not!"

"Well, then, smarty, Santa Claus will make boy dolls for me, and then there will be."

"He hasn't time to be bothered making special dolls for you. Who do you think you are?" Danny said.

"More than you."

"Children, if you quarrel, Santa Claus won't like it."

"Don't be fighting with me. I don't want to be punished by Santa Claus because of you," Danny said.

"Don't you pick fights with me."

"I ain't!"

"Don't talk to me! I don't want to talk to you, Daniel O'Neill," Little Margaret said, swinging around to face forward, watching Santa Claus as he sat benignly, meeting the children, one by one.

VII

"What is your name, my boy?" Santa Claus asked Danny in a rather hoarse and heavy voice, patting Danny's head with his right hand and looking him in the eye as he spoke.

"Daniel O'Neill. I'm seven, going on eight," Danny said, looking with awe at the false whiskers, painted face and almost watery eyes of Santa Claus.

"O'Neill. Are you the brother of the pretty little girl who just spoke to me here before you?"

"Yes, sir, I mean, yes, Santa Claus, I am."

"Your mother must be proud to have as fine a girl as your sister, and as fine a boy as you, Michael . . ."

"My name's Daniel, Santa Claus."

"Yes, I meant Daniel. Are you good to your little sister?"

Danny looked at Santa Claus, his eyes growing liquid. He didn't want to lie to Santa Claus, any more than he wanted to lie to God. But he was good at home, and he was good to Little Margaret. He tried to be, and he was better to Little

Margaret than she was to him. He wanted to say so, and the words just wouldn't seem to come out of his mouth.

"You don't mean to say that you haven't been good?" Santa Claus asked, leaning forward, patting Danny's head.

"I'm . . . good, and I do whatever . . . I'm supposed to," Danny answered tremblingly.

"Daniel, don't be so bashful. I'm not going to swallow you like a boogey man. Your sister who saw me just before you, she wasn't bashful and afraid of me. Now, you come close and tell me what you want me to bring you on Christmas Eve."

"Santa Claus, did you get my letter? I wrote you a letter and told you what I wanted, and my Aunty Margaret, she mailed it to you."

"I got it, but you tell me again."

"Well, I wanted a toy train set, with tracks, lots of tracks so I could run the train all around the house like it was a real train, and I want it to be an electric-train set instead of one with an engine you have to wind up all the time."

"That wouldn't be so hard to give you as long as you are a good boy."

"And I want some toy soldiers, and a right-handed fielder's glove for baseball, and if you bring me all these things, Santa Claus, I'll be awful good. Honest, I will!"

"All right, Daniel. I'll do it. And don't you forget, you obey your mother, and be good to your little sister, and I'll come down your chimney when you're asleep on Christmas Eve, bringing you your Christmas toys."

"Thank you, Santa Claus," Danny said, smiling, and his aunt led him away.

He couldn't wait until Christmas now when Santa Claus would bring his toys to him.

"Now we'll get out of this crowd, children. My feet are sore, and I'm very tired," Aunt Margaret said to them.

"I want to see the electric train run again," Danny said.

"If he can see the trains, I don't see why I can't see the dolls and doll houses again," Little Margaret said.

"Children, your aunt is so tired."

"Gee!" Danny exclaimed, half in tears.

"All right, come on!" Aunt Margaret said resignedly.

Lizz should do this herself. Margaret didn't see why she had all this trouble and responsibility put on her. Why couldn't Al do it, if Lizz wasn't able to? But, no, Al, he was too busy, and he could go blithely out of the house in the morning, saying to her, Peg, since you're off today, take the children down to see Santa Claus. He could. But always the burdens were put on her.

Danny pulled at one arm to lead her toward the trains. Little Margaret tugged to drag her to the dolls in the opposite direction. The Christmas crowd of milling, tired adults and shouting, exuberant children swirled all around them. Well, some day, some day, she wouldn't be bearing all these family burdens, Margaret assured herself, and Danny and Little Margaret continued to pull and yell at her.

33

I

His cheeks flushed, Danny dragged his sled up the snow hill in the prairie outside of his back yard. The hill was packed down and icy because all the kids had been using it, and, gee, tobogganing was fun.

"It's my turn, Dan," Bill said, detaching himself from a group of kids between the ages of seven and twelve.

Danny watched his big brother Bill, who could do anything and everything better than other kids could. Carrying the sled, Bill ran slowly with a limp, fell on top of the sled, slid down the slippery hill, and drew up against a snow bank. Gee, Danny wished that he could run better with a sled and handle and steer it like Bill could. Well, when he grew more he'd be able to do this, and he'd be able to do lots of things better than he could do them now. Bill limped up the side of the hill, dragging the sled by a rope. Danny watched Albie Goetz go down and spill. The kids laughed at Albie.

"My turn," Danny yelled, running up to Bill.

"That time didn't count. It wasn't so good because I didn't get off right. I ought to take my turn again," Bill said.

"But it's my turn," Danny said.

"You can have your turn when mine's finished. But if that time doesn't count, it's still my turn, isn't it? Yes, it is. And when my turn is finished, then it'll be yours."

"But you had your turn."

"Don't be so dotty! How can I have had my turn when that try didn't count? You'll get your turn next, when mine is finished."

"You did just have your turn," Danny said, feeling as if his heart were sinking.

"You go next."

"Can I have two turns straight?"

"We'll see."

Danny was almost in tears. He felt that Bill shouldn't do a thing like that. And this was the first time since Bill was hurt that his brother had come up to play with him without his crutches. He watched Bill limp over and stand behind Bull Young, waiting his turn to go down. Bull, blond-haired, twelve, a lefty, ran with his sled, shot down the hill nicely. He smiled as he trudged back up the side of the little hill. Danny stood trembling. Bill was going down again, when it wasn't Bill's turn. And whose sled was it? No, it was not right for Bill to go taking two turns in a row like that. He was so glad that his big brother Bill could come up and play with him again. And Bill was doing this to him. He hoped that Bill would fall in the snow and get himself all sloppy-wet worse than Bull had done when he'd taken a spill a little while ago. Bill fell on the sled, went down. He wished he could toboggan like Bill could. Bill slipped off into the snow. Good! The kids laughed at Bill. That made Danny sorry. He wanted his brother Bill to be the best darn tobogganer in the whole neighborhood. And Bill was the best, even if he was cheating on turns, even if he had just fallen off the sled. Maybe he had caused Bill to tumble by wishing that he would do it.

"Goddamn it!" Bill yelled, grinning as he limped up the hill.

"That was tough luck, Bill, and I'm sorry," Danny said.

"Oh, go to Hell!" Bill snapped at him.

Danny glanced aside. He wiped a tear with his mittened hand, streaking his face. He looked back at Bill. Would Bill give it to him? He watched Bill brushing his clothes off, afraid to ask, because Bill seemed like he was going to lose his temper. What would he do? And by rights, it was his turn. It was! Bill wasn't fair. But even so, he liked Bill. He stepped forward as if to take the sled.

"That the best you can do?" Bull Young sneered.

"It was just a damn shitty accident," Bill griped.

"An accident, my mother," laughed Cross-Eyed Bucky Haight.

"I'll show you it was! I'll go down again!" Bill said.

Bill was going down three straight times when they had agreed to take turns. He didn't want Bill to take his turn. But he did want Bill to show them that he was a better darn tobogganer than all of them put together. And he wanted to see Bill biff them all, and beat them up just like they had it coming to them.

"Can't there be an accident?" Bill said, standing in the midst of a vociferous group of kids.

"Sure! It'd be an accident if you went down without taking a spill," said Cross-Eyed Bucky.

"You guys don't know what you're talking about," Bill said weakly.

"You ain't so good as your baby brother here," Cross-Eyed Bucky said.

I'm not a baby, Danny told himself. And he didn't like Cross-Eyed Bucky, either.

"No?" said Bill.

"No!" Bucky said roughly.

Danny was afraid now that there might be a fight, and that Bill might be beat up because he was still limping a little from his broken leg. He didn't want to see Bill get beat up. But still he wanted there to be a fight and see his brother beat the hell out of them all. And he knew, too, that Bill could do it.

"Ah, tell it to Sweeney," Bull Young jeered at Bill.

"All right!" Bill said.

And now Danny didn't care that Bill was cheating him out of his turn, because Bill was going to show that he was the best darn tobogganer there was. Danny proudly watched his brother. Gee, some day he would be like Bill. There was Bill limping, dragging his sled, telling it to them good and plenty while they all yelled like crazy people. If they fought and beat up Bill, he'd pitch in and scratch and kick them. He would!

"Go ahead! I'm from Missouri. Show me!" Bull said.

"You took a tumble yourself, didn't you?" Bill said to Bull.

"It wasn't as bad as yours. You'll be puking up the snow you just swallowed for a whole week," Bull said to Bill.

"Yes, O'Neill, your tumble was worse than the Bull's," Cross-Eyed Bucky said.

"Anyway, I don't have to bat cross-handed when I hit a baseball," Bill said to Cross-Eyed Bucky.

"You ain't got enough sense to. If you did, you might hit at least half as many balls over that signboard as I do," Cross-Eyed Bucky said.

"Never mind that! It's winter now. Let's see you go down the hill without taking a tumble and washing your funny face in the snow," said Bull Young.

"I'm going to," said Bill.

"Well, go ahead!" Bull Young challenged.

"He will. He'll skunk you all at tobogganing or anything," Danny said with clenched fists, his voice throbbing.

"Say, punk!" said Cross-Eyed Bucky.

"Shut up, Dan!" Bill said in irritation.

"All right, what you stallin' for? We'll watch you stick your snout in the snow," Bull said.

Bill turned away from them. He gripped the sled in both hands. He ran, impeded by his leg. He fell on the sled.

"Now fall, you skinny bastard!" Bull hissed.

The sled shot down the hill, and on over level snow. Bill curved it about fifteen yards from the foot of the hill, and it gently eased against a snowbank. Bill got up and let out a proud yell. He limped back toward them, dragging his sled.

"Luck!" Bull Young loudly megaphoned through his cupped hands.

"Now say something, you wiseacres!" he said as he reached the top of the hill.

Danny told himself that it wasn't luck as Bull Young had yelled it was, no more than it was luck when Ed Walsh pitched a good game. These kids were the same as Bill was when he tried to argue that Three-Fingered Brown was a better pitcher than Ed Walsh. Why were kids like that, he wanted to know.

"Crap luck!" Bull Young said.

"Luck, my eye! I could do it all day," Bill bragged.

"Yeah, and I could be a flying machine if I wanted to," Bull said.

"And I could walk on my ears," Cross-Eyed Bucky said.

Now Bill would let him have his turn on the sled. He could slide down and have some fun himself. And maybe he wouldn't show them that he was pretty good himself for a kid his size!

He went to Bill. He put out his right arm for the sled rope. He drew it back. He waited. Bill didn't look at him.

"That a boy, Bill. That was swell," he said joyously when Bill looked at him.

"I told them I could do it," Bill said with a wide grin.

"It was swell and dandy, Bill," Danny said.

"I can toboggan. Goddamn right, I can!" Bill said.

"I know it," Danny said, as glad as if he had done it himself.

"You watch me do it again, Dan," Bill said.

"You can't do it twice in succession," sneered Cross-Eyed Bucky.

"But, Bill, it's my turn?"

"Watch me, Dan!"

In tears, Danny watched Bill go down the hill again.

II

Cross-Eyed Bucky Haight took out two large cigarette butts. Sneering at Bill, he handed one to Bull Young.

"Gee, this is swell," Bull Young said pointedly to Bill after having inhaled histrionically.

"I like nothin' better than to take a few drags on a nice big butt after I been exertin' myself like I just done," Cross-Eyed Bucky said, squinting at Bill.

"Where did you get 'em, Bucky?" asked Bull.

If they were going to be mean to Bill, let them! Some day he and Bill would fix them. Next year when they played ball and he came out with his Ty Cobb Louisville Slugger bat, he wouldn't let them even look at it.

"They're big ones, ain't they, Bull? I sniped 'em," Cross-Eyed Bucky said with pride.

"They're the next thing to being fresh fags," Bull said, and then he took a long and comfortable drag.

A grocery wagon clattered past them. Little Albie Goetz dragged his sled off home.

"I'm glad you guys like them," Bill said.

"Sure we do. When I snipe butts, I snipe good ones," Cross-Eyed Bucky said.

"I used to, too, when I was snipin'," Bill said.

"What do you mean?" asked Bull Young.

"What's the matter? Laid off smokin'?" asked Cross-Eyed Bucky.

"Yeah, he couldn't stand it. Yellow, because he thinks it might make him a midget," said Bull.

"Oh, I haven't particularly quit," said Bill, drawing a box of Melachrinoes from his pocket.

Very slowly, he took a cork-tipped cigarette from the box, examined it, put it in his mouth.

"I don't like the taste of it," he said.

He squashed it so that it couldn't be smoked. He pulled out another one. He again examined it with care. He put it between his lips, and stuck the box back in his pocket. He lit it and inhaled.

"This one tastes better," he said to the envious kids.

Danny smiled. He was so glad that Bill was putting it over on them.

"Where'd you get 'em?" Cross-Eyed Bucky said in a bullying voice.

Mort Young spilled in the snow. He brushed himself and dragged his sled uphill.

"Can't you understand English? Come on, where'd you get 'em?" Cross-Eyed Bucky asked.

"Where do you think I got 'em?" Bill replied.

"You stole 'em!" Cross-Eyed Bucky said.

"There's one thing I'll never be, and that's a thief. My old lady told me that there's nothin' worse than bein' a thief," Bull said.

"My brother ain't a thief," Danny said almost passionately.

"Shut up, punk!" Bull said.

"He ain't a thief," Danny repeated.

"He is, too, a thief. How'd he get the cigarettes?" Bull said.

"I got 'em! And there's more where these came from," Bill said.

"Give us one, will you, O'Neill?" Cross-Eyed Bucky asked.

"You got a butt. What more do you want?" Bill said, posing as he let the smoke out through his nose.

Danny stood marveling at the way Bill was showing them up.

"Keep them! I didn't want one anyway. I wouldn't take a stolen cigarette. Not on a bet!" Cross-Eyed Bucky said.

"And you can thank your big feet we don't tell a cop on you," Bull said.

"Snitcher!" Danny said.

"You little snotnose, it's the last time I'm going to tell you to keep your trap shut," Bull Young said, taking a step toward Danny.

"Pick on someone your own size," Danny said, retreating.

"Can it, Dan," Bill said conciliatingly.

"Well, gee whiz, they don't have to pick on me. I can talk, can't I?" Danny whiningly protested.

"No!" Bull barked at him.

"Come on, you! Tell us where you got 'em!" Cross-Eyed Bucky commanded.

"People that mind their business always keep out of trouble," Bill said.

"What do you mean?" Cross-Eyed Bucky challenged.

"I don't see how it's your business where I got these cigarettes. Say, but they're mild," Bill said.

"Come on, give us a fag!" Bull demanded.

"Who was your servant last year?" Bill replied.

"Don't talk to me that way!" Bull said, stepping close to Bill.

"Well, then, don't order me around and tell me I got to give you a cigarette that don't belong to you!" Bill said.

"Where the hell did you buy 'em?" jeered Cross-Eyed Bucky, stepping to the other side of Bill.

Danny trembled at Bill's side. He fought not to cry.

"I bought 'em in a cigar store. Where'd you think I'd get 'em, in a fish market?"

"Crap!" sneered Bull Young.

"You copped 'em!" said Cross-Eyed Bucky.

"I bought 'em!" said Bill.

"Crap! Crap!" said Cross-Eyed Bucky, seeming to like the sound of the word.

"Take that one, if you like," Bill said, shooting a small, unsmokable butt into the snow.

"All right, but don't ever come bellyaching to us for anything, ever," said Bull Young.

"Look out, Bill! Look out, Bill!" Danny shrieked.

His warning came too late. Cross-Eyed Bucky had dodged behind Bill, and bent down on all fours. Bull shoved him. Bill tumbled over Bucky and landed in the snow.

"Watch what the hell you're doing!" Cross-Eyed Bucky said, getting up and laughing at Bill who was sprawled out in the snow.

"Let's wash his face," Bull shrieked with glee, jumping on top of Bill.

"Help! Help! Let my brother alone!" Danny yelled as Bull managed to press down Bill's face.

Danny jumped on Bull's back. He tried to scratch. Cross-Eyed Bucky snatched him off and hurled him away roughly. Danny hit on his knees, and felt a burning sensation. His stocking was ripped and his knee was bleeding. He cried. He heard Bill yelling to be let alone, and he saw them mashing Bill's face in the snow. Mort Young came up and clawed at Danny. They went down and rolled over. Danny blindly struck at Mort.

"Let me get up!" Bill begged as Bull pushed snow down his back.

"Let him up, and I'll fight him!" Bull said.

They got off.

"Murder!" Mort Young screamed as Danny pursued him, shouting like a fiend.

Bull Young stood in front of his brother.

"He killed me!" Mort Young screamed.

Bull punched Danny in the jaw.

"Ooh!" Danny screamed, lying in the snow, holding his hand to his face.

"Come on, you, fight!" Bull said to Bill.

"I can't fight you in the snow with my broken leg," Bill said, already wincing from the punishment he had taken.

"You're a yellow belly," Bull said.

"When my leg is better, and I can fight on firm ground, I'll take on the two of you!" Bill said.

"Yellow belly!" Bull said.

"Come on, Dan, let's go!" Bill called.

Dazed, Danny got to his feet.

"No, you don't! No, you don't!" Cross-Eyed Bucky said, stepping in front of Bill.

"Ouch!" Bill cried in surprise after Bull caught him unexpectedly on the left side of the jaw.

He turned toward Bull whom he hadn't seen swing. Cross-Eyed Bucky caught his arms and held him. Bull poked him in the jaw a second time. Bill squirmed to free himself. Cross-Eyed Bucky released his hold and socked Bill. He and Bull piled into him at the same time, drove him to his knees, pushed him down, and again rubbed his face in snow. Danny ran screaming at them, and jumped on Bull's back. Bull swung him off, and washed his face in snow. Bill stumbled to his feet. Bull encircled him with his arms. Cross-Eyed Bucky searched him, and took a dime and his box of cigarettes. As Cross-Eyed Bucky stepped away from Bill, Bull punched him again. Bill fell, and his nose bled, staining the snow. Laughing, they ran away, Bull dragging his brother after him.

Bill got to his feet. His nose dripped blood. His face was dirty, swollen, half-recognizable.

"I'm sorry, Bill," Danny sobbed.

"Shut up!" Bill said in a whine.

Danny stood tense, sobbing. His face stung. He had a sick, throbbing head-ache. His knee burned.

"I'll fix them, the dirty c...........s! I'll get even!" Bill said, spitting his words out venomously.

"And so will I," Danny sniffled.

Bill limped away a few steps. His nose had stopped bleeding, and he was re-gaining some of his strength.

"Dan!" he called, and Danny ran to him.

He pointed to the sleds which Bull and Cross-Eyed Bucky had forgotten. He looked around the prairie but could find nothing. He went to the back yard and under the porch he found a chunk of lumber. Limping, he carried it back to the prairie.

"They'll never use these again," Bill said, beginning to smash Bull's sled.

Crying, he smashed both sleds. He turned them upside down. He pounded on the runners until he bent them.

"And, Dan, if they ever touch you or me again, I'm going to bring Big Ears Delaney and my gang from La Salle Street up here to get 'em," Bill said.

Bill limped across the alley to the back yard. Danny followed him.

34

I

The battered alarm clock, its glass cracked, slowly ticked off each loud, long second in the silent O'Neill household. Lizz with a shawl thrown around her shoulders, got herself a cup of tea and sat sipping it and reading a week-old newspaper by the dining-room lamp. Every few minutes she glanced at the clock. She set her paper on the table and went to the parlor window. La Salle Street was quiet, dark, deserted. Moonlight glittered on the trampled icy snow.

A train passed on the Rock Island tracks, ripping the silence to shreds. Then it was gone, and the quiet seemed more profound. She listened closely for the sound of footsteps from the corner. She heard the wind whistling in a low key. She turned from the window and again looked at the clock. It was almost five minutes after eleven. She wrung her hands. She picked up her newspaper and turned to the funny page. She set it down. She poured herself a hot cup of tea. She sipped it. She again went to the window. She turned from it. She looked at the clock.

She went into the boys' bedroom on tiptoe, and shook Bill.

"Son! Son!" she said gently as she continued to shake him.

"What?" he asked with the surliness of one who has been inexplicably awakened from deep and comfortable sleep.

"Son! Son! Wake up! Your mother wants to talk to you," she said.

"Huh!" he muttered drowsily.

"It's after eleven and your father isn't home yet."

"Aw, gee, Ma!" Bill exclaimed rubbing heavy eyes.

"I want you to get up and watch the house. I'm going down and notify the police."

"But, Ma, Pa's at work," Bill said.

"No, I'm sure something's happened to him."

"What time is it?"

"It's almost a quarter after eleven," Lizz said in a worried voice.

"Heck, Ma, don't worry. You go to bed. Pa'll be home. Last night, didn't he say that they were so busy that he didn't know what time he would be getting in until the Christmas rush was over?"

"But he said this morning that if he could, on his lunch hour, he was going to try to get over to Dinny Gorman's to collect the money that's coming from your leg."

"Please don't worry, Ma," Bill said.

"Oh, Son! Son! What will your mother do? I just know that somebody hit him over the head and took our money. Oh, my son, you'll be the man of the house if anything happens to your poor Pa," Lizz said.

"Ma, nothin' will happen to Pa. If anybody tries to hit him over the head, he'll sock them. Pa ain't afraid of burglars or nobody," Bill said like one whistling to keep up his courage.

"They might have sneaked up behind him and hit him before he knew what was happening."

"I'll get up and wait with you, Ma," Bill said.

As he got out of bed, he started to sneeze.

"No, Son, you stay in bed. You have a cold and it's chilly in the house now. I'll wait a little while," Lizz said.

"But, Ma, I can . . ." Bill sneezed again.

"Oh, those dirty stinkers that beat you up. My poor lame boy. Oh, wait until I go up to Mother's, I'll go out and find them! I'll pull the hair out of the heads of their dirty stinking mothers!" Lizz said.

"Ma, please don't. I'll fix them myself," Bill said.

"You poor lame darling. You sleep, and get over your cold," said Lizz.

"Ma, promise me that you won't tell Pa about the fight. I don't want Pa to think I got beat up. I didn't get beat up fair and square, either," Bill said.

"I won't tell him, Son! Oh, your poor Pa. Where is he?" Lizz said.

Bill sneezed. She set the covers over him and kissed him. She went back to the dining room. She sat by the lamp, her face wreathed in worry. In times like this, Mary, Holy Mary, She alone was a source of comfort. Lizz began fervently to pray to the Blessed Virgin.

And if anything happened to Jim? She was sure this time, too, that it wasn't a false alarm. She had fooled Jim about her curse this last time, so as not to have the poor man worrying. And he had been so busy, working these long hours all month, that he had not noticed. Half of the time the poor man had come home late, taken his supper, and tumbled into bed. Yes, Mary alone was a comfort to her now.

II

Jim got in around eleven-thirty. Lizz rushed to him, clasped him in her arms. She kissed him and cried with relief. He kissed her perfunctorily, and flung his cap and coat on a chair. She asked him if he wanted anything to eat, but he said that he had had supper and that all he wanted was a cup of tea and a slice of bread.

"I'm so glad that Papa's home. I was praying for fear that something had happened to him," Lizz said like a happy child as she placed warm tea before him.

"Only a few more days, and this damn Christmas rush is all over."

"You poor man!"

"I thought that I was going to get home around nine o'clock. But after I went in to the Atlantic Depot with a pickup, Pickles Hickman, the night dispatcher, grabbed me off and gave me a load for the New Jersey that had to make a train."

"Say, he has a nerve! I'll tell Patsy McLaughlin about him and he'll be fired."

"Lizz, the place was a madhouse. Nobody knew whether he was coming or going. Freight was falling off the platform. Christ, I thought I was in a lunatic asylum. They ought to have more wagons out on the streets, but they haven't. So we got to do more work. That's all. Even though I get fifty cents an hour overtime, I'll be glad when it's over!"

"Drink your tea, Jim, while it's warm."

"Lizz, aren't you going to ask me something? You know I was able to get to Dinny's office on my lunch hour," Jim said, his worn face breaking into a smile, his soft brown eyes twinkling.

"I knew you got it! I knew! I knew from the way you came in just now, tired as you were, that you had good news."

Jim pulled out a stack of bills which made Lizz's eyes pop. He seriously and slowly counted them.

"Three hundred and fifty dollars, Lizz. And it's ours."

"Is that all we get?" she said, her gaiety suddenly changing to disappointment.

"No, this is just the first payment. Dinny settled out of court with him. We're getting a thousand dollars. Starting next month, the fellow is going to pay us an installment every other month until June."

"My breadwinner! My breadwinner! We have more money than we ever had before since we were married. We only had a hundred and fifty when we were married. Do you remember, Jim?" Lizz said, going to him, flinging her arms around him, kissing him.

"Well, sometimes I feel that I'm not such a breadwinner," Jim said, taking a half a slice of bread at one bite and drinking tea. "A man comes to a hell of a pass when he has more money than he ever had before because his oldest son was run over by a wagon and got his leg broken. Why only for luck, we might have got this at the expense of a son who was crippled for life. And the poor bastard of a dago, he didn't do it intentionally. He's got a wife and kids, too, and he's trying to get along. Dinny said that we got the money that he was using to buy his own home. Well, maybe that's life," Jim said, his words tinctured with bitterness.

"Say, shit for him! He ran over my precious son. My poor boy laid there in the hospital, and it would break anyone's heart to see him suffer," Lizz said.

"Well, Lizz, we have a right to it. And let's not hang out a strip of crepe just when things are stacking up better for us than they ever did before," Jim said, smiling, reaching over to chuck Lizz under the chin.

"Papa's our money man," Lizz said gaily.

"Here, Lizz. Now you take care of it. We'll put it in the saving's bank down on Wentworth. You go there tomorrow."

"Yes, I will. I'll get it in both our names," she said.

"How will it feel, Lizz, to have our own bank account?" Jim smiled.

"But, Jim, can't you take the day off? You have to take Dennis down to see Santa Claus, and we got to buy so many things for Christmas," Lizz said.

"I can't, Lizz. I was off Monday, after I went to see Joe," Jim said, abashed.

"But with our fortune, Jim, we can afford to let you lay off and be docked another day," Lizz said.

"We got to guard it. It'll go soon enough. And we have to pay the hospital out of it. We can't be getting highfalutin' notions just because we got this little bit of money," Jim said.

"But, Jim, when are you going to take Dennis to see Santa Claus? He went around here all day saying that his Papa was going to take him to see Santa Claus," Lizz said.

"I'll be getting off at a respectable hour on Christmas Eve. I'll take him down then," Jim said.

"And when can you decorate the tree for the children?"

"I'll do it Christmas Eve. Also I'm getting the tree tomorrow. And when I take Denny down, why, I'll pick up a few more ornaments for it."

"Jim, I started cleaning the house today. I scrubbed the kitchen floor," Lizz said.

"Don't work too hard, Lizz," Jim said solicitously.

"I'm going to have the house all fixed up like a mansion for Christmas," Lizz boasted.

"Yes, this is going to be our best Christmas," Jim said, yawning.

"Here, I'll get you another cup of tea," Lizz said, taking his cup.

"Well, Lizz, things look like they're going to pick up for us. And even if I don't like political jobs—well, I might have Joe get me one if he is elected next year. Then, old girl, we'll be sitting on top of the world. Lizz, when we got hitched up, didn't I tell you that we'd pull through something grand?" Jim said.

"I'll say a novena that he wins. I always knew what my Jim would do for me," Lizz smiled, her decayed teeth showing.

"And, Lizz," Jim said, noticing her teeth, "you're going to a dentist."

"Oh, Jim, we can't afford it."

"What do you mean we can't afford it?" Jim said, pointing to the stack of money before her.

"That's our son's money. We ought to leave it in the bank, and when he grows up he can use it for an education. Maybe he can study to be a dentist, and then he'll fix his mother's teeth free," Lizz said.

"And she won't have any more teeth to be fixed, then. You're going to the dentist!"

"We'll need so many things."

"I said the final word on that! And in the spring, you're going to be togged out in such glad rags that nobody'll know you. Next Easter when I take my girl in the parade, she's going to be the belle of the walk," Jim said, getting up, taking Lizz in his arms, squeezing her, kissing her.

He heard Bill sneezing and coughing in his sleep.

"What's that? One of the kids sick?" Jim asked, worried, again sitting down.

"Today was the first day that Bill went up to play with Danny without his crutches. And, Jim, the kids up there, the dirty hooligans, beat up him and Danny. One of them held Bill's arm, and the others hit him. They threw them down in the snow. Bill came home with a black eye, and he has a cold from it."

"Did Bill fight back?"

"They wouldn't let him. And he, poor boy, with his lame leg."

"I'll have to teach Bill a few tricks about fighting. And when his leg gets stronger, I'm going to send him up there to paste the living hell out of them," Jim said.

"No, Jim, we'll do it! You get their fathers and knock their eyes out, and I'll say a thing or two to their dirty mothers," Lizz said.

"Is Bill's cold serious?"

"No. I'll give him Boucher's Cough Medicine, and I'll keep him in tomorrow."

"What about the other fellow? Did he stick with his brother?"

"Oh, Jim, Bill said Danny fought like a tiger, too. He wouldn't let anything happen to his brother."

"Something will come of that kid yet. I knew it, Lizz; I knew that he was an O'Neill, and they can't take that away from him, no matter how they try," said Jim with pride.

"Oh, I'm so rich," Lizz said, joyfully fondling the money.

"We'll move now, too, to a nicer place, Lizz. Next spring we'll go looking for a place some nice Sunday. But one thing, Lizz! We can't be using this money for high masses for all your dead relations. God doesn't want poor people to be doing that with the little money they've got," Jim said.

"Of course not, Jim. But we mustn't forget that it was God who gave us this windfall," Lizz said.

Jim yawned. His head began nodding.

"Come on, Jim, you got to get to bed. You have to be up early and out in the cold, working," Lizz said.

"Oh, well, only a few more days. And Lizz, old girl, this is going to be the best Christmas the O'Neills ever had," Jim said, patting Lizz.

III

Five minutes after Jim got under the covers, he was snoring. Lizz lay beside him. She sat up. She looked at him in the dark. He seemed to her like one of her children instead of her man. She kissed his forehead. She caressed his head. No, she couldn't tell him about it right now. She'd do it later. But she was certain that this time it wasn't a false alarm.

35

I

Things like snakes were going to eat him up. Something like a devil was going to kidnap him. All around the room, where it was all dark, there were things. He could see them. The Devil must be coming to get him and take him away before Santa Claus gave him any toys. He could see them, devils, awful things, snakes in every corner of the awful dark room. They were coming at him. What had he done? Why were they coming at him? What had he done? They were coming at him in the awful dark. Oh, he was afraid! God ought to help him now. He wished Santa Claus would come down the chimney right away quick, and chase the Devil and the snakes and all these awful things right out of the room. It was so dark. And there was nobody, nobody, nobody to help him. He could feel them all, coming, coming, coming right up on him in his bed. They were coming from every corner of the darkness, crawling on their bellies, and leaping and dancing, taking their time in coming, to make him more afraid, coming very slow, having hands that were some kind of awful claws with nails longer than Mother's toenails and fingernails when she didn't cut them for a long time. They were coming, slow, very slow, because they wanted to torture him before they killed him and drank his blood. They wanted him to know they were going to torture him, and then maybe kill him. Coming!

Danny tossed, sweated, curled and twisted himself up in a painful sleep.

"Let me 'lone! Go way! I done nothing!" he mumbled in a feverish whispered whine.

There they all were in the dark, making noises like they were hissing kinds of snakes and animals with poison coming at him out of their mouths like gas would if he turned on the gas to kill himself. Coming, coming, snakes and lizards and devils and awful things, coming, coming!

"Go way! Lemme 'lone!"

He hadn't done nothing to them. They didn't care. They were going to hurt him and do awful things to make him cry. And, oh, he couldn't move. He couldn't run. They had all left him. Nobody was going to help him here where he was all alone in some place where it was awful dark and lizards and awful things could all come at him the way they were coming, and do awful things to him, and make him cry, and kill him. They were coming. Coming!

"Go way! Don't hurt me!"

There was something awful, standing right over him! A beard! A black suit! Things were sneaking like a thief in the night behind the awful beard and the awful black suit that was standing right over him. Coming still! And the awful thing over him, it was black! And he could hear terrible moans worse than devils moaning in the wind at night. Moans worse than the wind, and more awful than dogs moaning over sick people the way Mother said the dogs did in Ireland. Moans like devils howling over souls they had stolen from God. Moans that were more awful than awful. And there it was, something standing right over him, a boy with a beard and a black suit, and he was bending over him, nearer, snapping his teeth to bite like a mad dog, leaning down over the bed with his beard, scaring him so that he could hardly breathe. He wanted to beg the boy, but he couldn't even talk. He wanted to scream and he didn't seem able to whisper. The boy with the beard was bending over him, his face getting closer. He was sticking out long fingernails like horns, ready to grab and scratch and kidnap and kill him.

Danny sprang out of bed. He ran screaming and barefooted down the hallway, into the dining room and around the circular table, the boy with the beard chasing him in the darkness. He ran around and around, shrieking at the top of his lungs, his cries shrill, piercing, expressive of some deep unutterable horror.

Suddenly, he opened his eyes. The dining room was lighted, and he found himself in Uncle Al's arms, with Mother and Aunty Margaret beside him, and Little Margaret standing timidly near her aunt. He was shivering cold, and he breathed in struggling gasps.

"What is it?" Uncle Al whispered.

Danny whimpered like a sick animal.

"There, there, now, Dan! You're all right. Buck up, now, you're all right! Here's Mother, and your aunt and your sister and I! And Santa Claus will come soon after you're asleep again, bringing you your Christmas toys."

"The poor thing, he must have been having a nightmare," Aunt Margaret said.

"He was chasing me, trying to hurt me, and kill me, and kidnap me, and stick his fingernails in me," Danny gasped whimperingly, tears streaming unwiped down his face.

"Who? What?" Uncle Al asked gently.

"What was it, Son?" asked the fretting grandmother.

"He was chasing me!"

"What did he look like?" the grandmother asked.

"He was a boy as big as Mother, with a beard like a dwarf and a black suit like the Devil. He came after me in bed to scratch me with his big fingernails. He chased me to hurt me and kill me and kidnap me. Is he gone? Chase him away!" Danny said, hiding his cowering head against his uncle.

"There's nobody after you now, Sport."

"He must be sick," Aunt Margaret said.

"The Devil got him! Good Jesus Mary and Joseph!" exclaimed the grandmother, rushing out of the dining room.

"Don't let anybody do things to my brother," Little Margaret said with indignation.

"Take it easy, Sport, easy, Sport! You're safe now."

"Begone, Satan! Begone before I stick pitchforks in you!" the grandmother monotoned, sprinkling Danny with holy water.

Danny crumpled onto the floor. Al picked him up and carried him back to bed, followed by Mrs. O'Flaherty, who shouted and danced about in worried incoherence. Margaret rushed to the telephone to call Doctor Geoghan. Little Margaret stood shivering by the dining-room table.

II

Margaret put Danny's bathrobe on and led him into the parlor by the hand. Al sat on a rocker, near the Christmas tree, smoking a cigar as he read a book. The mother was near the new victrola to the left of the piano, playing records. Little Margaret sat at the foot of the Christmas tree, fondling a new doll. Outside, the Christmas day was beginning to darken into twilight.

"How do you feel, Little Brother?" the aunt asked, while Danny weakly clutched her hand, lest he topple.

"He better get back to bed. With the O'Neill tribe coming here soon, there'll be enough excitement for him, sick as he is!" Al said, looking up from his book.

"I feel good. Oh, I feel very good. I'm getting better," Danny earnestly said.

"I thought that I would let him get up for just a minute to see the Christmas tree," Margaret said to Al coaxingly.

"Al! Al! Turn this music box off," Mrs. O'Flaherty said in excitement as the needle began scratching the record she had been playing.

"Brother, don't you feel bad because you missed the turkey today. As soon as your little tum-tum is better, your Aunty is going to cook another turkey, all for you. And, you little bugger, you learned something last night, didn't you?" Aunt Margaret said.

"Yes, I did," he said feebly.

"What did Little Brother learn?"

He looked at her, perplexed, asking.

"Ah, you did so. You learned that when you eat too many walnuts, and too much sweet candy on Christmas eve, you'll be too sick to have turkey and mashed potatoes and gravy and dressing for Christmas dinner."

"Oh, no, that didn't make me sick. I didn't eat very much candy. The boy as big as Mother with the beard and the fingernails like daggers, he made me sick," Danny said.

"You little angel. You ate too much candy, and now you have to get better."

"Aunty Margaret, I don't like Doctor Geoghan," Danny said.

"Why? He made you better."

"He made you give me castor oil, and I can still taste it."

"You had to take it, because you were sick. Doctor Geoghan is going to make you get over your little tummy-ache and your cold."

"Like the Christmas tree, Sport?" Uncle Al said.

"Yes."

"Peg, don't keep him up long. I can see by the way he talks and looks that he isn't up to par," Al said, watching Danny.

"Sure, the poor lad is pale as a ghost. We'll have to build him up with soups that will put some strength back into him," the grandmother said.

"Oh, I feel very good now, except for that castor oil that Doctor Geoghan made me take. It makes my stomach ache," Danny said with wistful earnestness.

"No, it doesn't, Sport. That candy last night did the trick. Now, you got to profit by your lesson. Don't hog a box of candy any more," Al said, smiling as he spoke.

"But I feel good now. I'm better," he said feebly.

"Hurry up and take a look at the Christmas tree, and then you better get back into bed. We had enough trouble with you as it is. You were very sick last night, Sport," Al said.

"Daniel! Daniel, look at what my son gave me. He paid a hundred dollars for it," the grandmother said, proudly pointing to the square-shaped boxlike victrola which was taller than Danny.

"When he's a man, he's going to buy a victrola like that for his aunty, aren't you, Brother?" said Aunt Margaret.

"Yes, I am."

"Danny, look at the doll I got from Santa Claus. It's got blue eyes and real hair. It closes its eyes and goes to sleep," Little Margaret said, holding up her doll for Danny to see.

"Aunty Margaret, when I go to see Santa Claus next year, I'm going to give him a piece of my mind," Danny said, ignoring his sister and her doll.

"Why, Brother, I never heard you talk like that," said the aunt.

"Well, he didn't keep his word to me. No, Santa Claus didn't, Aunty Marga-ret," Danny said.

"What's this?" Uncle Al said, his mouth popping open in surprise.

"He promised me an electric train, and I didn't get it."

"But I bought you a train when I took you to see Santa Claus, Brother."

"Yes, but he said he would give me an electric train, and he didn't. And he said that I could have a fielder's glove, and I didn't get it, either."

"He must have forgot, and he did bring you other things, Brother. He even left a two-dollar-and-a-half gold piece in your stocking."

"But he promised me, and he didn't keep his word."

"Hey! Hey! You got lots more than many children did. You shouldn't complain like that, Sport. If you do, you're liable to get less next Christmas. You want to learn never to be a hog. You were a hog last night with candy and walnuts, and that's why you're sick today," Al said.

"But he said he would give me those things, and he didn't."

"You got other things. You got more than lots of poor boys, more than your brothers got. I'm telling you, Sport, you can't have everything. You got to leave something for the next fellow."

"I know, but he did promise them to me, and he never kept his word."

"Well, you have to learn you can't have everything you want in this world, Sport, and that you must be thankful for what you do get."

"Come and look at the little manger, Brother," Aunt Margaret said, leading him closer to the tree.

"That's our Lord in the crib, and there's the sheep, isn't it, Aunty Marga-ret?"

"He was born such a poor little boy, Brother, and He never had the nice things you get. He never had any sleds, and any trains that run like yours, Brother. You must always think of that and be thankful for the nice things you do get. And there's Saint Joseph. And there's the three wise men who brought presents to our Lord," the aunt said, pointing at the crib and the statues that were dramatically arranged about the foot of the Christmas tree.

"And wasn't our Lord a boy like me, too, once?" Danny said, looking down at the statues of dogs, sheep, wise men, the infant Jesus, and Saint Joseph, and the shepherds.

"Yes," the aunt smiled.

"This is my Christmas tree, isn't it, Aunty Margaret?"

"It's mine, too," Little Margaret said.

"Yes, Dan, it's yours and your sister's," Al said.

"And those lights on it, they are electric, and they light up, don't they?" Danny said, pointing at the lights, looking up and down the tree which almost touched the ceiling, with its unlit colored lights, its gayly tinted ornaments, its silvery tinsel, its dabs of cotton, and the golden ornament shaped like a star at the top.

"Peg, even if they cost a little, I'm glad we got lights this year instead of the candles we used to have. Candles are a fire hazard," Al said.

"I'll put them on for you, Brother," the aunt said, bending down and pushing a button that lit the lights.

"Oh, that's beautiful, Peg," the mother said.

"Like that, Sport?" Al said.

"Yes, I do."

"Peg, better not let him stay up too long there," Al said, noticing the way Danny clung to his aunt for support.

"Brother, your aunt is going to put you back to bed now. The tree is going to be up all week, and you can see it when you get better," she said.

"Yes," Danny said, looking down at the small manger.

"Peg, you put the little fellow back to bed. He's as white as a sheet and he hasn't a leg to stand on. Poor thing, my heart bleeds when I see how weak he is," the grandmother said.

"Aunty Margaret, want to know what I'm calling my doll?" Little Margaret said, looking up at her aunt.

"What?"

"Margaret Mildred Elizabeth Mary, after you, and Mother, and my Aunt Mildred, and Mama," Little Margaret proudly said.

"Uncle Al, I'm all right now. Can I stay up?" Danny said.

"What do you think, Peg?" Al asked.

"Brother, I can see you're getting weak. Come, I'll put you to bed, and when you are stronger you can play all you want," she said.

"Yes, Sport, you better come back to bed," Al said, and he and Margaret took Danny's hands to lead him back to his bedroom.

He went with them meekly, and he moaned from a pain in his stomach as he left the parlor.

III

"With Little Margaret to talk to him for a while, he won't be so blue. He'll fall asleep, and that's good for him. I've never seen a child so sad as he seems today," Margaret said, back again in the parlor.

"We got to watch him. Ed Geoghan said it wasn't serious, but that we should just keep him resting and feed him a liquid diet for a day or so. But holy sailor, he was a sick boy last night. I was worried until I got reassurance from Ed," Al said.

"I'm so sorry to see him sick today. Christmas means so much to him," Margaret said.

"Christmas is a day when we all should be happy," Al said.

"You say the truth, Al," Mrs. O'Flaherty said.

"This is our first Christmas without poor Father and Louise. And Louise was so gay and so happy last year, Al, when she helped you decorate the tree. I tell you, I never would have believed it if anyone had said to me then that she was spending her last Christmas with us. And she said to me when we sat down to dinner, she said, 'Peg, I don't think any of us will ever be sitting down to another Christmas dinner with poor Father.' She almost had tears in her eyes. And to think of it! It was her last Christmas on this earth," Margaret said.

"Well, it was the will of God, Peg," Al said.

"And I tell you, there is no gainsaying the will of God," Mrs. O'Flaherty said as if she were personally enforcing a stern and drastic discipline.

"Well, we've had our burdens, Al, but I am sure that the Lord has good things in store for us now," Margaret said.

"Ah, Peg, that's the way I like to hear you talk. If we keep ourselves in that frame of mind, you watch and see how the sunshine pours in upon us. Come on, slip us a kiss on that sentiment," Al said, going over to Peg and embracing her while she gave him a smacking kiss on the cheek.

"Yes, Al, I believe that we get what we look for. When we look for the worst, we're liable to get it," Margaret said.

"Sure, you say the truth, Peg," Mrs. O'Flaherty said.

"This year that has passed has carried its crosses along with it. But still, it wasn't only crosses. We're getting along. Maybe next year is going to be better. From now on, I have a hunch that things are going to get better and better for us," Al said profoundly.

"Our Lord was born early on Christmas morning, wasn't He, Peg?" Mrs. O'Flaherty said.

"Yes, when the stars were out, and the wise men came to the little stable in the frosty early morning. Yes, it was early in the morning that He was born," Al said.

"The birth of the Christ child makes Christmas such a beautiful day, and it gives such a beautiful sentiment to Christmas," Margaret said.

"It certainly does. It makes it the most beautiful and wonderful day on the calendar. It's the day, above all days, when people should be happy. That's why I'm so glad that we are having such a lovely Christmas day, even if it is marred a little by the little lad's upset stomach. It's wonderful, Peg, to be happy on Christmas day. Peace on earth to men of good will, ah, that's the lovely sentiment of this day," Al said.

"And I'm so glad, Al, that you could get Mother such a lovely present as this victrola," said Margaret, looking from her mother to the shiny new victrola.

"Sure, a hundred dollars is much too much to be spending on me," Mrs. O'Flaherty said.

"Nix, nix on that, you great big beautiful doll. It's something that we all can take pleasure out of," said Al.

"And indeed we won't. I'm not letting every Tom, Dick and Harry play my machine," the mother said, staring directly at Margaret.

"Come, come, you, or we'll lock you in your bedroom on bread and water," said Al.

"That's all I had in the old country," Mrs. O'Flaherty said.

"Well, then, we'll just make it water," Al said, smiling.

"Al, of course we have lots of time, but do you think we should stay here, or should I think about looking for a new flat for when our lease is up in May?"

"Whatever you think, Princess," Al said.

"One place is good as another. Sure me mother didn't move in the old country for a hundred years," Mrs. O'Flaherty said.

"I just wanted to know. Now, of course, this place has its advantages, but maybe we could do better for fifty dollars a month," Margaret said.

"If you want to move, all right, and if you want to stay, it's O.K., Margaret," Al said.

"Of course, there's been a death here, and that might mean that we ought to leave," Margaret said.

"Would me own daughter be coming back to haunt us?" Mrs. O'Flaherty said indignantly.

"I don't know, Peg. Unless you really want to move, why, this place is satisfactory to me."

"Why, no, I thought that you might want to move."

"No, I like this place."

"Well, I will only say this then. We'll have to see that Little Brother makes less noise. About a week ago, I met the lady downstairs in the hall, and I said good morning to her, and do you know, she hardly spoke to me. I know that the reason is that Little Brother runs around here, and he has those baseball bats of his out on the back porch, and they're always rolling down off it. Of course, we can't say anything to him now when he's sick, but when he's up again you tell him to make less noise running up and down the hall, and shouting, and to watch so that those baseball bats of his don't roll off the porch. Why, they're liable to kill somebody sometime," Margaret said.

"When I'm here alone with him, why, he's as quiet as a mouse," the mother said.

372

"Now, Mother, this is not something where you should be sticking up for him. He does make too much noise, not meaning to, of course. He's just a child. He runs, you know, up and down the hall, and those darn old bats do roll off the porch, and they fall all the way down three stories to the back yard."

"I'll tell him as soon as he's better. But you know, holy sailors, that bat he bought. Say, he can't lift it. Why did you let him do that?" Al asked.

"I didn't know. My friend, Dick Smith, oh, he's the nicest man, Al, and I want you to meet him, Dick gave it to him. He didn't tell a soul. He just went down the street, and he came home with the bat. And he was smart, the little bugger, because he scratched the bat before he got home so we couldn't make him take it back."

"Well, that was a lulu. I tell you, he's a bird, getting himself a bat that he'll have to wait three or four years, before he can swing. Why, Peg, if I was playing in a ball game, I think I'd use a bat lighter than that," Al said.

"Well, what's done's done," the mother said.

"Listen, I'll talk to him. And when I'm away, and Peg is at work, Mother, don't forget, don't be soft with him! Don't let him make noise. We don't want trouble with the agent and the people downstairs."

"He doesn't make enough noise to scare a mouse when him and me is alone. He draws pictures, and he's there in a corner with his schoolbooks learnin' to be a scholar," the grandmother said.

"We have to discipline him now and then! We can't let him grow up wild like his brother," Al said.

"Lizz and Jim should be here soon now with their young ones," the mother said.

"They went to the O'Reilleys first. They'll be here after supper," Margaret said.

"And, Peg, when they come, you know how Lizz and Jim are. We want to handle them with tact. We don't want any defugalties spoiling our lovely Christmas day," Al said.

"They're happy today. With the money they got out of Bill's accident, they bought a lot of things they need."

"Fine! Fine! I want to tell Jim when he comes, to watch that money," Al said.

"You better tell it to Lizz. She told me over the phone that she's having high masses said for Pa and Louise, and for Mother's father and mother, and also for Jim's parents. And she said I shouldn't tell Jim," Margaret said.

"Ah, she's a good thing, my Lizz is," the mother said.

"Jesus Christ! She doesn't have to be doing that. The Lord doesn't want that," Al said.

"And also, Al, I forgot to tell you this. She's pregnant again. She hasn't told Jim yet, because she's afraid to worry him. But can you beat that?"

"I told her time and time again to restrain Jim!"

"And I've tried to teach her things, but it's no use. Al, we just better not say a word to her," Margaret said.

"I guess so. But damn it, Peg, I told her to restrain Jim," Al said, his voice almost injured.

"It's the will of God," Mrs. O'Flaherty said.

"And Peg, you try diplomatically to hint to them that we don't want Bill here so much, will you? Do it, you know, with tact and subtlety, so we don't have any defugalties. But see if you can't make it sink in just the same," Al said.

"Now, Al, I will not! I will not do a thing that will cause any fights today."

"I guess you're right. I won't say a word. I'll just mention once or twice that Bill will probably have a lot of studying to do to make up the time he lost in school. That ought to turn the trick," Al said.

"Al, I swear if there is any fighting here, I'll go out," Margaret said.

"There won't be. Don't worry. I'll handle everything," Al said.

"Sure, why in the name of God should we all be fighting on Our Lord's birth-day? Sure, we're all members of one family," Mrs. O'Flaherty said.

"You know, I asked Bill, and I've asked Danny four times about that ring. I can't get a word out of them. Little Brother wouldn't lie. I know that. He wouldn't know what it is to tell a lie. If Bill took it, he must have done it when Danny wasn't here."

"Maybe it will turn up, Peg. Did you pray to Saint Anthony?" the grandmother said.

"I've prayed, and I looked, and I sent money to the Poor Clares to pray that I find it. I don't know! I don't know!"

"Well, anyway, Peg, it's settled. We'll figure on this place for another year," Al said.

"All right. I'll speak to Mr. Shodroff, the agent, about decorating it, when he comes around for the rent after the first."

"Any kind of decorations you like will do for me," said Al.

"Ah, I was just thinking, Peg, isn't it wonderful the things we do be getting in America. Now me mother, she wouldn't ever have dreamed of getting music out of a box like that," the mother said, pointing at the victrola.

"Yes, Peg, just think of all the things that have come into the world since we were kids," Al said wistfully.

"Isn't it wonderful? And think, Al, of what there will be when Danny is a man. Why, it will be the most wonderful world you can imagine."

"Yes, and the Lord be willing, we'll all be on more than just Easy Street then. Just think, in twenty years from now, 1931, say, when Dan has become a lawyer, why, everybody in America who's worth his salt ought to be rich by then. All Lizz's kids will be grown, and you know, if I make enough money, I'm going to try and help them all to get an education. Now, you take Bill. You know what I'd like to do with him?"

"What, Al?"

"Send him to Culver Military Academy in Indiana. That's the place, by golly, for a boy who needs discipline. I tell you, if we could afford to send him there, he'd come back a perfect little gentleman. Now if I could do it, who knows, we might get him into West Point or Annapolis afterward."

"That would be lovely."

"Well, if I can't, I think we can manage to send Danny there when he graduates from Crucifixion school. But that's eight years off. No use crossing too many bridges before we come to them," Al said.

"Oh, in a few years, Al, we'll all be better off," Peg said.

"The Lord willing," Mrs. O'Flaherty said.

"That's the spirit. That's the optimistic way we should all look at things on Christmas day, with a new year dawning fresh for us," Al said.

"Peg, play some music in my new music box there," the mother said.

"Yes, let's have some Irish songs," Al said.

Margaret went to the victrola and began looking through records.

"It isn't every mother whose son will buy her such a fine present on Christmas. I tell you it isn't. Ah, Al, you're a good boy," the mother said.

"I'm glad, Mother, if we can make you happy," Al said reflectively.

Margaret wound the victrola, put on a record, set it going.

Oh, Kathleen Mavourneen. . . .

"That's lovely," Margaret said.

"There's nothing as beautiful as good music," Al said.

They sat listening. Outside, it was totally dark. The parlor was washed in shadows, the lights on the Christmas tree shone against the window. The mumbled talk of Little Margaret and Danny could be heard from the bedroom. They listened. Margaret's face was soft and moody. Mrs. O'Flaherty gazed with childlike awe and wonder upon the victrola. Al sank back in his chair, puffed contentedly, with perfect happiness, on a fresh cigar.

Oh, Kathleen Mavourneen. . . .

JAMES T. FARRELL, author of a prodigious volume of work, dedicated his career to depicting the Irish-American, urban world in which he had grown up. Best known for his Studs Lonigan trilogy, Farrell also wrote four large fiction cycles, several volumes of critical writings, and approximately 250 short stories.

CHARLES FANNING is a professor of English and history and director of the Center for Irish Studies at Southern Illinois University in Carbondale. Fanning is the author or editor of several books and articles, including Farrell's *Chicago Stories*.

The text for this edition of *A World I Never Made* was taken from the 1916 first edition from the Vanguard Press.

The University of Illinois Press is a founding member of the Association of American University Presses.

Composed in 10/13 Janson Text
with Hoefler Titling display
by Jim Proefrock
at the University of Illinois Press
Designed by Dennis Roberts
Manufactured by Sheridan Books, Inc.

University of Illinois Press
1325 South Oak Street
Champaign, IL 61820-6903
www.press.uillinois.edu